THE TRAUMATIC MEMORY OF THE GREAT WAR, 1914-1918, IN LOUIS-FERDINAND CÉLINE'S *VOYAGE AU BOUT DE LA NUIT*

18/5/2006

To Owen,

With all best wishes

and regards,

[signature]

THE TRAUMATIC MEMORY OF THE GREAT WAR, 1914-1918, IN LOUIS-FERDINAND CÉLINE'S *VOYAGE AU BOUT DE LA NUIT*

Tom Quinn

The Edwin Mellen Press
Lewiston•Queenston•Lampeter

Library of Congress Cataloging-in-Publication Data

Quinn, Tom, 1958-
 The traumatic memory of the great war [1914-1918] in Louis-Ferdinand Céline's Voyage au bout de la nuit / Tom Quinn.
   p. cm.
 Includes bibliographical references and index.
 ISBN 0-7734-5938-3
  1. Câline, Louis-Ferdinand, 1894-1961. Voyage au bout de la nuit. 2. World War, 1914-1918--Literature and the war. I. Title.

PQ2607.E834V6377 2005
843'.912--dc22

                                                                      2005054029

hors série.

A CIP catalog record for this book is available from the British Library.

Front cover photo: Louis-Ferdinand Céline
                    Courtesy of Fonds L.-F. Céline/Collection Destouches-Gibault/Archives IMEC
Author photo courtesy of Kinane Studio, Phibsboro, Dublin

          The Edwin Mellen Press   The Edwin Mellen Press
                Box 450   Box 67
          Lewiston, New York   Queenston, Ontario
          USA 14092-0450   CANADA L0S 1L0

                       The Edwin Mellen Press, Ltd.
                       Lampeter, Ceredigion, Wales
                       UNITED KINGDOM SA48 8LT

                    Printed in the United States of America

*This book is dedicated to
Professor Leslie Davis who
knows the secret of turning
base metal into gold*

TABLE OF CONTENTS

ACKNOWLEDGEMENTS

I wish, first of all, to acknowledge the assistance of the Irish Research Council for the Humanities and Social Sciences who awarded me a generous three-year Government of Ireland Scholarship to complete my research. In addition, the Council also awarded me a travel bursary enabling me to travel to Paris to do research there. I also wish to acknowledge the support of the Research Committee at Dublin City University (DCU) who provided me with a three-year research bursary. I would also like to thank the members of the Research Committee and the staff of the School of Applied Language and Intercultural Studies (SALIS) at DCU for their commitment and support throughout my research. I wish particularly to acknowledge the support of Dr David Denby of SALIS.

In the course of my research I have been in contact with many experts, not alone in the field of Céline studies, but also in relation to the Great War and the memory of the Great War. In the field of Céline studies, my particular thanks go to François Gibault, Henri Godard, Pascal Ifri, Ian Noble, and Frédéric Vitoux. In relation to the Great War, I have corresponded with historians Niall Ferguson, Richard Holmes, John Horne, and Jay Winter, all of whom responded generously to my questions. The historian to whom I am most indebted, however, is Jean Bastier, author of an important study of Céline in the Great War, and who answered many questions both about Céline and about the Great War.

In relation to the trauma of war, my reading was complemented by the commentary and insights of Lieutenant Colonel Colman Goggin, Head Psychiatrist with the Irish Army, now retired, and of trauma specialist and First World War historian, Yvonne McEwen.

I am indebted to the staff and services of quite a large number of libraries. My home library at Dublin City University gave me outstanding support and I wish to express particular thanks to Mags Lehane there. I also wish to acknowledge the staff and services of the Irish Army Library in the Curragh, County Kildare. The French Army National Archive at Vincennes provided a model of accessibility and support in allowing me to view the handwritten diaries of Céline's regiment in the Great War. The French National Library also greatly facilitated my research. I am particularly indebted to the library's manuscript department, in rue Richelieu, which allowed me access to the manuscript of *Voyage au bout de la nuit* acquired in 2001. The *Institut mémoires de l'édition contemporaine* (IMEC) in Paris provided access to its significant Céline archive and also provided the photograph of Céline used for the cover of this book.

I am indebted to Dr Peter Tame, and to Dr Rosalind Silvester, both of French Studies, Queen's University, Belfast, and to Dr Eamon Maher, of the School of Humanities at the Institute of Technology, Tallaght, Dublin, for reading preliminary versions of my manuscript and for showing interest and support at all times in my research.

Many friends listened with both interest and patience not just to accounts of my research but to the account of my experience of doing research, sometimes difficult and painful. Two persons, however, deserve special acknowledgement, Dr Niamh Chapelle, formerly of SALIS, who listened, supported and encouraged, and Alva Moloney, whose enthusiasm for endless conversations about Céline greatly sustained this writer on his own journey to the end of the night.

The importance of support and guidance to anyone embarking on a full-time research project cannot be overstated. In this respect, the figure of my good friend and fellow Célinian, Professor Leslie Davis, overshadows all others. His warmth, interest, enthusiasm, kindness and the unfailing reassurance of his personal presence, allied to his immense humanity, will not need emphasis for any who know him. This acknowledgement of his role in my research is accompanied by my warmest thanks and appreciation.

Last but by no means least, I wish to acknowledge the unfailing presence and support on every level of my wife, Joan Moore. Without whom nothing would be possible or even imaginable.

ABBREVIATIONS

The edition of Céline's writings used in this work is the four-volume *Pléiade* edition of Céline's novels, edited and annotated by Henri Godard.[1] In-text references will refer to the relevant volume. Thus, references to *Voyage au bout de la nuit*, which appears in Romans, I, or volume one of the *Pléiade*, will carry the abbreviation RI, plus the relevant page reference, in parenthesis.

Voyage au bout de la nuit, which is cited extensively throughout this work, is for the most part referred to as *Voyage*. Other titles, by Céline and other authors, may be similarly abbreviated, both in the main text and in the endnotes.

In-text referencing to Céline's pamphlets, which do not appear in the *Pléiade*, will carry the following abbreviations: *Bagatelles pour un massacre* (BM); *L'École des cadavres* (EC); *Les Beaux Draps* (BD), followed by the page reference.

---

[1]Louis-Ferdinand Céline, *Romans*, ed. by Henri Godard, Bibliothèque de la Pléiade, 4 vols (Paris: Gallimard, 1974-). A fifth volume of Céline's correspondence is in preparation.

FOREWORD

That's how it started. With the war. The Great War 1914–1918. After the initial war episodes, *Voyage au bout de la nuit* — Louis-Ferdinand Céline's masterpiece — takes flight: towards Africa and its colonies, America and its 'progress', Paris and the misery of its working class suburbs. Nonetheless, the reader never gets over the shock of the beginning, the initial seism: the first battles of 1914, the blind violence, the suffering, the deaths, the nightmare, the absurdity of all things, as if setting for once and for all the novelistic tone of the entire Célinian universe.

That's how it started. Yes. That's how it started for *Voyage*. But better — or worse — still, that's how it started for Céline too, after he enlisted in the cavalry, in 1912, while the young Louis Destouches was still innocent or happy — which amounts to the same thing. He still had his comforting illusions back then; he could still believe himself immortal. He lived in a protected world; a static world. The world embodied by his maternal grandmother. In his own words, he was 'a virgin to horror'. But alas! Caught up in the fighting of summer and autumn 1914, and eventually seriously wounded, young Destouches was to die in battle. And Céline was to be born there. A changed man. Or simply, a man. A writer, persuaded that 'this world's only truth is death'. No, it is not too much to say that everything in Céline has its roots in that apocalyptic war where Europe signed its own death warrant, and where one of the greatest novelists of the twentieth century was issued with his birth certificate.

All of this is to say that the theme chosen by Tom Quinn is an essential one. It is, indeed, *fundamental*. He has examined the decisive months Louis Destouches spent in combat. He has read, reread, understood and noted all that Louis-Ferdinand Céline has retained of this experience in his work. Make no mistake about it: the obsession, the recurrent anguish, the refusal, the delirium, the violence, the pacifism, the anti-Semitic aberration of the '30s, his philosophy of life, all, in Céline, starts with this experience. It is not too much to say, therefore, that the Great War 1914–1918 is an important theme for the writer. It is one of the keys — and without question the most valuable one — with which to penetrate to the heart of his work, and with which to dissipate the mists, the ambiguities, the contradictions and the mysteries which surround his troubling and controversial personality.

Let us thank Tom Quinn for offering us that key!

Frédéric Vitoux
Of the *Académie Française*

(Text translated from French)

PREFACE

When speaking of Céline, it is always necessary to journey back to that war which in France has been for a long time known as 'la Grande Guerre' [the Great War] and which nowadays is more often recalled as 'the 14–18 war' than the 'First World War' which features in the history books. In Céline's writing, the Great War maintains its presence to the very end, explicitly or implicitly, sometimes hovering just beneath the surface, but always there nonetheless as a point of reference. In his first novel, the one for which he is most remembered, *Voyage au bout de la nuit*, the war was the alpha and the omega: the opening chapters with the front and rear episodes; the closing scenes with the more or less provoked shooting of the narrator's alter ego, a character first encountered in the war and who ever since, in the course of the novel, has done little more than outlive it. From start to finish of the novel, the war provides the key to all of the experiences of peace time, in which the narrator inescapably discerns the common ground his world of peace shares with the world of war.

It is without doubt due to this interweave of all of the novel with this experience, even in its most recondite and least tangible aspects, that *Voyage au bout de la nuit* remains within European literature the great novel of this decisive period in the continent's history. It followed many other accounts of the war, when it appeared in 1932, but it went further and it went deeper than they had. Its richer resonance contributed greatly to the novel's initial impact. Its reverberation can still be felt today, at a time when the Great War, as we can observe from the many recent publications devoted to it, continues to be seen as the founding event, at every level, of the era in which we live.

It was not at all apparent that *Voyage au bout de la nuit* would become the Great War's great novel, given that Céline's personal experience of the war appeared, compared to that of many other participants, to have been rather limited in its duration and in its scope: only three months spent at the front, in a cavalry regiment belatedly engaged in combat, followed by a demobilisation due to wounds which, however grave, were far less dramatic and spectacular than the amputations and disfigurements the war had inflicted on so many others. His critics needed little more than this in order to question the authenticity of Céline's war experience, especially when his late-1930s' pamphlets made them especially eager to detect him in flagrant distortion of facts as early as his first novel.

And yet, Céline's experience of war was a very real one, and it can be considered legitimately as the origin of his work. This view represents Tom Quinn's starting point, and he has brought new facts and new perspectives to help establish its truth. Céline's contact with the reality of war, however brief, was nonetheless acute enough for it to penetrate deeply into his flesh and for it to be inscribed to an even greater extent in the mind of the young man of twenty who had been exposed to it. His wounds, while they were less severe than those suffered by other combatants, had nonetheless left ineradicable scars. Interestingly, they had been suffered in the course of a mission for which the young cavalryman had volunteered; that is, due to an act of heroism. With those wounds, however, an entire system of values, of which heroism was one of the crowning glories, was placed in doubt.

Due to a dearth of necessary documentation, we are only beginning to be aware of the change operated in Céline by those three months of war. The man who emerged from that experience was not the same one who had entered into it. In this regard, Céline's second novel, *Mort à credit*, warped our perspective. In this novel, the protagonist, who is to become a soldier, is depicted in his childhood and adolescence as a boy already at war with the moral values and social conformity — including the patriotism — of his parents. This vision, however, was the product of a reconstruction. When the letters young Céline addressed to his parents prior to 1914 are published it will be seen clearly that, on the contrary, he lived in perfect harmony with them. It was his experience of war which changed everything. What he lived through in the war was enough to convince him for good that he had discovered the hidden face of things, that he had seen the underlying reality of the reigning social hierarchies and in particular of those values and ideas which enabled those same hierarchies to perpetuate themselves. The scales had fallen from his eyes. He had in one fell swoop lost his innocence; or rather he had been, to use that French slang word best suited to express the change in him, 'affranchi' [disabused]. In words and actions, he was now unrecognisable. Where was the young man who, on the day war was declared, had written to his parents, 'Je suis persuadé que tout le monde fera son devoir. Jamais je n'ai eu le moral meilleur.' [I believe everyone will do his duty. I've never felt better]. And who, in mid-September, would write, 'Je crois qu'une grande bataille est imminente où le sang ne sera pas marchandé. Allons-y ! Sus !' [I believe a great battle is imminent where blood will not be spared. Let's get on with it! At them!]. After the shock of combat, the wounds, the news of a war which continues even if he himself has escaped it, his tone is completely altered.

> Voici aujourd'hui deux ans que je quittai Rambouillet pour la grande aventure, et depuis ce temps on a tué beaucoup, et on tue encore, inlassablement fastidieusement, la guerre commence à me faire l'effet d'une ignoble tragédie, sur lequel le rideau s'abaisserait et se relèverait sans cesse, devant un public rassasié ; mais trop prostré pour se lever et partir—
>
> [It is two years ago today that I left Rambouillet for the great adventure, and since then many have been killed, and the killing goes on, tirelessly tediously, the war is beginning to have the effect on me of an ignoble tragedy, on which the curtain goes endlessly up and down in front of a jaded public, too weary to get up and leave—]

It is tempting to situate the turning point of this change in him in an episode presented in *Voyage au bout de la nuit*, and in an attitude attributed to a comrade of the narrator, but which the correspondence now reveals was that of Céline himself. Amid the patriotic fever of the rear, an actress came to Val-de-Grâce hospital, in Paris, to visit the wounded. She stopped to talk to the brand new hero, wounded in his right arm now useless for war, and to console him she remarked that the wound would at least prevent him being returned to the front. His response to her was particularly heroic and she found it so beautiful, she wrote to him, that she had told it to one of her friends who then wrote a forty verse poem inspired by it, in which the soldier's 'quip' has become the principle refrain and which is repeatedly to be heard at the *Comédie française* theatre:

Mais lui se rengorgeant et le prenant de haut :
—Au feu ! j'espére bien y retourner bientôt.
Je suis dragon. Mon arme est le sabre qui fauche…
Je puis tenir mon sabre encor de la main gauche…

[But, his breast swelling, he let her know:
—To the front! I hope soon to go.
I'm a dragoon. My sword is my enemy's harm…
I can still wield my sword with my left arm…]

This expression of heroism is so outlandish that it denounces itself as parody. The sacred fire no longer burns, only words are left. Of the exaltation which implied self-sacrifice, there remains only a means of gaining advantage, especially where women are concerned.

The experience, however, is more complex than it seems. It will only become part of literature when Céline has found the angle which will allow him to catch its complexity and to create a new work from it. This is because Céline did not experience the war like any other young man of his age. At the time he knew or sensed that writing was his true vocation. The aspiration in no way undermines the authenticity or the traumatic nature of the experience, but it does subordinate it to demands which, without changing the nature of it, will transform it from a lived experience into a literary creation.

It is remarkable that the experience of war, which gives his work its shape, does not immediately make itself felt in Céline's first literary efforts. It will take fifteen years for it to come to the surface — something which may in itself be seen as proof of its depth. Even when, in 1926, Céline attempted to write a play by drawing on many of his experiences — of medicine in Africa, his experience of the United States, his work as a doctor in the Paris suburbs — the war did not yet feature. He needed to determine to use these experiences as material for a first-person narrative in order for the war to find its place within his story, which trigger allowed his other experiences to find their true meaning. And still he did not straightaway find the form which would do justice, speaking from a literary point of view, to the founding experience of the war. The *Voyage au bout de la nuit* manuscript come to light in 2001, which Tom Quinn has usefully drawn on and cited to support his arguments, has revealed the existence of an earlier version of the novel's initiating chapter which differs in one major respect from the published version. In the manuscript, the first-person voice, and consequently, the narration, was attributed, not to the character, Bardamu, presented as an anarchist — that is to say, someone who draws political conclusions from his disabused status — but to his interlocutor who embodies alongside him an attitude of naivety and conformity. It is this latter character who, at the end of the early manuscript sequence, marches off to war with a passing regiment. Given this division of roles and of discourses, it was Bardamu's companion who was destined gradually to lose his illusions and to discover the reality of the war, first of all, and later, of the social practices which ensure the continuation of war during peace time. Bardamu, the anarchist, was simply a more experienced figure and voice whose role was to open the hero's eyes. However, on the one hand, this progressive transformation did not really do justice to Céline's experience, and on the other hand, a similar denunciation of war and the evils of society already existed in literature: Voltaire's *Candide*. Relived in the twentieth century the experience called for a new artistic approach, one which would ensure its originality.

What we see in the correspondence and accounts left us is that the loss of faith in the principle values of society, and in particular, of heroism, was too sudden an experience for Céline for him to quickly 'put off the old man', to employ a biblical term. From one day to the next, he had become someone who no longer believed in the received values of his time, but this happened with such abruptness that he had not altogether stopped being the person who had believed in them. Perhaps it is the case that there can be no complete transformation, unless it is progressive. If not, within the 'new man', the 'old one' lives on, like a ghost, if only in his language. Moreover, the presence of the old self persisting in the background adds particular emphasis to the discourse of the disabused new self.

Rewriting the novel's first sequence, Céline has the idea of transferring the first-person voice to the 'anarchist', Bardamu, and so it is he, at the end of the rewritten sequence, who marches off to learn about the true nature of war. From this point on, two men, or rather, two discourses will coexist in him: that of the naïve companion, first of all, who little by little, and through his own astonishment at them, will bring to the fore and underline the truths he discovers and which scandalise him; but also, the complementary discourse of his knowing counterpart, who possesses in advance an awareness of the hidden reality of things. These two discourses, each enriching the other, were necessary in order to embrace and pin down the contradictions to which twentieth-century man is subject. They also had the advantage of bringing together in the same voice the two forms of language that traditional French usage had been careful to keep apart: the written language, correct, stylised, 'literary', with which French literature had contented itself until then; and the spoken language, popular, rich in slang, which the written form was determined to ignore, and which was, in fact, no less troubled by it.

Heroism was, in an ideal world, the acme of traditional values. When, through experience, it declared its own desuetude, an entire world changed. To cope with this upheaval, humans adapted to it as best they could, and their language adapted with them. By allowing no less than fifteen years for his experience of war to mature in him, Céline gave himself the means to little by little find the means of making *Voyage au bout de la nuit* one of the most significant novels of its time, one equal to that period in history which is its subject.

Henri Godard
Professor Emeritus of the Sorbonne

(Text translated from French)

INTRODUCTION

The Great War and Voyage au bout de la nuit

The memory of the Great War 1914–1918 has been remarkably persistent. Indeed, in the wake of the Cold War and the collapse of communism there has been renewed interest in a war which initiated the modern age and the modern mind. This renewed interest culminated in the massive 80th Great War Armistice commemoration in 1998 and it is gathering force again as the 90th anniversary of that same commemoration approaches. Memory continues to turn over the embers of the 'war to end wars'. In recent years a plethora of novels, memoirs, history books, Internet sites and TV series have all striven to recall and represent the truth of a conflict which shaped our world. It is still difficult, however, to look the Great War in the face and say just what its truth is. There are so many truths on offer. Louis-Ferdinand Céline's 1932 *Voyage au bout de la nuit* [*Journey to the End of the Night*] is one of those truths.

Céline's masterpiece made one of the most stunning debuts in literary history. An immense popular success, critically acclaimed and hailed by all shades of political opinion, *Voyage* was most notable for the introduction of a new voice in French literature. 'Il a inventé, en français, une rythmique inouïe' [He invented, in French, an unprecedented rhythmic], Philippe Sollers says of Céline.[1] 'Céline est entré dans la grande littérature comme d'autres pénètrent dans leur propre maison' [Céline entered great literature like other men enter their homes], wrote Trotsky.[2] Today Céline is recognised alongside Proust as the major French writer of the twentieth century.[3] The purchase by the French National Library, at a record price for a literary manuscript,[4] of the original manuscript of *Voyage*, which came to light in early 2001, underlines Céline's status and ensures his enduring reputation; a reputation which has survived despite Céline's own long-time marginal status as a result of his scabrous political and predominantly anti-

Jewish pamphlets published in the late 1930s. The release of François Dupeyron's planned film version of *Voyage* will do much to awaken new interest in one of French literature's most remarkable masterpieces and in Céline.

Louis-Ferdinand Céline

Céline, real name Destouches, was at twenty years of age a regular soldier in the French cavalry when war broke out in August 1914. He was among the first wave of French soldiers sent to confront the German invader, and while he was for a long time, in keeping with the cavalry's supporting role in the conflict, mainly an observer of the war's horror, he was by virtue of this role ideally positioned as witness on the cutting edge of modern warfare. The Great War was the swan song of the cavalry and the destruction of the cavalry regiments would mark one of the war's most notable transitions from traditional to modern warfare. Céline would live this transition in person. In late October 1914, he was a dismounted cavalryman fighting on foot under heavy bombardment during the first battle of Ypres. Delivering a message on foot to an embattled infantry regiment at Poelkapelle,[5] he was wounded and evacuated from battle. In December 1914, he was decorated for heroism.

Having left the war behind, Céline travelled to England, Africa and later to America. He trained as a doctor and worked with the League of Nations in Geneva before establishing himself as a general practitioner in the Paris suburb of Clichy. Some of these episodes in his life would provide substantial grist for the mill of *Voyage* and Céline's portrait of the post-Great War world. While for many years he maintained an implacable silence in relation to the war, in the late 1920s he broke that silence. His war experience provided the starting point for *Voyage*. *Voyage*'s fictional narrative, however, is at odds with the heroic reality of Céline's war past.

Voyage tells the story of one Bardamu, a Chaplinesque *picaro*, who leaves in a fit of enthusiasm for war before discovering that it is 'une immense, universelle moquerie' [an immense, universal mockery] (RI, 12),[6] in which cowardice and desertion are the only worthwhile values, 'dans une histoire pareille [...] il n'y a qu'à foutre le camp' [in a situation like this [...] the only thing to do is get the hell out of it] (RI, 12). Escaping the war, Bardamu, like Céline, travels to colonial Africa and to America, before returning to practise medicine in the fictional Parisian suburb of Rancy. While the war and home front episodes represent just one quarter of the novel's length, the presence of the Great War is felt at all times, thanks to a structure which repeats what has gone before. As Philip Stephen Day says, 'toute chose et tout lieu rappellent à Bardamu le traumatisme de la guerre' [every thing and every place remind Bardamu of the trauma of the war].[7] Bardamu is, indeed, haunted by his memory of war and on several occasions breaks down. In the very last pages of the novel he is once again on 'la route de Noirceur' [the Noirceur road] (RI, 503), the abandoned village he visited in the company of his alter ego, Robinson, during the war episode. The novel's structure of re-enactment ensures that the memory of war is ever present in Céline's portrait of Bardamu's post-war world. In this way, *Voyage* shadows forth the reality of a world which remembers the trauma of the Great War; a world, indeed, which cannot forget it.

Memory and Truth

This work treats *Voyage* as Céline's memory of the Great War. In doing so, it hurtles against a major truth problematic. Written over a decade after the war ended, and some fifteen years after Céline's own war experience, *Voyage* revisits Céline's war past in a fictional, pseudo-autobiographical setting. Céline's narrative of past and self, however, appears to owe little to the facts of his experience. Indeed, his fictional self-portrait as the coward and would-be deserter, Bardamu, is astonishing from someone who was a decorated hero of the Great War. In *Voyage*, Céline remembers, it seems, only to forget. As such, *Voyage* embodies in one site of memory Paul Ricœur's notion of modern memory sick with 'le trop de mémoire ici, le trop d'oubli ailleurs' [too much remembering in one place, too much forgetting in another].[8] This extraordinary novel, however, carries a force of conviction and an aspiration to truth-telling which is unmistakeable.[9]

So, what does Céline remember? How does he remember? And why does Céline remember the way that he does? What truth or truths of memory, if any, does *Voyage* have to offer in relation to the Great War and its consequence? What, indeed, is its value as witness? This is our subject.

The Contours of Trauma

This work examines Céline's rewriting of his memory of war and self in *Voyage* by placing it, first of all, within the context of a war that marked a transition from heroic to debased consciousness. Soldiers on all sides left for war with enthusiasm only to find themselves locked into a paradigm of murderous geopolitical stasis. The Great War was dominated by technology and marked the end of a 'vertical' mode of heroism which had endured since time immemorial. Forced into the ground for protection the soldier was no longer a hero standing, facing death, but a coward hiding from it. The Great War was unprecedented in its capacity for slaughter, killing ten million men, almost one and a half million of them French. Céline's own death encounter, when wounded in October 1914, initiates him into the very heart of this experience of death. His witness to war, expressed in *Voyage*, is the direct outcome of this initiation.

While this work is intent on illuminating the totality of *Voyage*'s relationship to the experience and memory of the Great War, any approach to *Voyage* as memory must take the trauma of Céline's encounter with death into account. *Voyage* is a novel haunted by death. *Voyage* 'peut être considéré comme la description des rapports qu'un homme entretient avec sa propre mort' [can be considered as the description of the rapport a man maintains with his own death], wrote Georges Bataille.[10] This 'description' brings us into the very core of Céline's memory, the memory of a soldier traumatised by war, and raises the question, given the pseudo-autobiographical nature of *Voyage*: how much of Bardamu's war trauma is, in fact, Céline's? For many Céline scholars the notion of a Céline traumatised by his war experience is readily acceptable. 'La guerre, c'est le souvenir écrasant de Céline' [The war is Céline's crushing memory], wrote Pol Vandromme in 1963.[11] For Maurice Rieuneau, perhaps the first commentator to focus on *Voyage* as a novel of the Great War, Céline's writing was born in its entirety out of his war experience. As Rieuneau writes:

> Retenons surtout que c'est à la guerre qu'il a dû son initiation à l'horreur et à l'absurde. Il n'est pas exagéré de dire que toute son œuvre est née de

là, y compris sans doute ce style incomparable décapé de toute convenance et de toute mesure, qui est la transposition littéraire, donc artificielle, du langage spontané des 'poilus', truculent, imagé et argotique, et qui, par la force d'authenticité qu'il lui emprunte, paraît jaillir des profondeurs d'une âme confrontée à l'épouvante.[12]

[Remember above all that it is the war which initiates him into the experience of horror and absurdity. It is not an exaggeration to say that all of his writing is born from that experience, including, without doubt, that incomparable style, stripped bare of all nicety and all measure, which is the literary, and as such artificial, transposition of the spontaneous language of the French 'poilus' [infantry soldiers], truculent, colourful and slangy, and which by the force of authenticity which Céline lends it, appears to surge from the depths of a soul confronted by horror.]

'La guerre explique tout' [The war explains everything], Céline's biographers, François Gibault and Frédéric Vitoux, propose without hesitation.[13] For his part, André Malraux, while not directly implicating Céline's war experience in his judgement, averred that, 'l'expérience humaine qui faisait la base solide du *Voyage* relève de l'intensité particulière de la névrose' [the human experience which constituted the solid base of *Voyage* derives from the particular intensity of a neurosis].[14] Still the gap between Bardamu and Céline does not close. One of the most notable commentators on *Voyage*, Marie-Christine Bellosta, states what is certainly the majority view on Céline and the representation of trauma in *Voyage*, when she argues that Bardamu's trauma is nothing other than a pretext or strategy employed by Céline 'pour se défaire du "réalisme"' [to rid himself of 'realism'].[15] Historian Jean Bastier is, indeed, the first Céline scholar, to our knowledge, to clearly affirm that Céline was 'shell-shocked' at Poelkapelle in 1914,[16] an affirmation of trauma this present work will build upon.

The assertion of trauma in Céline is, more often than not, presented in a general way as if war must always be traumatising, and there has been no real effort to examine the inner reality or nature of Céline's war trauma and its interplay with *Voyage* as this present work does. Indeed, the question of trauma is often confused by seemingly gratuitous remarks about Céline's mental stability. This is a tradition which began a long time ago, inaugurated by H.-E. Kaminski responding to Céline's pamphlet *Bagatelles pour un massacre* [*Bagatelles for a massacre*] by asking, 'Il est fou?... Probablement' [Is he mad?... Probably].[17] It is a tradition upheld by Milton Hindus who, visiting Céline in his post-Second World War Denmark hideout, described him as 'full-fledged *fou*' [*mad*].[18] A tradition supported by such as Pierre de Boisdeffre suggesting that 'il était sûrement un *peu dingue*' [he was certainly a *little crazy*].[19]

Other commentators have proven much more sophisticated. Jean-Pierre Richard identified what he called Céline's 'nausée' [nausea], an elemental malaise derived from the revelation of the body's 'manque de *tenue*' [lack of *consistency*], its tendency to disintegration and dissolution. The site of this revelation, Richard situates in 'le traumatisme déchirant de la guerre' [the terrible trauma of the war], without investigating the nature of this trauma in its context of war and the memory of war.[20] We shall, however, return to Richard's 'nausée' [nausea] in the course of this work. Julia Kristeva occupied similar territory to Richard when she made of Céline's 'abjection' an expression of almost biblical revulsion at existence. Kristeva's concept of the 'abject', central to her understanding of Céline, takes her into deep psychoanalytical waters: 'J'imagine un enfant ayant avalé trop tôt ses parents' [I imagine a child having swallowed his parents too soon], writes Kristeva, launching on her chosen theme, 'qui s'en fait "tout seul" peur et, pour se sauver, rejette et vomit ce qu'on lui donne, tous les dons, les objets. Il a, il pourrait avoir, le sens de l'abject' [who 'all alone' makes himself afraid and, to save himself, rejects and vomits what is given him, all the gifts, the objects. He has, he could have, a sense of the abject].[21] It is not the war, in other words, which has disturbed Céline, but rather his 'ayant avalé trop tôt ses parents' [having swallowed his parents too soon].

A number of notable 'psychocritical' studies of Céline have associated his trauma with a Freudian model of 'narcissistic infantile sexuality'. The Freudian model advances that trauma is revealed by war rather than produced by it.[22] As we shall see it is a model of combat trauma which has been seriously questioned and, indeed, contradicted since at least the Second World War. The result of the application of these theories to Céline is predictable with all roads in psychoanalysis leading back to infantile sexual frustrations and repressions.

Albert Chesneau was one of the first to adopt this approach in his study of the language of Céline's pamphlets. For Chesneau, Céline is the victim of a personal myth whose origin is a childhood feeling of illegitimacy. According to Chesneau, Céline controls the myth and so there is method in his madness. Madness does not inhabit Céline, but rather, inhabits the myth. 'C'est le mythe qui est fou' [It is the myth which is mad], not Céline, writes Chesneau.[23] In the 1990s, Chesneau found a worthy successor in Jack Murray who in his modernist study constructed his interpretation of Céline around notions of legitimacy and illegitimacy.[24]

Willy Szafran also subjected Céline to psychocritical study. For him, it is Céline's relationship with his mother which is crucial.[25] Szafran proposes that Céline identifies France with his mother, while his hated father becomes the Jew, and in another transformation, the German.[26] 'La relation avec les objets primitifs, père et mère,' he writes, 'est déterminante à chaque phase pour la relation avec les objets adultes et les objets symboliques' [The relation with the primitive objects, mother and father, is determinative at each phase for the relation with adult objects and symbolic objects].[27] Szafran also opts for a Hamlet style mad/not mad dichotomy in Céline.

The psychologist Isabelle Blondiaux has also entered this troubled area of Céline studies to 'analyse' Céline's text, which she characterises as 'une écriture psychotique' [a psychotic form of writing]. 'Céline n'est pas un banal psychotique, c'est un écrivain qui *négocie* avec la psychose pour construire son écriture' [Céline is not a banal psychotic, he is a writer who *negotiates* with psychosis in order to construct his writing], she declares.[28] For Blondiaux, it is Céline's writing which is crazy, rather than Céline. While she initially makes some promising noises in the direction of Céline's war experience — in her later work she presents Bardamu's trauma as an element in a clever satire by Céline of psychiatric discourses in WWI France[29] — she soon follows Kristeva and Szafran into the intimacy of Céline's infantile preoccupations with his mother. For Blondiaux, 'le rejet de la fusion avec la mère' [the rejection of fusion with his mother] in Céline leads to 'le refus de la guerre qui est rejet de la mère-patrie, le dégoût de la campagne qui est rejet de la mère-nature' [the rejection of war which is rejection of the mother-land, and disgust with the countryside which is rejection of mother-nature].[30] In other words, when all is said and done, Céline's pacifism owes nothing here to his war experience, but is the outcome of a failed infantile sexual fixation with his mother. On top of all this, Jean-Paul Mugnier, while noting that 'la sexualité de Céline présente un caractère post-traumatique' [Céline's sexuality presents a post-traumatic character],[31] has recently argued that Céline was sexually abused as a child, and by a key figure in his childhood, his grandmother no less, from whom Céline took his pen name. This is something which, whether true or not, can never be proven, while the war with all its glaring obviousness is passed over in silence.

All the while these writers push Céline's trauma away from his war experience. They appear to think like Robert Jay Lifton's trauma therapists who push their patients away from the uncomfortable recognition of horrendous real-life adult trauma back towards the safer waters of Freudian theory on the repressions of childhood. Lifton talks of:

> the all-too-frequent experience in therapy of people who have undergone extreme trauma of having that trauma negated [...]. I've heard accounts of this again and again in which the therapist insists that the patient look only at his or her childhood stress, or early parental conflicts, when that patient feels overwhelmed by Auschwitz or other devastating forms of trauma. [...] Adult trauma is still a stepchild in psychiatry and psychoanalysis.[32]

Commentators who have more directly questioned the possibility of war trauma offer little more. Some, such as Pierre Lainé and Patrick McCarthy, have adopted an extremely specious 'but other soldiers didn't suffer from trauma, so why should Céline?' argument (the question might so easily be turned on its head). Their approach to trauma in Céline falls well short of full recognition of the inherently damaging effects of war. They identify the problem without pursuing it to its logical conclusion. Pierre Lainé, for example, writes:

> Il faut [...] s'interroger sur la résurgence permanente d'un traumatisme qui envahit la vie et l'œuvre entière de l'écrivain. Parce qu'aussi douloureuse que fut l'expérience de CÉLINE, elle ne demeure malheureusement pas exceptionnelle et d'autres écrivains ont traversé les champs de bataille de 1914 — plus longuement d'ailleurs que Louis DESTOUCHES —[33]
>
> [The permanent resurgence of a traumatism occupying the life and entire production of the writer needs to be questioned. Because, no matter how

painful CÉLINE's experience was, it was unfortunately not exceptional, and other writers also spent time on the battle fields of 1914 — and, moreover, they spent more time there than Louis DESTOUCHES —]

Having thus sidelined the obvious source of trauma Lainé concludes, 'le drame pour CÉLINE repose sur un regard peut-être trop perçant' [CÉLINE's drama is due to a perhaps too piercing vision].

Patrick McCarthy, author of *Céline*, the first major English-language biography of Céline, insightfully recognises Céline's elaboration of selves as a response to trauma.[34] However, he too refuses the notion of war-related trauma, writing, in good company with Lainé:

> Thousands of men who were wounded in Flanders recovered and went on to lead normal lives. They were not haunted by ambivalent nightmares. They did not see every passer-by as a potential executioner. One can only conclude that Céline's nervous, melancholic temperament led him to dramatise his experiences.[35]

This tradition is alive and well in Céline studies. Philippe Alméras, writing of Céline's 1915 sojourn in London, dismissively comments, 'pas question dans tout cela du moindre malaise' [no question of the slightest malaise in all that].[36] In his extensive biography, Nicholas Hewitt devotes only four pages to Céline's First World War experience, a large part of which is devoted to minimising Céline's injuries at Poelkapelle.[37] Most recently, the Great War historian, Jay Winter has affirmed, 'there is no evidence that Destouches suffered from shell shock or that his wound was accompanied by any other trauma.'[38] Chapters Three and Four of this work will amply refute this affirmation. It is, indeed, our intention to fully restore to Céline his status as a wounded and traumatised soldier-survivor of the Great War.

Methodology

Our investigation of the 'truth problematic' at the heart of *Voyage* takes us into the troubled area which divides the novel as evocation of Céline's lived experience on the one hand and as fictional representation of that experience on the other. This area is fraught with difficulty. Nicholas Hewitt has warned, 'the novels cannot ever be used as evidence in the construction of the Célinian biography.'[39] Philippe Lejeune, for his part, excluded *Voyage* from

L'Autobiographie en France, ranking Céline among certain 'mythomanes avoués' [avowed mythomaniacs].[40] And yet what is clear is that the Célinian biography — his experiences in the war, at the rear, in Africa, in America, and working as a doctor in Paris — underpin Bardamu's tale.[41] *Voyage* is, indeed, a vibrant mixture of autobiography and fiction, of life and imagination, where the facts of Céline's life are never far from the surface. This dynamic interaction of fact and fiction is underlined by François Gibault who, commenting on the presence of elements of the war experience of Louis Destouches in Céline's *Voyage* narrative, reminds us, 'combien son œuvre est autobiographique, malgré ses transpositions et ses outrances' [the extent to which his work is autobiographical, despite its transpositions and excesses].[42] Henri Godard describes Céline's 'projet romanesque' [novelistic project] as one 'qui revendique contradictoirement la garantie du réel et le droit à l'imagination ; qui se veut à la fois autobiographie et roman' [which, in contradictory fashion, claims both the guarantee of the real and the right to imagination; which seeks to be both autobiography and novel].[43] The effect of this is to open up narrative to Céline's authorial presence. 'En même temps que dire qui est […] le moi qui exprime,' observes Godard, 'il lui faut encore faire place dans le texte à l'existence même de ce narrateur-auteur' [At the same time as saying who is […] the I who speaks, he needs to make space in the text for the existence of the narrator-author].[44] Godard adds, 'n'osant pas assumer l'histoire lui-même, Céline la prête au nommé Bardamu' [not daring to assume responsibility for the story himself, Céline assigns it to Bardamu]. 'Bardamu "parle", mais c'est Céline qui signe' [Bardamu 'speaks', but with Céline's signature], he comments.[45]

The analysis of Gibault and Godard reveals three levels of narration within *Voyage*: that of narrator and protagonist, Bardamu, that of the author, Céline, and finally, that of Destouches, the real-life model for Bardamu. This analysis acknowledges that within the different levels of narration in *Voyage* there is a real store of lived experience, a reality of lived memory, mediated, articulated and, indeed, transformed by the narrative 'interference' of both author and fictional protagonist.

Our approach to *Voyage*, as Céline's witness to the Great War and its consequence, is firmly based on our acknowledgement of it as a rewriting of memory in which there is a dynamic interaction between 'model', 'author', and 'narrator-protagonist', to create a supreme fiction rooted in a real life, however remote. Having recognised this, our examination centres on the necessities that underlie Céline's rewriting of life and self, necessities which draw *Voyage* inexorably from fact to fiction, from Destouches to Bardamu. We shall see that these necessities are manifold, but that centrally they are articulated around Céline's need to escape past trauma through creation of a new narrative of the past. This movement from 'traumatic past' to 'traumatic narrative' (see 5.1 *From Traumatic Memory to Traumatic Narrative*) encompasses the movement from autobiography to novel, from truth to untruth. It is the renewal of self which is at stake here. The requisite transformation — or 'transposition' as Céline calls it — cannot take place without the author's engagement with the real substance of his past life, that is, without engagement with his memory of the past. Fundamental to our unravelling of the mysteries of *Voyage*, therefore, is our understanding of it as the product of an engagement with a real experience of trauma in Céline's life.

Céline's trauma and his effort, through writing, to heal trauma and gain 'death mastery' — as Robert Jay Lifton terms it — in a world saturated with war and death are a central preoccupation of this work. However, this must be understood as part of an overall project to illuminate the totality of the relationship between *Voyage* and the Great War and its consequence. Céline's trauma exists within a paradigm of collective trauma, and *Voyage* is not just his effort to record and transcend personal disasters but to address the wider trauma and dangers flowing from the breach in the world made by the war. To concentrate solely on Céline's trauma would be to strip *Voyage* of its significant anti-war status and lose the vast and multifaceted character of its engagement with its artistic and societal inheritance. It would be to concentrate on its healing of self, when *Voyage*, as we shall see, wishes to heal both self and world.

An important premise of this work is that *Voyage* engages in a significant manner with its time and place. This inevitably draws us away from the text and takes us towards the world it inhabits. This is to say that an important key to understanding *Voyage* is found in its context and that knowledge of what is beyond the text is essential to a true reading of the novel. As such, *Voyage* is a document illuminating and illuminated by its time. Indeed, this interdependence of text and 'hors-texte' [what is outside the text] in *Voyage* is signalled — not just by *Voyage*'s autobiographical underlay, which calls us beyond the text — but also by one of the main strategies shaping Céline's composition: intertextuality. Céline's use of borrowed texts is rampant. As we shall see, however, intertextuality is not just a device exploited by Céline in the elaboration of a complex fiction, but a means to representing the 'totality' of his time, and most significantly, the cornerstone of his creation of witness to war and its consequence (see 5.3 *Intertextual Witness*). This character of witness is further enhanced through analysis of other stylistic features of Céline's novel — features by definition identified through textual analysis. *Voyage*'s characteristic circular patterns, its use of repetition, pleonasm, and interruption, are all significant aspects of its oral style. These aspects of Céline's oral style, however, take on a far deeper resonance when it is realised that the Great War saw a breakdown of faith in the written word and a renewal of the oral as the language of truth-telling (see 1.4 *Censorship*). Our reading of Céline's orality is further enhanced when we understand the extent to which these characteristic stylistic patterns provide a form of oral witness which, as we shall see, bring us closer to the pain and truth of the memory of trauma (see 8.1 *Oral Witness*).

To speak of *Voyage* as witness acknowledges that it has a truth claim. It acknowledges its relation to the world which has produced it. *Voyage*, however, does not just reflect the world, it interacts actively with it. The way in which *Voyage* challenges the values of the commemoration of the Great War — at its height in the late 1920s as Céline begins to write *Voyage* — cannot be fully grasped without some knowledge of how commemoration operated within Céline's war-torn world. *Voyage* is very much a novel that is '*engagé*' [committed], not just in terms of the witness that it offers to its time and place, but in its immense thrust to enact change in society, politics and memory, as well as in literature. Its aims, we shall see, are as much polemical and educational as literary. The reality of its time, caught in the midst of two cataclysmic wars, demands this. Consequently, *Voyage* is shaped as much by a need to address the disasters that have befallen and that threaten Céline's world as by his need to emerge from personal trauma.

Voyage is a novel which has an immense debt to experience. This work acknowledges this, not just by drawing on biographical sources, but by delving into a wide range of documents — personal, historical, literary — relating to the Great War and the memory of the Great War. These documents reveal the 'commonality' of Céline's voice. This is evidenced directly by Céline's use of intertextuality, but we will find this 'commonality' equally in the letters of the ordinary soldier and in the literary accounts of the war which have preceded *Voyage*. Our placing of *Voyage* in the context of writers such as Robert Graves, Erich Maria Remarque and Ernest Hemingway, shows many common strategies at work in relation to language, style, and voice (see 2.2 *The Writers of Modern Memory*).

In order to illuminate the richness of *Voyage*'s engagement with its world this work complements its use of biographical and literary studies of Céline and *Voyage* by drawing on a wide range of materials and disciplines relating to the Great War, to memory and trauma — in particular combat trauma — as well as a number of important general texts of literary analysis. The many insights produced by the application of such a broad range of texts and disciplines is ample justification of the 'totality' of our approach to what is, as we shall see, a 'total' novel of 'total' war.

Cultural studies of the Great War have much to offer to our understanding of Céline. Indeed, Céline can be readily placed within a paradigm of memory established by Paul Fussell. Fussell's *The Great War and Modern Memory* is one of the lenses through which we shall view *Voyage*. Examining the response of British writers to the Great War, Fussell identified the war as a starting point for a new form of consciousness.[46] The shape of Fussell's modern memory fits Céline like a glove. Its foremost elements of irony, obscenity, black humour, theatricality, its use of demonic and excremental imagery, all subsumed in an adversarial relationship to the surrounding world and imbued with an atmosphere of ritual and myth, are all prominent in *Voyage*. Even modern memory's fascination with the figure of the 'lad' or 'boy' is given striking expression in *Voyage*'s Bébert, described as 'une gaieté pour l'univers' [a gaiety for the universe] (RI, 242). Indeed, given the shift from heroic to debased consciousness represented by Céline's self-portrayal as Bardamu, *Voyage* offers striking support to Fussell's contention that a new form of consciousness emerged from the war. This shift from heroic Destouches to debased Bardamu is further emphasised by a comparison of Destouches' pre-war *Carnets*, full as they are of innocence and sensitivity, with the coarse howl of protest that is *Voyage*. Indeed, Céline and *Voyage* embody perfectly the notion of a caesura, a split from an heroic golden age and exile in a debased one, articulated around the disaster of the Great War. Given all of this, Céline can be seen as an exemplary literary representative of Fussell's modern memory. This work will amply bear this out.

If Fussell's modern memory throws light on the structure and content of Céline's Great War memory, it is the literature of trauma, however, which offers most to an understanding of the inner Céline. Robert Jay Lifton, in his study of the survivors of Hiroshima,[47] and particularly in his work with American veterans of the Vietnam War,[48] enlightens the psychology of Céline, the soldier-survivor, at every turn. Reading Lifton, it is impossible not to remark the relevance of his accounts of survivor experience and adaptation to Céline's experience. Lifton's insights into the survivor's struggle for 'death mastery' and the search for meaning attendant on a catastrophic 'death immersion' have immense resonance with Céline and with *Voyage*. Lifton's soldiers announcing their status as 'ghost',[49] or declaring their loss of faith in humanity — 'I'll never trust people like I did before'[50] — or expressing their astonishment at war's moral inversion, 'it's even... smiled upon, you know',[51] echo time and time again the experience of Bardamu, 'mi-revenant' [half-ghost] (RI, 74), declaring that 'je ne croirai plus jamais à ce qu'ils disent, à ce qu'ils pensent' [I will never believe again in what people say, in what they think] (RI, 15), or voicing his own astonishment at war's inversion, 'ce qu'on faisait à se tirer dessus [...] n'était pas défendu ! [...] C'était même reconnu, encouragé' [shooting like that at one another [...] wasn't forbidden! [...] It was even acknowledged, encouraged] (RI, 14). Their voice of survival confirms Bardamu's and so confirms Céline's, for whom Bardamu speaks.

While it is not the intention or, indeed, the competence of this work to lumber Céline with the label of clinical trauma, there is much in recent models of post-traumatic stress disorder that can be applied to him. Céline's restless life after the war, his difficulties with relationships and in his professional life, his alienation from the society he lived in, his raging anti-authority stance, all place him within an established paradigm of post-combat trauma of which *Voyage* is the resolute expression.[52] Céline's trauma, as we shall see, is very much a lived experience of division and turmoil at the heart of self and being, but this experience is heightened by circumstance. Its intensity gives the measure of the difficulty Céline faced in adapting to a world in crisis. This dual experience of trauma in self and world shapes *Voyage* from start to finish and ensures that while it embodies, on a literary level, the reality of traumatised self and memory, it also provides an invaluable document for understanding the trauma and anguish of the world which emerged from one war and which moved ineluctably towards another.

Céline's post-Great War world looked back towards unprecedented cataclysm. It derived much of its strange darkness, however, from the looming shadow of war to come. What shall emerge most forcefully in the course of our work is the way in which the prospect of war to come influences Céline's literary memory of war past. We shall clearly see that *Voyage* is a Janus, torn between two wars, whose cry of warning and despair echoes with educational and polemical intent. *Voyage*, we shall see, is more than just an anti-war novel, it is a novel whose aim is to rescue a world condemned to war and death. Its aesthetic innovations are driven by an ultimate desire for healing and 'death mastery' for Céline, for France and for a whole world at war with itself. Understanding

Voyage's aesthetic achievement in this light emphasises the profoundly moral character of Céline's genius and of *Voyage*.

Summary of Chapters

This work begins by acknowledging the experience which produced trauma in Céline and his world. Chapter One is an examination of the Great War shift from heroic to debased consciousness which is central to any understanding of *Voyage*. It traces the significant links between *Voyage* and the collective experience of the war and locates *Voyage*'s collective memory of the past in the event which defined the Great War for the French mind: Verdun. Chapter Two begins by examining the commemoration of the war and emphasises the ways in which traditional memory institutionalised a form of forgetting to be contested by Céline and the other writers of modern memory. The second half of Chapter Two will examine some of the major writers and works which preceded *Voyage* and examine the ways in which they overlap with *Voyage*. This section provides an important literary context for Céline's literary memory of the war and offers essential background to anyone wishing to understand how *Voyage* engages on a literary level with the world around it. Chapter Three examines Céline's family background and his entry into the army before examining his experience of war based on a reading of the handwritten wartime diary of his regiment: the 12th Cuirassiers. This chapter concludes by examining Céline's traumatic death encounter at Poelkapelle in 1914. Chapter Four follows Céline into hospital at Hazebrouck and provides further evidence of trauma. It traces the contours of Céline's trauma, before plunging into the aftermath of his war and the path to *Voyage*. Chapter Four concludes by showing how Céline's trauma is inscribed in the structure and language of *Voyage*. Chapter Five examines how Céline's traumatic memory of war becomes fictional narrative before examining in detail the character and meaning of the silence which invests *Voyage*. It concludes by examining the way in which Céline transposes his 'eye-witness' to war into a complex weave of fictional 'I-witness'. Chapter Six examines Céline's rewriting of self in *Voyage*, articulated around his protean effort to escape the stasis of traumatised memory and achieve healing 'death mastery'. Chapter Seven examines the themes of Céline's anti-memory or anti-commemoration of the Great War. Chapter Eight examines Céline's development of a new language of truth-telling in *Voyage* and the manner in which his oral style provides oral witness to war, before looking at the way in which the novel's imagery reflects the breakdown in the relation to symbols of self and world at the heart of the war's transition from heroic to debased consciousness. Chapter Nine reveals how Céline's artistic project is shaped through interaction with one of western civilisation's founding texts, Plato's *The Republic*. Understanding the nature of this engagement not only throws light on the nature of Céline's art but leads us towards an understanding of the immensely polemical nature of that art. Chapter Nine continues with an examination of *Voyage*'s anti-Enlightenment status before revealing Céline's vision of 'personal evil', against whom the savage irony and invective of *Voyage* is directed. It concludes by briefly looking at the persistence of Céline's memory of the Great War in the rest of his literary production after *Voyage*, including his controversial pre-Second World War pamphlets.

Conclusion

This work examines *Voyage au bout de la nuit* as the literary expression of Louis-Ferdinand Céline's memory of the Great War 1914–1918. It deals with the truth problematic posed by the transformation of Destouches the hero into Bardamu the coward, emblematic of the novel's vast discrepancy between fact and fiction, through examination of the Great War shift in consciousness from heroism to debasement and particularly through examination of Céline's traumatic encounter with death and the consequence of that encounter. The examination of Céline's memory of the war takes place in the context of how the Great War was remembered and commemorated, examination which provides an important dimension to understanding the shape and content of Céline's memory. This work then is triple in that it provides an account of the Great War, its commemoration, and its literary memory. It is the first major work devoted entirely to an examination of *Voyage* in the context of the Great War and the memory of the Great War. It is the first major work to fully engage with the structure and character of Céline's war trauma and to show how this trauma shapes *Voyage*. It will prove of interest to historians, to those involved or interested in memory studies, to all who are interested in the literature of the Great War and in literature in general and it will be of major interest, of course, to readers, students and scholars involved in or at the periphery of Céline studies and to all readers of *Voyage au bout de la nuit*.

---

[1] Philippe Sollers, untitled text, *L'Herne: L.F. Céline*, ed. by Dominique de Roux, Michel Beaujour, Michel Thélia (Paris: Cahiers de l'Herne, 1972), p.429. This publication is a reissue of numbers 3 (1963) and 5 (1965) of the Cahiers de l'Herne. It will be referred to throughout this work as *L'Herne*. The translation here and all translations used in this work are my own.

[2] Léon Trotsky, 'Céline et Poincaré', *L'Herne*, 434–435 (p.434).

[3] See Pascal Ifri, *Céline et Proust: Correspondances proustiennes dans l'œuvre de L.-F. Céline* (Birmingham, Alabama: Summa Publications, 1996), p.1. Ifri describes Céline as the 'Proust du pauvre' [Proust of the poor], p.243.

[4] See Raphaëlle Rérolle, 'Le Manuscrit du "*Voyage au bout de la nuit*" vendu pour 11 millions de francs', *Le Monde*, 17 May 2001, p.32. The total cost of the acquisition by the Bibliothèque nationale de France amounted to '12,184 millions de francs,' writes Rérolle, 'un record pour un manuscrit littéraire' [12,184 million francs, a record for a literary manuscript]. This sum represents approximately 2,000,000 Euro.

[5] For convenience sake the regular French spelling of Poelkapelle is the preferred choice in this work.

[6] The page reference is to Céline, *Romans*, I: *Voyage au bout de la nuit, Mort à Crédit* (1981).

[7] Philip Stephen Day, *Le Miroir allégorique de Louis-Ferdinand Céline* (Paris: Klincksieck, 1974), p.73.

[8] Paul Ricœur, *La Mémoire, l'Histoire, l'Oubli* (Paris: Seuil, 2000), p.1.

[9] A lecturer at one Paris University, in conversation with myself, remarked that her students believed implicitly in the truth of Céline's vision of war, even when told that his real life experience was greatly at odds with Bardamu's fictional adventure.

[10] Georges Bataille, 'Une signification humaine', in *Les Critiques de notre temps et Céline*, ed. by Jean-Pierre Dauphin (Paris: Garnier, 1976), pp.29–30 (p.29).

[11] Pol Vandromme, *Louis-Ferdinand Céline* (Paris: Éditions Universitaires, 1963), p.86.

[12] Maurice Rieuneau, *Guerre et révolution dans le roman français 1919–1939* (Paris: Klincksieck, 1974), p.313.

[13] Speaking in the course of separate interviews with myself in Paris.

[14] In Frédéric Grover, *Six entretiens avec André Malraux sur des écrivains de son temps* (Paris: Gallimard, 1978), pp.86–103 (p.86).

[15] Marie-Christine Bellosta, *Céline ou l'art de la contradiction: lecture de Voyage au bout de la nuit* (Paris: Presses Universitaires de France, 1990), p.127.

[16] See Jean Bastier, *Le Cuirassier blessé: Céline 1914–1916* (Tusson, Charente: Du Lérot, 1999), pp.337–343.

[17] H.-E. Kaminski, *Céline en chemise brune*, first published 1938 (Paris: Plasma, 1977), p.114.

[18] Milton Hindus, *The Crippled Giant* (Hanover, NH: University Press of New England, 1986), p.35.

[19] Pierre de Boisdeffre, 'Sur la postérité de Céline', *L'Herne*, 303–309 (p.308).

[20] Jean-Pierre Richard, *Nausée de Céline* ([Montpellier]: Fata Morgana, 1973), p.9.

[21] Julia Kristeva, *Pouvoirs de l'horreur: essai sur l'abjection* (Paris: Seuil, 1980), p.13.

[22] For an understanding of the Freudian view of war neuroses see Drs. S. Ferenzi, Karl Abraham, Ernst Simmel, Ernest Jones, *Psycho-analysis and the War Neuroses*, intro. by Sigmund Freud (London: The International Psycho-analytical Press, 1921).

[23] Albert Chesneau, *Essai de psychocritique de Louis-Ferdinand Céline* (Paris: Lettres Modernes, 1971), p.91.

[24] Jack Murray, *The Landscapes of Alienation: Ideological subversion in Kafka, Céline, and Onetti* (Stanford: Stanford University Press, 1991).

[25] Willy Szafran, *Louis-Ferdinand Céline: essai psychanalytique* (Brussels: Éditions de L'Université de Bruxelles, 1976), p.143.

[26] Szafran, pp.191–192.

[27] Szafran, pp.194–195.

[28] Isabelle Blondiaux, *Une écriture psychotique: Louis-Ferdinand Céline* (Paris: A.G.Nizet, 1985), p.14.

[29] See Isabelle Blondiaux, 'La représentation de la pathologie psychique de guerre dans *Voyage au bout de la nuit*', in *Roman 20-50: Revue d'étude du roman du xxe siècle*, dossier critique : *Voyage au bout de la nuit* de Louis-Ferdinand Céline, études réunies par Yves Baudelle, 17, June 1994, pp.105–115.

[30] Blondiaux, *Une écriture psychotique*, p.34.

[31] Jean-Paul Mugnier, *L'Enfance meurtrie de Louis-Ferdinand Céline* (Paris: L'Harmattan, 2000), p.108.

[32] See Cathy Caruth, 'Interview with Robert Jay Lifton', in *Trauma: Explorations in Memory*, ed. and intro. by Cathy Caruth (Baltimore: John Hopkins, 1995), pp.128–147 (p.142).

[33] Pierre Lainé, 'De la débâcle à l'insurrection contre le monde moderne: l'itinéraire de Louis-Ferdinand Céline' (unpublished doctoral thesis, Paris IV, 1984), p.72.

[34] Patrick McCarthy, *Céline* (London: Allen Lane, 1975), p.81.

[35] McCarthy, p.25.

[36] Philippe Alméras, *Céline: entre haines et passions* (Paris: Robert Laffont, 1994), p.45.

[37] Nicholas Hewitt, *The Life of Céline* (London: Blackwell, 1999), pp.25–29.

[38] Jay Winter, 'Céline and the Cultivation of Hatred', in *Enlightenment, Passion, Modernity: Historical Essays in European Thought and Culture*, intro. and ed. by Mark S. Micale and Robert L. Dietle (Stanford: Stanford University Press, 2000), pp.230–248 (p.234).

[39] Hewitt, p.xv.

[40] Philippe Lejeune, *L'Autobiographie en France* (Paris: Armand Colin, 1971), p.29.

[41] See Henri Godard's 'Les données de l'expérience', in *Romans*, I, 1179–1217.

[42] François Gibault, *Céline*, 3 vols (Paris: Mercure de France, 1985–1986), I: *1894-1932 Le Temps des espérances* (1986), 140.

[43] Godard, *Romans*, I, p.xxii.

[44] Henri Godard, *Poétique de Céline* (Paris: Gallimard, 1985), pp.307–308.

[45] Godard, *Poétique de Céline*, p.283.

[46] See Paul Fussell, *The Great War and Modern Memory* (Oxford: Oxford University Press, 1975), p.35.

[47] Robert Jay Lifton, *Death in Life: The Survivors of Hiroshima* (London: Pelican, 1971).

[48] Robert Jay Lifton, *Home from the War: Vietnam Veterans, neither Victims nor Executioners* (London: Wildwood House, 1974).

[49] Lifton, *Home from the War*, p.105.

[50] Lifton, *Home from the War*, p.116.

[51] Lifton, *Home from the War*, p.36.

[52] For a clinical description of post-traumatic stress disorder see *Diagnostic and Statistical Manual of Mental Disorders: DSM IV* (Washington: American Psychiatric Association, 1994), pp.428–429.

CHAPTER 1

4 MAI

From Heroism to Alienation

Introduction

To understand Céline's memory of the past, it is necessary to examine that past. This chapter initiates this through examination of the Great War experience in a manner which emphasises the dynamic correlation between it and *Voyage*. Modern, total and unprecedented, the Great War marked an ironic transition from heroic to debased consciousness. This transition was the product of changes in the nature of war itself. A new type of war reached its apotheosis in the Great War's greatest battle, the 1916 battle of Verdun. *Voyage* evokes Verdun by recalling the 'date fameuse ce 4 mai' [that famous date 4 May] (RI, 428), a date, as we shall see, inextricably linked with the meaning of Verdun. As such, '4 mai' is the key to *Voyage*. Indeed, it can be said that *Voyage* is written under the sign of '4 mai', under the sign of Verdun.

1.1 PRELUDE

Enlightenment and Revolution

The Great War took place against a background of three centuries of Enlightenment providing what John Cruickshank calls a 'secular faith of man in man'.[1] The central symbol of the Enlightenment was the rising sun of reason, triumphing over darkness at dawn.[2] The French revolutionary philosopher, Condorcet, saw history as ending in the dawn of Enlightenment.[3] The Enlightenment philosopher, Kant, saw peace as the natural outcome of the Enlightenment's supreme value: reason. Kant argued that the creation of republics, the growing power of commerce and money, and the establishment of a League of Nations, would lead to everlasting peace. The philosopher was to be the key figure in this new dispensation. Kant, echoing Plato's notion of the

Philosopher King, proposed a 'secret article for perpetual peace' whereby the views of philosophers on the waging of war would be heard in secret by the state.[4] It is, indeed, the philosopher-led French Revolution, the birthplace of the French Republic, which emerges as the Enlightenment's crowning achievement. The pantheisation of Voltaire in July 1791 demonstrates how the Enlightenment *philosophes*, Voltaire, Rousseau and Diderot chief among them, became part of Revolutionary hagiography.[5]

Rewriting history in the 1930s so that the Great War would not take place, the French writer, André Maurois, imagined away the French Revolution.[6] The French Revolution fundamentally changed the nature of war. The idea of putting the entire resources of the nation at the disposal of war emerged among the Parisian *sansculottes* in 1792. The new political entity was to be defended by an egalitarian army of patriotic citizens drafted into war. Already, in February 1792, 300,000 men had been conscripted. By summer, over 600,000 men had been mobilised. This Republican initiative culminated in August's *levée en masse* [mass conscription] which mobilised all Frenchmen between the ages of 18 and 25. All others were made subservient to the war effort. By September 1794 the Republic counted an army of well over 1,000,000 men, the largest Europe had ever seen.[7] The nation in its entirety, man, woman and child, was at war, and all its resources, cultural, economic and political were subservient to the war effort. The French Revolution had given birth to 'total war'. The defining characteristic of the Great War was in place.

The Memory of War

'In 1914 most people had no memory of war,' wrote historian George Mosse.[8] Britain's most recent wars had been the Boer War of 1899 and the Crimean war of 1854–55. These were localised wars and casualties, while significant, were few by comparison with the Great War. Less than eight thousand British troops died in action or of wounds in the Boer War.[9] France also fought in the Crimea. However, it was the disastrous Franco–Prussian war of 1870 which made the greater impact on French memory. The effect of this war on the French mind cannot be overstated. France was invaded, defeated, and Paris taken. The debacle resulted in the Paris Commune and its bloody repression.

The defeat of 1870 was the culmination of an eighty-year cycle of revolution and war in France. The French Revolution had changed the world. The Napoleonic Wars, an epic cycle of glorious victories and cataclysmic defeats, had lasted fifteen years before Napoleon was toppled from grace in 1815. Revolutions followed in 1830, 1848 and 1871. According to writers Ross Chambers and Richard Terdiman, French memory entered crisis around 1850 and destabilised the way in which French writers represented the world.[10] From 1793 on, French history can be seen as a series of blows to identity and to memory culminating in 1914. In 1914, failure to transcend the defeat of 1870 would clearly open another moral, intellectual and artistic wound on top of those already existing in French memory. *Voyage*, when it appears, will provide a most profound expression of this accumulation of wounds to French memory and identity.

Ernest Psichari

In France, in 1912, a survey of the attitudes of young people in higher education offered insights into the mind of the young intellectual elite prior to the outbreak of war.[11] The *Agathon* survey found that these youngsters were characterised by a taste for action and sport, by patriotic enthusiasm, a revival of fervent Catholicism, a return to traditional values of authority and discipline, disillusion with science, and a political realism which embraced the need for war. A writer who embodied this spirit was the soldier and novelist, Ernest Psichari. Captain Nangès, a character in Psichari's 1913 *L'Appel des armes* [*Call to Arms*], views war and soldiering as follows:

> Nangès ne pense qu'à la guerre et cette pensée harmonise tous ses actes. Avant tout, il veut faire des soldats de bataille, des soldats de sang et de victoire rompus à toutes les fatigues et toujours prêts au sacrifice.[12]

> [Nangès thinks only of war and that thought harmonises all his acts. Above all, he wants to make soldiers for battle, soldiers of blood and victory capable of withstanding all strains and at all times ready for sacrifice.]

Nangès aspires to war as a cleansing, sacrificial act, in which the ugliness of the world falls away. Declares Nangès, 'j'ai pensé à la guerre, à la guerre qui purifiera, à la guerre qui sera sainte, qui sera douce à nos cœurs malades' [I thought of the war, a war which would purify, a holy war, a war which would soothe our sick hearts].[13]

Psichari's deepest motive sprang from the desire and willingness to sacrifice his life. Invoking Calvary, he summoned the overt appeal of sacrifice for a young generation soon to leave for war:

> Un champ de bataille n'est-il pas l'image temporelle de la miraculeuse grandeur du sacrifice ? [...] Nous savons bien, nous autres, que notre mission sur la terre est de *racheter la France par le sang*.[14]

> [Is not the field of battle the temporal image of the miraculous grandeur of sacrifice? [...] We know well, we others, that our mission on this earth is to *reclaim France through blood*.]

For Psichari, boldness in the face of death is the supreme expression of soldierly valour. Léon Riegel comments:

> Il est choquant de constater que [Psichari] fait de la témérité une qualité militaire ; que rien ne lui semble plus digne d'admiration que le chef qui se dresse devant l'ennemi la poitrine nue, sabre au clair.[15]

> [It is shocking to observe that Pschari makes a military quality of temerity; that nothing appears more worthy of admiration to him than the chief who stands before the enemy, his breast exposed, his sword drawn.]

Psichari would die with this heroic vision. Two days before his death, he wrote, 'nous allons certainement à de grandes victoires et je me repens moins que jamais d'avoir désiré la guerre qui était nécessaire à l'honneur et à la grandeur de la France' [we are on our way to great victories and I regret less than ever having desired this war which was necessary for the honour and grandeur of France].[16] He was killed by a bullet to the head on 22 August 1914.[17] He was not alone. On this day, the old heroic vision of war met with the new mechanical reality of the Great War and 27,000 French soldiers died along with Psichari.[18]

In his writings, Psichari had exalted society's *trois ordres*: 'les militaires, les prêtres, les savants' [*three orders*: the military, the priests, the scientists].[19] They were 'le bras, le cœur et le cerveau de la nation' [the arm, the heart, and the brain of the nation]. *L'Appel des armes* was a paean to them and to the military in particular. But Psichari's work was more than just a celebration of military life; it was didactic and intended to inspire the young. Riegel comments: 'Plus que tout, l'auteur veut des garçons qui croient en leurs chefs, en leur armée, en la France, en eux-mêmes' [Above all, the author wants young men who believe in their leaders, in their army, in France, in themselves].[20] The *Agathon* survey findings suggest that Psichari found a ready audience for his appeal. We may wonder if a young Louis Destouches was part of it.

Enthusiasm

Raised on heroic stories of previous wars, and eager to embrace war as a testing ground of manhood, the expectation of those who left for war in August 1914 was seriously adrift of the reality they would face. The result was enthusiasm. As George Mosse has written, 'many of them saw the war as bringing both personal and national regeneration. [...] The war [...] was described as a festival.'[21]

Research by Jean-Jacques Becker indicates that, in France, enthusiasm for war was muted.[22] There is, however, ample evidence that enthusiasm existed. 'En 1914, les appelés ne s'étaient pas posé des questions ; tous partirent et, quand ils défilèrent, leurs visages disent dans quel esprit : ils rayonnaient' [In 1914, the soldiers called-up did not ask questions; all of them left for war and, as they marched away, their faces showed the spirit in which they were leaving: they were radiant], wrote historian Marc Ferro.[23] More direct testimony comes from historian Marc Bloch. 'Le tableau qu'offrit Paris pendant les premiers jours de la mobilisation demeure un des plus beaux souvenirs que m'ait laissé la guerre' [The tableau offered by Paris during the first days of the war remains one of the most beautiful memories the war has left me], he recalled in his 1914 memoirs.[24] 'Les armées nationales ont fait de la guerre un ferment démocratique' [The nation's armies made a democratic ferment of the war], he wrote, remembering the dawn of August 1914, while underlining the democratic nature of this 'war to end wars'.[25]

One witness remembered 2 August 1914 in the following manner, 'c'est inoubliable... c'était un spectacle extraordinaire... toute la population était dehors' [It's unforgettable... it was an extraordinary spectacle... everybody was outdoors...]. And another recalled requisitioned goods trains 'ornés de bouquets de fleurs' [decorated with bouquets of flowers] leaving with 'À Berlin' [To

Berlin] written on the sides.[26] It is in this atmosphere of enthusiasm for war that the young soldier, Louis Destouches, left for the front in August 1914.

The Hero

'The remarkable fact,' writes Terrence des Pres, 'is that while the business of living goes forward from day to day we reserve our reverence and highest praise for action which culminates in death.'[27] The meaning of heroism is inextricably intertwined with death. In the heat of war, standing face to face with death, the soldier became a man and more than a man. He saw himself transformed into a death-mastering hero. 'Parce qu'il est le seul à pouvoir regarder la mort dans les yeux, seul le soldat est un homme libre' [Because only he is able to look death in the eyes, the soldier alone is a free man], wrote one soldier in 1914.[28] German soldier Ernst Jünger caught this transcendent, heroic mood in his *Storm of Steel*:

> The war had entered into us like wine. We had set out in a rain of flowers to seek the death of heroes. The war was our dream of greatness, power, and glory. It was a man's work, a duel on fields whose flowers would be stained with blood. There is no lovelier death in the world.[29]

The heroic impulse in the writings of Jünger and others emerges from and tends towards mythology. In myth the hero is identified with the sun; like the sun the hero's trajectory rises and falls, and like the sun he enters and emerges from darkness, 'le héros semble toujours imaginé avec des traits empruntés au soleil. [...] Cette solarité se marque par certains traits physiques du héros, en particulier sa chevelure ou ses yeux' [the hero appears always to be imagined with features borrowed from the sun. [...] His sun-like nature is shown by certain of his physical features, in particular his hair or his eyes].[30]

'The mythological hero,' writes Joseph Campbell, 'is the champion not of things become but of things becoming; the dragon to be slain by him is precisely the monster of the status quo: Holdfast, the keeper of the past.'[31] 'The symbolism,' comments Robert Jay Lifton, 'is that of killing in the service of regeneration. [...] The Hero as Warrior [...] acts in the service of man's spiritual achievement.'[32] The redeeming power of the heroic myth, claims Lifton, comes from 'man's perpetual confrontation with death'.[33] 'Death,' he says, 'is not eliminated, or washed away, but rather transcended by a newly envisaged, enduring principle, by an activated sense of being part of eternal forms.' The hero, he suggests, confers immortality on his culture and on his race. The hero 'kills not to destroy life but to enlarge, perpetuate, and enhance life'. It is this dreamed-of, immortalising, power over death — death mastery — which intoxicates the would-be hero and his people.

The generation doomed to die in the Great War had no shortage of heroes. In England, Wellington and Nelson had long since entered the pantheon of heroes. In France, Napoleon formed a sacred trinity with Jeanne d'Arc and Charlemagne and had been celebrated in novels by Stendhal, Hugo and Balzac. Balzac represented the heroic invulnerability of Napoleon at the battle of Eylau, his head immune to the bullets that flew about him killing his men like flies.[34] The generation doomed to die in the Great War would enjoy no such immunity. The 1914 *mitrailleuse* [machine gun] would not afford them the legendary respect shown to Napoleon. In the first years of the war, wounds to the head would account for 60% of casualties, most of them fatal.[35]

1.2 THE GREAT WAR

Modern War

The Great War represents a dividing line in history. As historian Stéphane Audoin-Rouzeau writes:

> Avec la Grande Guerre est apparue une nouvelle forme d'affrontement armé, qui fait de 1914–1918 une rupture historique fondamentale, aux conséquences déterminantes pour toute l'histoire du XXe siècle.[36]

> [A new form of armed warfare appeared with the Great War, so that 1914–1918 represents a fundamental breach in history, whose consequences will shape all of twentieth-century history].

This breach in time he locates in one simple fact, 'le franchissement d'un seuil dans la violence de guerre' [the crossing of a threshold in the violence of war]. Historian, Pierre Miquel, spells out the war's 'pioneering' role:

> Les innovations 'scientifiques' de la civilisation industrielle ont permis d'envoyer sans crier gare de nombreuses victimes au fond de l'océan, dans les hôpitaux des gazés par milliers, dans les camps de concentration les premiers déportés et les populations 'déplacées'. De ce point de vue, la 'Grande Guerre' n'est pas du XIXe siècle, elle est bien du nôtre, de l'atroce XXe siècle.[37]

[The 'scientific' innovations of industrial civilisation allowed many victims to be sent without warning to the bottom of the ocean; consigned thousands of gassed to hospitals; created concentration camps for the first deportees and 'displaced' populations. From this point of view, the 'Great War' is not a nineteenth-century war; it belongs to our century, the atrocious twentieth century.]

The war confronted societies and individuals with the reality of a new technological era. The modern age had truly begun.

Unprecedented War

The Great War was not just modern, it was unprecedented. John Cruickshank indicates three factors that made it so: the mechanisation of war, the alienation of the individual soldier, and the scale of death.[38] With over ten million dead in total, death was undoubtedly the most impressive feature. 'It resulted from the application of new and increasingly sophisticated industrial techniques to warfare,' writes Cruickshank.[39] The use of the machine-gun, steel helmets, barbed wire, flame-thrower, the deployment of lethal gas and the introduction of the tank and aircraft were all characteristic of the Great War.[40] Soldiers were no match for this new material of war. 'On ne lutte pas avec des hommes contre du matériel' [You cannot use men to fight against machinery], declared the French General Pétain in January 1916.[41] However, it was this very struggle which was at the heart of the Great War experience.

Total War

There was something else which made the war unprecedented. The Great War was planetary. There had never been a World War. Writes Eric Hobsbawm:

> The First World War involved *all* major powers and indeed all European states except Spain, the Netherlands, the three Scandinavian countries and Switzerland. What is more, troops from the world overseas were, often for the first time, sent to fight and work outside their own regions.[42]

Russia was pitted against Germany on the Eastern Front while America and Canada fought with the Allies against Germany on the Western Front. Britain and France drew on their colonial reserves in India and Africa while the war itself was fought in Europe, Africa, the Middle East, and there were naval battles in the Atlantic. Within months of starting the war had become global and to some seemed about to embrace the entire Universe.[43]

It was not just manpower which was mobilised. Made in the image of the French Revolution's total war combatant nations mobilised all their resources, political, economic, cultural and human for the war effort. Women played a role, providing labour by replacing men away at the front, working as nurses or in munitions factories. The minds of children were enlisted.[44] The war, however, was not just total in its use of resources; it was also total in its logic and its aims. According to John Horne, 'the essence of the First World War [...] lay in a totalising logic, or potential', leading to a 'dizzying escalation' visible in the spiral of technology and casualties and in the tendency to describe the war in absolute terms.[45] As Eric Hobsbawm writes, 'this war, unlike earlier wars [...] was waged for unlimited ends.'[46] The reason for this, says Hobsbawm, was that, in the nineteenth century, politics and economics had fused and the economic model of competition and expansion now defined the war. In other words, the war was a product of capitalism.

Nothing serves to underline the profound relationship of *Voyage* to the Great War than the novel's representation of the war's totalising logic. As Bardamu walks along New York's Broadway, for example, the end of the street becomes 'le bout de toutes les rues du monde' [the end of all the streets in the world] (RI, 192). The war itself is described as 'une immense, universelle moquerie' [an immense, universal mockery] (RI, 12). This totalising logic is present from the first chapters of *Voyage*. The very first chapter intimates the totality of the novel to come, while in the first chapter of the war episode, the totalising tendency in Céline's language, what Michael Donley calls its 'force centrifuge' [centrifugal force] is eminently clear:[47]

> Serais-je donc le seul lâche sur la terre ? pensais-je. Et avec quel effroi !... Perdu parmi deux millions de fous héroïques et déchaînés et armés jusqu'aux cheveux ? Avec casques, sans casques, sans chevaux, sur motos, hurlants, en autos, sifflants, tirailleurs, comploteurs, volants, à genoux, creusant, se défilant, caracolant dans les sentiers, pétaradant, enfermés sur la terre, comme dans un cabanon, pour y tout détruire, Allemagne, France et Continents, tout ce qui respire, détruire [...] ! (RI, 13)

> [Was I the only coward on the face of the earth? I wondered. And with such panic!... Lost among two million heroic madmen armed to the teeth and set loose? With helmets, without helmets, without horses, on

> motorbikes, howling, in automobiles, whistling, sniping, plotting, flying, kneeling, digging, running for cover, skipping along paths, blasting, shut up on the earth as if it were a madhouse, ready to destroy everything in it, Germany, France and all of the continents, everything that breathes, destroy […]!]

This totalising logic is sustained throughout *Voyage* until the very last lines are reached:

> De loin, le remorqueur a sifflé; son appel a passé le pont, encore une arche, une autre, l'écluse, un autre pont, loin, plus loin... Il appelait vers lui toutes les péniches du fleuve toutes, et la ville entière, et le ciel et la campagne, et nous, tout qu'il emmenait, la Seine aussi, tout, qu'on n'en parle plus. (RI, 504–505)

> [In the distance, a tugboat whistled; its call passing a bridge, another arch, another, the lock, another bridge, distant, more distant... It was calling all of the barges on the river, all of them, all of the city, the sky and the countryside, and us, calling everything away with it, the Seine too, everything, let's talk no more about it.]

Thanks to Hobsbawm's analysis above, it is perfectly clear that Céline's language here not only reflects the totalising expansion of total war but that it also represents the spiralling economic model from which the war emerged. *Voyage*, in this sense, is a 'total novel'.

Union Sacrée

The war had another form of totalising logic, or rather, a unifying one. In Britain, France, and Germany, governments of national unity were formed at the outset of war. In France, Raymond Poincaré, mentioned bitterly in the very first lines of *Voyage*, called for a *Union Sacrée* [Sacred Union] on 4 August 1914. This was to unite hitherto opposed groups in French society and politics. The greatest beneficiary was the Catholic Church. The Great War saw the restoration of Psichari's 'heart' of the nation in France. Soldiers crowded churches, eager to receive communion before leaving for the front. Poincaré used the term 'foi patriotique' [patriotic faith] to describe how patriotism was informed by religious faith.[48] The Church made a significant contribution to the war effort. 25,000 priests were mobilised and seminaries were transformed into hospitals for the wounded. The Church was also prominent in the effort to finance the war.

'Donnez joyeusement votre or' [Give your gold joyously] it exhorted the populace. 'Dieu aime le don joyeux' [God loves the joyous gift].[49]

Gold

The war needed to be paid for. Initially it was considered the war would be a short one, as money would run out. The solution was credit. Credit paid for the Great War, credit sustained it. 'The modern system of credit is peculiarly adapted to facilitate the prolongation of war,' noted one commentator.[50] The war was good for credit. 'Success means credit,' Lloyd George told his war cabinet, underlining the fact that lenders would readily finance a war on its way to victory.[51] France's and Britain's war was financed mainly by loans from each other and from the United States. Death, in this new dispensation, was literally paid for on credit, a fact echoed in the title of Céline's second novel *Mort à credit* [*Death on Credit*].

Gold was the centre of the world economy in 1914. Britain and France were the leading players in the world of finance. Britain guaranteed international credit through the gold standard while France held vast reserves of gold. These reserves had grown immensely since the institution of the 'franc d'or' [gold franc] during the French Revolution.[52] The nineteenth century had been one of massive increases in the production of gold. Increasingly this gold had become the property of the banks. In 1889, 31% of the world's gold money supply was in official reserves, by 1910 almost 60% had been sucked in.[53] This trend increased with the coming of war.

Until 1914, notes could be converted to gold on demand and gold coinage still circulated. In August 1914, with the outbreak of war, convertibility was suspended. In France, banks hoarded gold while reserves there increased nominally by over 56% during the war itself.[54] To raise funds for the war governments demanded gold. In Britain 'give your money or give your blood' was the demand.[55] A French war loan poster carried the exhortation 'Versez votre or' [Pour out your gold] and 'l'or combat pour La Victoire' [Gold fights for Victory], while representing a French cockerel pecking at a subdued German soldier from a golden circle of coin bearing the Republican motto 'Liberté Égalité Fraternité' [Liberty, Equality, Fraternity].[56] Gold coinage was withdrawn from circulation and replaced by base metal.[57] Loss of gold and its replacement by base metal symbolised the Great War transition from an heroic to a debased world. It was indeed, quite literally, as gold coinage disappeared from circulation, the end of the world's Golden Age. At the end of the war, reserves of gold remained in the control of banks and governments.

Gold, as we shall see, is central to Céline's understanding and memory of the Great War. It will be the symbol of his loss of death mastery, and the guiding arrow of an accusation which characterises the war as a criminal financial manipulation whose goal is gold churned from the entrails of sacrificed heroes. The Great War was, for Céline, the theft of the world's gold.

1.3 DEATH, STASIS, REPETITION

The Trenches

After the opening flurry of the war, the soldiers stagnated, accompanied by rats and lice, in the trenches.[58] Frontline trenches were joined to support trenches by communication trenches and the soldiers lived in deep dugouts within the trenches themselves. The area between enemy trenches was known as 'no-man's-land'. War on the Western Front was defined by life in the trenches. 'Going to ground' was to be the emblem of the soldier's debasement. Hiding from death, the war succeeded in making 'cowards' of 'heroes'.

The inhabitant of the French trenches was 'le poilu', or infantry soldier, prototype of Bardamu, unwashed, unshaven. Living under the menace of imminent death 'le poilu' suffered greatly from 'le cafard', a deep and clinging depression, which the reader of *Voyage* will recognise in Bardamu. The following describes, in almost Célinian terms, 'le cafard':

> Le cafard est hideux, sans volupté : il a en lui quelque chose de mortel. Il est lourd à porter comme la pierre d'un sépulcre. Souvent, on rit, on s'agite, on est dans un moment d'oubli. Puis le cafard revient, tenace ... Et l'on songe à tous ceux qu'on aimait et qui sont loin... Et l'on songe à tous ceux qu'on aimait et qui sont morts... et quand même, on parle, et quand même, on rit [...]. Et dans le moment même qu'on plaisante, on a en soi, dans le cœur et dans les yeux, que le souvenir d'un mort qu'on aimait.[59]

> ['Le cafard' is hideous, without any pleasureable aspect: it carries something mortal with it. It is heavy as a tombstone to carry. Often, when one laughs, or moves about, one forgets for a moment. Then 'le cafard'

returns, tenacious... And one thinks of all those whom one loved and who are distant... And one thinks of all those whom one loved and who are dead... even so, one talks, one even laughs [...]. But at the very moment when one is joking, one carries inside, in one's heart and in one's eyes, the memory of a dead person one loved.]

'Intuition ou crainte de sa propre mort : telle est l'origine du "cafard"' [Intutition or fear of one's own death is at the root of 'le cafard'], writes Audoin-Rouzeau.[60] One remedy was laughter. According to one trench newspaper, one of the main causes of 'le cafard' was 'thinking about the Hundred Years War'.[61] The war seemed interminable.[62] It is clearly not for nothing that the Hundred Years War receives honourable mention in *Voyage* during Bardamu's anti-war outburst to Lola (RI, 65).

Soldiers had a vision of the war's end. Each had his own, but the commonest vision according to C.E. Montague 'was that of marching down a road to a wide, shining river'.[63] 'Once more,' he comments, 'the longing of a multitude struggling slowly across a venomous wilderness fixed itself on the first glimpse of a Jordan beyond.' Elias Canetti tells us, however, that the river is a crowd symbol, 'the symbol of a movement which is still under control'.[64] The vision of the river, therefore, suggests a desire for a return to order, to re-establish the crowd as it was before the war. Yet again, we may grasp the intimate relation of *Voyage* to the Great War when we recall that this vision of the 'war's end', the soldier wandering down to a river, is the one which closes Céline's novel (RI, 500).

It was some time before the military command came to terms with the trenches. The generals conducted the war as if it belonged to a previous century. They threw soldiers forwards in massed, hopeless attacks, against machine guns and heavy bombardment. The wastage of lives remains incredible. The first day of the Battle of the Somme was the worst day in British military history. Leaving the trenches, kicking footballs in front of them,[65] the British walked towards the German machine-gun emplacements. 20,000 were killed.[66] 40,000 were reported wounded or missing.

The impact of the trenches both on those within and beyond the war cannot be overstated. 'Trench warfare determined not only the perception of war of those who passed through it, but also how the war was understood by future generations,' says George Mosse.[67] Their impact on the literature of the war was profound and the long shadow of the trenches is also felt, as we shall see, throughout *Voyage*.

The Death of the Cavalry

Scale of death aside, the initial stage of the war, in which Céline fought, resembled a nineteenth-century war. 'In many respects,' writes Richard Holmes, 'the war's first campaign [...] had more in common with the Franco-Prussian War forty-four years before [...] than it did with First Ypres only six weeks later.'[68] This was the war of movement, Céline's war. Soldiers wore cloth caps, useless for protecting the head. The French were dressed in loud red pants providing an ample target for the enemy. Holmes, in his televised series *Western Front*, used an extract from *Voyage*, in translation, to make a point about the unsuitability of the French uniform at the outset of war:[69]

> J'avançais d'arbre en arbre, dans mon bruit de ferraille. Mon beau sabre à lui seul, pour le potin, valait un piano. Peut-être étais-je à plaindre, mais en tout cas sûrement, j'étais grotesque. À quoi pensait donc le général des Entrayes en m'expédiant ainsi dans ce silence, tout vêtu de cymbales ? Pas à moi bien assurément. (RI, 36–37)

> [I advanced from tree to tree, making as much noise as a hardware shop. My fine sword alone was as loud as a piano. Maybe I was to be pitied, but in any case, certainly, I was grotesque. What was General des Entrayes thinking of by sending me into that silence, all dressed in cymbals? He wasn't thinking of me, and that's for sure.]

The historian's choice of Céline in this instance underlines *Voyage*'s credibility as witness to war.

In 1914, the cavalry, to which Céline belonged, remained central to battle plans. 'It seems probable,' writes John Keegan, 'that there was more cavalry in the world in that year than in any before'.[70] The trench war, however, was a swan song for the cavalry. A static front destroyed cavalry mobility.[71] As Marc Ferro says, 'la cavalerie devint rapidement une arme anachronique [...] les tranchées n'avaient guère besoin de cavaliers' [the cavalry quickly became an anachronism [...] the trenches had no need of cavalrymen].[72] The dismounted cavalryman soon became commonplace as cavalry regiments joined the infantry. The cavalryman represented three thousand years of military tradition. High on his horse he had been the very embodiment of the vertical hero, erect, face to the enemy. The cavalryman's fall from grace was another decisive step downwards in the Great War transition from heroism to debasement. Céline, as we shall see in Chapter Three, would embody this fall from grace in his own person.

Death

Death was the war's most potent reality. The figures prove it. In the first five months of the war two thousand French soldiers a day were being killed. 'By the end of 1914 [...] 300,000 Frenchmen were dead [...].'[73] The heaviest casualties had been suffered by the youngest year-groups: 'between 27 per cent and 30 per cent of the conscript classes of 1912–1915'. That is, '30 per cent' or one third of Céline's generation.

At the end of the war the French counted 1,394,388 dead.[74] Added to these figures for deaths were three million wounded, of which one million were invalided and 60,000 amputees.[75] France had suffered the third greatest number of casualties, but as a percentage of population it was hardest hit. For France, the war was rightfully termed 'une véritable saignée' [a veritable blood letting].[76] The war had very nearly encompassed the death of a generation and threatened the death of France itself.

Behind the statistics, however, death had an even more appalling face. Death was everywhere, corpses, often horribly mutilated, lay unburied, often in an advanced stage of decomposition. The soldiers were literally saturated with death. In *Voyage*, Bardamu uses the verb 'habiller' [dressed in] to describe his own immersion in corpses (RI, 13). Contact with death produced a profound malaise. As Antoine Prost writes:

> Les combattants ont vécu des jours entiers, et souvent des semaines, dans une sorte de familiarité ou d'intimité avec la mort : menace ressentie de façon incessante et viscérale, émotion contre laquelle on ne s'aguerrit jamais totalement, image de tous côtés offerte à voir, et qui ébranle à la fois la raison, les sentiments et l'instinct le plus vital. Le 'vécu' des combattants [...] ce qu'ils ont éprouvé, ressenti et pensé, s'organise autour de cette présence constante.[77]

> [Combatants lived for days and sometimes weeks on end in a sort of familiarity or intimacy with death. It constituted a constant, visceral threat, an emotion from which one could never fully recover, an image visible on

all sides, unsettling reason, emotions, and the most vital of instincts. The lived reality of the combatants [...] what they experienced, felt and thought, was organised around this constant presence.]

This experience of death changed the soldier. His inability to communicate the 'incomprehensible' experience of death isolated him from those who had not shared it. Prost comments:

> Aucune autre expérience humaine ne se peut comparer à celle-là [...]. C'est dire qu'elle est impossible à comprendre [...]. Elle était radicalement incommunicable, intransmissible, sauf à ceux qui l'avaient partagée. [...] Au vrai, elle n'est pas seulement rupture entre combattants et non-combattants ; au sein de chaque existence individuelle, elle institue un avant et un après. L'expérience de la mort est une découverte inoubliable, qui laisse l'homme changé ; impossible ensuite de faire comme si cette rencontre n'avait pas eu lieu.[78]

> [No other human experience is comparable to the experience of death [...]. That is to say, it is impossible to understand [...]. It is radically incommunicable, intransmissable, except to those who have shared it. [...] In truth, it represents not only a breach between combatant and non-combatant; at the heart of each individual existence it creates a before and an after. The experience of death is an unforgettable discovery, which changes the soldier; it is impossible after this to carry on as if the encounter with death had not taken place.]

This rift in consciousness is central to the experience of the soldier and, of course, to Céline. It is central, as we shall see, to *Voyage*.

Audoin-Rouzeau in his study of trench newspapers has noted their fascination with death. This fascination was accompanied, he writes, by 'l'affaiblissement de certains interdits [...] transgressés avec une attirance morbide [...] prononcée' [the weakening of certain taboos [...] transgressed with a marked, morbid attraction].[79] He explains this transgression in the following manner:

> Cette omniprésence du thème de la mort et l'étrange complaisance dont ces journaux font preuve à son égard indiquent que leurs récits furent un point de passage par lequel la profonde angoisse des soldats s'est frayée un chemin. [...] Évoquer brutalement la mort et la souffrance, c'est tenter de se libérer un peu de la peur qu'elles inspirent. La dérision était l'ultime moyen d'y parvenir.[80]

> [The omnipresence of the theme of death and the strange complacency with which trench newspapers treated its subject indicates that accounts of death were a means of release for the profound anguish of the soldiers.

[...] The brutal evocation of death and suffering constitutes an attempt to free oneself of the fear they inspire. Derision was the ultimate means of achieving this.]

In almost all war accounts and narratives the horror of war is reduced to this one essential, the vision of death. As Samuel Hynes writes:

> Most young men [...] reach adulthood without ever having confronted death face-to-face [...]. Then they go to war, where death is the whole point, the truest truth, the realest reality; and they find that death, when you see it up close, isn't what you expected, that it's uglier, more grotesque, less human. And so astonishing death is a recurrent subject in the soldiers' tale.[81]

How true this is of Céline's soldier's tale in *Voyage*. It is the unforgettable experience of death which moulds Céline and which, as Antoine Prost would say, divides him past and future and makes it impossible for him to live as if nothing terrible had intervened. *Voyage* will ultimately testify to this experience when it embodies, in 1932, Céline's memory of death. When he writes his 'truest truth', his 'realest reality', 'la vérité de ce monde c'est la mort' [this world's truth is death] (RI, 200).

Verdun

If it is possible to sum up *Voyage* in one word, it is Verdun. By evoking the 'date fameuse ce 4 mai' [famous date of 4 May] (RI, 428) Céline places *Voyage* under the sign of one of the key moments in the Great War. Until now, Céline scholarship has not recognised the symbolic significance of this date. Marie-Christine Bellosta relates it to the French mutinies of 1917.[82] The date, however, is less a symbol of revolt than the expressed consciousness of the death of heroism in the new dispensation of modern war and of the threatened death of France itself as a result of its sacrifice; sacrifice of which Verdun and in particular '4 mai' provides the lasting image.

In 1916, the German Army Command decided it would provoke the death of the French Army. Attacking the sacred site of Verdun, 'le cœur de la France' [the heart of France],[83] the Germans drew the French into a year-long cycle of slaughter and attrition. The French decided to rotate their entire army through Verdun, creating what was known as the 'tourniquet',[84] or the 'noria'[85]: the wheel.

Verdun was of greater symbolic than strategic significance. The French were involved in an heroic fight to preserve an immortalising symbol, a sense of its own enduring truth as nation and race. Although ultimately victorious, the cost was terrible. More than any other battle, Verdun would represent the cycle of static, murderous re-enactment which characterised the Great War.

The battle of Verdun began on 21 February and ended on 18 December 1916. The battle was fought on what was 'un mouchoir de poche' [a handkerchief][86] compared to the total geography of the war. It was what Sun Tzu in his *Art of War* calls 'encircled' and 'desperate' ground, 'in which the army survives only if it fights with the courage of desperation'.[87] *Voyage* is made in the image of this enclosed, desperate ground: circumscribed, turning in circles, increasingly desperate, Bardamu's world is Verdun.

Verdun was an experience of total destruction 'genre Hiroshima' [Hiroshima style].[88] Over 302 days, 140,000 shells a day rained down on this patch of earth.[89] Here, Pierre Miquel writes, 'la guerre changeait de nature et d'échelle. Elle n'avait plus rien d'humain' [war changed in nature and in scale. It was no longer human].[90]

Verdun was an experience of exhaustion. The French won back the narrow land they had lost to the Germans but the cost was immense. By the end of 1916, over 61,000 French soldiers had been killed and 216,337 wounded. 101,151 were missing.[91] These latter were the disappeared, soldiers lost without trace in the slaughter and devastation; men lost to rituals of burial and grieving, like so many of the dead of the Great War; men lost to memory. Congeries of their bones, mixed with those of the enemy, would fill the Ossuary at Douaumont after the war.

On 4 May, *Voyage*'s 'famous date', the 6th company of the 60th infantry regiment counter-attacked at the hill known as *Mort-Homme* [Dead Man's Hill]. By the end of the attack 11 of 143 had survived.[92] The very resonance of the name *Mort-Homme* underlines the scale of the sacrifice and the irony of victory. The French sacrificed themselves here as elsewhere at Verdun. They sacrificed themselves conscious of the terrible price being paid. In an unheroic, inhuman war, however, the soldiers no longer rushed willingly to their own sacrifice. They had learned its futility and they now sacrificed themselves 'à contrecœur' [reluctantly]. A few days before he died at Verdun in November 1916, Captain Jean Vigier wrote:

> Je m'indigne de l'énorme inutilité de nos pertes. Tout disposé que je sois à me sacrifier, je voudrais du moins que le gaspillage des vies et des forces fût connu un peu plus chaque jour et que le péril qui nous menace, *Mourir de notre victoire*, soit entrevu et conjuré.[93]

> [I am angry at the immense futility of our losses. As ready as I am to sacrifice myself, I would at least want the wastage of lives and energies to be each day better-known, and the danger which threatens us, *To die by our victory*, to be foreseen and circumvented.]

Vigier's voice is the Great War voice of irony. His is heroism conscious of its own mortality, its own wastage; conscious too that the scale of sacrifice will drain victory of its virtue. The hero of Verdun dies with a sense of futility attending his own death, aware of the impossibility of transcendence, and oppressed by his consciousness that it is death itself which will prove the ultimate victor. This is the consciousness which imbues *Voyage* where every line resonates with the symbolism and meaning of *Mort-Homme* and the memory of '4 mai'.

Voyage's '4 mai' thus points the reader towards an experience which more than any other exemplifies the Great War death of heroism in a world of static, murderous re-enactment. Indeed, '4 mai' or *Mort-Homme* could provide alternative titles to Céline's novel. But '4 mai' tells us more about *Voyage*. The date declares that *Voyage* is indeed an act of memory (to recall a date is always to remember something about that date) and, because it is a date, it tells us something about the type of memory *Voyage* is. We are, indeed, in a dynamic of commemoration.

Commemorative rites, Paul Connerton tells us, employ a rhetoric of 'calendrical re-enactment'.[94] These are dates, such as Christmas Day, or 14 July, which provide a basis in memory for the constitution of a 'founding myth' or 'master narrative' about a society's origins and legitimacy. A society remembers its beginnings and celebrates its legitimacy annually on these dates. In *Voyage*, '4 mai', becomes the novel's calendrical focus and an emblem of 're-enactment'.

And *Voyage* itself becomes a 'master narrative' constituted around the 'founding myth' of Verdun. As memory act, *Voyage* is thus revealed as 'commemorative'. And what it commemorates is the inhuman sacrifice and futile re-enactments of *Verdun* and the Great War. *Voyage* is a rite of memory of a rite of sacrifice.

Céline's use of '4 mai' is ironic. By evoking '4 mai', Céline declares his own memory of Verdun and challenges his readers to remember. Indeed, he goes further. He accuses their loss of memory. Slipped almost unnoticed into the body of *Voyage*, the date addresses those who remember, and mocks and indicts those who do not. *Voyage* is revealed as an act of remembering opposed to forgetting.

That Verdun is, indeed, central to the meaning of *Voyage* is proven by indications given by Céline in the course of an interview in which he imagines the beginning and the end of a film version of his most famous work. The end of the film is not to be the same as that of the novel. Instead, Céline situates the end of the film close to an immense war cemetery 'aux environs de Verdun' [near Verdun].[95] No clearer signal is needed that Verdun, at the heart of France, and at the heart of the Great War, is also at the heart of *Voyage au bout de la nuit*.[96]

1.4 ALIENATION

Mechanisation

The war produced various forms of alienation which also underlie the psychological landscape of *Voyage*. The most immediate form of alienation came from the mechanisation of the war. According to Denis de Rougemont, Verdun marked a turning point in warfare. Baptised *Materialschlacht* (Battle of Material) by the Germans, Verdun, de Rougemont says, was where the mechanisation of total war destroyed the human dimension of warfare:

> Il ne s'agissait plus de violence du sang, mais de brutalité quantitative, de masses lancées les unes contres les autres non plus par des mouvements de délire passionnel, mais bien par des intelligences calculatrices d'ingénieurs. Désormais, l'homme n'est plus que le servant du matériel.[97]

> [War was no longer a question of the violence of blood, but rather, of quantitative brutality, of masses thrown each against the other, not through the delirium of passion, but rather through the calculating intelligence of engineers. From this point on, man is nothing more than the servant of machinery.]

De Rougemont saw relations between the sexes as providing a model for battle and warfare over the centuries. As long as war held on to some vestige of these relations it could remain humane. At Verdun, however, war finally outstripped the power of love. At Verdun, de Rougemont says, love itself would die:

> La technique de la mort à grande distance ne trouve son équilibre dans nulle éthique imaginable de l'amour. C'est que la guerre échappe à l'homme et à l'instinct; elle se retourne contre la passion même dont elle est née.[98]

> [The technique of long-distance death has no equivalent in any imaginable ethic of love. War has escaped man and his instincts; and it is turned against the very passion which gave birth to it.]

Of the inter-war period, he says, 'les relations individuelles des sexes ont cessé d'être le lieu par excellence où se réalise la passion' [individual relations between the sexes ceased to be the site *par excellence* where passion fulfilled itself].[99] The war, he says, led to 'generalised impotence' and 'chronic masturbation and homosexuality' in soldiers after the war.[100] The twentieth-century breakdown of marriage and the family represent, for him, the logical outcome of Verdun. Suffice it to say, at this stage, that the failure of love is a prominent theme in *Voyage* (see 7.5 *The Death of Compassion*).

Landscape

The very landscape of war was alienating. On the Western Front it was characterised by mud. 'The whole of one's world, at least of one's visible and palpable world, is mud in various stages of solidity or stickiness,' wrote Vera Brittain's fiancé, Roland.[101] Bombardment tortured landscape. Samuel Hynes terms landscape subjected to continual bombardment '*anti*-landscape, an entirely strange terrain with nothing natural left in it. It's the antithesis of the comprehensible natural world,' he says.[102] George Mosse says of it, 'the surrounding landscape was more suggestive of the moon than the earth, as heavy shelling destroyed not only men but nature.'[103] Reflected in *Voyage*, it will become what Leslie Davis calls Bardamu's 'anti-monde'.[104]

The landscape of war had its own smell too, one of rotting bodies and excrement. At Verdun, soldiers drank from pools of water in which corpses lay.[105]

Soldiers recovering dead comrades were guided by the stench of death. 'L'odeur nous guidait, la terrible odeur' [the smell guided us, that terrible smell], wrote one soldier of his nocturnal search for fallen comrades.[106] The landscape of war embodied death; it expressed it. In doing so, it alienated the soldier from nature itself.

Absurdity

In the world of broken heroism, of incomprehensible, incommunicable death, in a landscape the antithesis of natural landscape, lying under constant bombardment, a sense of absurdity took hold of the soldier. Ernst Jünger's *Storm of Steel* described what it feels like to be pinned down by a bombardment:

> You cower in a heap alone in a hole and feel yourself the victim of a pitiless thirst for destruction. With horror you feel that all your intelligence, your capacities, your bodily and spiritual characteristics, have become utterly meaningless and absurd. While you think it, the lump of metal that will crush you to a shapeless nothing may have started on its course. Your discomfort is concentrated in your ear, that tries to distinguish amid the uproar the swirl of your own death rushing near.[107]

Absurdity here has usurped transcendence. Sacrifice is no longer glorious. It is meaningless. The soldier too, in Jünger's account, has become, body and soul, meaningless and absurd. *Voyage* is imbued with this sense of absurdity, and Jünger's description indicates that Céline's experience of prolonged bombardment in the war has more than a little to do with it (see 3.3 *The Encounter with Death*).

Shell-shock

'There are strange hells within the minds war made,' wrote the poet Ivor Gurney.[108] Céline's was one such mind. It is our intention to show that Céline was traumatised by war. The following will, therefore, provide a backdrop to our later discussion of Céline's trauma.

The Battle of the Somme in 1916 brought home the reality of soldiers' mental vulnerability in modern, mechanised war.[109] The ceaseless attrition of Verdun, also in 1916, proved another site of soldier despair and collapse.[110] Soldiers suffering from shell-shock were given little sympathy. In September 1914, one month after the start of the war, the first British shell-shock victims began to arrive home to a less than enthusiastic reception:

> Many of them were regarded as insane [...]. It was believed [...] that their
> brains had been damaged by blast-concussion from exploding shells, as it
> was not yet realised that war psychosis was primarily a psychological
> disorder.[111]

Towards the end of 1914, long after Céline had been evacuated, a *Lancet* editorial made the link between battle stress and breakdown explicit.[112] Among the more prominent effects of shell-shock were forms of paralysis and violent tremors and the loss of sight and hearing.[113] In addition, shell-shock undermined the self. It was noted early on that the sufferer 'is cut off from his normal self and the associations that go to make up that self'.[114] The return of experience was also a prominent feature. 'Insomnia troubles him and such sleep as he gets is full of visions; past experiences on the battlefield are recalled vividly.'[115]

In 1915, a Dr Turner was asked by the British War Office to write a report on the increasing numbers of psychiatric casualties as a result of the war. He published some of his findings in an article in the *British Medical Journal*. Those affected were mostly young. Most of them were 22 or 23 years of age. 'Their condition had been caused [...] either by their proximity to shell explosions, or by nervous exhaustion due to physical strain, sleeplessness and other stressful circumstances.'[116]

Ahead of the United States entry into the war, an American physician, John T. MacCurdy, examined and described the condition of shell-shocked soldiers. The soldiers he examined showed:

> 'signs of fatigue' [...]. [They] looked as though they were under a great
> strain [...]. Their expressions denoted mental anguish [...]. A frequent
> complication was depression, taking the form of a feeling of hopelessness
> and shame for their own incompetence and cowardice. Sometimes this
> depression concluded with obsessive thoughts about the horrors they had
> seen on the battlefield and the horrors of war in general.[117]

French records of shell-shock victims are incomplete but, as in Britain, attitudes were highly sceptical. Soldiers were often seen as simply being hysterical, or malingering.[118] A report commissioned early in the war by the French government concluded that 'the amount of insanity caused by the war would be inconsiderable, and that cases of mental disorder among men worn out by the fatigue of a campaign were extremely rare.'[119] The authors did, however, acknowledge incidences of delirium among the troops, which they put down to over-indulgence in alcohol.

According to French military psychiatrist, Louis Crocq, many soldiers were not properly diagnosed as suffering from shock, simply because at the time the means were inadequate.[120] Soldiers were often returned to battle before they had been properly treated.[121] What was most missing from the WWI understanding of a traumatic response to warfare, Crocq says, was the awareness that war could go on in the soldier's mind when the war itself had ended. It was becoming apparent, however, that the horror of war haunted the soldier even at a remove from it. Siegfried Sassoon described the atmosphere at Craiglockhart hospital where he was recovering from his 'break down'. Sassoon might well be describing the atmosphere of *Voyage*:

> One became conscious that the place was full of men whose slumbers were morbid and terrifying — men muttering uneasily or suddenly crying out in their sleep. Around me was that underworld of dreams haunted by submerged memories of warfare and its intolerable shocks and self-lacerating failures to achieve the impossible.[122]

Even a brief and apparently well-tolerated experience of bombardment could have a delayed, shattering impact:

> Shell-shock. How many a brief bombardment had its long-delayed after-effects in the minds of these survivors, many of whom had looked at their companions and laughed while inferno did its best to destroy them. Not then was their evil hour, but now; now, in the sweating suffocation of nightmare, in paralysis of limbs, in the stammering of dislocated speech.[123]

We must remember this when we think of Céline. We might, indeed, ask ourselves how much of the nightmare and the broken speech of war's ongoing trauma found its way into *Voyage* and in what ways.

The condition of the shell-shocked soldier sums up the alienating effect of modern war and the way in which the war continued in the soldier's mind and nightmares provides an appropriate metaphor for the characteristic stasis and repetition of the Great War itself. The war, moreover, was driving men mad and if the illness in any way resembled its cause then it was just a short step in logic to see the war itself as mad.

Censorship

Censorship contributed to the soldiers' alienation. During the Great War, 'les consignes les plus sévères touchaient les informations militaires' [information on military matters was under the most severe control].[124] The rationale for censorship was clear, ensuring that information was kept safe from the enemy. Censorship was used, however, to create a favourable climate for the war itself. 'Il faut que la lecture du journal ne soit plus une source de pessimisme et découragement, mais de persévérance et d'enthousiasme' [Reading a newspaper should not be a source of pessimism or discouragement, but of perseverance and enthusiasm], demanded the French General Pétain.[125] Censorship helped prolong the war. One of the most important roles of censorship was to prevent the spread of pacifist ideas.[126]

Censorship did not just withhold or distort the truth; it made the truth itself appear unreliable. According to Marc Bloch:

> Le rôle de la censure a été considérable. Non seulement pendant toutes les années de guerre elle a bâillonné et paralysé la presse, mais encore son intervention, soupçonnée toujours alors qu'elle ne se produisait point, n'a cessé de rendre incroyables aux yeux du public jusqu'aux renseignements véridiques qu'elle laissait filtrer.[127]

> [Censorship played a considerable role. Not only did it, during the war years, gag and paralyse the press, but in addition, its application, suspected even where not present, made the most reliable information allowed to filter through appear incredible to the eyes of the public.]

France was the only combatant country in which it was forbidden to publish lists of casualties.[128] Jean Vigier's desperation at 'l'énorme inutilité de nos pertes' [the immense futility of our losses] during the battle of Verdun is vividly coloured by his awareness that censorship is preventing the truth being known (see 1.3 *Verdun*). The implication is that without censorship the heroes who fought the war could not have been sacrificed in the way that they were by the French Army Command. It was only in 1920 that the extent of France's human losses was acknowledged publicly and even then the figures proved unreliable.[129]

Truth had become a casualty of war. Belief in the written word collapsed and the war, says Marc Bloch, favoured 'un renouveau prodigieux de la tradition orale' [a prodigious renewal of the oral tradition].[130] This 'renewal' cannot fail to colour our reading of Céline's choice of an oral style with which to provide his witness to war in *Voyage*.

Cowardice, Desertion and Mutiny

Military executions provide a trenchant metaphor of alienation in a war that was comprehensively alienating. During the Great War the slightest breach of discipline was punishable by death. WWI combatant, Maurice Maréchal, in a letter home early in September 1914, reported seeing the body of a dead soldier behind a farm wall. He had been shot because he had stolen a chicken.[131] Another soldier described an execution in which he participated:

> Je verrai toujours devant mes yeux cet homme à genoux, les yeux bandés, les mains attachées au poteau ; un feu de salves, et c'en est fini de l'existence. Pourtant, ce n'est pas un crime qu'il avait commis [...]. On a voulu faire un exemple et cela est tombé sur lui.[132]

> [I will always see before my eyes that man kneeling, his eyes blindfolded, his hands tied to the post; a salvo of shots and his existence is over and done with. He had, however, committed no crime [...]. They wanted someone as an example and they picked on him.]

Such men, executed by their own army, were buried without honours, while their comrades often continued to visit and lay flowers on their graves, a practice the authorities tried to outlaw.[133] The families of victims of military executions suffered ostracism. Their wives could not find employers.[134] The gravest accusation that could be levelled against a soldier was cowardice. 'Il n'y a qu'un mot dans notre langue pour caractériser le pacifisme à outrance, et ce mot c'est: LÂCHETÉ !' [There is only one word in our language to characterise pacifism taken to extremes, and that word is: COWARDICE!], read one pre-war patriotic text.[135] The coward was the antithesis of the hero and any display of cowardice created a rift in the values that sustained the heroic ideal. Men had a deep fear of cowardice. 'N'importe quel homme se battra pour prouver qu'il n'est pas un lâche' [Any man will fight to prove he is not a coward], wrote the French philosopher and historian, Alain.[136] As a commanding officer, Marc Bloch made a point of displaying his revulsion at any show of fear in his men.[137] It is certain that fear of being considered a coward was a motivation in maintaining men at war, despite the imposed cowardice of the conditions of war itself. A would-be coward had little choice; refusal to fight or fear in the face of the enemy was punishable by death.

Most of the recorded 600 military executions by the French during the war took place between September 1914 and June 1915. Most were for the crime of desertion.[138] The figure, which does not include unrecorded summary executions, also at their high point during this period, indicates that military executions in the French army were at their high point during the period when Céline was fighting. Marie-Christine Bellosta is wrong, therefore, when she argues that Céline's preoccupation with military executions in *Voyage* derives from the repression of the 1917 mutinies.[139] It is part of his experience.[140]

The lesson of the 1917 mutiny would not have been lost, however, on Céline. April 1917 witnessed the Chemin des Dames debacle. After a series of disastrous offensives, led by General Nivelle, the French soldiers refused orders to go to the front.[141] Their protest was not against sacrifice but against the manner of the sacrifice. There would be no second Verdun. 'Nous avons manifesté pour attirer l'attention du gouvernement, lui faire comprendre que nous étions des hommes, non des bêtes que l'on mène à l'abattoir' [We protested to draw the attention of the government, to make it understand that we were men, not beasts to be led to the slaughterhouse], wrote J.-N. Jeanneney.[142] An estimated 40,000 soldiers were involved in the mutiny.[143] According to Marc Ferro, five hundred and fifty four soldiers were condemned to death as a result of the mutiny; forty nine were executed.[144]

Endurance

It did not take long for the initial enthusiasm of the soldiers to fade in war. Heroism was no longer viable; sacrifice no longer immortalising. The soldiers' letters testify to their changed mood. The following is a letter to his parents from a soldier in May 1916:

> Il est inutile que vous cherchiez à me réconforter avec des histoires de patriotisme, d'héroïsme ou choses semblables. Pauvres parents ! Vous cherchez à me remettre en tête mes illusions d'autrefois. Mais j'ai pressenti, j'ai vu et j'ai compris. Ici-bas, tout n'est que mensonge, et les sentiments les plus élevés, regardés minutieusement, nous apparaissent bas et vulgaires. A présent je me fiche de tout, je récrimine, je tempête, mais

dans le fond cela m'est complètement égal. Pour moi, la vie est un voyage! Qu'importe le but, près ou loin, pourvu que les péripéties en soient les plus agréables possible. [...]. Fernand.[145]

[It is pointless to try to comfort me with stories of patriotism, heroism, or suchlike. Poor parents! You wish to reawaken in my mind the illusions of the past. But I've felt, I've seen, and I've understood. Here, all is lies, and the most elevated sentiments, examined closely, seem low and vulgar to us. At present, I don't give a damn about anything, I recriminate, I rage, but deep down nothing at all matters to me. As far as I am concerned, life is a journey! What does the destination matter, whether near or far, as long as the journey itself should be as pleasant as possible. [...]. Fernand.]

To anyone familiar with *Voyage* the resonance of this letter is astonishing. Even the name signs off like a ghostly message from Céline himself (Fernand was his father's name). This letter alone, reminiscent too of Céline's 1916 letters from Africa (see 4.1 *Africa*), and employing *Voyage*'s central metaphor of the journey, shows again how deeply embedded Céline's novel is in the experience, and the *mentality*, of the Great War.

How, however, did this new spirit of scepticism and irony endure in appalling conditions of carnage? For Gérard Vincent it is '[la] ferveur patriotique [...] qui permit à la France de vaincre' [patriotic fervour [...] which allowed France to achieve victory].[146] But where does this leave Fernand's letter above with its clear anti-patriotism? Clearly not all French soldiers were sufficiently motivated by patriotism. One of the most powerful motivations, as we have seen, was the fear of being considered a coward. Another factor was hostility towards the enemy.[147] The Germans were clearly perceived as an enemy to be beaten. The alternative was intolerable. And could it be that simply losing face was another lethal factor? The close link to the rear, based on familial bonds, provided another strengthening force, says Audoin-Rouzeau. 'La population civile était en accusation,' he writes, 'mais c'était elle qui importait le plus' [the civilian population stood accused, but it mattered more than anything].[148]

For Gérard Vincent, a sense of solidarity stronger than social divisions is also a factor in soldiers' endurance.[149] But how strong was the spirit of comradeship? Writes Audoin-Rouzeau, 'les articles qui attestent une véritable fraternité sont en assez petit nombre, guère plus nombreux en tout cas que ceux qui, à l'inverse, témoignent de l'isolement et de l'égoïsme de chacun' [few articles in the trench newspapers bear witness to real comradeship; they are hardly more numerous than those which bear witness, on the contrary, to the isolation and egoism of each individual soldier].[150] Pity crumbles before the death of comrades. Writes one soldier, 'on en a tant vu que les sens s'émoussent, que le cœur se blase, heureusement !' [we have seen so much death that our senses are dulled and our heart has become indifferent, fortunately!].[151] 'La fraternité des tranchées fut en grande partie illusoire' [comradeship in the trenches was for the most part illusory], concludes Audoin-Rouzeau, arguing that the much-vaunted spirit of comradeship was a myth emanating from the middle-classes, reinforced by the newspapers, and taking full flight after the end of the war.[152] *Voyage*, as we shall see, will enact a determined rebuttal of this myth (see 7.4 *The Death of Camaraderie*).

Lyn MacDonald questions the general perception of the soldier of the Great War struggling with the horror of it. Having interviewed hundreds of veterans over the years she says she never once heard the word 'horror' mentioned. She suggests the soldiers enjoyed the war.[153] George Mosse felt that a low rate of desertions in the war was due to the 'brutalising' effect of 'killing and being killed'.[154] 'Men fought because they did not mind fighting [...],' writes Niall Ferguson. 'Killing aroused little revulsion [...]. Freud was close to the mark when he suggested that a kind of "death instinct" was at work'.[155] But surely such truths only serve to condemn the instincts of men? And to confirm Céline's judgement of his fellow soldiers, 'devenus incapables soudain d'autre chose [...] que de tuer et d'être étripés sans savoir pourquoi' [suddenly incapable of doing anything other than killing and having their guts spilled out, without knowing why] (RI, 34). And to further confirm his accusation, 'c'est à cause de ça que les guerres peuvent durer' [that's why wars can go on] (RI, 36). The heady drop from Enlightenment optimism, with its faith in reason and human progress, would seem to have here reached its nadir. The Great War revealed perhaps more of the mind and heart of man than it is good to see.

Conclusion

What began in heroic enthusiasm ended in alienation and death. In the Great War, heroism died and a worldview inherited from the Enlightenment was scuttled and lay dead in the water. At the heart of the war was Verdun and it is at the heart of *Voyage*. The modern world arrived with the Great War and with it the modern mind. As Will Hutton wrote on the occasion of the 80th Armistice commemoration, 'the degree of trauma associated with the Great War marked a departure not merely for the creation of new social forces but for the twentieth-century mind.'[156] This was mind born from unprecedented violence. This is the mind which will remember in Céline's *Voyage*.

This overview of the war experience, which will reverberate throughout our examination of *Voyage*, is only one half of the context for this work. The other half is how the war was remembered in the years that followed it. The memory of the Great War is the subject of the next chapter.

---

[1] John Cruickshank, *Variations on Catastrophe: some French responses to the Great War* (Oxford: Oxford University Press, 1982), p.34.

[2] For an account of the light imagery of the Enlightenment see the first pages of Ulrich Im Hof, *The Enlightenment*, trans. by William E.Yuill (Oxford: Blackwell, 1994).

[3] Marquis de Condorcet, *Esquisse d'un tableau historique des progrès de l'esprit humain* (Paris: Librairie Philosophique Vrin, 1970).

[4] Immanuel Kant, 'Toward perpetual peace', in *Practical philosophy*, trans. and ed. by Mary J.Gregor, The Cambridge edition of the works of Immanuel Kant (Cambridge, U.S.: Cambridge University Press, 1996), pp.311–351. For a view of Kant's role in the invention of peace 'as more than just a pious aspiration', see Michael Howard, *The Invention of Peace* (London: Profile Books, 2000), pp.29–31.

[5] See Roger Chartier, *Les Origines culturelles de la révolution française* (Paris: Seuil, 1990), p.111.

[6] See Niall Ferguson, *The Pity of War* (London: Penguin, 1998), p.457.

[7] See William Doyle, *The Oxford History of the French Revolution* (Oxford: Oxford University Press, 1989), pp.204–205.

[8] George Mosse, 'Two World Wars and the Myth of the War Experience', *Journal of Contemporary History*, 21 (1986), 491–513 (p. 494).

[9] These figures are taken from the *South African War Virtual Library* website at http://www.sawvl.com/stats.html, retrieved in September 2000.

[10] See Richard Terdiman, *Present Past: Modernity and the Memory Crisis* (Ithaca: Cornell University Press, 1993). Also, Ross Chambers, *The Writing of Melancholy: Modes of Opposition in Early French Modernism*, trans. by Mary Seidman Trouille (Chicago: Chicago University Press, 1993).

[11] See Cruickshank, pp.18–24, for an extensive analysis of the *Agathon* survey conducted by Henri Massis and Alfred de Tarde.

[12] Cited in Léon Riegel, *Guerre et Littérature* (Paris: Klincksieck, 1978), p.58.

[13] Cited in Riegel, p.54.

[14] Ernest Psichari, cited in *Anthologie des écrivains morts à la guerre 1914–1918*, published by l'Association des écrivains combattants, preface by José Germain, 5 vols (Amiens: Edgar Malfère, 1924–1926), II (1924), 598.

[15] Riegel, p.57.

[16] Cited in Cruickshank, p.12.

[17] For various accounts of Psichari's death on 22 August, see *Anthologie des écrivains morts à la guerre*, II, 599–600.

[18] This figure is taken from Jean-Jacques Becker and Serge Bernstein's *Victoire et frustrations 1914–1918* (Paris: Seuil, 1990), p.34.

[19] See Riegel, p.61.

[20] Riegel, p.57.

[21] Mosse, pp.492–493.

[22] See Jean-Jacques Becker, *1914 Comment les Français sont entrés dans la guerre* (Paris: Fondation Nationale des Sciences Politiques, 1977), pp.515–558.

[23] Marc Ferro, *La Grande Guerre* (Paris: Gallimard, 1969), p.12.

[24] Marc Bloch, *Souvenirs de guerre 1914–1915* (Paris: Armand Colin, 1969), p.9.

[25] Bloch, p.10.

[26] Both these accounts are taken from Hubert Knapp's televised documentary, *Ils ont tenu 1914–1918*, TF1, 1978.

[27] Terrence des Pres, *The Survivor* (New York: Oxford University Press, 1976), p.5.

[28] Letter of Richard Hoffman, soldier in the German army, in *Paroles de Poilus: Lettres et carnets du front 1914–1918*, ed. by Jean-Pierre Guéno and Yves Laplume (Paris: Librio, 1998), p.21.

[29] Ernst Jünger, *The Storm of Steel*, trans. by Basil Creighton (New York: Howard Fertig, 1975), p.1.

[30] Philippe Sellier, *Le Mythe du héros ou le désir d'être dieu* (Paris: Bordas, 1970), pp.18–19.

[31] Joseph Campbell, *The Hero with a Thousand Faces* (London: Abacus Books, 1975), p.337.

[32] Robert Jay Lifton, *Home from the War*, p.26.

[33] Lifton, p.27.

[34] Honoré de Balzac, *Le Médecin de campagne*, cited in Sellier, p.131.

[35] Pierre Miquel, speaking on *Bouillon de Culture*, Antenne 2, presented by Bernard Pivot, broadcast internationally on TV5 on 11 November 2000.

[36] Stéphane Audoin-Rouzeau, 'L'Épreuve du feu', *L'Histoire*, 225 (October 1998), 34–43 (p.34).

[37] Pierre Miquel, *La Grande Guerre* (Paris: Arthème Fayard, 1983), p.7.

[38] Cruickshank, pp.28–34.

[39] See Cruickshank, p.31.

[40] See Paul Fussell, ed., *The Bloody Game: An Anthology of Modern Warfare* (London: Scribners, 1991), p.29.

[41] Cited in André Ducasse, Jacques Meyer, Gabriel Perreux, *Vie et mort des Français 1914–1918* (Paris: Hachette, 1962), p.137.

[42] Eric Hobsbawm, *The Age of Extremes: The Short Twentieth Century 1914–1991* (London: Michael Joseph, 1994), p.23.

[43] View of Alfred Baudrillart, cited in Hew Strachan, *The First World War* (Oxford: Oxford University Press, 2001), p.1114.

[44] See Stéphane Audoin-Rouzeau, 'Quand les enfants font la guerre', *L'Histoire*, 169 (September 1993), 6–12.

[45] John Horne, 'Introduction: mobilising for "total war", 1914–1918', in *State, society and mobilisation in Europe during the First World War*, ed. by John Horne (Cambridge: Cambridge University Press, 1997), pp.1–17 (pp.3–4).

[46] Hobsbawm, p.29.

[47] Michael Donley, 'L'identification cosmique', *L'Herne*, 327–334 (p.328).

[48] Jean-Jacques Becker, with the collaboration of Annette Becker, *La France en guerre 1914–1918: la grande mutation* (Paris: Complexe, 1988), p.44.

[49] Cited in Becker, *La France en guerre*, p. 47.

[50] American diplomat, Lewis Einstein, cited in Ferguson, p.319.

[51] Strachan, p.818.

[52] See Pierre Vilar, *A History of Gold and Money 1450–1920*, trans. from the Spanish by Judith White (London: NLB, 1976), pp.307–308. The gold franc was established in 1793 and issued in April 1803. The French example was copied all over Europe during the following century.

[53] See Strachan, p.819.

[54] See Strachan, p.829.

[55] See Ferguson, p.325.

[56] Poster reproduced in Stéphane Audoin-Rouzeau and Annette Becker, *La Grande Guerre 1914– 1918* (Paris: Gallimard, 1998), p.50.

[57] R.A.G. Carson says of France, 'after the First World War, gold coinage ceased for all practical purposes and the smaller franc values were replaced by coinage in aluminium bronze.' See Carson, *Coins: Ancient, Mediaeval and Modern* (London: Hutchinson, 1962), p.294.

[58] Paul Fussell's *The Great War and Modern Memory* provides a comprehensive account of the trenches in a chapter called *The Troglodyte World*. For some account of rats and lice see pp.48–49.

[59] Cited in Stéphane Audoin-Rouzeau, *à travers leurs journaux: 14–18 Les combattants des tranchées* (Paris: Armand Colin, 1986), p.59.

[60] Audoin-Rouzeau, *Les Combattants des tranchées*, p.58.

[61] Trench newspaper *Le Canard des Boyaux*, cited in *France Soir* newspaper, 11 November 1999, p.8.

[62] For an account of the crystallisation of this feeling of a never-ending war see Fussell, *Great War and Modern Memory*, pp.71–74.

[63] C.E. Montague, *Disenchantment* (London: MacGibbon & Kee, 1968), p.130.

[64] Elias Canetti, *Crowds and Power*, trans. by Carol Stewart (London: Penguin, 1981), p.97.

[65] See Fussell, *The Great War and Modern Memory*, p.27.

[66] The figure is from Martin Gilbert, *The First World War* (London: Weidenfeld & Nicolson, 1994), p.541.

[67] George Mosse, *Fallen Soldiers: Reshaping the Memory of the World Wars* (Oxford: Oxford University Press, 1990), p.4.

[68] Richard Holmes, 'The Last Hurrah: Cavalry on the Western Front, August–September 1914', in *Facing Armaggedon*, ed. by Hugh Cecil and Peter Liddel (London: Leo Cooper, 1996), pp.278– 294 (p.280).

[69] Richard Holmes, *Western Front*, dir. by Albert Herman, BBC Television, 1999.

[70] John Keegan, *Soldiers: A History of Men in Battle* (London: Hamish Hamilton, 1985), p.94.

[71] See Keegan, p.94.

[72] Marc Ferro, p.168.

[73] John Keegan, *The First World War* (London: Hutchinson, 1998), p.6.

[74] Olivier Faron, 'Une catastrophe démographique', *L'Histoire*, 225, 46–48 (p.47).

[75] Faron, p.47.

[76] Faron, p.46.

[77] Antoine Prost, *Les Anciens Combattants et la société française 1914–1939*, 3 vols (Paris: Presses de la Fondation Nationale des Sciences Politiques, 1977), III: *Mentalités et Idéologies*, 6.

[78] Prost, III, 6–7.

[79] Audoin-Rouzeau, *Les Combattants des tranchées*, p.88.

[80] Audoin-Rouzeau, *Les Combattants des tranchées*, p.88.

[81] Samuel Hynes, *The Soldier's Tale: Bearing Witness to Modern War* (London: Pimlico, 1998), p.19.

[82] See Marie-Christine Bellosta, p.127.

[83] Term used in *1916 Année de Verdun*, preface by Alain Décaux, produced by the Service historique de l'armée de terre (SHAT) in collaboration with the Service d'information et de relations publiques des armées (Paris: Charles-Lavauzelle, 1986), p.16.

[84] Jean-Jacques Becker, 'Mourir à Verdun', *L'Histoire*, 76 (March 1985), 18–29 (p.21).

[85] Pierre Miquel, *Les Poilus: la France sacrifiée* (Paris: Plon, 2000), p.282.

[86] Pierre Miquel, speaking on *Bouillon de Culture*.

[87] Sun Tzu, *The Art of War* (Hertfordshire: Wordsworth Classics, 1998), p.45.

[88] Miquel speaking on *Bouillon de Culture*.

[89] Becker, 'Mourir à Verdun', p.20.

[90] Pierre Miquel, *Les Poilus*, p.241.

[91] These figures are taken from Gérard Canini, *Combattre à Verdun: vie et souffrance quotidienne du soldat 1916–1917* (Nancy: Presse Universitaire de Nancy, 1988), p.11.

[92] Jacques Meyer, 'Vie et mort du soldat de Verdun', *Verdun 1916: Actes du Colloque international sur la Bataille de Verdun 6–7–8 juin 1975* (Verdun: Association Nationale du Souvenir de la Bataille de Verdun, Université de Nancy, 1977), 187–196 (p.189).

[93] Cited in Becker, 'Mourir à Verdun', p.29.

[94] See Paul Connerton, *How Societies Remember* (Cambridge: Cambridge University Press, 1989), p.65.

[95] Interview with Jean Guenot and Jacques Darribehaude, 'Le voyage au cinéma', *L'Herne*, 52–54 (p.53).

[96] For a comprehensive overview of the place of Verdun in *Voyage* and in Céline's life and work see, Tom Quinn, '"Une immense, universelle moquerie" : mémoire démesurée de guerre démesurée — Céline, *Voyage au bout de la nuit* et la Grande Guerre', in *La Démesure: Actes du XIVᵉ Colloque international L.-F. Céline de Paris 2002* (Paris : Société d'études céliniennes, 2003), 217–231.

[97] Denis de Rougemont, *L'Amour et l'Occident* (Paris: Plon, 1939), p.225.

[98] De Rougemont, p.225.

[99] De Rougemont, p.227.

[100] De Rougemont, p.226.

[101] Vera Brittain, *Testament of Youth* (London: Virago Press, 1978), p.232.

[102] Hynes, p.7.

[103] Mosse, *Fallen Soldiers*, p.5.

[104] Leslie Davis, 'L'anti-monde de L.-F. Céline', *Céline: Actes du Colloque international de Paris (27–30 July 1976)* (Paris: Société d'études céliniennes, 1978), 59–74.

[105] Miquel, *Bouillon de Culture*.

[106] Cited in Audoin-Rouzeau, *Les Combattants des tranchées*, p.87.

[107] Ernst Jünger, p.180.

[108] Ivor Gurney, 'There are strange hells within the minds war made', in *The Bloody Game*, p.196.

[109] See Ben Shephard, 'Shell-Shock on the Somme', *RUSI*, 141 (June 1996), 51–56.

[110] See Becker, 'Mourir à Verdun', p.20.

[111] Anthony Babington, *Shell-shock* (London: Leo Cooper, 1997), p.43.

[112] See Babington, p.45.

[113] Babington, p.44.

[114] Cited in Shephard, p.52.

[115] Shephard, p.52.

[116] Babington, p.52.

[117] Babington, p.46.

[118] See Louis Crocq, *Les traumatismes psychiques de la guerre* (Paris: Odile Jacob, 1999), pp.38–40.

[119] Babington, p.48.

[120] Interview with Louis Crocq, 'Et puis, c'est vous qui montez à l'assaut...', recorded by Bruno Cabanes, *L'Histoire*, special issue, 'Les hommes et la guerre' [Men and War], 267 (July–August 2002), 68–69 (p.69).

[121] Crocq, *Les traumatismes psychiques*, p.50.

[122] Siegfried Sassoon, *The Complete Memoirs of George Sherston* (London: Faber and Faber, 1972), pp.556–557.

[123] Sassoon, p.557.

[124] *Histoire générale de la presse française*, ed. by Fernand Terrou, Claude Berranger, Jacques Godechot, Pierre Guiral, 5 vols (Paris: Presses Universitaires de France, 1969–1976), III, 1972: *De 1871 à 1940*, p.416.

[125] *Histoire générale de la presse française*, III, 423.

[126] See *Histoire générale de la presse française*, III, 416.

[127] Marc Bloch, *Réflexions d'un historien sur les fausses nouvelles de la guerre* (Paris: Allia, 1999), p.50.

[128] See *Paroles de Poilus*, p.8.

[129] See Antoine Prost on the Louis Marin reports on war casualties in, Prost, II: *Sociologie*, p.2 and following pages. Prost suggests that Marin's figures were undermined by the unwillingness of the French War Ministry to reveal the true extent of the nation's manpower losses. See also Becker, 'Mourir à Verdun', p.24.

[130] Bloch, *Réflexions*, p.50.

[131] *Paroles de Poilus*, p.39.

[132] *Paroles de Poilus*, p.92.

[133] See Nicolas Offenstadt, *Les Fusillés de la Grande Guerre et la mémoire collective (1914–1999)* (Paris: Odile Jacob, 1999), p.59.

[134] See Offenstadt, p. 84.

[135] General Bonnal, cited in Riegel, p.51.

[136] Alain, cited in Prost, I: *Histoire*, p.26.

[137] Marc Bloch, *Souvenirs de guerre*, p.50.

[138] See Offenstadt, pp.20–21.

[139] See Marie-Christine Bellosta, p.39.

[140] An interview with General André Bach of the French Army's history service, published in *Libération* newspaper, 11 November 2001, p.17, gives a figure of 550 French soldiers executed during the course of the war. Based on his own research in the French Army archives, Bach confirms that the majority of executions took place in the first months of the war. 60% of executions took place during this period, he says. Bach confirms that courts-martial ordered the execution of men to set 'an example'. He also confirms that in the early part of the war there were a number of summary executions not recorded in the archives.

[141] Guy Pedroncini, *Les Mutineries de 1917* (Paris: Presse Universitaires de Paris, 1983), is the definitive account of the mutiny in the French Army.

[142] Cited in Ferro, p.313.

[143] Pedroncini, p.308.

[144] Ferro, p.315. General Bach, in *Libération*, puts the figure at twenty-seven executions.

[145] *Paroles de Poilus*, p.121.

[146] Gérard Vincent, 'Guerres dites, guerres tues et l'énigme identitaire', in *Histoire de la vie privée*, ed. by Philippe Ariès and Georges Duby, 5 vols (Paris: Seuil, 1987), V: *de la Première Guerre mondiale à nos jours*, ed. by Antoine Prost and Gérard Vincent, 201–249 (p.208).

[147] Audoin-Rouzeau, *Les Combattants des tranchées*, p.216.

[148] Audoin-Rouzeau, *Les Combattants des tranchées*, p.214.

[149] Gérard Vincent, 'Guerres dites, guerres tues', p.208.

[150] Audoin-Rouzeau, *Les Combattants des tranchées*, p.54.

[151] Audoin-Rouzeau, *Les Combattants des tranchées*, p.55.

[152] Audoin-Rouzeau, *Les Combattants des tranchées*, p.56.

[153] Lyn MacDonald, *To the Last Man: Spring 1918* (London: Viking, 1998). Writes MacDonald in her foreword: 'The word "horror" has become inseparable from contemporary judgement of the First World War, but it is too glib an appraisal. In many years of conversing with former soldiers I can say with perfect honesty that I have never heard the word "horror" on their lips, though many of the experiences they spoke of were indeed horrific.' See p.xvi. MacDonald reproduces a poem by Somme Veteran, Jim Aldous, which she says sums up the experience of the ordinary soldier and which includes the line 'until the end rather enjoying it'.

[154] Mosse, 'Two World Wars and the Myth of the War Experience', p.507.

[155] Ferguson, p.447.

[156] Will Hutton, 'The Terrible Slaughter that changed the World', *The Observer*, 8 November 1998, p.14.

CHAPTER 2

REMEMBERING

From Myth to Anti-Myth

Introduction

'Commemoration was a universal preoccupation after the 1914–18 war,' writes Jay Winter.[1] Memory, however, was divided. Following the war, national commemoration was organised around traditional symbols of heroism and sacrifice — expressing a narrative continuity with the past — while beneath the surface a different, disenchanted memory of the war persisted. In 1929, following the massive 10th anniversary Armistice commemoration, the divide in memory opened wide. Traditional memory faltered. Ironic, modern memory surged from below. Chapter Two examines this paradigm of divided memory and provides further context for *Voyage*, Céline's own Great War memory.

2.1 TRADITIONAL MEMORY

Commemoration and Myth

Post-war society was a place of mourning. 'Among the major combatants, it is not an exaggeration to suggest,' writes Jay Winter, 'that every family was in mourning.'[2] In France, in July 1920, there were an estimated 700,000 widows as a result of the war,[3] and about one million children had become wards of state or 'pupilles de la nation'.[4] Mass mourning was swiftly orchestrated into a monumental expression of unprecedented grieving. The war began to be commemorated.

All commemoration ceremonies, Paul Connerton tells us, 'do not simply imply continuity with the past but explicitly claim such continuity'.[5] They do so by 'ritually re-enacting a narrative of events held to have taken place at some past time, in a manner sufficiently elaborate to contain the performance of more or less invariant sequences of formal acts and utterances'. The Great War commemoration's narrative continuity with the past was established mainly through the myth of the war experience.[6]

The myth, writes George Mosse, 'was a democratic myth centred upon the nation symbolised by all the war dead'.[7] It gathered together the 'themes' that had sustained men at different stages of the war: 'the spirit of 1914, the war as a test of manliness, the ideal of camaraderie and the cult of the fallen soldier'.[8] After the war, according to Mosse, 'the reality of the war was submerged into the myth.'

The myth trivialised the war and was accompanied by a host of trivialising supports: 'kitsch and trashy literature [...] picture postcards, toys and games, and battlefield tourism'.[9] In England and France, Thomas Cook captured the private market for battlefield tourism.[10] Soon there was a 'thriving battlefield industry' selling souvenirs found on the battlefield or bric-à-brac such as 'mugs and reproductions of trenches on cigarette cases'.[11] In this way, Mosse says, 'the reality of war was disguised and controlled.'[12]

Manifestations of the myth were widespread. In France, it was incorporated into religious form and imagery.[13] The fallen soldier became a Christ-like figure.[14] There was too a resurgence of traditional *Épinal* imagery, kitsch representations of military themes dating from Napoleonic times.[15] What made these trivialising images popular, writes Jay Winter, was that 'they spoke of a common past in terms which made sense of the present crisis.'[16] However, while these manifestations of traditional memory established narrative continuity with the past, they were inadequate to the present. Narrative continuity simply plastered over the fragmentation the war had brought with it. It projected a consoling image of historical and national wholeness. Structured around the myth of the war experience, traditional memory refused to acknowledge that the narrative link with the past had been broken. Worse still, it made a sacred virtue of this refusal. 'Through the myth which came to surround it,' confirms Mosse, 'the war experience was sanctified.'[17] The myth redeemed the war. In France, it redeemed it to the strains of the *Marseillaise*.

The Dead

At the centre of commemoration were the compliant dead. As Annette Becker writes:

> Les 1 400 000 morts français ont bien envahi tout l'espace symbolique et affectif de la nation. Les cérémonies grandioses, les constructions des monuments aux morts ont transformé ces millions de deuils, affaires privées, en une affaire d'Etat.[18]

> [The 1,400,000 French dead occupied all of the nation's symbolic and affective space. Grandiose ceremonies, and the construction of monuments to the dead, transformed millions of individual, private instances of grief into an affair of state.]

The keynotes of commemoration, provided by the myth, were commitment to remember, reverence for the dead, the exaltation of patriotism and sacrifice, and an implicit affirmation of the war. The French Republic became its chief beneficiary.[19] The Republic grew strong upon its dead. Those revered and remembered were subsumed into a collective which institutionalised a form of forgetting. Excluded from remembrance were any who challenged the myth. Missing were the mutineers, the deserters, the cowards, and the victims of military executions.

The Unknown Republican Soldier

The French Great War dead were buried in vast necropoli in the north of France, at the site of great battles such as the Somme, the Marne and Verdun. Inspired by an egalitarian consciousness dating from the French Revolution,[20] these cemetery sites were impressively organised as architectural landscapes with infinite alignments of identical crosses.[21] The appropriation of nature in this context reflected the Enlightenment ideal of nature associated with Rousseau, for example, whose tomb bore the inscription 'Nature et Liberté' [Nature and Liberty].[22] In these massive cemeteries, the Great War dead shared a perfectly egalitarian, democratic and patriotic camaraderie. Half a million of the French dead, however, were unidentifiable and were buried in anonymous graves or in mass sites such as the Douaumont Ossuary. How could these soldiers be remembered? The answer was ingenious. In 1920, the return of the Unknown

Soldier from the battlefields of the Great War was a symbolic high-point of commemoration in France and Britain.

In 1920, the French performed an unprecedented ritual at Douaumont Ossuary. On 10 November, a soldier, whose father was one of the war's disappeared, randomly chose one of eight coffins — by placing a bouquet of flowers taken from the battlefield on top of it — each containing unidentified remains brought from the major battlefields of the war.[23] The chosen remains were then transported to Paris and interred at the Arc de Triomphe. The manner of the interment, however, shows how commemoration in France was used to affirm the French Republic. The French Government chose to make the interment of the Unknown Soldier part of its commemoration of the 50th anniversary of the proclamation of the Third Republic in 1870. On arrival in Paris the Unknown Soldier lay in state at Place Denfert-Rochereau. The next day, the Unknown, draped in the tricolour, was taken first to the Pantheon for the interment of the heart of Léon Gambetta, who had proclaimed the Third Republic in 1870. The Unknown Soldier's remains then continued to the Arc de Triomphe.[24]

The interment was symbolically, profoundly Republican; the link with Gambetta had ensured this. It was also profoundly religious. 25,000 French priests had been mobilised in the war and almost 5,000 had been killed.[25] The war had allowed the Catholic Church to renew its position in France. The Church was already highly involved in the creation of the war cemeteries, including that of Verdun,[26] but the interment of the Unknown Soldier in November was to be the most overt expression of its renewal. The ceremony was attended by vast numbers of Catholics and the coffin of the Unknown was blessed before interment by the archbishop of Paris. This new alliance of Republic and Church was underlined by the re-establishment at the same time of official relations with the Vatican. In 1923, the inauguration of an 'eternal flame' at the site of the Unknown Soldier's grave was confided to the 'très catholique' [very catholic] Jacques Péricard'.[27]

Who owned the French commemoration? In 1929, as Céline began *Voyage*, national fundraising days were inaugurated for the completion of the four massive cemeteries in the North of France. These days were organised under the patronage of the President of the Republic, the Field Marshals of France, the cardinals and archbishops, the pastors and the Grand Rabbi.[28] From 14 to 28 July, they granted the right to street merchants to sell flags, insignia, postcards and other trivia to raise funds for the appeal. In France as a whole only the communists appear to have refused the values of commemoration, 'il s'agit de commémorer les morts et non la guerre ; comme on ne peut faire l'un sans l'autre, nous désapprouvons toute commémoration' [it is the dead who are to be commemorated and not the war, and as it is not possible to do one without the other, we disapprove of all commemoration], was the Lyon Communist Party's response to plans to erect a monument.[29] In general, George Mosse has signalled the 'inability of the Left [...] to enter into the myth of the war experience'. This inability enabled the Right, on the other hand, to 'exploit the suffering of millions for its own political ends'.[30] It is perhaps Céline's own inability to enter the myth which gave *Voyage* its original appeal to the Left.

The purposeful interment of the Unknown Soldier at the Arc de Triomphe transformed a vainglorious monument commemorating the victories of Napoleon's armies into a universal tomb for the nameless dead of the Great War. At the same time it subsumed the memory of all the unknown soldiers of the Great War into the greater narrative memory of Republican France. 'Commemoration was a political act,' writes Jay Winter, 'it could not be neutral.'[31] The Unknown Soldier was nothing if not a profoundly political statement about the continuity of the French Republic which transformed Armistice Day in France into a Republican feast. As Antoine Prost has written, the 11 November Armistice commemoration is the only republican cult to have to have excited popular unanimity in France.[32] The wholesale involvement of children in the commemoration ensured that commemoration, like the war itself, would be 'total'.[33]

Pour elle un Français doit mourir

In France, the tradition of commemorating dead soldiers began with the French Revolution. This tradition was amplified following the Franco-Prussian war, when metal or stone tableaux were used to commemorate the names of the dead in churches and cemeteries.[34] In 1870, an empty monument to the dead was erected in Père-Lachaise. It is this style of monument which will characterise the Great War commemoration of the dead. Philippe Ariès notes that after the Great War 'dans chaque commune de France, dans chaque arrondissement de Paris, on érigea aux soldats tués [...] un tombeau vide' [in every French commune, in every Parisian arrondissement, an empty tomb was erected to soldiers killed].[35] There are roughly 36,000 of these monuments to fallen soldiers in towns and villages throughout France.[36] Most of the monuments were erected between 1919 and 1924 and for reasons of economy are often simple stelae or obelisks. During Armistice Day commemorations the local authorities would gather round 'le monument aux morts' to remember and pay tribute. The Republican anthem, the *Marseillaise*, was invariably played. Ariès comments: 'les clairons sonnent, comme aussi le même jour à l'église, le chant funèbre : "Pour elle [la Patrie] un Français doit mourir"' [the bugles sound, and in the church the funeral hymn is sung: 'For France, a Frenchman must die'].[37] Here then was the meaning of the war and its unprecedented numbers of dead. They had died for France; they had died for the Republic. The monuments made this answer explicit. 60% of monuments proclaimed the dead, 'morts pour la France' [died for France]. 18% proclaimed them 'morts pour la patrie' [died for the fatherland].[38]

These monuments sanitised the war. Annette Becker describes them thus:

> Les plus nombreux louent le soldat en tant que combattant courageux et victorieux de la patrie républicaine. Ces braves incarnent un conflit aseptisé : ni boue, ni sang. Les sculpteurs insistent sur l'armement et l'uniforme, bandes molletières comprises. Souvent, au sommet, un coq représentant la patrie ; enfin, au pied du monument, les civils, femmes ou enfants.[39]

> [Most of them praise the soldier as a courageous and victorious combatant of the republican fatherland. These brave soldiers embody an aseptic conflict: no mud, no blood. The sculptors emphasise the weapons and the uniform, leg bands included. Often, on the summit, there is a cockerel representing France; finally, at the foot of the monument, one sees the civilians, women or children.]

These monuments deny the ugly reality of the war. Death is cleansed, given meaning and exalted through reverence for the heroic power of sacrifice, which is directly related to the life of the collective, of the Nation (see 1.1 *The Hero*). It is as if the Great War destruction of the heroic ideal had never happened and an unbroken connection with a pre-war narrative of redemption has been maintained. The dead, of course, were literally at a remove from these monuments and their pious inscriptions. Empty monuments fittingly represented the way in which public memory had emptied itself of the reality of warfare. The monuments were effectively monuments to forgetting.

1793

The ritual remembrance of dead soldiers was somewhat of an innovation. 'La guerre de 1914,' writes Philippe Ariès, 'a donné au culte civique des morts "de nos combats mémorables" une diffusion et un prestige qu'il n'avait jamais connus auparavant' [The 1914 war gave to the civic cult of the dead 'of our memorable battles' a diffusion and a prestige that it had never before known].[40] Ariès describes a long tradition preceding the Great War by which the mass of soldiers killed in battle was buried anonymously and indiscriminately in mass graves on or near the battlefield. Sometimes the bodies were simply burned en masse as happened in the wake of the battle of Sedan. Nothing proved more expedient, sure or economical than burning.[41] One understands immediately from this, the historical source of Bardamu's fear in *Voyage* that he will be burned, 'je ne veux surtout pas qu'on me brûle !' [Above all, I do not want my body to be burned!] (RI, 65). In addition, and as an example of the rich layers in *Voyage*, Bardamu's gesture is intrinsically unheroic. The Homeric hero was cremated.[42] Refusing cremation, Bardamu confirms the Great War breach with the heroic ideal.

The moment Ariès identifies as a turning-point in the remembrance of dead soldiers in France is highly significant for *Voyage*. As he writes:

> Les premiers soldats qui ont été honorés d'un tombeau-mémorial ont été les victimes des guerres civiles de la Révolution française : monument de Lucerne aux Suisses massacrés le 10 août 1792.[43]

> [The first soldiers to be honoured with a memorial tomb were the victims of the French Revolution's civil wars: the Luzerne monument to the Swiss Guard massacred on 10 August 1792.]

These of course are the same Swiss Guard of *Voyage*'s poignant *Chanson des Gardes suisses* which inaugurates the novel. *Voyage* thus begins with an act of memory, by remembering the first soldiers to have found a permanent place of honour in memory, soldiers brutally murdered at the inception of the radical revolution. By attaching the date 1793 to the *Chanson*, Céline adds blatant emphasis to what is a clear anti-Republican statement. And he identifies the cult of the dead soldier with the rise of Revolutionary France.

Date and *Chanson* should alert the reader to *Voyage*'s anti-Republican content. They announce *Voyage* as an act of dissenting memory. We have said that '4 mai' signals *Voyage*'s war memory as 'commemorative' (see 1.3 *Verdun*). This is true, but in the context it gives itself, of the massacre of '10 August', and of 1793, and in the context of the Republican commemoration of the Great War, it is more exact to describe *Voyage* as *anti*-commemoration and *anti*-Republican.

Silence

Traditional memory was inherently resistant to new narrative. Public performances of the myth were constructed around a restricted, static vocabulary of word and gesture.[44] For this reason, public commemoration of the Great War in the third millennium is little different from the commemoration of the 1920s. Commemoration is led in most countries by state, military and religious leaders. The great mass of people observe rather than participate in its structures. Public discourse is filled with set phrases, with prayers, poetry, song and hymns that are impervious to penetration from the outside. All possibility of new narrative, especially the possibility of dissent, is restricted, contained and finally sublimated by means of the commemoration's centrepiece, an emblematic and highly theatrical silence.

While it had its roots in the experience of the Boer War, the silence of the Armistice Day commemoration may be considered a significant innovation of the Great War. Its main aim was expressed in a memorandum by Sir Percy Fitzpatrick, who helped inaugurate it, when he said, 'it may help to bring home to those who come after us the meaning, the nobility and the unselfishness of the great sacrifice by which their freedom was assured.'[45] In other words, the silence would consolidate the myth. It was a great popular success.

The symbolic silence of remembering took place annually, at the eleventh hour of the eleventh day of the eleventh month, the hour when the Armistice was signed in 1918. At this time whole nations stopped in their work and fell silent. The silence was a highly theatrical expression of national unity. But it could not help be much more than that. The silence contained an essential irony. It commemorated a modern war through a gesture that was profoundly unmodern. Some believe the significance of the silence is the falling silent of the guns when the war ended. But on Armistice Day, the silence also meant the falling silent of machines in factories, of cars and buses, and other products of the modern age, in other words, the interruption of modern life and its constant noise of machinery. Perhaps unwittingly, and in spite of itself, the silence succeeded in representing the antithesis of war in the midst of a discourse that affirmed traditional narrative. The silence turned its back on modern society and allowed noiseless peace to reign. It is tempting to think that in the midst of battle, this silence is what the soldiers would have wished for most of all.

The silence ultimately symbolised assent, acceptance and reconciliation. That was the real problem with it. Whatever inner discourse it might contain, silence could never express open revolt against the war. Indeed, it silenced dissent and as such suited the architects of commemoration. If in France and Britain the silence was maintained in all its thrilling theatricality, in Germany, where war wounds were deeper, silence was problematic. It was 1924 before the Germans attempted a commemorative, public silence.[46] It did not work. A projected two minute silence was broken quickly by the shouted claims of the various groups attending the commemoration. It was not until the Nazis came to power in 1934 that a proper day of remembering, known as *Heldengedenktag*, or Heroes' Day, was instituted.[47]

Veterans

Veterans formed a large group within French society after the Great War. Over six million had survived the war and were its living legacy. Céline was one of them. The veteran occupied a privileged position of witness. 'Celui qui n'a pas compris avec sa chair ne peut vous en parler' [he who has not understood with his flesh cannot speak to you of the war], wrote Jean Bernier.[48] This privileged position was recognised by society at large. For example, the victory parade of 14 July 1919 on the Champs Elysées was led by a group of 'mutilés de guerre' [war disabled], reminding the onlookers of the price that had been paid for victory.

Veterans were haunted by the fear that their sacrifice would be forgotten and that the deaths of so many would count for nothing. They saw themselves as the guardians of memory. The moral commitment to remember was present even in the war itself. 'Hâtons-nous vers ces souvenirs que demain recouvrirait l'oubli' [Let's make haste to record those memories which tomorrow will be forgotten], wrote Raymond Jubert, urging his comrades to remember the war.[49] 'Il faut te faire toi-même un serment : ne pas oublier' [swear an oath to oneself, never to forget], wrote Léon Werth. 'Prends des repères dans l'horreur. Tel cadavre, tel blessé, telle pensée, telle pensée sous l'obus, telle pensée avant l'attaque. Retiens ces repères' [Take note of the horror: that corpse, that wounded soldier, that thought, the thought you had under bombardment, the one you had before the attack. Take note of these things and remember them].[50] Céline would echo this powerfully in *Voyage*:

> La grande défaite, en tout, c'est d'oublier, et surtout ce qui vous a fait crever, et de crever sans comprendre jamais jusqu'à quel point les hommes sont vaches. Quand on sera au bord du trou faudra pas faire les malins nous autres, mais faudra pas oublier non plus, faudra raconter tout sans changer un mot, de ce qu'on a vu de plus vicieux chez les hommes [...]. (RI, 25)

> [The great defeat, in all things, is to forget, and especially to forget that which has done for you, and to die without ever understanding the extent to which men are wicked. When we find ourselves on the edge of the grave, that's not the time for us to act the smart ass, but neither is it the time to forget. We've got to tell it all, the very worst we've seen of men, without changing a single word [...].]

Feeling a duty to remember, veterans were tormented by the frailty of memory. 'On oublie le bombardement de la veille... comme on oublie tout' [one forgets the bombardment of the day before... as one forgets everything], wrote Werth.[51] The importance of protecting memory was not alone to ensure that the real meaning of sacrifice endured but that the cruel truth gained in war was not lost. As Jules-Émile Henches wrote:

Plus que jamais la guerre me fait prendre le mensonge en horreur : faute, maladresse, faiblesse, crime... C'est peut-être une des rares choses que la guerre m'aura fait gagner : le désir plus ardent de la vérité.[52]

[More than ever before, the war causes me to view lies with horror: faults, blunders, weakness, crime... That is perhaps one of the rare things the war has given me: a most ardent desire for truth.]

Once, in another world, another lifetime, the veterans had left for the war young, enthusiastic, able-bodied. They had come back marked by death, damaged in body and mind, haunted by their experience, estranged by the world they found at the rear. 'Les hommes qui ont participé à la dernière guerre comprennent qu'ils ont passé d'un monde ancien à un monde nouveau, du monde d'avant-guerre à celui d'après-guerre' [The men who fought in the last war understand that they have gone from an old world to a new one, from a pre-war to a post-war world], wrote Henry Malherbe.[53] The war had changed the world and it had changed them:

Ils ne se reconnaissaient pas eux-mêmes. Marqués d'un 'signe secret', particulier, véritables 'revenants', un abîme séparait le vieil homme que chacun d'eux avait été avant guerre, de l'homme nouveau qu'il était devenu.[54]

[They did not know themselves. Marked with a private, 'secret sign', veritable 'ghosts', an abyss separated the man each one of them had been before the war from the new man he had become.]

While the civilian populations celebrated frenetically —'a loathsome ending to the loathsome tragedy of the last four years,' wrote Siegfried Sassoon [55] — for the soldiers returning from the trenches 'en ce 11 novembre, à 11 heures, une immense lassitude se superposait à la satisfaction d'être victorieux et d'en avoir fini' [on that 11 November, at eleven in the morning, an immense lassitude dampened the satisfaction of having been victorious and being done with the war].[56] The war had changed them and it had sapped them.

Reintegration into society was not easy. Divisions that had appeared during the war deepened on returning. The veterans felt their welcome home was often a cold one. 'Ils ont des droits sur nous' [we owe them a debt], declared French Prime Minister, Georges Clemenceau, but when veterans insisted on their rights: 'Le rappel [...] les fit passer bientôt pour des importuns. Des gêneurs :

ainsi, déjà, l'arrière les considérait parfois pendant la lutte. Gêneurs ils demeurèrent après la victoire' [When they reminded people of their rights [...] they were soon treated as troublesome. Trouble-makers; even during the war the home front had sometimes thought of them as trouble-makers. In victory, they remained trouble-makers].[57]

On a logistical level the sheer number of returning soldiers created a problem:

> Ce gigantesque mouvement d'hommes provoqua de très difficiles problèmes de transport, d'habillement [...] et surtout de réinsertion dans le marché du travail : un grand nombre de démobilisés se retrouvèrent chômeurs.[58]

> [The massive movement of men caused serious problems in respect of transport and clothing [...] and above all in relation to their re-entry into the labour market. A large number of demobilised soldiers found themselves unemployed.]

Add to the numbers of unemployed those who had lost limbs, faces, minds and it becomes clear that on returning to society the veterans constituted a severely marginalised group. This marginalisation, some thought, should have inevitably led to change in society but it did not. The French government circumvented veteran dissatisfaction and dampened down dissension by offering substantial pensions and absorbing most veterans into the conservative *Union nationale des combattants*.[59]

Veterans were prominent in all aspects of commemoration. Respect for the Republic was part of their upbringing. Perhaps most significantly, in contributing to the maintenance of the status quo, the majority of veterans felt the need to redeem the war and the sacrifice of lives made. 'Condamner sans nuances ce qui venait de se passer, c'était nier les sacrifices des Français au front. [...] Le fond commun de leur pensée alliait l'horreur de la guerre et la conscience d'avoir fait ce qu'il fallait' [To condemn without reserve what had happened was to betray the sacrifices of French soldiers at the front. Their common attitude mixed horror at the war with a sense of having done what was needed].[60] The attitude towards war adopted by the majority of veterans was one of 'patriotisme pacifiste' [patriotic pacifism], which 'n'était en rien la négation de la guerre qui avait eu lieu ; il était la négation des guerres futures' [was not at all the negation of the war which had taken place, but rather, it represented the negation of future wars].[61] Such an attitude was inherently contradictory and established a level of complicity among veterans with the Great War and the myth of the war experience. This attitude could only mean that inevitably the veteran would be neutralised and his voice increasingly diminished within society.

In spite of their commitment to remember, the perceived 'dominant characteristic of veterans of the First World War,' states Eric J. Leed, was 'silence'.[62] In 1928, in his preface to Jacques Meyer's *La Biffe*, Henry Malherbe confirms this, describing the situation of the veteran ten years after the war, just as Céline began writing *Voyage*:

> Depuis l'armistice [...] les mutilés et les anciens combattants ont subsisté à l'ombre. Ceux qui ne mouraient pas étaient ensevelis dans un silence profond comme la mort. La fatigue, la fierté, ne leur ont pas encore permis de sortir de leur long évanouissement. Trahis par des chefs dérisoires, tenus par leurs anciennes leçons de soumission et de discipline, ils ne se vengeaient plus que par la modération de l'insultante légèreté dont on les traitait.[63]

> [Since the armistice [...] the war disabled and veterans have lived in the shadows. Those who did not die were buried in a silence as profound as death itself. Fatigue, pride, have not yet allowed them to emerge from their long effacement. Betrayed by their derisory leaders, kept in line by their old habits of submission and discipline, their only vengeance has been the moderation of the insulting levity with which they have been treated.]

The efforts they made to contribute to society through their associations, such as writer Henri Barbusse's *Association républicaine des anciens combattants,* began to weaken.

> Si résolus qu'ils aient été, les 'héros' étaient diminués et fatigués. Ne demeuraient-ils pas tous 'des blessés de guerre'... des convalescents qui souffraient encore 'comme d'une plaie', comme de 'milles plaies intérieures', mal fermées ? [...] Ainsi, les anciens combattants sentirent peu à peu faiblir leur volonté et leur résolution.[64]

> [No matter how resolute they had been, the 'heroes' felt weakened and fatigued. Were they not all 'war wounded'... convalescents still suffering from 'a wound', from 'a thousand internal wounds' poorly healed? [...] And so, the veterans felt their will and their determination weaken little by little.]

Soon their role was limited to marching in commemorative parades and basking in the reflected glory heaped on their dead comrades; yet, they embodied still the living remnants of war and the living rests of memory. Theirs was the responsibility for maintaining the eternal flame that burned over the tomb of the Unknown Soldier. Each day the flame was renewed. Each day memory was carefully maintained 'avec piété et ferveur' [with piety and fervour].[65] Each day the promise was kept not to forget. Céline, veteran, 'à l'ombre' [in the shadows], 'blessé' [wounded], 'enseveli dans un silence profond' [buried in a profound silence], would keep that promise in his own way.

11 November 1928

The 10th Armistice Anniversary of November 1928 represented a turning-point in memory. A massive effort of commemoration should have been the time for memory to move on from the disasters of the war. Instead, the commemoration revealed the emptiness of ritual memory and its platitudes. It would be followed within a year by the greatest cry of protest ever uttered by literature.

In Paris, that November, there was yet another ministerial crisis as the country stumbled towards the economic depression which would mark the end of 'les années folles' [the roaring twenties]. And there was a further novelty on the horizon of memory. The war was back on the cinema screen. Léon Poirier's film *Verdun* was a cinematic event.[66] Poirier's film was a mix of documentary footage and reconstituted scenes based on the witness of survivors. A veteran of the war and committed pacifist, Poirier's film was openly didactic and featured 'd'abord une mise en scène des combats, de cette violence qu'il a lui-même vécue et dont il entend montrer les ravages' [a vision of battle, of the violence he had himself experienced and whose destruction he wanted to show].[67] Poirier succeeded. *Verdun* would run in Paris cinemas during and in the wake of the Armistice commemoration, as Céline was embarking on his *Voyage*. Poirier had managed to provide 'la représentation de la guerre plus radicalement portée à l'écran que dans toute œuvre précédente' [a more radical screen representation of the war than in any previous work].[68] Those who crowded to see it could witness for themselves what *Le Figaro* called 'le spectacle de la Guerre telle qu'elle fut', adding, 'la voici dans sa vérité terrifiante et simple' [the spectacle of the war as it really was, seen here in all its terrifying and simple truth].[69] Its scenes were indeed so terrible that the French right-wing writer, Pierre Drieu La Rochelle, a veteran of the massacre at Charleroi in 1914, cowered in his seat in the cinema.[70] Poirier's film ensured that as the November commemoration took place realistic images of the war would accompany the words and gestures of commemoration in the public mind, and that Verdun itself would loom large and terrible in memory.

1928 was a year of commemoration, but it was in November that traditional memory raised itself to an unprecedented fever pitch. As usual, silence would form the centrepiece of the commemoration. On 10 November *Le Figaro* issued its call to memory for the following day, announcing in traditional tones of reverence and duty, 'l'hommage d'une minute de silence fervent [...] à la sainte mémoire des héros qui, par leur sacrifice, ont illustré et sauvé la Patrie' [the homage of a minute's fervent silence [...] dedicated to the sacred memory of those heroes who, by their sacrifice, adorned and saved France].[71]

Memory's dissenting voice, however, was not far away. On the morning of 11 November, Henry Vidal, writing on the front page of *Le Figaro*, accused memory while evoking the disenchantment and isolation of the veteran. 'Héros d'un temps légendaire [...] ce sont des condamnés, d'anciens bannis' [Heroes of a legendary time [...] they live now under a sentence, as former outcasts].[72] His accusation becomes a condemnation of post-war Republican France. 'Ils commémorent cette date dans l'anarchie et la corruption triomphante' [They commemorate Armistice Day in an atmosphere of anarchy and triumphant corruption], he writes. His accusation finds root in the emptiness of the words for which the soldiers fought and died and by which they are remembered. 'La justice... liberté,' he writes, 'depuis dix ans ils ont appris que les mots étaient creux' [Justice... freedom, over the last ten years they have learned how empty these words are]. This dissenting language would never be heard in the heart of the commemoration itself, which despite its commanding solemnity was making its way, that very day, towards revealing farce.

The commemoration was massively supported. On 12 November, *Le Figaro* reported that crowds attending the remembrance ceremonies were greater than ever before. The now traditional silence had been as impressive as ever. 'Durant une minute [...] la vie suspendit son cours' [For one minute [...] life stopped in its course]. *Le Figaro* described the veterans' parade in terms that represent traditional memory at its most effusive, evoking:

> le déchirant cortège des victimes, l'interminable cortège de ceux que la tourmente a meurtris. Les mutilés, les amputés... les aveugles... les 'gueules cassées'... tragiquement belles.[73]

> [the heart-rending cortege of victims, the interminable cortege of those stricken by the war. The war disabled, the amputated... the blinded... the 'broken faces'... so tragically beautiful.]

However, at a reception organised for the end of the parade in the Hôtel de Ville the whole commemoration turned to parody. 'Des grands mutilés, des blessés de face, beaucoup de ceux pour qui [...] la réception était donnée, n'avaient pu entrer' [the severely war disabled, the facially disfigured, many of those for whom [...] the reception had been organised, could not get in].[74] They had quite simply been forgotten. The veterans gathered outside the reception hall. There were voices of protest followed by embarrassment and apologies from the organisers. Eventually a compromise was reached and some of the veterans were allowed in to the reception. It was all too late. The massive structure of traditional commemoration had been reduced to this single microscopic moment where it was found singularly wanting. Who could blame the veterans for feeling they had been cheated? That the entire commemoration was a fraud? The next few years would reveal the extent of the breach now apparent in the façade of traditional memory.

2.2 THE WRITERS OF MODERN MEMORY

1929

Traditional memory, whatever its merits, had been a site of fake reconciliation. Traditional memory held together with the glue of silence and its silences were finally crumbling. Siegfried Sassoon's memory of silence was the following:

> I remember a man at the C.C.S. with his jaw blown off by a bomb [...]. He lay there with one hand groping at the bandages which covered his whole

head and face, gurgling every time he breathed. His tongue was tied forward to prevent him swallowing it. The War had gagged him — smashed him — and other people looked at him and tried to forget what they'd seen...[75]

In 1929, the silence of traditional memory could no longer contain this horror of broken speech and traumatised forgetting.[76] The new narratives of memory that emerged were told mostly in autobiographies, in poems and in stories, in that age-old space of paradox where memory meets imagination. 'The history of the war may never be written,' said veteran and poet, Herbert Read, 'but if it is written, it will be written by the poets who took part in it. [By] a man with an eye for significant detail.'[77] And Read knew what the books of such poets would be like:

> There are two possible categories. The first is the plain narrative — the journal or diary of day-to-day experiences. [...] The second category is made up of those books in which the narrative has been arranged for imaginative or persuasive effect. No detail is false; the perspective is true. But the result is not a diary, but a work of art. This type of war-book is very rare, because normally the events are too violent to be easily subdued for the purposes of art. They are a hard kind of rock to hew into shape.[78]

It is, indeed, here, in narrative arranged for imaginative effect, that the twentieth-century memory of the Great War found its most resonant and enduring representations. In 1929, the major literary accounts of the Great War broke through the barrier of silence erected by traditional memory. The books of such as Erich Maria Remarque, Ernest Hemingway, Robert Graves and others, carried voices from the heart of the war itself. Theirs was a voice of persisting trauma shared by Céline. They heralded *Voyage*. They are indeed its master models, intermediaries between the Destouches of war and the Céline of *Voyage*, and they foreshadow the themes, methods and narrative voice of *Voyage*. They are presented here for their value in illustrating the transition from traditional to modern memory and to establish the literary context from which *Voyage* will eventually emerge.

It has been said that the writers who emerged in the late 1920s did so as a result of the world economic recession at that time.[79] This is simply not the case. Edmund Blunden, for example, began writing his autobiographical *Undertones of*

War in the early 1920s and it appeared in 1928. The Wall Street Crash of 1929 took place in October long after disenchanted accounts of the war appeared. The effects of recession were not fully felt in France until the last quarter of 1931, two years after Céline began writing *Voyage*.[80] The real catalyst is the failure of traditional memory.

Graves

For Robert Graves the war had been an attractive alternative to college. 'I wanted to be abroad fighting,' he wrote.[81] He had his wish. His 1929 *Goodbye to All That* is the most popular of all Great War autobiographies. It is Graves's valediction not just to the war but a scathing, formal farewell to the England which had died with the war. He wrote it, he said, for 'forgetfulness, because once all this has been settled in my mind and written down it need never be thought of again'.[82] He was wrong. Graves would remain tormented by his war experience for the rest of his life.[83]

Interestingly, Graves had initially attempted to write a novel of the war but had failed:

> I […] made several attempts during these years to rid myself of the poison of war memories by finishing my novel, but I had to abandon them. It was not only that they brought back neurasthenia, but that I was ashamed at having distorted my material with a plot, and yet not sure enough of myself to retranslate it into undisguised history.[84]

His experience neatly expresses the dilemma of the writer torn between history and fiction, between a sense of moral obligation to the past and the affirmation of imagination. However, in spite of his 'fidelity' to his war memories Graves was always going to produce a 'yarn'. A born storyteller, like Céline, his storytelling talent constantly pulled him away from the world of literal fact and towards invention.

In the context of *Voyage*, *Goodbye* is interesting for a number of reasons. First of all there is its outrageous humour which is an integral part of its appeal as Graves pokes fun at the war and at death. Examples are numerous. One scene shows the soldiers preparing for an attack. As the ridiculous operation order is read the soldiers collapse in laughter. They are then told the attack is merely a diversion for the real thing taking place elsewhere. The commander comments,

'"Personally, I don't give a damn either way. We'll get killed whatever happens." We all laughed.'[85] A further passage, omitted from the 1929 edition, offers an account of the trial of a soldier for 'committing a nuisance' on the barrack square.[86] The scene is funny but, in relation to *Voyage*, the use of excrement and humour to ridicule the army, its language and ritual, is what is important. That the passage was expurgated underlines how constraints on theme and language hindered memory's efforts to express its savage discontents.

Graves's humour often anticipates Céline's, as does his theatricality. *Goodbye* is composed largely of a series of sketches or 'caricature scenes' drawing on the tradition of music hall and pantomime. It is not insignificant that before writing *Voyage*, Céline had produced two unsuccessful plays. The theatrical instinct obviously ran deep and it is reflected, as we shall see, in the structures and patterns of *Voyage* (see 7.3 *The Theatre of Patriotism*). Paul Fussell's description below of Graves's art could equally apply to *Voyage* and its portraits of Bestombes (RI, 86 and 92–94), Puta (RI, 105–106), Baryton (RI, 423–426), and Princhard (RI, 66–71) among others. The opening scene of the war episode with the colonel impervious to German fire (RI, 11) — Bardamu sees him 'dans un music-hall' [in a music hall] (RI, 19) — or the later *Amiral Bragueton* scene, when Bardamu is subjected to an impromptu court-martial (RI, 119–123), should particularly be kept in mind:

> [Graves's] wry anecdotes take the shape of virtual playlets [...]. They present character types entirely externally, the way an audience would see them. The audience is not vouchsafed what they are or what they think and feel or where they were last Thursday, but only visible or audible signs of what they do and say, how they dress or stand or sit or move or gesture. Their remarks are not paraphrased or rendered in indirect discourse: they are presented in dialogue. Many of these playlets have all the black-and-white immediacy of cartoons with captions.[87]

The entire effect, Fussell says, is enhanced by the use of 'pithy lines'[88] similar to Céline's indulgence in epigrams, or witty one-liners. With both Graves and Céline, the reader is in the presence of comic masters, drawing on common experiences and employing similar techniques to the same derisive end. Both push satire to the point of parody, but Céline is the one who most clearly reaches towards parody's extreme: invective. Moreover, Céline is noteworthy for his ability to encompass not just the humour of Graves, but the denunciation of a Hemingway and the anguish and solitude of a Remarque, establishing a shared imagery with them while all the while pushing the frontiers of style, language and imagination, into unknown territory. That is Céline's genius.

One can see too that Graves's basic approach to writing his autobiography was also used by Céline in the construction of his fiction. As Graves explained:

> [I have] more or less deliberately mixed in all the ingredients that I know are mixed into other popular books…[such as] food and drink… murders … ghosts […] mothers […] millionaires and pedlars and tramps and adopted children […] foreign travel […] love affairs (regular and irregular) […] wounds […] severe illnesses, suicides. But the best bet of all is battles.[89]

Voyage's replication of several of the most prominent genres of the 1920s, including war novels, the resurgent picaresque tradition, the vogue for travel books and exotic literature, hamletism, the populism of Eugène Dabit, even surrealism,[90] and its appropriation of preceding and often quite recent texts, as well as its reliance on stock characters and situations, such as the Madelon/Robinson/Bardamu love triangle and the novel's climactic *crime passionnel* [crime of passion], together with its exploitation of the resources of music hall and theatre, all confirm Céline's deliberate intention to fill his book with successful 'ingredients'. The apparent superficiality of this approach, however, should not be underestimated, as it has a much farther-reaching consequence, particularly true of *Voyage*, in that it embeds the work in the culture of its time and becomes its all-encompassing representation. It is yet another facet of *Voyage*'s totalising logic (see 1.2 *Total War*). Nonetheless, it is as fascinating as it is surprising to discern a common storytelling instinct at work in writers as different as Graves and Céline.

Another aspect of *Goodbye* relevant to *Voyage* is its ahistorical character. Graves's book, writes Paul Fussell, is rich 'in fatuous, erroneous, or preposterous written "texts" and documents, the normal materials of serious "history" but here exposed in all their farcical ineptitude and error'.[91] Fussell adds:

> The point of all these is not just humankind's immense liability to error, folly, and psychosis. It is also the dubiousness of a rational — or at least a clear-sighted — historiography. The documents on which a work of

'history' might be based are so wrong or so loathsome or so silly or so downright mad that no one could immerse himself in them for very long, Graves implies, without becoming badly unhinged.[92]

This is exactly the point as Céline undermines the official discourse of war, psychiatry, and memory in *Voyage*. Like Graves, through careful selection, Céline enables these discourses to satirise themselves. In addition, both *Goodbye* and *Voyage* demonstrate a flagrant disregard for 'fact'. They refuse to take 'fact' seriously but mock it. This perhaps is why historian Jay Winter says of *Voyage* that 'no one, Céline suggests, could possibly take all this literally, or totally seriously.'[93] As with *Goodbye*, however, the outrageous humour of *Voyage* in no way undermines its seriousness. Indeed, it enhances it, expressing as it does a fundamental disrespect for war, the army, history, memory, even reader.

When *Goodbye* was published Graves was accused of telling 'falsities'. His reply is immensely relevant. He wrote:

> Great latitude should [...] be allowed to a soldier who has [...] got his facts or dates mixed. I would even paradoxically say that the memoirs of a man who went through some of the worst experiences are not truthful unless they contain a high proportion of falsities.[94]

Graves adds, with perhaps more truth than he realised, that 'high-explosive barrages will make a temporary liar or visionary of anyone.' His statement underlines the close connection between traumatic experience and the lie of fiction and provides an important insight into *Voyage*'s truth/untruth problematic. Indeed, Graves's paradox reconciles truth and untruth in a new locus of 'truthfulness' and argues for a broader understanding of 'truth' than what is purely 'factual'. These views are important for our understanding of Céline.

Finally, if we consider *Goodbye* as representing a breakdown in the autobiographical mode, insisted on by Graves, we gain a further understanding of the elaborate autobiographical fiction that is *Voyage*. The gravitational pull exerted by imagination, irony and laughter on Graves's 'autobiography' is fully embraced by Céline who can no more write an 'autobiography' than Graves can write a 'novel' of the war.

Hemingway

'Force, hatred, history [...]. That's not life for men and women, insult and hatred,' Leopold Bloom says in Joyce's *Ulysses*. 'Everybody knows that it's the very opposite of that that is really life [...]. Love [...] I mean the opposite of hatred.'[95] Hemingway's 1929 *A Farewell to Arms* is a love story, opposing the possibilities of renewal and rebirth through sexual love to the Great War's rampant, destructive, intercultural hatred. In 1918, an eighteen-year old Hemingway volunteered as an ambulance driver on the Italian Front. He was badly wounded and twice decorated. While convalescing he fell in love with a nurse. The infatuation was not reciprocated.

Farewell is a fictional account of Hemingway's war experience in which the unrequited infatuation becomes the inspiration for the novel's love story. It describes the death of love in a war which killed love (see 1.4 *Mechanisation*). It symbolically attempts to resuscitate the heroic, immortalising aspect of sexual love in an atmosphere of war which has abandoned seduction for murderous brute force. But, just as the war kills the object of its desire in its effort to possess it, so sexual love — in Hemingway's novel — results in death. In the wake of the Great War, *Farewell* asks 'is love possible?' It answers that it is not. *Voyage* too asks this question.

Many of the themes elaborated in *Voyage* are present in Hemingway's characteristically telegraphic account of the War. For example, the notion of a war which begins over and over, 'next week the war starts again';[96] theatricality, 'I'm leaving now for a show up above Plava';[97] resentment of the military police and coercion, 'were you there, Tenente, when they wouldn't attack and they shot every tenth man?'[98] Present also is the theme of the 'lie' of the war, contrasted with love as the possibility of truth: 'you don't have to pretend you love me'; 'let's not lie when we don't have to.'[99] Presented in contrast with a language of love, seeking simplicity and truth, is the collapse of a war-centred system of language embodying now moribund values, a collapse made memorably explicit by Hemingway:

> I had seen nothing sacred, and the things that were glorious had no glory
> and the sacrifices were like the stockyards at Chicago if nothing was done

with the meat except to bury it. There were many words that you could not
stand to hear and finally only the names of places had dignity. Certain
numbers were the same way and certain dates and these with the names of
places were all you could say and have them mean anything. Abstract
words such as glory, honor, courage, or hallow were obscene beside the
concrete names of villages, the numbers of roads, the names of rivers, the
numbers of regiments and the dates.[100]

Hemingway's emphasis on the importance of dates cannot fail to remind
us of *Voyage*'s '4 mai' and make us ask: is '4 mai' the only truth in *Voyage*? If
Voyage's language, obscene and excremental, provides a cry of protest at the
words 'you could not stand to hear' — the words that structure traditional
memory's ritual commemoration — it is the *meaning* of '4 mai' which opposes
their meaninglessness.

Symbolically present throughout *Farewell*, as in *Voyage*, is the river,
dividing two armies, war from peace, life from death, man from man, dividing
consciousness, one world from another, one self from another, the self who
embraced the war from the self who refuses it, dividing past from present, and
ultimately embodying the bright, cold symbol of the dream of the war's end noted
by C.E. Montague (see 1.3 *The Trenches*). In Hemingway's novel, the river
becomes the site where the hero's commitment to the war is washed away after
his own army has tried to kill him. 'Anger was washed away in the river along
with any obligation. [...] That ceased when the carabiniere put his hands on my
collar.'[101] The symbolism of Hemingway's fictional alter ego deserting in the fall
of 1917, at a time when American enthusiasm for entry into the war was at a fever
pitch, rather than in July 1918 when Hemingway himself was wounded, needs
little underlining. Here, narration allows Hemingway to re-enter the 'river' of time
and reconfigure the past to include his voice of dissent from years ahead. This
aspect of his novel has obvious resonances with Céline's own rewriting of self as
the coward, Bardamu. Like Hemingway, Céline will seize on the possibilities of
re-narrating his past to declare, after the fact, his dissent from the war.

Céline, as we shall see, was intent on retelling the stories of others in his
own story of the war (see 5.3 *Intertextual Witness*). *Farewell* is certainly a book
he is likely to have read. Indeed, that novel's explosion scene, recording its hero's

symbolic death, bears a strong resemblance to the equivalent scene in *Voyage* (RI, 17) and it is possible that Céline had it in mind as he was writing *Voyage*:

> There was a flash, as when a blast-furnace door is swung open, and a roar that started white and went red and on and on in a rushing wind. I tried to breathe but my breath would not come and I felt myself rush bodily out of myself and out and out and out all the time bodily in the wind. I went out swiftly, all of myself, and I knew I was dead and that it had all been a mistake to think you just died. Then I floated, and instead of going on I felt myself slide back. I breathed and I was back.[102]

This resemblance underlines the importance of contextualising Céline, not just to emphasise the immensity of shared memory in *Voyage*, but also to point out how Céline's memory encompasses the memory of others in order to represent in one site a totality of memory greater than the sum of its parts.

Hemingway's 'hero' seeks to escape from his war identity (the destructive hatred of self for other) through the creation of new identity (the desire of self for other) founded in the ecstatic union of lovers. 'I want you so much I want to be you too'. 'You are. We're the same one.'[103] The keynote of the novel, however, remains tragedy and the impossibility of new creation. The war sweeps everything away with it, including the possibility of redemption through love. Hemingway's novel ends with a death which erases the future. The final death of baby and mother at the end of *Farewell* — 'that was what people got for loving each other'[104] — is perhaps the most despairing image produced in any of the novels of the Great War:

> I could see nothing but the dark and the rain falling across the light from the window. [...] The baby was dead. [...] Now Catherine would die. That was what you did. You died. You did not know what it was about. You never had time to learn. They threw you in and told you the rules and the first time they caught you off base they killed you. Or they killed you gratuitously like Aymo. Or gave you the syphilis like Rinaldi. But they killed you in the end. You could count on that. Stay around and they would kill you.[105]

Hemingway lived a tempestuous life. In the short, strong sentences characteristic of his writing style he sought to revivify the masculine principle so damaged in the war.[106] His work embodies the confrontation and struggle against death. His passion for bull-fighting and big-game hunting expresses a will to death mastery based on heroic ritual confrontation.[107] All his life he was prone to deep and violent depressions and outbursts. On 2 July 1961, one day after the death of Céline in Paris, Hemingway shot himself.

Remarque

One writer above all would embody the shift from traditional to modern memory, the German veteran, Erich Maria Remarque. Remarque's 1929 *Im Westen nichts Neues* (literally *Nothing New in the West*), famously translated as *All Quiet on the Western Front*, was to become the best-known novel of the Great War and one of the most successful books of all time.[108] The effect of this book when it appeared was quite simply tremendous. In its first year of publication it sold a million copies in Germany alone and one and a half million copies in translation world wide. It was translated into thirty or more languages. It is still widely read today and has been filmed three times, the first time in 1930 as an award-winning Hollywood war classic. The success of the book and film made its author an internationally renowned and wealthy figure. Remarque and *All Quiet* are undoubtedly one of the most important reference points for Céline and *Voyage*. If, of the war books examined in this section, Graves's book is the closest to *Voyage* in terms of approach, Remarque's is the closest in terms of voice.

Remarque had been drafted into the German army in 1916. He served on the Western Front as a member of a sapper unit, laying wire and building bunkers and dugouts. He was wounded in July 1917 and was hospitalised until October 1918. The war ended before he could return to it. Remarque, speaking in a voice we will hear in Céline's 1916 letters from Africa to his childhood friend, Simone Saintu (see 4.1 *Africa*), said of his experience of war:

> At that time I was brimming over with enthusiasm and animated [...] by a great feeling of patriotism. [...] But afterward, afterward! The war was too terrible and too long for me not to learn to think otherwise. After it was all over I saw all its hideousness, but there was one thing I could not accept; I saw my best friend lying in the mud, his abdomen torn open. That is what is really insupportable and incomprehensible and what is no less comprehensible is that it required so many post-war years and so much reflection for me to realise the full atrocity of these occurrences.[109]

Remarque's novel struck a chord with almost everyone, not least the veterans. Herbert Read recognised it as the work of art the memory of the war had been waiting for. He wrote:

> [Remarque's] book is alone. It makes all other war books seem unnecessary. It achieves [...] the communication of experience. It is experience translated directly into terms of art and made universal. [...] It is the greatest war book that has yet appeared. [...] It is not a pacifist book; it is not a humanitarian book; it is the truth.[110]

Another veteran and poet, Richard Church, echoed Read's judgement: 'this is no literary trope; it is true.'[111]

All Quiet tells the story of the young German soldier, Paul Baumer, and his comrades. On its very first page the novel produces a scene which is emblematic of the war experience and which recalls '4 mai' at Verdun. A company of one hundred and fifty men have occupied a quiet sector of the front. As they prepare to move back they are caught by long range artillery. Only eighty of them survive. Ironically, the survivors enjoy extra rations as a result of the slaughter. This is the authentic voice of irony and disenchantment.

In the course of the novel Baumer loses all of his close comrades. The novel gives an account of each painful loss until eventually Baumer himself is killed. The loss of Baumer's illusions is swift. In the war he *sees* the truth, and the world he has left behind, the world of school and family, vanishes across an immeasurable gulf of true witness:

> In our minds the idea of authority [...] implied deeper insights and a more humane wisdom. But the first dead man that we saw shattered this conviction. [...] Our first experience of heavy artillery fire showed us our mistake, and the view of life that their teaching had given us fell to pieces under that bombardment.[112]

The value system that structured and sustained that world has collapsed with it. Says Paul bitterly of the war's hospitals and wounds:

> Everything must have been fraudulent and pointless if thousands of years of civilisation weren't even able to prevent this river of blood, couldn't stop these torture chambers existing in their hundreds of thousands.[113]

The only reality is the war itself. Everything else has been swallowed up. And the war itself is death. This is where *All Quiet* is closest to *Voyage*:

> Shells, gas clouds and flotillas of tanks — crushing, devouring, death. Dysentery, influenza, typhus — choking, scalding, death. Trench, hospital, mass grave — there are no other possibilities.[114]

All Quiet is the most significant intermediary between Céline's 1916 African letters and *Voyage*, if intermediary is needed. It is very likely that Céline recognised his own experience in Remarque's novel. It is likely too that Céline's choice of pen name is an acknowledgement of Remarque. Remarque assumed his mother's name Maria, Céline his grandmother's name.[115] Both names symbolically distance the holder from the patronym, and if the father is strikingly absent from Remarque's novel, appearing only in the guise of a French soldier who is also a printer like Baumer's father, and who is killed by Baumer,[116] he is equally absent from *Voyage* and appears in *Mort à crédit* only to be symbolically killed by a typewriter-bearing Ferdinand (RI, 822–823). Nothing could better represent the sense of betrayal felt by the young soldiers experiencing the war and their resentment at the older generation who led them to it. 'What would our fathers do if one day we rose up and confronted them, and called them to account?' asks Baumer.[117]

Reading *All Quiet*, Céline would have returned to his world of twenty. Indeed, as with Hemingway, particular passages in *Voyage* seem directly inspired by Remarque. For example, the scene where Baumer sees a poster of a beautiful girl:

> For us, the girl on the poster is a miracle. We have forgotten completely that such things exist, and even now we can scarcely believe our eyes. At any rate, we haven't seen anything like this for years, nothing remotely approaching this for light-heartedness, beauty and happiness.[118]

This immediately suggests the scene where Bardamu examines the cinema posters in New York, 'de véritables imprudences de beauté, ces indiscrétions sur les divines et profondes harmonies possibles' [veritable imprudence as far as beauty is concerned, indiscreet variations on all of the divine and profound harmonies possible] (RI, 201). When Remarque adds about the girl, 'this is what peace must be like', we are accorded an astonishing insight into the true nature of the hymn to the female form that resonates throughout *Voyage*.

Céline would have empathised as Remarque's novel becomes a lament for a generation lost to war — 'the war swept us away'[119] — whose possibilities of youth have been swallowed up by death:

> I am young, I am twenty years of age; but I know nothing of life except despair, death, fear [...]. Our knowledge of life is limited to death. What will happen afterwards. And what can possibly become of us?[120]

Life at the front in *All Quiet* is lived in a manner of exceptional frankness. As the soldiers play cards sitting on a circle of thunder-boxes in the open air, Baumer comments:

> A soldier is on much closer terms with his stomach and digestive system than anyone else is. Three-quarters of his vocabulary comes from this area and, whether he wants to express delight or extreme indignation, he will use one of those pungent phrases to underline it. It is impossible to make a point as clearly and as succinctly in any other way.[121]

This language will be their badge of experience. When they return home, 'our families and our teachers will be pretty surprised [...] but out here it's simply the language that everyone uses.'

The novel's deepest impression, however, is of strength of camaraderie. Here it differs most from *Voyage*, where camaraderie is implicit, hidden, subterranean. Remarque's scenes of camaraderie have a lasting pathos, and when Baumer's last comrade Katczinsky dies the passage that follows captures the essence of post-war memory and the negation of memory:

> Am I walking? Do I still have legs? I look up. I look about me. And then I turn right around, and then I stop. Everything is just the same as usual. It's only that Private Stanislaus Katczinsky is dead.
> After that I remember nothing.[122]

Perhaps this is Remarque's greatest truth of memory. How many of those who had lost fathers, sons, brothers, husbands, lovers, friends and comrades in the war, including Céline, read those lines and felt their truth within themselves? And for how many did memory begin and end with the war and its irreparable losses? If *All Quiet* is primarily the story of grieving memory, for one's own losses as well as the losses of others, its novelty is in giving back to memory, on a massive scale, its notes of disillusion and protest at these losses. With *All Quiet* the war, and war in general, ceased forever to be an episode of heroic grandeur. By maintaining camaraderie as the supreme value of wartime, however, Remarque had left a bridge for the world to cross over from traditional memory, whose core was silence and acceptance, to modern memory, which encompassed disenchantment and protest. In other words he created a broad space in memory for pain, futility and condemnation and at the same time left the door open for meaning and redemption.

The Battle for Memory

All Quiet divided memory. Although a major success with the public, Remarque found himself, in common with other war novelists, criticised on a number of fronts. Like Graves he was accused of falsehood. He was also accused of writing and sensationalising his story for money. Such attacks place these books of the late 1920s at the heart of a battle between the two forms of memory — traditional and modern — exalted and redemptive on the one hand, ironic and disenchanted on the other.

In his 1929 opus *Témoins* [*Witnesses*] the French War veteran, Jean Norton Cru, famously put the novels of the Great War on trial. His shorter *Du témoignage* [*Of witness*], published in 1930, offered a condensed, more pointed, account of his criticisms. Cru believed the truth of the war could be represented as scientific fact:

> La vérité de la guerre est une réalité aussi tangible à l'intelligence que la vérité de tout autre phénomène observable, vérifiable, où nos actions et nos émotions entrent en jeu [...]. La guerre eut même l'avantage de durer plus longtemps et de faciliter, par la répétition des expériences, le rajustement des impressions aux faits.[123]

> [The truth of the war is a reality as tangible to the intelligence as the truth of any other observable, verifiable phenomenon, where our actions and our emotions are in play [...]. The war even had the advantage of lasting longer and of facilitating by the repetition of experiences, the adjustment of impressions to the facts.]

He launched a blistering attack on the popular war novelists of the late 1920s. His critique became a denunciation of the role of imagination and story in the process of remembering:

> Les romanciers célèbres dont nous avons critiqué [...] les inexactitudes et les inventions illégitimes nous dénient le droit de contrôle en s'abritant derrière l'indépendance de l'art, en invoquant une vérité esthétique supérieure à la vérité des faits. Il est évident qu'ils ne se rendent pas compte de l'énormité de leurs erreurs ni de l'énormité du privilège qu'ils réclament. [...] C'est le droit à l'absurde.[124]

[Those famous novelists whose inexactitude and illegitimate inventions I have criticised deny us the right to criticise by taking cover behind the independence of their art, invoking an aesthetic truth superior to the facts. It is obvious that they have no idea of the enormity of their errors nor of the immensity of the right they claim. [...] It is a right to the absurd.]

Ironically, it was the 'absurdity' of war that writers like Graves and later, Céline, were targeting.

Indignantly, Norton Cru dismissed the major French war novelists while singling out Remarque because of the great success of *All Quiet*:

> L'utilité des romans de Barbusse et de Dorgelès, l'utilité du roman de Remarque — livre dont le cas est encore plus significatif — est à peine plus réelle que l'utilité de l'étude médicale fantaisiste.[125]

> [The utility of the novels of Barbusse and Dorgelès, the utility of Remarque's novel — the case of this book is even more revealing — is hardly any more real than the utility of fantastical medical writing.]

He argues that the novelist's desire to succeed commercially causes him to portray the war in a sensational manner guaranteed to please the morbid tastes of the reading public. Of course, this criticism not alone questions the writer's motive but also attacks his sincerity. The novelist is transformed into some Machiavellian prince of memory. According to Cru:

> L'écrivain dont la préoccupation première est, non pas de servir, mais d'imposer son œuvre au public, tombe inévitablement dans la fantaisie, le sensationnel gratuit, trop souvent le sadisme.[126]

> [The writer, whose primary preoccupation is, not to serve, but to impose his work on the public, falls inevitably into the trap of fantasy, gratuitous sensationalism and, too often, sadism.]

It is the tarnished image of the war and its soldiers which is most resented by him:

> Les romans qui ont eu le plus de succès ne flattent pas la guerre [...]. Le formule du succès est de présenter la guerre sous les apparences les plus sanglantes et les plus viles.[127]

> [The most successful novels do not flatter the war [...]. The formula of success is to present the most bloody and vile image of the war.]

He indicts the novelist's 'mind', indicts imagination, indicts art:

> La difficulté réside moins dans l'objet que dans l'esprit de l'artiste hanté par la mode littéraire, les procédés, le désir d'obtenir des effets, d'autre part obsédé par les légendes dont il n'a pas su conjurer l'emprise.[128]

> [The problem is less in the object than in the mind of the artist obsessed, on the one hand, with literary fashion, with literary method, and the desire

to obtain effects, and on the other hand, with the impact of rumour and legends he has been unable to withstand.]

He attacks the very means by which novelists compose their portrait of the war. For Norton Cru these means derive from a 'tradition menteuse' [lying tradition].[129] He explicitly affirms the adequacy of the nineteenth-century novel's 'realist' mode as a means of portraying the truth of an unprecedented twentieth-century experience of mass death.[130] He accuses 'pacifist' writers of subverting their literary models of the past, without seeming at all aware himself that the Great War has occasioned a fundamental shift in perception. He fails to see that the memory of the war is changing and that the core of that shift lies in the collapse of the heroic ideal and its supports in memory, and in the return of memory itself to imagination as a means of mediating the war experience. His attack on novelists becomes ever more scathing:

> Boucheries héroïques [deviennent] sous leur plume boucheries démentes et inhumaines. [...] Leurs poilus ont des goûts d'apaches et s'adonnent au meurtre avec un brio imité des brutes héroïques de nos fastes militaires apocryphes. C'est la plus révoltante calomnie de ces braves gens, le soldat français et le soldat allemand. La belle œuvre que voilà, pour des pacifistes! La belle vérité qu'ils nous révèlent ! Ils ne l'ont certes pas puisée dans leur expérience personnelle du combat.[131]

> [In their writing heroic slaughters become demented and inhuman. [...] Their soldiers behave like apaches and give themselves over to murder with a brio inspired by the heroic brutes featured in our apocryphal military annals. They perpetrate the most revolting calumny against those courageous figures: the French and German soldier. That's fine work for the pacifists! That's the wonderful truth they reveal! They certainly didn't learn it through their own experience of combat.]

This last quote defines Norton Cru, and *his* truth. He is firmly within the myth of the war experience, finding redemption in the traditional images of heroism and sacrifice of the ordinary soldier. His work is more than historical; it is redemptive and cloaks all combatants on all sides in a mantle of redemption. Thus, he later hopes for more modesty, and more justice with regard to their comrades, from those he calls the 'enfants gâtés de la réclame' [advertising's spoiled children], the writers of pacifist novels, Remarque *et al.*[132]

Norton Cru's work, cogent and persuasive if read on its own terms, above all denies the right to imagination and its value as an indispensable dimension of memory. He concludes:

> Ceux qui souhaitent que la vérité de la guerre se fasse jour regretteront qu'on ait écrit des romans de guerre, genre faux, littérature à prétention de témoignage, où la liberté d'invention, légitime et nécessaire dans le roman strictement littéraire, joue un rôle néfaste dans ce qui prétend apporter une déposition.[133]

> [Those who would like the truth of the war to be known will one day regret that war novels have been written, constituting a false genre, literature claiming to be witness, where the freedom to invent, legitimate and necessary in the strictly literary novel, plays a nefarious role in what claims to provide a testimony.]

Norton Cru's was not the only work of its kind. In 1930, in England, Douglas Jerrold's *The Lie about the War* took over where Norton Cru left off. Jerrold chose Barbusse, Hemingway, and Remarque among his particular targets. Jerrold complained of the lack of truth in these writers and of their:

> obsession of futility [...] which accounts for the piling up of the individual agony to so many poignant climaxes remote from the necessities or even from the normal incidental happenings of war.[134]

Bernard Bergonzi insightfully commented on the divide between Jerrold and the writers he attacks. His insight holds good for Norton Cru:

> The ultimate difference between them is that Jerrold remains secure in traditional habits of mind, which the others have abandoned. He regarded the war as both necessary and significant; they see it as meaningless.[135]

For mind read memory and the divide is revealed in its full significance. Neither Norton Cru nor Jerrold could at heart accept the role of imagination in the memory of the war. The shift towards imagination of 1929, however, is a shift away from the 'literal' towards another means of mediating memory, a new means of trying to understand the past. That some should not wish, or not be able, to make that transition is understandable.

The efforts of Norton Cru and Jerrold did nothing to limit the public demand for war novels and the popularity of these works has never waned. The memory of the Great War can never now be separated from the names of Graves, Hemingway, Remarque, and Céline.

The Anti-Norton Cru

Céline is aware, as he writes *Voyage*, of the debate that surrounds the literary memory of the Great War and aware of the accusations launched against the major war novelists such as Barbusse and Remarque. When he enters the arena of memory in 1932 he disarms criticism with one of literature's most ironic and challenging epigraphs:

> Notre voyage à nous est entièrement imaginaire. Voilà sa force. [...] Hommes, bêtes, villes et choses, tout est imaginé. C'est un roman, rien qu'une histoire fictive. Littré le dit, qui ne se trompe jamais. (RI, epigraph)
>
> [Our journey is entirely imaginary. That's its strength. [...] Men, animals, towns and objects, are all imagined. It's a novel, nothing but a fictional story. Littré says so, and he's never wrong.]

Céline would make a virtue of all the criticisms marshalled by Norton Cru against Remarque and others. He would claim that he wrote *Voyage* for money; that he was following a fashion, nothing more.[136] He effectively placed himself beyond criticism and had the first and last laugh at any would-be detractors. Coming hot on the heels of Cru's work, *Voyage* usurps and mocks Cru. It makes of Céline an anti-Cru, doing everything Cru says he should not do to arrive at the truth, and success.[137]

Conclusion

In 1928, as traditional memory massively commemorated the Great War, its silences began to crumble. In 1929, a series of literary accounts of the war appeared, whose voices, breaching traditional memory, allowed pain, disillusionment and protest to be heard. These narrative accounts favoured imagination and story over direct telling and revealed a public need for story as a means of remembering and mediating the experience of war. The works of Remarque, Hemingway and Graves were a site of shared memory of war and forerunners of *Voyage*. Their books, to a greater or lesser extent, offered a dissenting counterpoint to the way the war was remembered within the exalting framework of official commemoration. *Voyage*, when it appears in 1932, enters this dynamic of dissent.

[1] Jay Winter, *Sites of Memory, Sites of Mourning* (Cambridge: Cambridge University Press, 1995), p.28.

[2] Jay Winter, 'The Great War and the Persistence of Tradition', in *Modernity and Violence*, ed. by Bernd Hüppauf (Berlin: De Gruyter, 1997), pp.33–45 (p.34).

[3] Olivier Faron, 'Une catastrophe démographique', p.47.

[4] Faron, 'Les pupilles, enfants chéris de la nation', *L'Histoire*, 225, p.48.

[5] Connerton, p.45.

[6] See Mosse, 'Two World Wars', p.492.

[7] Mosse, *Fallen Soldiers*, p.99.

[8] Mosse, 'Two World Wars', p.492.

[9] Mosse, *Fallen Soldiers*, p.127.

[10] Mosse, *Fallen Soldiers*, p.152.

[11] Mosse, *Fallen Soldiers*, p.154.

[12] Mosse, *Fallen Soldiers*, p.127.

[13] See Annette Becker, *La Guerre et la Foi: de la mort à la mémoire 1914–1930* (Paris: Armand Colin, 1994).

[14] See Jean-Pierre Blin, 'Le Christ au champ d'honneur', *L'Histoire*, 225, p.52.

[15] For an extended exploration of the use of *Épinal* imagery in the Great War, see Winter, *Sites of Memory*, pp.122–133. See also Tom Quinn, 'La Gloire guerrière et les images d'Epinal', *The Irish Journal of French Studies*, 3, 2003, 79–93.

[16] Winter, *Sites of Memory*, p.129.

[17] Mosse, *Fallen Soldiers*, p.7.

[18] Annette Becker, 'Aux morts, la patrie reconnaissante', *L'Histoire*, 225, 50–53 (p.50).

[19] According to Niall Ferguson, 'the First World War turned out to be a turning point in the long-running conflict between monarchism and republicanism; a conflict which had its roots in eighteenth-century America and France [...]. The war led to a triumph of republicanism undreamt of even in the 1790s.' See Ferguson, pp.434–435.

[20] See Mosse, *Fallen Soldiers*, p.40. According to Mosse, 'the revolutionary emphasis on collectivity, even in death, foreshadows the rows upon rows of identical graves in military cemeteries.'

[21] See Philippe Ariès, *L'Homme devant la Mort* (Paris: Seuil, 1977), p.543.

[22] See Mosse, *Fallen Soldiers*, p.41.

[23] See Prost, III, 37.

[24] See Becker, *La Guerre et la Foi*, p.112.

[25] See Jean-François Sirinelli, ed., *La France de 1914 à nos jours* (Paris: Presses Universitaires de France, 1993), pp.21–22.

[26] See Becker, *La Guerre et la Foi*, p.114.

[27] See Becker, 'Aux morts, la patrie reconnaissante', p.53.

[28] Becker, *La Guerre et la Foi*, p.115.

[29] Cited in Becker, *La Guerre et la Foi*, p.115.

[30] Mosse, *Fallen Soldiers*, p.106.

[31] Winter, *Sites of Memory*, p.82.

[32] Prost's view is cited in Gérard Vincent, 'Guerres secrètes, guerres tues', p.211.

[33] See Prost, III, 55–56.

[34] Ariès, p.542.

[35] Ariès, p.543.

[36] Becker, 'Aux morts, la patrie reconnaissante', p.51.

[37] Ariès, pp.543–544.

[38] Prost, III, 43.

[39] Becker, 'Aux morts, la patrie reconnaissante', pp.51–53.

[40] Ariès, p.543.

[41] See Ariès, pp.541–542.

[42] See Peter V. Jones' introduction to Homer, *The Odyssey*, trans. by E.V. Rieu (London: Penguin, 1991), p.xxxi.

[43] Ariès, p.542.

[44] Connerton, p.60.

[45] Adrian Gregory, *The Silence of Memory: Armistice Day 1919–1946* (Oxford: Berg, 1994), p.9.

[46] Robert Whalen Weldon, *Bitter Wounds: German Victims of the Great War 1914–1939* (London: Cornell University Press, 1984), p.33.

[47] See Whalen Weldon, p.184.

[48] Cited in Jean Norton Cru, *Témoins* (Nancy: Presses Universitaires de Nancy, 1993), p.575.

[49] Cru, p.330.

[50] Cru, p.655.

[51] Cru, p.655.

[52] Cru, p.523.

[53] Henry Malherbe, preface to Jacques Meyer, *La Biffe* (Paris: Albin Michel, 1928), p.xvi.

[54] See Ducasse and others, *Vie et mort des Français*, p.470.

[55] Cited in Fussell, *The Bloody Game*, p.36.

[56] Jean-Jacques Becker, 'Plus jamais ça !', *L'Histoire*, 225, 56–59 (p.57).

[57] Ducasse and others, pp.471–472.

[58] Becker, 'Plus jamais ça !', p.57.

[59] 'Plus jamais ça !', p.57.

[60] 'Plus jamais ça !', pp.57–58.

[61] 'Plus jamais ça !', p.58.

[62] Eric J.Leed, *No Man's Land: Combat and Identity in World War One* (London: Cambridge University Press, 1979), p.208.

[63] Malherbe, p.x.

[64] Ducasse and others, p.471.

[65] Ducasse and others, p.473.

[66] Léon Poirier, dir., *Verdun*, Gaumont, 1927, 1928, 1930. Only copy extant consulted courtesy of the Cinémathèque Française at the Fort de St. Cyr, near Paris.

[67] Michel Cadé, 'La Grande Guerre dans le cinéma français : une mise à distance', retrieved from http://www.ags.fr/d3/actesducolloque/frame325139.html on 19 September 2000. Text originally published in *Traces de 14–18: Actes du Colloque international tenu à Carcassonne du 24 au 27 avril 1996*, ed. by Sylvie Caucanas and Rémy Cazals (Carcassonne: Les Audois, 1997), pp.91–101.

[68] Cadé.

[69] *Le Figaro*, 10 November 1928, p.2.

[70] See Jean Bastier, p.274.

[71] *Le Figaro*, 10 November 1928, p.2.

[72] Henry Vidal writing in *Le Figaro*, 11 November, 1928, p.1.

[73] *Le Figaro*, 12 November, 1928, p.2.

[74] *Le Figaro*, 12 November, p.2.

[75] Sassoon, pp.652–653.

[76] The breakdown in the narrative of traditional memory is recognised by Eric Hobsbawm when he writes, 'in spite of the trauma of the First World War, continuity with the past was not so obviously broken until the 1930s'. See Hobsbawm, p.190. Hobsbawm makes *All Quiet on the Western Front* a key moment in this break with continuity.

[77] Herbert Read, 'Why War Books Are Popular', in *Readings on All Quiet on the Western Front*, ed. by Terry O'Neill (San Diego: Greenhaven Press, 1999), pp.34–38 (pp.36–37).

[78] Read, p.37.

[79] This in particular is Modris Eksteins's view of Remarque and *All Quiet* and the other novels of disenchantment. 'Nineteen twenty-nine was a critical year,' writes Eksteins, invoking international recession as a reason for the 'war books' boom. See Eksteins, *Rites of Spring: The Great War and the Birth of the Modern Age* (London: Papermac, 2000), p.294.

[80] See Sirinelli, pp.108–109.

[81] Robert Graves, *Goodbye to All That* (Oxford: Berghahn, 1995), p.75.

[82] Graves, p.11.

[83] See Martin Seymour Smith, *Robert Graves: His Life and Work* (London: Bloomsbury, 1995). Smith, who knew Graves, records delusional episodes when Graves was in his eighties and writes

that guilt over killing people haunted Graves until the end of his life. 'I am certain that war-guilt caused him the most intense grief,' he writes. See Smith's introduction, pp.xviii–xix.

[84] Graves, p.297.

[85] Graves, p.136.

[86] The offending passage is featured in Fussell, *The Great War and Modern Memory*, pp.210–211. It is also to be found in the later 1957 edition of *Goodbye to All That*.

[87] Fussell, pp.208–209.

[88] Fussell, p.209.

[89] Robert Graves, cited in preface to *Goodbye to All That*, p.xi.

[90] See Philip Stephen Day, *Le Miroir allégorique*, pp.120–123.

[91] Fussell, p.216.

[92] Fussell, p.217.

[93] Jay Winter, 'Céline and the Cultivation of Hatred', p.238.

[94] Cited in preface to *Goodbye to All That*, p.xvii.

[95] James Joyce, *Ulysses* (New York: Vintage Books, 1961), p.333.

[96] Ernest Hemingway, *A Farewell to Arms* (London: Arrow Books, 1994), p.11.

[97] Hemingway, p.39.

[98] Hemingway, p.45.

[99] Hemingway, p.30.

[100] Hemingway, p.165.

[101] Hemingway, p.208.

[102] Hemingway, p.50.

[103] Hemingway, p.266.

[104] Hemingway, p.283.

[105] Hemingway, p.289.

[106] According to Stanley Cooperman, 'in the work of Hemingway death is less a threat to a man's existence than to his *cojones*.' See Cooperman, *World War I and the American Novel* (Baltimore: John Hopkins University Press, 1967), p.188.

[107] See Cooperman, pp.186–187.

[108] *All Quiet on the Western Front* was reputed to be the second most read book in history after the Bible. See introduction to *Readings on All Quiet on the Western Front*, pp.10–13 (p.11).

[109] Cited in 'Erich Maria Remarque: A Biography', in *Readings on All Quiet on the Western Front*, pp.14–29 (pp.16–17).

[110] Read, pp.37–38.

[111] Richard Church, '*All Quiet* Perfectly Transmits the Experience of War', in *Readings on All Quiet on the Western Front*, pp.39–43 (p.39).

[112] Erich Maria Remarque, *All Quiet on the Western Front*, trans. by Brian Murdoch (London: Vintage, 1996), p.9.

[113] Remarque, p.186.

[114] Remarque, p.199.

[115] See Frédéric Vitoux, *La Vie de Céline* (Paris: Grasset, 1988), p.24.

[116] Remarque, pp.153–159.

[117] Remarque, p.186. One thinks of Edward Thomas expressing his hatred for 'one fat patriot', his father, when he writes 'God how I hate you!' Edward Thomas, 'This is No Case of Petty Right or Wrong', *Poets of the Great War*, Naxos, CD, NA 210912, 1997.

[118] Remarque, p.102.

[119] Remarque, p.14.

[120] Remarque, p.186.

[121] Remarque, p.6.

[122] Remarque, p.205.

[123] Jean Norton Cru, *Du témoignage* (Paris: Allia, 1997), pp.23–24.

[124] *Du témoignage*, pp.105–106.

[125] *Du témoignage*, p.110.

[126] *Du témoignage*, pp.110–111.

[127] *Du témoignage*, pp.108–109.

---

[128] *Du témoignage*, p.107.

[129] *Du témoignage*, p.106.

[130] *Du témoignage*, pp.112–113.

[131] *Du témoignage*, p.111.

[132] *Du témoignage*, p.114.

[133] *Du témoignage*, p.99.

[134] Cited in Bernard Bergonzi, *Heroes' Twilight: A Study of the Literature of the Great War* (London: Constable, 1965), p.196.

[135] Bergonzi, pp.196–197.

[136] See, for example, as early as February 1933, 'Propos recueillis par Élisabeth Porquerol', *Cahiers Céline*, 1: *Céline et l'actualité littéraire 1932–1957*, ed. by Jean-Pierre Dauphin and Henri Godard (Paris: Gallimard, 1976), 43–49 (p.46), 'A-t-il vu dans la littérature un moyen de s'en tirer, de faire fortune ? En partie, certainement' [Had he seen in literature a means to advance himself, to make his fortune? In part, certainly]. Private remarks in letters to Joseph Garcin show Céline in more trenchant form, almost in Norton Cru pose: 'mentir et survivre [...] suivre la mode comme les midinettes, c'est le boulot de l'écrivain très contraint matériellement, c'est la condition sans laquelle pas de tirage sérieux (seul aspect qui compte)' [to lie and survive [...] to follow the fashion like a midinette, that's the job of a writer experiencing material difficulties, and without which he cannot hope to sell (all that matters)]. See Lainé, p.632. This sort of remark soon becomes part of Céline's public persona as a writer.

[137] Céline mentions Cru in a letter to Milton Hindus dated 2 October 1947. Philippe Alméras notes a distinct rapport between Cru's analysis of war accounts and Céline's representation of war in *Voyage*. See Alméras, *Dictionnaire Céline: Une œuvre, une vie* (Paris: Plon, 2004), pp.226–227. See also the full text of this letter in *L'Herne*, 127–128.

CHAPTER 3

CÉLINE AT WAR

From Rambouillet to Poelkapelle

Introduction

As Céline's memory was shaped by his encounter with death, it is necessary to be attentive to the detail of this encounter. As we have seen in Chapter One, the experience of death creates a duality (see 1.3 *Death*). Beginning with early childhood and those experiences which will constitute the ground for future trauma, this chapter takes us with Céline into the Great War towards the discovery of his own mortality, discovery which divides him before and after, past and present. In doing so, this chapter uses a number of factual sources: Céline's own pre-war *Carnets* [notebooks];[1] the regimental *Journal des marches et opérations*, a handwritten day-to-day record of his regiment's involvement in the war; and the official *Historique du 12e Cuirassiers*, the regimental history. These sources will enable us to measure the distance between the lived reality of Céline at war and the fictional portrait of that reality in *Voyage*.

3.1 CHILDHOOD EXPERIENCE

Separation

Hendin and Haas in their study of trauma in Vietnam veterans tell us:

> While the traumatic experience of combat is at the heart of the disorder, neither the subjective perceptions of combat, nor the subsequent reactions to it, are the same for all veterans. The unique personal and social characteristics that each individual brought to combat played a role in shaping his combat experiences, in influencing his perceptions of traumatic combat events, and in determining the specific meanings that such events had, and continue to have, for him.[2]

Elements highlighted in this first section which will later influence Céline's response to the traumatic conditions of combat are the death of his grandmother, his experience of bereavement, his religious education, and a degree of resentment in his decision to join the army due to tension with his father.

Céline was born under a star of separation and dislocation. He was born on 27 May 1894 at Courbevoie near Paris, and christened Louis-Ferdinand Destouches, the only child of Fernand, an insurance clerk, and Marguerite, the owner of a boutique specialising in the sale of lace items.[3] Because of his mother's suspected tuberculosis the child was sent to live with a nurse. Family visits were few. Louis was three when eventually taken to live with his parents in Paris.[4] Life remained unsettled. In Paris, the family moved twice before, in 1899, settling in the Passage Choiseul, a long, narrow, gas-lit shopping gallery, Céline would later describe as 'une cloche à gaz' [a bell jar filled with gas].[5] The pattern of separation also continued. Having finished his regular schooling and obtained his *certificat d'études*, Louis was sent, in August 1907, to Germany, to learn German for use in the business career intended for him. He returned home in December 1908. His education abroad was not finished however. In February 1909 he left for boarding school in England, remaining there until November.

Death

Young Destouches, a solitary child with few friends, was particularly close to his maternal grandmother, Céline Guillou. He would later choose her name as his pen name. She looked after him while his mother worked. She fed his imagination, taking him on excursions, introducing him to the theatre and the cinema, providing him with copies of *Les Belles Aventures illustrées*.[6] Her demise in December 1904 was Céline's most significant experience of death prior to the war. He discovered nature, he later said, when taken 'au cimetière, pour aller voir la tombe de ma grand-mère, quand elle est morte' [to the cemetery, to see my grandmother's grave, after her death].[7]

As for Céline's first experience of death, he would later write of his grandmother's demise in *Mort à crédit*:

> Elle a voulu me dire quelque chose... Ça lui râpait le fond de la gorge, ça finissait pas... Tout de même elle y est arrivée... le plus doucement qu'elle a pu... 'Travaille bien mon petit Ferdinand !' qu'elle a chuchoté... J'avais pas peur d'elle... On se comprenait au fond des choses... (RI, 598)

[She wanted to tell me something... It rasped at the back of her throat, endlessly... All the same she managed to get it out... as gently as she could... 'Work hard my little Ferdinand!' she whispered... I wasn't afraid of her... Deep down we understood each other...]

What is remarkable in this passage is the description, not of Caroline's death itself, which remains hidden — Caroline sends the family into the next room — but of her attitude towards death, her *pudeur* [reserve], and the closely observed attitude of her bereaved family.[8]

> On a fermé notre boutique. On a déroulé tous les stores... On avait comme une sorte de honte... Comme si on était des coupables... On osait plus du tout remuer, pour mieux garder notre chagrin... On pleurait avec maman, à même sur la table... On n'avait pas faim... Plus envie de rien... On tenait déjà pas beaucoup de place et pourtant on aurait voulu pouvoir nous rapetisser toujours... Demander pardon à quelqu'un, à tout le monde... On se pardonnait les uns aux autres... On se suppliait qu'on s'aimait bien... On avait peur de se perdre encore... pour toujours... comme Caroline... (RI, 598)

> [We closed the shop. We pulled down the blinds... We felt a sort of shame... As if we were to blame... We didn't dare budge, the better to hold back our grief... We cried along with mama, face down on the table... We had no appetite... No appetite for anything... We already occupied such little space, and yet we would have liked to occupy even less... To ask forgiveness of someone, of everyone... We forgave each other... We pleaded with each other to go on loving each other... We were afraid of losing each other... forever... like Caroline...]

The passage provides a pen-portrait of bereavement within a specific social context, that of middle-class shop-keepers in Paris before the Great War. And there is little edifying here, beyond the silent modesty of Caroline's surrender. Ferdinand's mother falls prostrate with anguish. Grief is accompanied by a falling away of the appetite, of desire for the world. Grandmother Caroline's death taints the bereaved with fear of their own death, together with a sense of irreparable loss and separation. This, it can justly be claimed, is the paradigm of loss and bereavement which informs *Voyage*.

Family, Work and Army

Marcel Brochard, a friend of Céline's from medical school, lunched occasionally with Céline's parents. Brochard remembered them as 'braves gens tranquilles, petits bourgeois, effacés' [honest, quiet folk, lower middle-class, self-effacing].[9]

'On en sortait éberlué à la pensée que Louis était leur enfant' [We were astonished to think that they were Louis's parents], he wrote.[10] Céline's father he remembers as physically a round man, jovial and frank. Céline's parents, he says, loved each other and got on well together. Brochard recalled Céline's childhood, perhaps based on conversations with Céline's parents, 'il est exact Louis que tu étais un enfant endiablé, indiscipliné, ivre de liberté, et que tu as reçu des gifles et des fessées sûrement bien méritées' [it's true, Louis, that you were a frightful child, undisciplined, drunk with freedom, and that you were often on the receiving end of surely well-deserved corporal punishments].[11] Céline himself would later comment, 'j'ai été élevé dans les gifles' [I was raised by slapping];[12] a practice, as we shall see, which would prepare a profound psychological mark after his experience of bombardment in the war.

Céline attended a state school where he received a purely lay education. Although his mother was religious, his religious education was scant. In 1905, following the death of his grandmother, and at a time when anti-clericalism was at its height in France, he was enrolled at his mother's wishes in St. Joseph's catholic school to enable him to make his First Communion.[13] This he did on 18 May 1905. A year later he was moved again, his father insisting on a 'republican' education. Lack of religious formation would possibly contribute to Céline's inability to transcend death.[14]

In 1909, Céline started work. He held various positions between 1910 and 1912, draper's assistant and later, jeweller's assistant. Eventually he worked with the jeweller, Lacloche, also spending some time at a branch of Lacloche in Nice. There he attended an immense military pageant to commemorate Queen Victoria. The sight intoxicated him.[15] In 1958, asked why he had enlisted Céline responded that, among other reasons, he felt:

> Un certain goût [...]. Je voyais ça très brillant, et puis l'histoire des cuirassiers de Reichshoffen, cela me paraissait quelque chose de très brillant je dois dire. Et puis c'était très brillant parce que c'était le ton de l'époque.[16]
>
> [A certain taste for it [...]. I saw it as something quite brilliant, and then the history of the Reichshoffen cuirassiers seemed quite marvellous to me,

I must admit. It was all quite brilliant because that was the tone of the time.]

Within days of returning to Paris, Louis's future was settled. His father wrote to Lacloche:

> Quelques jours après son retour de Nice il nous a déclaré qu'après en avoir référé à ses Patrons et à vous-même en particulier il en avait conclu qu'il était de l'intérêt de son avenir dans votre bonne maison de se libérer le plus rapidement possible de ses obligations militaires, ainsi s'explique que j'ai consenti à son engagement au 12e Cuirassier.[17]

> [Some days after returning from Nice he declared that after having consulted with his employers and with you in particular he had reached the conclusion that it was in the interests of his future in your fine company to acquit himself as rapidly as possible of his military obligations, which explains why I have consented to his enlisting in the 12th Cuirassier regiment.]

This letter suggests that Céline's decision to join the army was a practical one. That the youngster received the encouragement of his employer and his father is obvious. Céline's father, Fernand, had served four years in an artillery regiment in the 1880s and was no doubt proud to see his son enlist.[18] François Gibault tells us that Fernand, resolutely patriotic, republican and 'revanchard' [avid to avenge the French defeat in the 1870 Franco-Prussian war] assailed the child Louis with vivid evocations of the 'revanche' [revenge] to come.[19]

Fernand would later joke that he had made his son join the army because he did not know what else to do with him.[20] This flippancy reveals some truth in Marcel Brochard's testimony that 'à 18 ans, tu te heurtes à des parents excédés, et excédé toi-même tu t'engages dans l'armée par coup de tête' [at 18, your outraged parents will have no more of your excesses and outraged yourself you get carried away and join the army].[21] This provides an important element in the contextualisation of Céline's joining the army in 1912 and it is likely that some tension with his father figured in Céline's decision to enlist. Along with a certain attitude to death absorbed from his social and cultural background, this resentment provides a significant element in Céline's traumatic response to war and its eventual expression in *Voyage*.

3.2 BEFORE THE WAR

The 12th Cuirassiers

On 28 September 1912, Céline joined the 12th Cuirassier cavalry regiment. The 12th Cuirassiers formed an elite cavalry regiment with a prestigious history. If Céline's military dream was for something 'brilliant', the 12th Cuirassiers could certainly provide it. It was 'un régiment pour la parade où la discipline était de fer, les traditions immuables, les corvées sans limites et les préoccupations morales inexistantes' [a show regiment whose discipline was ironlike, traditions immutable, where chores were limitless and moral preoccupations inexistent].[22] Entering this world, Céline began a process of personal transformation that would culminate in his experience of war two years later.

Arrival at Rambouillet

The young soldier Céline kept a notebook in which he recalled his life at Rambouillet. In these *Carnets*, Céline describes his arrival at Rambouillet and the company he found there:

> 3 octobre — Arrivée — Corps de garde rempli de sous-offs aux allures écrasantes. Cabots esbroufeurs. Incorporation dans un peloton le 4e Lt Le Moyne bon garçon, Coujon méchant faux comme un jeton — [...] C'est entouré de cet état-major bigarré que je fais mes premiers pas dans la vie militaire. Sans oublier Servat, un ancien cabot cassé... faux et brute.[23]

> [3 October — Arrival — Guardroom full of non-commissioned officers of shocking demeanour. Coarse braggarts. Incorporated into the 4th platoon Lieutenant Le Moyne a good sort, Coujon wicked and false — [...] Surrounded by this motley crew I take my first steps in military life. Not to forget Servat, an experienced old recruit... false and brutish.]

The world Céline had entered was far different from the world of Parisian jewellers and lace-makers. Céline's comrades were mostly Breton peasants. This is how he remembered them in 1939, 'En 14, nos gars étaient des culs-terreux. Le service ne changeait pas le rythme de leur existence passée à la ferme au cul des chevaux. [...] Ils étaient ignorants comme des bœufs d'herbe' [In '14, our soldiers were peasants. Military service did nothing to change the rhythm of their lives on the farm whose boundaries were set by the horses' backsides. [...] They were as ignorant as the grazing cattle.][24]

The distance between the uneducated Breton peasants and the Parisian shop-keeper's son, educated in England and Germany, is all too clear. In 1950, he returned to the attack, describing his doomed, rustic comrades in a frank letter to Henri Nimier:

> Absolument breton — ah ! pas proustiens du tout — même pas de sensualité élémentaire— [...] Une petite érection vers la cantinière... vague... à peine — Tristes gens — *mystiques.* Je les ai vu foncer dans la mort — sans ciller — les 800 — comme un seul homme... et chevaux — une sorte d'attirance — pas une fois, dix ! comme d'un débarras. Pas de sensualité — pas un sur dix parlait français — doux et brutes à la fois — des purs cons en somme — [25]

> [Breton through and through — ah! not at all Proustian — not even a basic sensuality— [...] A faint erection in honour of the canteen lady... vague... barely — Sad men — *mystical.* I saw them throwing themselves at death — without blinking — all 800 of them — as one man... and their horses too — a sort of attraction — not just once, but ten times! As if getting rid of something. No sensuality — not one in ten spoke French — gentle and brutish at the same time — in brief, pure idiots —]

This striking statement of his comrades' attitude to death provides a confirming echo of Bardamu's bitter depiction of his comrades in *Voyage.* Céline's astonishment remains undiluted over the years as the letter ends in brusque dismissal.

If Céline had little in common with his comrades, he may have found solace among the officers. The lieutenant Dugué Mac-Carthy seems an untypical soldier. He organised a choir and theatre group at Rambouillet.[26] We shall later see his sensitivity in dealing with Céline at a time when his military future was in some doubt. Another officer who would play a significant part in Céline's military life was Colonel Blacque-Belair who took command of the 12th Cuirassiers in May 1914 and who led the regiment into the Great War.[27] His death in 1930, when Céline was writing *Voyage,* may have contributed to the novel's pessimism.[28]

Barrack Life

The *Carnets* gives us some insight into life at Rambouillet. It is imbued with a melancholy akin to the December darkness in which it was composed. 'Qu'est-il au monde de plus triste qu'un après-midi de décembre un dimanche au quartier ?' [What could be more miserable than a Sunday afternoon in the barracks?].[29]

Army life here seems anything but 'brilliant'. The young soldier is rudely awakened at dawn. 'Que de réveils horribles [...] que aux sons si faussement gais du trompette de garde vous présentent à l'esprit les rancœurs et les affres de la journée d'un bleu' [So many horrible mornings which [...] waking to the falsely gay sound of the bugle, present you with the trials and tribulations of a new recruit's day]. [30]

The day begins early with the cleaning out of the stables, where army life seems to reach its lowest ebb:

> Ces descentes aux écuries dans la brume matinale. La course sarabande des galoches dans l'escalier la corvée d'écurie dans la pénombre. Quel noble métier que le métier des armes. Au fait les vrais sacrifices consistent peut-être dans la manipulation du fumier à la lumière blafarde d'un falot crasseux ?...[31]

> [Going down to the stables in the morning mist. The saraband of boots running on the stairs the stable cleaned out in near-darkness. What a noble calling that of arms. Perhaps the real sacrifices consist of shovelling shit in the pale light of a filthy lamp?...]

The tone here is ironic. Enthusiasm, if there was enthusiasm, has given way to humiliation. There is further humiliation during riding lessons. Horses frighten Céline. The city boy's attempts at riding provoke laughter:

> Au cours des élèves brigadiers pris en grippe par un jeune officier plein de sang en butte aux sarcasmes d'un sous-off abruti ayant une peur innée du cheval, je ne fis pas (longtemps) long feu.[32]

> [During the brigadier training course picked on by a fierce young officer the butt of a brutal non-commissioned officer having an innate fear of horses, I did not (for very long) make much of an impression.]

Barrack life, however, had other less trying aspects. Surviving fragments of *Casse-pipe* recall escorting the President of the Republic during his visits to Rambouillet: 'Nous parcourions [...] tous les abords de la forêt, à très noble allure, au trot somptueux des attelages' [We rode through the forest, looking very noble, matching the sumptuous trot of the carriages] (RIII, 68).

The pageantry of 14 July 1913 at Longchamp where Ferdinand parades in front of the French President would remain in memory as something 'brilliant'. The cuirassiers charge to the front of the tribune:

Ça fait un mouvement d'amplitude sept mille cavaliers au galop... Faut entendre ça comme résonance. Faut voir aussi tout l'éventail, les cuirassiers... le flot hérissé des dragons... la légère à tombeau ouvert qui prend la corde à l'aile marchante. Il en mugit dans l'avalanche, le sol cavalé... jusqu'aux gradins ça carambole et ça gronde. Voilà le travail ! Les batteries éclatent leurs gargousses. (RIII, 70)

[Seven thousand cavalrymen at the gallop offers quite a spectacle... You should hear the reverberation. You should see the way they fan out, the cuirassiers... the flood of dragoons with lances raised... the light cavalry charging hell for leather on the flank. The ground, beaten by hooves, groans under the avalanche... rolling and thundering all the way to the stands. What a piece of work! The batteries let fly.]

There was pride too on his visits home. Splendidly arrayed in uniform, Céline liked to impress.[33] However, the joy of these moments seems lost on the young man who in the winter of 1913 composed his solitary notebook.

Cuirassier Céline

What sort of young man was Céline before the war? Can we approximate him to the young intellectuals of 1912's *Agathon* survey? (see 1.1 *Ernest Psichari*) Yes, to an extent. He seems to share their patriotic enthusiasm, infatuation with the military and a taste for action (while dislike of science and reason will certainly be characteristic of an older Céline). Does this extend to a desire for war? The *Carnets* do not lead us to believe so but they do reveal a Céline who expected the army to make a man of him. Instead, barrack life depresses him. This stage in his life, he writes, is 'la première vraiment pénible que j'ai traversée [...]. Depuis mon incorporation j'ai subi de brusques sautes physiques et morales' [the first really painful period I have known [...]. Since joining I have endured both physical and moral shocks].[34] Army life is 'ce calvaire' [this calvary].[35] He feels 'une nostalgie profonde de la liberté' [a profound nostalgia for freedom].[36] Céline's solitude is matched only by a sensitivity astonishing to anyone familiar with the virulent style of Céline's novels and pamphlets. Indeed, the *Carnets* reveal a Céline never to be seen again in his writing. 'Je suis de sentiments complexes et sensitif la moindre faute de tact ou de délicatesse me choque et me fait souffrir' [I am made of complex feelings and sensitive the least lack of tact or delicacy shocks me and makes me suffer].[37]

The young soldier Céline appears childlike, crying alone on his bed, struggling to become a man, unable to believe that he is one, at grips with a sense of his own lack of character:

> Que de fois je suis remonté du pansage et tout seul sur mon lit, pris d'un immense désespoir, j'ai malgré mes dix-sept ans pleuré comme une première communiante. Alors j'ai senti que j'étais vide que mon énergie était de la gueule et qu'au fond de moi-même il n'y avait rien que je n'étais pas un homme je m'étais trop longtemps cru tel [...] alors là vraiment j'ai souffert, aussi bien du mal présent que de mon infériorité virile et de la constater.[38]

> [How many times have I returned from grooming the horses, and gripped by an immense despair, and despite my seventeen years, cried like a girl making her First Communion. I have felt then that I was empty and that my energy was a boast and that at heart there was really nothing to me I wasn't the man I had for so long believed I was [...] at these times I truly suffered, as much from the awfulness of my present condition as from the observation of my virile inferiority.]

Céline's military dream was a dream of becoming a man. If his experience has placed a question mark over this ambition — one that will be tested even more in the war — it has, however, taught him valuable lessons: 'C'est alors dans le fond de mon abîme que j'ai pu me livrer aux quelques études sur moi-même et sur mon âme que l'on ne peut scruter je crois à fond lorsque elle s'est livrée combat.' [It is at these times in the depths of my own abyss that I have been able to study myself and my soul which one can only scrutinise I believe in depth when it is engaged in struggle].[39] This self-knowledge has shown him the distance separating discourse from experience. Knowledge which cruelly and completely deflates him:

> J'ai senti que les grands discours que je tenais un mois plus tôt sur l'énergie juvénile n'étaient que fanfaronnade et qu'au pied du mur je n'étais qu'un malheureux transplanté ayant perdu la moitié de ses facultés et ne se servant de celles qui restent que pour constater le néant de cette énergie.[40]

> [I felt that the great discourse I had maintained a month earlier on the energy of youth was nothing but a boast and that when push came to shove I was nothing other than an unhappy interloper who has lost half of his faculties and who cannot make use of what is left of them to do anything other than note the void of this energy in himself.]

Céline's image of himself is darkened by these insights into the vanity of his own nature. The suspicion of his lack of real value is expressed in strikingly anti-heroic terms:

> De même dans les catastrophes on voit des hommes du meilleur monde piétiner les femmes et s'avilir comme le dernier des vagabonds. De même j'ai vu mon âme se dévêtir soudain de l'illusion du stoïcisme dont ma conviction l'avait recouverte.[41]

> [As in the midst of catastrophe the very best of men can be seen to trample on women and disgrace themselves like the worst of vagabonds, I too have seen my soul shed the illusion of stoicism in which my conviction had dressed it.]

Perhaps this lack of stoicism is a reference to plans Céline had earlier made to desert his regiment. Army life, it seems, had got the better of him. This brings us to what is the most significant episode in Céline's life at Rambouillet with regard to *Voyage*.

Desertion

Céline notes it in his notebook. Following the incident during his training with horses, when he is laughed at, 'je commençais sérieusement à envisager la désertion qui devenait la seule échappatoire de ce calvaire' [I began seriously to envisage deserting as the only escape from this calvary].[42]

This plan to desert was real. It was uncovered by his father who became furious. It is probably the incident referred to when he wrote to Lacloche:

> Je n'ai pas besoin de vous rappeler l'incident survenu depuis son arrivée au régiment puisqu'il s'en est ouvert paraît-il à vous-même et que c'est sur vos sages conseils qu'il s'est ressaisi et qu'il est revenu à plus de sang-froid.[43]

> [I do not need to remind you of the incident which has taken place since his entry into the regiment, as it appears he has opened himself to you on that account and that it is due to your sound advice that he has managed to get a grip of himself and restore himself to calm.]

He adds, 'depuis son arrivée au régiment son attitude me cause de sérieuses appréhensions' [since his incorporation into the regiment his attitude has given me serious cause for worry].

According to one testimony Céline drew his sword on an officer, Jozan. This could have led to court-martial. François Gibault discounts this testimony but that an incident did occur is beyond doubt. Céline's mother eventually went to see the aforementioned Dugué Mac-Carthy and the incident was passed over.[44] While barrack life appears to have done little to diminish his native rebelliousness, Céline's military career continued with more equanimity.

La Réussite

Was Céline disposed to melancholy? The evidence suggests that he was:

> Suis poétique non ! je ne le crois pas seul un fond de tristesse est au fond de moi-même et si je n'ai pas le courage de le chasser par une occupation quelconque il prend bientôt des proportions énormes au point que cette mélancolie profonde ne tarde pas à recouvrir tous mes ennuis et se fond avec eux pour me torturer en mon for intérieur.[45]

> [Am I poetic no! I don't believe so just a touch of sadness deep down which if I have not the courage to rid myself of it through some occupation suddenly takes on immense proportions to the point where a profound melancholy in no time covers over all of my anxieties and joins with them to torture me in my heart of hearts.]

This tendency to melancholy made life at Rambouillet difficult. It also impelled him to write just as later his trauma will drive him to write *Voyage*. 'Je ne saurais dire ce qui m'incite à porter en écrit ce que je pense' [I cannot say what impels me to write down my thoughts], he writes, as he plunges into his notebook.[46] How this melancholy character would react to the shock of war, we shall later see, but as far as life at Rambouillet is concerned, it is clear that Céline did have the inner strength to rise above it. During his time there he was promoted twice, achieving the rank of *Maréchal des logis* [Sergeant]. The last entries in his notebook are astonishing. He still retains his dream of manliness and of freedom: 'Je veux que plus tard ou le plus tôt possible être un homme complet [...]. Je veux obtenir par mes propres moyens une situation de fortune qui me permette toutes mes fantaisies' [I want sooner or later to be a complete man [...]. I want to obtain by my own means a situation of fortune which will allow me all my dreams].[47] He resorts to near-heroic terms in the face of an unknown future:

> Mais ce que je veux avant tout c'est vivre une vie remplie d'incidents que j'espère la providence voudra placer sur ma route [...] si je traverse de grandes crises que la vie me réserve peut-être je serai moins malheureux qu'un autre car je veux connaître et savoir en un mot je suis orgueilleux est-ce un défaut je ne le crois et il me créera des déboires ou peut-être *la Réussite*.[48]

[But what I want above all is to live a life full of incident which I hope providence will place in my path [...] if I endure the great crises which life reserves for me perhaps I will be less unhappy than others because I want to experience and to know life in a word I am proud is that a fault I don't think so and it will create difficulties for me or perhaps bring *Success*.]

Céline's *Carnets* end with a strong yearning for life. His proud spirit has remained intact throughout his barrack life and we can imagine him still imbued with it when just months later he faces into the first of the 'great crises' he foresees. But how will this eagerness to live life respond to the demand that he sacrifice that very life for his country? Asked in 1959 if he was afraid to die in the war, Céline responded, 'j'avais des raisons encore de vivre, n'est-ce-pas. [...] A ce moment-là j'avais encore des illusions. Pas des illusions, l'instinct de vivre' [I had reasons for living, did I not. [...] At that time I had illusions. Not illusions, the instinct to live].[49] Here, as we shall see in the following chapter, is another of the keys to Céline's death encounter and the trauma that emerges from it.

3.3 WAR

Mobilisation

The *Historique du 12ᵉ Cuirassiers* records the moment when war entered Céline's life:

> Un peu après la soupe du soir, vers les quatre coins du quartier et jusqu'à ce qu'il perdît haleine, la trompette du corps de garde sonna 'la Générale'. C'était la guerre. Il y eut quelques instants de fièvre, des cris de jeune enthousiasme et puis le régiment se prépara au départ.[50]

> [A little after supper, the bugler sounded the General Assembly to the four corners of the barracks until he was out of breath. It was war. There were a few moments of fervour, cries of youthful enthusiasm, and then the regiment began to prepare for departure.]

Céline described his own reaction to war in a letter to his parents. He is conscious of the uniqueness of the moment and of his feelings. There is pride too when he writes, 'c'est une impression unique que peu peuvent se vanter d'avoir éprouvée' [it leaves a unique impression few can boast of having experienced].[51] He describes the mood of the camp, 'Tout le monde est à son poste confiant et tranquille cependant la surexcitation des premiers moments a fait place à un silence de mort qui est le signe d'une brusque surprise' [Everyone is at his post confident and tranquil, however, the overexcitement of the first moments has given way to a deathly silence which is the sign of a sudden shock].[52]

This 'silence de mort' [deathly silence] is premonitory, but Céline's lack of any real knowledge of what death in war could mean is shown by a sudden effusion of heroic sentiment and filial affection:

> Quant à moi je ferai mon devoir jusqu'au bout et si par fatalité je ne devais pas en revenir... soyez persuadé pour atténuer votre souffrance que je meurs content et en vous remerciant du fond du cœur. Votre fils.[53]

> [As for me I will do my duty to the end and if by some accident I should not return... persuade yourselves so as to assuage your suffering that I died happy and thanking you from the bottom of my heart. Your son.]

The discontented brigadier of the *Carnets* has been transformed on the instant into an heroic warrior but this 'je meurs content' [I die happy] is surely Céline's last expression of pre-war innocence.

North

Céline's squadron took the train on the morning of 1 August. As they rode through the streets, civilians hailed them. Women reached out their hands to the passing soldiers.[54] The 12th Cuirassiers formed part of the 6th Brigade of Cuirassiers and the 7th Cavalry Division under General Gillain. During the first two months of the war the regiment's role was one of support, cover, reconnaissance. This is the war that will figure largely in *Voyage*. 'Les pertes furent légères, mais la fatigue immense' [Losses were few, but the fatigue was immense], notes the *Historique*. 'Il fallait sans cesse avancer, retourner en arrière, avancer de nouveau et revenir encore. Epuisantes randonnées dans un secteur qui ne compte pas plus de 100 kilomètres de l'Est à l'Ouest' [It was necessary to ceaselessly advance, pull back, advance again and pull back again. Exhausting journeys in a sector no more than 100 kilometres from East to West].[55] At the heart of this sector stood Verdun.

During the first days of August the regiment moved northwards. On 11 August, at three in the morning they were called to assist infantry under attack at Mangiennes. The Germans having retreated, the regiment returned to camp without having seen action. This established a pattern. Meanwhile, the regiment fulfilled its reconnaissance role. A reconnaissance unit could be away from the main regiment for up to six days. The cavalry was in constant movement. An exhausted Céline wrote home:

> Nous dormons par bribes de droite et de gauche et au point tel que l'on peut dormir jusqu'à dix fois dans la journée par fractions de 10 minutes à 2 heures c'est du reste la seule façon car il n'existe pas de repos continu.[56]
>
> [We snatch sleep here and there to the extent that we can sleep up to ten times a day for anything from 10 minutes to 2 hours there is moreover no other way of getting sleep because continuous rest does not exist.]

He has not lost his heroic poise, however, adding in a naïve and grandiose flourish, 'la marée allemande monte toujours mais nous l'étranglerons' [the German tide is rising but we will strangle it].[57]

Withheld from direct action the cuirassiers were obliged to observe the war from a distance. On 22 August, the day Ernest Psichari died, they are called to support advancing troops. The attack proves catastrophic for the infantry. The cavalry, however, instead of lending support, are pulled back by General Gillain.[58] The regiment halts to witness the bombardment of Murville-Malavilliers before being pulled back even further, the farce repeating itself over the next few days. On 24 August, the regiment is again called on to support an attack, and once again ordered to retreat.[59] Next day the regiment is called to support an attack at Conflans; once again it is ordered to retreat.[60] Inevitably, Gillain is replaced on 26 August by General d'Urbal, *Voyage*'s 'général des Entrayes' to be.[61] The cuirassiers are exhausted. Men and horses both suffer. A brigadier, seven cuirassiers and twenty horses are evacuated. On 29 August, a further seventeen horses are evacuated.

Horses suffered terribly during the Great War. More than half a million died in the war zones, while 15,000 drowned on their way to them.[62] At Verdun, 7,000 horses were killed in a single day by long-distance shelling, including ninety-seven from a single shell.[63] As a cavalryman, *Maréchal des logis* Destouches was particularly well-placed to note the impact of the war on horses. We shall see their suffering in *Voyage*, evidence of the psychological mark it made on Céline:

> Mon cheval [...] rien que deux plaques de chair qui lui restaient à la place, sous la selle, larges comme mes deux mains et suintantes, à vif, avec des

grandes traînées de pus qui lui coulaient par les bords de la couverture jusqu'aux jarrets. [...] On ne pouvait plus le laisser qu'au grand air. Dans les granges, à cause de l'odeur qui lui sortait des blessures, ça sentait si fort, qu'on en restait suffoqué. (RI, 25)

[My horse only had two pieces of flesh remaining, under the saddle, as big as my two hands and seeping, raw, with two immense streams of pus running from the edge of the saddle-cloth down to his hocks. [...] All that could be done was to leave him in the open air. In the barns, the smell of his wounds was so strong it was suffocating.]

The Enemy

The power of modern weaponry made the Germans a distant enemy:

Le plus souvent, les combattants ne se voyaient que de très loin, à cause de la portée des armes à feu. Un fusil d'infanterie pouvait tuer à 1800 mètres, une carabine de cavalerie à une distance un peu moindre.[64]

[More often than not the combatants could only see each other in the distance, because of the range of their weapons. An infantry rifle could kill at a distance of 1800 metres, a cavalry carbine could kill at a slightly shorter distance.]

The war for Céline was a landscape of ruined or burning villages, civilians in flight, and a constant ritournelle of troops to and from the combat zones.[65] However, in September, direct contact with enemy cavalry reconnaissance units was frequent. 'Nos postes et nos patrouilles sont sans cesse en contact avec l'ennemi' [Our posts and our patrols are in constant contact with the enemy], records the Historique.[66] On 4 September, a skirmish occurred which would find its way into the pages of Voyage. Sub-lieutenant Daubon encountered a unit of enemy cavalry. The regiment's Journal des marches et opérations records the encounter with brutal frankness:

Daubon et un sous-officier de chasseurs pointent chacun un adversaire. Daubon vient d'en sabrer un second au cou quand arrive le cuirassier de 1ère classe, Lebas, qui pointe à son tour. La lance sort de 20cm par la bouche du dragon allemand qui tombe.

[Daubon and a non-commissioned officer each strike an enemy soldier. Daubon had just pierced another in the neck with his sword when the 1st class cuirassier, Lebas, arrived and struck with his lance. The lance emerged 20cm from of the mouth of the German dragoon, and he falls.]

The Historique, written in the 1920s, remains slightly more discreet on this episode but Céline in Voyage chooses no such reticence:[67]

Un matin en rentrant de reconnaissance, le lieutenant de Sainte-Engence invitait les autres officiers à constater qu'il ne leur racontait pas des blagues. 'J'en ai sabré deux !' assurait-il à la ronde, et montrait en même temps son sabre où, c'était vrai, le sang caillé comblait la petite rainure, faite exprès pour ça. (RI, 31)

[One morning on returning from reconnaissance, lieutenant Sainte-Engence invited the other officers to observe that he did not speak in jest. 'I ran two of them through with my sword!' he assured his audience, while showing them the sword where, it was true, congealed blood filled the small groove running down it, made expressly for that purpose.]

Captain Ortolan happily supports Sainte-Engence's claims. 'Je n'ai rien perdu de l'affaire ! Je n'en étais pas loin ! Un coup de pointe au cou en avant et à droite !... Toc ! Le premier tombe !...' [I saw it all! I wasn't far from it! One thrust to the neck forward and to the right!... Toc! The first one is done for!...] (RI, 32).

The *Journal*, providing information not in the *Historique*, establishes Céline's position as witness to war and confirms the truthfulness of his fiction. Episodes like this oblige us to take *Voyage*'s representation of war seriously and remind us that behind it there is a significant store of lived experience.

The Battle of the Marne

In September 1914, the French were being pushed back towards Paris. The 12th Cuirassiers, with the Germans 'sur nos talons' [on our heels], covered the retreat. It looked as if the Germans were about to break through and force their way to Paris. 'Les jours suivants [...] sont, pour la France, les plus angoissants de toute la guerre' [the following days [...] are, for France, the most agonising of all the war], notes the *Historique*.[68] One can only imagine the state of mind of soldiers already at the limits of endurance. On 8 September, the regiment suffered its first fatality when cavalryman Dupuis was killed during reconnaissance. The suffering of the horses continued. The next day, with the regiment once again at Verdun, twenty-six horses were evacuated. On 10 September, at three in the morning, the regiment is ordered to cover the retreating 6th corps which has suffered heavy losses. The *Journal* notes laconically, 'la situation semble très grave' [the situation seems very serious]. It was.

'On est puceau de l'Horreur comme on l'est de la volupté' [You can be a virgin in horror as in sex], wrote Céline in *Voyage* (RI, 14), and it is here at the

Battle of the Marne that he first experiences the horror of modern warfare. Note how the word 'horror' echoes down the years in *Voyage* from when Destouches wrote home in September 1914:

> La lutte s'engage formidable, jamais je n'ai vu et verrai tant d'horreur [...] depuis 3 jours les morts sont remplacés continuellement par les vivants à tel point qu'ils forment des monticules que l'on brûle et qu'à certain endroit on peut traverser la Meuse à pied ferme sur les corps allemands.[69]

> [The struggle is formidable, I have never seen and never will see so much horror [...] for 3 days the dead have been replaced continually by the living to such a point that they form heaps to be burned and that in certain places the Meuse can be crossed on foot by walking on the bodies of German soldiers.]

According to Jean Bastier, this last assertion is an example of 'rumeur et fausse nouvelle' [rumour and legend][70] — how could the bodies of German dead form a bridge across the Meuse? —this does not mean, however, that Céline is writing a deliberate falsehood. Soldiers do not leave their imaginations behind when they go to war and so imagination must be part of how the experience of war is told. Destouches records not just his vision of war but the state of mind which accepts that vision as real. He is here the soldier pushed to the limit of endurance where imagination takes over and truth occupies the limit of what can be said, believed or imagined about the war. As Eric J. Leed comments, 'One must see illusion in general, and the myth and fantasies of war in general as an attempt to dissolve and resolve the constraints upon vision and action that define the reality of war.'[71] The distortion here becomes itself a *truth of war* — that part of war in which the imagination is plunged and from which it may never fully emerge. Robert Graves's view that the memoirs of a man who had seen the worst of war are 'not truthful unless they contain a high proportion of falsities' is especially relevant in this instance (see 2.2 *Graves*). Indeed, in *Voyage*, it is imagination which will once again, as in wartime, colour the memory of war until its truth once again hovers on the edge of hallucination. *Voyage* is indeed proof that, years after, Céline's imagination remains organised around war just as much as his mind does.

Céline ends his letter to his parents with a premonitory remark which anticipates Jean Vigier's despair two years later at Verdun (see 1.3 *Verdun*). Like

Vigier, young Destouches is only too aware that the scale of sacrifice of heroes may result in the death of France itself. He writes, in what is as good a definition of 'attrition' as any, 'La bataille laisse l'impression d'une vaste fournaise où s'engloutissent les forces vives de deux nations et où la moins fournie des deux restera la maîtresse' [The battle leaves the impression of a vast furnace into which the living force of two nations is being poured and where the least depleted will prove master].[72]

The French won the Battle of the Marne and it has remained ever since a synonym for legendary victory in the French collective mind. For those who were there it was an unforgettable experience. Marc Bloch wrote of it, 'il est probable que tant que je vivrai, à moins que je ne finisse mes jours dans l'imbécillité, je n'oublierai jamais le 10 septembre 1914' [it is unlikely that as long as I live, unless I end my days in senility, I will ever forget 10 September 1914].[73] His memory is vivid. 'Les blessés criaient ou râlaient. [...] Une odeur de sang flottait dans l'air' [The wounded cried out or groaned. [...] The smell of blood hung in the air].[74] The experience of the individual soldier in the midst of a great battle is limited, subjective. He has not the point of view of the historian who sees the grand scale. The soldier only knows what he sees and this often remains incomprehensible. They called it the *Victoire de la Marne* [Victory of the Marne]. 'Je n'aurais pas su la nommer' [I would not have known what to call it], Bloch writes.[75] Significantly, in *Voyage*, Céline does not even mention it.

On 12 September, Céline's regiment is ordered to follow the retreating Germans. Leaving camp at one in the afternoon, after an arduous journey it arrives once more at Verdun at eleven that night. Many horses die en route. One *Maréchal des logis*, four brigadiers and fifteen ordinary soldiers are evacuated. On 15 September, the regiment, fighting on foot, is forced to fall back on Mageville, 'village complètement saccagé et abandonné' [a village completely looted and abandoned].[76] Next day the regiment enters woods at Spincourt to flush out enemy troops. Four cuirassiers are wounded. Is this where Céline first feels fear? With death waiting behind every tree as in *Voyage*, 'des arbres, je m'en méfiais [...] depuis que j'étais passé par leurs embuscades' [trees, I was wary of, ever since I had endured their ambushes] (RI, 57)?

These are days of constant skirmishing. Fatigue continues to take its toll. Nine more men are evacuated. There follows a substantial reinforcement of the regiment: five *Maréchaux des logis*, thirteen brigadiers, one hundred and thirty one cavalrymen, one hundred and seventy three horses, an indication of how exhausted and depleted it has become. On 23 September, the regiment suffers its second fatality. *Maréchal des logis* Renard is killed when a reconnaissance unit is surprised by Germans. At the end of the month a brigadier, sixteen men and twenty-seven horses are evacuated. On 1 October, the regiment is embarked for Flanders.

Flanders

The situation in Flanders is different. The Race to the Sea is on and the face of battle has greatly changed. The regiment finds itself fighting more and more on foot, 'il s'opposa à la marche de l'ennemi par d'incessants combats à pied' [it opposed the enemy's advance by incessant fighting on foot], notes the *Historique*.[77] On 4 October, brigadier Bouteloup is killed. The regiment is sent to guard the river Lys, including the Bout-du-Monde bridge. 'Toute la jeunesse est allée mourir déjà au bout du monde dans le silence de vérité' [All our youth has left already to die at the end of the world in the silence of truth], Céline will write in one of *Voyage*'s most significant passages (RI, 200). Here, the cuirassiers await the inevitable attack. On 5 October, it comes and the regiment is forced to fall back. Cuirassier Ach is killed in an explosion. The following day the regiment retakes the bridge. Céline takes part in a reconnaissance patrol to Comines in the wake of the Germans. Comines, as we shall see, will become Noirceur-sur-la-Lys in *Voyage*. In the course of a patrol Lieutenant Jozan is wounded as is cuirassier Luart. The trumpeter Chaligue is killed, shot through the head. The regiment is involved in close fighting and falls back 'ne cédant le terrain que pied à pied' [only yielding terrain inch by inch].[78] On 11 October, while attacking Richebourg-l'Avoué, brigadier Trelat and cuirassier Jouan are killed, lieutenant Tourout and seven others wounded. Céline, deeply affected by the loss of his comrades, writes to his parents in what is his most eloquent expression of camaraderie; expression which will contrast starkly with the anti-camaraderie of *Voyage*:

> Nous déplorons la perte de pas mal d'entre nous: Lt Tourout, Jozan, Doucerin, Legrand, Brigadier Trelat et pas mal de nos pauvres camarades. [...] J'apprends les blessures de pas mal d'entre nous, j'ai appris aussi que ce pauvre Max Linder avait été tué à Estemay.[79]

> [We regret the loss of quite a few among us: Lt Tourout, Jozan, Doucerin, Legrand, Brigadier Trelat and many of our poor comrades. [...] I've learned that many among us have been wounded, I've also learned that poor Max Linder was killed at Estemay.]

The truth is certainly that, whatever divided them, Céline could in no way have remained indifferent to the suffering and loss of men whose life, anxieties and dangers he shared. In spite of these losses his tone remains resolutely heroic, assuring his parents 'continuons quand même et vaincrons sûrement' [we will carry on none the less and we are sure to achieve victory]. And yet with striking premonition — surely a sign of his deep agitation — Céline can look beyond the war to its consequence, 'c'est effrayant ce qu'il y en aura après cette guerre maudite' [it is frightening to think what the aftermath of this accursed war will bring]. His own war will not last for very much longer.

On 14 October, the regiment attacked at Pont-Richon. 'Le combat est très violent' [the fighting is very violent], records the *Historique*.[80] One officer and three cuirassiers are wounded, ten horses killed or wounded. The regiment needs rest but the situation is critical. The Germans must not be allowed to cross the Ypres canal. In an effort to stop them the 7th Division is thrown to the north of Ypres. Two days later the regiment, again on foot, holds back the Germans, but eventually it is forced back to Poelkapelle. On 20 October, at dawn, the regiment is thrown forwards. It fights all day to hold back the German line but again is forced back and Poelkapelle surrendered. That night the Germans attack Langemarck and the cuirassiers are moved to the trenches to support the infantry there. On 22 October, the regiment takes part in a massed attack on Bixschoote, aided, bizarrely, by the division cyclists and a regiment of kilted Scotsmen.[81] None of this will figure in *Voyage*.

The Encounter with Death

The battle in which Céline takes part in late October 1914 is the first battle of Ypres, a battle which, according to Jean Bastier, 'surpasse en violence et en acharnement les combats de la Marne' [surpasses in violence and intensity the fighting of the battle of the Marne].[82] Battle rages around Poelkapelle and Langemarck. On 25 October, the regiment is ordered to cover the left flank of the 66th infantry regiment attacking Poelkapelle. It is of the utmost importance to assure the liaison between the 66th and the 125th infantry regiment attacking Poelkapelle from the east. These are days of constant bombardment and artillery fire. The 66th infantry regiment loses over six hundred men during the next four days.[83] In these conditions the regular liaison officers hesitate to carry messages over the flat, exposed terrain. Céline volunteers to do it. On foot he carries a message to the colonel of the 66th infantry regiment.

There is a possibility that, at this point, Céline may have suffered a head injury. The evidence comes from a medical note he wrote in 1946 where he mentions 'ma première blessure lorsque je fus projeté par un éclatement d'obus contre un arbre' [my first injury when I was thrown against a tree by an explosion].[84] Is this the scene recalled in *Voyage*, 'le feu est parti, le bruit est resté longtemps dans ma tête' [the fire died down, the noise remained a long time in my head] (RI, 17)? In any case, it is here that Céline has his solitary encounter with death. Céline's father described what happened:

> Il a été frappé [...] au moment où sur la ligne de feu il transmettait les ordres de la division à un Colonel d'Infanterie. La balle qui l'a atteint par ricochet était déformée et aplatie par un premier choc ; elle présentait des bavures de plomb et des aspérités qui ont occasionné une plaie assez large, l'os du bras droit a été fracturé.[85]

> [He was hit [...] while he was transmitting a divisional order to an infantry colonel. The ricochet bullet which hit him was damaged and flattened by its first impact; its blunt, jagged edges made a fairly large wound, his right arm was broken.]

A letter from his Captain Schneider expands on the circumstances of Céline's wound. Céline's courage in the face of death appears either heroic or reckless:

Il a été atteint d'une balle dans les circonstances suivantes : le 27 courant, chargé avec quelques cuirassiers du régiment d'établir la liaison entre des éléments d'infanterie et le commandement, à l'attaque de Poelkapelle, traversant à plusieurs reprises des zônes les plus dangereuses, il a été, ce jour-là à 18 h frappé d'une balle au bras.[86]

[He was shot in the following circumstances: on 27 October last, attempting with other members of the regiment to establish a liaison between some infantry positions and the command position, during the attack on Poelkapelle, while traversing repeatedly the most dangerous areas of the battlefield, he was, at 1800 hours on that same day, hit by a bullet in the arm.]

Schneider emphasises Céline's bravery:

Ce que je tiens surtout à vous redire, c'est combien le courage de votre fils a été admirable. Depuis le début de la guerre on le trouve d'ailleurs partout où il y a du danger, c'est son bonheur, il y est plein d'entrain et d'énergie ! Le 27, il marche sans compter, même quand ce n'est pas son tour, sous un feu formidable qui depuis quatre jours est un roulement de tonnerre ininterrompu. Fusillade, mitrailleuses, obus, rien ne l'arrête.[87]

[What I insist on repeating to you is the extent to which your son's courage has been admirable. Since the start of the war he is to be found everywhere there is danger, that's what makes him happy, he is full of action and energy in such a situation! On 27 October, he set off without hesitation, even when it wasn't his turn to do so, under intense fire which had created a constant rolling of thunder for four days. Shooting, machine guns, shells, nothing could stop him.]

Those four days of fire and bombardment give the lie to those who seek to minimise Céline's experience of war.[88] Céline's wound, however, was only the beginning of his trauma. His father describes the circumstances of his evacuation from the battlefield:

L'action était tellement chaude, le nombre de morts et de blessés tellement grand que le premier échelon des ambulances ne put le panser, les tentes étaient remplies de morts et de mourants, il a dû faire 7 kilom à pied [...]. Pendant tout ce trajet son bras fracturé était maintenu par son ceinturon disposé en baudrier, c'est à dire passé autour de son cou ; il devait aller d'Ypres à Dunkerque dans un convoi mais il n'a pu aller jusqu'au bout du trajet tellement la douleur était vive, il lui a fallu descendre à Hazebrouck.[89]

[The fighting was so intense, and the number of dead and wounded so great that the first line of ambulances could not treat him, the tents were full of dead and dying, he had to walk for 7 kilometres [...]. During the journey his broken arm was held in place by his belt used as a sling tied around his neck. He had to go from Ypres to Dunkirk in a convoy but he could not finish the journey because the pain was too acute. He had to stop at Hazebrouck.]

On 29 October 1914, by order of Colonel Blaque-Bélair, the name of Louis Destouches is inscribed in the regimental *Journal*. The entry records the special 'mention' accorded Céline and his fellow-cuirassiers by the Commander of the 66th infantry regiment, 'ils se sont conduits comme des héros' [they acted like heroes]. The entry is later copied to the *Historique*.[90] History records that Louis Destouches was a hero of the Great War. *Voyage*, as we shall see, will have none of it.

The End of the War

François Gibault tells us that Céline's arm wound was initially treated at the field ambulance number 3.[91] Céline refused to allow his arm to be amputated and was transferred to the auxiliary hospital at Hazebrouck. Here, two days after receiving his wound, the bullet was finally removed. Fearing his arm would be amputated, Céline refused an anaesthetic. A month later he was transferred to the hospital of Val-de-Grâce in Paris. Here, on 4 December, Céline was awarded the French *médaille militaire* [military medal]. The citation he received reads as follows:

> En liaison entre un régiment d'infanterie et sa brigade, s'est offert spontanément pour porter sous un feu violent un ordre que les agents de liaison de l'infanterie hésitaient à transmettre. A porté cet ordre et a été grièvement blessé au cours de sa mission.[92]

> [In liaison between his brigade and a regiment of infantry, he volunteered to transmit under intense fire an order which the infantry liaison agents hesitated to carry. He transmitted the order and was grievously wounded in the course of his mission.]

Céline's heroism had earned him the ultimate imprimatur.

The Death of the 12th Cuirassiers

Three months after it had begun, Céline's war was over. The rest of the war he would follow from afar. The war was changing. After the battle of Ypres the new lines of trenches consolidated and the war was no longer a war of movement. The cavalry lost its usefulness. On 9 December 1914, the 12th Cuirassiers cavalry regiment went into the trenches. The war and its cavalry had gone to ground. Over the next three years, fighting as infantry, the 12th Cuirassiers would become part of the war's lethal pattern of cyclical re-enactment, constantly drained of its manpower, constantly renewed by reinforcements.

Figures from the last months of the war give some idea. From 2 to 11 April 1918: 74 cuirassiers dead, 332 wounded, 33 missing.[93] Between 12 April and 3 June: 43 cuirassiers dead, 355 wounded and 41 missing. In the period 4 June to 14 June: 54 cuirassiers dead, 391 wounded, 184 missing. Casualties remained heavy for the last period of the war. From 15 June to 19 September 1918, the regiment lost 16 men dead, 103 wounded, 4 missing. From 20 September to 11 October: 37 men dead, 106 wounded, 6 missing.

The cycle of re-enactment continued to turn. In July 1918, the regiment was moved back towards its 1914 positions and was stationed once again in the region of Verdun, at the famous hill known as *Mort-Homme*, with all its resonance of '4 mai'. Did Céline read the *Historique*? Did he identify the fate of his regiment with that 'famous date'? It is possible. The *Historique* was published in the early 1920s and according to Jean Bastier was 'in principle' distributed to members of the regiment.[94] If Céline did have a copy, and we cannot be sure, it is possible that he used it as the basis for the war episode in *Voyage*. It is tempting to believe that, dropped into Céline's silence of the mid to late twenties, the *Historique* contributed to the crisis in memory which will cause him to embark on *Voyage*.

Conclusion

Céline's encounter with death was multiple, cumulative. The Great War itself, heralding a new, modern, industrialised age, would produce the death of the world that had existed before it, the world of his grandmother, the world in which Destouches had grown-up, been happy, and to which he belonged, the heroic pre-war world of France's and Céline's Golden Age. At the cutting edge of modern warfare, he witnessed the deaths of his own comrades in the 12th Cuirassiers and of those soldiers of the French regular army who were being killed at a rate of 2,000 men a day during the bloodiest period of the war, from August to November 1914. He witnessed the death of his generation as one third of those, like him, born in 1894, were lost on the battlefield (see 1.3 *Death*). He witnessed the death of an age-old concept of war based on movement and the emergence of an unprecedented experience of war as long lines dug in the earth produced stasis, debasement and alienation. He witnessed the death of the Cavalry and was part of its ironic fall from grace, obliged to 'faire les mille pattes' [become centipedes], [95] crawling on the ground under bombardment from an enemy he could not see. As modern warfare took hold of his world and prepared to kill it, he encountered death first-hand, caught by the ricocheting bullet that maimed him. He left the battlefield a hero, but this unheroic war was not finished with him. The 12th Cuirassiers itself, as the *Historique* informs us, would die over and over in unending cyclical re-enactment during the war, before being dissolved soon after it. When the war ended, it was as if France itself had suffered a deathblow. The size of the effort, the numbers sacrificed, represented a scale of defeat rather than of victory. Memory, as we have seen, would never be a place for celebration, rather a place for mourning. In a very real sense, death had won and would dominate memory. In Chapter Four we will turn our attention to Céline's traumatic memory of war as it moves to the startling irony of its expression in *Voyage*.

---

[1] The *Carnets* of cuirassier Destouches were written towards the end of 1913. Céline took them to war with him and when he was wounded gave them to a fellow cuirassier for safe-keeping. The *Carnets* were eventually restored to him in the 1950s. See 'Les Carnets du cuirassé Destouches', *L'Herne*, 10–12.

[2] Herbert Hendin and Ann Pollinger Haas, *Wounds of War: The Psychological Aftermath of Combat in Vietnam* (New York: Basic Books, 1984), p.10.

[3] Much of the detail of this section on Céline's early life is indebted to the first volume of François Gibault's *Céline*.

[4] See Gibault, I, 38–41.

[5] In 'Interview avec Louis Pauwels et André Brissaud', *Cahiers Céline*, 2: *Céline et l'actualité littéraire 1957–1961*, ed. by Jean-Pierre Dauphin and Henri Godard (Paris: Gallimard, 1976), 119–129 (p.122).

[6] Gibault, I, 50–51.

[7] 'Interview avec Louis Pauwels', p.123.

[8] Céline's own death in 1961 would recall the death of his grandmother. Writes François Gibault, 'il ne voulait personne. [...] Le vieux cavalier voulait mourir comme il avait vécu, en solitaire' [he wanted nobody. [...] The old cavalryman wanted to die as he had lived, alone]. See Gibault, III: *1944–1961 Cavalier de l'Apocalypse* (1986), 346–347.

[9] Marcel Brochard, 'Céline à Rennes', *L'Herne*, 203–206 (p.203).

[10] Brochard, p.204.

[11] Brochard, p.204.

[12] 'Interview avec Louis Pauwels', p.122. The French word 'gifle' specifically indicates a slap to the face.

[13] Gibault, I, 59.

[14] Asked by Louis Pauwels if he believes in God, Céline's response is an emphatic 'non, je ne crois pas du tout, non, non, je ne crois pas du tout, non, non, non, non, je ne crois pas en Dieu' [no, not at all, no, no, I don't believe at all, no, no, no, no, I don't believe in God]. See, 'Interview avec Louis Pauwels', p.127.

[15] See Gibault, I, 114–115.

[16] 'Interview avec Louis Pauwels', p.124.

[17] Gibault, I, 118.

[18] Gibault, I, 21.

[19] Gibault, I, 57–58.

[20] Gibault, I, 117.

[21] Marcel Brochard, 'Céline à Rennes', p.204.

[22] Gibault, *Céline*, I, 124.

[23] 'Les Carnets du cuirassé Destouches', 10–11.

[24] 'Le Baptême du feu de 1914 raconté par Céline en 1939' [Recorded in writing by P. Ordioni], in *Romans*, III: *Casse-pipe, Guignol's band I, Guignol's band II* (1988), 77–79 (p.79).

[25] 'Lettre à Roger Nimier', in *Romans*, III, 76.

[26] See Gibault, I, 129.

[27] Gibault, I, 133.

[28] 'Mon colonel de 14 a disparu l'an dernier. Que de fantômes...' [my colonel in 1914 died last year. So many ghosts...], wrote Céline to his friend Joseph Garcin. Letter of 6 January 1931, in Lainé, p.624. Céline's letters to Garcin have been published separately in a volume edited by Pierre Lainé, *Lettres à Joseph Garcin: 1929–1938* (Paris: Monnier, 1987).

[29] 'Carnets', p.11. The punctuation in these passages is as appears in *L'Herne*.

[30] 'Carnets', p.11. 'Le bleu' is the newly enlisted soldier with most of his service before him. See Henri Godard's 'Notice', in *Romans*, III, 863–894 (p.884).

[31] 'Carnets', p.11.

[32] 'Carnets', p.11.

[33] Gibault, I, 131.

[34] 'Carnets', p.10.

[35] 'Carnets', p.11.

[36] 'Carnets', p.11.

[37] 'Carnets', p.11.

[38] 'Carnets', p.11.

[39] 'Carnets', p.11.

[40] 'Carnets', p.11.

[41] 'Carnets', p.11.

[42] 'Carnets', p.11.

[43] Gibault, I, 128.

[44] Gibault, I, 129.

[45] 'Carnets', p.11.

[46] 'Carnets', p.10.

[47] 'Carnets', pp.11–12.

[48] 'Carnets', p.12.

[49] 'Interview avec Louis Pauwels', p.125.

[50] *Historique du 12ᵉ Cuirassiers: au danger mon plaisir*, ([n.p]: [n. pub.], [n.d.]), p.3. Jean Bastier reckons the date of publication of the *Historique* to be between 1920 and 1925. See relevant bibliographical entry in Bastier, p.421.

[51] Cited in Gibault, I, 136–137.

[52] Gibault, I, 137.

[53] Gibault, I, 137.

[54] See photo of Céline's regiment riding through the streets of Paris to the Gare de l'Est in Bastier's *Le Cuirassier blessé*.

[55] *Historique*, p.4.

[56] Gibault, I, 139.

[57] Gibault, I, 138.

[58] For an account of this infamous retreat, see Bastier, pp.59–67.

[59] See Bastier, p.73.

[60] See Bastier, pp.86–87.

[61] Bastier, p.91.

[62] See Martin Gilbert, p.xx.

[63] See Gilbert, p.235.

[64] Jean Bastier, in correspondence with myself, letter dated 4 December 2000.

[65] Jean Bastier speculates that Céline may have witnessed villages burning as early as 9 August. See *Le Cuirassier blessé*, p. 46.

[66] *Historique*, p.6.

[67] The *Historique*'s account of this episode reads as follows: 'Le sous-lieutenant Danbon avait derrière lui 4 cuirassiers et 3 chasseurs ; il charge les cavaliers ennemis. Ceux-ci font demi-tour, mais trop tard pour éviter les nôtres. L'officier pointe un adversaire, en sabre un autre ; un sous-officier de chasseurs pointe à son tour ; enfin un dragon allemand tombe en avant, le corps traversé par le sabre du cavalier Lebas, un vrai cuirassier' [Sub-lieutenant Danbon has 4 cuirassiers and 3 chasseurs at his back; he charges the enemy cavalry. They perform a half-turn but too late to avoid our men. The officer strikes an enemy soldier, and strikes another with his sword; a non-commissioned officer with the chasseurs also strikes at the enemy; finally, a German dragoon falls forward, his body pierced by the sword of cavalryman Lebas, a true cuirassier]. See *Historique*, p.6. It is to be noted that the *Historique* records the name of Danbon while the regimental diary appears to read Daubon. The name Danbon is retained by François Gibault, while Daubon is retained by Jean Bastier. It is obviously the same person in question.

[68] *Historique*, p.6.

[69] Gibault, I, 140.

[70] Bastier, p.161.

[71] Leed, p.116.

[72] Gibault, I, 140.

[73] Bloch, *Souvenirs de guerre*, p.14.

[74] *Souvenirs de guerre*, p.17.

[75] *Souvenirs de guerre*, p.18.

[76] Recorded in the *Journal des marches et opérations du 12ᵉ Cuirassiers*.

[77] *Historique*, p.9.

[78] *Historique*, p.10.

[79] Cited in Bastier, p.219.

[80] *Historique*, p.11.

[81] See Bastier, p.278.

[82] Bastier, p.304.

[83] See Bastier, p.308.

[84] See Gibault, I, 161–162. François Gibault accepts the possibility of 'une première blessure' [a first wound], but having studied Céline's medical records for 1914–1915 he finds 'ni trépanation ni même trauma crânien' [neither trepanation nor even injury to the head], see p.159. Jean Bastier, p.337, lends considerable credence to Céline's medical note and uses it as an important element in his argument that Céline suffered shell-shock. See also 4.2 *The Trepanation Myth*.

[85] Gibault, I, 147.

[86] Gibault, I, 151.

[87] Gibault, I, 151–152.

[88] Describing Céline's wound as 'la bonne blessure' [a lucky wound], Philippe Alméras says of him, 'son courage a consisté à tuer l'imagination, c'est fait d'orgueil' [his courage consisted of killing imagination, it consisted of pride]. See Alméras, p.41. Jay Winter writes, 'he had been hit accidentally, wandering around in the darkness. [...] He had received what British soldiers called a 'Blighty', the best kind of wound — honourable but in no sense dangerous. He was out of the real war.' See Winters, 'Céline and the Cultivation of Hatred', p.234.

[89] Gibault, I, 148.

[90] *Historique*, pp.12–13.

[91] See Gibault, I, 153. This, of course, is to be compared with Céline's father's account.

[92] Gibault, I, 149.

[93] These figures and those that follow are calculated from the *Journal des marches et opérations du 12ᵉ Cuirassiers*.

[94] In correspondence with myself, letter dated 4 May 2001.

[95] 'Mille-pattes', as well as being a character in *Guignol's Band* is the mocking description of the dismounted cuirassier in Robert Desaubliaux's memoir, *La Ruée: étape d'un combattant*, cited in Jean Bastier, p.284. Desaubliaux served in the 11th Cuirassiers during the war and his itinerary was very much Céline's. His *La Ruée* appeared in 1920 (see also 5.3 *Intertextual Witness*).

CHAPTER 4

RE-ENACTMENT

From Hazebrouck to Voyage

Introduction

This chapter traces Céline's trauma from Hazebrouck in 1914 to Paris in 1929 where Céline will suffer the crisis in memory from which *Voyage* emerges. By examining his trauma in the light of our present awareness of combat disorders this chapter will construct its profile. Central to this examination is Robert Jay Lifton's description of the 'death imprint'. Céline, we shall see, is the 'death-imprinted' survivor, living in a state of recurrent trauma. Céline's trauma will influence in a fundamental way the structures and language of *Voyage*, most tangibly in its all-pervading *duality* and in the circular, repetitive patterns of its *cycle of re-enactment*.

4.1 MEMORY

Shock

'There is no evidence that Destouches suffered from shell shock,' affirms Jay Winter, 'or that his wound was accompanied by any other trauma.'[1] But there is. It is not in the medical records but rather in the observations of his father who visited him at Hazebrouck. He found Céline delirious and obsessed by visions of death. He wrote to his brother:

> Nous l'avons trouvé assez déprimé moralement sous le coup de la réaction des fatigues continuelles et excessives de ces 3 derniers mois et surtout de tout ce qu'il a vu sous ses yeux ; la mort de plusieurs bons camarades l'a particulièrement affecté.[2]

> [We found him quite depressed in reaction to the continual and excessive fatigue of the last 3 months and in particular to all that he has seen before him; the death of several good comrades has particularly affected him.]

In Hazebrouck, Céline's earlier agitation over the wounding and death of his comrades is renewed and intensified (See 3.3 *Flanders*). His memory relives the past as an hallucinatory flux. His father records it, 'la vision de toutes les horreurs dont il a été le témoin traverse constamment son cerveau...' [the vision of all the horrors that he has witnessed traverses constantly his mind].[3]

Yet again we encounter the word 'horror' in relation to Céline. The word is indeed charged with significance for Céline and helps us to understand his experience of war. Louis Crocq, a specialist on war trauma, tells us:

> L'horreur [...] désigne un sentiment complexe où l'on saisit que les limites de ce qui est tolérable à voir sont dépassées et où les valeurs morales les plus sacrées sont bafouées. [...] L'horreur apporte avec elle quelque chose d'incompréhensible, d'inexplicable et d'indicible. En ce sens, c'est elle qui nous paraît le mieux adhérer au vécu traumatique.[4]

> [Horror [...] describes a complex feeling where it is perceived that the limits of what it is tolerable to see have been transgressed and that the most sacred moral values have been flouted. [...] Horror carries with it something of the incomprehensible, inexplicable and unspeakable. In this sense, it appears to us to be closest to the lived experience of trauma.]

What lucidity remains to Céline allows only a troubled awareness of past danger and of escape from death:

> Il se demande encore par quel miracle il se trouve encore de ce monde ; la présence du danger aigu de jour et de nuit auquel il a conscience seulement maintenant d'avoir échappé a provoqué chez lui [...] une surexcitation nerveuse.[5]

> [He asks himself by what miracle he is still of this world; the presence day and night of grave danger he is only now conscious of having escaped has provoked in him [...] a nervous agitation.]

His father's observations match forcefully the description of shell-shock victims offered by Drs John T. MacCurdy and Turner (see 1.4 *Shell-shock*). In addition, Céline's condition was complicated by infection from his ricochet wound. Infection raised temperature, causing a severe headache. But infection also intensified the breakdown not just of Céline's body, but also of his personality, his self.[6] Nurse Vera Brittain described what happens:

> Wounded men kept their personalities even after a serious operation, whereas those of the sick became so quickly impaired; the tiny, virulent microbe that attacked the body seemed to dominate the spirit as well. Why

was personality so vulnerable, why did it succumb to such small, humiliating assailants?[7]

How many days did this delirium last? We cannot tell, but his father's visit came one whole week after Céline had been wounded. This is a most significant period for Céline and *Voyage*. It is here in these days of delirium that Céline's heroic self is lost. And it is here that we find the original memory loss on which *Voyage* is founded and around which it and all of Céline, words and deeds, orbits in ceaseless circles.

Infection humiliated Céline. But there was further humiliation. In the enforced inactivity of hospital, reduced to helplessness, Céline was possessed by fear, the fear he had felt in the wood at Spincourt (see 3.3 *The Battle of the Marne*). And there is nothing he can do. Frightened, a subversive seed of cowardice grows in his mind.[8] Céline's heroism ends in Hazebrouck. A hero at Poelkapelle, he wakes from his delirious forgetfulness in Hazebrouck, to find he is changed radically in his innermost being. He is afraid of death. He has become a coward. Struggling with this new self, he is torn by conflicting feelings. He feels guilt because he is away from the war, feels guilt that he has deserted his comrades, and at the same time is relieved that he has escaped. This latter awareness brings its own humiliating self-knowledge and guilt.[9] But above all, he is glad to be out of the war and from here on he is characterised by a determination never to return to it.[10]

Val-de-Grâce

After a month at Hazebrouck, Céline was transferred to Val-de-Grâce hospital in Paris. Here he made friends with Albert Milon, *Voyage*'s Branledore.[11] Writing to Milon's widow in 1947, Céline recalled Val-de-Grâce while offering a homage to his deceased comrade:

> Il emporte aussi nos pauvres espoirs nos douloureuses illusions si blessées... nos sacrifices nos héroïsmes si inutiles... Vous voyez Renée l'agonie a vraiment commencé au Val-de-Grâce, ce n'était qu'un répit un sursis ce n'était pas la vie ni le bonheur... Ce n'était déjà plus possible... Une fatalité atroce était sur nous...[12]

> [He also takes with him our poor hopes our so wounded painful illusions... our so useless sacrifices and heroism... You see, Renée, the agony really began at Val-de-Grâce, it was a respite only a pause it was

neither life nor happiness... That was no longer possible... A terrible fatality hung over us...]

In Val-de-Grâce, the heroic revealed itself definitively as futile and gave way to a new, unheroic, debased consciousness. Here Céline developed and consolidated his deep repugnance for the war. On the evidence of *Voyage* it is in the hospitals at the rear that a deep disenchantment with the war and with the French Republic emerges and takes hold in the minds of the wounded. Yet, ironically it was here that Céline's heroism was consecrated by that very same Republic. Here, in early December 1914, he was awarded the *médaille militaire*.[13] A photograph was taken to commemorate the occasion. The medal is recalled with theatrical irony in *Voyage*:

> En convalescence, on me l'avait apportée la médaille, à l'hôpital même. Et le même jour, je m'en fus au théâtre, la montrer aux civils pendant les entractes. Grand effet. C'était les premières médailles qu'on voyait dans Paris. Une affaire ! (RI, 49)

> [While convalescing, they brought me my medal, in the hospital itself. The very same day I went to the theatre, to show it off to the civilians during the interval. What an effect it made! It was one of the first medals to be seen in Paris. What a sensation!]

In January 1915, Céline was transferred to a hospital at Villejuif, in the care of Gustave Roussy, the future Docteur Bestombes of *Voyage*.[14] He was operated on and spent some time at home convalescing. In February, he was again hospitalised for painful electrical treatment to his wounded arm involving '[un] courant continu et chocs galvaniques' [a continuous current and electric shocks],[15] a 'medical advance' he will satirise in *Voyage* (See RI, 89–90 and 94).

London

In May 1915, still in the army, Céline was posted to the French consulate in London. A colleague, Georges Geoffroy, recalled days and nights of freedom, girls, and music halls, lived in the wings of an expatriate underworld of French pimps.[16] As recalled in *Guignol's band*, this expatriate society would complete Céline's anti-war education. This latter novel is the finest expression of Céline's 'délire' [delirium]. Hallucinatory in style, its hero, Ferdinand, in an atmosphere provided by the war, repeatedly breaks down and sees visions of the dead. Years later Céline recalled his London sojourn in a letter to Joseph Garcin, dated April

1930, 'j'avais 20 ans et trop de souvenirs du front' [I was 20 years of age with too many memories of the front].[17] Written two years before the publication of *Voyage* this letter confirms the weight of memory of war clouding Céline's London sojourn. Trauma, as we shall see, is characterised by the cyclical return of experience. That the twenty-year old survivor of war was happy to be alive does not exclude the recurring anguish of a persistent memory of death. Indeed, the sheer joy of finding himself alive and far from war, may well have thrown into stark relief that anguish, as in *Guignol's band*.

Africa

Céline was demobilised in December 1915.[18] In May 1916, he sailed from Liverpool to work for a forestry company in the Cameroon. However, while the war continued, he remained subject to military control, just as Bardamu does. From Africa, Céline wrote letters to his childhood friend, Simone Saintu, to his parents, and to Albert Milon. In these letters memory of the war dominates Céline. The twenty-two year old already speaks with the tone of the disenchanted veteran:

> Presque tous ceux avec lesquels je suis parti en campagne, sont tués, les rares qui subsistent sont irrémédiablement infirmes, enfin quelques autres comme moi, errent un peu partout, à la recherche d'un repos et d'un oubli, que l'on ne trouve plus—[19]

> [Almost all of those with whom I left for the war have been killed, those who have survived are irremediably weakened, some like me wander everywhere a little, seeking a respite and forgetfulness which cannot be found.]

Here, self-portrayed as 'irremediably weakened' and unable to forget, is the solitary, alienated spirit of the future Bardamu, whose life is lived as a perpetual past shadowed by war. Henri Godard is indeed right to say that these letters contain 'l'essentiel de la vision de la guerre et des hommes dans la guerre que mettra en œuvre *Voyage au bout de la nuit*' [the essence of the vision of war and men at war which will be implemented in *Voyage*].[20] The war Céline remembers here anticipates the war of *Voyage*, theatrical and incessantly re-enacting itself (see 7.3 *The Theatre of Patriotism*). His voice carries a stern if weary note of denunciation:

> Voici aujourd'hui deux ans que je quittai Rambouillet pour la grande aventure, et depuis ce temps on a tué beaucoup, et on tue encore,

inlassablement fastidieusement, la guerre commence à me faire l'effet d'une ignoble tragédie, sur lequel le rideau s'abaisserait et se relèverait sans cesse, devant un public rassasié ; mais trop prostré pour se lever et partir—[21]

[It is two years ago today that I left Rambouillet for the great adventure, and since then many have been killed, and the killing goes on, tirelessly tediously, the war is beginning to have the effect on me of an ignoble tragedy, on which the curtain goes endlessly up and down in front of a jaded public, too weary to get up and leave—]

He remembers the moment at nightfall when he was wounded:

Il y a aujourd'hui très exactement 2 ans que je fus amoché [...]. Je me rappelle qu'à ce moment, entre la première ligne de tranchée et le poste de commandement il n'y avait pas de boyaux, à la nuit tombante on pouvait aussi chercher pendant les heures, à l'aveuglette le poste du commandant qu'aucune lumière ne révélait naturellement.
On appelait ça, garder les vaches—
C'est en gardant les vaches que je fus numéroté—[22]

[Exactly 2 years ago today I was wounded [...]. I remember that at that moment, between the first line of trenches and the command post there were no communication trenches, in the night you could spend hours blindly searching for the post which was of course in darkness.
That was called, minding the cows—
It was while minding the cows that my number was taken—]

Memory here is full of darkness and blindness, essential metaphors of *Voyage*. A sense of comical absurdity frames the moment and strips it of any appeal to heroism as the 'agent de liaison' wanders in darkness, unable to find his way. The body too, a site of memory, is stripped of its grace, 'amoché' [made ugly], an appropriate word indeed to describe Céline's memory of war and its literary expression in *Voyage*.

There is rage here too. In a movement of anger, Céline takes Saintu to task for her theatrical enthusiasm for the war's offensives:

Chaque fois que j'entends parler d'offensive... Je me représente, un soldat quel qu'il soit, mort, tué, sanglant, râlant, dans la boue rouge —
Et mon enthousiasme disparaît — Représentez vous ce petit tableau et si vous avez deux sous de sens commun, je vous défis à l'avenir d'applaudir aux offensives —[23]

[Each time that I hear talk of an offensive... I imagine some soldier, dead, killed, bleeding, groaning, in reddened mud—

And my enthusiasm disappears — Imagine that little scene and if you have tuppence worth of common sense, I defy you to applaud offensives in future—]

Imbued with this 'imagination of death', Céline's memory of the war has taken shape. 'J'éprouve un profond dégoût pour tout ce qui est belliqueux. [...] Je n'ai plus d'enthousiasme que pour la paix' [I feel a profound disgust for everything to do with war. I only have enthusiasm for peace], he tells Saintu.[24] He openly detests the war. 'Je ne vous cache pas que la guerre me répugne' [I will not hide from you that I find the war repugnant].[25] And in a style and language again anticipating *Voyage* he attacks the notions of heroism and sacrifice. 'Je prétends que la plupart des malheureux qui font acte de courage, accusent une pénurie tout au moins de représentation de l'idée de la mort' [I claim that most of those unfortunates who perform courageous acts suffer a lack at the very least of any imagination of the idea of death].[26]

This passage glitteringly reveals an essential element of Céline's truth of and witness to war. It will find its full expression in *Voyage* when Bardamu accuses his comrades of lacking 'l'imagination de la mort' [the imagination of death] (RI, 36). These letters reveal a certain insight on Céline's part into man's attitude faced with death, insight owing nothing to the theories of Freud as has been claimed within Céline scholarship.[27]

The following passage from a letter to Saintu might well be Céline's assessment of his own heroism:

J'ai vu, étudié, malaxé de mes yeux, la figure de l'homme qui va se faire tuer, lorsqu'il n'est pas illuminé, déterminé — il est résigné, il ne *comprend plus*, tout ce qu'on pourra vous raconter, d'avance je le réfute, ceux qui ont vu ont voulu *voir* quelque chose, là où il n'y a rien à voir, la figure de l'homme ordinaire devant la mort, reflète je le maintiens l'atonie passive, et ceux qui font froidement le sacrifice de leur vie sachant exactement l'étendue et la portée de leur geste — ont pris simplement le parti-pris de jouer bien ou mal, le rôle qui leur est échu, mais ne font en aucun cas participer leur conscience et leur concept à l'abandon total de leur instinct de conservation.[28]

[I have seen, studied, and scrutinised the man who is about to get himself killed, when he is not illuminated, determined — he is resigned, he *no longer understands*, all that anyone can tell you about this, I refute it in advance, those who have seen something have wanted to *see* something, there where there is nothing to see, the face of the ordinary man faced with death reflects I maintain passive acceptance, and those who coldly sacrifice their lives knowing exactly the scope of their gesture — have simply decided to play, well or badly, the role which has fallen to them, but in no way is their consciousness or their intellect involved in the total abandonment of their instinct for survival.]

The letters establish Céline's position of witness — his 'I have seen' guarantees witness — and reveal a strong sense of being in possession of the truth. The war has been a site of revelation. Ironically, the express desire of the *Carnets*, 'savoir et connaître' [to know and to experience] (see 3.2 *La Réussite*), has been fulfilled by experience. As Céline writes to Saintu, 'il me fallait cette grande épreuve pour connaître le fond de mes semblables sur lesquels j'avais de grands doutes —' [This great test was necessary for me to know the depths of my peers about whom I had many doubts—].[29]

Knowledge of his fellow man, however, 'je sais ce que je vaux, je sais ce qu'ils valent' [I know what I am worth, I know what they are worth], has isolated Céline, or rather, confined him within a certain group whose experience has set them apart: disenchanted veterans. 'Les "errants" qu'aura causé la guerre seront nombreux—' [the 'wanderers' caused by this war will be many], he predicts, prefiguring the dislocation and alienation of veterans in post-war society.[30] This alienation, Céline suggests, is the corollary of witness:

C'est pourquoi, je parcours et parcourrai encore le monde, dans des occupations fantaisistes, c'est pourquoi aussi beaucoup d'autres qui ont *vu* nous joindront, c'est pourquoi le régiment des dévoyés et des 'errants' se renforcera de nombreuses unités, transfert fatal de la désillusion, bouée de l'amour propre, rempart contre la servitude qui avilit et dégrade, mais contre qui personne ne proteste, parce qu'elle n'a que notre cerveau comme spectateur —[31]

[That is why I travel and will continue to travel this world, in fantastical occupations, it is why many others who have *seen* will join us, it is why the regiment of displaced and 'wanderers' will be strengthened by many units, the inevitable product of disillusion, safeguard of vanity, rampart against vilifying and degrading servitude, against which no one protests, because it has only our brain as spectator—]

Céline announces here his own alienated and rootless condition and ranks himself among those who have *seen*, who have witnessed. The word 'errants' evokes an army of ghosts, of which he is one, and anticipates *Voyage* and its 'fantômes' [phantoms]. The last twist of this tortuous sentence is noteworthy, emphasising the subjective nature of witness, a clear starting point for the subjectivity of *Voyage*.

The letters reveal Céline's ardent desire for peace before he returns to Europe and a latent mistrust of mankind, 'je me berce souvent du doux espoir que la paix sera signé avant que je revienne près des hommes' [I comfort myself often with the sweet hope that peace will be signed before I return to live among men], he writes.[32] However, in a letter to his parents, he foresees that this peace when it comes, will be a deeply troubled one, 'des plaies sociales d'origine profondes issues de la guerre seront encore pendant de longues années, des sources de purulence qu'il sera—, je crois, difficile de tarir —' [deep social wounds caused by the war will be a source of purulence for years to come and will—, I believe, prove difficult to stem—].[33] There is no Enlightenment dawn here, no progress justifying the war's slaughter. The death of France — 'mon pauvre pays que j'aime quand même' [my poor country which I love nonetheless][34] — as a result of the war, continues to haunt him. He asks:

> Qui nous restera-t-il pour représenter l'idée française dans ce pays où la saignée pratiquée sur un rigoureux pied d'égalité n'aura pas épargné plus le docteur ès/science que le dernier des illettrés.[35]
>
> [Who will remain to represent the idea of France in this country where blood letting practised on a rigorous egalitarian basis will no more have spared the doctor of science than the least of illiterates.]

This statement is of capital importance for *Voyage*. Here, side by side, is Céline's express concern with the degeneration of France — 'l'idée française' drained of its lifeblood — and an accusation aimed at the 'democratic' nature of the war. 'Les principes égalitaires sont à peu près inapplicables en temps de paix, mais leur application est facilitée en temps de guerre et ils deviennent désastreux' [egalitarian principles are almost inapplicable in times of peace, but their application is facilitated in times of war and they prove disastrous].[36] Behind this accusation lies the shadow of the French Revolution.

Here too, in the year of Verdun, is an express and poignant awareness of the meaning of Verdun, of the changed nature of warfare and of the wastage of heroism. This voice cannot fail to remind us of Jean Vigier (see 1.3 *Verdun*):

> Nous faisons la guerre selon le mode qui nous est imposé, mais à contre cœur, nous gardons malgré nous l'empreinte des temps de notre apogée à nous, nous avons le courage d'il y [a] deux siècles, et eux, font la guerre d'aujourd'hui —Tout est là...[37]

> [We fight the war in the manner which has been imposed on us, but we do so reluctantly, we have kept in spite of ourselves the imprint of our apogee, we have the courage of two centuries ago, while they, they fight today's war— That explains everything...]

This statement embodies one of the principle qualities of Paul Fussell's modern memory, an adversarial view of social relationships, as 'nous' [we] opposes 'eux' [them]. This 'them' extends to all that supports the architecture of the war, including the press. Railing against French newspapers' coverage of the war, Céline defends his own truth, truth which is, in a manner characteristic of Céline, dangerous to speak. He writes:

> Toutes les vérités ne sont pas bonnes à dire. [...] Il a coûté fort cher à Gallilée au xve S de maintenir que la terre tournait, il est presque aussi dangereux de notre temps de prétendre que la roue tourne.[38]

> [All truths are not good to say. [...] It cost Galileo quite a lot in the fifteenth century to maintain that the world turned, it is almost as dangerous in our times to claim that the wheel turns.]

This is an excellent example of how the war shaped a consciousness characterised by an experience of alienation from truth itself. The war silenced truth (see 1.4 *Censorship*). And truth becomes dangerous to speak once it is subject to control and punishment. *Voyage* will be heavily conditioned by this aspect of Céline's memory, while it will give expression in symbolic form to Céline's truth, which here remains implicit: 'the wheel turns'. The phrase is simple but, as *Voyage*'s cycle of re-enactment will reveal, 'the wheel' is the central image of Céline's trauma and an important key to his understanding of the Great War. It is the emblem of both trauma and war, emblem of Verdun, the 'noria', of '4 mai' and, as we shall see, of the origin of Republican France: the French Revolution. It will echo throughout his writing and in his pamphlets.

If Africa was in any way a refuge from the war it was not so for long. Céline's African sojourn ended, as his war did, in a debacle of fever and excrement. As *Voyage* testifies, Africa was an alienating re-enactment of Céline's war experience. In April 1917, Céline was shipped home with chronic enteritis.[39]

He will, therefore, be back in France to witness the last year of the war and its aftermath.

Silence

On 11 November 1918, Céline was in Dinan, on an educational mission with the Rockefeller Foundation. The end of the war was celebrated here, as elsewhere, with uninhibited joy. We do not know Céline's reaction, his inner thoughts, his remembrances. It was Céline's work with the Rockefeller Foundation which brought him to Rennes where he completed his *baccalauréat* and began his training as a doctor.[40] In Rennes he met and married Edith Follet.[41] These were years of silence about the war. When asked about his war experience, 'read Barbusse' was all Céline would answer.[42] However, the trauma of memory persisted. More than sixty years later, Edith Follet insisted on Céline's trauma, remembering his silence and unhappiness whenever the war was mentioned.[43] 'Louis ne savait pas être heureux' [Louis did not know how to be happy], she said.[44]

Sometimes the silence broke. Follet recalled that in 1919 Céline told her father that he had been afraid during the war and that he saw this fear as a proof of cowardice.[45] Years later he would repeat this to Elizabeth Craig.[46] Céline's memory of war was tainted by a suspicion of his own lack of courage, born of a recognition of his own fear in war — perhaps originating in the wood at Spincourt — and enlarged by an access of fear during his breakdown in Hazebrouck. Fear compromises masculinity and Céline's confessions confirm that the war, acting on his doubts over his own virility, damaged his sense of being a man (see 3.2 *Cuirassier Céline*). As such, Céline's experience recalls the crisis in masculinity caused by the war and noted particularly by Denis de Rougemont (see 1.4 *Mechanisation*).

Semmelweiss

In 1923, Céline completed his medical training. He wrote his doctoral thesis on the Hungarian doctor, Semmelweiss, the father of antisepsis. Although he always had an ambition to write,[47] *Semmelweiss* marks a turning point for Céline. It is his first important literary work. Elaborating Semmelweiss's story from other texts,

Céline invests himself in its patterns while enlarging and distorting the truth. The work is in reality a fictional biography in which the author invests himself in the character of his protagonist, evidence of a tendency in modern literature, termed the 'existential fallacy' by Northrop Frye.[48] Semmelweiss, in anticipation of Bardamu and Robinson, becomes Céline's double.[49]

If the Great War appears absent from *Semmelweiss*, the work is profoundly marked by a consciousness shaped by the traumatic experience of the war. Death and truth are central. And Céline's essential metaphors are present. The journey to truth is a journey through darkness, 'dans l'ombre il trouvera la clef de mystères' [in the darkness he will find the key to mysteries].[50] Semmelweiss struggles to 'faire sortir [la vérité] du silence' [make the truth emerge from silence],[51] opposed by colleagues who collaborate with death. 'Ils ont pactisé avec la Mort' [they have made a pact with Death], writes Céline.[52] The doctoral thesis is the first site of Céline's enunciation, 'la Vérité c'est la Mort' [the Truth is Death],[53] a formula which will return in *Voyage*. And it is the setting for a vision of history and of humanity which will underlie *Voyage*, a vision whose key is 1793, and whose keynote is sacrifice:

> En 93, on fit les frais d'un Roi. [...] Il fut sacrifié [...]. L'Homicide est une fonction quotidienne des peuples, mais, en France tout au moins, le Régicide passait pour neuf. On osa. Personne ne voulait le dire, mais la Bête était chez nous [...]. On trouva que la Bête avait du génie. Et ce fut dans la boucherie une surenchère formidable. On tua d'abord au nom de la Raison [...]. La foule voulait détruire et cela suffisait.[54]

> [In '93, a King paid the price. [...] He was sacrificed [...]. Homicide is a daily function of nations, but, at least in France, regicide passed for something new. We dared. No one wanted to say it, but the Beast was among us [...]. We found that the Beast was ingenious. There followed a formidable excess of butchery. Killing took place, first of all, in the name of Reason [...]. The crowd wanted to destroy and that sufficed.]

Semmelweiss anticipates here the anti-Enlightenment and anti-Republican views of Princhard in *Voyage* (RI, 67–70). The whole pattern of history appears traumatised. Humankind is murderous, hypocritical; reason is a lie, a pretext. The evocation of 'la Bête' [the Beast] anticipates *Voyage*'s elaboration of a sustained metaphor based on the image of the monstrous.[55] The vision of 'la foule' [crowd] as a murderous horde will haunt not just *Voyage* but all of Céline's work. The passage gives way to a denunciation of sentimentality, 'assez vite on se mit à pleurer sur le malheur des tourterelles avec des larmes aussi réelles, aussi sincères que les injures dont on criblait, la veille, la charrette des condamnés' [quite quickly one began to lament the misfortune of turtledoves with tears as real and sincere as the insults with which one had, the evening before, inundated the carts carrying the condemned],[56] heralding a determined anti-sentimentality in *Voyage*.

Semmelweiss reveals a Céline equipped with a mature, if savagely disenchanted reflection on humanity, war and history. Lurking at the back of this description is the Great War and the lessons Céline has learned from it. These lessons will provide a solid foundation for the intersection of memory and imagination that is *Voyage*. Apart from that, *Semmelweiss*'s literary importance is that, as a doctoral thesis, it provides Céline with the rudiments of a literary method based on the exploitation of existing texts and awakens him to the possibilities inherent in the literary rewriting of self.

Marriage

By this time, Céline's marriage was foundering. It effectively ended when Céline left Rennes to work with the *Société des Nations* [League of Nations] in Geneva. In a letter to his wife, Céline ended their marriage with all the venomous angst of Robinson towards Madelon in *Voyage* (RI, 493–494). Céline wrote:

> Il m'est impossible de vivre avec quelqu'un — Je ne veux pas te traîner pleurarde et miséreuse derrière moi, tu m'ennuies, voilà tout — ne te raccroche pas à moi. J'aimerais mieux me tuer que de vivre avec toi en continuité — cela sache-le bien et ne m'ennuie plus jamais avec l'attachement, la tendresse — mais bien plutôt arrange ta vie comme tu l'entends. J'ai envie d'être seul, seul, seul, ni dominé, ni en tutelle, ni aimé, libre. Je déteste le mariage, je l'abhorre, je le crache ; il me fait l'impression d'une prison où je crève.[57]

> [It is impossible for me to live with anyone — I do not want to drag you snivelling and miserable behind me, you bore me, that's all — don't cling to me. I would prefer to kill myself than to live with you on a continuous basis — know as much and don't bother me any longer with attachment, or tenderness — but rather organise your life as you intend. I want to be alone, alone, alone, not dominated, not in someone's care, not loved, but free. I detest marriage, I abhor it, I spit on it; it is like a prison in which I am dying.]

The letter reveals yet again how much of Céline is invested in *Voyage*, in those doubles, Bardamu and Robinson, who speak in his name.

La Société des Nations

In June 1924, Céline began working as a hygienist for the League of Nations in Geneva. The job allowed him to travel. In the next number of years he visited Cuba, America, Canada and returned to Africa. His first impressions of New York show his memory of war hovering beneath the surface of even the most novel experience. 'Tout ce que je vois ne ressemble à rien' [everything I see is like nothing on earth], he writes, 'c'est insensé comme la guerre' [it's senseless like the war].[58] Céline's experience in Geneva is critical with regard to memory. The post-war League of Nations was established to create world peace. Vera Brittain was a lecturer with the League in the early twenties and attended its Geneva Assemblies. 'I felt [the League] to be the one element of hope and progress contained in the peace treaties,' she wrote.[59] This hope was to be disappointed. The League, Brittain wrote, was destined to be used as a 'stage on which [the Foreign Ministers of the Great Powers] could play the skilled game of the Old Diplomacy circumspectly dressed up in international costume'.[60] This is *L'Église* [*The Church*].[61] Brittain's 'stage' metaphor shows how appropriate Céline's use of theatre was for the representation of the League's failure.

Less than ten years after the Great War, the League's death-mastering potential had proven vain. Céline would get an insider's view. His unsuccessful 1926 play, *L'Église*, in which Bardamu makes his first appearance, is the result. Like *Mea culpa* ten years later, *L'Église* records a collapse in belief. It announces the crisis in memory which will lead to *Voyage*. As will prove his wont, Céline responds to this failure by supporting memory with vibrant tones of satire, mockery and anti-Semitism.

Céline's experience of the League of Nations was disastrous. While he lived an extravagant, indebted lifestyle, his position there deteriorated quickly and ended suddenly when he was accorded four months' sick-leave at the end of 1927, apparently due to symptoms related to his old African fever.[62] The cycle of fever and collapse had once again been set in motion. At the end of 1927, Céline left the

League and returned to Paris. He will be there in 1928 as the 10th Anniversary Armistice commemoration takes place and the collective memory of the Great War reaches fever pitch.

The Crisis in Memory

In Geneva, Céline met the American dancer, Elizabeth Craig.[63] They began a passionate love affair. They enjoyed life together. 'In Geneva, we used to go skiing,' Craig remembered. 'He taught me how to ski and ice skate, we had a great time.'[64] This changed when they went to live in Paris. More precisely, she remembered, it changed when they moved to an apartment in Montmartre. This was in August 1929. Céline announced that he was going to write a book. 'I need one little room for myself,' he told Elizabeth, 'that's all I need, because I'm going to write a book.'[65] This is when Céline, revisiting memory, breaks his silence about the war. As of late 1929, Céline is at work on *Voyage*. Writing it changed him visibly in the eyes of those around him. 'I can't understand why he changed so much,' said Elizabeth Craig. Adding, 'even my parents noticed how much he had changed when they came back for a visit.'[66] The reason was, simply, that he remembered.

At this time Céline's professional life was in turmoil. In early 1928, in the wake of the Geneva debacle, he opened a general practice in Clichy. The practice failed. Towards the end of 1928, Céline obtained a post as part of a medical team in Laennec Hospital. Robert Debré, a member of the team, remembered meeting Céline. François Gibault reports his impressions, 'il eut tout de suite l'impression d'avoir en face de lui un homme malheureux, qui avait dû souffrir et avait l'air battu par la vie' [he had the impression that he was meeting an unhappy man, one who had suffered and who had an air of having been beaten by life].[67] According to Debré, Céline 'parut alors accablé par tout ce qu'il voyait à Clichy, par la misère ouvrière qu'il côtoyait quotidiennement et par la tuberculose dont il constatait chaque jour les ravages' [seemed distressed by what he saw at Clichy, by the poverty of the workers he saw daily and by the ravages of tuberculosis which he witnessed from day to day]. Elizabeth Craig also testifies to Céline's obsession with the poor. 'We'd go back to the old streets, walk the cobblestones

to some God-forsaken place, and he seemed to believe that he belonged there.'[68]
Céline as an ex-soldier felt a natural kinship with the poor.[69] Significantly, it
provides him with the point of view he will lend Bardamu in *Voyage*. As such,
Bardamu expresses on Céline's behalf a profoundly troubling experience of self.

Céline announced the beginning of *Voyage* in letters to a fellow-veteran,
Joseph Garcin. These letters offer direct insights into Céline's state of mind as he
undertook *Voyage*. Céline claimed a shared understanding of the past with Garcin,
an understanding rooted in the 'hell' of war:

> Nous avons en commun cette expérience de 1914 *dont je ne parle jamais*
> *sauf aux initiés*, très rares... Vous avez compris que nous sommes en
> sursis depuis quinze ans, que nous avons côtoyé l'enfer dont il ne faudrait
> pas revenir.[70]

> [We have in common the experience of 1914 *of which I never speak*,
> except to those very rare initiates... You understand that we have been in
> suspension for fifteen years, that we have experienced that hell from which
> we were not meant to have returned.]

In March 1930, having come out of his fifteen-year state of 'suspension', Céline
refers directly to *Voyage*:

> Vous le savez j'écris un roman, quelques expériences personnelles qui
> doivent tenir sur le papier, la part de folie, la difficulté aussi, labeur
> énorme... D'abord la guerre, dont tout dépend, qu'il s'agit de exorciser.[71]

> [You know I am writing a novel, some personal experiences which should
> take hold on paper, the madness, the difficulty, an immense task... First of
> all, the war, on which all else depends, which must be exorcised.]

There can be no doubt. Céline's main aim is to evoke 'le charnier des
Flandres' [the Flanders slaughterhouse],[72] the madness of war, and in doing so
transfer the nightmare of memory from his mind to his text. He writes to Garcin:

> J'ai en moi mille pages de cauchemars en réserve, celui de la guerre tient
> naturellement la tête. Des semaines de 14 sous les averses visqueuses,
> dans cette boue atroce et ce sang et cette merde et cette connerie des
> hommes, *je ne me remettrai pas*, c'est une vérité que je vous livre une fois
> encore, que nous sommes quelques-uns à partager. Tout est là. Le drame,
> notre malheur, c'est cette faculté d'oubli de la majorité de nos
> contemporains...[73]

> [I have in me a thousand pages of nightmare in reserve, those of the war
> naturally come first. Weeks in '14 under heavy showers, in that atrocious
> mud and that blood and that shit and that stupidity of men, *I will never get*
> *over it*, it is a truth I wish to offer you once again, a truth shared by just a

few of us. It's all there. The drama, our unhappiness, is the faculty for forgetting of the majority of our contemporaries…]

This letter is immensely significant, expressing a profound sense of alienation and marginalisation — 'our unhappiness' — in a society which has forgotten, which has cleansed itself of the truth of 'that blood and that shit and the stupidity of men'. In this context, where 'forgetting' is opposed to 'truth', *Voyage* becomes an act of truthful remembrance. In other words, it is Céline's unforgettable nightmare, his trauma, his *Voyage*, which is true; and the exaltation of commemoration which is false.

Writing, Elizabeth Craig recalled, was at first enjoyable for Céline but soon it became an obsession. Although initially he wrote for just a couple of hours, later as momentum increased, he wrote morning, noon and night. 'He *had* to write, he *had* to correct, he *had* to rewrite it.'[74] He became depressed and was depressing company for the young American. The worst part was how much he had changed. Watching him writing, Elizabeth Craig, saw him suddenly aged, as if he had become an old man:

> As soon as he closed the door to his studio he became a different man. […] Hunched over his papers, he looked like an old man, his face looked old, everything about him looked old. It made me wonder: *Is that Louis?* [75]

Lost in a frenzy of writing, of memory, Céline became prey to the despair that had sheltered for long years inside him. 'He'd go in his study,' Elizabeth Craig remembered, 'and come out an entirely different person, staring with a desperate look on his face that would make you want to cry.'[76] His writing opened a breach between them. How could she understand what Céline was carrying inside him? 'He'd look at me as if to say, *Well, you don't understand anything, you just don't know how tragic life is!*'[77] She tried to reason with him, life isn't all sad, she argued. 'He'd look at me as if to say: *You'll never understand!*'[78]

What was happening to Céline as he wrote *Voyage*? Writing trauma is to engage trauma. It is to confront trauma in an effort to quell it. The writing of trauma, however, is fraught with danger. Jorge Semprun has described what happens. For Semprun, writing about the experience of death is to construct a life from death itself:

> Je ne possède rien d'autre que ma mort, mon expérience de la mort, pour dire ma vie [...]. Il faut que je fabrique de la vie avec toute cette mort. Et la meilleure façon d'y parvenir, c'est l'écriture.[79]

> [I possess only my death, my experience of death, to speak my life [...]. I must make my life with all that death. The best way to do this is through writing.]

The effort to write becomes the effort to transform death *into* life. However, Semprun tells us, it is an effort doomed to failure:

> Le bonheur de l'écriture [...] n'effaçait jamais ce malheur de la mémoire. Bien au contraire : il l'aiguisait, le creusait, le ravivait. Il le rendait insupportable. Seul l'oubli pourrait me sauver.[80]

> [The happiness of writing [...] never effaced the unhappiness of memory. Quite the contrary: it sharpened it, deepened it, revived it. It made it unbearable. Only forgetting could save me.]

Here Semprun introduces us to the very core of Céline's experience as he wrote *Voyage*.

Céline entered memory only to become trapped there. 'At the beginning it was more like a loving trust,' remembered Elizabeth Craig. 'Toward the end, it became more like a duty, he had to harness himself down to keep going. [...] It became an occupation, a frantic occupation.'[81] It was not what Céline had hoped for. *'I'll be a different man when I get it out of me,'* he told her.[82] Through writing he sought his own transformation. *'It's been cooking inside of me for a long time,'* he said. But writing only made the past's sway over him more complete. *'Please forgive me,'* Céline pleaded, *'but at times I can't think of anything else.'* Craig saw that writing, far from helping Céline to release himself from the pain of the past, was entrenching him in it. Even his laughter was dying:

> He would get so immersed in his work, I would tell myself, 'I've got to yank him out of that thing, he's getting ridiculous.' I would bring him out of this sombre mood by pushing him to do normal things, by making him laugh. He loved to laugh.[83]

In an interview with Jean Monnier, Craig recalled walks to the Sacré-Cœur sitting under the stars. 'Je vois... je vois la mort' [I see... I see death], Céline told her.[84] And then as they watched the stars in the night-sky above Paris, 'je me sens mieux' [I'm feeling better]. Here clearly is the origin of the passage in *Voyage* where Bardamu, accompanied by Tania, sees the dead rising in the night-sky above Montmartre (RI, 366–369). Did Céline really have visions of the dead? Why not? If Siegfried Sassoon saw the streets of London littered with corpses, why could not Céline, haunted by death, have experienced something similar? The evidence of *Guignol's band* suggests that he did. Céline really was afraid of death, Craig said. He spoke of death as of something 'imminent'.[85]

Elizabeth Craig lost her battle to save Céline. Remembering his horrible mental crises, she wondered how she managed to live so long with that sense of death at her side.[86] 'He didn't have the kind of hope I had,' she remembered.[87] Their life together became unbearable:

> The more Louis immersed himself in the book the worse it got. *If he has to be like this in order to write, it's pretty awful.* It's horrible to think that he couldn't create without going through those dreadful crises.[88]

In 1933, Craig returned to America.

4.2 THE TRAUMA OF THE SOLDIER

The Stress of Combat

Bardamu's story is the story of the traumatised soldier. The insights that form this fictional portrait of the damaged soldier are drawn from Céline's own experience. We have seen ongoing trauma in Céline's life culminating in the crisis of memory as he writes *Voyage*. In examining that trauma, however, Céline is seen chiefly from the outside. This section will elucidate Céline and his double, Bardamu, by entering into the substance of trauma itself, and describing what is on the inside.

Since the Second World War it is widely acknowledged that the conditions of battle itself produce breakdown.[89] Zahava Solomon, in his study of breakdown among Israeli soldiers during the Lebanon war, *Combat Stress Reaction* (CSR), affirms:

> by whatever name it is called and however difficult it is to define, [Combat Stress Reaction] is a pathology with a consistent set of symptoms and expressions. [...] Essentially it is a war-induced pathology wherever and whenever that war takes place and whoever the fighters are.[90]

Solomon's study established a taxonomy of CSR.[91] This analysis presents us with a modern picture of what 'shell-shock' was and continues to be. Solomon recognised the polymorphic, labile nature of CSR. His analysis showed that anxiety and depression were its most common characteristics. Solomon's analysis identified six main factors involved in a CSR:

> *Distancing* [...] the term assigned to [...] psychic numbing, fantasies of running, and engaging in thoughts about civilian life. [...] *Anxiety* [including] paralysing anxiety, fear of death, and thoughts of death. [...] *Guilt* about poor performance and exhaustion [...]. *Loneliness and vulnerability* [...]. Loneliness [...] from the recognition that [...] in death one is alone. [...] Vulnerability [...] from the reality that the soldier [...] often [...] has no place to hide and take shelter [...]. *Loss of self-control* [...], weeping, screaming, [...] vomiting, wetting and diarrhea. [...] *Disorientation*, fainting and trembling [emphasis added].[92]

Almost all of these are recognisably part of Céline's disintegration in Hazebrouck. In addition, all are features in *Voyage* of Bardamu's response in the aftermath of the explosion in which his colonel is killed (RI, 17–21), conferring these pages with an extraordinary degree of psychological truth. The following cursory examples confirm this. First: distancing. As Bardamu leaves his dead colonel behind, he dreams of returning to Place Clichy, 'on repasserait peut-être place Clichy en triomphe [...] on passerait sous l'Arc de Triomphe...' [we would return perhaps to Place Clichy in triumph [...] We would march under the Arc de Triomphe...] (RI, 18). Secondly: loneliness and vulnerability faced with death. 'Pendant longtemps je n'ai rencontré personne [...]. De temps en temps, je ne savais d'où, une balle [...] me cherchait [...] entêtée à me tuer, dans cette solitude, moi' [For a long time I did not meet anybody [...]. From time to time, from where I don't know, a bullet [...] sought me [...] determined to kill me, in that solitude, me] (RI, 19). Thirdly: thoughts of death. 'Étais-je donc le seul à avoir l'imagination de la mort dans ce régiment ?' [Was I the only one in the regiment who was capable of imagining death?] (RI, 19). Fourthly: anxiety over performance. 'On m'aurait fusillé : douze balles, plus une' [They would have shot me: twelve bullets, plus one] (RI, 19). Finally, there is loss of self-control and disorientation in the chapter's final pages. 'J'ai dû céder à une immense envie de vomir, et pas qu'un peu, jusqu'à l'évanouissement' [I had to give way to an immense desire to vomit, and not just a little, right until I passed out] (RI, 21).

That is not all. Examining depression among veterans, Solomon offers this finding: 'the descriptions of our soldiers reveal that the seeds of their depressive reactions are often planted when they witness absurd losses and destruction.'[93] He adds that one soldier who 'could not shake off the psychic numbing he had tried to use as a defence, broke down when he saw stables piled with the corpses of dead Arabian horses'. This explains why Bardamu breaks down at the sight of the regimental butchers at work and not before. Faced with this evidence how can *Voyage* in this instance be anything other than the transcription of a personal experience of CSR?

There is yet more. For Jean-Pierre Richard this scene in *Voyage* is one of epiphany. Richard calls Bardamu's sickness 'nausée exemplaire' [exemplary nausea], provoked by the brusque revelation that 'la chair n'est en réalité que viande' [flesh in reality is nothing other than meat].[94] This insight, he writes, determines 'la grande maladie du corps célinien [...] le manque de *tenue*' [the great malady of the célinian body [...] its lack of *consistency*].[95] In other words, this scene is at the core of Céline's obsession with death and decay. We can now see this 'nausea' as part and parcel of a CSR.

The Aftermath

It is now known that the trauma of war can linger long after the war has ended. Even those soldiers who do not break down during war can suffer long-term traumatic effects. They remember and re-experience combat in intrusive flashbacks and nightmares. They can suffer extremes of anxiety and depression. Soldiers from the Second World War were breaking down for the first time in 1995, on the occasion of the 50th Commemoration of the end of that war.[96] A 1985 study claimed that as many as 35,000 Vietnam veterans had committed suicide since returning from the Vietnamese war.[97]

In recent years the syndrome known as post-traumatic stress disorder (PTSD) has received much attention. This disorder was first recognised in Vietnam veterans. Its diagnosis was established in the American Psychiatric Association's *Diagnostic and Statistical Manual: Version Three* (DSM-III).[98] The DSM-III diagnosis centred on three groups of symptoms: intrusion, constriction and avoidance, and arousal — including insomnia and irritability. These symptoms represent a dysfunctional response to an event 'outside normal human experience'. The diagnosis was seen by many to be too narrow and it was argued that criteria such as 'nomadism' and 'antisociality' should have been included.[99] All in all, research into PTSD indicates that 'there is probably a spectrum of stress response problems varying from subtle forms to severe, chronic disorder.'[100] Which is to say that there is no straightforward PTSD diagnosis, but rather an array of symptoms that appear both varied and changeable.

The Trepanation Myth

The purpose of this work is not to label Céline with PTSD or any form of clinical trauma or neurosis. CSR and PTSD are only evoked in so far as they throw light on Céline's experience. Indeed, as we have seen, established PTSD criteria fall short of the full range of traumatic effects observed in soldiers. Antisociality and nomadism, for example, are terms that could easily be applied to Céline in the decade and a half that follow the war and beyond. In particular, lacking from the PTSD spectrum of criteria are two traumatic responses apparent in Céline. The first, the crisis in masculinity, derives from the emasculating effect of the Great War. There is evidence that Denis de Rougemont's assertion that the war had produced an effect of 'generalised impotence' and 'chronic onanism and homosexuality' in males was true to some extent of Céline (see 1.4 *Mechanisation*). While Elizabeth Craig testifies to Céline's insatiable sexual appetite,[101] this may be true only of the early part of their relationship. There is evidence from Marcel Brochard that *circa* 1930, as he lost himself in writing *Voyage*, and his crisis of memory deepened, Céline suffered from some degree of impotence.[102] In addition, François Gibault has noted Céline's propensity for masturbation, 'même lorsqu'il eut de nombreuses aventures et liaisons avec de très belles femmes' [even when he had numerous adventures and liaisons with very beautiful women].[103] Henri Mahé claimed that Céline masturbated even while writing.[104] *Voyage* is littered with references to masturbation, with characters who masturbate, such as Bébert and Pomone, and with references to homosexuality. The persistent homophobia of Céline's pamphlets completes this picture of disrupted maleness concomitant with the collapse of the heroic ideal.

The other, and certainly the most intriguing, manifestation of trauma is the trepanation myth. Céline claimed that he had been trepanned during the war but he had not been. 'Nous autres tes copains de Rennes, nous le savons bien, tu n'as jamais été [...] trépané !' [We, your Rennes companions, know quite well that you were never trepanned], wrote Marcel Brochard.[105] Associated with the trepanation myth were lifelong incapacitating headaches and a condition resembling tinnitus.[106] However, the imaginary trepanation does have an anchor in the reality of post-combat trauma. One study of Vietnam veterans with PTSD found that a 'high incidence of head injury [...] was reported [...] but electroencephalographic studies gave unexpectedly normal results'.[107] The trepanation myth becomes Céline's way of trying to express the paradoxical reality of a sense of having being damaged in the head, where medical investigation reveals nothing.

Erik Erikson also throws light on Céline's headaches. In the case study of a traumatised veteran he noted incapacitating headaches. Like Céline, Erikson's soldier when evacuated from combat contracted fever. Erikson comments, 'from the physiological viewpoint the fever and the toxic state had justified his first headache, but only the first one.'[108] Erikson concludes that the soldier was suffering from psychosomatic 'over-compensation':

> Once evacuated, many men felt, as it were, unconsciously obligated to continue to suffer and to suffer somatically, in order to justify the evacuation, not to speak of the later discharge [...]. The Second World War experience has indicated insight into what might be called an *over* compensation neurosis — i.e., the unconscious wish to continue to suffer in order to over-compensate psychologically for the weakness of having let others down; for many of these escapists were more loyal than they knew. Our conscientious man, too, repeatedly felt 'shot through the head' by excruciating pain whenever he seemed definitely better.[109]

The 'shot through the head' metaphor recalls Céline's own 'j'ai une balle dans la tête' [I have a bullet in my head] in his 1957 interview with Madeleine Chapsal.[110] Erikson describes this as a common 'neurosis', which can be activated by memory and in which, significantly, the contours of time, space and truth are distorted. According to Erikson:

> There have been many war neuroses of this kind. Their victims were in a constant state of potential panic. [...] Childlike anger and anxiety without reason were provoked by anything too sudden or too intense, a perception or a feeling, a thought, or a memory. [...] They would find themselves unable to remember certain things; in their own neighbourhoods they would lose their way or suddenly detect, in conversation, that they had unwittingly misrepresented things. They could not rely on the characteristic processes of the functioning ego by which time and space are organised and truth is tested.[111]

Voyage's acts of misrepresentation,[112] its confused references to truth,[113] its time lapses, and its enclosed or labyrinthine spaces all have part of their origin here in trauma. Time and truth 'out of joint', Erikson's text reveals how much of Céline 'mythomane' [the mythomaniac] is in fact a condition of his ongoing trauma of war.

It is hardly surprising that Céline's 'over-compensation' for evacuation from the war should represent itself as a head wound or injury both in his life and work. We have, indeed, seen that he was repeatedly struck on the head by his father as a child (see 3.1 *Family, Work and Army*). In particular, we have seen that in the early part of the war 60% of injuries suffered were to the head (see 1.1 *The Hero*). Céline's traumatic or imaginary head wound is, in the light of experience, an appropriate expression of his witness to war. It captures both his sense of having been 'wounded' to the head, and his sense of the experience in its totality as being effectively a 'wounding' to the head. This is also true of his tinnitus complaint. If we remember Ernst Jünger's comment that under bombardment a sense of 'absurdity' concentrates in the ear, it is but a short step in logic to recognise Céline's symptom as the literal 'transposition' of this sense of absurdity (see 1.4 *Absurdity*). If it is also borne in mind that the etymology of 'absurd' is rooted in whatever is 'unbearable to the ear', the living metaphor of Céline's tinnitus becomes a fitting expression of the Great War's 'unspeakable' or 'unlistenable' nature.

The Nightmare of Memory

Post-traumatic stress disorder is a disease of memory and of time. In abnormal life-threatening situations the mind simply cannot absorb what is happening. Writes Zahava Solomon, describing the inscription of trauma:

> People are flooded by an excess of aversive stimuli that are difficult either to block out or integrate. Thus, after a war ends on the field, it still continues in the men's minds.[114]

He adds:

> Practically all the soldiers I know are to some degree still haunted by their war experiences [...]. Even men without PTSD may wake up from nightmares of exploding tanks or find themselves ruminating about lost buddies in the middle of a business meeting.

Nightmares can be horrifically real. A soldier dreamed of being in a dark room sifting with his fingers through human remains, 'I could feel human intestines... brain... I was picking up.'[115] 'Many of the nightmares and flashbacks represent an accurate reliving of actual experience,' notes Solomon.[116] The soldier may even dream of his own death:

> One common dream is the dream of being dead, of being mistaken for dead, or of being buried alive or mourned as dead. [...] Dreams of swollen or burnt corpses and of bodies missing the head or limbs are also common.[117]

This last description suggests that in *Voyage*, Céline has written his personal nightmares into passages such as the war episode's decapitating explosion (RI, 17) and its recapitulation (RI, 260). This anchors the 'rêve éveillé' [waking dream] style of *Voyage* in the reality of Céline's own dreams and nightmares. It is worth remembering in this respect that Léon Daudet, when using the phrase 'rêve éveillé', linked it directly to the experience of the Great War.[118] According to Solomon, dreams about death represent not just anxiety but also 'symbolic enactments of that state'.[119] The dream reactivates the soldier's own experience of death on the battlefield. Insomnia, from which Céline was a lifelong sufferer, becomes the soldier's way of warding off such dreams. Bardamu too has difficulty sleeping (RI, 199).

The Death Imprint

For the depressed soldier, it is the encounter with death which is most significant. In this regard, Zahava Solomon's remarks are of the utmost importance for understanding Céline and *Voyage*. He writes, 'what distinguishes the depressed PTSD casualty from the others is that he has internalised the deaths he encountered.'[120] The consequence of this is far-reaching:

> In the more seriously affected soldiers, it leads to an identification with death. This identification often shows itself in images and dreams of the dead that the soldier finds difficult to throw off, as well as in a pervasive inner sense that one is not quite alive oneself.

Soldiers, says Solomon, mourn what they experience as their own death, a phenomenon described by Robert Jay Lifton who calls it the 'death imprint'. Those afflicted by the death imprint 'live as though they are dead, denying themselves pleasure and curtailing their own vitality'.[121] Anger often appears, violent outbursts and attacks, directed either at the world or at oneself. For Lifton, survivor anger and rage are 'directly related to an inner sense of death' and represent a 'desperate effort at vitality [...] a way of holding onto a psychic lifeline when surrounded by images of death'.[122] In other words, for the 'death imprinted' survivor, anger becomes a way of shaking off death and feeling alive.

Lifton describes the death imprint as 'the radical intrusion of an image feeling of threat or end of life'.[123] Important factors that determine the intensity of the death imprint are: 'the degree of unacceptability of death contained in the image — of prematurity, grotesqueness and absurdity'; 'the impossibility of assimilating the death imprint', due to, among other reasons, 'its association with the terror of premature, unacceptable dying'; and 'one's vulnerability to death imagery — not only to direct life threat but also to separation, stasis and disintegration — on the basis of prior conflictual experience'.[124] It is clear from Céline's ongoing preoccupation with death in his work and life that he suffered a form of 'death imprint'. He unites all the preconditions for it. His youth and his dream of a life full of incident are the primary mental characteristics which render death absurd and unacceptable to him. Céline's experience of his grandmother's death, as well as his own solitary upbringing, provides the source in early childhood of his vulnerability to 'separation, stasis and disintegration'. Included in this predisposition to trauma is his latent resentment of army life and of his father who encouraged, if not obliged, him to enlist. This provides a critical element of 'prior conflictual experience' which will influence the shape of *Voyage* and also, as we have seen, of *Mort à crédit* (see 2.2 *Remarque*).

The Search for Meaning

Robert Jay Lifton has argued for a move away from seeing trauma in terms of 'neurosis'.[125] He believes the search to find meaning in the experience of death is at the root of traumatic memory. 'The survivor's overall task,' writes Lifton, is to evolve 'new inner forms that include the traumatic event, which in turn requires that one find meaning or significance in it so that the rest of one's life need not be devoid of meaning or significance.'[126] There has been a break in the survivor's lifeline which must be re-established on a 'new basis'. The survivor 'seeks vitality both in immediate relationships and ultimate meaning'. The 'ultimate dimension', Lifton affirms, 'the struggle for resurgent modes of symbolic immortality, is crucial [...], though rarely recognised as such.' In Lifton's terms, therefore, the writing of *Voyage* is a search for meaning intended to repair a broken lifeline through reconnection with 'symbolic immortality'. The aim, we can clearly see, is to achieve a newfound heroic death mastery. *Voyage* itself, founded on a creative, immortalising dynamic, becomes 'heroic'. Breaking free of the past, however, is not easy. Lifton defines the response of the death-imprinted survivor, seeking to free himself of his own sense of 'inner deadness' in terms of a three-stage process of 'confrontation, reordering, and renewal'. A major obstacle in the way of this process of return and renewal, he says, is the:

> literalism the survivors impose upon themselves in viewing their death encounter. [...] They may bind themselves to what they take to be its absolutely unaltered reality.[127]

This view, which also enables us to understand the point of view of a Jean Norton Cru, offers a remarkable insight into the way in which Céline confronted his trauma by straying from the 'absolutely unaltered reality', in his attempts to 'reorder and renew' his experience of death. Furthermore, Lifton implicitly makes a case for trauma as a driving force towards the expansion of consciousness, the goal of which is to place overwhelming, unacceptable death within a new configuration of meaning, to elaborate new terms of death mastery. This too is *Voyage*.

4.3 THE SITE OF RE-ENACTMENT

Duality

Chapter One described the breach in consciousness due to the Great War, the breach made in the world and in the individual soldier by death (see 1.3 *Death*). This fracture is visible in the underlying patterns of *Voyage*, in particular the novel's fundamental *duality*, what Jean-Pierre Dauphin calls its '*mode binaire*' [binary mode].[128]

Voyage is a world broken in two. According to Dauphin, it is composed of two halves, divided into three episodes each.[129] Each episode, he writes, is further divided in two. For example, the war episode is divided in two sections, 'front' and 'rear'. The front is further divided into two halves, 'operations' and 'reconnaissance', with the reconnaissance section comprising two further episodes, those of Barbagny and Noirceur.[130] The remaining episodes are similarly constructed. Dauphin finds duality too in the way characters in *Voyage* re-enact each other. Examples of these *duplicata* are Lola/Musyne, Bestombes/Baryton, but by far the greatest example of duality in *Voyage* is Bardamu's double, Robinson. These 'dual' relationships ultimately reflect *Voyage*'s most significant split in consciousness, the one that divides its creator, Céline, from his creation, Bardamu, and the further one that divides Céline from his heroic self, Destouches. All of these 'splits' reflect an elemental and ultimately antagonistic break in consciousness flowing from the trauma of the Great War and refracted artistically through the traumatised consciousness of Céline himself.

Destouches/Céline, Céline/Bardamu, Bardamu/Robinson are the initiating models for the development of 'dual' relationships within *Voyage*. From these models flow a whole series of diametrically opposing 'dualities': above/below, big/small, rich/poor, heroism/cowardice, remembering/forgetting, speech/silence, autobiography/fiction, literature/orality, reason/emotion, male/female, life/death, truth and untruth. As such, *Voyage* negotiates a world of paradox where duality is the structural and symbolic representation of a broken time, a broken world and a broken consciousness whose origin is the Great War. Duality, however, is only one in a series of overlapping patterns in *Voyage*. Other patterns are provided by the inversion of heroic myth and the novel's key pattern, the cycle of re-enactment, of which '4 mai' is the burning emblem.

The Breach in Consciousness

Trauma in *Voyage* can be read through its impact on narrator, language, structure and even on inherited mythical patterns. Paul Fussell has pointed out how most war novels and memoirs re-enact the tripartite form of the heroic quest: journey to battle, confrontation with the monster, return.[131] *Voyage* is no exception. Bardamu represents the modern warrior-hero who sets off to confront the beast and returns armed with knowledge. The beast is death and the knowledge gained is expressed in the formula 'la vérité de ce monde c'est la mort' [the truth of this world is death] (RI, 200). The particularity of *Voyage* is that it re-enacts this tripartite narrative within each episode. The novel becomes a series of successive journeys in which the monster of war appears and is confronted by Bardamu. Thus escaping from the war, Bardamu finds that the rear, Africa, New York, Paris, Toulouse and the asylum at Vigny provide re-enactments of his war experience.

The tripartite structure of *Voyage*'s episodes reproduces the basic cyclical pattern of the heroic myth; a cycle, as Fussell puts it, of 'innocence, death, rebirth'.[132] In *Voyage*, however, the content of the myth is inverted. The Célinien hero, unlike the hero of myth, does not resemble the sun (see 1.1 *The Hero*). The mythical hero is blonde and bright-eyed; Bardamu is spectral, dark. Indeed the mythical hero's solarity, a clear symbol for the heroic spirit, is so subverted in *Voyage* that the sun is presented as antagonistic to Bardamu. This is most evident in the African episode but it is immediately apparent in the war episode when Bardamu comments, 'jamais je ne m'étais senti aussi inutile parmi toutes ces balles et les lumières de ce soleil' [I had never felt myself to be so useless as in the midst of all those bullets and the light of that sun] (RI, 12). If the mythical hero's voyage is a solar one, from horizon to horizon across a limitless sky, Bardamu's is a journey through successive underworlds. Bardamu is not the hero who regenerates his race, but rather, his lack of death mastery becomes one of the reasons for its fall from grace. This is why Bardamu says, 'je n'arrivais jamais à me sentir entièrement innocent des malheurs qui arrivaient' [I could never feel entirely innocent of the misfortunes that happened] (RI, 279). The degeneration of France is ultimately felt as the consequence of Céline/Bardamu's own lack of heroic transcendence. In the same way, Erik Erikson notes in his aforementioned case study how the trauma of a veteran can be linked to his family's economic decline.[133] The implications for Céline's depiction of his family background in *Mort à crédit* need no emphasis.

'It is logical,' Northrop Frye tells us of the romantic hero's series of adventures, 'for it to begin […] with some kind of break in consciousness.'[134] And so it is with Bardamu. Returning to camp he is confronted by the regimental butchers dismembering the carcass of a pig hanging from a tree. Sickened, he collapses:

> J'ai eu le temps encore de jeter deux ou trois regards sur ce différend alimentaire, tout en m'appuyant contre un arbre et j'ai dû céder à une immense envie de vomir, et pas qu'un peu, jusqu'à l'évanouissement. (RI, 21)
>
> [Leaning myself against a tree, I just had time to shoot a few glances toward that alimentary argument, before giving way to an immense desire to vomit, and not just a little, but right until I passed out.]

Bardamu's collapse provides an essential element of heroic myth: forgetting. In heroic myth, Frye tells us, the break in consciousness 'involves actual forgetfulness of the previous state'.[135] This, Frye calls, 'the motif of amnesia'. 'Such a catastrophe,' he continues, 'may be internalised as a break in memory.' The 'motif of amnesia' recurs in *Voyage*'s many lapses and the silences that divide its episodes. As Frye says, they do indeed represent 'forgetfulness of the previous state', but in *Voyage* the myth is once again inverted. What is forgotten is the heroism of Destouches; and the past heroic identity of France itself. This is part of what Céline means when in his letter to Garcin he accuses 'the faculty for forgetting' of his contemporaries (see 4.1 *The Crisis in Memory*). *Voyage* thus embodies this forgetfulness at the same time as it accuses it. And a striking literary metaphor has been created.

Each lapse into silence in *Voyage* is effectively a repetition of the 'motif of amnesia', and an effort to remember, to recall a previous, heroic, death-transcending identity which is at one and the same time Céline's past heroism and

France's own, heroic, death-mastering past. It is an effort equally to forget one's present domination by death, which *Voyage* presents as the condition of Republican France. Each effort to forget, however, results in failure and leads ironically to *persistent memory* of death itself, the cycle of trauma. *Voyage* is, in this way, both remembering and forgetting. As Bardamu says, 'je me suis réveillé dans une autre engueulade du brigadier. La guerre ne passait pas' [I woke up in the midst of a rollicking from the brigadier. The war was still going on] (RI, 21).

The war simply will not go away. In *Voyage*, therefore, the breach in consciousness is represented as forgetfulness of the previous, heroic, death-mastering state, and as prelude to the stasis and repetitions of traumatised memory. Indeed, the 'motif of amnesia' denotes a condition of traumatised memory whose re-enactments represent a form of 'working through' resistance to remembering. Freud described how memory is compelled to repeat, in a process of 'working through', until what is forgotten is recovered.[136] All of *Voyage* is subsumed in this dynamic of 'working through', or the effort to recall a forgotten, heroic, death-mastering previous state. This indeed is the dynamic by which Céline hopes to release himself from trauma through writing *Voyage*. This too is the dynamic which produces *Voyage*'s key pattern, the cycle of re-enactment.

The Cycle of Re-enactment

'Possession by the past', is the term used by Cathy Caruth to describe post-traumatic stress disorder where 'the overwhelming events of the past repeatedly possess, in intrusive images and thoughts, the one who has lived through them.'[137] Bardamu's traumatic past possesses him. Whether it be Africa, New York or Paris, the war is always present, returning throughout the novel like an 'idée fixe' [fixed idea]. Indeed, the strength of this effect is shown inadvertently by Milton Hindus, when he recalls the remark of a friend concerning *Voyage* that he had found the first fifty pages tremendously exciting but that as Céline had merely gone on repeating himself he had 'grown bored'.[138] Hindus himself refers to 'the narrowness of Céline's inspiration'.[139] And Nicholas Hewitt has also pointed to the 'sameness' of *Voyage*, its 'circularity' — Dauphin refers to 'une série de cercles' [a series of circles][140] — and 'inescapable repetition', insightfully remarking that the psychocritical concept of 'fantaisies à répétitions' [repetition of fantasies] applied by Albert Chesneau to Céline's pamphlets could be just as well applied to *Voyage*.[141] Céline's inspiration is indeed narrow, but for a very good reason, as the novel is shaped by the return of its own themes and motifs. In doing so it gives rise to a cycle of re-enactment whose origin and inspiration lies in both the repetitive experience of the Great War and in the cycle of traumatised memory.

Bardamu experiences the war in an endless and circular series of recapitulations. For example — examples are myriad — in the *Amiral Bragueton* episode, a hostile soldier confronts Bardamu. 'Cet homme,' he says, 'me faisait l'effet d'un morceau de la guerre qu'on aurait remis brusquement devant ma route, entêté, coincé, assassin' [that man had the effect on me of finding a fragment of the war suddenly set before me on my path, stubborn, determined, murderous] (RI, 119). Africa he describes as 'la guerre en douce' [the quiet war] (RI, 127), where nearly naked natives engage in absurd military drills with imaginary equipment and bayonets (RI, 150). In his New York hotel, the bellboy reminds Bardamu of a 'très jeune général de brigade' [very young brigadier general] (RI, 197), while the elevated metro hurtles past his window 'comme un obus' [like a shell], precipitating yet another crisis (RI, 199–200). In the Ford factory in Detroit, the noise of the machines absorbs and possesses him as did the explosion in wartime, so that he becomes 'un nouveau Ferdinand' [a new Ferdinand] (RI, 226). Working as a doctor in Paris, Bardamu watches helplessly as a young woman bleeds to death, 'je ne savais que faire' [I didn't know what to do], he says. 'Ça faisait "glouglou" entre ses jambes comme dans le cou coupé du colonel à la guerre' [The bleeding 'guggled' between her legs like it had from the neck of the colonel decapitated in the war] (RI, 260).

Bardamu, 'attaqué par le cauchemar' [attacked by the nightmare] (RI, 461), is condemned to relive his trauma of war. 'J'avais beau essayer de me perdre pour ne plus me retrouver devant ma vie, je la retrouvais partout simplement. Je revenais sur moi-même' [I had tried in vain to lose myself so as never to find myself faced with my life again, I simply found it everywhere. I kept coming back to myself] (RI, 500). Cyclical re-enactment of trauma returns him again and again to where he started. 'C'était à recommencer' [it was to begin over again], he says, realising he cannot escape the war (RI, 18). 'C'était à recommencer entièrement' [it was entirely to begin over again], he repeats, losing his composure when a child he is treating starts to cry (RI, 274). The child's mother rages at him. 'C'était la guerre !' [It was war!], Bardamu thinks. The return of the *Tir des Nations* [Shooting Gallery of Nations], with its noise of gunfire, to the *Fête Foraine* [Fun Fair], also sets the cycle in motion again. 'C'était tout à recommencer' [it was all to begin over again], Bardamu comments (RI, 311). 'Tout était à recommencer' [It was all to begin over again], he says of Madelon's arrival at the asylum in Vigny (RI, 470).

Voyage is orchestrated around this pattern of return of experience so that a 'noria', 'tourniquet', or wheel effect is produced. That is, *Voyage* is structured like the Great War, like Verdun, just as it equally represents the static and repeating pattern of trauma to memory. The effect of this pervasive recurrence of motifs is to enclose Bardamu within a décor of symbols, reminders of the war, from which he cannot escape. The dynamic is one of inescapable trauma in a world of perpetual war.

The Function of Rappel

The cycle of re-enactment of trauma in *Voyage* is imprinted not just on the story but also on the main element of popular speech Céline uses to create *Voyage*'s unique linguistic style: 'rappel' [recall]. 'Rappel', or pleonasm, is characterised by the return of the subject in phrases such as, 'il a dormi, le père' [he slept, the father].[142] The very first sentence of the novel, impossible to properly translate into English, 'ça a débuté comme ça' [here is how it began] (RI, 7), points to circular re-enactment not just at the level of narrative, but also at the level of language itself. 'Rappel' provides an instant flashback, or intrusion of language upon itself. Past language erupts in present language and language too produces a 'noria'. As Danièle Racelle-Latin has observed, 'rappel' represents 'le processus d'une reprise mémorielle [...] inlassable et fastidieuse redite d'une expérience déceptive qui ne peut s'instaurer en Histoire ou en Raison' [a process of reprise of memory [...] tireless and tedious repetition of a disappointing experience which cannot find its place in History or in Reason].[143] 'Rappel' provides the perfect linguistic expression of Bardamu's trauma, and of Céline's. Speech re-enacting itself tells a story that re-enacts itself. Through its language *Voyage* becomes a closed system of re-enactment, endlessly turning upon itself, a novel trapped within the inexorable return of traumatic memory and of history.

But 'rappel' does much more. First of all, it signals something which has been surprisingly lost to Céline scholarship. It, indeed, gives the game away. As if the narrative voice's retrospection were not enough, 'rappel' clarifies *Voyage*'s function as memory. This is clear from the very meaning of the word 'rappel' as to begin with, recall or evocation of past facts and, furthermore, as a 'reminder' of what has happened. Céline here, in what is a most exciting insight into the role of *Voyage* as memory, clearly embraces Socrates' view, expressed in the *Phaedrus* (275a), that the written word cannot be the memory of what is past, but only a 'reminder' of it. *Voyage*, as we already know, is not the memory of what has taken place, but it is a reminder. That is, indeed, what it is intended to be.

'Rappel' indicates that *Voyage* is both an effort to commit past events to memory through repeated evocation of those events and that it is also a reiteration of past events directed as a 'reminder' at others. But who are these others? Well, clearly, they are, to begin with, the readership of *Voyage*, primarily the French. Another usage of 'rappel', however, is to recall someone who has been sent into banishment or exile. This might be Céline himself who has ceased to be 'in suspension' as he wrote to Joseph Garcin. But it is equally true of all soldiers and veterans of the Great War (see 2.1 *Veterans*). 'Rappel' has the added and highly significant sense of a mobilisation or call-up. It is a *call to arms*. *Voyage* reminds soldiers of the wrong done to them during the war and since their return from battle and summons them to mobilise against their real enemy: the French Republic. The figure of Belisarius, evoked early on by Céline (RI, 16), certainly points in this direction. This Byzantine general was unjustly blinded by Emperor Justinian and was often depicted as a beggar, holding out his upturned helmet to gather alms. Céline makes him a symbol of the condition of the veteran in post-war France, and a reminder to the veterans of their wrongs. Céline's memory is thus a battle cry directed towards his fellow veterans, whose basis is the evocation of their common memory of war and whose emblem is the novel's most distinguishing linguistic feature 'rappel'.

In addition, a further use of 'rappel' is in the locution 'rappel à l'ordre' [call to order]. Together with the recurrent symbol of the river with its meaning of an orderly and *linear* crowd (see 1.3 *The Trenches*) this suggests that Céline is demanding that the crowd that is France return to an orderly sense of itself from the death-engendering chaos of its Republican identity.

The Cycle of Commemoration

'Rappel', of course, has a limiting effect on the action and language of *Voyage*, as the same images, the same scenes, the same words wind constantly back into view. It is easy to see the link between these re-enactments and '4 mai', the calendrical focus of *Voyage*. '4 mai', as we have seen, is evidence that *Voyage* behaves like commemoration. The use of 'rappel' reinforces this view. Paul Connerton tells us that commemorative rites employ a '*rhetoric of re-enactment* [...] calendrical, verbal and gestural'. These commemorative narratives employ fixed and limited sequences of speech acts constantly re-enacted (see 2.1 *Silence*). Through 'rappel' and its other re-enactments *Voyage* once again places itself in a dynamic of commemoration or *anti*-commemoration and in so doing announces itself as a 'master narrative' of Republican France in the inter-war years.

The Cycle of Revolution

Voyage's 'master narrative' of Republican France is one of anti-commemoration (see 2.1 *1793*). As such, *Voyage* sends back a blackened, inverse image of the official commemoration, opposing '4 mai' to '14 juillet' [14 July], identifying the Great War dead with the massacred Gardes suisses, supplanting Republican France's linear claims to historical legitimacy with the circular re-enactments of Verdun. The French Revolution, Paul Connerton tells us, transformed the meaning of the word revolution 'from a circularity of movement to the advent of the new'.[144] The Revolution, an event which Kant said could never be forgotten,[145] provided an historical beginning. Writes Connerton:

> Throughout the nineteenth century it was common to interpret every violent upheaval in terms of the continuation of the movement begun in 1789, so that the times of restoration appeared as pauses during which the revolutionary current had gone underground only to break through to the surface once more, and on the occasion of each upheaval, in 1830 and 1832, in 1848 and 1851, in 1871, adherents and opponents of the revolution alike understood the events as immediate consequences of 1789.[146]

Céline places 1914 as the culmination of this enumeration. He finds the image of his own circular re-enactments of trauma in the repetitions of Verdun. He sees Verdun in the image of the French Revolution, in the circularity of the original meaning of revolution. And he identifies his *inability to forget*, that is *his trauma*, with the event that cannot be forgotten, 'la guerre ne passait pas' (RI, 21). Céline's trauma, the trauma of the Great War, and the trauma of the French Revolution are identified as one and represented in a single image of trauma by the cycle of re-enactment. Here once again we see the dynamic of anti-commemoration, the dynamic of Céline's dissenting 'master narrative', at work as *Voyage* presents French history since the Revolution as a series of cyclical re-enactments of trauma and disruption of memory in which the true identity of France is forgotten (see also 1.1 *The Memory of War*).

It is not just France, however, which is condemned in this analysis. The modern world began with the French Revolution. Céline's 'circle' is the image of that world, the image of an entire world given over to the static, democratic and egalitarian, re-enactment of war in a post-heroic age. By virtue of the cycle of re-enactment, and of Bardamu's journeys, war in *Voyage* extends to embrace the entire world, so that the very concept of war, in *Voyage*, is planetary. *Voyage*'s war is truly a world war. The world has become as a consequence — in a further expansion of the 'circle' motif — a 'wheel' of torture or fire on which the victim is tied and broken. If the stasis of the cycle of re-enactment suggests a state of imprisonment, this last image of 'the wheel' not only contradicts the Revolutionary principle of 'liberté' [freedom], but expresses the unbearable, unending anguish of the tortured prisoner who turns upon the wheel. The wheel of the world. That the narrative voice of *Voyage* is the voice which emanates from the prisoner of 'the wheel' gives some idea of the depth of anguish of Céline's trauma. It is a voice sharpened and conditioned by awareness of the traumatic return of experience.

The Return of Experience

Céline was acutely conscious of the return of experience. He mentions it in his 'Hommage à Zola' [Homage to Zola] public speech – his only one ever – in 1932, at the same time giving a vivid clue to the inner dynamic of *Voyage*. 'Nous n'existons plus que par d'insipides redites' [we no longer exist except by insipid repetitions], he says:

> Peut-être [...] les 'civilisations' subissent-elles le même sort ? La nôtre semble bien coincée dans une incurable psychose guerrière. Nous ne vivons plus que pour ce genre de redites destructrices.[147]

> [Perhaps [...] civilisations endure the same fate? Our one seems caught up in an incurable war psychosis. We live only for this type of destructive repetition.]

Already, in March 1930, in a letter to Joseph Garcin, he says of the war, 'hélas nous verrons mieux encore dans le sinistre' [we will see better yet in the way of disaster].[148] In August of the same year, he writes:

> L'Europe est folle. [...] L'hystérie s'installe et va bientôt sans doute nous contraindre au pire. J'ai vu en Europe centrale ce qu'on ne veut pas voir, la catastrophe est imminente, plus précisément sadique que tout ce que nous avons connu — Les hommes dansent et sont aveugles et sourds.[149]

> [Europe is mad. [...] Hysteria is taking hold and will soon no doubt force us to the worst. I have seen in Central Europe what people do not wish to see, the catastrophe is imminent, more precisely sadistic than anything that we have known — Men dance and are blind and deaf.]

This knowledge is written into *Voyage*. As Philip Stephen Day writes of the final carnival scene (RI, 481), 'il ne fait pas de doute que le carnaval et le tir sont un microcosme du voyage de Bardamu et qu'ils contiennent la prédiction des guerres à venir' [there is no doubt but that the carnival and the firing range are a microcosm of Bardamu's journey and that they contain the prediction of wars to come].[150] Bardamu himself predicts, 'quand la guerre elle reviendra, la prochaine' [when the war comes again, the next one] (RI, 240).

The world between two wars was caught in its own cycle of re-enactment. The narrative and language of *Voyage* is, therefore, not just the narrative and language of Bardamu or of Céline's experience of cyclical, repetitive trauma, it is also the narrative and language of a world where war has its own cyclical return. *Voyage* is, in relation to the world it inhabits, a wheel within a wheel, a novelistic re-enactment of war in a world that re-enacts war.

This means that *Voyage* is as much a work of *foresight* as of *hindsight*. Its circular patterns are *prophetic*. Any analysis of it must be conditioned by this awareness of its Janus quality. This lends a whole other meaning to Bardamu's:

> Je me décidais à risquer le tout pour le tout, à tenter la dernière démarche, la suprême, essayer, moi, tout seul, d'arrêter la guerre ! Au moins, dans ce coin-là où j'étais. (RI, 15)

> [I decided to risk everything for everything, to make the ultimate effort, the supreme one, to try, me, all by myself, to stop the war! At least, in that corner of the world where I found myself.]

And to his later, 'quand il s'agit d'éviter le grand écartelage il se fait dans certains cerveaux de magnifiques efforts d'imagination' [when it's a question of avoiding the great dismemberment some brains embark on magnificent efforts of imagination] (RI, 64). *Voyage*, directed towards war to come, as towards past war, is the result of these magnificent efforts. This, indeed, is supported by what Céline originally wrote in the corresponding passage of the original *Voyage* manuscript:

> Ce serait le plus formidable et le plus intéressant document sur la guerre et les hommes celui où serait fidèlement décrit en vérité tout ce que les hommes de tous les côtés de l'enfer et de toutes couleurs ont tenté, inventé, ont osé […] pour échapper à l'étripade générale.[151]

> [The most formidable and interesting document on war and men would be the one where all that men of every species and from every region of hell have attempted, invented, dared […] in order to escape the general disembowelling would be faithfully and truthfully set down.]

Voyage is truly then a novel of 'between the wars', facing backwards and forwards, both post-war and *pre-war*, preoccupied as much by what is to come, as by what has been. It is written not just to 'exorcise' past war — as Céline tells Garcin — but as a charm against future war.

The knowledge that Céline was aware of a second impending catastrophe sets the writing of *Voyage* firmly between an unmastered past and a threatening future. In other words, Céline's ability to master death and emerge from trauma is undermined and taken away by the perceived inevitability of the Second World

War. This is a major key to *Voyage*'s inconsolable anguish, its Sisyphean futility and its failure to find redemption.

The Voice of the Wound

Some fifty years before PTSD was recognised,[152] Céline offered, in *Voyage*, a detailed portrait of the return of traumatic experience, using language to body forth the mind of a young soldier who had survived war. But *Voyage* offers more than a portrait of the PTSD sufferer. It is much more real than any mere description. In 'Beyond the Pleasure Principle', Freud illustrates the return of trauma through the legend of Tancred and Clorinda.[153] Tancred accidentally kills his lover Clorinda and later passing through a wood, frightened, he strikes at a tree. Clorinda's soul, imprisoned in the tree, cries out that Tancred has wounded her again. Cathy Caruth has reinterpreted this legend, emphasising not just the *return* of trauma, the striking of the wound, but also the *voice* of trauma as Clorinda cries out in pain.[154] This interpretation is applicable to *Voyage*, which represents not just the re-enactment of the wound, but also the crying out of the wound. *Voyage* is both the wound and its voice.[155] The cycle of re-enactment, which begins as soon as Céline sets pen to page, is one dimension of its hurt, another is the inconsolably grieving plaint that issues ceaselessly from it, until in the end it finds silence. That voice of pain and grief, of inescapable, circular re-enactment, ultimately belongs to Céline, his trauma, and his truth. It is to be argued that the intensity of wound and of voice derives ultimately from the anguish laid upon anguish which is the particularity of French memory since 1793 and which having come through the greatest war in history faces forwards, in 1932, towards yet greater disaster (see 1.1 *The Memory of War*).

Conclusion

Chapter Four has established that Céline was traumatised by his war experience. The origin of this trauma is in Céline's death encounter at Poelkapelle and its aftermath at Hazebrouck. This is where the old heroic self, Destouches, dies. *Voyage* is Céline's effort to forget trauma and recover, or *remember*, his lost condition of death-mastering heroism. *Voyage* seeks to 'work through' Céline's resistance to remembering, creating a dynamic of repetition, most visible in the novel's cycle of re-enactment. In the process *Voyage* becomes more than just the representation of Céline's struggle to transcend trauma, it becomes a metaphor for the state of the nation, a statement of France's loss of memory — its forgetfulness of its past heroic identity — and a metaphor for the condition of history itself, imprinted since 1793 with the circularity of the French Revolution. Pierre Drieu La Rochelle recognised this when he wrote in a letter to a friend:

> Je suis navré à l'idée que tu ne peux pas comprendre Céline [...] c'est tellement l'Europe d'après la guerre, l'Europe de la crise permanente, l'Europe de la Révolution, l'Europe qui crève, qui va faire n'importe quoi pour ne pas crever.[156]

> [I am saddened at the idea that you cannot understand Céline [...] it is so much the Europe of after the war, the Europe of the permanent crisis, the Europe of the Revolution, the Europe which is dying miserably, the Europe which will do anything so as not to die miserably.]

Voyage is made in the image of its time. Caught in a world traumatised by war and condemned to cyclical re-enactment of disaster it voices an unyielding, humiliated plaint. This is the voice of a wounded world. This is Céline's voice.

---

[1] Winter, 'Céline and the Cultivation of Hatred', p.234.

[2] Letter from Hazebrouck, 5 November 1914, of Fernand Destouches to his brother Charles, cited in Gibault, I, 147.

[3] Gibault, I, 148.

[4] Crocq, pp.236–237.

[5] Gibault, I, 148.

[6] For a description of the gravity of the ricochet wound see Bastier, p.340.

[7] Brittain, p.394.

[8] In the case history of a US Marine hospitalised during wartime, Erik H. Erikson notes, 'he was immobilised, unable to move, and, much worse, unable to help. Here for the first time he felt fear, as so many courageous men did at the moment when they found themselves on their backs, inactivated.' See Erikson, *Childhood and Society* (London: Vintage, 1995), p.34.

[9] See Zahava Solomon, *Combat Stress Reaction: The Enduring Toll of War* (New York: Plenum Press, 1993), p.33: 'Once out of danger, casualties could hardly escape the thought that they owed their lives more to fear than courage. This is a humiliating, guilt-provoking conclusion. [...] The end result of such unwelcome self-knowledge seems to be a radical loss of self-esteem and ensuing depression.'

[10] This work here finds some common ground with Philippe Alméras when he writes of Céline, 'à partir de ce moment, il prend son destin en main, il échappe à l'organisation militaire' [as of this moment, he takes his destiny in hand, and escapes the army]. See Alméras, p. 40.

[11] Gibault, I, 155.

[12] Gibault, I, 155.

[13] Gibault, I, 154.

[14] Gibault, I, 158.

[15] Gibault, I, 166.

[16] See Georges Geoffroy, 'Céline en Angleterre', *L'Herne*, 201–202 (p.201).

[17] Cited in Lainé, p.618.

[18] Gibault, I, 171. The period between demobilisation and departure for the Cameroon is veiled in mystery. However, it is known that on 19 January 1916 Céline married a Frenchwoman, Suzanne Nebout, in London. It appears that Suzanne Nebout was a prostitute and that she supported Céline for a time. She could, therefore, be a model for Molly in *Voyage*. The marriage in any case did not last. See Gibault, I, 169–170.

[19] Letter to Simone Saintu, 31 July 1916, *Cahiers Céline*, 4: *Lettres et premiers écrits d'Afrique 1916–1917*, ed. by Jean-Pierre Dauphin (Paris: Gallimard, 1978), 60–67 (p.61).

[20] See Henri Godard, 'Notice', in *Romans*, I, 1131–1288 (p.1185). This goes some way to contradict Nicholas Hewitt's view that 'Céline in 1916 was certainly not the Bardamu of *Voyage au bout de la nuit*.' See Hewitt, *The Life of Céline*, p.29.

[21] Letter to Saintu, p.60.

[22] Letter to Saintu, 29 October 1916, *Cahiers Céline*, 4, 140–142 (p.140).

[23] Letter to Saintu, 22 August 1916, *Cahiers Céline*, 4, 76–79 (p.78).

[24] Letter to Saintu, 11 December 1916, *Cahiers Céline*, 4, 156–157 (p.156).

[25] Letter to Saintu, p.78.

[26] Letter to Simone Saintu, dated 27 September 1916, in *Cahiers Céline*, 4, 104–105 (p.104).

[27] Marie-Christine Bellosta is a prominent exponent of this view. She argues that Céline's description of Bardamu's 'neurosis' is plundered from Freud and his disciples (Bellosta, pp.122–133). This argument of necessity leads to the conclusion that Bardamu's mental trauma is nothing other than an instrument Céline has chosen for literary purposes. However, this affirmation is undermined by Nicholas Hewitt who, in *The Life of Céline*, declares Freud's influence on *Voyage* to be minimal, 'there seems to be little direct Freudian influence on the novel' (p.122). Bellosta supports her thesis by maintaining that Céline was aware of and is simply repeating Freud's views in his letters to Simone Saintu (see Bellosta, p.115, note 1 and p.121, note 13).

[28] Letter to Saintu, pp.104–105.

[29] Letter to Saintu, p.63.

[30] Letter to Saintu, p.61.

[31] Letter to Saintu, pp.63–64.

[32] Letter to Saintu, 4 July 1916, *Cahiers Céline*, 4, 44–45 (p.45).

[33] Letter to Céline's parents, 1 January 1917, *Cahiers Céline*, 4, 166–168 (p.167).

[34] Letter to Céline's father, 30 August 1916, *Cahiers Céline*, 4, 83–88 (p.88).

[35] Letter to father, pp.86–87.

[36] Letter to father, p.86.

[37] Letter to father, p.86.

[38] Letter to father, p.88.

[39] Céline's medical condition was the subject of a report reproduced in *Cahiers Céline*, 4, p.184. See also Gibault, I, 189–190.

[40] See Gibault, I, 212–213.

[41] The marriage took place on 19 August 1919. See Gibault, I, 223.

[42] Gibault, I, 235. Henri Barbusse's *Le Feu* (Paris: Flammarion, 1916) was one of the first literary accounts of the war and was notable for its graphic, often grotesque, quality.

[43] See Lainé, p.53.

[44] Cited in Gibault, I, 237.

[45] Lainé, pp.52–53.

[46] See Jean Monnier, *Elizabeth Craig raconte Céline: entretien avec la dédicataire de Voyage au bout de la nuit* (Paris: Bibliothèque de Littérature française contemporaine, 1988), p.78. Craig says Céline hated himself for his cowardice.

[47] Céline wrote short stories and a number of poems when in Africa. One story, *Des Vagues*, which recalls the United States' entry into the war, and two poems are published in *Cahiers Céline*, 4. Céline's letters to Simone Saintu and his parents also contain several references to his efforts to write and be published.

[48] Northrop Frye, *The Anatomy of Criticism* (London: Penguin, 1990), p.63. Allen Thiher, *Céline: The Novel as Delirium* (New Brunswick: Rutgers University Press, 1972), p.85, dates this tendency as of Céline's prologue to *Guignol's band*. It is clear, however, that the author's

identification with his work is an incipient feature of Céline's literary project as early as *Semmelweiss*.

[49] See also Denise Aebersold, *Céline, un démystificateur mythomane* (Paris: Lettres Modernes, 1979), p.10.

[50] 'La Vie et l'œuvre de Philippe Ignace Semmelweiss', *Cahiers Céline*, 3: *Semmelweiss et autres écrits médicaux*, ed. by Jean-Pierre Dauphin and Henri Godard (Paris: Gallimard, 1977), 13–79 (p.41).

[51] 'Semmelweiss', p.45.

[52] 'Semmelweiss', p.40.

[53] 'Semmelweiss', p.28.

[54] 'Semmelweiss', p.20.

[55] On this theme of the monster and the monstrous in *Voyage* see Leslie Davis, 'L'anti-monde de L.-F.Céline'.

[56] 'Semmelweiss', p.21.

[57] Gibault, I, 270.

[58] Letter of 24 February 1925 cited in Gibault, I, 256.

[59] Brittain, p.538.

[60] Brittain, pp.556–557.

[61] Louis-Ferdinand Céline, *L'Église* (Paris: Gallimard, 1952).

[62] Gibault, I, 277.

[63] Céline met Craig outside a bookshop in Geneva. See Alphonse Juilland, *Elizabeth and Louis: Elizabeth Craig talks about Louis-Ferdinand Céline* (Stanford: Montparnasse Publications, 1991), pp.385–386.

[64] Juilland, p.460.

[65] Juilland, p.465. According to Elizabeth Craig, she and Céline always spoke English together.

[66] Juilland, p.460.

[67] Gibault, I, 282.

[68] Juilland, p.505.

[69] Vera Brittain, in England, shared Céline's empathy with the poor whom she describes as living in 'grim chaos'. She sees a kinship between them and 'the Tommies whom I had nursed for four calamitous years'. See Brittain, p.576.

[70] Letter to Joseph Garcin, 1 September 1929, in Lainé, p.615.

[71] Letter to Garcin, 21 March 1930, in Lainé, p.617.

[72] Letter to Garcin, 18 June 1930, in Lainé, p.619.

[73] Undated letter to Garcin, September 1930, in Lainé, p.621.

[74] Juilland, p.472.

[75] Juilland, p.503.

[76] Juilland, p.460.

[77] Juilland, p.460.

[78] Juilland, p.461.

[79] Jorge Semprun, *L'écriture ou la vie* (Paris: Gallimard, 1994), p.215.

[80] Semprun, p.212.

[81] Juilland, p.472.

[82] Juilland, p.472.

[83] Juilland, p.373.

[84] Monnier, p.61.

[85] Monnier, p.72.

[86] Monnier, p.81.

[87] Juilland, p.442.

[88] Juilland, p.454.

[89] Abraham Kardiner is credited with being the 'first psychoanalyst to depart from the assumption of a predisposition on etiology'. Kardiner believed that the neurosis originated in the 'event itself'. See Erwin Randolph Parson, 'Post-Traumatic Self Disorders', in *Human Adaptation to Extreme Stress*, ed. by John Preston Wilson, Zev Harel and Boaz Kahana (New York: Plenum Press, 1988), pp.245–283 (p.246).

[90] Solomon, pp.37–38.

[91] Solomon, pp.31–38.

[92] Solomon, pp.34–36.

[93] Solomon, p.93.

[94] Richard, p.8.

[95] Richard, p.9.

[96] See *Shell Shock*, television series prod. and dir. by Julia Harrington, Blakeway Productions, Channel 4, 1998. This series was accompanied by a Wendy Holden book, *Shell Shock*, from Channel 4 books.

[97] Report cited in Solomon, p.97.

[98] *Diagnostic and Statistical Manual of Mental Disorders: Version III* (Washington: American Psychiatric Association, 1984).

[99] Roland M.Atkinson, Michael E.Reeves, Michael J.Maxwell, 'Complicated Postcombat Disorders in Vietnam Veterans', in *Human Adaptation to Extreme Stress*, pp.357–375 (pp.358–359).

[100] Atkinson and others, p.357.

[101] See Juilland, p.174.

[102] See Brochard, p.206.

[103] Gibault, I, 100.

[104] See Lainé, p.509.

[105] Brochard, p.204.

[106] For an account of Céline's spurious trepanation see Gibault, I, 158–164. For Céline's general health see his self-penned report while in Denmark, in Gibault, I, 161–162.

[107] See D. J. Power, *Military Psychology including Terrorism* (Chichester: Barry Rose Law Publishers, 1991), p.126.

[108] Erikson, p.34.

[109] Erikson, p.38.

[110] 'Interview avec Madeleine Chapsal', *Cahiers Céline*, 2, 18–36 (p.24).

[111] See Erikson, p.35.

[112] Milton Hindus in *The Crippled Giant*, p.66, refers to Céline's inaccuracy with facts and dates, saying 'he was forever making slight mistakes about things and people and events. These mistakes were not about matters of opinion but about matters of fact.' Elsewhere, Hindus writes, 'Céline suffers from what may be called *overconviction* about perfectly inaccurate facts.' See Hindus, p.26.

[113] See Jean-Pierre Dauphin on *Voyage*'s varied and confusing references to truth, '*Voyage au bout de la nuit*: étude d'une illusion romanesque' (unpublished doctoral thesis, Paris IV, 1976), p.378.

[114] Solomon, p.74.

[115] Soldier interviewed in the military training video, *The Mind at War: Post-traumatic stress disorder*, dir. and prod. by Anne Carroll, Services Sound and Vision Corporation Production, for the British Ministry of Defence, 1993.

[116] Solomon, p.75.

[117] Solomon, p.75.

[118] See Henri Godard, 'Notice', in *Romans*, I, 1390.

[119] Solomon, p.94.

[120] Solomon, p.94.

[121] Solomon, p.95.

[122] See Robert J.Lifton, 'Understanding the Traumatized Self', in *Human Adaptation to Extreme Stress*, pp.7–31 (p.26).

[123] Lifton, 'Understanding the Traumatized Self', p.18.

[124] Adds Lifton, 'the survivor retains an indelible image, a tendency to cling to the death imprint — not because of release of narcissistic libido, as Freud claimed, but because of continuing struggles to master and assimilate the threat [...] and around larger questions of personal meaning.' Lifton, 'Understanding the Traumatized Self', p.19.

[125] Lifton, 'Understanding the Traumatized Self', p.18.

[126] Lifton, 'Understanding the Traumatized Self', p.26.

[127] Lifton, 'Understanding the Traumatized Self', p.27.

[128] Dauphin, 'Étude d'une illusion romanesque', p.160.

[129] See Dauphin, 'Étude d'une illusion romanesque', p.155. With regard to the basic dual structure of *Voyage*, Frédéric Vitoux has described the novel as having a double structure, being to begin with a novel of initiation before becoming a character-based novel. See Frédéric Vitoux, *Misère et parole* (Paris: Gallimard, 1973), p.166. A.-C. and J.-P. Damour have noted a further structure 'en forme d'arche' [in the form of a boat] in *Voyage*. See *L.-F. Céline: Voyage au bout de la nuit*, Études littéraires (Paris: PUF, 1994), pp.14–16. The idea of *Voyage* as a boat 'en route pour l'Infini' [en route for the Infinite] (RI, 473) is a very attractive one and this last structure, as we shall see in Chapter Eight, does indeed have some very real substance.

[130] Dauphin has mapped the dual structure of *Voyage* in diagrammatic form. See Dauphin, 'Étude d'une illusion romanesque', pp.156–159.

[131] See Fussell, *The Great War and Modern Memory*, pp.125–131.

[132] Fussell, p.128.

[133] Erikson, p.37.

[134] Northrop Frye, *The Secular Scripture: A Study of the Structure of Romance* (Cambridge: Harvard University Press, 1976), p.102.

[135] Frye, *The Secular Scripture*, p.102.

[136] See Sigmund Freud, 'Remembering, Repeating and Working Through', in *The Standard Edition of the Complete Psychological Works*, ed. and trans. by James Strachey, in collaboration with Anna Freud, assisted by Alix Strachey and Alan Tyson, 24 vols (London: Hogarth Press and the Institute of Psycho-analysis, 1955, 1958, repr. 1964), XII, 145–156.

[137] Cathy Caruth, 'Introduction to Part II: Recapturing the Past', in *Trauma: Explorations in Memory*, ed. and intro. by Cathy Caruth (Baltimore: John Hopkins, 1995), pp.151–157 (p.151).

[138] Hindus, p.63.

[139] Hindus, p.63.

[140] Dauphin, p.193.

[141] Hewitt, *The Golden Age of Louis-Ferdinand Céline*, p.81.

[142] See Léo Spitzer, 'Une habitude de style, le rappel chez Céline', *L'Herne*, 443–451.

[143] Danièle Racelle-Latin, '*Voyage au bout de la nuit* ou l'inauguration d'une poétique "argotique"', *Revue des Lettres Modernes*, 4 (1976), 53–78 (p.65).

[144] Connerton, p.6.

[145] See Connerton, p.7.

[146] Connerton, p.18.

[147] Céline, 'Hommage à Zola', *L'Herne*, 22–24 (p.23).

[148] See letter of 21 March 1930, in Lainé, p.617.

[149] Letter of 4 August 1930, in Lainé, p.620.

[150] Philip Stephen Day, p.98.

[151] *Voyage* manuscript, fol. 90.

[152] Lt Col Ian Palmer, speaking on Channel 4 television's *Shell Shock* had this to say: 'It seems very difficult to understand why we didn't understand that there was a hangover effect after wars, that wars had a psychological consequence for some individuals. But the feeling abroad, until 1980, was that if you could deal and adjust to the battlefield, you could adjust very easily to peacetime.'

[153] Sigmund Freud, 'Beyond the Pleasure Principle', in *The Standard Edition of the Complete Psychological Works* (1955, repr.1964), XVIII, 7–64 (p. 22).

[154] Cathy Caruth, *Experience: Trauma, Narrative, and History* (Baltimore: The John Hopkins University Press, 1996), pp.2–3.

[155] In this context it is interesting to read the passage in *Voyage* where Bardamu assumes the character of Tancred as he walks with Lola in the Bois de Boulogne. 'Un mort derrière chaque arbre' [a dead man behind each tree], he says, frightened of the trees (RI, 57).

[156] Cited in Paolo Carile, *Louis-Ferdinand Céline: Un allucinato di genio* (Bologna: Pàtron, 1969), p.34.

CHAPTER 5

TRUTH AND UNTRUTH

From Silence to Witness

Introduction

Rewriting his past Céline rewrites himself back into the trauma of that past. Nonetheless, *Voyage* remains a novel shaped on every level by the effort to achieve death-mastering healing. Chapter Four has shown how trauma shaped *Voyage*. This chapter will show how it has shaped *Voyage*'s witness to war. *Voyage* is a novel characterised by a will to witness. This witness is the outcome of a triple movement: from traumatic memory to traumatic narrative; from silence to speech; and from *Eye-witness* to *I-witness*. Each section of this chapter will explore one aspect of this movement, which brings Céline's witness to war from truth to untruth and back again.

5.1 FROM TRAUMATIC MEMORY TO TRAUMATIC NARRATIVE

The Site of Remembering and Forgetting

According to Paul Ricœur, modern memory is sick with 'le trop de mémoire ici, le trop d'oubli ailleurs' [too much remembering in one place, too much forgetting in another].[1] *Voyage* embodies this sickness in one site of remembering and forgetting. *Voyage*, as we have seen, is a work characterised both by an inability to forget and an inability to remember. What cannot be forgotten is the cyclical trauma of war; what cannot be remembered is the heroic past. Much of Céline's war is missing from *Voyage*. Missing, for example, are the major battles. Missing too is the heroism of Destouches. Bardamu, a coward, is his opposite. Yet *Voyage* is closely modelled on Céline's own life. Why does *Voyage* remember the way that it does? And why does it forget the way that it does? The answer lies not just in Céline's desire to provide a metaphor for his own or for France's loss of heroic identity, but in how memory deals with trauma. That is, through the elaboration of a new narrative.

Traumatic Memory

Céline's letters to Garcin are unequivocal. *Voyage* is intended to 'exorcise' the trauma of the war (see 4.1 *The Crisis in Memory*). He will do this by exploiting memory's capacity to re-narrate past events. Memory is not fixed. Rather, it is a malleable narrative whose relationship to the past is problematical. As Harold Pinter observed, 'the past is what you remember, imagine you remember, convince yourself you remember, or pretend you remember.'[2] Memory uses narrative to establish continuities of past and identity. As researchers Antze and Lambek affirm, 'in forging links of continuity between past and present [...] memory operates most frequently by means of the threads of narrative.'[3] Trauma, however, undermines memory's ability to create coherent narrative. This is because trauma itself constitutes a breach in continuity. *Voyage*'s lapses and silences, which undermine its narrative continuity, are evidence of trauma's disruption.

French psychologist, Pierre Janet, recognised the role of narrative in healing trauma. Janet thought of his patients as 'accrochés' [hooked] to an *idée fixe* [fixed idea]. This *idée fixe* was not a single idea but 'constituée de tout un ensemble de souvenirs [...], d'images, de sensations [...] s'annexant par association une foule d'autre images' [made up of an ensemble of memories [...], of images and sensations [...] drawing to it by association a host of other images].[4] The trauma sufferer, unable to move on from this *idée fixe*, finds himself 'contre un mur' [against a wall],[5] the very situation of Bardamu 'au bas de la muraille' [at the bottom of the wall] (RI, 200). At the origin of this 'accrochage', Janet says, is a failure of language or narration, what he calls 'langage intérieur' [interior language]. Trauma can, therefore, only be remedied through a response which encompasses:

> les paroles que nous nous adressons à nous-mêmes, par l'organisation du récit de l'événement (à l'intention de nous-même comme à l'intention des autres) et par la mise en place de ce récit comme un chapitre de notre propre histoire.[6]

[the words we address to ourselves, through the organisation of the story of the event (for ourselves as much as for others) and by the placing of the story as a chapter in our own history.]

A description which recalls Bardamu 'me faisant une espèce de scène brutale à moi-même' [making an ugly scene intended for myself] (RI, 274). Of equal interest here, however, is Janet's use of the image of the 'sentinel', sent forward to reconnoitre enemy positions and report back on them, to illustrate his thesis. The sentinel masters the danger of his situation outwardly by concealing his movements and inwardly by preparing an account of his mission. Faced with an external danger he cannot combat physically, the sentinel thus masters the situation mentally through the words he uses to 'objectivise' it, that is, through language and narration. It is difficult to imagine a more apt image for the 'agent de liaison' Destouches/Céline confronting his trauma of memory than this image Janet provides of the sentinel mastering his trauma through the elaboration of narrative.

Traumatic memory, therefore, strives towards healing through narrative transformation and, most significantly, through transformation of language. In the words of researchers, Van der Kolk and Van der Hart, 'traumatic memories [...] need to be [...] transformed into narrative language.'[7] For this to succeed, they say, echoing Freud's notion of 'working through' memory, 'the traumatised person has to return to the memory often in order to complete it.' This 'return' provides the essential dynamic of *Voyage*'s cycle of re-enactment. Return leads to the creation of what Laurence J. Kirmayer calls 'a specific narrative landscape', a reconstruction of what happened. According to Kirmayer:

Reconstructions of traumatic memory involve the building up of a landscape of local coherence to better manage or contain it, to present it convincingly to others and, finally, to have done with it.[8]

This is what Céline does. His re-writing of war and self is an attempt to heal trauma by creating a narrative which will enable him to integrate and control his traumatic past. Writing *Voyage*, he returns to the past. This return is undertaken in hope. For Paul Ricœur it is the hope of realising the lost potential of one's past. The work of healing memory, Ricœur says, is to 'défataliser le passé' [undo the inevitability of the past], 'oublier la suite pour nous replacer dans un passé ouvert' [forget what followed in order to reposition ourselves in a past which remains open] and 'sauver les promesses non-tenues du passé' [redeem the unkept promises of the past].[9] Jorge Semprun revisiting Buchenwald after many years expressed this effort to restore 'promise' in the following way:

> Je revenais chez moi, je veux dire dans l'univers de mes vingt ans : ses colères, ses passions, sa curiosité, ses rires. Son espoir, surtout. J'abandonnais toutes les désespérances mortelles qui s'accumulent dans l'âme, au long d'une vie, pour retrouver l'espérance de mes vingt ans qu'avait cernée la mort.[10]
>
> [I was returning home, I mean to say to the universe of myself at twenty years of age, with its rages, its passion, its curiosity, its laughter. Its hope, above all. I was letting go of all the deadly despair which accumulates in the soul during a lifetime, to rediscover the hope I had at twenty and which had been ringed round by death.]

It is Céline's return to 'l'univers de ses vingt ans' [his universe of twenty] — 'je n'avais que vingt ans d'âge à ce moment-là' [I was no more than twenty at that time], Bardamu will say (RI, 12) — which gives *Voyage* its autobiographical dimension, its quality of remembering a lived past. The new narrative he creates of that past is what lends *Voyage* its quality of forgetting. This is how it must be. Forgetting is necessary to narrative construction. As Ricœur says, in one of his English-language texts:

> The best use of forgetting is precisely in the construction of plots, in the elaboration of narratives concerning personal identity or collective identity; that is, we cannot tell a story without eliminating or dropping some important event according to the kind of plot we intend to build. Narratives, therefore, are [...] the occasion for manipulation [...] but also the place where a certain healing of memory may begin.[11]

Thus, the healing of memory necessitates forgetting, and forgetting leads to an affirmation of imagination central to the healing process. This affirmation represents the movement away from the literalness of the past demanded by Robert Jay Lifton. It reaffirms the creative power of trauma in the search for meaning (see 4.2 *The Search for Meaning*). The prize at the end of the day is healing.

Forgetfulness and manipulation... The two go together in *Voyage*. This explains the impression of many Céline scholars that they were dealing with a writer in control of his 'personal myth', his 'paranoia', or his 'madness' (see

Introduction, *The Contours of Trauma*). What they had stumbled on was memory healing its wounds through its capacity to create narrative. Or Céline immersed in the substance of his own trauma and making a novel out of it.

From one Narrative to Another

In Céline's account of his war past, what happened, fixed forever in time, is overwritten by a narrative of what might have been. Entering the possibilities of narrative Céline seeks to recall the *irrevocable* and reverse the *irreversible*. Through memory he re-enters time (another facet of *Voyage*'s river symbol with its promise of linear continuity or memory healed) to reorganise or, indeed, to overthrow it. He seeks, like Martin Amis in his anti-Holocaust *Time's Arrow*,[12] to reverse time and so revive its ousted 'infinite possibilities'.[13] He exploits narrative to 'défataliser le passé' [undo the inevitability of the past] as Ricœur says, and to restore 'les promesses non tenues' [unkept promises] of that past. His movement from traumatic memory to traumatic narrative is, therefore, a movement away from stasis towards redeeming possibility.

This movement towards possibility explains why Céline, at first, enjoyed writing *Voyage* so much. His traumatic past was now the subject of liberating playfulness. The balance of trauma shifted from the past into his hands. Through 'manipulation' of narrative — of remembering, of forgetting — he was taking control of what had been and settling accounts with the 'unspeakable'. However, the pain of returning to the site of trauma, as well as the knowledge that war was preparing to re-enact itself soon acts to shut down narrative and returns liberating possibility to cruel stasis.

Céline, however, has created new narrative because he must. And there is no turning back. 'Mentir et survivre, et pas autre chose, foutre non !' [Lie and survive, and nothing else, hell no!], he writes to Garcin,[14] acknowledging that there is only one way out of trauma. The movement from one narrative to another obeys this imperative. 'Il faut choisir, mourir ou mentir' [you have to choose, to die or to lie] is its expression in *Voyage* (RI, 200). Life itself demands forgetting, imagination and manipulation of narrative. And so what happened is replaced by what might have been. Fact by fiction. Destouches by Bardamu. Truth by untruth.

The past becomes a story, 'un roman [...] une histoire fictive' [a novel [...] a fictional story] (RI, epigraph), or 'une espèce de scène brutale à moi-même' [an ugly scene intended for myself].

Céline's traumatic narrative has a logic: reversal. Indeed, reversal constitutes a strategy which came to Céline in a flash of inspiration. The original *Voyage* manuscript reveals what happened. Writing the first chapter Céline situated Bardamu and Arthur in a Place Clichy café. They exchange pleasantries, 'ces vérités utiles' [those useful truths] (RI, 7). However, their roles are the reverse of what they will become in the finished *Voyage*. It is, indeed, naïve Arthur who represents the first-person voice and who, at the end of the chapter, marches off to join the passing regiment on its way to war. Bardamu is simply his knowing companion. But then Céline has his inspiration. Returning to the manuscript he makes Bardamu the 'I' who speaks, and it is Arthur who now watches aghast as Bardamu leaves to join the war. Bardamu now embodies the contrary of his original position. This sudden movement, Henri Godard tells us, creates the 'dualité constitutive' [constituent duality] which will power *Voyage*.[15] It is, therefore, the essence of all *Voyage*'s duality, determining what Leslie Davis calls Bardamu's 'anti-monde' [anti-world], 'où toutes les certitudes sont mises en question' [where all certainties are placed in doubt].[16]

Where does Céline's inspiration for this reversal come from? Not surprisingly, it comes directly from experience. It comes from the traumatic encounter with death on 27 October 1914, when Destouches is catapulted from the heroic self, braving death at Poelkapelle, into humiliating self-knowledge at Hazebrouck, where stripped of his heroism he is the opposite of what he was before. It comes from the irony of his own situation. The irony, that Paul Fussell tells us, is the hallmark of modern memory.

Céline realises that the dynamism between past and present has become one of irony, of duality, of opposition, of contradiction. Stating the contrary, as he does when he reverses roles in the novel's introductory chapter, enables him to embody this dynamism. It is too his acknowledgement of a breach in the world, of a transition from one form of consciousness to another, and a statement of narrative discontinuity with his own past.

Stating the contrary, Céline moves from traumatic memory to traumatic narrative; from silence to witness; from Destouches to Bardamu. And he moves from commemoration to anti-commemoration. It is here then within the dynamic of stating the contrary that *Voyage* shifts from being a record of individual trauma to being a statement of dissent. But before being anything at all, there is a major obstacle which must be overcome. This obstacle is Céline's moral commitment to silence.

5.2 FROM SILENCE TO WITNESS

The Temptation of Silence

Voyage emerges from Céline's silence about the war. Silence informs both the structure and content of *Voyage*, occupying its beginning, 'moi, j'avais jamais rien dit' [I had never said anything] (RI, 7), and ending, 'qu'on n'en parle plus' [let's talk no more about it] (RI, 505), the broad gaps between episodes, the space behind and beyond words and the interstices of words. *Voyage* makes explicit its relationship to silence from the very outset, and thus orients the reader towards its silent spaces. Without recognition of these silent spaces the reader will lose much of what makes *Voyage* the solemn expression of memory that it is.

For George Steiner, what he calls 'the most honest temptation to silence in contemporary feeling' dates from 'c. 1914'.[17] There, he says, began a process of 'linguistic devaluation' linked to the dehumanising process of the war itself. After the war, it was impossible to use language as it had been used before. For Steiner, the writer whose confidence in language has been eroded has two choices. One is to make language reflect the 'general crisis', 'to convey through it the precariousness and vulnerability of the communicative act'. The other is to 'choose the suicidal rhetoric of silence'. *Voyage* is torn between these two choices, creating a duality exemplified in the struggle between speech and silence. Céline never fully renounces silence and throughout *Voyage* aspires to return there. This inevitably establishes a constant to and fro between speech and silence — between the text of *Voyage* and what lies beyond it. Céline clings to his moral silence and *Voyage* is a novel that ideally would like to say nothing at all.[18] Céline's Flaubertian preoccupation with style undoubtedly has its beginnings here, in his moral silence about the Great War.

The Silence of Memory

Céline's silence has its roots in his experience of war. As war is announced at Rambouillet he writes home to his parents, 'la surexcitation des premiers moments a fait place à un silence de mort' [the overexcitement of the first moments has given way to a deathly silence].[19] This premonitory 'silence de mort' would soon be all too real. Soldiers would experience it as they discovered the horrors of the battlefield. Many would founder in hysterical mutism, their loss of voice symbolising perfectly the unspeakable nature of the war. The silence of the soldier-witness echoed the silence of the dead. The dead were everywhere, a silent counterpoint to the mechanised violence that had silenced them. Over all this, the silence of censorship ensured not only that the war remained in the realm of the unspeakable but, in addition, made speaking the truth a fundamental act of military disobedience.

All of these silences coalesced for Céline at Hazebrouck in the days of delirium and forgetfulness which swept his heroic identity away. And it is this silence which constitutes the 'dark star' around which *Voyage* orbits (see 4.1 *Shock*).

Céline's silent memory, like that of other veterans, is multifaceted and complex. If silence was, to begin with, an effort to find an 'oubli' [forgetting], it remains the emblem of Céline's forgetting in *Voyage*, the sign of his lost heroic identity, a statement too of his intent to turn his attention from the past to the future (see 4.3 *The Return of Experience*). It is too, however, the product of a raft of moral imperatives derived from the experience of the war itself. It was, as we have seen, an act of soldierly submission, acceptance of the censor's command not to speak the truth. It is, indeed, in this sense, a space of 'non-dit' [what remains unsaid], complicit with the war itself. It was too an emblem of his horror at the war, acknowledgement that the war was unspeakable. At its deepest level, however, Céline's silence expressed 'union' with the war dead. It was the outward sign of his 'inner deadness' and is the most tangible evidence of his 'death imprint' (see 4.2 *The Death Imprint*). Having gone furthest in 'knowing' the war, the dead, through silence, represented war's 'true witness'. By being silent, Céline could obviate his survivor guilt and be one with them. Their death was his, his death theirs, their silence mutual.

The Breach of Silence

The war was, for Céline, 'cette expérience de 1914 *dont je ne parle jamais* sauf aux initiés, très rares...' [that experience in 1914 *of which I never speak* except to those initiates, very rare...].[20] This silence was part of *L'Église*. Bardamu's name signals it. A composite of *Bard*, a Celtic poet singing of the deeds of heroes, *barda*, a soldier's kit, and the old French adjective *mu* signifying silence,[21] the name tells us that here is someone who has been to war and who remains silent. By refusing to speak the unspeakable in *L'Église*, which has no war episode, Céline remains true to his silence and faithful to the dead. The problem is that this silence proves unliveable and leads directly to the crisis of memory of late 1928 onwards. As traditional memory broke down, war simply could not be left to silence and a new formulation of memory — one which broke with silence — needed to be found. Céline is forced into speech. He decides to write it all, 'raconter tout' [tell everything] (RI, 25), and when he has said all, to return to silence. This is a fundamental premise of *Voyage* confirmed in Céline's letters to Garcin (see 4.1 *The Crisis in Memory*). As Bardamu says:

> Il n'y a de terrible en nous et sur la terre et dans le ciel peut-être que ce qui n'a pas encore été dit. On ne sera tranquille que lorsque tout aura été dit, une bonne fois pour toutes, alors enfin on fera silence et on aura plus peur de se taire. Ça y sera. (RI, 327)

> [There's nothing terrible inside us or on earth or in heaven perhaps except what hasn't been said yet. We'll not be at peace until everything has been said, once and for all, and then we'll be silent and we won't be afraid any longer to say nothing. That'll be that.]

The tension that exists between Céline's moral commitment to silence and his need to speak provokes the violence of *Voyage*'s beginnings. *Voyage* is an outburst. Not only is speech abandoned, it is ruptured by a flood of recrimination. Its broken silence, however, remains like an accusation. Céline has resisted

Steiner's temptation to silence. He has broken the rule of censorship. He has abandoned a stance which acknowledged the unspeakable nature of the war. Most of all, he has broken his survivor's pact with the dead. Speaking, he acknowledges that he has survived. And speech, as Camus wrote, is betrayal.[22] *Voyage* is transgression. It is betrayal.

Silence and Witness to War

Céline assuages betrayal by creating as great a space as possible for silence in *Voyage*. *Voyage* opens and closes on silence, and proceeds through a series of ellipses, most notably at the end of each episode. Céline breaks silence by brusquely recognising his own transgression, 'j'avais jamais rien dit' [I had never said anything] (RI, 7), before going on to establish a commitment to speak and bear witness, 'la grande défaite, en tout, c'est d'oublier [...]. Faudra raconter tout sans changer un mot' [the great defeat, in everything, is to forget [...]. Everything must be told, without changing a word] (RI, 25). Here is the conflicting core of *Voyage*, containing both commitment to silence and to witness. However, it is in his commitment to witness that Céline finds the strength to break his silence. He then assuages guilt by making silence the emblem of his witness. At the end of the war episode, for example, Bardamu abruptly returns to silence, saying, 'et puis il s'est passé des choses et encore des choses, qu'il est pas facile de raconter à présent, à cause que ceux d'aujourd'hui ne les comprendraient déjà plus' [and then things happened and then more things, which are not easy to tell about, because already people nowadays wouldn't understand them] (RI, 47). Here, made explicit, is the silence of a war incomprehensible both to the soldier who fought it — 'la guerre en somme c'était tout ce qu'on ne comprenait pas' [the war in brief was everything one couldn't understand] (RI, 12) — and to the public at a remove from it. Here too is the silence that divides them, the silence that divided front from rear and which divides writer from reader. This silence is immense. It subsumes almost the entirety of the Great War — never explicitly mentioned in *Voyage* — and most of the personal detail of Céline's war, thus providing the substance of his forgetting. However, it also enables him to retrieve a 'truthful' stance in relation to the war. Once again he refuses to speak and atones for the guilt of having spoken. His return to silence recognises the futility of speech and acknowledges the incomprehensible, incommunicable and unspeakable nature of the war. It obeys the law of censorship. Most importantly, it allows Céline to restore faith with the dead. The silence speaks for itself and finally, as in the Armistice commemoration, it allows the dead a voice. The all-pervading silence that echoes through *Voyage* is ultimately neither more nor less than the silent presence of the Great War dead. This makes of *Voyage* a site of memory whose silent outer reaches are populated by the decimated hosts of Republican France, observers of Bardamu's adventures. *Voyage* becomes a chaplinesque comedy offered by Céline to the war dead. And it is to them, as much as to the living, that Céline's 'rappel', his mobilising battle-cry is directed (see 4.3 *The Function of Rappel*). Their silent witness is, indeed, the answer to his call.

Silence pervades *Voyage*. Céline's treatment of the war is typical. He says as little about it as possible. The episode at the front is the shortest (RI, 11–47). However, if we remember that Céline's original stance in relation to the war is one of silence, it is not surprising that he should strive to keep the war episode short. In addition, *Voyage* is alert to war's seductions. Using a minimalist approach, Céline ensures that *Voyage*'s war scenes cannot be read for thrills. The death scenes are stripped of pathos and laced with black humour. The unspeakable remains unspoken, unglamourised. The war is crushed with ridicule as it is diminished through silence. Indeed, Céline's silence, through which the war is effaced, is perhaps *Voyage*'s greatest anti-war quality.

Silence Against Silence

Céline's silence was intensely moral, a sign of his own 'inner deadness' and the emblem of 'true witness'. But in the paradoxical paradigm that is *Voyage*, Céline's silence is also dissent and contestation. Silence, as we have seen, occupied the heart of the Armistice commemoration. This is not, however, the same silence as informs *Voyage*. Indeed, the logic of 'reversal' tells us it is its antithesis.

Contrasted with Céline's private, personal silence, the silence of official commemoration had one over-riding quality: it was public and, therefore, highly theatrical. It provided the crowd with a unique frisson of emotion and this was the danger of its appeal. Cut off from the crowd by his experience of war Céline decried its silence. A line in *Voyage* provides a veiled satirical reference to the public silence of remembering. Bardamu imagines the nurses remembering the dead after the war. The irony is unmistakeable:

> Elles vous auraient alors des soupirs remémoratifs spéciaux de tendresse qui les rendraient plus attrayantes encore, elles évoqueraient en silences émus, les tragiques temps de la guerre, les revenants… (RI, 88)

> [They would heave for you then especially tender sighs of remembrance which would made them appear even more attractive, they would evoke in moving silences, the tragic time of the war, the ghosts…]

Their silence, satirised as the equivalent of the simpering sentimentality of the trivial heroines of romantic novels, is a silence, not just of assent, but of complicity. It collaborates with death. By provocatively attacking this silence, Céline refuses it any of the redemptive quality many commentators find in it.[23] For Céline the entire commemoration of the war, even to its very core of silence, is a lie to be denounced. It is a lie which covers in silence the sacrifice of countless soldiers. It is a lie of memory.

Silence and Self

Céline's silence seeks to restore truth to witness. The more Céline directs his text towards silence the more successfully he restores faith with the war dead, the more trenchantly he underlines his own and France's 'memory loss'. For this reason, the most striking use of silence in *Voyage* is Céline's erasing of his own heroism. This is the moral equivalent of throwing away one's medal, a protest against the futility of heroism and a declaration of a loss of heroic identity. With this gesture, Destouches is all but obliterated, made silent, in favour of Bardamu. And Bardamu, as fictional inversion of Destouches, protects Céline's moral silence while at the same time providing a conduit for speech.

Carl Jung told how he identified 'essential matters' among American Indians by their silent response to certain questions.[24] Céline's heroism is consigned to this essential zone by Céline's unwillingness to speak about it. It indicates that his past heroic identity has become taboo. Indeed, we shall see that the hero in *Voyage* has been transformed into a monster — 'condamné à porter un masque monstrueux' [condemned to wear a monstrous mask], as Leslie Davis says[25] — and that his monstrosity is defined by collaboration with death.

But there are other areas of Céline's life left to silence, other 'essential matters'. Notably, there is silence in relation to his father. His absence is noteworthy in a novel whose mode is disguised autobiography. The explanation is that Céline identifies his father with the war. An ex-soldier, Céline's father fed his dreams of military life and encouraged him to enlist. In addition, the blows he rained down on his son's head were precursors to the blow to the head given by the war (see 3.1 *Family, Work and Army*). This identification is not unusual. It can also produce extreme rage. Robert Lifton reports a traumatised Vietnam veteran's desire to kill his father.[26] We will yet see Céline's own version of killing his father in *Mort à crédit* (RI, 822–823).

With Céline this identification of father and war has another dimension. Céline's father was staunchly republican. Fernand was, therefore, identified with the French Republic. Belief in both collapsed with the debacle of heroism. 'Je ne croirai plus jamais à ce qu'ils disent, à ce qu'ils pensent' [I will never again believe in what people say, in what they think], marks the moment in *Voyage* (RI, 15). The profound reverberations of this collapse are explicit in what follows. 'C'est des hommes et d'eux seulement qu'il faut avoir peur, toujours' [It is of men, and men alone, that one needs to be afraid, always]. Father and state are both identified with an army which sacrificed its sons to slaughter while inciting them to a heroism which had no place in modern war. Rather than fulfilling their protecting, death-mastering role they have become sources of death. Fernand becomes, like the war, like the Republic, unspeakable. He is taboo and, like the French Republic, like Céline's own heroism, like the war itself, he remains hidden in one of *Voyage*'s most resonant silences. It is, indeed, likely that Céline's virulent anti-republicanism grew to some extent from this seed of hatred felt towards his father.

None of this is surprising. It is part of the psychology of the traumatised soldier. Robert Lifton, writing of Vietnam veterans, underlined the direction of their rage:

Rage could be directed towards any figures or symbols of authority, especially official authority — political leaders, the Veterans Administration, representatives of the establishment or ordinary middle-class society, or of the older generation. [...] There was a special kind of rage reserved for the military.[27]

Lifton quotes one soldier saying:

I wanted to become a communist. I wanted to assassinate the president. I wanted to organise some kind of uprising that would swoop down on the Pentagon — [and] save the world.

Céline's rage is animated by feelings like these. Ironically, the silence reserved for his father gives the measure of Céline's annihilating rage for him.

Beyond Silence

Silence is a natural response to the horror of war. However, Lieutenant Colonel Colman Goggin, former Chief Psychiatrist with the Irish Army, emphasises the need for traumatised soldiers to talk about the event which has traumatised them as a necessary first step to recovery.[28] The soldier's comrades, he believes, must help him to break through the wall of silence — Janet's failure of language — that follows trauma. Goggin believes silence would have increased the stranglehold of traumatic memory on Céline. Inside this stranglehold is Céline's lived experience of the war.

The creation of a space of silence within *Voyage* is the principal means of repairing the breach in silence. *Voyage*'s silence assuages Céline's guilt over speech, over betrayal, and it restores Céline's union with the war dead. It remains the badge of his inner deadness even while his speech pours forth. Silence offers the dead a voice and provides 'true witness' throughout the novel, one that accuses the memory loss of Republican Commemoration and indicts the unspeakable nature of the war and the Republic. However, Céline's 'temptation to silence' is too the point of departure for an unprecedented linguistic project. It marks Céline's own heightened uncertainty about language, his awareness of Steiner's 'general crisis', and his rebuttal of pre-war linguistic values. It represents the dividing line between traditional and modern narratives of memory and thus provides the starting point of new consciousness. And it is, in counterpoint to the savage torrent of words that flood *Voyage*, Céline's final commentary and most profound witness to the unprecedented experience of death that was the Great War.

5.3 FROM EYE-WITNESS TO I-WITNESS

The General Picture

Bardamu's war is grafted on Céline's own. Like Céline, Bardamu is in the cavalry. Like Céline, his war is limited to the war of movement in the Marne and Flanders. The 'petty detail' of Céline's war, the suffering horses, the burning villages, the weather, the fatigue, the aimless reconnoitring, is all present. Yet, the main events are missing. Céline's representation of his three months of war remains a general one. He provides just enough information to establish that he was there. That is, he provides himself only with a basis for rewriting the war. But it is this basis which will enable him to draw memory and imagination towards witness. As Paul Ricœur says:

> Testimony is the ultimate link between imagination and memory, because the witness says 'I was part of the story, I was there.' [...] Testimony would be a way of bringing memory and imagination together.[29]

In other words, testimony is the basis for the creation of *Voyage*.

Eye-Witness

Céline places his own eye-witness at the core of *Voyage*. The most striking example of this is the scene already evoked where 'le lieutenant de Sainte-Engence' has killed two German soldiers (3.3 *The Enemy*):

> 'J'en ai sabré deux !' assurait-il à la ronde, et montrait en même temps son sabre où, c'était vrai, le sang caillé comblait la petite rainure, faite exprès pour ça. (RI, 31)

> ['I ran two of them through with my sword,' he assured his audience, while showing the sword, where, it was true, congealed blood filled the narrow groove running down it, made on purpose for that.]

The 'c'était vrai' [it was true] in the middle of this last sentence is by no means incidental. It is one instance where Céline's claim to truth leads us back to verifiable fact. The eye-witness claim to truth, here proven, substantiates all other claims to truth and the novel's truth claim as a whole. It is this which lends *Voyage*'s fictions their stamp of conviction. Indeed, this 'c'était vrai' and its often ludic variants throughout *Voyage* constitute the resilient motto or battle-cry of Céline's narration, his witness.

Narrative Voice

The Sainte-Engence passage provides a good example of how narrative voice adds to Céline's eye-witness. His 'c'était vrai' resonates throughout all of the passage. Not only is it true that Sainte-Engence has killed two German soldiers, but it is also true that the cavalryman's traditional weapon, his sword, is grooved to channel the enemy's blood. The 'petite rainure' [narrow groove] is offered as an horrendous, if understated, example of human ingenuity at warfare and killing. Because the sword is one of humankind's earliest examples of weaponry, Céline is also drawing the reader's attention to an age-old propensity for organised mass murder. This, of course, is Céline's view of war, one of the building blocks which lead him eventually to declare, 'c'est tuer et se tuer qu'ils voulaient' [to kill and get themselves killed is what they wanted] (RI, 270). This pessimistic voice is an indispensable part of Céline's witness and one which opposes him to all who exalt the war. It is this voice which introduces him into the body of his own text.

Narrative voice gives Céline's witness its distinct character. It makes *Voyage* what it is. It is the voice of modern memory, the voice of the war writers of 1929. It is the voice of Céline's trauma, the voice of the wound (see 4.3 *The Voice of the Wound*). It is ultimately Céline's own voice. Again and again Bardamu speaks for him. For example, when he says that he does not like the countryside (RI, 13). Or when he evokes his fear in the woods at Spincourt, 'un mort derrière chaque arbre' [a dead man behind each tree] (RI, 57). Or when he describes his resentment towards his mother, authenticated by Lucette Almansor, who remembered:

> Plus que tout, il ne pouvait admettre qu'elle ait pu penser : 'si mon fils est tué au front, eh bien tant pis ! Il sera mort pour la France', qu'elle l'accepte comme une fatalité parmi d'autres, il ne pouvait le comprendre. La mort d'un homme jeune restera pour lui l'injustice suprême, l'inacceptable.[30]
>
> [More than anything, he could not accept that she could think: 'if my son is killed at the front, ah well, that's too bad! He will have died for France', that she could accept it as a fatality among others, he could not understand

it. The death of a young man remained the supreme, unacceptable injustice for him.]

Her memory confirms *Voyage*, 'elle acceptait l'accident de ma mort, non seulement elle consentait, mais elle se demandait si j'avais autant de résignation qu'elle-même' [she accepted the accident of my death, not only did she consent to it, she wondered if I had as much resignation as she did] (RI, 96).

From this real wound in experience flows the systematic degradation of the mother in *Voyage*, from the mother of the child murdered by the Germans (RI, 39), or the mother of Robinson's dying captain (RI, 42), to the mother who tortures her own child in Rancy (RI, 266–267).

Above all, *Voyage*'s narrative voice reports Céline's encounter with death and its traumatic consequence. Bardamu's 'je ne veux plus mourir' [I do not want to die anymore] (RI, 65) voices the absurdity and unacceptability of violent death for Céline, as well as his desire to reconnect with immortalising modes, and this short sentence must be considered as *Voyage*'s despairing emblem. 'Je ne veux plus mourir', with its clear desire for death mastery, explains Céline's breach of silence, explains *Voyage*. Opposed to 'la vérité de ce monde c'est la mort' [the truth of this world is death] (RI, 200), 'je ne veux plus mourir' drives *Voyage*'s narrative voice and guides Céline's traumatic reworking of memory. Memory which, we must not forget, is a Janus, with one face to past war and one face to future war.

War Narrative

Voyage's narrative voice is that of a soldier. Bardamu's tale could be any soldier's tale. Samuel Hynes describes the typical war narrative as 'something like travel writing, something like autobiography, something like history'.[31] *Voyage* eminently fits this description and so assumes the character of a 'true' war narrative. If we allow Hynes to expand we can see just how true this is:

> The men who were there tell a different story [from historians], one that is often quite ahistorical, even anti-historical. Their narratives are indifferent to the exact location of events in time (they rarely put dates to their actions) or in space (either they never knew exactly where they were or they have forgotten the names). But that seems right for the soldiers' tale they tell. [...] They aren't even interested in victory or defeat, except as it affects them personally; survival is their happy ending.[32]

The protagonist of the war narrative stands outside history, in the midst of an absurd and threatening world which only serves to underline his mortality. Céline's rejection of 'history', however, is more than just an affirmation of the witness of the 'man who was there', it is part of his anti-war, anti-Republican agenda, and provides an implicit denunciation of the historian's role in sustaining the Great War and in legitimising the French Republic. As Marie-Christine Bellosta observes:

> On sait [...] que pendant la Grande Guerre, la République mit ses historiens à contribution, et particulièrement le plus prestigieux d'entre eux, Ernest Lavisse, pour galvaniser les énergies nationales.[33]
>
> [We know [...] that during the Great War, the French Republic called on its historians, in particular the most eminent one, Ernest Lavisse, to galvanise national energies.]

Princhard's speech, Bellosta says, offers a sustained parody of 'tous les clichés de l'histoire républicaine telle qu'on l'enseignait dans les manuels inspirés par l'*Histoire générale* de Lavisse' [all the clichés of republican history as it was taught in manuals inspired by Lavisse's *General History*].[34]

Céline is in full combat not just against Lavisse but against an entire historiography which offered a cleansed and exalted view of the war (see also 2.2 *Graves*). Writing of the war's 'non-dits' [unspoken realities] of violence and brutality, historians Stéphane Audoin-Rouzeau and Annette Becker reveal the historians' role in occluding the truth of the Great War:

> Il nous semble que l'historiographie du conflit a longtemps 'aseptisé' ce volet de l'histoire de la Grande Guerre, au risque de nous la rendre pour une part incompréhensible. [...] Le témoignage combattant [...] a durablement culpabilisé les historiens de la Première Guerre mondiale.[35]
>
> [It appears to us that for a long time the historiography of the conflict 'aseptisised' the history of the Great War, at the risk of making it to an extent incomprehensible. [...] The witness of the combatant [...] provides a lasting indictment of the historians of the First World War.]

Céline thus writes in opposition to the historian who complements the war's official commemoration and who sustains 'cette faculté d'oubli de la majorité de nos contemporains' [the faculty for forgetting of the majority of our contemporaries] (see 4.1 *The Crisis in Memory*).

Céline does, however, have an historical vision. His opening reference to Raymond Poincaré (RI, 7), points to Poincaré and the leadership of Republican France as not just the architects of war, but also of a post-war peace which is characterised as excremental. As Bardamu says:

> En somme, tant qu'on est à la guerre, on dit que ce sera mieux dans la paix et puis on bouffe cet espoir-là comme si c'était du bonbon et puis c'est rien quand même que de la merde. (RI, 234)

> [In short, when you are in the war, you tell yourself things will be better when peace comes, and you swallow up that hope as if it were a piece of sweet cake and of course it's nothing in the end only a piece of shit.]

The *Voyage* manuscript, significantly, calls it 'notre paix dégueulasse' [our disgusting peace].[36]

Céline's occlusion of the Germans as the enemy in *Voyage* is in direct contradiction to the tenor of the Versailles Treaty which indicted them.[37] Poincaré was firmly anti-German and in 1923 ordered the occupation of the Ruhr valley. Treaty and occupation, particularly in the context of commemoration, would provide essential elements in sustaining a war logic leading towards the Second World War. While *Voyage*'s structure of forgetting is open to criticism as 'false witness' for political or ideological ends,[38] Céline's witness nonetheless stands apart from:

> les générations de l'entre-deux-guerres [qui] n'ont pas perçu l'irradiation du monde par la culture de violence issue de la Grande Guerre. [...] Brutalisation [...] désormais inscrite au cœur des sociétés occidentales.[39]

> [the inter-war generations [who] did not see the irradiation of the world by a culture of violence issued from the Great War. [...] A brutalisation [...] from that point on written into the heart of western societies.]

Witness, suggest Audoin-Rouzeau and Becker, involves more than just perception of the event. It involves perception of its 'conséquences profondes' [profound consequences].[40] Céline's witness is a function not just of the war, but of its consequence, and it is implicated entirely in its historical context. That side of memory which faces towards future war is the proof of the rounded and aware character of Céline's witness.

It is the case also, that the achronology and ahistorical character of the typical war narrative is particularly appropriate to represent the First World War and to inform witness. In war narrative the subjective expresses a commonality of experience. All war narratives are different, says Hynes, but:

> behind those variables there is always one story — the individual's journey from innocence into experience, the serial discovery of what had before been unimaginable, the reality of war.[41]

The telling of this reality is never easy. Hynes delves into *Voyage*'s truth problematic when he writes that 'the man-who-was-there asserts his authority as the only true witness of his war; but the truth that he claims to tell is compromised by the very nature of memory and language.'[42] Finally, when Hynes says of war writing that it is 'a genre without a tradition to the men who write it',[43] we are offered an insight into why it was a novel conceived in war, *Voyage*, which broke so dramatically with French literary tradition to revolutionise that tradition and the French language itself.

Intertextual Witness

Céline seeks to bolster his eye-witness by drawing on other witness. In doing so, he shifts his position from eye-witness to I-witness. This shift is a moral one and reflects the movement from silence to speech. As Michael Lambek writes, 'memories are eyewitness accounts [...] only if the emphasis is put on the witnessing, a moral act, rather than on the eye.'[44] The most striking way Céline creates this emphasis is through intertextuality.

Intertexuality in *Voyage* serves several purposes. It maintains Céline's essential silence. It provides confirming voices to *Voyage*'s witness to war. It supports memory. And, in a work which is characterised by disconnection, by a breach with past literary forms, intertextuality enables Céline to remain connected to earlier narrative while subverting and transforming it.

Intertextuality in *Voyage* starts from two main sources, the 12th Cuirassiers' *Historique*, and a war journal called *La Ruée: étapes d'un combattant* [*The Stampede: Itinerary of a Combatant*]. We have seen already how the *Historique* — which Céline may have read — confirms Céline's witness. Its importance, however, is not that it confirms, but that it exists, freeing Céline to provide a different order of witness. Indeed, while confirming the truthful, eye-witness nature of the Sainte-Engence/Daubon scene, the *Historique* underlines the moral superiority of Céline's enriching fiction, whose narrative voice provides, as we have seen, a far-reaching commentary on the incident.

The second source, Robert Desaubliaux's *La Ruée*, was published in 1920 and highly praised by Norton Cru.[45] Desaubliaux was one of the 11th Cuirassiers, who fought the war alongside the 12th. His war resembled Céline's. Indeed, this is so much the case, that Jean Bastier uses long passages from *La Ruée* to reconstitute Céline's war in his study of Céline's war experience. The similarity of characters' names in Desaubliaux's book to characters in both *Voyage* and *Casse-Pipe* indicates that Céline had read or was familiar with *La Ruée*.[46] The *Historique* and *La Ruée* thus provide significant foils for *Voyage*, the official history and the journal forming a triptych of war with *Voyage*'s supreme fiction in the middle.

Given Norton Cru's endorsement, *La Ruée* frees Céline from the moral obligation to be factual, and underwrites his right to imagination. With regard to the war he lived, both *Historique* and *La Ruée* speak for Céline. They provide a starting-point for and confirmation of *Voyage*. They tell Céline's story and so allow him the moral commitment to silence he will invest in *Voyage*. They make *Voyage* possible. Céline's intertextual sources, however, are far more extensive than this.

Henri Barbusse

'Read Barbusse,' was Céline's usual response when asked about the war.[47] Unsurprisingly then, Céline makes Barbusse part of his witness. However, he does not stop there. Marie-Christine Bellosta has described how the work of other war novelists is woven into *Voyage*.[48] Bellosta argues that Céline borrowed not just Barbusse's oral style and made it the dominant stylistic motif of *Voyage* but that he also borrowed scenes, incidents and metaphors from Barbusse, among others. Céline's war represents the 'totalité' [totality] of the war as seen by Barbusse, Dorgelès, Duhamel, Genevoix, and others, she says.[49] However, she recognises Céline's purpose in this. 'Ecrire ainsi [...],' she says, 'c'est écrire pour se situer par rapport à du déjà écrit, en réécrivant *pour* ou *contre*' [To write like this [...] is to situate oneself in relation to what has already been written, in rewriting *for* or *against* it].[50] That is, Céline uses other writers to support his witness. In a further example of *Voyage*'s totalising logic — Bellosta's use of the word 'totalité' is significant — these writers confirm his memory, he theirs. Moreover, they allow him silence. By presenting extraneous texts, Céline saves the illusion of silence and assuages guilt for speech. He once again points the reader towards *Voyage*'s silent spaces where 'true witness' lies.

Voyage's intertextual scope is very wide. Bardamu's arrival in New York, for example, draws directly on the work of Paul Morand and Georges Duhamel.[51] Witness too Bardamu's reading of a letter by Montaigne, recreating it in Céline's unique oral voice (RI, 289). There is too, for example, a clear echo of Chateaubriand's ironic 'ce fut une esclave qui me reçut sur la terre de la liberté' [it was a slave who welcomed me to the land of freedom] on arrival in America,[52] when Bardamu discovers on his own arrival in the new world, 'les pauvres de partout' [the poor from everywhere] (RI, 191). While its use derives from Céline's need to maintain silent witness — and while it is also the natural outcome of a literary technique developed while writing that most intertextual of texts: the PhD (see 4.1 *Semmelweiss*) — intertextuality is the critical point in *Voyage* where past narrative meets new. It is where Céline announces his breach with past literature.

By rewriting existing texts, Céline points to their desuetude, while underlining his own achievement in bringing a 'modern' tone and style to them. Significantly, however, while subverting past narrative, Céline remains connected to it and becomes part of the vast tapestry of French literature. Indeed, in *Voyage*, it is Céline who is making the tapestry anew, stitching the threads of other writers into his fabric, as when he parodies Proust:[53]

> Proust, mi-revenant lui-même, s'est perdu avec une extraordinaire ténacité dans l'infinie, la diluante futilité des rites et démarches qui s'entortillent autour des gens du monde, gens du vide, fantômes de désirs, partouzards indécis attendant leur Watteau toujours, chercheurs sans entrain d'improbables Cythères. (RI, 74)

> [Proust, a half-ghost himself, lost himself with an extraordinary tenacity in the infinite, the diluent futility of rites and rituals which wind around the people of the fashionable world, people of the void, phantoms of desire, undecided orgiasts waiting still for their Watteau, lacklustre searchers after improbable Cythereas.]

In this way, Céline becomes the sum and the summit of all that he has read. He draws on the immortalising possibilities of French literary tradition while signalling his own death-mastering renewal of that very same tradition. Indeed, the intertextual in *Voyage* becomes the site of a resuscitated heroic struggle to revitalise France — nation and race — through renewal of its language and literature (see 1.1 *The Hero*). In the process, intertextuality becomes one of the chief aspects of *Voyage*'s duality, representing the divide between past and present literatures, between old and new consciousness, as well as providing the point from which Céline looks both forwards and backwards in the hope of establishing dual death mastery through literary connection and disconnection.

Marcel Lafaye

One of *Voyage*'s most striking intertextual sources is Marcel Lafaye. Lafaye, a Parisian, from Montmartre, was born in 1897.[54] He fought in the Great War, in the infantry, and was wounded twice in 1917. Transferred to the air force as a pilot, his plane was shot down and he was badly disfigured. After the war, he worked for a time as foreman of a plantation in the Cameroon. He also worked in America, as a mechanic in the Ford Factory at Detroit and later worked in the Statistics Office of a firm in New York. The resemblance with Bardamu is clear.

Lafaye, something of a poet and writer, lived in Montmartre and formed part of a bohemian circle there. It was there, in 1928, that he met Céline.[55] Lafaye's daughter, Noëlle, recalls that her father was introduced to Céline as someone who could help him with his novel.[56] The two ex-veterans established a ready intimacy based on their war past. Pierre Lainé notes in Lafaye the same trauma, the same reticence, the same hatred of the war to be found in Céline.[57] In the 1930s, Lafaye would also turn to outspoken anti-Semitism as Céline did. This empathy made it easy for Céline to adapt elements of Lafaye's biography to the telling of Bardamu's tale. Undoubtedly, Lafaye provided Céline with much of the source material for Bardamu's time in Detroit and New York. Lafaye's daughter Noëlle confirms this. She says:

> Les similitudes entre les aventures et les commentaires de Bardamu et ceux de mon père sont frappantes. Les réflexions faites par mon père sur les États-Unis rejoignent presque en tous points celles de Bardamu.[58]

190

[The similarity between the adventures and observations of Bardamu and those of my father is striking. The comments made by my father in relation to the United States match Bardamu's in almost every detail.]

Of the African episode in *Voyage*, she adds, 'l'aventure de Bardamu ressemble point par point à celle vécue par mon père' [Bardamu's adventure resembles point for point the experience of my father].[59]

Lafaye was also a source for Céline's war portrait. He had written an unpublished novel, *Mon ami Labiffe, histoire d'un soldat* [*My friend, Labiffe, a soldier's story*].[60] Says Lainé, Lafaye's war, with its 'angoisse de la boue' [agony of mud] and its officers who 'ressemblent souvent à des brutes cherchant le malheur des soldats' [often resemble brutes seeking the unhappiness of their soldiers], became Bardamu's.[61]

According to Lainé, many elements in Lafaye's book found their way into *Voyage*. There is a Dorothée encountered in New York who serves as a model for the prostitute, Molly (RI, 228–236). Bardamu's debacle in the fast-food restaurant near Times Square, with its memorable evocation of the 'tarte lumineuse' [luminous tart], also comes from Lafaye (RI, 206–208). As does Musyne's 'Théâtre aux Armées' [Army Theatre] (RI, 79–80) and the entire episode of 'la belle subventionnée de la Comédie' [the lovely actress from the Comédie Française Theatre] (RI, 98–101).[62]

The debt is extensive but Lafaye's utility is not just in providing Céline with a double or with theatrical set-pieces to enliven his narrative. It is in enabling him to maintain his moral commitment to silence. Lafaye's tale becomes Céline's elaborate disguise, a means of deflecting guilt for the transgression of silence. At the same time, as with other intertextual sources, his tale complements Céline's witness, so that the site of memory in *Voyage* is duplicated and thus stronger. 'On est deux' [One becomes two], as Bardamu says (RI, 63).

I-Witness

In *Voyage*, different levels of witness ultimately merge together to become I-witness. Céline's I-witness can be summed up as the uniquely personal, fictional witness that is *Voyage*. Marie-Christine Bellosta has shown how Céline weaves different strands of witness together, focusing on the war episode's culminating scenes when Bardamu travels to Noirceur-sur-la-Lys.[63] Noirceur-sur-la-Lys (RI, 44–46) has been identified as Comines, a town occupied by the Germans during the war. 'Le pont Rouge' (RI, 38), where the young boy in sailor's outfit is lanced through the middle by a passing German cavalryman, recalls Pont-Rouge, the site of fierce fighting from 15 to 30 October 1914. 'La maison du Passeur' [the boatman's house], where Bardamu and Robinson halt (RI, 46),[64] recalls combat that took place at 'la maison du Passeur', a terrain situated near the Yser canal near Ypres, and the site of particularly fierce fighting, also in late 1914. By evoking these placenames, Céline addresses the collective memory of the war. Bellosta shows too how Céline's fictional witness emerges from disparate elements *remembered* by Céline. Interestingly, from an aesthetic point of view, he is here in the act of producing the 'synthesis of the war' denounced by Norton Cru, 'synthesis' which, in the event, is perfectly representative of *Voyage*'s totalising logic. Again note Bellosta's use of the word 'totalité':

> L'auteur fabrique un objet nouveau par l'assemblage d'objets non imaginés ; rassemblant en un épisode trois souvenirs historiques séparés dans le temps, il propose une image de la guerre qui est la synthèse symbolique d'expériences variées. Errant en une seule nuit de Pont-Rouge à Comines et à la Maison du Passeur, Bardamu prend d'un seul coup la mesure de la totalité de la guerre : les deuils des habitants (Pont-Rouge), la lâcheté des responsables civils (Comines) et la mort de soldats inconnus dans des lieux perdus (la Maison du Passeur) composent une image unique de la 'noirceur' de la guerre et de l'humanité.[65]

> [The author makes a new object through assembling non-imagined objects; drawing together three separate historical memories in one episode, he offers an image of the war which is the symbolic synthesis of varied experiences. Wandering in one single night from Pont-Rouge to Comines and to the Maison du Passeur, Bardamu takes all at once the measure of the totality of the war: the grief of the people (Pont-Rouge), the cowardice of the civil authorities (Comines) and the death of unknown soldiers in remote places (the Maison du Passeur), compose a unique image of the 'blackness' of the war and of humanity.]

This 'unique image' belongs to Céline's personal geography of wartime. La Maison du Passeur, Comines and Pont-Rouge were all in the region of Poelkapelle. These names, forming the map of his personal past, are part of Céline's direct witness to war, on which he proceeds to graft the substance of collective experience and memory. His own eye-witness authority supports the moral character of the collectively authenticated, fictional portrait. It is difficult in view of this, and in the context of her own insights, to understand why Bellosta denies *Voyage* its character of witness. '*Voyage* n'est ni un roman réaliste, ni un témoignage' [*Voyage* is neither a realist novel, nor a testimony], she writes.[66] This is to misunderstand the essential character of Céline's witness, to limit it purely to eye-witness, when Céline has enlarged the 'moral' scope of his witness to become an I-witness.

Jean Bastier has also identified Comines as the model for Noirceur-sur-la-Lys. According to Bastier, however, the atmosphere of Comines is directly borrowed from that of Lille in 1914, and the efforts of the mayor of Lille to ensure the safety of the city. Worried by the examples of Louvain and Reims, attacked by the Germans, the mayor wanted to avoid the same fate for Lille.[67] 'Les mesures de défense que l'autorité militaire a prises... sont malheureusement suffisantes pour attirer la foudre sur notre grande cité' [The defence measures taken by the military authorities... are unfortunately sufficient to draw the fire of the enemy down on our great city], he complained.[68] Noted the town prefect, 'la présence de nos soldats [...] inquiète l'Hôtel de ville. Le maire vient aux nouvelles. "Vous allez nous faire bombarder !" s'écrie-t-il dans un geste désespéré !' [the presence of our soldiers [...] is worrying the Mayor's office. The mayor comes for news. 'You are going to get us bombarded!' he cries with a despairing gesture].[69] Bardamu offers the following witness, 'il s'épuisait en de touchants efforts, le maire de Noirceur, ardent à nous persuader que notre Devoir était bien de foutre le camp' [the Mayor of Noirceur was wearing himself out by his moving and ardent efforts to persuade us that our Duty was to get the hell out of his town] (RI, 45). Lille was eventually declared 'ville ouverte' [open city] and evacuated. The Germans occupied it on 13 October 1914, two weeks before Céline was wounded. Historian Bastier has described Céline's rendering of this episode of the war in *Voyage* as 'd'une vérité psychologique et historique qui nous paraissent admirables' [having a psychological and historical truth which I find admirable].[70] Praise indeed for the truthful nature of Céline's witness.

The Community of Telling

Céline's witness extends to the personalities who people his war. As noted in the *Historique*, the 12th Cuirassiers' Captain de Malmusse, for example, shares a passion for the race course with *Voyage*'s Ortolan (RI, 32).[71] We have also seen that General d'Urbal, the commander of the 7th Cavalry division, is the model for General des Entrayes.[72] General des Entrayes is the occasion for some bitter satire on Céline's part:

> Le général des Entrayes, dans la maison réservée, attendait son dîner. Sa table était mise, la lampe à sa place. [...] Il en avait de trop à bouffer le général, puisqu'il touchait d'après le règlement quarante rations pour lui tout seul ! (RI, 25–26)

> [General des Entrayes, in the house reserved for him, was waiting for his dinner. His table was set, the lamp in its place. [...] He had too much to eat, the General, as he received by regulation, forty rations all for himself!]

The general is exigent, 'il engueulait tout le monde [...] si son ordonnance ne lui trouvait pas dès l'arrivée à l'étape [...] un lit bien propre et une cuisine aménagée à la moderne' [he roared at everyone [...] if his orderly didn't find him, as soon as he had arrived where he was to spend the night [...] a clean bed and a modern kitchen] (RI, 22).

D'Urbal published his war memoirs in 1939. Jean Bastier observes that it seems his 'souvenirs des repas ou des désagréments d'intendance aient servi de points d'ancrage à la mémoire de ce général' [memories of meals or problems with supplies served to anchor the memory of this General].[73] His memory *and* Céline's. *Voyage*, of course, which appeared years earlier in 1932, anticipated D'Urbal's memoirs. His portrait of d'Urbal/des Entrayes would undoubtedly have provoked many a wry smile among ex-combatants, who would have recognised the truth of the caricature. No doubt, Céline's portrait of d'Urbal would have echoed the sort of sharp banter surrounding the figure of the general in wartime. This is a highly significant aspect of Céline's war witness, creating a special type of 'community of memory' around shared experience. This specific memory is addressed primarily to veterans like Joseph Garcin and Marcel Lafaye. It may well be that this witness is accessible only to those who share it, those who were part of the experience, who remember, and whose mentality is in tune with the soldier's distortion, enlargement and mockery of reality. It is perhaps this aspect of Céline's memory which inspires Jay Winter's dismissal of *Voyage*'s 'truth' as a 'semi-sober barroom conversation between two buddies'.[74] It would be a mistake, however, to underestimate the 'seriousness' of what is in fact a form of camaraderie surviving in a novel which appears devoid of it.

The same process is at work as Céline weaves the memories of his friend, Lafaye, into *Voyage*. Once again, he establishes a community of memory and telling while raising Lafaye's stories to extraordinary literary heights. One can only strive to imagine the intense togetherness enjoyed by these men as they shared in the irreverent retelling of their war experience.

Another thread in this community of memory, as well as an important dimension of the novel's intertext, are the allusions to songs throughout *Voyage*, from 'No more worries' (RI, 264),[75] to the disastrous Tarapout 'chanson d'amour' [love song] (RI, 363), and the dreamlike 'Ferme tes jolis yeux' [Close your lovely eyes] (RI, 401), which also features notably in Dorgelès *Les Croix de bois*. In Dorgelès, this latter is sung by a company of soldiers who, while they sing, forget the war. 'On ne veut plus rien voir : les soldats, la guerre…' [we did not want to see anything anymore: the soldiers, the war…].[76] The song, in *Voyage*'s Toulouse 'péniche' [barge] dream scene, also indicates healing forgetfulness, but the song's primary function, and the function of all song and music in *Voyage*, is as a vector for memory. The inherently repetitive and circular nature of song makes it ideal for *Voyage*'s mnemonic process, its work of 'recollection' or 'recall'. While retaining deeply personal associations, the songs cannot fail to address popular memory. In this context, it should not be forgotten that Madelon's name recalls a French song popular with the soldiers in wartime. Céline's ironic portrait of Madelon, as the young, love-besotted killer of Robinson, is thus accompanied by a silently remembered, bittersweet musical soundtrack which carries the reader/listener back to the war. Céline's 'faut entendre au fond de toutes les musiques […] l'air de la Mort' [you have to hear at the bottom of all music […] death's melody] emphasises the link between these songs and his wartime experience (RI, 297). Music and song are, therefore, not just a support to memory, but an integral part of both Céline's eye-witness and his I-witness to war made in the image of the novel's cycle of re-enactment.

Voyage's unforgettable colonel who, under fire, initiates the war episode, is yet another example of Céline's community of memory (RI, 11). Céline based him on a General Grossetti. According to Jean Bastier, Grossetti distinguished himself in Flanders in October 1914 by sitting under a bombardment for a whole half-hour in an effort to rally his troops.[77] His act was widely reported. Céline would have read an account of it while convalescing. The reader of *Voyage* whose memory served him well, most likely a veteran, would have readily recognised and enjoyed the caricature.

Céline exploits Grossetti, or rather the colonel, to make him an initiating and emblematic figure of an absurd and blind war. 'Le colonel, c'était donc un monstre ! À présent, j'en étais assuré, pire qu'un chien, il n'imaginait pas son trépas !' [The colonel was a monster! I was sure of it now, worse than a dog, he couldn't imagine his own demise!] (RI, 13). Bardamu considers this blindness to one's own mortality an implacable part of 'la sentence des hommes et des choses' [the sentence of men and things] (RI, 13), and a reason for the very existence of the war. Thus, the episode is again enriched by Céline's narrative voice, which not alone remembers but says what it thinks about what it remembers, adding its retrospective voice to witness, by virtue of which all the various elements of witness are heightened to a unique intensity as they become fiction. It can indeed be said that Céline's 'transposition' is the means by which diverse forms of witness and remembering are unified as fiction. That is, Céline's 'transposition' of reality is the means by which traumatic memory becomes traumatic narrative, silence becomes speech, and eye-witness becomes I-witness.

From Truth to Untruth

At the start of Camus's *La Peste*, Rieux sets out the manner in which he will constitute his witness to disaster, 'son témoignage d'abord, celui des autres ensuite [...] et, en dernier lieu, les textes qui finirent par tomber entrer ses mains' [his witness first of all, then that of others [...] and, lastly, the texts which had fallen into his hands].[78] This is, indeed, the basic model for Céline's witness in

Voyage. It is the model, from eye-witness to I-witness — a model which also contributes to the novel's logic of expansion — which will shape all of *Voyage*'s episodes. I-witness, therefore, comprises different forms of witness, legitimised by eye-witness. It also comprises different levels of witness which emerge from the I's awareness of the process of witnessing. Dori Laub, writing of the Holocaust, names these as:

> the level of being a witness to oneself within the experience, the level of being a witness to the testimonies of others, and the level of being a witness to the process of witnessing itself.[79]

Céline's awareness of his own act of witness begins with his self-conscious breach of silence, 'ça a débuté comme ça' [this is how it started] (RI, 7), immediately shadowing forth its subject through linguistic evocation of the repetitive circularity of memory dominated by the traumatic return of the unspeakable: 'ça' [it]. This awareness initiates a process of, in Laub's words, 'facing loss', 'of going through the pain of the act of witnessing, and of the ending of the act of witnessing'.[80] 'Qu'on n'en parle plus' [let's talk no more about it], writes Céline (RI, 505), signalling not that the process of witnessing is ending, but rather that it has returned to silence, or true witness. Céline's journey thus accomplishes a circular movement from silence to silence, from truth to untruth and back again, in which the process of witnessing and, therefore, the pain of witnessing, of 'facing loss', never ends.

Conclusion

'No one should read war literature to find out "what the war was really like",' writes historian, Jay Winter. Adding that 'this is especially so in reading Céline'.[81] At first sight, *Voyage*, which all but erases Céline's own personal past to construct an impersonal form of witness, would seem to confirm Winter's view. And yet if we consider the significant witness of *Voyage*'s silent spaces and the many levels of witness brought together to form Céline's I-witness account of war we may readily concur with Richard Holmes' view that 'there is a powerful case for offering the novel as a quest for a truth deeper than that which even the best historians can reach.'[82] *Voyage* is, indeed, nothing more nor less than this 'quest' for a deeper truth. A quest which starts from traumatised memory and the need to rewrite the past, which hurtles against the obstacle of silence, which forgets as it remembers, but which never diminishes its will to witness, its commitment to 'tout dire' [say everything]. 'One of the central problems of fiction writing [...] is that of legitimacy and the arrival at the truth on a crooked route,' opined W.G. Sebald.[83] *Voyage* takes that crooked route, the crooked route of memory, and while it may never have the 'legitimacy' of conventional historical narrative, it will nonetheless retain its place as witness to the Great War, and to its consequence. It was not for nothing that Claude Lévi-Strauss wrote of *Voyage* that it contained 'les pages les plus véridiques, les plus profondes et les plus implacables qui aient été jamais inspirées à un homme qui refuse d'accepter la guerre' [the most truthful, the most profound and the most implacable pages ever inspired in a man who refuses to accept war].[84]

Founded on an essential silence, and driven by moral commitment to offer testimony, *Voyage* is for all time the war as Céline wanted to remember it and as he wanted it to be remembered.

---

[1] Paul Ricœur, *La Mémoire, l'Histoire, l'Oubli*, p.1.

[2] Cited in Barbie Zelizer, 'Reading the Past Against the Grain: The Shape of Memory Studies', *Critical Studies in Mass Communications*, 12, 2 (June 1995), 214–239 (p.235).

[3] Paul Antze and Michael Lambek, 'Introduction: Forecasting Memory', in *Tense Past: Cultural Essays in Trauma and Memory*, ed. by Antze and Lambek (London: Routledge, 1996), pp.xi–xxxvii (p.xvii).

[4] See Crocq, p.240.

[5] Crocq, p.241.

[6] Cited in Crocq, p.241.

[7] Bessel A. Van Der Kolk and Onno Van Der Hart, 'The Intrusive Past: The Flexibility of Memory and The Engraving of Trauma', in *Trauma: Explorations in Memory*, pp.158–182 (p.176).

[8] Laurence J. Kirmayer, 'Landscapes of Memory: Trauma, Narrative and Dissociation', in *Tense Past*, pp.173–196 (p.182).

[9] Speaking on video, *Mémoire, oubli, histoire,* dir. Stéphane Ginet, Arts et Éducation, France, 1995.

[10] Semprun, p.373.

[11] Paul Ricœur, 'Memory and Forgetting', in Kearney and Dooley, eds., *Questioning ethics: debates in contemporary philosophy*, pp.5–11, p.9.

[12] Martin Amis, *Time's Arrow* (London: Penguin, 1992).

[13] James Joyce, *Ulysses* (New York: Vintage, 1961), p.25.

[14] Letter of 13 May 1933, in Lainé, p.632.

[15] Henri Godard, 'Une nouvelle lumière sur le "Voyage au bout de la nuit"', *Le Monde*, 11 May 2001, p.14. See too Godard's preface to this book, pp.x–xii.

[16] Davis, 'L'anti-monde de L.-F.Céline', p.73.

[17] George Steiner, 'Silence and the Poet', in *Language and Silence: Essays 1958–1966* London: Faber and Faber, 1985), pp.55–74 (p.69).

[18] *Voyage*, as Frédéric Vitoux has shown, privileges silence. Through the silence of certain characters, of Molly, Alcide, Bébert's aunt, Céline brings a clear moral dimension to the role of silence in the novel. See Vitoux, *Misère et Parole*, pp.57–70.

[19] Gibault, I, 137.

[20] Letter of 1 September 1929, cited in Lainé, p.615.

[21] See *Le Petit Robert* (Paris: Le Robert, 1989), p.1241.

[22] 'Speaking always implies a treason', cited in Lifton, *Death in Life*, p.565.

[23] Patrick Wright, for example, in a television programme broadcast for Armistice Day in 1999, said of the Armistice silence, 'the two minute silence stands out as a blessed moment [...]. It's like a crack in time, a profound fissure that runs back through the century.' See *A Day to Remember*, dir. Ian McMillan, Illuminations, Channel 4, 1999.

[24] Carl G. Jung, *Memories, Dreams, Reflections*, recorded and ed. by Aniela Jaffé, trans. by Richard and Clara Winston (London: Fontana Press, 1995), p.279.

[25] Davis, 'L'anti-monde de L.-F. Céline', p.73.

[26] Lifton, *Home from the War*, p.149.

[27] Lifton, *Home from the War*, p.142.

[28] Interviewed by myself in summer 2000.

[29] Ricœur, 'Imagination, Testimony and Trust', in *Questioning ethics*, pp.12–17 (p.16).

[30] In Véronique Robert with Lucette Destouches, *Céline secret* (Paris: Bernard Grasset, 2001), pp.52–53.

[31] Hynes, pp.4–5.

[32] Hynes, p.11.

[33] See Bellosta, p.256.

[34] Bellosta, p.256.

[35] Stéphane Audoin-Rouzeau and Annette Becker, *14–18: retrouver la guerre* (Paris: Gallimard, 2000), p.50.

[36] *Voyage* manuscript, fol.111.

[37] See Audoin-Rouzeau and Becker, *14–18: retrouver la guerre*, pp.259–261.

[38] See Cathy Caruth, 'An Interview with Robert Jay Lifton', p.139, where Lifton remarks 'false witness tends to be a political and ideological process.'

[39] Audoin-Rouzeau and Becker, *14–18: retrouver la guerre*, p.259.

[40] Audoin-Rouzeau and Becker, *14–18: retrouver la guerre*, p.259.

[41] Hynes, pp.16–17.

[42] Hynes, p.25.

[43] Hynes, p.4.

[44] Michael Lambek, 'The Past Imperfect: Remembering as Moral Practice', in *Tense Past*, pp.235–254 (p.248).

[45] See Norton Cru, *Témoins*, pp.126–129.

[46] Bastier, pp.20–21.

[47] See Gibault, I, 235.

[48] See Bellosta, pp.38–51.

[49] Bellosta, p.51. For an itinerary of the intertextual sources of Céline's war portrait see Bellosta, pp.41–46. For a comparison with Barbusse in particular, see pp.74–80.

[50] Bellosta, p.46.

[51] See Dauphin, 'Étude d'une illusion romanesque', pp.307–314.

[52] Chateaubriand, *Mémoires d'outre-tombe*, preface by Julien Gracq, ed. by Maurice Levaillant, 4 vols (Paris: Flammarion, 1982), I, 275.

[53] For a treatment of themes common to both Céline and Proust, see Pascal Ifri, *Céline et Proust*.

[54] See Lainé, p.116 and following pages.

[55] In a letter to Joseph Garcin dated 6 January 1931, Céline writes, 'Je vois LAFAYE, c'est un ami précieux et discret et fidèle—' [I see LAFAYE, he's an invaluable friend, discreet and loyal—]. See Lainé, p.624.

[56] Lainé, p.119.

[57] See Lainé, pp.121–122.

[58] Lainé, footnote 14, p.119.

[59] Lainé, p.121.

[60] See Lainé, p.116.

[61] Lainé, p.128. According to Lainé, even Bardamu's name was inspired by Lafaye. See Lainé, p.126.

[62] On this episode see Henri Godard's preface to this book, pp.ix–x.

[63] Bellosta, pp.47–50.

[64] Actually reads 'maison du Pasteur' in the Pléiade edition, but correctly reads 'Passeur' in the 1952 Gallimard folio edition.

[65] Bellosta, p.49.

[66] Bellosta, p.38.

[67] See Bastier, p.210.

[68] Bastier, p.210.

[69] Bastier, p.211.

[70] Bastier, 'L.-F.Céline en 1914, d'après les archives de l'armée', *Actes du Colloque international de Paris 1992* (Tusson: du Lérot and Société des études céliniennes, 1993), 35–50 (p. 45).

[71] See *Historique*, p.5.

[72] Bastier, *Le Cuirassier blessé*, p.138.

[73] Bastier, *Le Cuirassier blessé*, p.202.

[74] Winter, 'Céline and the Cultivation of Hatred', p.238.

[75] Henri Godard suggests that this song is in reality 'Pack up your troubles', popular in English music halls during Céline's London sojourn in 1915. See Godard, 'Notes et variantes', in *Romans*, I, 1290–1308 (p.1302). The song had a strong association, in tandem with *Tipperary*, with British troops marching to war, of which Céline would have been aware.

[76] Roland Dorgelès, *Les Croix de bois* (Paris: Albin Michel, 1919), p.148.

[77] See Bastier, *Le Cuirassier blessé*, pp.359–360.

[78] Albert Camus, *La Peste* (Paris: Gallimard, 1947), p.16–17.

[79] Dori Laub, 'Truth and Testimony: The Process and the Struggle', in *Trauma: Explorations in Memory*, pp.61–75 (p.61).

[80] Laub, p.74.

[81] Winter, 'Céline and the Cultivation of Hatred', p.238.

[82] In correspondence with myself by e-mail on 25 October 1999.

[83] Cited in *The Questionable Business of Writing*, interview published at amazon.co.uk, retrieved 24/01/00. Website address: http://www.amazon.co.uk/exec/obidos/tg/feature/-/21586/026-3158445-1515666. The use of the word 'crooked' cannot fail to remind us of Céline's own metaphor of a broken stick plunged in water to make it look straight to describe his art. See *Entretiens avec le professeur Y*, in *Romans*, IV: *Féerie pour une autre fois I, Féerie pour une autre fois II, Entretiens avec le professeur Y* (1993), 489–561 (p.546).

[84] Claude Lévi-Strauss, January 1933 review of *Voyage* in *L'Étudiant socialiste*, in *70 critiques du Voyage au bout de la nuit 1932–1935*, ed. by André Derval (Paris: IMEC, 1993), pp.119–121 (p.121).

CHAPTER 6

REWRITING THE SELF

From Destouches to Céline

Introduction

In *Voyage*, the experience of self, made in the image of the Great War, is circular and inescapable. Says Bardamu:

> Tout notre malheur vient de ce qu'il nous faut demeurer Jean, Pierre ou Gaston coûte que coûte pendant toutes sortes d'années. [...] Notre torture chérie est enfermée là, atomique, dans notre peau même, avec notre orgueil. (RI, 337)

> [All our unhappiness comes from the fact that we must remain Jean, Pierre or Gaston no matter what, year after year. [...] Our beloved, atomic, torment is shut up there, inside our very skin, along with our pride.]

Without the courage to end it all, the self remains locked within its own recurrent failure to transcend stasis. 'On éclaterait si on avait du courage, on faille seulement d'un jour à l'autre' [We'd burst right open if we only had the courage, but from one day to the next we just can't manage it]. This stasis is the condition of the debased self, shut out of the death-mastering possibilities of heroic myth. Enclosed in circular stasis, the traumatised Célinian self strives to re-enter myth through protean change. As Patrick McCarthy says:

> When Céline goes into his hallucinated, creative fit he brings out of himself other selves. It is a process of self-transformation, of projecting one part of himself into the realm of his imagination.[1]

In this process the self is rewritten over and over to create a protean self, striving towards wholeness. This chapter examines that protean struggle.

6.1 THE CIRCLE OF STASIS

Circles

Carl Jung described the circle as a symbol of the self. Serving in the army towards the end of the Great War he began sketching circles in his copy-book.[2] This activity puzzled him until he realised that the circles reflected his state of mind and that they imaged forth a desire for self-protecting wholeness. A young child will draw circles in an effort to maintain psychic integrity in response to painful experiences such as bereavement.[3] We may wonder if the young Louis Destouches drew protecting circles in his copybooks in the wake of the death of his grandmother, Céline Guillou (see 3.1 *Death*). We may do so not only because, as we have seen, *Voyage* is characterised by its circularity, but also because there is evidence, preceding *Voyage*, of Céline's own obsession with circular patterns.

As with Jung, Céline's fascination with circles follows on his experience of war. Writing to Simone Saintu from Liverpool in May 1915, he described his favourite pastime by the river Mersey, 'qui consiste à cracher dans l'eau et d'obtenir par ce moyen des cercles sans cesse grandissants' [which consists of spitting in the river so as to create by this means ever-increasing circles].[4] Already the shape of *Voyage*, sixteen years in the future, is reflected in Céline's idle leisure. At the end of July 1916, a letter from Africa reveals other, more deadly, circles. In a village, the natives treat him to a strange demonstration:

> Vous faites un cercle avec des lianes, d'environ 50 centimètres de diamètre vous posez ce cercle sur le sol vous posez au milieu de [ce] cercle un scorpion — et vous mettez le feu aux lianes, le scorpion se trouve donc environné, circonscrit par le feu, il cherche immédiatement à sortir mais en vain — tourne retourne, va et vient mais ne peut sortir il s'immobilise alors à l'intérieur du cercle, et se piquant lui même, et longuement au dessus du corsellet, s'empoisonne et meurt presque aussitôt—[5]

> [Using some creepers you make a circle of about 50 centimetres in diameter and you place it on the ground with a scorpion in the middle — then you set the creepers on fire, the scorpion finds itself surrounded, encircled by the flame, it immediately endeavours to escape but in vain — it turns returns, comes and goes, but cannot get out, and so stops moving inside the circle, and stinging itself, at length above the corselet, it poisons itself and dies almost immediately—]

Céline is impressed by this struggle in nature culminating in suicide. He is impressed too no doubt by the ritual nature of the drama with its circle of fire and its ring of spectators. Did these circles of fire remind Céline of the war? Undoubtedly they did. They emerge years later in *Voyage* as Bardamu watches villages burning:

> Tous les soirs ensuite vers cette époque-là, bien des villages se sont mis à flamber à l'horizon, ça se répétait, on en était entourés, comme par un très grand cercle […]. (RI, 29)
>
> [Every evening around then, any number of villages began blazing up on the horizon, one after the other, until we were surrounded by them, as inside a very large circle […].]

Bardamu's position in the Great War is that of the scorpion, surrounded by fire, caught between the instinct to live and the will to sacrifice — or suicide. In Céline's letter, the description of the scorpion enclosed by fire comes just a page or two after he has recalled leaving for war two years earlier. The juxtaposition tells its own story. The war has left Céline feeling encircled by fire.

The image of Bardamu trapped by fire as he turns in circles throughout *Voyage* is a poignant one. The problem he faces of how to master death could equally be one of how to master fire. His repetitive circling becomes a sort of ritual fire dance designed to protect him from the flames, from *le feu* [the fire], France's term for the Great War. Indeed, the last act of *Voyage*, set in a canal bistro, is Gustave Mandamour's enraged and catastrophic 'la véritable danse du Feu' [veritable Fire Dance], under the malevolent gaze of 'le patron […] un sournois, Vaudescal ; […] avec des chemises toujours bien trop propres pour qu'il soye tout à fait honnête' [the owner […] a sly sort, Vaudescal; […] with shirts far too clean for him to be altogether honest] (RI, 504). The positioning of the scene underscores its significance. As *Voyage*'s all but final gesture it emphasises a further aspect of its inner dynamic, a ritual fire dance, frowned upon by 'le patron' [the owner].

The Debased Self

Bardamu's problem is that he is trapped in circular stasis. This stasis is the product of his loss of heroic identity. The heroic self derived its strength from its immortalising participation in heroic myth. The debased self on the other hand has no such immortalising possibilities. Distinguished from the heroic self by what Bardamu calls 'l'imagination de la mort' [the imagination of death] (RI, 19), the debased self experiences death as a violation. 'Quand on a pas d'imagination,' he says, 'mourir c'est peu de chose, quand on en a, mourir c'est trop' [Death is a small matter, if you have no imagination, but if you do have some, dying is just too much] (RI, 19). Where the heroic self desires death, the debased self shuns it. 'Bientôt on serait en plein orage,' remembers Bardamu, 'et ce qu'on cherchait à ne pas voir serait alors en plein devant soi et on ne pourrait plus voir qu'elle : sa propre mort' [Soon we would be in the thick of the storm, and the very thing we did not want to see would be set right in front of us and we would be able to see nothing but it: our very own death] (RI, 33). The debased self confesses its inability to master death. 'Je n'ai jamais pu me tuer moi' [I never had what it takes to kill myself], Bardamu says (RI, 200). Lacking death mastery it is oppressed by its own inner deadness, 'assassiné en sursis' [waiting to be assassinated], living an 'espèce d'agonie différée, lucide' [a sort of deferred, lucid, death throe], 'dans la vérité jusqu'au trognon' [up to the eyeballs in truth], 'ma propre mort me suivait pour ainsi dire pas à pas' [my own death followed me, so to speak, step by step]. 'Il faut l'avoir endurée pour savoir à jamais ce qu'on dit' [You have to have endured it, to be qualified forever to talk about it], (RI, 52). 'Toutes les pensées conduisent à la mort' [every thought leads to death], Bardamu says (RI, 326). But this awareness of his own death is no help. 'Même pas bon à penser la mort qu'on est' [no good even thinking of the corpse you are], he says (RI, 332). 'Je ne veux plus mourir' [I don't want to die anymore], is his despairing cry (RI, 65).

The debased self experiences itself as a prisoner, 'cet enragement à persévérer dans notre état constitue l'incroyable torture' [that rage to persevere in our current state constitutes an unbelievable torture] (RI, 337). Its image is the circle; its emblematic date is '4 mai'. It moves in circles turning upon itself. 'J'avais beau essayer de me perdre pour ne plus me retrouver devant ma vie, je la retrouvais partout simplement' [I had tried in vain to lose myself so as never to have to come face to face with my life again, but I simply found it everywhere], says Bardamu, unable to escape himself (RI, 500). 'Je revenais sur moi-même' [I kept coming back to myself]. This static turning upon self expresses a profound dissatisfaction with self. It is, however, a function not just of the memory of death, which is its negative pole, but also of the restless quest for an ideal self, which is its positive pole:

> Chacun possède ses raisons pour s'évader de sa misère intime et chacun de nous pour y parvenir emprunte aux circonstances quelque ingénieux chemin. Heureux ceux auxquels le bordel suffit ! (RI, 426)[6]
>
> [Each of us has our own reasons to escape from our personal, intimate misery and each of us avails of whatever ingenious route circumstances allow. Happy are those for whom the brothel suffices!]

The restless quest for the ideal self produces protean transformation in and outside *Voyage*. The movement from Destouches to Céline to Bardamu and on to Robinson is the clearest statement of this protean flight from old to new identity underlying *Voyage*.

The Mask

The protean struggle begins with the death of the heroic self, Destouches, in war. The loss of heroic identity demands that a new identity be forged with which to address the world while encompassing the protean effort of transformation. This new identity leads the ghost of Destouches to don a mask of self, an authorial presence, Céline, and the protean 'je' [I] of *Voyage*. Nominally this 'je' is Bardamu, but as Bardamu is a vehicle for transformation, his 'je' reveals itself as something more complex. It is, indeed, a mask used by Céline which, while it guarantees his moral silence about the war, is also deeply implicated in *Voyage*'s ritual structure.

There was one group of veterans who more than any other represented the idea of lost identity: 'les gueules cassées' [broken faces]. There were fifteen thousand 'gueules cassées' in France after the war, men whose faces had been shattered by bullets or exploding shells. Five of them were symbolically present at the signing of the Versailles Treaty that ended the war.[7] Their wounds were often so serious that they could not be integrated socially and they were resettled in rural houses. These men provided much of the impetus behind the development of plastic surgery in the war. Many wore masks modelled on their original features.[8] Marcel Lafaye was disfigured during the war; his face needed seventeen skin grafts to restore it (see 5.3 *Marcel Lafaye*).[9] This painful procedure of restoring a face to its former likeness, using borrowed skin, is an appropriate metaphor for the creation of Bardamu.

Céline, having been 'disfigured' by the war, borrows a 'likeness' from Lafaye to create a semblance of self. Doing so, he reveals the impossibility of returning to the original. The damaged or destroyed past self needs to be doctored before it can stand viewing and before it can negotiate with the world. Lafaye, of course, is just one element used in the making of Céline's mask. The vast intertextual weave that is *Voyage* also helps to make it. Elias Canetti says that the mask sets a limit to transformation and encloses the wearer in an unbreakable duality.[10] The originality of Céline's mask, however, is that it is intrinsically protean and thus enables him to transcend duality and any limits the mask poses to transformation.

Donning the Mask

We have already described *Voyage* as behaving like ritual commemoration through both calendrical and verbal repetition. The donning of the mask provides a most astonishing enlargement of this view. By adding *gestural* re-enactment to calendrical and verbal it completes the three main aspects of Paul Connerton's *rhetoric of re-enactment* central to commemorative practices. Here, in a staggering movement from one self to another, Céline reaches into the primitive core of ritual re-enactment to summon and re-enter the presence of the dead. Drawing on archaic ritual, Connerton describes how actors wear masks that identify them with their dead. The wearers of the masks represent ghosts. According to Connerton:

> To wear a mask is to have immediate and direct contact with the beings of the unseen world; during the time of such direct contact [...] the actor and [...] the spirit he represents are one. [...] Gestural repetition enacts the idea of bi-presence; the inhabitants of the other world can reappear in this one without leaving their own.[11]

This extraordinary insight into the dynamic of memory in *Voyage* beautifully enlightens Nicholas Hewitt's view that *Voyage* is a song sung by ghosts.[12] But the singer of this 'ghost-song' is Céline himself, whose inner deadness confers him with the status of ghost, and who by donning the mask identifies himself with the ghosts of the Great War. He not just speaks for them, he *becomes* them. Céline's 'je', his mask, Bardamu, is his identity with the war dead. Connerton confirms this when he says of archaic ritual, 'elders use the first person singular when speaking for their dead predecessors.'[13] This 'identification through utterance' culminates, Connerton writes, when the 'individual elder ceases to exist [...] and is replaced by "another"'. As this is a form of possession, we can say that beneath the mask, Céline is inhabited by the war dead. This makes sense of his assertion, through Bardamu, that one finds the dead 'du dedans et les yeux presque fermés' [from inside and with eyes near closed] in the scene where the dead fill the sky above Montmartre (RI, 366).

The Effort to Break Free

Voyage has a ritual structure, thanks to its triple aspect of calendrical, verbal and gestural repetition. It is a ritual of memory performed by a masked dancer, moving in circles, who begins his performance by closing his eyes, 'il suffit de fermer les yeux' [all that is needed is to close your eyes] (RI, epigraph), and who trance-like passes from this world into another, 'c'est de l'autre côté de la vie' [it's on the other side of life]. Shaman-like, this entranced figure provides a bridge to the other world for his audience, introducing them to their ghosts and speaking on behalf of the dead themselves. *Voyage*, in this sense, responds to the public need in the 1920s to establish contact with the dead, which saw a marked increase in spiritualism.[14]

The ritual commemoration that is *Voyage* directly reflects a society saturated by commemoration, organised around commemoration and structured by it. This seems to indicate that the memory of *Voyage* is bound to the past in the same way as the organised public commemorations of the 1920s and that Céline's novel does no more than reflect an inverse mirror image of official commemoration. Céline's effort, however, is intrinsically different from commemoration because of its protean determination to escape the cyclical re-enactments attendant on static ritual.

The protean is intrinsically part of Céline's literary production. In his career he writes poems, songs, plays, scenarios, ballets, pamphlets, novels, while producing a massive volume of correspondence. The protean shift from the failed play *L'Église* to the successful novel *Voyage* is one of Céline's most successful protean adaptations. *Voyage* is resolutely protean, evidenced not just by the

aforementioned shift in identity from Destouches to Bardamu to Robinson, but by
the use of multivalent symbols, rampant intertextuality and the protean richness of
Céline's language which, as we shall later see, draws from a wide gamut
comprising slang, conventional literary language, medical terms and that most
protean of language forms: the neologism (see 8.1 *Protean Language*). We have
seen too that *Voyage*'s structure is protean, being at once dual, circular and,
according to one theory, shaped like a boat.[15] There is too the protean presence of
myth in *Voyage*, so that the story being told shifts, as we shall see, from one myth
to another, from Orpheus to Sisyphus to Proteus. Myths, of course, are 'universal'
stories and together with the other protean elements they tend towards
establishing a universality in *Voyage*, reflecting a Universe of which it is the
central point. The protean in *Voyage* is indeed, in part, the product of the novel's
totalising or universalising logic.

It is not surprising, given this protean dynamic, that we find further traces
of ritual in *Voyage*. Indeed, as Leslie Davis has written, 'tout prend les dimensions
d'un rituel' [everything becomes ritual].[16] Bardamu's war and subsequent journey
becomes a ritual of initiation,[17] at once moral and sexual, 'j'étais dépucelé' [I had
been deflowered] (RI, 14), while the war itself is characterised as ritual sacrifice
by the reference to the Aztecs '[qui] éventraient couramment [...] dans leur
temples du soleil, quatre-vingt mille croyants par semaine' [who as a matter of
course eviscerated [...] in their sun temples, eighty thousand believers a week]
(RI, 37). On board the *Amiral Bragueton*, Bardamu himself is prepared for
sacrifice (RI, 118). Bardamu touching Lola's bottom represents nothing other than
the enactment of a fertility rite, expressing his desire for birth in the midst of a
death-saturated wasteland (RI, 54).[18] In New York's 'caverne fécale' [faecal
cavern] the occupants also perform a ritual, 'c'était le rite' [it was a rite] (RI, 195).
And we have seen Mandamour's attempt to perform a protecting fire dance ritual
and how this ritual is also part of the shape of *Voyage*. The return to myth and
ritual is, indeed, a characteristic of Paul Fussell's modern memory of the Great
War, a psychic and creative response to the war's ravages.[19]

Bardamu's turning in circles defines his existence as a product of ritual. In this dispensation, the self itself is structured in the manner of a ritual and becomes a creature of 'invariant sequences' (see 2.1 *Commemoration and Myth*). It is, however, on the level of self, that we find the most exciting transformations taking place as Bardamu tries to find his ideal self. As Philip Stephen Day comments:

> Bardamu cherche à se transformer en un être invulnérable, étanche. À défaut de pouvoir sortir du corps, il se donne l'illusion d'une protection contre le dehors en transformant sa personnalité.[20]

> [Bardamu seeks to become invulnerable. Unable to escape his body, he creates an illusion of protection against the outside world by transforming his personality.]

From civilian to soldier to convalescent patient during the war, to agent in a colonial forestry company after it; from flea-counter, casual tourist and illegal immigrant in New York to factory worker in Detroit; from doctor in Paris to stage extra in the Tarapout music hall to tourist again in Toulouse and eventually to asylum manager at Vigny, Bardamu embodies his author's propensity for change and provides a vehicle for the rich protean experimentation of *Voyage*.[21] It is not for nothing that Claude Lévi-Strauss wrote of *Voyage*, 'on se demande parfois, lisant un paragraphe, si c'est bien le même homme...' [you ask yourself sometimes, reading a paragraph, if it could be the same man...].[22] '[Céline] a commencé à suggérer,' writes Henri Godard, 'qu'en tout homme il y a plusieurs voix qui dialoguent' [Céline began to suggest that inside every man there are several voices engaged in dialogue].[23] Indeed, Elizabeth Craig recalled Céline's voice changing as he read *Voyage* in progress, as if there were several distinct personalities inside him, a Céline who became his characters.[24] The second half of this chapter will examine some of the chief aspects of the transformation of self taking place in *Voyage*.

6.2 THE PROTEAN SELF

Towards the Protean [25]

'One self per novel is not enough for Céline,' writes Patrick McCarthy, 'he splits himself up.'[26] This series of selves, beginning with *Voyage*, represents the discontinuous nature of the traumatic self.[27] As Erik H. Erikson wrote of his work with soldiers suffering from war neurosis:

> What impressed me most was the loss in these men of a sense of identity. They knew who they were; they had a personal identity. But it was as if, subjectively, their lives no longer hung together — and never would again. There was a central disturbance of what I [...] started to call ego identity. [...] This sense of identity provides the ability to experience one's self as something that has continuity and sameness, and to act accordingly.[28]

Indeed, the episodic nature of *Voyage* represents this sense of a self not 'hanging together'. Its reiterated 'falls from narrative' symbolise, in Robert Jay Lifton's words, 'radical discontinuities in life story',[29] the reiterated breaching of the narrative of self. Each return to narrative signals a renewed attempt to restore self. In this way, narrative in *Voyage* embodies at one and the same time the rift made by the trauma of war in the self-process and the ongoing effort to create a viable, unified self.

Lifton has characterised the self as 'a symbol of one's organism'.[30] For Céline, the experience of the war destroyed this symbol in its heroic guise. The protean self, as it moves towards 'many possibilities', is dependent, Lifton says, 'upon the existence of relatively established corners of the self'.[31] It is Céline's need to build on these 'established corners' which creates an autobiographical setting for his tale. It is his use of fiction as a vehicle for the protean which makes of *Voyage* a pseudo-autobiography, or a 'protean' one, an autobiography broad enough to encompass the transforming potential of fiction, to encompass different levels of identity, of 'je' [I]. In *Voyage*, the most striking result of this interaction of fiction and autobiography is, of course, one of the novel's foremost examples of duality: the transformation of the hero, Destouches, into the coward, Bardamu.

The Self as Coward and Deserter

Céline's mocking self-depiction as the coward Bardamu is one of his most potent protean symbols. As Robert Jay Lifton writes:

> Mockery and self-mockery, irony, absurdity, and humour enable the protean self to 'lubricate' its experiences and to express the absence of 'fit' between the way the world presents itself and the way one actually feels about it.[32]

The transition from hero to coward is a perfect example of this process of 'lubrication' at work. Bardamu's cowardice implies a sustained mocking of Destouches' failed heroism. More than any other transformation it emphasises the debasement of the hero.

The coward in *Voyage* is a complex creation. On one level it is an expression of the war's debasement of the hero, a metaphor for the Great War transition from heroic to debased consciousness. As well, however, as recognising that the Great War had turned aspiring heroes into cowards, Céline followed Alain in recognising how fear of cowardice could make men fight, and so sustain war. His self-portrait as coward in *Voyage* springs too from this perception and so he makes cowardice the emblem of his anti-war statement. It is his adoption *in extremis* of a stance of 'pacifisme à outrance: LÂCHETÉ !' [pacifism taken to extremes: COWARDICE !] (see 1.4 *Cowardice, Desertion and Mutiny*).

To depict oneself as coward and deserter is perhaps the greatest insult the debased, ironic self can offer to its former heroic self. 'Serais-je donc le seul lâche sur la terre ?' [Could I be the only coward on the face of the earth?], asks Bardamu (RI, 13). Inversion functions as a form of dissent, a means of distancing oneself from the absurdity of the war. 'Dans une histoire pareille, il n'y a rien à faire, il n'y a qu'à foutre le camp' [In a situation like this, there is nothing to do, except to get the hell out of it], says Bardamu (RI, 12). It also ridicules the heroic self. Bardamu, 'qui ne voyais pas du tout pourquoi je l'aurais été brave' [who could not see at all any reason to be brave] (RI, 23), views the war unheroically from 'derrière un arbre' [behind a tree] (RI, 12) having acquired enough practical sense 'pour être lâche définitivement' [to be a coward for good] (RI, 36). Cowardice, however, does not help him to escape the war. His attempt to desert also turns to ridicule. Ironically, coward and hero exit the war via the same route, a wound, reduced almost to silence in Céline's fictional memory.

Céline's coward faces towards both private and public memory. If cowardice is an affront to Céline's own war past, it is also an affront to a public memory based on the myth of the war experience. Bardamu's cowardice is a direct challenge to the myth's exaltation of heroism and as such undermines the solemnity and reverence of collective memory. Indeed, the coward undermines not just heroism but also the myth's other values. Cowardice directly challenges the notions of patriotism and sacrifice. It negates camaraderie. Bardamu's anti-war speech culminating in his poignant 'je ne veux plus mourir' [I don't want to die anymore] functions within *Voyage* as a coward's charter (RI, 65). Lola's 'c'est impossible de refuser la guerre' [it's impossible to say no to war] represents the combined weight of history, collective memory and public opinion supporting the heroic ideal and the monolithic war myth. Her 'il n'y a que les fous et les lâches qui refusent la guerre' [only madmen and cowards say no to war] is the expression of an implacable public will to war and also provides a *raison d'être* for Bardamu's double depiction as coward and unbalanced.

Céline's role as 'noircisseur' [blackener] is seen in this context as a critical aspect of his own memory work.[33] Céline takes charge personally of his own sense of debasement and heightens it through the development of a literature made of the very stuff of debasement. The choice of oral language can be seen as a debased tongue reflecting the debasement of its protagonist, just as the recurrent underground motif provides an appropriate *topos* of debasement. When Bardamu asks, 'pourquoi n'y aurait-il pas autant d'art possible dans la laideur que dans la beauté ?' [why shouldn't there be as much art in ugliness as in beauty?], he acknowledges his own debasement as his artistic material (RI, 78). His affirmation, 'c'est un genre à cultiver' [it's a genre to be cultivated], expresses Céline's commitment to making literature from debasement.

In this light, Céline's self-portrayal as coward can be seen as a symbol of his art. It is too the appropriate symbol of his own private memory of the Great War, one which captures the transition from heroic to debased self which takes place at Hazebrouck (see 4.1 *Shock*). And, in so far as it represents the breakdown and failure of the myth of the war experience to mediate the trauma of the war, it is a symbol of a collective memory of debasement. Seamus Deane has described the great novel as one which 'marks a connection between the consciousness of the individual and the condition of the nation'.[34] One measure of *Voyage*'s greatness is the way in which the private symbol of Céline's debasement also symbolises the debasement of his people and of his nation, France.

The self as coward is a primary aspect of the protean transformation of Destouches. It is a flagrant contradiction of the heroic self; yet, if we remember Robert Lifton's view that the protean is built upon 'established corners of the self', we can at the very least assume that Céline's self-portrait as coward is built on the discovery of the very real possibility of cowardice within himself. Here, however, there is room for more than assumption. We have seen Céline's own self-lacerating accusation of cowardice recalled by Edith Follet (see 4.1 *Silence*). We have seen too the emergence of fear at Spincourt (3.3 *Flanders*), and Hazebrouck (4.1 *Shock*). Céline's self-portrayal as coward and deserter, however, reaches right back prior to his war experience and is part of his return to 'l'univers de ses vingt ans' [his universe at twenty years of age] to save 'les promesses non-tenues du passé' [the unkept promises of the past] (see 5.1 *Traumatic Memory*).

As we have seen, Destouches' pre-war *Carnets* reveal his desire to desert the army (see 3.2 *Desertion*). This desire, springing from his pre-war self, becomes the starting point in *Voyage* for the recreation of the hero, Destouches, as the coward, Bardamu. Céline's traumatic narrative of his past connects to the one possibility that might redeem the redundant hero, Destouches: cowardice. In this way Céline acknowledges belatedly the possibilities that lay within the heroic self. He seizes on an aspect of self which, prior to the war, acted against his own latent heroism, against the army and its values, society and its values, in short, against war and against death. Cowardice is the emblem of Destouches's debasement, but it is too a pre-existing fragment of self. Rescued from the disaster of his past, it is the founding stone on which he rewrites self and on which he builds his protest.

Here, once again, we must remind ourselves that Céline's memory is two-sided and that his protestation of cowardice announces both his dissent from past and from future war.

Robinson: The Broken Self

Céline's self-portrait as coward belatedly acknowledges his own duality, and reverses the medal to show the underside of the hero. As we have seen, *Voyage* is invested with duality (4.3 *Duality*). Without duality, Céline cannot image forth a broken world nor practise the reversals which signal his own inner divisions. This sense of divided self is perhaps the most powerful force operating within *Voyage*'s circle of self. The sense of fracture is very deep.

In trauma, as we have seen, the self begins to break down (see 1.4 *Shell-shock*). According to Louis Crocq:

> Beaucoup de personnes traumatisées relatent avoir vécu, au moment du surgissement du trauma et dans les moments qui ont suivi, le sentiment bizarre de ne plus reconnaître le monde comme familier, ni même réel. [...] Elles avaient l'impression d'êtres autres [...] de vivre un rêve ou un cauchemar [...] une sensation de monde et de moment factices [...]. Cette déréalisation et cette dépersonnalisation [...] on les retrouverait [...] dans tout vécu traumatique. [...] Le changement de personnalité [...] semble bien s'initier [...] au moment même du surgissement du trauma.[35]

> [Many traumatised persons tell of having experienced, at the moment in which the trauma occurred and in the moments following it, the bizarre feeling of no longer recognising the world as familiar, or even real. [...] They had the impression of being other than themselves [...] of living a dream or a nightmare [...] a sensation that the world and the moment were artificial. This derealisation and this depersonalisation [...] are found in every experience of trauma. [...] The change of personality [...] seems to begin [...] in the very moment when the trauma occurs.]

Those who were most vulnerable to this disruption of self were younger men. It has been noted that 'young people whose personalities are in the process of maturation but not yet "set" at the time of the trauma and who return to an unstable home environment, suffer most.'[36] Men like cuirassier Céline aged twenty, whose war would continue for four years after his evacuation from the battlefield.

The more extreme the trauma the more extreme the consequences to the self. Writes Robert Lifton, 'extreme trauma creates a second self. [...] Recovery from posttraumatic effects [...] cannot really occur until that traumatised self is reintegrated.'[37] This makes the self-process fundamental to *Voyage*. *Voyage* becomes the site of return where Céline seeks to repair the damage done to self in the Great War.

The second self which emerges in traumatic experience can be a protective one, which suffers in place of the first. As such the second self embodies those experiences or qualities that the first cannot successfully integrate. In *Voyage*, Robinson fulfils this role. He is, of course, a literary construct, or metaphor, but just as the loss of memory exemplified in *Voyage*'s silences is a metaphor built on a very real sense of memory and identity loss incurred at Hazebrouck, so Robinson has emerged from Céline's real sense of being *other* since the war, a breakdown in personality found, as Louis Crocq has told us, 'dans tout vécu traumatique' [in every experience of trauma].

From the start of *Voyage* to its culmination the destinies of Bardamu and Robinson are intertwined. Their relationship begins in wartime, and fills a void in comradeship deeply felt by Bardamu. 'J'en aurais fait mon frère peureux de ce garçon-là !' [I would have made my brother in fear of that young man], Bardamu has already said of the 'agent de la liaison'. 'Mais on n'avait pas le temps de fraterniser [...]' [but we didn't have the time to fraternise] (RI, 14). The more Bardamu is isolated from his comrades, the greater his need to be 'à deux' [as two]. 'À deux on y arrive mieux que tout seul' [as two you manage better than when all alone], he later says (RI, 15). Alone in the night time, on a dangerous reconnaissance mission, this desire is realised when he meets Robinson on his way to surrender to the Germans. Robinson appears as the underside of Bardamu, voicing Bardamu's own inner thoughts and emotions. 'Il cachait rien' [he concealed nothing], Bardamu says (RI, 41). Together they attempt to desert, but fail miserably. Their problem is simply being who they are. The two engage in self-transforming fantasy, 'si seulement t'avais été un Allemand toi [...] tu m'aurais fais prisonnier' [if only you had been a German [...] you would have taken me prisoner], complains Robinson bitterly (RI, 45–46). The desire for transformation of self, however, is not so easily realised. 'On a du mal à se débarrasser de soi-même en guerre !' [it's not at all easy to rid oneself of oneself in wartime!], Robinson adds.

Bardamu and Robinson lead parallel lives. They meet in the war, in Paris, in Africa, America, Rancy and Toulouse. They even share the attractions of the same woman, Madelon, and eventually find refuge together in Baryton's asylum at Vigny. Although at first Bardamu likes Robinson, 'je ne pouvais m'empêcher d'avoir un peu confiance en lui' [I couldn't help trusting him], he says (RI, 41) and later seeks him in Africa (RI, 176) and America (RI, 199), the relationship between the two becomes an adversarial one. This happens after Bardamu has established himself as a doctor at Rancy. Robinson's return signals a collapse back into Bardamu's traumatised self. 'Avec sa gueule toute barbouillée de peine, ça me faisait comme un sale rêve qu'il me ramenait et dont je n'arrivais pas à me délivrer depuis trop d'années déjà' [With his face all daubed with suffering, I felt he was returning to me with a bad dream I had been trying to escape from for far too many years already] (RI, 270).[38] Bardamu is even afraid to leave home in case he will meet Robinson (RI, 271).

Une espèce de scène brutale à moi-même

The passage that follows makes explicit the theme of confrontation with self. Bardamu is called to tend a sick child. In the course of his examination the child becomes agitated, 'il en eut assez l'enfant de mes doigts tripoteurs et de mes manœuvres et se mit à hurler' [he had had enough of my manoeuvres and of my dabbling fingers and he began to howl] (RI, 273). The child's agitation provokes a strange reaction from Bardamu, a reaction he relates to Robinson. 'Depuis le retour de Robinson, je me trouvais devenu bien étrange dans ma tête et mon corps et les cris de ce petit innocent me firent une impression abominable' [Since the return of Robinson, I had been feeling strange in my head and in my body and the cries of this little innocent made an abominable impression on me] (RI, 273). Bardamu launches on a violent tirade. Astonished, the child's parents rescue him from Bardamu's arms and Bardamu is shown the door.

In this scene, Robinson is the real cause of Bardamu's unease. He is also the object of Bardamu's tirade:

> J'avais espéré me délivrer par un état de franchise, trouver dans le scandale volontaire la résolution de ne plus le recevoir celui-là, en me faisant une espèce de scène brutale à moi-même. (RI, 274)
>
> [I had hoped to free myself through my frankness, to find in voluntary scandal the determination never to receive him again, by making a sort of ugly scene intended for myself.]

Here, in the absence of Robinson, Bardamu takes his place, and identifies himself not just *with*, but *as* Robinson: 'moi-même' [myself]. Bardamu's tirade is presented as an effort to rid himself of Robinson in his own person. The scene marks the interdependence of the two characters and clearly unites them within the same, if dual, order of self. Bardamu's disquiet, 'c'était la pagaïe dans mon esprit' [my mind was a shambles], he says (RI, 271), is directly related to the existence of his double, and his future peace of mind depends on ridding himself of Robinson.

Bardamu's tirade fails and Robinson remains at Rancy. Bardamu's attitude to him is ambiguous, secretly wanting to get rid of him but also fascinated by his machinations to kill 'la mère Henrouille' [grandmother Henrouille]. Bardamu feels both implicated in and complicit with Robinson's actions. 'Je me sentais coupable quand même,' he says. 'J'étais surtout coupable de désirer au fond que tout ça continue' [I felt guilty all the same. I was guilty in particular of deep down wanting it all to continue] (RI, 331). When Robinson's murderous enterprise disastrously fails, leaving him blind, Bardamu tends him and keeps him company. Later, the result of a shabby monetary transaction, he rids himself of Robinson, packing him off to Toulouse (RI, 344). However, Bardamu's expectation that this will improve his own state of mind is not realised (RI, 345). Eventually, he follows Robinson to Toulouse:

> Aller à Toulouse c'était en somme encore une sottise. […] Mais à suivre Robinson comme ça, parmi ses aventures, j'avais pris du goût pour les machins louches. À New York déjà quand j'en pouvais plus dormir ça avait commencé à me tracasser de savoir si je pouvais pas accompagner plus loin encore, et plus loin, Robinson. (RI, 381)

> [Going to Toulouse was a further stupidity. […] But following Robinson like that, on his adventures, I had developed a taste for shady business. Already in New York, when I couldn't sleep, it really bothered me to know if I'd be able to follow him still further, and further still, Robinson.]

This pursuit of Robinson, the ongoing confrontation with self, eventually leads Bardamu towards death.

The Death of Robinson

It is Bardamu who provokes Robinson's death. 'C'est à cause de moi qu'on s'est reparlé' [It was my fault that we began talking again], he says (RI, 487). The words he has initiated lead directly to Robinson's murder. As Bardamu's double dies, Bardamu measures himself against death and discovers his own lack of death mastery. 'J'étais pas grand comme la mort moi. J'étais bien plus petit' [I was not big like death. I was much smaller] (RI, 496–497). On the other hand, in death, Robinson achieves his apotheosis. By dying, he assumes mastery over death, unlike Bardamu, 'c'était pas à envisager que je parvienne jamais moi, comme Robinson, à me remplir la tête avec une seule idée, mais alors une superbe pensée tout à fait plus forte que la mort' [I couldn't envisage that I would ever manage, like Robinson had, to fill my head with just one idea, but a truly superb one altogether stronger than death] (RI, 501). Robinson's death mastery redeems him and restores him to hero status, 'c'était comme s'il essayait de nous aider à vivre à présent nous autres' [it was as if he was trying now to help the rest of us to live] (RI, 497). Try as he might, Bardamu cannot find what he is seeking, 'une entière idée de courage' [an entire idea of courage] (RI, 501), in the face of death. Redemption of the self through the conquest of death, through dying, remains impossible for him. Separated at last from his double, Bardamu struggles down towards the Seine, towards that singular vision of an end to the war (see 1.3 *The Trenches*).

Double Trouble

Bardamu and Robinson had precedents. Famous literary doubles already existed in the work of Dostoevsky, Maupassant, Stevenson, Wilde, and many others. Otto Rank's celebrated psychoanalytical study of the double appeared a short number of years before *Voyage*. Rank traced the double motif to its origins in folk belief that the immortal soul was contained in the shadow or mirror image of the individual. Loss of either shadow or image meant a loss of the immortal self. This belief makes the figure of Robinson the clearest indication within *Voyage* that Bardamu's quest, his pursuit of Robinson, is ultimately one to recover his immortality.

For Rank, the double in literature assumes a clear 'death meaning' and confrontation with the double is confrontation with the death of the self. Rank enumerated the characteristics of the classic literary double:

> We always find a likeness which resembles the main character down to the smallest particulars [...]. This double works at cross-purposes with its prototype; and, as a rule, the catastrophe occurs in the relationship with a

woman, predominantly ending in suicide by way of the death intended for the irksome persecutor. In a number of instances this situation is combined with a thoroughgoing persecutory delusion [...] assuming the picture of a total paranoiac system of delusions.[39]

Rank also looks beyond the creation to the creator. Turning his attention to the 'identical psychic structure' of those authors who have created doubles, Rank finds that they were 'decidedly pathological personalities [...]. They suffered — and obviously so — from psychic disturbances or neurological and mental illnesses.'[40]

This suggests that Robinson, as *literary invention*, offers evidence of mental trauma in Céline. For Rank, the root of this trauma lies in a narcissistic relation to self. Of Wilde's *Dorian Gray* he writes, 'fear and hate with respect to the double-self are closely connected with the narcissistic love for it and with the resistance of this love.'[41] Rank's conclusion, in effect, is that the self is in love with itself and cannot contemplate its own demise. The double, therefore, is a form of surrogate who dies on the protagonist's behalf. Rank traces the narcissistic attachment to self back to childhood experience and the relationship with the mother. We can here, however, recognise the propensity in psychoanalysis, recognised by Robert Jay Lifton, to assign trauma to theoretical complexes associated with childhood (see Introduction, *The Contours of Trauma*).

Nowhere in *Voyage* is its essential duality more explicit than in the figure of the double. In creating Robinson, Céline acknowledges the effects of war on self. Moreover, he creates space in which the dissociative experience of war can be explored and in which the debased self can be confronted. The whole of *Voyage* can be seen as the enactment of that 'espèce de scène brutale à moi-même' [sort of ugly scene intended for myself] which confronts Bardamu with his self. This 'ugly scene' is enacted primarily on the level of memory. It represents Céline's violent effort to exorcise his past, to transcend the return of trauma and escape the persistence of his debased, death-imprinted, war-divided self.

The Self as Voyager

The war made home intolerable. 'I hated England,' Vera Brittain wrote of wartime England, from which she escaped to war work in France.[42] Paul Fussell traced this change in attitude to home as a result of the war. To its writers, says Fussell, post-war England seemed decayed and paralysed.[43] We can readily imagine that something of the same feeling drove Céline away from France to England and to Africa during the war and remained at the root of his restlessness after the war.[44] Céline himself foretold it; the war would displace people and turn them into wanderers. Writing to Simone Saintu in 1916 he predicted, 'les "errants" qu'aura causé la guerre seront nombreux' [the 'wanderers' caused by this war will be many].[45] He himself would provide living proof of this, and it is no surprise that *Voyage* retails a seemingly endless series of movements with Place Clichy at its core and Africa and America at its furthest reaches.

The voyager self in *Voyage* has three main aspects, all of which reflect debasement: refugee, exile, and immigrant. Together they confer Bardamu with *picaro* status and add the picaresque to *Voyage*'s already protean range of styles. The picaresque reflects the experience of the self at a remove from any stable centre, a world experiencing fragmentation and dispersal. This portrait of the self as *picaro* places *Voyage* at the nexus of a twentieth-century experience of war-generated movements and migrations beginning with the Great War.

Through travel, Bardamu seeks to reconstitute a habitable self. Stasis of self has become associated with stasis of place and transformation is sought through movement, 'se chambarder d'un flanc sur l'autre, c'est tout ce qu'on peut faire et tout ce qu'on a trouvé comme défense contre son Destin' [shifting from one place to another is all we can do and the only thing we've come up with to protect us from our Destiny] (RI, 346). The self, however, remains static and inescapable, 'faut pas espérer laisser sa peine nulle part en route' [mustn't expect to leave one's suffering behind anywhere on the journey] (RI, 346). The traumatised self remains a condition of mind and body and can only be forgotten in the dissolution of these latter. The transcendence or forgetting of self implicit in Bardamu's desire to 'sortir de soi-même' [get out of oneself] is achieved ultimately, not through movement from place to place, but through his experience of delirium.

Sex Tourism

In *Voyage*, it is Lola who first inspires Bardamu with the desire to travel.[46] 'Je reçus ainsi tout près du derrière de Lola le message d'un nouveau monde' [I received the message of a new world direct from Lola's bottom], he tells us (RI, 54). The perfect appeal of her body is easily understood in an ex-soldier whose experience of war has been one of bodily fragmentation. Lola's body becomes a site of discovery, a foreign land, foreign to self, offering infinite possibilities for travel. 'Son corps était pour moi une joie qui n'en finissait pas. Je n'en avais jamais assez de le parcourir ce corps [...]' [Her body was a constant joy to me. I never tired of journeying around it [...]] (RI, 53). Travel, in *Voyage*, is configured as a journey out of time, out of self, out of the world. Like sex, it provides an entry into the eternal and as such is death-mastering.[47] This wish is what lies behind Bardamu's hunger-sharpened, quinine-fuelled ecstasy at the sight of New York's midinettes. 'Je touchais au vif de mon pèlerinage' [I had reached the heart of my pilgrimage], he utters (RI, 193). Bardamu is ready to leave self behind, 's'il était possible de sortir de sa peau j'en serais sorti juste à ce moment-là, une fois pour toutes' [if it was possible to leave one's body, I would have left mine, just at that very moment, once and for all] (RI, 194). Female wholeness opens a gateway to 'le monde du Rêve' [the world of Dream] (RI, 194) where the broken male self is forgotten.

One of *Voyage*'s most beautiful images unites the dream of sexual transcendence with the concept of travel. When Bardamu describes Sophie as 'Trois-mâts d'allégresse tendre, en route pour l'Infini' [a three-master of tender sweetness, en route for the Infinite] (RI, 473) her body is presented, like Lola's, as a death-mastering excursion into the eternal. In the 'New World', however, this dream is destined for disappointment as women prove in general inaccessible or destined only for the rich (RI, 200). Bardamu's time in America becomes an odyssey of sexual loneliness, alleviated only by masturbation, the cinema, and the company of a prostitute, Molly. Nor does love offer the transformation of self Bardamu seeks and so he must remain on the move, a debased, 'homeless' Eros. 'J'aimais encore mieux mon vice,' he says, 'cette envie de m'enfuir de partout, à la recherche de je ne sais quoi' [I loved my vice even better, that desire to flee from everywhere, looking for I don't know what] (RI, 229). But he does know what he is looking for and as he leaves Molly he says exactly what it is, 'le plus grand chagrin possible pour devenir soi-même avant de mourir' [the greatest sadness possible so as become oneself before dying] (RI, 236).

Baryton Voyager

If Bardamu's journey offers Céline an opportunity to ironise the popular escapist and exotic literature of the 1920s, Baryton allows him to satirise the burgeoning culture of twentieth-century tourism and its search for the protean. 'Nos récits de voyages l'enchantaient' [our travel stories enchanted him], says Bardamu (RI, 416). Baryton's protean transformation begins with his English language lessons. 'Après huit mois de progrès assez anormaux, il était presque parvenu à se reconstituer entièrement sur le plan anglo-saxon' [after eight months of quite abnormal progress, he had managed to reconstitute himself almost entirely on the Anglo-saxon model] (RI, 434). He becomes strangely other. 'En vérité Baryton n'était plus du tout lui-même' [To tell the truth, Baryton was no longer himself] (RI, 436). The prospect of transforming his self fills Baryton, like a soldier leaving for war in search of heroic death mastery, with enthusiasm. 'Je vais renaître Ferdinand ! Tout simplement ! Je pars !' [I am going to be reborn, Ferdinand! Quite simply! I'm leaving!], he announces (RI, 438). This rebirth involves discarding the self that has trammelled him:

> Je veux, Ferdinand, essayer d'aller me perdre l'âme comme on va perdre son chien galeux, son chien qui pue, bien loin, le compagnon qui vous dégoûte, avant de mourir... Enfin bien seul... Tranquille... soi-même...
> (RI, 439)
>
> [I want, Ferdinand, to try to leave to lose my soul as one leaves to lose one's lousy dog, one's stinking dog, far, far away, like the companion who disgusts you, before dying... Finally, all alone...calm... oneself...]

Travel becomes a means to the ideal self. However, Baryton, the tourist, is left with no more substance than the various postcards that arrive from Finland and other places. The tourist self stands condemned as picturesque, trite and futile. The search for the ideal self is mocked.

Displaced Persons

The influence of travel literature is discernible in all of Céline's novels, writes Andrea Loselle.[48] She notes Paul Morand as a particular influence. Almost always, however, travel in Céline takes place against a backdrop of war. In *Voyage*, the movement of individuals and of groups is characterised as 'leur déroute' [their rout] (RI, 435). 'On dirait à les voir tous s'enfuir de ce côté-là, qu'il leur est arrivé une catastrophe du côté d'Argenteuil, que c'est leur pays qui brûle' [You would think to see them fleeing like that from over there, that some catastrophe had taken place in Argenteuil, that their world was on fire], observes Bardamu of the hordes filling Rancy's trams and métro (RI, 239). War's reverberations echo loudly in *Voyage*'s various modes of transport. The *Amiral Bragueton* is flotsam of war hovering above the equator. In New York, the elevated metro rattles past Bardamu's hotel window like a shell (RI, 198). In this way, *Voyage* recalls the modern world's first mass movements of soldiers and civilians using mechanised transport at the outbreak of world war in 1914. Escaped from the war, Bardamu's flight to distant continents also acts as an ironic commentary on one of the origins of twentieth-century tourism: battlefield tourism. The first Michelin travel guides were, indeed, guides to the battlefields of northern France.[49] Bardamu, of course, is travelling in the opposite direction.

The Self as Storyteller

The storyteller self is the one which most unites Céline and Bardamu. Both tell stories and both use stories to ensure survival. This self is closely related to another protean transformation: the theatrical self. The two are present in *Voyage* when Bardamu, inspired by Branledore, invents heroic tales to entertain staff and visitors. The stories he invents are complemented by the theatrical *mise en scène* of his own heroic impersonations. Later, he is forced to reprise this role-play to save his skin aboard the *Amiral Bragueton*. In both cases, Bardamu's stories are necessary to ward off death. That is, the self as victim lurks within Bardamu's storytelling self who offers protection from the outside world and its dangers.

Throughout *Voyage*, Bardamu spins tales, beginning with his excursion to St.Cloud accompanied by Lola, where he imagines the time before the war for her, conjuring up events that no longer exist and which he has never seen, a past from which he is doubly exiled (RI, 56). He is not, however, the only storyteller. Musyne, Branledore and Robinson all join him so that the novel teems with stories transacted for advantage or, as we have seen, for life itself. The storytelling self is the most protean of all possible selves. The very essence of story is its protean quality and *Voyage* itself as traumatic narrative of a traumatic past is built on the inherently transforming possibilities of story (see 5.1 *From One Narrative to Another*).

The 'je' [I] of *Voyage* is the origin of the story of *Voyage*. The story told by this 'je' gives rise to all the other storytellers and stories which populate the novel. Protean Céline contained all his characters, surging from the void where once the heroic self had been. What Northrop Frye called the 'existential fallacy' seems unusually marked in Céline. He slips in and out of characters, his own and other people's, real or fictional, starting with Semmelweiss, continuing with Bardamu, and Robinson, fitting them on like so many suits (see 4.1 *Semmelweiss*).[50] Ironically, this writer, driven in search of the ideal story and the ideal storytelling self, is also the one who ultimately seems most rooted in a self defined by trauma, anguish and stasis. But then this, of course, is the *sine qua non* of the protean in Céline.

The Self as Doctor

In his first interviews, Céline was at pains to present himself to the world as a doctor. He was interviewed more often than not in his Clichy clinic. The symbolism was clear: the author of *Voyage* heals. The object of his healing power was also clear: the ordinary man, the poor. 'C'est ici, dans ce dispensaire, qu'on pratique la vraie médecine, avec les pauvres, les travailleurs !' [It is here, in this dispensary, that real medicine is practised, with the poor, the workers!], he told one journalist.[51] The manipulation of his image may be disingenuous but it is not gratuitous. Nor is the presentation of Bardamu in the first lines of *Voyage* as 'un carabin' [a medical student] (RI, 7). The first half of *Voyage* is the story of an essential trauma, the loss of heroic immortality and a protean effort to escape stasis and recover the ideal state of death mastery. The second half of the novel is dominated by Bardamu's medical practice in the impoverished Parisian suburb of Rancy. The focus is now as much on his efforts to heal the world as on his effort to heal self.

Doctor Bardamu lives in a world which resists healing. Despised because he is poor, his clients call on him as a last resort. When not openly hostile to him, they refuse his advice, resist his healing. A young woman bleeds to death while her parents refuse Bardamu's urging to get her to hospital (RI, 259–263). Another woman suffers through her husband's inertia (RI, 300–304). The whole of Bardamu's medical career is marked by futility and helplessness, 'moi j'étais bien déçu par tout ce qui était arrivé [...] et bien fatigué en plus' [me, I was so disappointed with all that had happened [...] and so tired to boot] (RI, 304). In his room he listens as a young girl's parents torture her. He can do nothing, 'je ne pouvais rien faire' [I could do nothing] (RI, 267). His attempts to find a vaccine to save Bébert end in failure (RI, 276–291). Bébert's death epitomises the scale of medical failure in a world where even the innocence and hope of childhood is condemned to death. This is a world where healing is impossible. And yet the effort to heal, in the face of futility and the wilful malevolence of his clientele, underpins Bardamu's practice as it underpins Céline's intention throughout *Voyage*.[52]

Voyage, as we have seen, is Céline's effort to heal his trauma of memory. This effort involves return to the past and the creation of a new narrative of that past. First and foremost, this new narrative involves the application of a particular kind of medicine prescribed by Pierre Janet. Janet saw the problem of healing the trauma of the past as a problem of language and of the story we tell of the past. In the image of Janet then, Céline creates a story which he represents as part of his own personal history, 'une espèce de scène brutale à moi-même' [a sort of ugly scene intended for myself]. More significantly, however, he creates the new language Janet's treatment demands. Janet's prescription sounds a clear appeal to the protean and nothing more clearly denotes the protean in Céline than his breach with previous language to create a language all of his own (5.1 *Traumatic Memory*).

Janet's renewal of language was intended to rectify the past and in so doing heal the present. But Céline, in *Voyage*, has other 'medical' means at his disposal to produce health. Chiefly, he has dreams. This is not surprising as dreams were at the very origin of medicine. In the world's first hospital, the Asklepion on the Greek island of Kos, there was a special room where patients would spend the night. There, they were visited in their dreams by the God of Medicine, Asclepius. The dreams he brought had the power to heal them.[53]

Dreams have remained part of medicine. In the Middle Ages, doctors also used dreams to cure their patients.[54] In the modern age, psychoanalysis draws on dreams to understand and to treat the trauma of patients. If Freud at first understood dream as a form of wish-fulfilment, his work with shell-shocked soldiers of the Great War led him towards a new understanding of dreams. The soldiers' recurrent nightmares were so terrible they could not be seen as wish fulfilment. In his essay, 'Beyond the Pleasure Principle', Freud developed his original theory of dreams and suggested that the nightmares of traumatised soldiers represented an ongoing effort to master a traumatic experience.[55]

Céline gave one of the keys to *Voyage* when he told Léon Daudet, 'j'écris dans la formule *rêve éveillé*' [I write in the *waking dream* style]. *Voyage* as 'rêve éveillé' becomes a dream whose root is the death encounter (see 4.2 *The Nightmare of Memory*). It represents the recurring nightmare Céline or Bardamu, the veteran soldier, suffers from, while also acting as a metaphor for the recurring nightmare of war his society suffers from.[56] It is, in Freudian, terms an effort to master past trauma. It is too an effort to uncover meaning. 'The dream is the gateway to the meaning of our prehistoric past on which our sense of continuity and the totality of history depends,' affirms Laurens Van Der Post.[57] By recording his dreams and fantasies Céline hopes to find the meaning that underlies his troubled world and self. 'History is nothing' if not illuminated by dream, writes Van Der Post, and it is recognition of this truth which pulls Céline beyond causes and consequences, away from what happened towards the meaning of what happened. Through the dream that is *Voyage*, he offers that meaning to the world around him in a language accessible to all. The dream itself becomes the doctor's means to healing and Céline offers it to French society of the inter-war years as medicine, just as he uses it to heal himself.

Story, language and dream are all part of Céline's literary medicine. Their constituent parts, however, also have the power to heal. Oral storytelling was primarily the retelling of myth, and myth was played out against ritual as it is in *Voyage*. Paul Connerton describes myth as differing from ritual in that it is open to reinterpretation, to possibility.[58] Myth is, therefore, intrinsically protean. Céline uses his oral style to invoke the possibility of myth. He uses myth, in a dynamic relation to static ritual, for its healing protean value, but also in obedience to Janet's command to appropriate story and make it his own. Drawing on the myths of Er, Eros, Proteus, Sisyphus and Orpheus, among others, Céline employs the most powerful stories known to humankind. He uses the strongest medicine.[59]

When it comes to language, Céline is equally assiduous. 'Tout cela est danse et musique' [it is all dance and music], he told his translator, John Marks.[60] Renewing the French language, Céline invests it with the healing, energising properties of music and dance. He becomes a witchdoctor dancing in circles, moving to his own internal rhythms and song, and using the repetitions of his language to provide ritual incantations directed at the world around him. Céline is as primitive as he is modern in his desire to heal.[61]

The world, however, remains against him. As a doctor Bardamu is dominated by a sense of futility — and so is Céline. Despite the powerful remedies united in *Voyage* the possibility of healing a world abandoned to death remains remote. In a world which remains unable to re-enter immortalising heroic myth, and which remains threatened by new war, the protean effort to escape the stasis of memory and restore the ideal heroic self must continue.

The Quest for Gold

'The novel tells of the adventure of interiority,' writes György Lukács. 'The content of the novel is the story of the soul that goes to find itself.'[62] The novel, says Lukács, is a journey to 'clear self-recognition' towards attainment of an 'ideal' which 'irradiates the individual's life as its immanent meaning'.[63] It is this search which takes Bardamu from the battlefields of Flanders to Africa, New

York and back to Paris. On three occasions, in Paris, New York and finally in Toulouse, Bardamu descends into underground caverns. These descents are also part of *Voyage*'s store of myth. In this case a myth is evoked which directly allows Céline to mediate his experience of death and survival. Bardamu's descents recall the journey of the poet and musician Orpheus to Hades to rescue Eurydice.

Bardamu's descents have a further significance. Pluto was the God of the Underworld and of the dead. But Pluto was also the God of treasure, traditionally buried deep in the earth.[64] According to Northrop Frye, the quest in literature is, commonly, a treasure hunt.[65] Bardamu's quest then is a search for treasure.[66] This treasure is gold, the gold he has lost in wartime, the ideal state of heroic immortality, the perfect self. Significantly, Bardamu's underground caverns yield only dead meat, silent corpses and excrement. The only real gold in *Voyage* is hidden away in banks to where it has been spirited away in the course of the war (see 1.2 *Gold*).

The search for gold leads us to the origin of much of the symbolic content of *Voyage*: alchemy. Alchemy was Céline's own term for his artistic creation.[67] The aim of alchemy was the transformation of base metal into gold. Serious alchemists, however, sought the 'philosophical gold' of psychic transformation.[68] Céline's aim is to transform the debased self into the heroic, immortal golden self. *Voyage* is the process.[69]

Female Céline

Who was Céline? The pseudonym connects him positively with his mother's family, making it an affirmation of his former self. It links him particularly to his grandmother, Céline Guillou. His portrait of 'la mère Henrouille' is undoubtedly a homage to his grandmother. 'Ce regard allègre animait tout alentour, dans l'ombre, d'une joie jeunette, d'un entrain minime mais pur comme nous n'en avons plus à notre disposition' [that bright look enlivened all around her, in the shadows, with a youthful happiness, with a scant but pure energy, such as we no longer have among us] (RI, 254). Indomitable, she resists death. Belonging to Céline's golden age, prior to Great War debasement, Céline's choice of his grandmother's name represents an intense desire to confer himself with the immortalising qualities of that age.

The pen name, however, is typically protean. Perhaps most notably it is a woman's name. It lends Céline a bi-sexual quality like the blind seer, Tiresias. The union of male and female, Northrop Frye suggests, represents desire for fertility in a wasteland whose symbolism is directly related to the age and impotence of a king or of authority.[70] As an essential feminisation of self, Céline's pen name rejects war as a masculine enterprise, sustained by a preoccupation with male values, such as the fear of cowardice. This would seem to contradict Céline's painstaking view in *Voyage* that women are as much implicated in war as men are. What he is after, however, is the creative potential of the female, or of the union of the male and female, potential which he draws on to create new language and to give birth to a new death-mastering self.

Of all the different forms of the protean self it is Céline who is the most resilient. When, haunted by trauma, the moment comes to disturb silence, it is Céline who emerges from the debris of the heroic self to orchestrate the shape-shifting forms that inhabit *Voyage*. Céline is not, however, the first step in the recreation of self following the demise of the heroic Destouches. Céline is the end of an itinerary traced with hindsight in *Voyage*. He is the culmination of the broken hero's flight from memory, embracing Destouches' journeys to Africa and America, and his transformation into healing doctor. Céline, the result of a startling self-transformation from shattered hero to self-seeking and soul-seeking artist, is empowered to speak, to disrupt time, memory and truth. He is the architect of the transformation of memory which will give birth to Bardamu and *Voyage*. Céline orchestrates the protean struggle going on in *Voyage*. In other words he directs the search for gold. This gold is the stuff of his immortality and it is ultimately his art.

Céline Cellini

Speaking of gold inevitably suggests a new interpretation of Céline's protean pen name, one which gives a startling clue to the true nature of his artistic enterprise: Benvenuto Cellini. Cellini was a celebrated goldsmith and sculptor of the Italian

Renaissance.[71] He suggests some comparison with Céline, not least because a house Bardamu visits in Montmartre, at 12 rue Saint-Vincent (RI, 271) — just a stone's throw from rue Lepic where Céline lived — points us directly towards the actual site of the house the composer, Hector Berlioz, lived in (at 12 rue St. Denis, now the corner of 11 bis rue Saint-Vincent and 24 Mont-Cenis) and where he composed his famous opera: *Benvenuto Cellini*. Cellini, who also spent time in France — in the court of François I, who, significantly, undertook an important renewal of the French language, ousting Latin to make French the language of court and judiciary, thereby establishing Middle French — wrote a famous autobiography in which he recalled an eventful, often violent, life of wanderings from Florence to Rome to Paris, disrupted by wars and imprisonment. The autobiography contains tales of magic ritual, incantations and necromancy. Notably, on a literary level, Cellini achieved a stylistic shift, employing a robust vernacular style inspired by the language of the young men employed in his workshops. It is very likely that his autobiography is one of the protean elements in *Voyage*'s own pseudo-autobiographical status, which echoes, in a further aspect of Céline's intertextuality, the famous autobiographies of writers as diverse as Rousseau and Chateaubriand. According to Guido Davico Bonino, Cellini's autobiography has its origin in 'uno stato di sofferenza acuta' [a state of acute suffering],[72] and its structure is one of 'alienazione' [alienation]. In his uprootedness and estrangement from the world he lives in, says Bonino, Cellini anticipates the voice of the modern artist. Writes Bonino:

> La *Vita* infatti è la prima Autobiografia dell'Intellettuale Moderno nella misura in cui l'alienazione dell'artista ne è la struttura: e la ribellione del protagonista all'alienazione ne è il tema.[73]
>
> [The *Life* is in fact the first autobiography of the modern intellectual in so far as the alienation of the artist provides its structure, and the revolt of the protagonist against alienation provides its theme.]

The tone of Cellini's book is solitary, misanthropic, and excremental.[74] According to Bonino, it reveals traces of neurotic narcissism and fantasies of persecution, all qualities which suggest a parallel with Céline. But the greatest parallel relates to the culmination of Cellini's lifework, his Perseus, commissioned by Lorenzo di Medici.

The Perseus myth has much relevance for Céline. Perseus was born of the union of his mother, Danae, and Zeus in the form of a shower of gold. It is Perseus who slays the dreaded Medusa. Armed with invisibility conferred by Pluto, flight given by Mercury, and the mirror-like shield of Minerva which allows him to look on Medusa — that is, using 'appearance' as his weapon against her — Perseus finds the Medusa in a land of darkness and slays her. The myth, indeed, represents Céline's journey into darkness and his own efforts to slay the Gorgon of the French Republic using the fictional mirror of 'appearance'.

Bonino says of Cellini's Perseus that it is his 'doppio binario' [binary double].[75] It reveals the goal of Cellini's life and artistic effort in '[la] construzione di un Ideale dell'Io, o [...] la sublimazione dell'ego in un Io ideale' [the construction of an Ideal of the I, or [...] the sublimation of the ego in an ideal I].[76] This too is Céline's goal, the creation of an ideal self. But it is in the most famous pages of *La Vita*, where Cellini struggles to save himself and his Perseus from 'death' that we find the most exciting resonance for Céline.[77]

Working on the Perseus, a fire breaks out in Cellini's workshop, which Cellini fights to bring under control. Eventually he succeeds but suffering from the strain of his exertion he collapses in a fever in which he foresees his own death. 'Io non sarò mai vivo domattina' [I will not be alive tomorrow].[78] Cellini's struggle with death is assimilated with his struggle to create when in his fever he has a vision of a mysterious stranger who enters his room to tell him that the Perseus is being ruined and cannot be saved. The stranger's voice seems to Cellini to announce his own death. On hearing this, Cellini rises in a rage from his deathbed to rescue his Perseus. After a monumental battle with the furnace, in which all the works found in Cellini's workshop are added to the fire, the Perseus is saved. Seeing that he has 'risuscitato un morto' [resurrected a dead man], Cellini finds that he has 'piu febbre o piu paura di morte' [no more fever and no more fear of death].[79] It is in these lines that his identity with Céline is most emphatic.

If Cellini, like Céline, experiences death in the midst of a fever following on his struggle with fire, his sudden death mastery is the product of a violent will to artistic creation. Creation which assures his own immortality through creation of an heroic and immortal double, Perseus. Céline too is fighting against fire — his intertextuality offers the literary equivalent of Cellini adding the diverse works in his workshop to the flames — to overcome death through creation of his own ideal, heroic, immortal double, whose golden self, emerged from the flames, is embodied in his own art, which will heroically combat the Gorgon of authority and death.[80] The construction of this heroic self is concomitant with the creation of his art. Céline's art is, indeed, his true self. This self is resolutely protean, and Benvenuto Cellini is one of its models, yet another double of Louis-Ferdinand Céline, who through identification with Cellini transforms himself into 'un satané authentique orfèvre de langue' [an almighty authentic goldsmith of language].[81]

A second work by Cellini gives us a further invaluable insight into the nature of Céline's artistic enterprise. This is the famous saltcellar he made for François I.[82] This is an allegorical piece, symbolising the immortality of France itself, where the interlaced Earth and Neptune, representing the union of male and female, ride on the ocean. The saltcellar itself is in the shape of a golden boat and this is where a most exciting parallel with Céline begins to emerge.

The critics A.C. and J.P. Damour have shown that *Voyage*, a novel full of journeys and boats, is itself shaped like a boat, so that the novel's thematic matches its structure. This boat structure, however, is also the shape of a chalice. This is evident from Cellini's saltcellar, which is boat and chalice. This means that if *Voyage*, on a concrete level, is structured like a boat, it is structured on an imagined or symbolic level as a chalice. This is not really that surprising as the chalice, in the shape of the immortalising Holy Grail, replete with healing, fertilising, female virtue, is traditionally the goal of the heroic quest.[83] So, on this level too, *Voyage*'s structure also matches its thematic, and the Holy Grail of immortality is revealed as the ultimate aim of Bardamu's quest and, indeed, of Céline's own artistic quest. This means that *Voyage* is an heroic novel in the very deepest and truest sense.

Conclusion

In his effort to escape the stasis and debasement of self, resulting from his encounter with death, Céline engages in a protean struggle to recover his heroic self and ideal state of immortality. This state is symbolically represented as gold and the novel's journey disguises a restless quest for buried treasure. While Bardamu's protean incarnations return him always to his own debasement and the consciousness that he is shut out from heroic myth, Céline is at work on what is his gold, his art, out of which he intends to wrest a final death mastery. While *Voyage* is characterised by pessimism and a sense of futility, it is highly successful aesthetically. Its innovations of style and language ensure that Céline does, indeed, through the alchemy of his art, enter into possession of gold with the commercial and critical success of his novel: the literal gold which he will make from sales of *Voyage* and that other gold, the ideal state of gold, which comes with the assurance that *Voyage* has made him immortal.

---

[1] McCarthy, p.81.

[2] Jung, *Memories, Dreams, Reflections*, p.220.

[3] See M.-L. Von Franz, 'The process of individuation', in Carl Jung, M.-L. von Franz, Joseph L. Henderson, Jolande Jacobi, Aniela Jaffé, *Man and his Symbols*, ed. by Carl Jung (London: Aldus, 1979), pp.158–229 (p.165).

[4] Letter of 8 May 1916, to Simone Saintu, *Cahiers Céline*, 4, 24–26 (p.24).

[5] Letter of 31 July 1916 to Saintu, p.66.

[6] The phrase 'ingénieux chemin' here offers a surprising echo of W.G. Sebald's fictional 'crooked route' to truth (see 5.3 *Conclusion*).

[7] See Sophie Delaporte, '15 000 Gueules cassées', *L'Histoire*, 225, p.40.

[8] Lyn MacDonald writes that photographs taken for wives and girlfriends before soldiers left for the front were used to model masks which would later conceal their disfigurement. See MacDonald, *The Roses of No Man's Land* (London: Penguin, 1980), p.157. MacDonald gives an interesting account of the work of the 'Tin Noses Shop' or 'Masks for Facial Disfigurements Department'. See pp.153–159.

[9] Lainé, p.116.

[10] See Canetti, p.437.

[11] Connerton, p.69.

[12] See Hewitt, *The Life of Céline*, p.120.

[13] Connerton, p.68.

[14] Jay Winter in *Sites of Memory,* provides a chapter on the Great War and spiritualism. 'The enduring appeal of spiritualism,' writes Winter, '[...] was related directly to the universality of bereavement in the Europe of the Great War and its aftermath.' See Winter, p.77.

[15] See A. -C. and J.-P. Damour, pp.14–16.

[16] Davis, 'L'anti-monde de L.-F. Céline', p.62.

[17] See Erika Ostrovsky, 'Mythe et subversion de mythe chez L.-F. Céline', *Céline: Actes du Colloque international de Paris (17–19 juillet 1979)* (Paris: Société d'études céliniennes, 1980), 83–91 (pp.84–85).

[18] See Jolande Jacobi, 'Symbols in an individual analysis', in Carl Jung and others, *Man and his Symbols*, pp.272–303 (p.286).

234

[19] See Fussell, *The Great War and Modern Memory*, p.131.

[20] Philip Stephen Day, 'Le Héros picaresque dans *Voyage au bout de la nuit*' (unpublished M.A. in French Language and Literature Dissertation, University of Toronto, 1963), p.24.

[21] See Philippe Alméras's presentation of a protean, multiple Céline in *Dictionnaire Céline*, p.7.

[22] Lévi-Strauss, p.121.

[23] Henri Godard, 'Une nouvelle lumière sur le *Voyage*'.

[24] See Monnier, p.90.

[25] The notion of the protean self presented in this work is informed by Robert Jay Lifton's *The Protean Self: Human Resilience in an Age of Fragmentation* (Chicago: The University of Chicago Press, 1999). 'Tendencies towards multiplicity to the point of fragmentation are rampant in both the modern and the postmodern, but the latter embraces these tendencies,' writes Lifton, p.8.

[26] McCarthy, p.81.

[27] Writes Eric J. Leed, 'the psychic problems caused by the experience of war often lay in a profound sense of personal discontinuity.' See Leed, p.2.

[28] Erikson, p.36.

[29] Lifton, *The Protean Self*, p.30.

[30] Lifton, *The Protean Self*, p.5.

[31] Lifton, *The Protean Self*, p.5.

[32] Lifton, *The Protean Self*, pp.5–6.

[33] Robert Poulet, *Mon ami Bardamu: entretiens familiers avec L.-F. Céline* (Paris: Plon, 1971), p.78.

[34] Speaking at a public lecture in Dublin City University, 18 February 2000.

[35] Crocq, p.238.

[36] Power, p.128.

[37] See Caruth, 'An Interview with Robert Jay Lifton', p.137.

[38] The *Voyage* manuscript at the Bibliothèque nationale de France, Paris, contains a long passage in which Bardamu is called to treat a sick man working in a local factory. This man is Robinson.

[39] Otto Rank, *The Double: A Psychoanalytic Study*, ed., trans. and intro. by Harry Tucker, Jr. (New York: New American Library, 1978), p.33.

[40] Rank, p.35.

[41] Rank, p.73.

[42] Brittain, p.367.

[43] See Paul Fussell, *Abroad: British Literary Traveling Between the Wars* (New York: Oxford University Press, 1980), p.16.

[44] Céline's and Bardamu's attraction to Africa was not gratuitous. Writes Fussell, 'the "tropical" motif becomes a widespread imaginative possession of all in the trenches who were cold, tired, and terrified.' See *Abroad*, p.5.

[45] Letter of 31 July 1916, p.61 (see also 4.1 *Africa*).

[46] In a letter to his parents from Africa on 29 July 1916, Céline expresses the desire to travel to New York when he leaves Africa. See *Cahiers Céline*, 4, 59–60 (p.59). Céline ends this short letter abruptly by recalling the war, 'il y a bientôt 2 ans de guerre demain — C'est atroce—' [nearly 2 years of war tomorrow — It's awful —].

[47] Writes Andrea Loselle, 'death is consistently worked into the structure of travel as a movement in the direction of death.' See Loselle, 'Traveling in the Work of Louis-Ferdinand Céline' (unpublished doctoral thesis, Columbia University, 1990), pp.91–92.

[48] Loselle, pp.34–35.

[49] See Loselle, p.4.

[50] Isabelle Blondiaux has coined the term 'rétrofiction' [retrofiction] to describe a process whereby Céline elaborates a pseudo-biography from his fictions. See Blondiaux, 'Louis-Ferdinand Céline et le diagnostic de paranoïa', *Actes du Colloque international Louis Ferdinand Céline de Paris 1992*, 79–90 (p.87).

[51] See 'Interview avec Max Descaves I', *Cahiers Céline*, 1, 22–26 (pp.23–24).

[52] Nicholas Hewitt provides valuable context for Bardamu's medical practice in his *Les maladies du siècle: the image of malaise in French fiction and thought in the inter-war years* (Hull: University of Hull, 1988). Hewitt more than justifies Céline's portrait of the doctor struggling with

adversity. He places the portrait of Bardamu as doctor against a background of 'the erosion of the humanist concept of medicine' (pp.53–55).

[53] See Carl Jung, 'Approaching the unconscious', in *Man and his Symbols*, pp.18–103 (p.76).

[54] Jung, 'Approaching the Unconscious', p.78.

[55] See Freud, 'Beyond the Pleasure Principle', 12–14.

[56] 'L'Europe est visiblement malade de la guerre, en cette fin d'années 20 : son narrateur est malade de la guerre' [Europe is visibly sick with war towards the end of the '20s; his narrator is also sick with war], observes Marie-Christine Bellosta, describing Céline's choice of a traumatised narrator as 'résolument moderne' [resolutely modern], 'posture créatrice' [a creative posture], and 'parti pris' [bias]. See Bellosta, pp.128–129.

[57] Laurens Van Der Post, *The Voice of the Thunder* (London: Penguin, 1994), p.167.

[58] See Connerton, pp.54–57.

[59] Modern memory's tendency towards myth has been noted by Paul Fussell. He notes, the 'movement towards myth, towards a revival of the cultic, the mystical, the sacrificial, the prophetic, the sacramental and the universally significant. In short towards fiction.' See Fussell, *The Great War and Modern Memory*, p.131. Ritual, adds Fussell, 'comes easily to those whose experience of life and death has undergone [...] drastic simplification'.

[60] Gibault, II: *1932–1944 Délires et persécutions* (1985), p.79.

[61] In the world of transformation that is *Voyage* it is quite possible that we are in the presence of a magical text in which some type of spell is being cast. One possibility, suggested by the novel's preoccupation with blood and excrement, is that a death-spell is being directed at the French Republic. African witch doctors casting death-spells mixed the blood of sacrificed animals with the excrement of their enemies. The mixture was then thrown into fire or buried in the ground. This resonates powerfully with *Voyage*. Given *Voyage*'s protean nature, it is indeed likely that a number of spells are being performed. See Rollo Ahmed, *The Black Art*, intro. by Dennis Wheatley (London: Arrow Books, 1966), p.178. Paul Connerton notes 'curses' among the most common verbal utterances that feature in rites. Connerton, p.58.

[62] György Lukács, *The Theory of the Novel*, trans. by Anna Bostock (London: Merlin Press, 1971), p.89.

[63] Lukács, p.80.

[64] See H.A. Guerber, *The Myths of Greece and Rome* (Ware, Hertfordshire: Wordsworth Editions, 2000), p.115.

[65] See Frye, *Anatomy of Criticism*, p.193.

[66] Nicholas Hewitt has justly likened *Voyage* to Baudelaire's poems 'Le Voyage' and 'Un Voyage à Cythère', 'in which death, frustrated journeys and the search for Eldorado dominate.' See Hewitt, *The Golden Age of Louis-Ferdinand Céline*, p.63. 'The both mystical and concrete power of gold,' says Hewitt, '[...] appears constantly in Céline's work.' See, *Golden Age*, p.59.

[67] See Erika Ostrovsky, *Céline and His Vision* (London: University of London Press, 1967), p.201. Interestingly, Carl Jung notes his own obsession with alchemy which emerges in the late 1920s. Jung's encounter with alchemy is signalled by a dream in which the war is a significant key. The dream begins in wartime Italy with shells falling from the sky. 'The shells falling from the sky,' writes Jung, 'were, interpreted psychologically, missiles coming from the "other side". They were, therefore, effects emanating from the unconscious, from the shadow side of the mind. The happenings in the dream suggested that the war, which in the outer world had taken place some years before, was not yet over, but was continuing to be fought within the psyche. Here, apparently, was to be found the solution of problems which could not be found in the outer world.' Through their interest in alchemy, both Jung and Céline are seeking solutions to the problem of the war which is ongoing in 'the psyche'. See Jung, *Memories, Dreams, Reflections*, pp.228–232.

[68] See Aniela Jaffé's note on *aurum philosophicum* [philosophical gold] in Carl Jung, *Memories, Dreams, Reflections*, p.237.

[69] See Philip Stephen Day, *Le Miroir allégorique*, p.123. Day dismisses *Voyage*'s function as 'alchemy'. 'Céline ne croit évidemment pas aux vertus de la "pierre philosophale" et encore moins à celles de l'or' [Céline apparently does not believe in the virtues of the 'philosopher's stone', and believes even less in the virtues of gold], writes Day. In reality, as we have shown, *Voyage* is a quest for gold, not just real gold, but the philosophical gold of self-transformation and

this represents its ultimate goal and meaning. Day does, however, recognise in Céline a belief, 'peut-être' [perhaps], in 'l'esprit alchimique qui promet à l'homme, au créateur surtout, un pouvoir sur la matière, un renouveau de jeunesse par la création de nouvelles formes et une sorte d'immortalité conférée par la connaissance intime des choses' [the spirit of alchemy which promises man, and the creator in particular, a power over matter, a renewal of youth through the creation of new forms and a sort of immortality conferred by the intimate knowledge of things].

[70] Northrop Frye, *Anatomy of Criticism*, p.189 and p.193.

[71] Benvenuto Cellini was born in Florence in 1500 and died there in 1570.

[72] Benvenuto Cellini, *La Vita*, intro. by Guido Davico Bonino (Turin: Giulio Einaudi, 1973), p.viii. Bonino sees the work as Cellini's response to a crisis, 'un brusco mutare di *status* professionale' [a sudden change of professional status] (p.ix), which reminds us of how Céline's own professional difficulties, his departure from the *Société des Nations* in Geneva, and his later difficulties establishing himself as a doctor in Paris have contributed to the opening of the wound which is *Voyage* (see 4.1 *La Société des Nations* and *The Crisis in Memory*). Reading Cellini, this fact would undoubtedly have intensified Céline's identification with him. In addition, as we have seen, professional difficulties belong to the profile of the traumatised veteran. See diagnostic profile of post-traumatic stress disorder, in *Diagnostic and Statistical Manual IV*, pp. 428–429.

[73] Cellini, p.x.

[74] See Cellini, p.xvi.

[75] Cellini, p.xvii.

[76] Cellini, p.xvi.

[77] These pages from Cellini were often published separately. Céline may, however, have become acquainted with Cellini through Berlioz's opera *Benvenuto Cellini*. As pointed out in the text, Berlioz lived in Montmartre, in 12 rue Saint Denis, which following rebuilding now occupies the corner of rue Mont-Cénis and rue Saint Vincent, a street mentioned in *Voyage* (RI, 271) where it has been changed from rue Saint Vincent de Paul in the manuscript version (fol. 404). As with *La Vita*, much of Berlioz's *Cellini* resonates powerfully with Céline. The Perseus scene is outstanding, while its crowd scenes recall Céline's own fascination with the crowd. The work in its entirety is a stunning celebration of gold and the goldsmith. Lizst called it 'at once gorgeous metal work and original sculpture' and said of its carnival scenes, 'for the first time in music the mob speaks with its raging voice'. See David Cairns, Notes to *Benvenuto Cellini*, BBC Symphony Orchestra, Chorus of the Royal Opera House, cond. by Sir Colin Davis, Philips CD 416 955-2 PH3, pp.19–30 (p.20 and p.30).

[78] Cellini, p.425.

[79] Cellini, p.428.

[80] In this context, the parallel with Cellini is given great pungency by Karl Epting's remark that, 'Céline a l'œil qui voit par-dessus et par-derrière, le deuxième visage qui sait à travers le masque de l'apparence extérieure découvrir la tête de gorgone de la vérité' [Céline sees above and below, the face behind the face which knows how, by using the mask of appearance, to uncover the gorgon head of truth]. This remark identifies Céline with Perseus, his double and, as we have seen, Cellini's. Cited in Philip Stephen Day, *Le Miroir allégorique*, p.219.

[81] 'Orfèvre de langue' is Céline's description of Paul Morand, in a letter from Denmark to Milton Hindus on 11 June 1947, *L'Herne*, 114–115 (p.115).

[82] Cellini's resplendent saltcellar is reproduced on quite a large number of easily consultable Internet sites.

[83] Cellini's saltcellar features male and female allegorical figures of Earth and Neptune riding on a sea filled with phatasmagorical animals. A boat rides beside them. The boat itself forms a 'hollow vessel' or 'chalice' of gold. Hollow vessels, Northrop Frye tells us, have 'female sexual affinities', and so the image of *Voyage* as an empty chalice further defines Céline and his creation as 'female', expressing a desire for fertility, birth and regeneration, also symbolised by the union of the male and female figures. See Frye, *Anatomy of Criticism*, p.194. Significantly, Carl Jung speaks of the Holy Grail as the 'healing vessel'. See Jung, *Memories, Dreams, Reflections*, p.313.

CHAPTER 7

BEYOND REDEMPTION

From Accusation to Denunciation

Introduction

In *Voyage*, Céline revolts against silence, against his heroic past, and against the official war commemoration. Commemoration was articulated around values which redeemed the war. Through exploitation of the myth of the war experience, it enshrined the French Republic and became the celebration of a political system whose legitimacy was founded in sacrifice. Céline's revolt inverts the myth. By dragging the symbols of Republican commemoration into 'the mud and blood and shit' of the war Céline debases them. In doing so, not alone does he represent the Great War debacle of heroism — his own and France's — but he indicts the memory of the French Republic. Leaving behind the consolations of commemoration, however, he moves the war, and his own memory of the war, beyond redemption.

7.1 ACCUSATION

Revolt

Transgressing silence, Céline engages in an act of military disobedience and claims identity with the 1917 mutineers. Their revolt against the futility of sacrifice was punished by death. It was punished too by exclusion from the structures of memory (see 1.4 *Cowardice, Desertion and Mutiny*). Engaged in a logic of anti-commemoration, it is natural that Céline would recount his memory of the war from the point of view of someone whom commemoration has anathematised. Rewriting himself as coward and deserter, however, he not only adopts a position of dissent, he formulates a precise accusation directed against the French Republic. Not only did it murder its own soldiers, the accusation goes, it murdered those who, willing to sacrifice their lives for France, questioned the

Army's rage to sacrifice them. In other words, Céline accuses the French Republic of collaboration with death.

Céline goes much further than the mutineers. They mutinied, not against the war itself, but against the reckless manner in which their lives were being sacrificed. Céline, however, voices a complete refusal of the war driven, not just by a belief that the Republic wilfully sacrificed the courage of its soldiers, but also by his awareness that the same drama was about to be replayed. As such, *Voyage* constitutes a real attempt to undermine the myth of the war experience and its concomitant discourses as they prepare another hecatomb.

This makes of *Voyage* a true anti-war novel in the sense that it is not just *against* war, it is also actively trying to stop a major war before it has even started.

Denunciation

Voyage begins with a denunciation of the war itself. The war is 'une formidable erreur' [a formidable error] (RI, 12),[1] 'une croisade apocalyptique' [an apocalyptic crusade], 'cette abomination' [that abomination], 'le meurtre en commun' [collective murder] (RI, 14), 'la monstrueuse entreprise' [the monstrous enterprise] (RI, 33), '[le] cimetière ardent des batailles' [the ardent cemetery of battles], 'l'abattoir' [the abattoir] (RI, 50). Denouncing the war, Céline prepares the ground for a denunciation of those who organised and led it.

Céline's accusation of collaboration is clear from the very first pages of *Voyage*. Watching his colonel read the orders received from General des Entrayes, a disbelieving Bardamu comments:

> Dans aucune d'elles, il n'y avait donc l'ordre d'arrêter net cette abomination ? On ne lui disait donc pas d'en haut qu'il y avait méprise ? Abominable erreur ? Maldonne ? Qu'on s'était trompé ? [...] Mais, non ! 'Continuez, colonel, vous êtes dans la bonne voie !' Voilà sans doute ce que lui écrivait le général [...] notre chef à tous. (RI, 14)

> [Did not one of them contain an order to straightaway stop that abomination? Wasn't someone in command telling him that there had been some mistake? An abominable error? A misunderstanding? That they'd got it wrong? [...] Not at all! 'Carry on, colonel, you're on the right track!' That no doubt was his order from the General [...] the chief of us all.]

The abomination is, of course, the 'mille morts' [thousand dead] of the preceding page, the slaughter of not German, but French soldiers. The pun on the name

Entrayes [Entrails] says it all. Entrayes is more concerned with his own food and comfort than the slaughter of his troops. He is 'une sorte de dieu précis' [a sort of precise little god], with the same disregard for the lives of his soldiers as the Aztecs '[qui] éventraient couramment [...] quatre-vingt mille croyants par semaine' [who as a matter of course disembowelled [...] eighty thousand believers a week] (RI, 37). The accusation of sacrifice is clear, as is the parallel with another gold-obsessed society organised around the production of death, while Céline's figure speaks for itself. 'C'est des choses qu'on a du mal à croire avant d'aller en guerre. Mais quand on y est, tout s'explique' [It's the sort of thing you find hard to believe before you go to war, but once you are in it, it becomes easy to understand], Bardamu says (RI, 37).

Entrayes is just one in a series of portraits of the French command that dominate the war episode. There is to begin with Bardamu's death-defying colonel, 'un monstre ! [...] Il n'imaginait pas son trépas !' [a monster! [...] He couldn't imagine his own death!] (RI, 13), who remains indifferent to his own death and the deaths of his soldiers. Then there is Pinçon:

> Cette gueule d'État-major n'avait de cesse dès le soir revenu de nous expédier au trépas [...]. Si on [lui] avait dit [...] qu'il n'était qu'un sale assassin lâche, on lui aurait fait un plaisir énorme, celui de nous faire fusiller [...] par le capitaine de gendarmerie [...] qui, lui, ne pensait précisément qu'à cela. (RI, 24)

> [Our bloody commanding officer never tired as soon as night fell of sending us off to be killed [...]. If you told him [...] that he was nothing but a dirty, cowardly assassin, it would only have given him the immense pleasure of having us shot [...] by the captain of the military police [...] who thought of nothing else.]

It is the gendarmerie [military police] who will later be seen to assassinate their soldiers 'par escouades' [by squadrons] (RI, 30). Significantly, this is where Céline writes 'la grande défaite, en tout, c'est d'oublier' [the great defeat, in everything, is to forget]. When he continues, 'surtout ce qui vous a fait crever' [especially the thing that has done you in] (RI, 25), a significant dimension of *Voyage*'s inner dynamic is firmly established: memory (*rappel*) and accusation. 'Je me demandais quelle rage d'envoyer crever les autres le possédait celui-là ?' [I wondered what rage to send others off to be killed possessed him?], Bardamu asks of Pinçon, but he could be asking it of the entire army command (RI, 27).

Next in this gallery of portraits is Ortolan. Says Bardamu, in his most succinct indictment of the French army leadership, 'il nous aurait envoyés prendre du feu à la bouche des canons d'en face. Il collaborait avec la mort. On aurait pu jurer qu'elle avait un contrat avec le capitaine Ortolan' [he would have sent us to get a light from the mouth of the cannons opposite. He collaborated with death. You would have sworn that he had a contract with death, our Captain Ortolan] (RI, 32). The accusation of collaboration with death could not be more explicit.

The rogues' gallery of the opening chapters is completed by the portrait of the adjutant. 'Dans la nuit du village de guerre, l'adjudant gardait les animaux humains pour les grands abattoirs qui venaient d'ouvrir. Il est le roi l'adjudant ! Le Roi de la Mort !' [In the night of the war village, the adjutant shepherded the human animals for the great abattoirs which had just opened. He is the King, the adjutant! The King of Death!] (RI, 35). Depicting the ordinary soldiers as animals led to slaughter, Céline throws his accusation at the feet of their military leaders, who do the work of death itself. This is anti-commemoration at its finest, laced with humour and irony, light years from the po-faced, exalted tones of official remembrance.

The Breach of Contract

Nowhere is Céline's accusation more pointed than in the evocation of military executions. Céline shows the threat of being murdered by one's own troops as a condition of the war. 'Il n'y avait guère d'imprévu dans cette histoire que l'uniforme de l'exécutant' [There was nothing unforeseen in this tale apart from the uniform of the executioner] (RI, 27). Which is what happens to the Breton, Kersuzon, whose fate once again spells out clearly Céline's accusation, 'tué qu'il a été [...] par des Français' [shot he was [...] by Frenchmen] (RI, 28). Céline's war is in reality a civil war. The emphasis he wishes to place is on the murder and wastage of French soldiers by the French themselves, so bent on killing their own troops that they will execute them if they dare to question the manner of their own death. 'On a bien le droit d'avoir une opinion sur sa propre mort' [One certainly has the right to have an opinion on one's own death], as Bardamu protests (RI, 19). In what is a high point of indictment, and echoing his earlier 'ça venait des profondeurs' [it had come from the depths] (RI, 14), Céline calls this war of attrition against one's own troops 'la profonde, la vraie de vraie' [the deep down war, the truly true one] (RI, 30). This is the war then that should be remembered.

Bardamu is haunted by this reality, that his own army — on behalf of his society — seeks his death, 'si les gendarmes [...] m'avaient pincé en vadrouille [...] on m'aurait fusillé' [if the military police [...] had caught me rambling about like that [...] they would have shot me], he says (RI, 19). Even convalescing at the rear he recognises that he has not one enemy but two:

> J'étais en sursis de mort [...]. Des millions d'hommes [...] m'attendaient pour me faire mon affaire et des Français aussi qui m'attendaient pour en finir avec ma peau, si je ne voulais pas la faire mettre en lambeaux saignants par ceux d'en face. (RI, 82)

> [I was living under a suspended sentence of death [...]. Millions of men [...] were waiting to do me in and Frenchmen too were waiting to have my skin, if I wasn't eager to have those on the other side cut it to bloody ribbons for me.]

The *Amiral Bragueton* scene, where a party of soldiers subject Bardamu to a kangaroo trial, is the theatrical effusion of Bardamu's haunted awareness (RI, 111–124). This passage is, far from evidence of Céline's supposed paranoia, the brilliant *mise en scène* of one of the war's most disturbing realities. When Bardamu, taking 'l'escalier de départ' [the exit stairs], jumps ship, leaving behind his 'dangereux compagnons du bord' [dangerous voyage companions], he announces the definitive breaking of a contract (RI, 124), just as Hemingway does when the hero of *A Farewell to Arms* jumps in the river to escape summary execution. Céline's breach of contract is the one between him and the French Republic, between him and French society. It is not for nothing that this chapter ends the entire war episode, front and rear, in *Voyage*.

7.2 THE DEATH OF THE HERO

Je l'avoue

Voyage is a savage memorial to Céline's loss of heroic identity. As Robert Llambias observes:

> Le patriotisme et l'héroïsme dont a fait réellement preuve le brigadier Des Touches sont complètement effacés par le romancier Céline ; loin de lier l'attribution de sa médaille à un acte de bravoure, celui-ci évoque la réforme de Ferdinand comme les suites d'un dérangement mental causé par la peur, et 'oublie' purement et simplement les circonstances qui ont valu au jeune homme d'être décoré.[2]

> [The patriotism and heroism demonstrated by brigadier Destouches are completely effaced by the novelist, Céline; far from linking his medal to an act of bravery, he presents Ferdinand's demobilisation as the result of a mental disturbance caused by fear, and 'forgets' purely and simply the circumstances which had earned the young man his decoration.]

This 'oubli' [forgetfulness], *Voyage*'s memory loss, stands for Céline's own loss of heroic identity and for that of France. Céline's eliding of his heroic past, however, and the excision of all nostalgia or ambiguity towards it, is more than just a metaphor for identity loss, it is also a condemnation of his heroism to the realm of the unspeakable (see 5.2 *Silence and Self*). By writing his heroism into the war's silences, Céline announces his share of guilt in the war itself, made quite poignantly explicit when Bardamu evokes 'cette incroyable affaire internationale, où je m'étais embarqué d'enthousiasme... Je l'avoue' [that incredible international affair on which I had embarked with enthusiasm... I admit it] (RI, 27). Céline's own collaboration with death will provide an important dynamic in *Voyage*. It is evident, for example, when Bardamu acknowledges in the lead-up to Robinson's murder, 'c'est à cause de moi qu'on s'est reparlé et que la dispute a repris' [it was my fault that we began talking again, restarting the argument] (RI, 487). It is, undoubtedly, the springboard for much of Céline's self-denigration throughout the novel.

The Monster

Céline's silence about his own heroism is only one aspect of an equation which anathematises the heroic. By rewriting himself as coward and deserter, Céline heaps opprobrium and mockery on his own heroic past. The attack on the heroic self begins early in *Voyage*, 'moi crétin' [me the cretin] (RI, 15), is Bardamu's early self-judgement on the battlefield. Later he says, 'j'étais grotesque' [I was grotesque] (RI, 36).

For Céline heroism has no place in modern war. This is clear as early as his letter of 30 August 1916 to his father (see 4.1 *Africa*). It is not courage, however, that Céline deplores in *Voyage*. Indeed, in what is an important evocation of the debacle of Hazebrouck, the loss of courage or domination by fear is presented as an important aspect of Bardamu's trauma when he says, 'je suis tombé malade, fiévreux, rendu fou [...] par la peur' [I fell sick, fevered, maddened [...] by fear] (RI, 60). What Céline attacks is a heroism which shares blindly in its own destruction, which collaborates with death.

In *Voyage*, the hero is transformed into a monster.[3] The colonel, Bardamu says, 'était donc un monstre !' [was a monster!] (RI, 13). The colonel, however, is merely representative of a war driven by the heroic ideal, one of 'ces monstres' [those monsters] (RI, 15). 'Je conçus [...],' says Bardamu, 'qu'il devait y en avoir beaucoup des comme lui dans notre armée, des braves' [I saw [...] that there must be a lot like him in our army, brave types] (RI, 13). He sees himself 'perdu parmi deux millions de fous héroïques et déchaînés et armés jusqu'aux cheveux' [lost among two million heroic madmen set loose and armed to the teeth] (RI, 13). 'L'horreur' [horror], Bardamu discovers, resides here in 'la sale âme héroïque et fainéante des hommes' [the foul, idle, heroic soul of men] (RI, 14). 'L'horreur' comes from a lack of imagination. This is the source of the colonel's death. 'Le colonel n'avait jamais eu d'imagination lui. Tout son malheur à cet homme était venu de là' [The colonel had no imagination. That was the cause of all his misfortune] (RI, 19). Commemoration, Céline suggests, is itself built upon this blindness to death. *Voyage* becomes an effort to place 'l'imagination de la mort' [the imagination of death] at the heart of memory. *Voyage* is thus Céline's attempt to open the eyes of society to the reality of death through evocation of 'the imagination of death'.

Throughout *Voyage* the heroic is mocked. Heroism is part vanity, part theatre, part ignorance. Heroes, 'adorant leur rage' [adoring their rage] (RI, 13), are narcissistic. Their courage is suspect. 'Y a que la bravoure au fond qui est louche' [Deep down only bravery is suspect] (RI, 49). This is because bravery no longer means anything, 'lâche ou courageux, cela ne veut pas dire grand-chose' [to be a coward or courageous no longer means very much] (RI, 83). Heroic models are futile. Even Napoleon becomes 'ce fou' [that madman], 'pas sérieux en somme' [not to be taken at all seriously] (RI, 353).[4]

The False Promise of Immortality

Céline attacks the heroic ideal on three fronts. Firstly, it is a vector of man's mortality. The heroic makes war possible and prolongs it, 'avec des êtres semblables, cette imbécillité infernale pouvait continuer indéfiniment' [with such beings in it, this infernal stupidity could go on forever], Bardamu says (RI, 13). Rather than conferring the soldier with protection against death, the heroic ideal leads him blindly to it.

Secondly, Céline targets the notion that heroism is rewarded by society. This underlies Bardamu's ironic fantasy of heroic return from the war:

> On nous couvrirait de décorations, de fleurs, on passerait sous l'Arc de Triomphe. On entrerait au restaurant, on vous servirait sans payer, on payerait plus rien, jamais plus de la vie ! On est les héros ! qu'on dirait au moment de la note... Des défenseurs de la Patrie ! Et ça suffirait !... On payerait avec des petits drapeaux français !... (RI, 18)

> [We'll be covered in decorations, in flowers, we'll parade under the Arc de Triomphe. We'll enter restaurants and be served with no need to pay, we'll never pay again, never as long as we live! We're heroes! we'll say when the bill arrives... Defenders of the Fatherland! That will do!... We'll pay with little French flags!...]

The irony here derives from a contrast between Bardamu's fantasy, with its evocation of the promises made to the soldiers fighting the war and the harsh post-war reality they found (see 2.1 *Veterans*). The hero's fate, Céline says, is to be 'dupés jusqu'au sang' [duped right to his blood] (RI, 34). In this sense, Bardamu embodies the aftermath of the heroic myth. In his post-war alienation, he represents the reality of the soldier returned from war, no hero, but traumatised, frightened, forgotten, and alone. His portrait is part of *Voyage*'s function of 'rappel', a reminder to veterans of their betrayal.

Part of the attraction of the heroic ideal was sexual reward, the female who made herself available to the conquering hero. This too Céline suggests is a lie, as the death of the hero ensures it can never be a reality. The dead soldier will be forgotten. The soldier who survives will be demeaned. Bardamu makes this clear as he reads the minds of Bestombes' nurses:

> Vous serez vite oubliés, petits soldats... Soyez gentils, crevez bien vite... Et que la guerre finisse et qu'on puisse se marier avec un de vos aimables officiers... Un brun surtout !... Vive la Patrie dont parle toujours papa !... [...] Il sera décoré notre petit mari ! [...] Vous pourrez cirer ses jolies bottes le beau jour de notre mariage si vous existez encore à ce moment-là, petit soldat... (RI, 88)

> [You'll be quickly forgotten, little soldiers... Be good, die soon... And let the war finish so we can marry one of your lovely officers... A dark-haired one please! Long live the Fatherland about which Papa always speaks!... He'll have medals our little husband! [...] You can polish his fine boots on our wedding day if you're still alive then, little soldier...]

Céline's third point of attack is on the immortalising claim of the heroic ideal (see 1.1 *The Hero*). Heroes end up violently, grotesquely dead, he says, they have no immortality and no future other than that of the corpse. 'Invoquer sa postérité, c'est faire un discours aux asticots' [Invoking posterity is like making a speech to the worms], Bardamu says (RI, 35). Only the promise of memory, it seems, can offer the hero any immortality. There is tremendous irony implicit in the very notion that those who sacrifice their lives will be rewarded by being remembered by the living. Heroes, Céline insinuates, are duped by the promise of remembrance. They will always be dead, while the living will inevitably revel, 'par contraste' [in contrast], in being alive:

> Pendant des funérailles soignées on est bien tristes aussi, mais on pense quand même à l'héritage, aux vacances prochaines, à la veuve qui est mignonne [...] et à vivre encore, soi-même, par contraste, bien longtemps, à ne crever jamais peut-être... Qui sait ? (RI, 48)

> [At a well-conducted funeral, you naturally feel sad, but that doesn't stop you thinking of your inheritance, of your next holiday, of the pretty widow [...] or of going on living, yourself, in contrast, for quite a long time yet, and never dying perhaps... Who can tell?]

Princhard who, having become a thief to escape the war, finds he is nonetheless to be returned to the front for the honour of his family, takes up this theme at its most virulent, foreseeing how he will be remembered after the war:

> Tenez, je la vois d'ici, ma famille, les choses de la guerre passées... Comme tout passe... Joyeusement alors gambadante ma famille sur les gazons de l'été revenu, je la vois d'ici par les beaux dimanches...

Cependant qu'à trois pieds dessous, moi papa, ruisselant d'asticots et bien plus infect qu'un kilo d'étrons de 14 juillet pourrira fantastiquement de toute sa viande déçue... (RI, 68)

[Look, I can just see it, my family, when the war is ended... As everything must end... I can see my family gambolling joyously on the lawns of summers returned, I can just see them on sunny Sunday afternoons... While three feet under, I, Papa, riddled with worms and more putrid than a kilo of turds on 14 July will be rotting fabulously away, me and all of my disappointed flesh...]

Juxtaposing the image of his rotting corpse with the joyful forgetting of Princhard's family, Céline carries the 'imagination of death' to the core of remembrance and commemoration. The physical reality of death brutally challenges the very meaning of remembrance and is given immense, polemical, purpose through the evocation of 14 July. The official promise of remembrance is if anything even more debased than this familial remembrance. What place in official memory will heroes have won through the sacrifice of their lives, suggests Princhard, other than:

le droit magnifique à un petit bout d'ombre du monument adjudicataire et communal élevé pour les morts convenables [...] et puis aussi [...] le droit de recueillir un peu de l'écho du Ministre qui viendra ce dimanche encore uriner chez le Préfet et frémir de la gueule au-dessus des tombes après le déjeuner... (RI, 70)

[the magnificent right to a small piece of shade given by the monument commissioned and erected for the respectable dead [...] and also [...] the right to hear the echo of the Minister who will come yet again of a Sunday to urinate in the Prefect's house before shouting his mouth off over the graves after lunch...]

Bardamu, who has himself become 'devant tout héroïsme, verbal ou réel, phobiquement rébarbatif' [faced with all heroism, verbal or real, phobically resistant] (RI, 50), goes even further and launches a direct attack on the commemorative focus on remembering the names of fallen soldiers. Railing at the lie of immortalising remembrance he asks Lola:

Vous souvenez-vous d'un seul nom par exemple, Lola, d'un de ces soldats tués pendant la guerre de Cent Ans ?... Avez-vous jamais cherché à en connaître un seul de ces noms ?... [...] Vous n'avez jamais cherché ? Ils vous sont aussi anonymes, indifférents et plus inconnus que le dernier atome de ce presse-papier devant nous, que votre crotte du matin... Voyez donc bien qu'ils sont morts pour rien, Lola ! Pour absolument rien du tout, ces crétins ! (RI, 65–66)

[Do you remember a single one of the names, Lola, of any one of the soldiers who died during the Hundred Years War? Have you ever tried to discover any one of their names?... [...] You've never tried? They are as anonymous, as indifferent and unknown to you as the least atom of the paperweight here in front of us, as the turd you leave in the toilet in the morning... You see then, don't you, that they died for nothing, Lola! For absolutely nothing at all, those cretins!]

Bardamu goes on to attack the hero's promised place in history:

Dans dix mille ans d'ici, je vous fais le pari que cette guerre [...] sera complètement oubliée... À peine si une douzaine d'érudits se chamailleront encore par-ci, par-là, à son occasion et à propos des dates des principales hécatombes [...] C'est tout ce que les hommes ont réussi jusqu'ici à trouver de mémorable au sujet les uns des autres à quelques siècles, à quelques années et même à quelques heures de distance... (RI, 66)

[In ten thousand years from now, I bet you that this war [...] will be completely forgotten... At most a couple of dozen scholars here and there will argue over its cause and the dates of its greatest massacres [...] Until now, that's all men have succeeded in finding to remember about each other, once a few centuries, years, or even a few hours have gone by...]

Bardamu's denunciation echoes with real despair. Despair induced by the 'faculté d'oubli' [faculty for forgetting] Céline evoked in his letter to Joseph Garcin (see 4.1 *The Crisis in Memory*). Despair derived from his awareness that 'la grande défaite, en tout, c'est d'oublier' [the great defeat, in everything, is to forget]. Despair drawn too from the failure of the immortalising promise of his own heroism. Heroism failed Céline. Rather than protecting him from death, it plunged him into the anguished experience of his own mortality. Céline's trauma begins with the failure of his heroism. This failure carries the whole structure of his world with it. Gone is his youth, his innocence, his faith in his family, in society, in the world. Gone is his faith in the human. 'Jamais je n'avais senti plus implacable la sentence des hommes et des choses' [Never had I felt so implacably the sentence of men and things], Bardamu will say (RI, 13). From this wound in the fabric of existence, and intensified by the increasing anguish of his trauma, flows Céline's essential pessimism. 'C'est des hommes et d'eux seulement qu'il faut avoir peur, toujours' [It is of men and men alone that you must be afraid, always] is its corollary (RI, 15). Countering this pessimism is his ongoing search for new immortalising modes which will feed both his vehement pacifism and the development of an artform which is in essence heroic (see 6.2 *Céline Cellini*). It is, indeed, through literature that he will strive to heal the broken connection to his own immortality.

7.3 THE THEATRE OF PATRIOTISM

The Theatre of Trauma

War, Paul Fussell says, is eminently theatrical (see also 2.2 *Graves*). According to Fussell, 'if killing and avoiding being killed are the ultimate melodrama, then military training is very largely training in melodrama.'[5] Inevitably, the soldier sees himself and the war itself as theatrical creations. For Fussell this sense of theatre is enhanced by the utter unthinkableness of war. It is impossible for a participant to believe that he is taking part in such murderous proceedings in his own character. The whole thing is, 'too grossly farcical, perverse, cruel, and absurd to be credited as a form of real life'.[6] Seeing the war as theatre, Fussell argues, allows the soldier an important psychic escape route for his real self and his belief in the world as a rational place.

The perception of the war as theatre is part and parcel of the experience of trauma where, as Louis Crocq reminds us, the self experiences 'déréalisation et dépersonnalisation' [derealisation and depersonalisation].[7] Self and world are suddenly strange and unfamiliar. The theatrical motif, as Fussell says, is one way of making sense of it.

Another aspect of this experience of trauma is what Robert Jay Lifton calls the 'counterfeit universe'.[8] The world is robbed of its sense of order and its truth and suddenly appears a lie. Belief in the values of sincerity and compassion is undermined, while people, government and society all appear inauthentic, false, and theatrical. The world has become a series of impersonations or performances.

Theatre is one of the most important metaphors in *Voyage*. Indeed, so acute is Céline's sense of theatre, that the metaphor is inflated to its maximum to arrive at an effect of grotesqueness. Robert Llambias recognises this when, invoking Jarry, he refers to Céline's evocation of 'l'absurdité de la guerre sur un mode que l'on peut qualifier d'hyper-théâtral' [the absurdity of war using a mode which might be called hyper-theatrical].[9] The war in *Voyage* often appears to be nothing more than a cruel farce whose blackly comical aspect is reflected even in the names of its characters. In *Voyage*, the war itself is a stage. The colonel in the middle of the road becomes 'un spectacle à remplir l'Alhambra' [a show to fill the Alhambra music hall] (RI, 19). Bardamu himself is an 'accessoire figurant' [walk-on extra] (RI, 27). The theatrical metaphor runs through almost every page before culminating in the Robinson/Madelon murder scene, described as 'une vraie comédie' [a real comedy] (RI, 491). Where it is most potent, however, is in shadowing forth the lie of patriotism, particularly in Céline's portrait of the rear.

The war is heralded by the musical fanfare of the passing regiment which leads Bardamu away (RI, 10). He is now part of the theatre of patriotism, complete with its cheering spectators, 'des civils et leurs femmes [...]. Il y en avait des patriotes !' [civilians and their wives [...]. There were lots of patriots!] (RI, 10). As the war draws closer, however, this patriotism is revealed as a theatrical sham. 'Et puis il s'est mis à y en avoir moins des patriotes...' [And then there were fewer and fewer patriots...]. The soldier is cheered to his death but must face it alone. Bardamu sees himself duped and trapped, 'on était faits, comme des rats' [we were caught like rats in a trap]. At the end of the first chapter of *Voyage*, Céline directly accuses civilian society of sly collaboration in the deaths of soldiers, 'ils avaient refermé la porte en douce derrière nous les civils' [they had shut the door quietly behind us, the civilians] (RI, 10). This accusation will remain a keynote of his depiction of civilian life throughout the novel.

Lola

Returned from the war, Bardamu finds nothing has changed. Life, and the war, goes on in the shadow of 'des journaux délirants d'appels aux sacrifices ultimes et patriotiques' [newspapers delirious with calls for ultimate and patriotic sacrifices] (RI, 73). War fever mounts. 'Les journaux battaient le rappel de tous les combattants possibles' [The newspapers demanded the call-up of every last combatant] (RI, 82). Patriotism turns to pure melodrama. '"Des canons ! des hommes ! des munitions !" qu'ils exigeaient sans jamais en sembler las, les patriotes' ['Cannon! Men! Munitions!' they demanded, without ever seeming to tire of it, the patriots] (RI, 84). He is constantly exposed to the theatre of patriotism. The rear episode is a series of portraits of the characters who walk its stage. To begin with, the young American nurse, Lola, with, 'son petit air Jeanne d'Arc' [her little Joan of Arc air] (RI, 50). Lola's theatrical vocabulary has been scripted by the patriotic press. 'Elle traversait mon angoisse avec la mentalité du *Petit Journal* : Pompon, Fanfare, ma Lorraine et gants blancs...' [She passed through my anguish with the mentality of the *Petit Journal*: all pompom, fanfare, oh my Lorraine and the white gloves of the young officers...] (RI, 55). She has learned her part, but not perfectly. Lola 'ne connaissait du français que quelques phrases mais elles étaient patriotiques : "On les aura !...", "Madelon, viens !..." C'était à pleurer' [only knew a few French phrases, but they were patriotic: 'We'll get them!...' 'Come, Madelon!...' It was enough to make you cry] (RI, 54). The theatre ghosts of women cheering men to war hovers in Bardamu's portrait of Lola. 'Elle se penchait ainsi sur notre mort avec entêtement, impudeur, comme toutes les femmes d'ailleurs, dès que la mode d'être courageuse pour les autres est venue' [She attended to our deaths with stubborness and immodesty, like all women moreover, as soon as the craze for being courageous on behalf of others has come] (RI, 54). All the distance between theatre and reality, between life and death, separates them. After all, it is he who is going to die, not she. Like the nurses in Bestombes' clinic she simply plays her part, 'chacun son rôle... chacun sa mort...' [To each his role... To each his death...] (RI, 88). It is through Lola that Bardamu's condemnation comes when he confesses his cowardice. 'Vous êtes donc tout à fait lâche, Ferdinand ! Vous êtes répugnant comme un rat...' [And so you are a complete coward, Ferdinand! You are as repugnant as a rat...], she tells him (RI, 65), before leaving him, in a vividly theatrical *dénouement*.

Musyne

Musyne replaces Lola in Bardamu's affections. Like Lola, like his mother, Musyne's patriotism readily embraces the idea of Bardamu's death. Musyne 'désirait fort aussi [...] que je retourne au front dare-dare et que j'y reste' [also wanted me [...] to return double-quick to the war and to stay there] (RI, 82).

Musyne is the theatre of patriotism incarnate. 'Implacable dans son désir de réussir sur la terre' [implacable in her desire to succeed in this world] (RI, 76) she plays her patriotic role with verve. Musyne, 'violoniste de guerre si mignonne !' [such a pretty little war violinist] (RI, 80), is a music hall artiste subsumed appropriately into 'le *Théâtre aux Armées*' [the Army Theatre]. Through Musyne, war and patriotism take on quite literally the status of a music-hall turn in *Voyage*:

> Elle y détaillait, aux armées, la sonate et l'adagio devant les parterres d'État-major, bien placés pour lui voir les jambes. Les soldats parqués en gradins à l'arrière des chefs ne jouissaient eux que des échos mélodieux. (RI, 80)

> [She performed sonatas and adagios for the army in front of the serried ranks of the high command, who got the best seats to view her legs. The soldiers in the uncomfortable back rows behind them had to make do with melodious echoes of her performance.]

If for Lola, heroism consisted of tasting 'des beignets' [fritters] — 'elle eut en peu de temps aussi peur des beignets que moi des obus' [in no time at all she was as terrified of fritters as I was of shells] (RI, 51) — Musyne's heroism is acquired with theatrical aplomb. 'Un jour elle m'en revint toute guillerette des Armées et munie d'un brevet d'héroïsme, signé par l'un de nos grands généraux, s'il vous plaît' [one day she returned in sprightly mood from the Army Theatre with a certificate of heroism, signed by one of our great generals, if you please] (RI, 80). Musyne's certificate of heroism becomes the stamp of authenticity of her stage-patriotism, perfectly complemented by her talent for invention. Musyne, 'avait su se créer [...] un petit répertoire très coquet d'incidents de guerre et qui, tel un chapeau mutin, lui allait à ravir' [had been able to create a small but quite attractive repertoire of war stories which suited her beautifully, just like an impish hat] (RI, 80). The effect is irresistible. Admirers flock to her. As Bardamu comments, 'la poésie héroïque possède sans résistance ceux qui ne vont pas à la guerre et mieux encore ceux que la guerre est en train d'enrichir énormément. C'est régulier' [the poetry of heroism easily takes possession of all those who have no experience of war and better still of all those whom the war is making fabulously rich. It's only to be expected] (RI, 80). Evidently, Musyne is not the only one for whom the theatre of patriotism is a sound commercial proposition.

Bardamu recognises it for what it is, but unlike Musyne he does not yet know how to exploit it, 'je n'étais en fait de bobards qu'un grossier simulateur à ses côtés' [when it came to tall tales I was nothing but a shoddy pretender compared to her] (RI, 80). Destined one day to keep body and soul together as impromptu 'Pacha' on the Tarapout stage, he will learn (RI, 355).

Puta

A visit to Bardamu's ex-employer Roger Puta allows Céline to offer his most scathing portrait of a patriot. Puta has even had his German shepherds put down, a theatrical gesture if ever there was one. The Putas directly represent 'ceux que la guerre est en train d'enrichir énormément' [those whom the war was making immensely rich], 'sa femme,' says Bardamu, 'ne faisait qu'un avec la caisse' [his wife was inseparable from the cash desk] (RI, 103). Their jewellery business is thriving. 'Plus on avançait dans la guerre et plus on avait besoin de bijoux' [the more the war went on, the more need there was of jewellery], explains Bardamu (RI, 103). Any sympathy the Putas feel for the war-bereaved is tempered by patriotic stoicism. 'Ne faut-il pas que la France soit défendue ?' [Mustn't France be defended?], asks Roger. (RI, 104). Stoicism itself tempered by money. 'Ainsi bons cœurs, mais bons patriotes par-dessus tout, stoïques en somme, ils s'endormaient chaque soir de la guerre au-dessus des millions de leur boutique, fortune française' [Good-hearted, but good patriots above all, stoics, in a word, they went to sleep each night of the war above the millions in their jewellery shop, a French fortune] (RI, 104). Roger, in patriotic mode, reminds Bardamu and his fellow soldier, Voireuse, how lucky they are:

> Vous en avez de la veine [...] vous autres ! on peut dire ce que l'on voudra, vous vivez des heures magnifiques, hein ? là-haut ? Et à l'air ? C'est de l'Histoire ça mes amis, ou je m'y connais pas ! Et quelle Histoire ! (RI, 105)

> [You're so lucky [...] you fellows! Say what you like, but you are living through some magnificent moments, eh? Out there? In the open air? That's History, my good friends, or I know very little about it! And what History!]

Puta compares his own night service driving across blacked-out Paris to the dangers faced in the trenches. 'Ah ! c'est dur, j'en conviens, les tranchées !...

C'est vrai ! Mais c'est joliment dur ici aussi, vous savez !...' [Ah! They're hard, the trenches, I accept... It's true! But it's hard here too, you know!...] (RI, 105). The gap between front and rear has never been more farcical. 'Ah ! les rues de Paris pendant la nuit ! Sans lumière, mes petits amis [...] Vous pouvez pas vous imaginer !... C'est à se tuer dix fois par nuit !...' [Ah! The streets of Paris at night! Without any street lighting, my friends [...] You just can't imagine!... It's enough to get you killed ten times over each night] (RI, 106). Finally Bardamu and Voireuse leave, some money in pocket, with Puta's motto, 'Défense Nationale avant tout' [National Defence above all], ringing in their ears. 'À ces mots de Défense Nationale, il se fit tout à fait sérieux, Puta, comme lorsqu'il rendait la monnaie...' [At those words of National Defence, he became entirely serious, like when he was giving you back your change...] (RI, 106). There is more than a hint of swindle in the air.

The Patriotic Psychiatrist

It is no wonder that Bardamu has become one of 'ces soldats [...] dont l'idéal patriotique était simplement compromis ou tout à fait malade' [one of those soldiers [...] in whom the patriotic ideal was simply impaired or altogether sick] (RI, 61), a condition for which he is treated by Doctor Bestombes, *Voyage*'s most eloquent spokesman for the patriotic ideal and an opportunity for Céline to bring psychiatric discourse on to the stage of the theatre of patriotism. The scene where Bestombes catechises Bardamu would adorn any stage. Man is a mixture of egoism and altruism, argues Bestombes, but 'chez le sujet d'élite' [in the elite subject] altruism is stronger:

> — Et chez le sujet d'élite quel peut être, je vous le demande Bardamu, la plus haute entité connue qui puisse exciter son altruisme et l'obliger à se manifester incontestablement, cet altruisme ?
> — Le patriotisme, Maître !
> — [...] Vous me comprenez tout à fait bien... Bardamu ! Le patriotisme et son corollaire, la gloire, tout simplement, sa preuve !
> — C'est vrai ! (RI, 93–94)

> [—And for the elite subject what might be, I ask you, Bardamu, the highest notion known which may excite his altruism and oblige him to manifest it unquestioningly, this altruism?
> —Patriotism, Master!

— [...] You understand me completely... Bardamu! Patriotism and its corollary, glory, quite simply, its proof!
— How true!]

Father and Mother

Significantly, Bestombes speaks to Bardamu with 'une voix devenue paternelle' [a paternal voice] (RI, 94), evoking the absent figure of Céline's supreme patriot: his father. Immediately after this scene, Bardamu's mother makes her only real appearance in the novel. She recovers Bardamu like a bitch recovering her puppy, 'elle demeurait cependant inférieure à la chienne parce qu'elle croyait aux mots elle qu'on lui disait pour m'enlever' [however, she was inferior to the bitch because she believed in the words they had used to take me away from her] (RI, 94–95). Patriotic discourse has corrupted her mother's love and taken away its power to protect Bardamu, 'elle acceptait l'accident de ma mort' [she accepted the accident of my death], he says disconsolately (RI, 96). And it has made of her a particularly hapless character in a deadly farce played out on the stage of patriotism.

Abandoned by his mother, as by Lola and Musyne, on the pyre of 'les viandes destinées aux sacrifices' [meat destined for sacrifice] (RI, 97), there is nothing for Bardamu to do now but assume his role in the Theatre of Patriotism. As he says, 'les jeux étaient faits' [the die was cast] (RI, 97). Branledore is his mentor. The result is purest farce.

The Theatre of Survival

Branledore teaches Bardamu an important lesson, 'comme le Théâtre était partout il fallait jouer' [as the Theatre was everywhere you needed to play your role in it] (RI, 90). Like Siegfried Sassoon, who 'playing the part of a wounded young officer for various visitors to the hospital [...] alters the role to make it effective with different audiences',[10] Branledore cries out 'entre deux étouffements' [between two stifling coughs] whenever a nurse or doctor is near, 'Victoire ! Victoire ! Nous aurons la Victoire !' [Victory! Victory! We will have our Victory!] (RI, 90). He usurps the theatre of patriotism to enact the theatre of survival. Bardamu follows suit and the theatrical motif reaches its climax in Voyage.

Branledore, Bardamu and the other patients create an atmosphere of patriotic fervour in Bestombes' clinic. They receive visits from the great and famous, 'des évêques, [...] une duchesse italienne, un grand munitionnaire, et bientôt l'Opéra lui-même et les pensionnaires du Théâtre-Français' [bishops, [...] an Italian duchess, a great munitions manufacturer, and soon after, the performers from the Paris Opera and the French National Theatre] (RI, 98). Bardamu happily becomes the protégé of 'une belle subventionnée de la Comédie' [a lovely actress from the Comédie Française theatre] (RI, 98). Competition flourishes among the patients. 'Nous vivions un grand roman de geste, dans la peau de personnages fantastiques' [We were acting out a great, heroic novel, transformed into fantastical characters], says Bardamu (RI, 99). Their part in the theatre of patriotism has transformed them, 'devenus présentables et pas dégoûtants du tout moralement' [we had become presentable, and not at all repulsive from a moral point of view] (RI, 98). This theatrical interlude culminates when a poet friend of the 'belle subventionnée' renders Bardamu's invented heroism in epic poetry to be performed appropriately at the 'Comédie-Française'. All of France has become a theatre. When the 'belle subventionnée' appears draped in the French flag, reducing the most potent of patriotic symbols to the level of theatre, 'ce fut le signal dans la salle entière, debout, désireuse, d'une de ces ovations qui n'en finissent plus' [it was the moment for the entire audience to stand erect and to launch ardently into one of those never-ending ovations] (RI, 100). She declaims Bardamu's exploits in verse. The heroism is far-fetched but the crowd patriotically gullible. 'Heureusement, rien n'est incroyable en matière d'héroïsme' [Luckily, when it comes to heroism, nothing is unbelievable], comments Bardamu (RI, 101), before being cheated of the plaudits by Branledore.

This scene attains its true significance, however, when it is recalled that this theatre of patriotism really existed during the war. It was a theatre where an actress draped in the French flag could declaim:

> *Tomber pour la Patrie et pour la liberté,*
> *C'est la plus belle mort, c'est l'immortalité !*[11]
>
> [*To fall for the Fatherland and to be free*
> *Is the loveliest death, it's immortality!*]

This knowledge lends conviction and truth to one of *Voyage*'s most extraordinary scenes as, indeed, to the whole of Céline's theatre of patriotism (see also 5.3 *Marcel Lafaye*).

7.4 THE DEATH OF CAMARADERIE

The Denial of Camaraderie

If the most striking aspect of Céline's rewriting of his war past is his conversion from hero to coward, the most troubling aspect is his denial of camaraderie. We have seen Audoin-Rouzeau's assertion that camaraderie was largely illusory and it is easy to claim that lack of camaraderie in *Voyage* is a dramatisation of this fact (see 1.4 *Endurance*). Indeed, this is part of the multiplicity of motives that can be ascribed to Céline; the denial of the revolutionary ideal of 'fraternity' is another. It is also true that anti-camaraderie belongs to *Voyage*'s logic of anti-commemoration. We have nonetheless seen that Céline was deeply affected by the suffering of his comrades during the war (see 3.3 *Flanders* and 4.1 *Shock*). By not acknowledging comradeship, therefore, he fails, in Christopher Coker's words, 'to testify to the meaning of his own experience'.[12] Indeed, he does more than this. Turning his back on his comrades, Céline betrays them. This section explores the meaning of this betrayal which, perhaps more than any other aspect of *Voyage* pushes the war beyond redemption and Céline beyond consolation.

Ironically, *Voyage* opens on an evocation of failed camaraderie. 'J'en aurais fait mon frère peureux de ce garçon-là !' [I would have made my brother in fear of that young boy], Bardamu says of the 'agent de la liaison'. Adding, 'mais on n'avait pas le temps de fraterniser non plus' [we didn't even have the time to fraternise] (RI, 14), he points to one reason why camaraderie is denied in *Voyage*. Céline's brief experience of war may have prevented him from forming the strongest bonds of camaraderie. This was Malraux's analysis. Noting, 'l'absence de toute collectivité dans le *Voyage*' [the absence of all collectivity in *Voyage*], he remarked of Céline that 'il était très peu de temps au front' [he wasn't at the front for very long].[13] In addition, we have seen that the bond between the young, worldly wise and cultured Parisian and his Breton comrades was not to begin with a strong one. Language itself divided them. This alone, however, cannot resolve *Voyage*'s anti-camaraderie.

Through his anti-camaraderie, Céline once again enters a dynamic of accusation. Bardamu heaps insult after insult upon his comrades, calling them 'des dégueulasses' [disgusting types] and 'des abrutis' [brutes] when they remain indifferent to his news of the colonel's death (RI, 20). This is fundamental to Céline's accusation. Soldiers' indifference to their own death and that of others, their lack of any imagination of death, allows the slaughter to continue. 'Le canon pour eux c'était rien que du bruit' [the cannon were nothing but noise to them], Bardamu rails. 'C'est à cause de ça que les guerres peuvent durer. Même ceux qui la font, en train de la faire, ne l'imaginent pas' [That's why wars go on. Even those soldiers who are fighting a war, in the very thick of it, just cannot imagine it] (RI, 36). Céline's view is consistent here with those expressed in his letters to Simone Saintu (see 4.1 *Africa*). In *Voyage*, Céline raises this view to a system.

The Destruction of Solidarity

There are two clear dimensions to Céline's anti-camaraderie: collective and personal. On the collective level, his purpose is not so much to deny that solidarity exists among soldiers, but to show it in a new light, not as a protecting or consoling force against death, but as an element in crowd formation. The war is rendered as the movement of a crowd:

> Avec casques, sans casques, sans chevaux, sur motos, hurlants, en autos, sifflants, tirailleurs, comploteurs, volants, à genoux, creusant, se défilant, caracolant dans les sentiers, pétaradant, enfermés sur la terre, comme dans un cabanon, pour y tout détruire, Allemagne, France et Continents... (RI, 13)

> [With helmets, without helmets, without horses, on motorbikes, howling, in cars, whistling, sniping, plotting, flying, kneeling, digging, marching, running for cover, skipping along paths, blasting, shut up on the Earth, as if it were a madhouse, ready to destroy everything in it, Germany, France and all of the continents...]

Cohesive camaraderie is the battlefield image of national solidarity and by attacking it Céline attacks the claim that war produces solidarity. For Céline, there is no national solidarity, only 'cette foutue énorme rage qui poussait la moitié des humains [...] à envoyer l'autre moitié vers l'abattoir' [that immense bloody rage which impelled half of humanity [...] to push the other half into the slaughterhouse] (RI, 50). For him, the end of a war waged by a society is as much the death of its own citizens as that of the enemy state. Society and power within that society legitimises itself by producing death, just as the French Republic has legitimised itself thanks to 'les viandes destinées aux sacrifices' [meat destined for sacrifice] (RI, 97).[14] The wilful slaughter of its own citizens, however, contradicts the state's claim to national solidarity. And indifference to, acceptance of, and collaboration in the death of comrade by comrade equally contradict the ideal of camaraderie. In Céline's terms, both are lies which hide the truth of murder.

The Failure of Camaraderie

The personal denial of camaraderie is, however, what is most unsettling. Céline's attack on camaraderie appears weakened in the context of his own experience. The seeds for the reversal are, however, to be found in that experience, in Céline's traumatic death encounter. This is where his heroic self dissolves; and it is here, in the moment of isolating separation from the crowd, that the bond with his comrades is broken. At Poelkapelle, Céline discovers the unacceptable absurdity and grotesqueness of his own death. Significantly, he discovers it while he is alone (see 3.3 *The Encounter with Death*). What he also discovers is that in death he *is* alone. One of the functions of the war crowd — we might say of *camaraderie* — writes Elias Canetti, is to protect the cowardice of the individual who does not wish to face death alone.[15] Céline's encounter with death, by isolating him, imposes cowardice upon him. He realises that the crowd does not share his death. He makes this very point when he writes 'mais on ne partage la mort de personne' [you do not share anyone's death] (RI, 88). Camaraderie has failed him and *Voyage* is the record of its failure.

The bond of comradeship offered Céline no protection against death; indeed, it led him towards the solitude of his own sacrifice. On the strength of this discovery, Céline breaks his contract with his comrades. He, indeed, is the one who feels betrayed by them, just as he feels betrayed by his family, by his society and by his past heroic self. The breach is not a clean one, however, and one senses the aching nostalgia for comradeship in *Voyage*, most particularly in the figure of Robinson, but also in Céline's 'community of telling' and his sustained use of 'soldier speech' (see 5.3 *The Community Of Telling* and 8.2 *Soldier Speech*). It is the solitude-melting companionship which is most missed. 'À deux on y arrive mieux que tout seul' [as two you manage much better than all alone], as Bardamu says (RI, 15). This, indeed, is the real crux of the denial of comradeship in *Voyage*, the manner in which it isolates Céline within his own memory of trauma.

7.5 THE DEATH OF COMPASSION

L'amour impossible

There is another root leading to the death of camaraderie. It pushes Céline even further beyond consolation. Yet again, it is part of his inescapable trauma of war. A statement made by Céline in 1932, when asked the meaning of *Voyage*, points to it. 'Personne ne l'a compris,' answered Céline. 'C'est l'amour [...]. L'amour impossible aujourd'hui' [No one has understood it. It is the impossibility of love nowadays].[16] Indeed, there is no love lost in *Voyage*'s post-war world. Céline's 'amour impossible' [impossibility of love] is not, however, just the summation of his failed relationships to Suzanne Nebout, Edith Follet and Elizabeth Craig.[17] It is an evocation once again of the horror of Verdun where love itself had died (see 1.4 *Mechanisation*). How could, Céline is asking, Verdun have happened if love, if compassion, were real? Indeed, he makes this clear in the same interview saying, 'c'est l'amour dont nous osons parler encore dans cet enfer, comme si l'on pouvait composer des quatrains dans un abattoir' [it's the love we dare yet to speak of in this hell, as if it were possible to go on composing quatrains in a slaughterhouse].[18] The question is not an unusual one in the aftermath of holocaust.[19] The evocation of Verdun, however, hides a more troubled and private reality. Indeed, 'l'amour impossible', is integral to Céline's war trauma. It is the expression of his inner deadness (see 4.2 *The Death Imprint*).

War contradicts compassion. The good soldier must kill efficiently without pity, and soldiers to survive must cut themselves off from compassion in a process known as psychic numbing. Robert Jay Lifton describes psychic numbing as a 'diminished capacity to feel, a useful defence mechanism for dealing with immediate threat but subsequently a problem in living'.[20] This process involves the death of compassion on a literal level and, while we have seen Céline's distress at death and injury to his comrades, it is still likely that psychic numbing was a very necessary part of his experience of war. It is likely, therefore, that the ongoing experience of the death of compassion as part of Céline's psychological make-up informs this theme in *Voyage*.[21]

In *Voyage*, compassion is undermined to begin with by the conditions of military command. Soldiers are nonchalantly sent to their deaths by their superiors. It is not surprising then that Bardamu's first pitiless encounter with death is reserved for his commanding officer. Following an explosion Bardamu contemplates his dead colonel:

> Le colonel avait son ventre ouvert, il en faisait une sale grimace. Ça avait dû lui faire du mal ce coup-là au moment où c'était arrivé. Tant pis pour lui ! S'il était parti dès les premières balles, ça ne lui serait pas arrivé. (RI, 17–18)

> [The colonel's stomach was cut right open, and you could tell from his face that he wasn't happy about it. It must have really hurt him, the explosion, when it caught him. Pity about him! If he'd left when the first bullets began flying about, nothing would have happened to him.]

Maman ! maman !

Robinson carries this lack of compassion even further. Deserting from his regiment he comes across his dying captain:

> Il était appuyé à un arbre, bien amoché le piston !... En train de crever qu'il était... Il se tenait la culotte à deux mains, à cracher... Il saignait de partout en roulant des yeux... Y avait personne avec lui. Il avait son compte... 'Maman ! maman !' qu'il pleurnichait tout en crevant et en pissant du sang aussi...
> 'Finis ça ! que je le lui dis. Maman ! Elle t'emmerde !'... (RI, 42)

> [He was lying against a tree, he was a real mess!... About to kick it, so he was... Holding his trousers with both his hands, spitting blood... He was bleeding from everywhere and rolling his eyes... There was no one with him. He was done for... 'Mama! Mama!' he snivelled as he was dying and pissing blood too...
> 'You can forget about that!' I told him. 'Mama! She doesn't give a shit about you!']

This scene — which indirectly reflects Céline's anguished disappointment in his own mother — is harrowing. Robinson's refusal of compassion has erased him as an agent of human sympathy. 'Y avait personne avec lui' [there was no one with him], is a commentary on his own not being there, his own death of compassion, as well as on the loneliness of the captain's death.[22] This scene should invite pity but instead Céline uses its blackly humorous potential to destroy pity.[23] He refuses to allow compassion redeem the war. But there are other facets to the death of compassion here. The above scenes recall Robert Lifton's observation that traumatised soldiers indulge in sadistic fantasies about 'those in the military who had abused them'.[24] This means that the above scenes, drained of compassion as they are, draw on a reality of warfare.

In addition, David Denby has shown how sentimental literary tableaux, soliciting the compassion of the observer, expressed a utopian Enlightenment view of human relations.[25] Compassion was central to the Enlightenment view of humanity. 'Though men do not universally rejoice with all whom they see rejoice [...] they naturally compassionate all [...] whom they see in distress,' wrote Samuel Butler.[26] Céline drains his particular tableaux of compassion to contradict this Enlightenment view of the human and announce a modern war-engendered literary vision free of sentimentality.[27] The experience of the death of compassion is, therefore, used by Céline as an important contradiction of Enlightenment values.[28]

The following scene exemplifies Céline's usurping and subversion of the literature of sentiment and projects the death of compassion into the very heart of human relations. Bardamu enters a house where there is the corpse of a young boy killed by the Germans:

> Et j'aperçus — c'était vrai — au fond, le petit cadavre couché sur un matelas, habillé en costume marin ; et le cou et la tête livides autant que la lueur même de la bougie, dépassaient d'un grand col carré bleu. Il était recroquevillé sur lui-même, bras et jambes et dos recourbés l'enfant. Le coup de lance lui avait fait comme un axe pour la mort par le milieu du ventre. Sa mère, elle, pleurait fort, à côté, à genoux, le père aussi. Et puis, ils se mirent à gémir encore tous ensemble. Mais j'avais bien soif. (RI, 39)

> [And I saw — it was true — at the back of the room, a little corpse lying on a mattress, dressed in a sailor suit, whose head and neck, pallid as the light of the candle, just showed above the big blue check collar. He was curled up on himself, with arms and legs bent, the child. The lance had made an axis for death through the middle of his body. His mother was

crying her eyes out, kneeling beside him, his father too. And then they all began to moan together. But I was very thirsty.]

This scene appears designed to solicit a compassionate response from the reader. Yet, faithful to his anti-compassion, anti-Enlightenment theme, Céline uses it to create the opposite effect. Bardamu asks for a bottle of wine, the mother's tears dry up, and they begin to haggle. Compassion disappears and the family's grief is revealed as a fiction. It is the money transaction which is real and it contradicts compassion. Confronted by 'l'amour impossible' Bardamu finds refuge in self-protecting hate:

> J'étais pas content d'avoir donné mes cent sous. Il y avait ces cent sous entre nous. Ça suffit pour haïr, cent sous, et désirer qu'ils en crèvent tous. Pas d'amour à perdre dans ce monde, tant qu'il y aura cent sous. (RI, 40)

> [I was not content to have paid my few pennies. Those few pennies had come between us. A few pennies is enough to make you hate them and want to see them done in the lot of them. No love lost in this world, as long as there are a few pennies left in it.]

Compassionating the distress of others

In *Voyage*, Céline is committed to telling all of 'ce qu'on a vu de plus vicieux chez les hommes' [the worst seen of men] (RI, 25) but redeeming goodness is also intimated. In the African episode, the revelation that Alcide, Bardamu's colleague, is sacrificing his life in the jungle for his orphaned niece astonishes Bardamu:

> Pudique Alcide ! Comme il avait dû en faire des économies sur sa solde étriquée... sur ses primes faméliques et sur son minuscule commerce clandestin... pendant des mois, des années, dans cet infernal Topo !... (RI, 159)

> [Modest Alcide! How he must have saved on only his miserable salary... his lousy bonuses and his few clandestine trading deals... for months, for years, in that hellish Topo!...]

This evidence of human goodness shames Bardamu and accuses his own emptiness:

> Je ne savais pas quoi lui répondre moi, je n'étais pas très compétent, mais il me dépassait tellement par le cœur que j'en devins tout rouge... [...] Je n'osais plus lui parler, je m'en sentais soudain énormément indigne de lui parler. (RI, 159)

> [I did not know how to answer him, I wasn't very competent to do so, and he was so much better than I was, that it made me blush... [...] I didn't

dare speak to him, I felt myself suddenly immensely unworthy of speaking to him.]

'L'amour impossible' has shifted to the very centre of Bardamu. Compassion, he has discovered, exists but not in him. It is hidden away in the silent, inaccessible depths of such as Alcide.

Bardamu is seldom offered love. Molly, the Detroit prostitute, 'un cœur infini vraiment, avec du vrai sublime dedans' [a truly infinite heart, full of something truly sublime] (RI, 230), is an exception. Molly, like Alcide, is prepared to sacrifice herself for others. 'Molly lui envoyait régulièrement, à sa sœur photographe, cinquante dollars par mois' [Molly regularly sent fifty dollars a month to her photographer sister] (RI, 230). Molly falls for Bardamu, gives him money and buys him a suit. 'Elle voulait que je soye heureux. Pour la première fois un être humain s'intéressait à moi, du dedans si j'ose le dire' [She wanted me to be happy. For the first time a human being was interested in me, from the inside dare I say] (RI, 229). Her capacity for love and compassion, however, only reveals Bardamu's incapacity. His youth over, 'j'y croyais plus!' [I didn't believe in it anymore], he says, leaving her (RI, 229). 'L'amour' proves 'impossible' yet again.

As signalled by the scene with the dead child in 'sailor costume' the suffering of children is a constant in *Voyage*. In one cruel scene, a child is tortured by her parents while Bardamu listens helplessly. 'Je n'étais bon à rien. Je ne pouvais rien faire. Je restais à écouter seulement comme toujours, partout' [I was good for nothing. I could do nothing to help. I could only listen as usual, no matter where I was] (RI, 267). When the ghost of compassion appears, it is nearly always taken over by an inability to act. When Bardamu does manage to act, compassion is destined to failure. In one of *Voyage*'s most poignant passages Bardamu, now a doctor, makes desperate and futile efforts to save the child, Bébert, from typhoid:

> Une espèce de typhoïde maligne c'était, contre laquelle tout ce que je tentais venait buter, les bains, le sérum... le régime sec... les vaccins... Rien n'y faisait. J'avais beau me démener, tout était vain. (RI, 277)

[A sort of malignant typhoid it was, against which everything I tried foundered, the baths, the serum... the dry diet... the vaccines... Nothing worked. I'd struggled for nothing, it was all useless.]

This death of compassion leaves Bardamu feeling as if he too has died in one of the most poignant expressions of this theme:

Je cherchais quand même si j'y étais pour rien dans tout ça. C'était froid et silencieux chez moi. Comme une petite nuit dans un coin de la grande, exprès pour moi tout seul. [...] J'ai fini par m'endormir [...] dans ma nuit à moi, ce cercueil. (RI, 291)

[I asked myself all the same if it had not all been my fault in some way. It was cold and silent in my house. It was like a little night in a corner of the big night, put there for me alone. [...] I eventually fell asleep [...] in my very own night, that coffin.]

L'amour de la vie des autres

Scenes such as these, with Alcide, Molly and Bébert, appear to contradict the theme of the death of compassion and to introduce sentiment in a text which is anti-sentiment. It is this paradoxical quality which leads to divergent views even among the most distinguished readers. Jack Kerouac considered Céline the most compassionate of novelists,[29] but Goncourt winner, Jean Rouaud, has expressed an opposing view. Said Rouaud of Céline, 'il n'aime pas ses personnages... on trouve vraiment un manque de compassion... je ne crois pas à sa compassion quand il parle de Bébert...' [He does not like his characters... there is really a lack of compassion... I do not believe in his compassion when he speaks of Bébert...].[30] This divergence in opinion is clarified by a close reading of the novel's final scenes where the theme of the death of compassion is most explicit. Robinson has been shot and Bardamu watches him die. Despite wanting to, Bardamu feels no compassion. 'Et je restais, devant Léon, pour compatir, et jamais j'avais été aussi gêné. J'y arrivais pas...' [And I remained, before Leon, to show him compassion but I had never felt so awkward. I just couldn't manage it] (RI, 496).

Robinson too seeks the saving grace of compassion. One of his final human acts is to look for pity from Bardamu. Bardamu is not up to it:

Il devait chercher un autre Ferdinand, bien plus grand que moi, bien sûr, pour mourir, pour l'aider à mourir plutôt, plus doucement. [...] Mais il n'y avait que moi, bien moi, moi tout seul, à côté de lui, un Ferdinand bien véritable auquel il manquait ce qui ferait un homme plus grand que sa simple vie, l'amour de la vie des autres. De ça, j'en avais pas, ou vraiment si peu que c'était pas la peine de le montrer. (RI, 496)

[He must have been looking for another Ferdinand, a lot bigger than me, certainly, to die, or rather to help him to die, more gently. [...] But there was only me, just me, me alone, there beside him, an all too real Ferdinand lacking all of that which makes a man bigger than his life, the love of others. That, I had nothing of, or so little really that it was hardly worthwhile showing it.]

Here there is recognition that it is love which makes us fully human. But what if love proves impossible? The dehumanising death of compassion in wartime clings to Bardamu and possesses him. Lacking compassion Bardamu is, like the war, beyond redemption:

On manque de presque tout ce qu'il faudrait pour aider à mourir quelqu'un. [...] On l'a chassée, tracassée la pitié qui vous restait, soigneusement au fond du corps comme une sale pilule. On l'a poussée la pitié au bout de l'intestin avec la merde. Elle est bien là qu'on se dit. (RI, 496)

[Almost everything needed to help someone to die is lacking. [...] What pity there was has been painstakingly chased and harried like some horrible pill into the very depths of the body. It's been driven as far as possible down into the gut, where the shit resides. That's where it belongs, we tell ourselves.]

Excremental imagery signals the scale of the defeat. The incapacity to feel dehumanises Bardamu. It has left him beyond compassion. Rouaud appears vindicated here, but only incidentally. He does not see that the lack of compassion he denounces is the direct product of Bardamu's struggle with the death of compassion itself. On the other hand, the acknowledgement of compassion in *Voyage*, no matter how rare or ineffectual, and the struggle towards it, leaves a reader like Kerouac with a deep impression of compassion at work while combating its obstacles. Bardamu states the case much more eloquently:

Je ne retrouvais rien de ce qu'on a besoin pour crever, rien que des malices. Mon sentiment c'était comme une maison où on ne va qu'aux vacances. C'est à peine habitable. (RI, 497)

[I couldn't find anything of that which you need to help you die, I had nothing but slyness. My heart was like a house you only visit on holidays. It was barely habitable.]

In its final scenes the true dynamic of compassion in *Voyage* is made explicit. *Voyage* struggles against the death of compassion at the same time as it records it. Bardamu struggles to overcome the death of compassion in himself. His story recounts his effort to recover the essential of his own lost humanity but it is a story characterised by a failure to believe in and to feel compassion. It is a story which begins with Verdun and with the death of compassion in wartime. Significantly, *Voyage* ends with a reiteration of the death of compassion. 'C'était raté !' [What a fiasco!], says Bardamu (RI, 501). Love remains impossible.[31]

7.6 THE ANTI-PSICHARI

Les Trois Ordres

Céline's inversion of the myth of the war experience ensures that *Voyage* becomes the anti-image of official commemoration. He is not content, however, to debase the content of commemoration, he debases its architects. Céline directs his attack at three main groups, the army, the Church and the scientific establishment. As we have seen, before the war these groups constituted Ernest Psichari's 'trois ordres' [three orders], 'les militaires, les prêtres, les savants' [the soldiers, the priests, the scientists], the arm, heart and brain of the nation (see 1.1 *Ernest Psichari*).[32] It is these groups who lead France into war and who emerged strengthened from the slaughter. In *Voyage*, Céline drags these groups into 'cette boue atroce, ce sang et cette merde' [the atrocious mud, the blood and the shit] of his own war memory and in so doing creates an anti-image of Psichari's pre-war world. He creates a series of anti-portraits in which Psichari's 'trois ordres' are exposed as complicit with war, bloodthirsty, venal and ridiculous.

The Military

Céline by denouncing the war itself, the military, and the myth of the war experience, makes of *Voyage* a sort of anti-*L'Appel des armes* and makes of himself an anti-Psichari. We have seen the substance of Céline's attack on the military in his varied portrait gallery of the French army command (see 7.1 *Denunciation*). In *Voyage*, the army is not a source of death mastery, but the source of death itself. The irony is that this reign of death extends first and foremost to its own soldiers. The *Amiral Brageton* scene is the culmination of

Céline's army portrait. Bardamu, fallen foul of his fellow passengers, is designated for sacrifice and despite his efforts at evasion is cornered by the soldiers on board, in their best military attire for the occasion. Here the desire to kill, although dressed in theatre, is naked. The scene is presented as a symbolic reprise of the war. As Bardamu fears, 'une exécution lente et douloureuse' [a slow and painful execution] (RI, 119), the novel's cycle of re-enactment takes hold once again. 'Cet homme me faisait l'effet d'un morceau de la guerre qu'on aurait remis brusquement devant ma route, entêté, coincé, assassin' [that man had the effect on me of a fragment of the war placed in my path, stubborn, determined, murderous]. Bardamu talks his way out of trouble as the whole scene becomes a sustained satire on the soldier. 'Tant que le militaire ne tue pas, c'est un enfant,' he says. 'N'ayant pas l'habitude de penser, dès qu'on lui parle il est forcé pour essayer de vous comprendre de se résoudre à des efforts accablants' [As long as the soldier isn't killing anyone, he's like a child. Not used to thinking, as soon as you speak to him he is obliged to make truly strenuous efforts to understand you] (RI, 121). Far from the monkish, aesthetic militarism of Psichari, the soldier in *Voyage* is a murderous child incapable of an intelligent act. The effect is to heap ridicule on Psichari's pre-war ideal.

Bardamu having saved himself repairs to the ship's bar with his would-be assassins. As a prelude to his arrival in Africa and the beginning of *Voyage*'s colonial episode, he directly addresses the theme of colonial heroism dear to Psichari in *L'Appel des armes* while continuing to heap ridicule on the military:

> Je demandais et redemandais à ces héros chacun son tour, des histoires et encore des histoires de bravoure coloniale. C'est comme les cochonneries, les histoires de bravoure, elles plaisent toujours à tous les militaires de tous les pays. (RI, 122)

> [Over and over I asked each of these heroes to tell me more and more stories of colonial acts of bravery. Stories of bravery, just like dirty stories, are greatly enjoyed by soldiers of all nations.]

The novel's colonial episode continues this satire on Psichari's colonial romanticism. Bardamu becomes the anti-Nangès (see 1.1 *Ernest Psichari*). His world is Nangès' world, or rather Psichari's, held in abomination. There is perhaps no better way of demonstrating the changed consciousness that emerged from the disaster of the Great War than by looking at *Voyage* and *L'Appel des armes* divided as they are by the war itself. Indeed, Psichari is now considered to be unreadable, while Céline resonates powerfully with a modern audience.

Le Savant

'L'Institut Bioduret Joseph' [Joseph Bioduret Clinic] (RI, 279), where Bardamu goes 'à la recherche d'un savant' [looking for a scientist], is the spiritual home of the 'savant' in *Voyage*. By situating it 'derrière La Villette' [behind La Villette], Paris's slaughterhouse, Céline makes his most striking commentary on the role of the 'savant' in the Great War.[33] Their laboratories fittingly are 'en grand désordre' [in great disarray] and full of 'des petits cadavres d'animaux éventrés' [the small corpses of disembowelled animals] (RI, 279). The 'savants' themselves Céline describes bitingly as 'de vieux rongeurs domestiques, monstrueux, en pardessus' [monstrous old domestic scavengers, in overcoats] (RI, 280).

Bestombes is the best example of Céline's 'savant', of whom Parapine and Baryton are also shining examples. We are left in no doubt that Bestombes is one, 'c'était un savant, apprîmes-nous' [he was a scientist, we learned], says Bardamu (RI, 89). He is a pre-eminently theatrical one at that. Later, Bardamu tells us, 'nous jouions tous en somme dans une pièce où il avait choisi lui Bestombes le rôle du savant bienfaisant et profondément, aimablement humain' [in short, we were all playing a role in some play in which he had chosen for himself, Bestombes, the role of the benevolent and profoundly and amiably human scientist] (RI, 90). 'Ce savant' [this scientist], Bardamu repeats, as if he needed to (RI, 91). The role of 'ce savant' is to sustain the war by repairing the minds of soldiers no longer willing or able to sacrifice themselves for France and by sending them back as soon as possible to the front. His science is backed up with the most eloquent of patriotic discourses. Addressing his 'incapables héros' (RI, 85) he tells them:

> Notre science vous appartient ! [...] Toutes ses ressources sont au service de votre guérison ! Aidez-nous [...] ! Et que bientôt vous puissiez tous reprendre votre place à côté de vos chers camarades des tranchées ! [...] Vive la France ! (RI, 86)

[Our science is yours! [...] All our resources are at the service of your recovery! Help us [...]! So that soon you will be able to rejoin your dear comrades in the trenches! [...] Long live France!]

It is backed up too with electricity:

C'est ainsi que j'entends traiter mes malades, Bardamu, par l'électricité pour le corps et pour l'esprit, par de vigoureuses doses d'éthique patriotique, par les véritables injections de la morale reconstituante ! (RI, 94)

[That's how I intend treating my patients, Bardamu, with electricity for the body, and for the mind, vigorous doses of patriotic principles, with veritable injections of moral restorative!]

Bestombes becomes the epitome of the mad scientist, or a beautiful Groucho Marx with 'les plus beaux yeux du monde, veloutés et surnaturels' [the most beautiful eyes in the world, velvety and otherworldly] (RI, 86).

The Church

The Church receives far less of Céline's scathing attention than the military but fares no better. The tone is set by Bardamu's 'prière vengeresse et sociale [...] Les Ailes en Or' [avenging social prayer [...] The Wings of Gold] where God is 'un Dieu qui compte les minutes et les sous [...] un cochon' [a God who counts minutes and pennies [...] a pig] (RI, 8–9). The Church is associated throughout Voyage with money. In the New York episode, Manhattan is 'le quartier précieux [...] le quartier pour l'or [...]. Plus précieux que du sang' [the rich district [...] the district for gold [...]. More precious than blood] (RI, 192). The precious quality of the gold equates it with the 'precious blood' of the sacrificed Christ and by extension with the notion of sacrifice itself. Jesus, it is implied, serves as a model to incite the soldier to sacrifice so that his blood can be miraculously transformed into gold or 'le Dollar' [the Dollar]. Céline launches on a sustained metaphor where the modern bank is seen as a church. The metaphor is subtly wrought; Manhattan is full of gold, 'un vrai miracle' [a true miracle]; 'le Dollar, un vrai Saint-Esprit' [the Dollar, a true Holy Spirit]; the clients are 'les fidèles' [the faithful] (RI, 193). Money becomes the sacred host, symbol of the sacrificed body. It is not eaten, however, but used to fatten the wallets of the faithful. 'Ils ne l'avalent pas la Hostie. Ils se la mettent sur le cœur' [They don't swallow it, the Host. No, they place it right over their heart] (RI, 193). The interweave of symbols is articulated around the notion of sacrifice and reflects one of *Voyage*'s preoccupations, that the sacrifice of the soldiers produced massive wealth for those in a position to profit from it. Its impact would be greatly lessened, however, if it were forgotten that the Church re-established itself in France during and after the war, or that while claiming ownership of the war dead it was one of the architects of commemoration. As we have seen, the discourse of commemoration was firmly based on the founding notion of sacrifice (see 2.1 *Commemoration and Myth* and *The Dead*). Céline thus sees the Church as one of the chief promoters and beneficiaries of the war.

Protiste

Robert Jay Lifton tells us that Vietnam veterans reserved a very special tone of 'ironic rage' for 'chaplains and "shrinks"'.[34] For them, 'the only thing worse than being ordered by the military authorities to participate in absurd evil is to have that evil rationalised and justified by guardians of the spirit.'[35] The Great War veteran, Céline, shares their very special rage, visible in his portraits of *Voyage*'s 'shrinks', Bestombes and Baryton, and of its priests. 'Je n'aimais pas les curés' [I didn't like priests], confesses Bardamu (RI, 335). Already he has been sold into slavery by one priest — 'une longue croix dorée oscillait sur son ventre et des profondeurs de sa soutane montait [...] un grand bruit de monnaie' [a long, golden cross swayed over his belly and from the depths of his soutane could be heard [...] a great din of coins] (RI, 180) — when another arrives with a devilish transaction to propose. Protiste collaborates with death. 'Il avait comme honte de cette collaboration,' says Bardamu, but 'une espèce de sale audace s'était emparée de lui [...] avec l'argent' [He appeared somewhat ashamed of his collaboration, but a shabby daring had taken hold of him [...] because of the money] (RI, 339). Protiste has become an accomplice to the Henrouilles, covering up the botched attempt to kill 'la mère Henrouille' [grandmother Henrouille]. His solution to the problem has an advantage, 'il comportait une commission' [it involved a commission] (RI, 341). This advantage appeals to Bardamu. 'Mille francs d'espérance !' he says. 'J'avais changé d'avis sur le curé' [A thousand francs in prospect! I'd changed my mind about the priest] (RI, 342–343). Bardamu here adopts the role of debased, conniving 'savant', and priest and doctor collaborate to spirit Robinson and 'la vieille' [the old woman] away to Toulouse, where they will work as curators of a crypt. The crypt itself symbolises the Church's foundation in death, its promise of death mastery, and its venal exploitation of the same. 'C'est pas tous les jours qu'on peut faire travailler les morts' [It's not everyday you can put the dead to work], comments Bardamu (RI, 342). Protiste hovers reticently while Bardamu talks Robinson into accepting the arrangement. Bardamu cannot withhold his admiration. 'Ces curés ils savent tout de même vous éteindre les pires scandales' [Those priests know how to cover up the worst scandals], he says (RI, 342). It is, of course, the Church's role in the war commemoration that Céline is calling to mind.

Céline's knowing portrait of Protiste completes a sacred and conspiratorial trinity of army, Church and scientific establishment. Through his attack on this triumvirate he completes his condemnation of the official commemoration but also extends it to the pre-war world of which *Voyage* is now the anti-image and Céline the anti-Psichari.

Typically of Céline, he allows Robinson the last word. '"Ils me trompent ! Ils me trompent tous !" qu'il gueulait' ['They're cheating me ! They're all cheating me !' he roared] (RI, 343). Announcing to all and sundry that it is his role as ex-soldier to be duped and duped again, by everybody.

Conclusion

What, it might be asked, does Maurice Rieuneau mean when he writes that *Voyage*'s witness to war 'dépasse infiniment celle des témoignages [...] rencontrés dans la décennie 1920–1930' [infinitely surpasses that of those testimonies [...] which appear in the 1920s]?[36] We have seen that a significant part of this witness is the enlargement of Céline's circular vision of war from the battlefield to the entire planet, so that war in *Voyage*, is truly a *world* war (see 4.3 *The Cycle of Revolution*).[37] In *Voyage*, the whole world is organised around the production of death. Indeed, it is hard, looking back at the reality of world conflict in the first half of the twentieth century, not to recognise real truth in Céline's vision. However, while Céline's war is a global one and while, as the portraits in this chapter have illustrated, his condemnation is also global, embracing a whole world at war, and all of humanity, including himself, the strength of his witness to war has a further significant dimension, which may have contributed to a painful intensification of his trauma.

Speaking about the Holocaust, Saul Friedländer raised the problem of looking for redemption in past catastrophe, saying 'there is no redemptive message in [the Holocaust] at all.'[38] The most difficult task facing the survivor, Friedländer says, is 'precisely *not* to look for redemption'.[39] This is what Céline does in *Voyage*.[40] The death of camaraderie, of compassion, and of the redeeming values of commemoration push the war beyond redemption and push Céline beyond consolation. Indeed, this is what makes it possible to say of *Voyage* that it is made in the image of the young cuirassier who, fearing his arm would be amputated, refused an anaesthetic (see 3.3 *The End of the War*). *Voyage* is, indeed, a vision of war beyond redemption and beyond consolation. It is literature without the anaesthetic.

---

[1] Céline's description of the Great War as 'une formidable erreur' anticipates by seventy years historian Niall Ferguson's conclusion to his *The Pity of War*, calling the war 'the greatest *error* of modern history'. See Ferguson, p.462.

[2] Robert Llambias, 'Guerre, histoire et langage dans le récit célinien', *Revue des Sciences Humaines*, 204 (October–December 1986), 89–105 (p.91).

[3] For a detailed study of the image of the monster and the monstrous in *Voyage*, see Leslie Davis, 'L'anti-monde de L.-F. Céline'.

[4] On *Voyage* and Napoleon, see Nicholas Hewitt, *Les maladies du siècle*, p.12. According to Hewitt, 'Céline's use of Napoleon is completely in keeping with the ethos of the "nouveau mal du siècle": unable to live according to the heroic Napoleonic model.' 'Nouveau mal du siècle' [new century malaise].

[5] Fussell, *The Great War and Modern Memory*, pp.192–193.

[6] Fussell, p.192.

[7] Crocq, p.237.

[8] Lifton, *Home from the War*, pp.186–187. Lifton describes Vietnam veterans' concern with the counterfeit as occupying the 'centre of their survivor struggle'. This concern with the counterfeit extends to the individual himself. Lifton cites Philip Kingry, 'I am a lie. What I have to say is a lie. But it is the most true lie you will ever hear about a war.' See Lifton, p.187. Kingry's sentiments could certainly be ascribed to Céline and *Voyage*.

[9] Llambias is thinking particularly of 'la *Légende du Roi Krogold*', which features in *Mort à crédit*. See Llambias, p.89.

[10] Fussell, *The Great War and Modern Memory*, p.193.

[11] See Bastier, p.376. See also Henri Godard's preface to this book, pp.ix–x.

[12] Christopher Coker, *War and the 20ᵗʰ Century* (London: Brassey's, 1994), p.154.

[13] In Grover, p.97.

[14] See Elias Canetti on the anxiety of command, pp.546–547. According to Canetti, the ruler fears his people will recoil against his command and so he sends them to war as a means of annihilating them.

[15] Canetti, p.84.

[16] 'Interview avec Merry Bromberger', *Cahiers Céline*, 1, 29–32 (p.31).

[17] Céline's relationship with Craig was ending, indeed practically finished, at the time of this interview. For a note on Nebout, see endnote 18, p.163, of this work.

[18] 'Interview avec Merry Bromberger', p.31.

[19] Lawrence L. Langer in his *Holocaust Testimonies* offers the survivor testimony of Edith P. In a train leaving Auschwitz she raises herself to view a station platform. The scene is perfectly normal, but idyllic in the circumstances. The sun is bright, the station clean. She sees a woman waiting with a child. Everything is normal, representing a normality shattered in Auschwitz, where the sun was never beautiful. This normal world now seems like paradise for Edith P. Enchanted by what she sees, the sun, the woman and the child, she asks 'is there such a thing as love?' Langer, *Holocaust testimonies: the ruins of memory* (New Haven: Yale University Press, 1991), p.55.

[20] Lifton, *The Protean Self*, p.82.

[21] François Gibault, in conversation with myself, has stressed Céline's compassion as a medical practitioner. This does not preclude, however, that compassion should be problematic for Céline on both an individual and on a general human level. Indeed, the experience of the war ensures that it is.

[22] When asked the meaning of this scene Céline cynically replied, in full anti-Norton Cru mode, 'trente mille exemplaires de plus de vendus' [thirty thousand more copies sold], which if nothing else, recognises that the commercialisation of the memory of disaster has little to do with the development of compassion. See 'Interview avec G.Ulysse', *Cahiers Céline*, 1, 70–72 (p.70).

[23] In the Robinson scene, the captain's crying for his mother is emblematic. His helpless *Maman !* was familiar to soldiers returned from the battlefields. Blaise Cendrars described it in the following manner:

> Mais le cri le plus affreux que l'on puisse entendre et qui n'a pas besoin de s'armer d'une machine pour vous percer le cœur, c'est l'appel tout nu d'un petit enfant au berceau : '— Maman! maman !...' que poussent les hommes blessés à mort qui tombent et que l'on abandonne entre les lignes après une attaque qui a échoué [...]. Et ce petit cri instinctif qui sort du plus profond de la chair [...] est si épouvantable à entendre que l'on tire des feux de salve sur cette voix pour la faire taire [...] par pitié... par rage...par désespoir... par impuissance... par dégoût... par amour...

> [But the most awful cry you can hear which does not need the help of a machine to pierce your heart is the naked appeal of a small child it its cradle: '—Mama! Mama!...' called out by fatally wounded men who have fallen and been abandoned after an attack has failed [...]. And this instinctive little plaint which rises from the deepest part of flesh [...] is so awful to hear that shots are fired at it to silence it [...] out of pity... out of anger... out of despair... out of powerlessness... out of disgust... out of love...]

Note the strong compassion of Cendrars' rendering of this primeval cry. It has a poignancy transgressed in Céline where the death of compassion is paramount. See Cendrars, *La main coupée* (Paris: Denoël, 1946), p.431. Léon Poirier's film *Verdun*, which Céline may have seen in Paris when he was writing *Voyage*, also contains a scene where a dying soldier cries out for his mother (see 2.1 *11 November 1928*).

[24] Lifton, *Home from the War*, p.142.

[25] See David Denby, 'Civil War, Revolution and Justice in Victor Hugo's *Quatrevingt-treize*', *Romance Studies: Images of War*, 30 (1997), 7–17.

[26] Samuel Butler, 'On Compassion', in *The Age of Enlightenment*, ed. by Simon Eliot and Beverley Stern, 2 vols (London: Ward Lock Educational, in association with The Open University Press, 1979), I, 37–43 (p.38).

[27] A quality acknowledged and applauded by André Malraux who said, 'le *Voyage* [...] n'était pas sentimental et c'est sa force' [*Voyage* [...] was unsentimental and that is its strength]. Cited in Grover, p.88.

[28] In this context, see Marie-Christine Bellosta on Céline's 'anti-Rousseauism'. Bellosta, pp.235–248.

[29] Kerouac, *L'Herne*, p.423.

[30] Remarks made in the course of a public lecture at Trinity College Dublin, 12 December 1998. Rouaud more generally denounced 'une sorte de faux-semblant dans l'écriture même célinienne qui m'agace' [a sort of falseness in Céline's writing style which annoys me].

[31] Much of the material in this section on compassion has appeared previously in Tom Quinn, 'The Death of Compassion in Louis-Ferdinand Céline's *Voyage au bout de la nuit*', *The Irish Journal of French Studies*, 1 (2001), 67–74.

[32] Léon Riegel quotes Psichari's Nangès in *L'Appel des armes*, 'à ce point de vue, de l'ensemble de la société, nous ne sommes guère comparables qu'au prêtre et au savant' [from this point of view, taking society as a whole, we are comparable only to the priest and to the scientist]. Riegel, p.61.

[33] See Hewitt, *The Golden Age of Louis-Ferdinand Céline*, p.69.

[34] Lifton, *Home from the War*, p.163.

[35] Lifton, *Home from the War*, p.166.

[36] Rieuneau, p.308.

[37] Hew Strachan writes that the First World War gave shape to Clausewitz's abstract concept of 'absolute' war. *Voyage* gives literary shape to the reality of 'absolute' war. See Strachan, *The First World War* (London: The Historical Association, 1993), p.5. This work is a pamphlet, not to be confused with Strachan's major First World War study already cited. See also 1.2 *Total War*.

[38] Saul Friedländer, contribution to 'Roundtable Discussion', in *Writing and the Holocaust*, ed. by Berel Lang (New York and London: Holmes & Meier, 1988), pp.287–289 (p.287).

[39] Saul Friedländer, p.289.

[40] Friedländer envisages an art reaching beyond redemption as an art arriving at 'that deepest ironic vision which is tragic-ironic, in the sense of that total chaos and senselessness referred to by Paul Fussell in his account of the "Great War in modern memory"'. See Friedländer, p.289. It is, of course, our view that Céline is the supreme voice of Fussell's 'modern memory' (See Introduction, *Methodology*). It is, indeed, Céline's willingness to go beyond redemption which makes him so.

CHAPTER 8

ORAL WITNESS

From the Oral to the Demonic

Introduction

'La guerre n'est-elle pas [...] d'abord le mal du langage?' [The war, is it not [...] first of all a malady of language?], asks Robert Llambias of *Voyage*.[1] Indeed, Céline's war is very much a product of language, of the discourses which shaped the war itself and which continued to shape its memory. Seeing these 'sick' discourses as complicit with war and as shaping a coming cataclysm, Céline seeks to challenge them by evolving a new, healing language of truth-telling. In doing so, he creates a new voice in French literature and provides an unprecedented form of witness to an unprecedented war. This chapter examines Céline's language as oral witness. It explores *Voyage*'s irony, humour and obscenity before examining the manner in which the novel's 'demonic' imagery represents the experience of the war itself while providing evidence of the collapse of a previous 'symbol system'.

8.1 THE DEATH OF LITERATURE

A New Style

Voyage introduced a new style in French literature. This style is oral. *Voyage* was the first novel in the French language written entirely in oral form and as such it transgresses its literary past. Writes D. Racelle-Latin, 'le style naît du désir de renverser et le langage connu et la langue littéraire existante' [the style is born from the desire to overturn both language as it is known and existing literary language].[2] As such, *Voyage* marks one of those turning points where literature returns to what Laurence Van Der Post calls the 'living and immediate word'.[3]

The Living Word

Where does this renewal of language begin? Céline claimed he was reaching back to Rabelais' attempt to introduce popular speech into literature.[4] For Céline, conventional literary language was dead. As he said, 'les mots sont morts, dix sur douze sont inertes. Avec ça, on fait plus mort que la mort' [words are dead, ten out of twelve are inert. With them, you appear more dead than death itself].[5]

We have observed how Céline's silence, while expressing symbolic union with the war dead, also represented a collapse in the artist's faith in language (see 5.2 *The Temptation of Silence*). Céline remedies this through the creation of new rhetorical forms which express an unprecedented event using unprecedented means, and which embody a modern consciousness emerged from the war itself. In a life-affirming mode of protean transformation, he writes in opposition to his own literary past. Furthermore, he reaches after truthfulness by striving to capture the natural speech of someone who had experienced the war and whose language echoed it: the soldier. As we have seen, the soldier privileged the oral as a new locus of truth-telling (see 1.4 *Censorship*). In *Voyage*, the language of the soldier and veteran becomes Céline's language of truth.

The Language of Truth-Telling

The oral not just challenges Céline's literary past, it represents a striving for authenticity and, as such, it assuages guilt for transgressing silence. Significantly, through evoking his own language and the language of his comrades in battle, Céline's oral style represents a return to his origins in the Great War, and so represents a real act of memory, as well as a form of reconstituted comradeship. It is the language of a soldier speaking to soldiers (see 5.3 *The Community Of Telling*). More than anything, however, it is Céline's attempt to heal self and the murderous stasis of his world through creating the shift in language called for by Janet (see 5.1 *Traumatic Memory*).

Céline's language, however, is an invented one, an approximation to popular speech, not the real thing. Maurice Rieuneau recognises the artificiality of Céline's oral style, but also its authenticity. When Rieuneau comments that Céline's language 'paraît jaillir des profondeurs d'une âme confrontée à l'épouvante' [appears to surge from the depths of a soul confronted by horror][6] he acknowledges the truth of the narrating voice, the voice of witness to horror, Céline's voice. Through the creation of a uniquely oral style, Céline attempts to communicate the horror of war to the ordinary man and woman. Céline's embrace of the demotic, however, leads to one of *Voyage*'s greatest ironies in that, through its language, it represents the reality of its time, an age of democracy, in a novel — and an author — which is supposedly profoundly anti-democratic. Céline's orality together with his totalising intertextuality offers a comprehensive representation of the culture and society of his time. His choice is driven, however, by a need to speak to the generality of people, to couch his message about past and future war, delivered from a circumscribed present, in a language which is their language and which, at the same time, bears the stamp of truth. The creation of a new language with which to speak to the world about its disasters is evidence of Céline's commitment to healing his world and is a powerful, redeeming contradiction of the novel's apparent metaphysic of futility.

Protean Language

Céline's language is protean and as such is determined by his need to break out of the static rhetoric of re-enactment. Like self, language in *Voyage* adopts a multitude of changing forms.[7] This is immediately felt through the apparent hesitations and uncertainties which mark Céline's use of grammar. Henri Godard has noted, in *Voyage*, the use of 'passé simple' [simple past] and 'passé composé' [composite past] in a 'mélange anarchique' [anarchic mix] occurring even at the level of the individual sentence.[8] Philippe Lejeune has identified this confusion as part and parcel of certain 'procédés du "vécu"' [processing of 'lived experience'], marking a contrast between 'les temps du discours' [the tenses of discourse] and 'ceux de l'histoire' [those of the story].[9] In *Voyage*, the effect is wonderfully representative of Céline's linguistic shape-shifting, as well as marking a movement between two modes of consciousness and, as we shall see, two modes of writing. In addition, it marvellously evokes an experience of time where there exists a messy overlap of distant past and recent past intruding on a present of traumatised recall. Ultimately, however, it is one of Céline's emblems of the protean, a refusal of stasis, and a fierce and inspired assault on 'les mots [...] inertes' [inert words].

The protean confers *Voyage* with a rich polyphony. Léon Daudet said of it:

> Ce livre n'est pas écrit en argot [...]. Il est écrit en bagout parisien, langue à part, vadrouillarde en ses apparences, et savante en ses profondeurs [...]. Les inversions latines y abondent. On y trouve des composés de forme grecque, des salmigondis demeurés syntaxiques, du rire franc et de la pestilence.[10]

> [This book is not written in argot [...]. It is written in Parisian slang, a language apart, streetwise in appearance, and knowing deep down [...]. Latin inversions are rife. There are Greek-style composites, hotchpotches that remain grammatical, frank laughter and pestilence.]

The protean variety of Céline's language needs emphasis.[11] Argot is frequent, as is popular speech, often rooted in the obscene or scatological. There are archaisms, medical terms and neologisms. Perhaps more than any other feature, neologisms emphasise the protean effort of Céline's language to escape stasis through re-invention of itself.

Notably, Céline employs a range of philosophical terms, suitably capitalised — 'Infini' [Infinite], 'la Mort' [Death], 'Éthique' [Ethics], 'Fatalité' [Fate] — which lend *Voyage* the aura of a philosophical treatise, an effect which, as we shall soon see, is not at all gratuitous (see 9.1 *Céline's Philosophies*).

Voyage is layered too with rich strata of literary language. It is surprising, indeed shocking, to find this high style juxtaposed with Céline's debased one, but the ultimate effect is of new form erupting from old in a protean movement of transgression and disintegration. Two examples show this process at work. The first is the evocation of the 'prairie d'août [...] ombrée de cerisiers et brûlée déjà par la fin d'été' [August field [...] shaded by cherry-trees and scorched already by the end of summer] (RI, 20). The classical literary tone here is in stark contrast to the rest of the scene where 'il y en avait pour des kilos et des kilos de tripes étalées' [there were kilos and kilos of guts spilled out] and 'des moutons éventrés avec leurs organes en pagaïe' [gutted sheep whose inner organs were a shambles]. The scene exemplifies Céline's anti-nature and, given the Enlightenment reverence for nature, his anti-Enlightenment stance, but its supreme value is as a confrontation with an earlier style of writing whose linguistic and symbolic content he is in the process of destroying.

Céline's depiction of the African sunset goes further (RI, 168).[12] Here his destruction of the romantic image of the sunset accuses the tradition which has exalted it. In a sustained passage of incredible tension, the romantic sweep of 'toutes les couleurs retombaient en lambeaux, avachies sur la forêt comme des oripeaux après le centième' [all the ribbons of colours, falling flaccid over the forest like rolls of coloured paper marking a hundredth performance] contrasts starkly with the brutality of 'la nuit' [the night] with its 'mille et mille bruits de gueules de crapauds' [myriad noises of croaking toads] or 'des arbres entiers bouffis de gueuletons vivants' [whole trees choke-full with uproarious feasting]. Céline's new style here cannibalises the pre-existing one whose death it proclaims. What is ultimately taking place here, however, is a paradoxical pattern of connection and disconnection we have already seen in *Voyage*'s intertextuality, through which Céline affirms his place within a literary tradition at the same time as he enacts a profound realignment and revaluation of it. Once again he declares the moribund nature of what has preceded him and points to his own status as the sum and summit of French literature. The transgression, however, is what matters most. Here, indeed, is Céline's most exciting and successful attempt to break out of static circularity. That is, it is in his innovative style that we most clearly see the author in search of his own immortality.

Emotion

Charles-François Ramuz influenced Céline's spoken style. Ramuz had, prior to Céline, evolved a 'style parlé' [spoken style].[13] For him standard written French, 'la langue apprise' [learned language], was 'en définitive une langue morte' [a dead language]. Written French was for Ramuz 'une *"traduction"*' [a translation] of spoken French. 'Il y avait en lui comme un principe d'interruption' [there was a form of interruption in it], he claimed. As a translation it lacked authenticity. 'L'homme qui s'exprime vraiment ne traduit pas. [...] L'homme qui parle n'a pas le temps de traduire' [the man who truly expresses himself does not translate. [...] The man who speaks does not have the time to translate]. Here then, in its untranslated immediacy of emotion, is the chief animating ingredient of Céline's oral style.

For Céline, writing *Voyage* released the emotion pent-up in silence. Orality allowed this. Robert Lifton's lifeline of rage is, in Céline, verbal. Writing becomes an exercise in reanimating emotion directed against his experience of death. For Céline, the absence of emotion is synonymous with death. Other writers, lacking emotion, are moribund. 'Tous les autres écrivains sont morts...' [All the other writers are dead...] Céline would say in his treatise on style *Entretiens avec le professeur Y* [*Conversations with Professor Y*], 'ils pourrissent à la surface [...] momies... momies tous !... privés d'émotions !' [they're rotting on the surface [...] mummies... all mummies... lacking emotions !] (RIV, 530).

Describing his technique to Milton Hindus, Céline said, 'je suis bien l'émotion avec les mots je ne lui laisse pas le temps de s'habiller en phrases... je la saisis toute crue ou plutôt toute poétique' [I follow the emotion with the words, I don't leave it time to dress itself in sentences... I seize it in its crude, or rather, in its poetic form].[14] Merlin Thomas said of him, 'Céline achieved a manner of writing which was *emotionally* rather than intellectually based.'[15] Céline's emotive style is vitalising. It struggles against the death of compassion in *Voyage* and against his own inner deadness. Céline's emotion is a defensive weapon. It tends towards hate. As he said, 'c'est la haine qui fait l'argot' [it is hate which makes argot].[16]

If emotion is a lifeline, then the more extreme it is, the more viable the lifeline. The more emotion Céline succeeds in transmitting through language the more alive he feels. In pushing back death in this way, Céline's language achieves a form of death mastery. He himself suggested that the vitalising emotion in his language is directly inspired by the experience of death. Speaking once again of Rabelais he said, 'la mort le guettait, et ça inspire, la mort ! c'est même la seule chose qui inspire, je le sais, quand elle est là, juste derrière' [death was looking out for him, and that inspires, death ! It's indeed the only thing that inspires, I know well, when it's there, right behind you].[17]

Oral Witness

What art is needed to show the 'sights, faces, words, incidents' of war? 'The art,' Edmund Blunden opined, 'is [...] to collect them in their original form of incoherence.'[18] In *Voyage*, this 'original incoherence' is embodied in Céline's oral language and marks an effort on his part to offer 'oral witness'.

Although *Voyage* is not a *real* oral narrative, that is, a *spoken* one, it strives to be one. 'Le lecteur qui me lit ! il lui semble [...] que quelqu'un lui lit dans la tête !...' [The reader who reads me! It seems to him [...] that someone is reading to him in his head!], Céline said in *Entretiens* (RIV, 545). Moreover, the testimony of Elizabeth Craig reveals that Céline spoke his text repeatedly as he wrote it.[19] In this way, *Voyage*'s spoken quality reveals a Céline caught within the circular dynamic of oral witness as, through re-enactment, he tells his story over and over again.

There is a marked difference between literary and oral testimony. Lawrence L. Langer has explored this difference. Oral testimonies, says Langer, 'do not function in time like other narratives, since the losses they record raise few expectations of renewal or hopes of reconciliation'.[20] On the other hand, 'when literary form, allusion, and style intrude on the surviving victim's account, we risk forgetting where we are and imagine deceptive continuities.'[21] That is, in literary witness, order and continuity are substituted for disorder and discontinuity. Literary witness, in other words, tends towards redemption, while oral narrative, as happens in *Voyage*, remains beyond it.

If speech represents untranslated thought or emotion, oral testimony represents untranslated memory. According to Langer:

> Oral testimony is a living commentary on the limits of autobiographical narrative [...]. It [...] reveals the limits of memory's ability to re-create that past. The issue is not merely the unshareability of the experience but also the witness's exasperated sense [...] of a failure in communication.[22]

Oral narratives struggle openly with the limits of words and the appeal of silence. 'Oral testimonies pause in a variety of ways,' writes Langer.[23] They hesitate and leave gaps 'as if in pursuit of controlled *in*accuracy, not as a calculated breach of truth, but as a concession to what words cannot do'.[24] 'The initial problem surfacing in these oral testimonies [...],' he says, 'is [...] whether *any*thing can be meaningfully conveyed.'[25] He comments, 'the anxiety of futility lurks beneath the surface.'[26] All of these tensions are evident in *Voyage*.

Reading *Voyage*, we are face to face with a text where many literary conventions, of form, dialogue and characterisation obtain. However, *Voyage* is constantly pulled away from its 'literariness' by its tendency towards orality. Oral narrative, as we have seen, disrupts literary narrative. Moreover, through the oral, Céline challenges our *reading* of his testimony and undermines the reassuring, consolatory nature of the literary construct. He obliges us to grapple with the unprecedented, inchoate, absurd nature of the war itself. He brings us closer than ever to the psychological state of the survivor.

Through the oral, Céline seeks to abolish the distance between the novelist and his witness. Furthermore, he seeks to abolish the distance between novelist-witness and the reader, by transforming the former into *speaker* and the latter into *listener*. In doing so, Céline exposes us, and himself, to the real confusion and pain of remembering. It is a price paid for truthfulness. Writes Langer of oral witness to a later holocaust:

> The raw material of oral Holocaust narratives, in content and manner of presentation, resists the organising impulse of moral theory and art. Does this keep these narratives closer to their source in the pain of persecution? A kind of unshielded truth emerges from them.[27]

Protean *Voyage*, however, is both oral and literary, and literary witness also has its merits. 'No oral testimonies so far equal the *art* of writers like Primo Levi,' affirms Langer.[28] Céline strives for the best of both worlds, a symbiosis in which oral narrative assures the authenticity and believability of its literary face.

The tension between oral and literary witness creates a further duality in *Voyage*. At the root of this duality is Céline's need to grasp the immortalising lifeline of literature and to transcend his own ultimately imprisoning oral narrative, as one consequence of the oral, with its characteristic 'rappel', is to keep narrative turning upon itself. It is this circularity which perhaps leads to Langer's description of oral witness as 'endless remembering'.[29] Once again, we see that in *Voyage*, there is no real end to witness (see 5.3 *From Truth to Untruth*).

8.2 SOLDIER SPEECH

Humour

'*Il faut être plus qu'un petit peu mort pour être vraiment rigolo*' [*you have to be more than a little bit dead to be truly funny*], Céline said, juxtaposing laughter and death (RIV, 519). In *Voyage*, humour occupies the same plane as emotion and is an indispensable part of soldier speech. 'Le rire de Bardamu,' as Jean Bastier says, 'est identique à celui des *Poilus* de 14' [Bardamu's laughter is identical to that of the 1914 *Poilus*].[30] Laughter enables Céline to keep the horror of war, death and memory at bay and to escape from his own sense of inner deadness. 'La mort m'habite. Et *elle me fait rire* !' [Dead inhabits me. And *it makes me laugh*], he said.[31]

Humour was a weapon against the war, its discourses and values. As Terrence des Pres comments, 'the comic spirit proceeds in an antimimetic mode that mocks *what is*, that deflates or even cancels the authority of its object.'[32] 'Laughter revolts' and enacts 'resistance', Des Pres writes, refusing to take what has happened on its 'own crushing terms'.[33]

'In war, even humour is different, because it is full of death,' writes Samuel Hynes.[34] *Voyage* is full of such humour. Robinson's sadistic scorn towards his dying officer (RI, 42) or 'la mère Henrouille' exhibiting her 'mummies' to the tourists (RI, 390) are good examples of this, but the darkness of *Voyage*'s humour is unrelenting. Even such a stern moralist as Lord Moran recognised the value of humour in war, writing:

> Only humour helped. Humour that made a mock of life and scoffed at our own frailty. Humour that touched everything with ridicule and had taken the bite out of the last thing, death.[35]

Céline's humour is ultimately directed at this 'last thing'. Through vitalising humour he strives to loosen death's grip on him.

It was not easy, however, to be funny about the war. 'It is really hard to be funny about the war,' says historian John Horne. 'Yet the second chapter of *Voyage* is the funniest written about the war.'[36] But Céline is not just being funny about the war. He is being funny about the way the war was remembered.

The memory of the Great War, like the later memory of the Holocaust, was kept, as it still is, with extreme solemnity. To laugh at the war and the memory of the war was to infringe a taboo. Céline's laughter thus disturbs the sanctity of the collective war memory. He uses humour to strip it of its redemptive layers. Céline is once again, through humour, distancing himself from the supports to memory that appeared to work for the majority of the population. Or did they?

The use of soldier speech, laden with black humour and irony, was undoubtedly part of the appeal of *Voyage* to its vast international readership in the 1930s and beyond. This language was rooted in the experience of war and in particular in the soldier's experience of death. Black humour was particularly widespread during the war.[37] Its qualities helped the soldier to master or counteract death. These were the qualities needed by memory at the end of the 1920s, still haunted by one cataclysm, and facing into another visible on the horizon. Ironically, they were provided in *Voyage* by a form of scathing anti-memory, a bitter humour that mocked the values and institutions of commemoration. That *Voyage* was received with such broad enthusiasm indicates that its rhetorical adventure had found an echo in the hearts and minds of very many. The irruption of humour into the collective memory of the Great War can, therefore, be seen as one further example of the failure of traditional memory, not just to mediate death, but to draw on those resources that could best do so. Traditional memory could never use laughter to shake off death. It was simply incapable of being funny.

Irony

If irony is the keynote of the modern, as Paul Fussell maintains, then *Voyage* is one of its finest exemplars.[38] What could be more ironic than the real-life hero portraying himself as fictional coward? Or a breach of silence where the failure of language is a major theme? The dual nature of *Voyage*, its movement from heroism to cowardice, from truth to untruth, from silence to speech, epitomises irony. This is not surprising as *Voyage* has emerged from the most ironic of wars. Soldiers leaving with enthusiasm on an heroic adventure only to discover horror and slaughter could not escape the irony of their condition. The Great War as an induction to irony is fully reflected in the mirroring anti-domain of *Voyage*.

Voyage is deeply ironic. The depiction of the war hero, Destouches, as the coward, Bardamu, ensures this, but such irony is sustained throughout the novel. Here is a war novel in which the conventional enemy is all but missing. The Germans never fully materialise. Indeed, the concept of 'enemy' is transformed in *Voyage* where the Republican army sends its own troops to the slaughter, where comrade executes comrade, and where both armies become ironically 'les ennemis' (RI, 46) of Bardamu and Robinson. Bardamu's war continues in his mind. Ironically, the war is not over for him, even though it has ended on the field.

Voyage offers a succession of ironic characters defined by an ironic war. For Princhard, the irony is that petty thievery cannot exempt him from the war:

Jusqu'ici cependant, il restait aux petits voleurs un avantage dans la République, celui d'être privés de l'honneur de porter les armes patriotes. Mais, dès demain, cet état de choses va changer, j'irai reprendre dès demain, moi voleur, ma place aux armées... (RI, 68)

[Until now, petty thieves had one advantage in the Republic, that of being denied the honour of carrying the arms of a patriot. But, as of tomorrow, that's to change. Tomorrow, I, a thief, am going to resume my place in the army...]

Supreme lesson in irony for the history teacher! The irony is that the world is never as expected. Even the goodness of Alcide and Molly is ironic because it is so unexpected. When Bardamu travels to the New World he finds 'les pauvres de partout' [the poor from everywhere] (RI, 191). And just as soldiers are shot by their comrades, children are tortured by their parents, and parents are assassinated by their children. Love too is ironic. Lola and Musyne leave Bardamu because he refuses the glorious death they demand of him. Robinson is shot by the woman who loves him. Bardamu, a prisoner of irony, leaves Molly and later regrets her love.

The very structure of *Voyage* is ironic. Céline speaks while maintaining silence. He makes a literary text out of oral speech patterns. He offers oral witness in written form. He uses untruth to undo the truths of the past, and strives for authenticity while embracing liberating inauthenticity. An exercise in memory, *Voyage* enacts a form of fictionalised forgetting, in turn founded on an ironic inability to forget. The subversive intertexuality of *Voyage* provides further irony. By providing ironic notes to extraneous texts, Céline modernises them. He kits them out with a new, ironic frame of consciousness, illuminating them from an ironic post-war angle. He underlines that in the wake of war, they can only be read with irony.

 Voyage is ironic in an even deeper sense. For Northrop Frye, the ironic is the last in a cyclical series of five literary modes beginning with myth. 'Myth,' says Frye, 'is the imitation of actions near or at the conceivable limits of desire.'[39] This field of action is the province of the Gods who enjoy limitless power. Frye describes this world of myth as 'apocalyptic [...] as though it were all inside a single infinite body'.[40] Myth is a world of wholeness. The ironic occupies the opposite end of the scale. This is the province of the anti-hero whose world is at the limit of the undesirable. 'In irony,' Frye says, 'the wheel of time completely encloses the action.'[41] Irony thus represents a world of 'cyclical return'. Rather than 'apocalyptic' this enclosed world, he says, is 'demonic'.[42]

 Voyage's irony is protean, comprising tragedy and comedy, satire and invective. Irony, tragedy and comedy are 'episodes in a total quest-myth,' writes Frye.[43] Tragedy, he says, contains 'a mimesis of sacrifice'.[44] Tragedy is thus the memory of a ritual. As we have seen, *Voyage*'s re-enactments enact a ritual of memory. But Frye's insight tells us that not only is *Voyage* ritual memory, it is ritual memory of ritual sacrifice. 'Nous sommes les sacrifiés' [we are the sacrificed] the French soldiers sang at Craonne in 1917. Sacrifice which was ritualised in 'la Noria', the implacable wheel of repetitive stasis, of '4 mai' and Verdun. But *Voyage*'s ritual memory reaches right back in time to the origins of the French Republic in revolution sanctified through sacrifice, through ritual, public decapitation. This, certainly, is one reading of the decapitation of the 'cavalier' in *Voyage*'s war episode (RI, 17). Yet again, *Voyage*'s form reveals wheels within wheels.

Ultimately, says Frye, 'tragedy and tragic irony take us into a hell of narrowing circles' leading to 'demonic epiphany', a 'vision of the source of all evil in personal form'.[45] Unsurprisingly, Céline's evil vision has a human face. We have seen one aspect of it in the novel's anti-Republican portraits of Pinçon, des Entrayes, and others (see 7.1 *Denunciation*). In the next chapter, we shall see another aspect of it.

Because Céline's irony has a target, it inevitably moves towards satire. Satire, says Frye, is 'militant irony'.[46] Satire, he says, necessitates two things, 'one is wit or humour founded on fantasy or a sense of the grotesque or absurd, the other is an object of attack'.[47] As satire, *Voyage* fulfils both these requirements. According to Frye, the less humour employed the more a work becomes pure denunciation. Céline's humour constantly displays this tendency to reach towards opprobrium as it is usurped by emotion and the lure of a more vitalising literary form. 'Invective is one of the most readable forms of literary art,' says Frye.[48] This drive towards invective lends *Voyage* much of its force and lends it the fierceness of a pamphlet. Ironically, that is one of the qualities which make it so readable.

Against Censorship

How much of Céline's silence following the war emerged from a military training that inculcated silence, the silence of obedience, silence of censorship? It may have been his experience of military postcards that caused him to send a postcard to his parents from Cameroon with just the single word 'Louis' on the back.[49] By remaining silent he effectively reinforced the military practice of censorship. All this changes with *Voyage*. 'On ne sera tranquille que lorsque tout aura été dit' [We won't be calm until everything has been said], says Bardamu, refusing silence (RI, 327). *Voyage* is against censorship.

As we have seen, censorship was complicit with war. In his attack on the war, and in keeping with the logic of ironic reversal, Céline inverts the values of censorship, substituting pessimism and defeatism for the perseverance and enthusiasm demanded by Pétain (see 1.4 *Censorship*). 'Bas les cœurs ! que je pensais moi' [Hearts down! that's what I thought], as Bardamu says, offering his unspoken, uncensored thought (RI, 19).

When Céline adopts an anti-literary style he moves away from a censorious tradition to include what previously could not be said. In doing so, he escapes the structures, and strictures, that distorted the reality of the war and undermined truth. He gives himself the freedom to grapple with the war with the language best adapted to doing so. This allows him to get closer to the substance of war itself. This substance, we remember, is made of 'cette boue, ce sang et cette merde' [that mud, that blood and that shit]. And this is the substance out of which *Voyage* is made.

The Excremental

'Genius seems to have led practically every great satirist to become what the world calls obscene,' wrote Northrop Frye.[50] *Voyage*'s relentless satirising of war and the world which produces war exists under the sign of the obscene and, most particularly, the excremental. When Bardamu's Breton comrade, Kersuzon, says that all he can see before him is 'tout noir comme un cul' [as dark as an arsehole] he symbolises the war as an anus (RI, 28). Anything the war produces must by extension be excrement. 'Il m'a répété ça encore deux ou trois fois à propos du noir et du cul et puis il est mort' [he repeated that two or three times about the dark and the arsehole and then he died], says Bardamu, commenting Kersuzon's ironic shooting by French soldiers. Death is also excrement. 'Ce qui guide encore le mieux, c'est l'odeur de la merde' [the best thing for finding your way is the smell of shit], says Bardamu, finding his way in the dark (RI, 35). It is the excremental in *Voyage* which orients both narrator and reader towards the war and death. In the context of *Voyage* as past recalled, it is clear that Céline's memory is also guided by the smell of excrement.[51]

Paul Fussell concludes his *Great War and Modern Memory* with the following:

> It is the virtual disappearance during the sixties and seventies of the concept of prohibitive obscenity, a concept which has acted as a censor on earlier memories of 'war', that has given the ritual of military memory a new dimension. And that new dimension is capable of revealing for the first time the full obscenity of the Great War. The greatest irony is that it is only now, when those who remember the events are almost all dead, that the literary means for adequate remembering and interpreting are finally publicly accessible.[52]

This may, indeed, be the case as far as Anglo-American literature is concerned but ironically Fussell's 'it is only now' was pre-empted many years earlier in French literature by Céline. Fussell's point, however, is important. The obscenity of war demands obscenity in language (see 2.2 *Graves*).

It is now almost a cliché to describe war as 'shit'. Stanley Kubrick's film *Full Metal Jacket* fully exploited excremental imagery to get that idea across. A suicide scene in a training camp toilet underlined the point. The army too was 'shit'.[53]

The representation of war has come a long way from Remarque's 'latrine scene' (see 2.2 *Remarque*). Ironically, Remarque's scene is one of 'natural innocence'. 'Out here [...] it is beautiful,' Baumer says as his soldiers relieve themselves in open-air camaraderie.[54] The point is not missed, however, that Remarque has infringed a taboo.[55] His text acknowledges this.[56] However, while he shows that the war represents a collapse of normal values and appearances, he does not use this to condemn the war but rather to reaffirm openness and solidarity among soldiers.

In *Voyage*, the faecal theme achieves its apotheosis in the New York 'caverne fécale' scene. Bardamu enters an underground toilet. What he finds there horrifies him.

> Une espèce de piscine, mais alors vidée de toute son eau, une piscine infecte, remplie seulement d'un jour filtré, mourant, qui venait finir là sur les hommes déboutonnés au milieu de leurs odeurs et bien cramoisis à pousser leurs sales affaires devant tout le monde, avec des bruits barbares. (RI, 195)

> [A sort of swimming pool, but emptied of all its war, a fetid pool, filled only with a filtered, dying daylight, which had come to its end there among men with loosened trousers cramped in the midst of their smells and crimson with the effort of pushing their filthy business out for all to see, accompanied by barbaric groans.]

Here, as in the war, the true nature of men is revealed. The men are 'bien débraillés, rotant et pire, gesticulant comme au préau des fous' [half-undressed, belching and worse, gesticulating like in a madhouse] (RI, 195). Their jokes are 'dégueulasses' [disgusting]. Here, in the 'débauche soudaine de digestions et de vulgarité' [sudden debauchery of digestions and vulgarity], in the 'communisme joyeux du caca' [joyous communism of shit] (RI, 196), Céline's 'humanisme à rebours' [inverted humanism] is at its most disingenuous.[57] 'Tout ce débraillage intime, cette formidable familiarité intestinale et dans la rue cette parfaite contrainte !' [All of that intimate unloosening, that formidable intestinal familiarity contrasting with the perfect constraint shown in the street above], Bardamu comments, apparently incapable of understanding what he sees. 'J'en demeurais étourdi' [I was astounded] (RI, 196). But the reader is left with the impression, as indeed is Bardamu, that the men are being their true selves and that it is their behaviour in the world above ground which is false. The word 'contrainte' [constraint] carries that unavoidable connotation.

The underlying military imagery and the shadow of the trenches upon this scene should not be forgotten. Céline effectively transfers a widely recognised — thanks to Remarque — image of war to post-war society, Remarque's liberating outdoor scene, to an imprisoning New York subterranean one, and depicts man in terms of his excrement.[58] War is shit, Céline is saying, and so is society, and so is man, even in the New World. However, man has an added capacity for unhappiness. 'L'ordure elle, ne cherche ni à durer, ni à croître. Ici, sur ce point nous sommes bien plus malheureux que la merde' [Filth for its part does not seek to endure, nor to multiply. On that point we are much unhappier than shit], he writes (RI, 337).

Céline excels in the excremental. As Stanford Luce says:

> No aspect of man's excretion has been slighted: shit, vomit, piss, sweat, pus, drool, spittle, snot, cum, curse, fart, burp, stench. Rare indeed is the writer with a broader command of such vocabulary.[59]

The excremental is part of his linguistic array, part of the armour of soldier speech. 'They are weapons,' writes Luce, 'a barrage to hurl back at the grossness of life.'[60] And, of course, death.

Céline's unrelenting obscenity never allows the reader to escape his vision. When Bardamu says that 'la pitié' [pity] is 'au bout de l'intestin avec la merde' [in the bottom of our guts where the shit is] (RI, 496) he explicitly links the death of compassion to his excremental theme. War as 'shit' reduces all human values to its level. Human love collapses into it. Even the act of speech is reduced to the excremental. 'C'est plus compliqué et plus pénible que la défécation notre effort mécanique de la conversation' [Our mechanical effort at conversation is more complicated and more painful than defecation] (RI, 337). Exploiting the excremental, Céline is like the witness to holocaust in Langer who 'intentionally seeks to offend our sense of order, reason, and civilised behaviour, so as to break us out of patterns of thought that desensitise us to the implications of his camp experience'.[61]

Céline uses the excremental to convey the experience of war, but also to portray the debasement of the post-war world and express his dissatisfaction with peace time. 'Tant qu'on est à la guerre, on dit que ce sera mieux dans la paix et puis on bouffe cet espoir-là comme si c'était du bonbon et puis c'est rien quand même que de la merde' [while you are in the war, you tell yourself that things will be better in peacetime and you swallow that hope as if it were a sweet cake but all it turns out to be is shit], insists Bardamu (RI, 234). Through dislocating obscenity Céline confronts the reader not just with the obscenity of the war itself but with the obscene character of memory. It is useless, in the presence of memory violated in this way, to demand good taste. Toning down Céline's work, as happened with the Marks' translations in the 1930s, violates memory and its truth. It is to try to redeem literature, redeem the war and redeem memory. Céline's excremental obscenity, however, is yet a further step beyond redemption, and towards Fussell's 'full obscenity' of war.

8.3 IMAGERY

The Demonic

As the ironic mode of writing returns to myth, writes Northrop Frye, it seizes upon 'demonic imagery'.[62] As Paul Fussell points out, this imagery 'comes close to delineating the literal Western Front'.[63] Demonic imagery describes the real and imagined landscape of the Great War but also images forth the psychological imprint left by the war. It delineates not just the Western Front but also Céline's memory of it. Frye calls the world of demonic imagery:

> the world that desire totally rejects: the world of the nightmare and the scapegoat, of bondage and pain and confusion [...] the world also of

perverted or wasted work, ruins and catacombs, instruments of torture and monuments of folly.[64]

Is this not Bardamu's world? A closer look at Frye's demonic world shows just how much it resembles Bardamu's.

For Frye, the world of demonic imagery is 'closely linked with an existential hell [...] or with the hell that man creates on earth'.[65] *Voyage* fulfils Frye's demonic description in many ways, not least in its elements of parody. 'One of the central themes of demonic imagery,' says Frye, 'is parody, the mocking of the exuberant play of art by suggesting its imitation in terms of "real life".' *Voyage* is parody. The parody theme is signalled at the very beginning when Céline announces 'tout est imaginé [...] rien qu'une histoire fictive' [it's all imagined [...] nothing but a fictional story] (RI, epigraph). Indeed, Céline acknowledges here that representation can only ever be parody. *Voyage* is at once parody of what was, past and present, and parody of the artistic means of representing it.

Frye describes five worlds invested by demonic imagery: the divine world; the human; the animal; the vegetable; and the mineral.[66] The 'divine world' is characterised by 'the inaccessible sky' representing 'inscrutable fate or external necessity'.[67] We think, for example, of Bardamu in New York where the sky is shut out and the light arrives 'malade comme celle de la forêt' [sickly like in the forest] (RI, 192). Also the sky above Detroit and above Rancy, 'du jus de fumée' [a damp smoke] (RI, 238), where 'pour voir le soleil, faut monter au moins jusqu'au Sacré-Cœur, à cause des fumées' [to see the sun, you need to climb at least as high as the Sacré-Cœur, because of the smoke] (RI, 241).

The demonic human world, according to Frye, is dominated by two poles. The first pole is 'the leader-tyrant, inscrutable, ruthless, melancholy, and with an insatiable will'. General des Entrayes as Aztec God no less; or Pinçon, collaborating with death. The second pole is that of Bardamu, 'the *pharmakos* or sacrificed victim, who has to be killed to strengthen the others'.[68] This is the logic behind the demands of Lola, Puta, Musyne and others that Bardamu die on the battlefield. The social relation in the demonic human world, explains Frye, 'is that of the mob [...] looking for a *pharmakos*'.[69] Here we return to the notion of

Voyage as ritual memory of ritual sacrifice. The *Amiral Bragueton* passage, where Bardamu becomes 'un sacrifice !' (RI, 118) perfectly illustrates this.

In Frye's demonic animal world there are 'monsters or beasts of prey'.[70] Fussell evokes lice, rats and wild dogs, all familiar from the pages of *Voyage*. There is too Bardamu's colonel, described as 'un monstre', and the consistent use of the 'monster' motif throughout the novel, to depict a world and a humanity which is monstrous. Africa too has its monstrous creatures: scorpions, hyenas and monstrous evil-smelling snails, in what is a further contradiction of Psichari's colonial exaltation (see 7.6 *The Anti-Psichari*).

Frye's demonic vegetable world is a 'sinister forest' or 'waste land', appearing in the Bible in its 'concrete universal form in the tree of death',[71] reminding us of '4 mai''s hidden evocation of *Mort-Homme*, whose etymology is 'mort-orme' [dead elm] or 'dead tree', as well as Bardamu's perception of 'un mort derrière chaque arbre' [a deadman behind each tree] (RI, 57).[72] The Val-de-Grâce hospital where Bardamu recuperates is also 'barbue d'arbres' [fringed with trees] (RI, 84). Most striking are the trees in Africa, 'des arbres entiers bouffis de gueuletons vivants, d'érections mutilées, d'horreur' [whole trees choke-full with uproarious feasting, with mutilated erections, with horror] (RI, 168). Trees also represent the death and, indeed, concealment of memory, as the growth of trees covers over past terrains of battle. As early as 1930 there were plans to plant trees on the battlefields of Verdun.[73] Céline's use of tree imagery in *Voyage* is informed by this awareness of the menace of forgetting or concealment.

It is in the anti-Psicharian African episode that the vegetable world is most demonic devouring new roads in less than a month (RI, 134). This is the world of 'cet enfer africain' [that African hell] where the sunsets are 'comme d'énormes assassinats du soleil' [like tremendous murders of the sun] (RI, 168). The African episode might almost exist to demonstrate the movement from Frye's apocalyptic vision of the garden or the landscape veneration of traditional romantic pastoralism in the nineteenth century to the twentieth-century demonic world of nature.

Frye's demonic inorganic world is characterised by 'waste land', 'cities of destruction and dreadful night' — New York, Detroit, Paris in *Voyage* — and by 'images of perverted work [...]: engines of torture, weapons of war'.[74] The shape of this world is 'the labyrinth or maze, the image of lost direction [...] catacombs',[75] like a trench system, says Fussell.[76] This, significantly, is the world of the 'sinister circle, the wheel of fate or fortune' with which *Voyage* is stamped, and where it has become the wheel of self, memory, and a world of perpetual war. In this demonic world there is too the 'prison or dungeon, the sealed furnace of heat without light', recalling in particular *Voyage*'s underworld motif; recalling too the industrial nightmare of the Ford factory (RI, 223–227). *Voyage*'s cycle of re-enactment organises demonic imagery into a repetitive structure that is itself circular, labyrinthine and imprisoning.

Frye's demonic fire is a 'world of malignant demons' and appears as 'burning cities' (RI, 29) or in the form of the '*auto da fe*', in *Voyage* symbolised by Bardamu's own conversion to fire in the war episode (RI, 17). 'The world of water is the water of death, often identified with spilled blood,' says Frye. Water is nearly always, inescapably, foul in *Voyage* (RI, 19, 173). The recurrent image of haemorrhaging makes the image of spilled blood explicit (RI, 17, 260, 497).

What is most interesting, as Fussell points out, is the way in which Frye's 'demonic world' resembles the world of the war experience. With this in mind, *Voyage*'s all-pervading demonic imagery shows the clear relation of every episode of the novel to the experience of war. *Voyage* is defined by demonic imagery, proof of the grip of war on Céline's mind and imagination.

Underworlds

The demonic imagery of the underground is one of the most powerful symbols in *Voyage*. If the underground can be read as a direct evocation of the trenches its symbolism has prior roots in Céline's childhood. The 1900 Exposition in Paris announced the modern industrial era and foreshadowed industrial warfare.[77] To accompany the Exposition the first line of the new Paris metro was inaugurated. The line passed close to the Passage Choiseul and could not have escaped the notice of the boy Destouches. The shell through which the train would pass was constructed above ground. It was as high as the surrounding buildings. Later it was sunk deep into the earth. The new 'metro' suggested a modern world going to ground, whose journeys would take place under the earth, rather than above it. The underground world of the trenches was only a few years away.

In *Voyage*, the underground presents itself as a refuge, like the trenches, but one which Bardamu refuses because of its association with death.[78] During a night time Zeppelin alert Bardamu follows Musyne into the earth. 'Elle insistait pour que je me précipite avec elle au fond des souterrains, dans le métro, dans les égouts, n'importe où, mais à l'abri et dans les ultimes profondeurs et surtout tout de suite !' [She insisted that I hurry with her deep into the underground, the metro, the sewers, anywhere, once it was sheltered and deep in the deepest depths and without delay!] (RI, 83). Ironically, the butcher's cellar is chosen as the ideal shelter, 'on prétendait qu'elle était située plus profondément que n'importe quelle autre de l'immeuble' [it was claimed to be further down than any other cellar in the building]. Bardamu resists Musyne's entreaty. He recognises the odour of death. 'Dès le seuil il vous parvenait des bouffées d'une odeur âcre et de moi bien connue, qui me fut à l'instant absolument insupportable' [As soon as we reached the threshold a bitter odour well-known to me assailed us, which I found completely unbearable]. 'J'ai des souvenirs' [I have memories], he says, refusing to go down into the 'voûte odorante' [odorous vault]. Bardamu's first encounter, therefore, with the underground is to refuse to enter it. Nonetheless, its symbolism is clear, as a happy refuge for the citizens of Republican France, overseen by the butcher and his wife, and far from any real danger. It is the very image of the 'rear'.

The next occurrence of the underground motif is more explicit. It is the 'caverne fécale' [faecal cavern] scene. Here the underground once again appears as a refuge as Bardamu seeks to escape the attentions of a policeman. Once again the metro is evoked. 'À droite de mon banc s'ouvrait précisément un trou, large, à même le trottoir dans le genre du métro de chez nous. Ce trou me parut propice' [To the right of my bench there was a big hole in the pavement, like the entrance to the metro back home. The hole seemed auspicious to me] (RI, 195). The entrance to the underground is vaginal, 'tout en marbre rose' [all in pink marble], luring Bardamu, already sexually exalted by New York's midinettes (RI, 193), to enter. Reassuringly, the men who descend come back up again. This time we are given a description of the underground. The cavern is tomb-like and presents itself as the site of the unspeakable. 'En marbre aussi la salle où se passait la chose' [In marble too, the room where it took place] (RI, 195). Recalling Frye's demonic water imagery, Bardamu calls it 'une espèce de piscine, mais alors vidée de toute son eau, une piscine infecte' [a sort of swimming pool, but emptied of all its water, a fetid pool]. Light is shut out. The underground space is 'remplie seulement d'un jour filtré, mourant' [filled only with a filtered, dying daylight] (RI, 195). Having confronted the underground world of death Bardamu returns appalled to the world above. He has confronted death but has not mastered it.

A third occurrence of the underground motif appears during Bardamu's visit to Toulouse. This is one of *Voyage*'s most positive episodes. For once, the novel's demonic imagery tends back towards the apocalyptic, most particularly in the dreamlike 'belle péniche' [beautiful barge] scene with its Lethe-like intimations of forgetfulness, the whole, however, invested with Céline's unrelenting irony (RI, 400–407). In Toulouse, the underground is not only inviting but highly promising as Bardamu descends into the catacombs guided by Madelon (RI, 385). He is aware that the crypt contains the dead but Bardamu is no longer afraid. He has gotten used to it, 'on s'enfonce, on s'épouvante d'abord dans la nuit, mais on veut comprendre quand même et alors on ne quitte plus la profondeur' [you plunge into it, afraid at first in the darkness, but you want to understand all the same and then you remain there in the depths] (RI, 381). In this passage Bardamu exerts mastery over death. He flirts with Madelon. 'C'était bien bon' [it was good and fine], he says, once inside 'le caveau' [the crypt] (RI, 386). Bardamu is so indifferent to death he makes love to Madelon inside the crypt. He examines the dead. 'Une à une leur espèce de tête est venue se taire dans le cercle cru de la lampe. Ce n'est pas tout à fait de la nuit qu'ils ont au fond des orbites, c'est presque encore du regard mais en plus doux, comme en ont des gens qui savent' [One by one their strange faces emerged into the crude light of the lamp to be silent there. It's not altogether night which lies at the bottom of their eye sockets, it's almost as if they are looking at us but more gently, like you see in the eyes of people who know] (RI, 388). Here is death stripped of its horror, detached from reality, become theatrical, a circus turn for tourists. On one level the passage functions as a wry commentary on the rise of battlefield tourism in the 1920s (see 6.2 *Displaced Persons*). 'La mère Henrouille [...] les faisait travailler les morts comme dans un cirque' [Old mother Henrouille [...] set the dead to work like in a circus], Bardamu says (RI, 388). Yet, murder lurks in the apparent innocence of this scene and in the dreamlike tranquillity of the entire Toulouse episode as Bardamu will soon discover.

In *Voyage* the source of death is hidden, underground, in the depths of the human mind.[79] 'Ça venait des profondeurs et c'était arrivé' [It had come from the depths and it was among us], says Bardamu of the war (RI, 14). For Bardamu the war is a discovery of those depths and his journey of initiation takes him through them. His own experience of death is characterised by a descent, a symbolic burial (RI, 17). Each confrontation with death re-enacted in the three underground episodes demands a descent. In the first Bardamu fails to enter the cavern but each succeeding episode is a step closer to death mastery. Mastering death necessitates descent into the cavern.

Falling, as Jane Carson has pointed out, triggers 'the metamorphosis of a protagonist into a narrator'.[80] This makes 'falling' the sign of Céline's donning the mask where he speaks for the dead (see 6.1 *Donning the Mask*). For Carl Jung, 'the unconscious corresponds to the mythic land of the dead, the land of the ancestors.'[81] Donning the mask Céline 'falls' into his own underground, his unconscious. Writing itself becomes a descent where Céline, in the words of Laurens Van Der Post, 'goes down into an underworld of mind and time'[82] in a journey towards wholeness. Journey in which he is surrounded on all sides by the ghosts of the dead.

The metro sunk in the Paris underground announced an age gone to ground. For Céline, it came to symbolise a modern age of war and death and it is evoked in *Voyage* (see RI, 239–240) and in his later work. However, when he characterised his writing as 'le métro émotif' [an emotive metro], Céline made the metro the supreme symbol of his own, 'emotive', narration (RIV, 533–543). He took command of the underground, transforming a symbol and experience of death into an animating symbol of his art.

Mythologies

In his journey into the underground Céline uncovers myth. Myth underlies trauma. We have seen the myth of Proteus in Bardamu's efforts to re-enter heroic myth. Louis Crocq has evoked other myths we can see in *Voyage*, the myth of Sisyphus for example, visible in *Voyage*'s cycle of re-enactment.[83] Sisyphus escaped death at the hands of Thanatos, before capturing him, and thus stopping the spread of death on the planet. Punished for this by Zeus, Sisyphus escaped death by telling his wife not to perform his funerary rites. In the underworld he could thus persuade Hades to allow him rejoin the world of mortals in order to punish her. When he finally died Zeus condemned him to the endlessly, repetitive task of pushing a large boulder to a summit from whence it fell back down and so Sisyphus needed always to recommence. The presence of these myths can be directly related to Céline's experience of trauma. As Crocq observes:

> Sisyphe [...] symbolise avec évidence le syndrome de répétition des traumatisés. [...] Sisyphe personnifie aussi la confrontation avec la mort, car Thanatos a pourchassé et manqué le héros, comme la mort a manqué le rescapé qui demeure fasciné par cette expérience effrayante. Enfin, Sisyphe incarne l'expiation de la faute, car il est puni [...] pour avoir réussi à s'extraire de l'enfer.[84]

> [Sisyphus [...] clearly symbolises the syndrome of repetition of traumatised individuals. [...] Sisyphus also personifies the confrontation with death, because Thanatos pursued but failed to take the hero, just as death failed to take the survivor who remains fascinated by the frightening experience. Finally, Sisyphus embodies the expiation of a fault, because he is punished [...] for having succeeded in getting himself out of hell.]

The myth encapsulates the trauma of the death encounter as well as the reality of survival guilt. Sisyphus is condemned to an absurd destiny defined by circular and repetitive stasis, the very condition of Bardamu. His escape from hell is echoed by Céline himself when he writes to Garcin, 'nous avons côtoyé l'enfer dont il ne fallait pas revenir' [we have been to that hell from which one mustn't return] (see 4.1 *The Crisis in Memory*). It must not be forgotten either, that

Sisyphus is punished too for having stopped the work of death, Thanatos. This lends a clear Sisyphean tone to Bardamu's own effort to do so, 'je me décidais à risquer le tout pour le tout, à tenter la dernière démarche, la suprême, essayer, moi, tout seul, d'arrêter la guerre !' [I decided that I, myself, all alone, would risk all for all, attempting the ultimate, the supreme feat, that of stopping the war!] (RI, 15).

Orpheus

Also visible in *Voyage* is the myth of Orpheus, with its descent into the underworld (see 6.2 *The Quest for Gold*). Orpheus was a poet and musician whose singing created harmony in nature and in his fellow beings. When Eurydice dies, Orpheus enters the underworld and is allowed to leave with her on condition that he does not look back. This he does and so loses her a second time. Inconsolable, he retires to the top of a mountain. Crocq notes:

> Les traumatisés [...] incarnent [...] le destin d'Orphée, puisqu'ils ont voyagé aux enfers et qu'ils en sont revenus inconsolables, fascinés par leur malheur et coupés du commerce normal avec les humains.[85]
>
> [Traumatised individuals [...] embody [...] the destiny of Orpheus, since they have journeyed to hell and have returned inconsolable, obsessed with their misfortune and cut off from normal intercourse with humans.]

Like Orpheus, says Crocq, the sufferer from trauma, 'est obsédé et dominé par une activité incoercible de "reviviscence"' [is obsessed and dominated by an uncontrollable activity of "reliving"], comprising 'souvenir de l'enfer' [the memory of hell] and 'enfer du souvenir' [the hell of memory], a pattern we recognise in Céline's rewriting himself back into his trauma (see 4.1 *The Crisis in Memory*).

Voyage takes Bardamu on a mythic journey into the underworld. This journey, while drawing on the myth of Orpheus and others embedded in the patterns of trauma, already has an illustrious literary model in the demonic world of Dante's hell with its 'dark wood' [86] and its 'starless air',[87] its 'timeless night that [...] in dizzying circles sped'.[88] The parallel does not end there however. Dante's work enacted a return to vernacular language to tell its story of the afterlife and so does *Voyage*. And while it is commonplace to describe the Great War as hell on earth, it is this hell of war that Céline recreates in *Voyage*, offering a Dantesque vision of it and the world which made it from the depths of his own demonic memory.[89]

Conclusion

Voyage is Céline's oral witness to war. As oral witness it expresses all the inchoate and troubled nature of true witness. This witness directly captures the breakdown of memory, language and narrative attendant on the pain of witness itself. Orality in *Voyage* functions as an appropriate vector for debasement. Robert Jay Lifton has noted that trauma can lead to a 'complete breakdown of the symbol system by which a person has lived'.[90] This is shown, in Céline's case, by the collapse of the values of the myth of the war experience in *Voyage* and by his orality, but its real extent is underlined by Céline's use of demonic imagery. Céline's use of the obscene and excremental fully denotes the scale of the trauma attendant on this 'breakdown' in a mind caught between history's two greatest wars. Where, one might ask, could the mental life of such a man lead? Chapter Nine will reveal how Céline's rewriting of self in *Voyage* is accompanied and powered by one of the most virulent acts of condemnation in literature, directed towards a group who embody Céline's vision of 'personal evil'.

---

[1] Llambias, p.92.

[2] Danièle Racelle-Latin, p.53.

[3] Laurens Van Der Post, *The Voice of the Thunder*, p.60.

[4] Ian Noble has pointed out the relative positions of Céline and Rabelais in relation to the 'dominant code' within French: 'they are, historically, at opposite ends of that dominant code; [Rabelais] experimenting before the convention was formed, [Céline] writing in the period of its decline.' See Noble, *Language and Narration in Céline's Writings: The Challenge of Disorder.* (London: Macmillan, 1987), p.6.

[5] See 'Interview avec Pierre-Jean Launay', *Cahiers Céline*, I, 21–22 (p.22).

[6] Rieuneau, p.313.

[7] Paul Nizan, writing of Céline, noted that 'il est très remarquable que le roman français s'oriente visiblement vers la recherche d'un style parlé, chez des écrivains comme Giono, comme Aragon et comme Céline' [It is quite noteworthy that the French novel is visibly orienting itself towards a spoken style, in writers like Giono, Aragon, and Céline]. See Nizan, 'Au royaume des artifices symboliques', in *Les critiques de notre temps et Céline*, pp.55–60 (p.57).

[8] See Godard, *Poétique de Céline*, pp.309–311.

[9] Philippe Lejeune, *Je est un autre* (Paris: Seuil, 1980), p.219.

[10] Léon Daudet, 'Voici un livre étonnant', in *Les critiques de notre temps et Céline*, pp.21–26 (p.25).

[11] For a brief inventory of Céline's lexical resources see Christine Combessie-Savy, *Voyage au bout de la nuit de Céline* (Paris: Nathan, 1993), pp.111–114.

[12] See the analysis of this passage in A.-C and J.-P. Damour, pp.123–125.

[13] See Henri Godard, 'Notice', *Romans*, I, 1235–1236 for this and further Ramuz quotations.

[14] Letter to Milton Hindus, 16 April 1947, *L'Herne*, 110–111 (p.111).

[15] Merlin Thomas, *Céline* (London: Faber and Faber, 1979), p.80.

[16] Céline, 'L'argot est né de la haine', *L'Herne*, p.39.

[17] Céline, 'Rabelais, il a raté son coup', *L'Herne*, 44–45 (p.45).

[18] Edmund Blunden, *Undertones of War* (London: Penguin, 1982), p.182.

[19] See Monnier, p.90.

[20] Langer, p.xi.

[21] Langer, p.45.

[22] Langer, p.61.

[23] Langer, p.160.

[24] Langer, p.105.

[25] Langer, p.21.

[26] Langer, p.xiii.

[27] Langer, p.204.

[28] Langer, p.208.

[29] Langer, p.159.

[30] Bastier, p.322.

[31] In Poulet, p.164.

[32] Terrence Des Pres, 'Holocaust *Laughter?*', in Berel Lang, ed., *Writing and the Holocaust*, pp.216–233 (p. 220).

[33] Des Pres, 'Holocaust *Laughter?*', p.220.

[34] Hynes, p.11.

[35] Lord Moran, *The Anatomy of Courage*, 2nd edn (New York: Avery, 1987), p.144.

[36] In conversation with myself in May 1999.

[37] See view of Philip Gibbs on black humour, in Fussell, *The Great War and Modern Memory*, p.8. Journalist Gibbs' own energetic writing on the war in many ways resembles Céline's.

[38] See Fussell, *The Great War and Modern Memory*, p.35. Fussell's fundamental thesis is that there is a dominant form of 'modern understanding' which is 'essentially ironic' and which 'originates largely in the application of mind and memory to the events of the Great War'.

[39] Frye, *Anatomy of Criticism*, p.136.

[40] *Anatomy*, p.136.

[41] *Anatomy*, p.214.

[42] See *Anatomy*, p.147.

[43] *Anatomy*, p.215.

[44] *Anatomy*, p.214.

[45] *Anatomy*, p.239.

[46] *Anatomy*, p.223.

[47] *Anatomy*, p.224.

[48] *Anatomy*, p.224.

[49] This postcard is in the possession of Frédéric Vitoux.

[50] Frye, *Anatomy*, p.235.

[51] Jorge Semprun recalling the smell of burning flesh at Buchenwald powerfully echoes *Voyage*'s epigraph. Semprun writes: 'Il suffirait de fermer les yeux […]. Il suffirait […] d'une distraction de la mémoire remplie à ras bord de balivernes, de bonheurs insignifiants, pour qu'elle réapparaisse. Il suffirait de se distraire de l'opacité chatoyante des choses de la vie. […] Se distraire de soi-même, de l'existence qui vous habite […]. Il suffirait d'un instant de vraie distraction de soi, d'autrui, du monde' [It's enough to close your eyes […]. It's enough […] to be distracted from a memory full of idiocies, of insignificant happy moments, for it to reappear. It's enough to be distracted from the shimmering opacity of the things in life. […] To be distracted from oneself, from the existence which inhabits you […]. It's enough to be truly distracted an instant from oneself, from others, from the world]. See Semprun, p.17.

[52] Fussell, *The Great War and Modern Memory*, p.334.

[53] *Full Metal Jacket*, dir. Stanley Kubrick, Metrodome, 1987.

[54] Remarque, p.6.

[55] See Eksteins, p.288, for an account of critical reaction to the latrine scene in *All Quiet*. Remarque, says Eksteins, was known as 'the high priest of the "lavatory school" of war novelists'. The toilet scene was deleted from the American edition.

[56] See Remarque, p.6, 'Our families and our teachers will be pretty surprised when we get home.'

[57] The term 'humanisme à rebours' is from Erika Ostrovsky, *Céline and his vision*, p.85.

[58] Céline is part of a strong tradition here. Voltaire, for example, was also of the view that man is shit. See Bettina Knapp, *Céline: Man of Hate* (Alabama: University of Alabama Press, 1974), p.75. Interestingly, Knapp writes that alchemists sought the *prima materia* in excrement which they connected with gold, 'juxtaposing the "lowest" and the "highest" values' (see 6.2 *The Quest for Gold*).

[59] Stanford Luce, 'Increment and Excrement: Céline and the Language of Hate', in *Maledicta*, I (1977), 43–48 (p.44).

[60] Luce, p.45.

[61] Langer, p.28.

[62] Frye, *Anatomy*, p.147.

[63] See Fussell, *The Great War and Modern Memory*, pp.311–314, for his application of Frye's descriptions to the Western Front. Most of Frye quoted here is also to be found in the Fussell text.

[64] See Frye, *Anatomy*, p.147.

[65] *Anatomy*, p.147.

[66] *Anatomy*, p.141.

[67] *Anatomy*, p.147.

[68] *Anatomy*, p.148.

[69] *Anatomy*, p.149.

[70] *Anatomy*, p.149.

[71] *Anatomy*, p.149.

[72] J.G. Frazer, in his *The Golden Bough*, provides examples of belief that the souls of the dead inhabited trees. Bardamu's 'un mort derrière chaque arbre' expresses this belief in direct fashion. See Frazer, *The Golden Bough: A Study in Magic and Religion* (London: The Macmillan Press, 1983). It must be remembered, however, that symbols in *Voyage* are protean, multiple. This is the nature of the symbol. Céline's trees, for example, undoubtedly contain an echo of 'les arbres de la liberté' [trees of freedom] that greeted Louis XVI on 15 July 1793 on his return from Versailles. The revolutionary 'arbre de la liberté' was usually a poplar, symbol of the people. *Voyage*'s 'peupliers' (RI, 13) is an example of how Céline's representation of the Great War exploits symbols which refer it constantly backwards towards the French Revolution.

[73] See Prost, III, 237. These forests would become a reality. Prost presents them as time effacing the traces of the past.

[74] *Anatomy*, p.150.

[75] *Anatomy*, p.150.

[76] Fussell, *The Great War and Modern Memory*, p.312.

[77] See Céline's own hair-raising description of the 1900 Exposition in *Mort à crédit* (RI, 579-580). Also in his 'Hommage à Zola', p.22.

[78] Gilbert Schilling notes four main occurrences of the underground motif including Bardamu's descent into the basement of the Hotel Paritz to taste Lola's 'beignets' (RI, 50-53). See Schilling, 'Les "descentes" de Bardamu', *Céline: Actes du Colloque international de Paris (27-30 juillet 1976)*, 41-57.

[79] See Céline's declaration in 'Hommage à Zola', p.23, where he says: 'Le goût des guerres et des massacres ne saurait avoir pour origine essentielle l'appétit de conquête, de pouvoir et de bénéfices des classes dirigeantes. [...] Le sadisme unanime actuel procède avant tout d'un désir de néant profondément installé dans l'homme et surtout dans la masse des hommes, une sorte d'impatience amoureuse, à peu près irrésistible, unanime, pour la mort' [The taste for wars and massacres is not rooted essentially in an appetite for conquest, power or profit on the part of the ruling classes. [...] The current unanimous sadism comes above all from a deep desire in man and especially in the mass of men for the void, a sort of amorous impatience, practically irresistible, unanimous, for death].

[80] See Jane Carson, *Céline's Imaginative Space* (New York: Peter Lang, 1987), p.81.

[81] Carl Jung, *Memories, Dreams, Reflections*, p.216. Jung describes the confrontation with his own unconscious in an effort to grasp the stream of fantasies unleashed by the war. 'In order to seize hold of the fantasies, I frequently imagined a steep descent,' he says. See Jung, p.205. Jung's own descent into his unconscious involved him in conversations with the dead, the result of which was a book called *Septem Sermones*. With time, the dead became increasingly distinct to Jung 'as the voices of the Unanswered, Unresolved, and Unredeemed'. See Jung, p.217. One may speculate as to how much Jung's psychic turbulence, at this time, reflects Céline's. Whatever the case may be, it is increasingly clear that Jung illuminates Céline as much, if not more, than Freud.

[82] Van Der Post, p.151.

[83] André Smith traces the Sisyphean motif in Céline from *Voyage* to the pamphlets, suggesting that it forms the image of '[une] lutte […] d'avance vouée à l'échec' [a struggle destined from the beginning to end in failure]. See Smith, *La Nuit de Louis-Ferdinand Céline* (Paris: Grasset, 1973), p.118.

[84] Crocq, p.355.

[85] Crocq, p.356.

[86] Dante, *The Divine Comedy*, 3 vols (London: Penguin Books, 1949), I: *Hell*, 71.

[87] Dante, I, 85.

[88] Dante, I, 86.

[89] Céline's allusions to and affinity with Dante have already been extensively noted, particularly in relation to the German trilogy. See the last chapter of Philippe Muray, *Céline* (Paris: Denoël, 1984) and also D.L.Pike, 'Céline and Dante: From Golden Bough to Charon's Oar', *Lectura Dante: A Forum for Dante Research*, 12 (1993), 65-74. Pike suggests that Céline uses Dante as a 'negative vision of modernity' (p.73) and for less worthy purposes of autobiographical mystification.

[90] In Solomon, p.91. Northrop Frye, in the context of heroic myth, speaks of the hero's amnesia as a 'catastrophe' representing 'a collapse in the rightful order of the mind' (see 4.3 *The Breach in Consciousness*). This would seem to approximate to the collapse of Lifton's 'symbol system'.

CHAPTER 9

THE ANTI-REPUBLIC

From Voyage to Journey's End

Introduction

As a major anti-war novel, *Voyage* represents not just an attack on the values of the myth of the war experience, not just a condemnation of the commemoration of the Great War, it attacks the political system which produced the war. It attacks the very core values of this system by turning savagely on the Enlightenment culture which has animated it since its inception. In *Voyage*, Céline attacks the Enlightenment as the instigator of the French Revolution, the French Republic and, ultimately, the Great War. He does this through subversion of the key symbols of the Enlightenment, but more than anything, he does it through engagement with a work which was not just central to the Enlightenment but which was a founding text of Western civilisation: Plato's *The Republic*.

Voyage is Céline's anti-Republic. However, the extreme virulence of its denunciation is, ultimately, directed beyond the Republic as a system of government, towards its leaders, 'les maîtres' [the masters], those whom Céline accuses as ultimately responsible for the death of heroic France and for the slaughter of courage that was Verdun and '4 mai'.

The Chapter will conclude by tracing the memory of the Great War in Céline's writing after *Voyage*, including his controversial pamphlets.

9.1 CÉLINE'S PHILOSOPHIES

The Anti-Plato

Voyage is a world of myth, containing the ones we have seen, those of Sisyphus and Orpheus and more. Theseus and the Minotaur are also present (RI, 238). Louis Crocq also evokes the anti-authority myth of Oedipus as part of his description of patterns of war trauma. Its importance in the matrix of myths common to Céline is readily perceived if we recall the significance of the silence of the father, which is a symbolic form of murder. It is a 'silent' or implicit myth in *Voyage* but finds full expression in *Mort à crédit*. One further myth evoked by Crocq, however, is critical to our understanding of Céline and *Voyage*. It is the myth of the soldier Er told in Plato's *The Republic*.

Voyage's value as a 'réplique' [reply] to Plato has been overlooked. If the presence of a substantial philosophical vocabulary (see 8.1 *Protean Language*) and mocking references to Bardamu's 'philosophies' (RI, 380) were not enough, Céline himself gave a clue to the 'philosophical' nature of his work when he referred to his 'philosophies si originales' [so original philosophies] in an early draft of the 1949 preface to *Voyage*.[1] The year before he died he stressed the point when he described *Voyage* as having a philosophical 'signature'.[2] This signature is nothing other than a sustained confrontation with Plato's *The Republic*, with which *Voyage* shares many themes and symbols, such as the Sun and the Cave.[3] While the political system described by Plato is far removed from the one attacked by Céline in *Voyage*, one can readily see how the title (a mistranslation as it happens) of Plato's work would have interested him, and how its imagery and general tenor would have justified him in seeing it as a blueprint both for the Enlightenment and for the French Republic.

Voyage is organised like a work of philosophy through its very circularity. Philosophers disdained the linearity of storytellers who aimed for surprise effects in their work. The philosopher on the other hand set out his arguments and then repeated them,[4] which is what Céline does most particularly in his first chapter, which functions as a musical overture to *Voyage* and which the rest of the novel reiterates. Presented as a 'philosophical' conversation between Bardamu and Arthur Ganate it even mimics Plato's style and method.[5]

Plato's work sets out the basis for a form of democratic society, but also provides a meditation on justice, truth, beauty, art and the role of the artist. He views the world and its reality as mere reflections, apparitions or 'ghosts' — the word has immense significance for *Voyage*'s 'fantômes'[6] — of truth. His preferred form is the dialogue. Several chapters provide a defence of censorship, while he also attacks art as 'imitation'. At the same time Plato argues for education through 'fictions' and argues the necessity of a 'noble lie' so that society can function. His ideal state is ruled over by a 'Philosopher King' — an idea adapted in more modern times by Kant, who gave the philosopher a secret, advisory role in the running of his republics (see 1.1 *Enlightenment and Revolution*).

Most significantly, Plato's ideal state is organised around a citizen army — the Guardians, his watchdogs[7] — motivated by heroic myth, philosophy and the notion of immortality achieved through sacrifice. To a great extent, and one can see here its immense relevance to Céline, Plato's *Republic* is a handbook for the formation of good soldiers. Having prescribed appropriate modes of education and art for his Guardians, including allowing their children to see battles,[8] Plato describes how society shall honour those who 'die bravely on active service', to be reckoned as 'men of gold':

> We shall bury them with whatever special ceremonies Delphi prescribes [...] for men of such divine and heroic mould. [...] And [...] treat their tombs with reverence and worship them as Guardian spirits.[9]

It is not difficult to see the immense resonance Plato's views must have had for Céline in his commemoration-saturated world where the blood of sacrifice had been converted to gold (see 1.2 *Gold* and 7.6 *The Church*). If Plato's republic is far removed politically from the one Céline lives in, Plato nonetheless has gathered together many of the principles which underlie the functioning of the Third Republic, such as the exaltation of sacrifice within commemoration.

Voyage is, deep down, a meditation on society, on art, on mortality, engaging with Plato at every turn. *Voyage* is, as we have seen, anti-censorship. Indeed, *Voyage* simply must be read against the background of Plato's ideas on censorship. The resonances are fabulous, especially if one keeps in mind Plato's intention to use art to educate his 'Guardians'. In the course of a long passage Plato signals out episodes to be excluded from Homer, which together form a description of Bardamu's condition and of *Voyage*. 'We cannot have stories told about the transformations of Proteus,' he says,[10] as he proceeds to cut passages from Homer.[11] He demands that poets produce work to inspire soldiers to bravery and sacrifice, asking them to:

> stop giving their present gloomy account of the after-life, which is both untrue and unsuitable to produce a fighting spirit [...]. We must get rid too of [...] the ghosts and corpses [...]. We are afraid that the thrill of terror they cause will make our Guardians more nervous and less tough than they should be.[12]

Plato cuts out 'pitiful laments by famous men', Achilles 'wandering distraught',[13] or Priam imploring the gods while he grovels 'in the dung' (see 8.2 *The Excremental*).[14] 'And surely we don't want our Guardians to be too fond of laughter,' says Plato, outlawing humour (see 8.2 *Humour*).[15]

By rigorously countering Plato's censure of Homer, Céline makes his art in *Voyage* reflect Homer's. As anti-Plato, Céline transforms himself into a modern Homer, blind like him, 'il suffit de fermer les yeux' [you just have to close your eyes] (RI, epigraph), and given Homer's mythical and plural identity, unknown and composite like him by virtue of his qualities of silence and intertextuality. Like Joyce, Céline on this level is engaged in rewriting Homer, translating him to the modern age. In the process *Voyage* becomes a twentieth-century *Iliad*, a tale of war, followed by the *Odyssey*, a tale of exile in a world shattered by war.

What Plato says next shows the personal meaning his philosophy must have had for Céline:

> We must value truthfulness highly [...]. Falsehood is no use to the gods and only useful to men as a kind of medicine, it's clearly a kind of medicine that should be entrusted to doctors and not to laymen.[16]

Providing the healing Doctor Destouches and his medicinal fictions with Plato's imprimatur, this statement may well be the single most important point of inspiration for Céline's artistic project.[17]

Plato continues by outlawing lies except, significantly, by the state itself, and insists that the guilty party be punished for 'introducing a practice likely to capsize and wreck the ship of state'.[18] But there is another risk seized on by Céline and which takes us right to the heart of the unique symbiosis between aesthetic form and ideological intent that is *Voyage*:

> You should hesitate to change the style of your literature, because you risk everything if you do; the music and literature of a country cannot be altered without major political and social changes.[19]

This passage alone underlines the immense political and social impetus underlying Céline's renewal of French literature. It is, indeed, the measure of Céline's genius that, given Plato's warning, he sets out to and succeeds in changing the literature of his country.

Plato embarks on a long critique of 'representation', saying of Homer that he is 'merely manufacturing copies at third remove from reality'.[20] This receives its most striking riposte in *Voyage* when, in what is a further denunciation of a whole tradition of philosophy, Bardamu renders in his own oral voice a letter he finds from Montaigne to his wife consoling her on the death of their child (RI, 289), which letter is in itself a copy of an earlier letter from Plutarch to his wife consoling her on the death of *their* child, thereby producing a mocking representation of the original letter at a third remove from its origin.

The poet, Plato insists, should specialise, adopting one form of narration or representation, 'someone who has the skill to transform himself into all sorts of characters and represent all sorts of things [...] we [...] shall tell him that he and his kind have no place in our city.'[21] To which view, *Voyage*'s protean multiplicity and polyphony are the subversive reply. Plato concludes that, because the artist can only represent the 'ghosts' of things, he 'knows little or nothing about the subjects he represents and that the art of representation is something that has no serious value'.[22]

If any doubt exists that Céline has shaped his art, and his thinking about art, around a contradiction of Plato, it is surely removed by Plato's use of the image of the stick which looks bent in water, an image adapted by Céline to describe his own artistic method in *Entretiens pour le professeur Y* (RIV, 546). Because the stick appears bent in water, Plato concludes that appearances, or representations, are 'removed from reason, in a fond liaison without health or truth'.[23] Consequently, says Plato, the poet, is refused admission to:

> a properly run state, because he wakens and encourages and strengthens the lower elements in the mind to the detriment of reason, which is like

giving power and political control to the worst elements in a state and ruining the better elements.[24]

Céline's statement that he breaks the stick before plunging it in water, to make it look *straight* in the water, underlines that he is, indeed, engaged in a contradiction of Plato.

Ironically, Plato's strictures provide Céline with the artistic means for an attack on the French Republic. Through rampant intertextuality and borrowing of the styles of populism, hamletism, exoticism, travel literature and surrealism, he makes 'imitation' and 'falsehood' core strategies of his art. He eschews dialogue and depicts conversation as useless or even impossible (RI, 15–17). Céline turns Plato's views and practices to his own end. Given the correlation between the two works, it is certain that Plato's view that fiction should be used as a medium for education figured in Céline's awareness and that he intended *Voyage* to have an 'educational', as well as a 'polemical', value. 'It is in education that disorder can most easily creep in,' Plato warned.[25] In addition, by writing in opposition to his own lived truth, Céline employs a form of censorship. In doing so, he enacts Plato's 'noble lie' as *Voyage* itself.

Voyage mirrors Plato, just as it mirrors the war commemoration, while distorting, undermining and lampooning him. It is composed of the same substance as *The Republic*, philosophical in structure and character, and dealing with the same themes, yet it is radically different in its outcome. If Plato provides a handbook for the training of soldiers, Céline composes *Voyage* of all its antagonistic elements. Céline's art is made in the image of Plato's bad art, and he uses it not only to arrive at a truth in opposition to Plato's, but for all the purposes Plato decries: the discouragement of soldiers, to attack reason, and ultimately to 'capsize the ship of state'. But where the parallel between the two works is most exciting is in how Céline adapts the final chapter of Plato to *Voyage*. If Bardamu has a single model in myth it is as Plato's Er, the soldier returned from the dead and released from forgetting to tell his story of the afterlife.

Er

Er died in battle but came back to life as he was about to be burned on the pyre. Thus returned from the afterlife, he told the story of his dead soul which had journeyed with the souls of the other dead to a prairie existing within a heavenly system of eight circles joined by a column of light. In this prairie there were four chasms, two into and out of the earth and two towards and from heaven. Those who returned from the underground were covered in filth and dust, but the vilest souls were prevented from returning by demons of fire, which fact struck terror into Er and the others waiting. Er and the other souls were judged before being presented with a model for their life to come. Each soul chooses for itself, so that responsibility for its future life is its own. The souls, having chosen their destiny, then cross a torrid plain to Lethe where they drink of forgetfulness. Only Er is allowed not to drink. Then a thunderclap sends the souls towards their new lives. And Er returns from the dead to remember and tell his tale.

Er brings to his mythical world the promise of immortality, a promise designed to encourage the Guardians to sacrifice. In Céline's 'Anti-Republic', however, the soldier is a debased, duped figure, duped by the false promise of immortality — no longer achievable through heroic sacrifice on the modern field of battle — and violently and grotesquely sacrificed for the edification of the Republic itself and the enrichment of its leaders. Bardamu's world is a world whose immortality has been stolen away. In his anti-Platonic world, Bardamu, who also wanders with the 'dead' in a world circumscribed by eight circles — if we count each episode of *Voyage* as a circle — brings his own message to potential Guardians, 'la vérité de ce monde c'est la mort' [the truth of this world is death] (RI, 200). Bardamu remembers and enacts and re-enacts the failure of heroic myth to announce there is no more immortality in battle, only absurd death, and to ensure there will be no more sacrifice, no more 'men of gold'.

Er, says Louis Crocq, epitomises the experience of those traumatised by war. 'Comme lui, ils ont vécu la mort, et avec elle le mystère de l'effacement de la vie et l'échappée mystérieuse de l'âme dans le chaos des enfers' [like him, they have lived through death, and in death have experienced the mystery of life effaced,and the mysterious escape of the soul from the chaos of hell].[26] The myth offers hope, however, as through witness, 'énoncé, pour sa propre aperception autant que pour l'édification de ceux qui l'écoutent' [spoken, as much for his own apperception as for the edification of those who listen to him], Er achieves catharsis. But what needs real emphasis here is that the hope offered to and by Er is that memory can, indeed, be rescued from oblivion and that the story of the dead can be told. This, indeed, is where Céline and Er are one, as the soldier who has been dispensed from forgetting to tell his experience of death. And this is where Céline's own memory of war finds a possibility of redemption, in the act of remembering itself.

The myth of Er offers a further possibility of redemption, underlined by Crocq, that by choosing a right mode of existence, death itself can be overcome. This is the logic of Céline and Bardamu's protean transformations, but it is also part of the message Céline seeks to transmit to his readers, the essence of his 'rappel à l'ordre' [call to order] (see 4.3 *The Function of Rappel*). It is his hope and call for a new France, which by becoming an anti-Republic, can escape stasis, avoid the repetition of past disasters and ultimately recover its lost heroic identity, its lost death mastery.

Céline's Cosmogony

The Er myth with its systems of circles reveals elements of Plato's cosmogony and provides a clue to another aspect of *Voyage*'s protean structure. Er's afterworld is bound by eight circles representing the fixed stars, Saturn, Jupiter, Mars, Mercury, Venus, the Sun and the Moon.[27] Henri Godard divides *Voyage* into eight episodes, Front, Rear, Africa, America, Rancy, Paris, Toulouse and Vigny, with the first chapter providing an introduction. The length of each of these episodes corresponds proportionately to the width of Plato's planetary circles,[28] although the nature of a more precise correspondence between them remains to be explored. What correspondence there is provides rich ground for speculation. For example, Plato's planets as they moved made a music which could not be heard, 'the harmony of the spheres',[29] corresponding to *Voyage*'s silences which separate episode from episode. Furthermore, in the Er myth, the band of light which held the circles together is referred to as a 'swifter', a rope tied longitudinally around a boat to prevent the timbers coming apart. This has a special resonance if we recall the view of A.-C. and J.-P Damour that *Voyage* is structured like a boat. The Er connection does indeed confirm this thesis. It is, therefore, likely that Céline imagined *Voyage* itself as a 'Trois-mâts […] en route pour l'Infini' [Three-master […] en route for the Infinite] (RI, 473) whose journey is bound by the dawn. In this way, Céline's 'cosmogony' is the modern literary counterpart of Er's or Plato's, just as Bardamu's story is that of a modern Er.

9.2 THE ANTI-ENLIGHTENMENT

The Dawn

'Light is a precious thing,' says Plato, making the sun the metaphor of his eternal good.[30] That the sun was also the central image of the Enlightenment shows the more than two-thousand year old continuity of this imagery in Western Civilisation. *Voyage* challenges this continuity. One of the ways in which it does so is through a reversal of Enlightenment imagery. *Voyage*'s demonic view of nature demonstrates Céline's revolt against the apocalyptic Enlightenment view.

All of *Voyage*'s imagery, from the title onwards, tends towards the creation of an anti-Enlightenment metaphor which accuses the Enlightenment of leading to the slaughter of the Great War. This is most clearly seen in Céline's treatment of the central symbols of the Enlightenment: Condorcet's dawn of history and Immanuel Kant's sun of reason (see 1.1 *Enlightenment and Revolution*). *Voyage*'s circular movement is towards the dawn where ultimately the novel ends. It clearly echoes the journey of Er to rebirth, whose plain of orbs was bounded by a band of light.[31] It more directly echoes Céline's own experience of war, however, and the repetitive early alerts of the 12th Cuirassiers. Soldiers had a special relationship to the dawn. Morning stand-to in the trenches left an indelible impression on them. The daily stand-to emphasised the ritual and sacrificial aspect of the war, as soldiers awaited the signal to leave the trenches, their death sentence.[32]

The ritual, sacrificial aspect of dawn was enshrined in military practice. Military executions took place at dawn. Waiting for dawn, journeying towards dawn, became synonymous with waiting for or journeying towards one's own death. As usual, however, Céline's symbolism has endless layers. Elias Canetti tells us that in some cultures, the souls of dead ancestors entered the world through the dawn.[33] *Voyage*'s orientation towards the dawn, therefore, signifies not only Céline/Bardamu facing towards his own death, but towards the memory of the Great War dead. And this, Céline ultimately suggests, is the finality of Condorcet's history, a uniquely resonant symbol and vision of death itself.[4]

The Sun

Voyage is a world void of reason, characterised by delirium and madness. If the sun is the ultimate symbol of reason, it is not surprising that it is corrupted in *Voyage*. In *Voyage*, Pierre Verdaguer writes, 'la chaleur n'est pas simple cause d'accablement [...]. Elle est aussi assimilable au danger et à la violence latents' [the heat is not just oppressive [...]. It is also identified with danger and latent violence].[34] Significantly, *Voyage* begins as Bardamu and Arthur Ganate seek shelter from the hot sun in a Place Clichy café. The circularity of Place Clichy announces the novel's cycle of re-enactment, and it is also, by virtue of its circularity, an emblem of the sun itself. At the heart of this circle is the embattled hero, Moncey, 'qui défend' [who defends], as Céline does, 'la Place Clichy [...] contre des souvenirs et l'oubli' [Place Clichy from memories and forgetting] (RI, 350). Significantly, it is from the heart of this image of the sun that Bardamu leaves for war. Symbolically, war and sun are the same, as Bardamu stands 'parmi toutes ces balles et les lumières de ce soleil' [amidst all those bullets and the light of that sun] (RI, 12). The description of the war as 'le feu' [the fire] (RI, 14) extends this imagery of the war as a product of the Enlightenment sun of reason and truth. Perhaps *Voyage*'s most striking image of the war is as a circle of fire (RI, 29). Light itself announces death. 'La première lumière qu'on verrait ce serait celle du coup de fusil de la fin' [the first light seen would be the rifleshot that finishes you off] (RI, 27).

'Dans le *Voyage*,' writes Verdaguer, 'le symbolisme bienfaisant [...] du soleil est systématiquement mué en son contraire' [In *Voyage*, the benign symbolism of the sun is systematically changed into its opposite].[35] Nowhere is this more evident than in the demonic African episode. As the passengers on the *Amiral Bragueton* approach the equator the sun becomes a malefic force dissolving their veneer of civilisation:

> Dans le froid d'Europe [...] on ne fait, hors les carnages, que soupçonner la grouillante cruauté de nos frères, mais leur pourriture envahit la surface dès que les émoustille la fièvre ignoble des Tropiques. (RI, 113)

> [In the cold of Europe [...] you would never suspect, slaughters aside, the seething cruelty of our brothers, but as soon as the ignoble fever of the Tropics begins to titillate them, their corruption comes right to the surface.]

Here the tropical sun reveals the true nature 'des Blancs' [of Whites], 'la vérité [...] la charogne et l'étron' [the truth [...] decayed meat and excrement]. Here Céline opposes the humanist basis of the Enlightenment through corruption of its central image. In the full glare of the sun, he says, man is revealed as nothing more than excrement and decay. At this point, Céline is as far removed from the Enlightenment vision of man and progress as he could be, where the very image of the sun serves to contradict its 'secular faith of man in man' (see 1.1 *Enlightenment and Revolution*).

In Africa, Céline's subversion of the Enlightenment sun reaches its zenith, in a bloody destruction of the romantic symbolism of the sunset. The African sunsets resemble 'd'énormes assassinats du soleil' [tremendous murders of the sun], an image of the war itself in all its sacrificial glory (RI, 168). Through use of conventional romantic lyricism in this passage, Céline suggests a culture steeped in the poetry of blood and sacrifice, reminiscent of 'les Aztèques' [the Aztecs] and their sacrifices in 'leurs temples du soleil' [their sun temples] (RI, 37). What *Voyage* does retain of past symbolism of the sun is ultimately this, its bloody echo of ritual sacrifice, its demonic and murderous nature 'd'écarlate en délire' [of delirious scarlet] (RI, 168).

Perpetual War

The Enlightenment promised peace but it brought revolution and war. Kant's Enlightenment vision of perpetual peace was based on three assumptions: the rise of democracy — by virtue of the establishment of republics —, technological and economic development, and the establishment of a League of Nations (see 1.1 *Enlightenment and Revolution*). The evidence of the Great War contradicted him and Céline seizes on that contradiction. In *Voyage*, war is democratic. Lola, Musyne, the actress from the *Comédie Française*, the Putas, and even Bardamu's mother, are as much the face of war as Pinçon or des Entrayes. War in *Voyage* is total, global, a product of culture, theatre and newspapers, as much as technology, the Ford Factory in Detroit where 'on cède au bruit comme on cède à la guerre' [you surrender to the noise like you surrender to the war] (RI, 226). Ultimately, Céline's war is a war to produce gold from the blood of soldiers, Plato's 'men of gold'. Thus, Céline's Great War is precisely the result of democracy, of the institution of the French Republic, of technology and of economic interests. And there is no international saviour (see 4.1 *La Société des Nations*).

Voyage, as we have seen, is oriented as much towards war to come as war past and so, through its cyclical prolongation of war, Kant's 'perpetual peace' becomes Céline's 'perpetual war', technological and economic, democratic and global. It is hard not to accept that the evidence of history during the inter-war years is on Céline's side and conclude that, at that juncture at least, the values of the Enlightenment had resulted in the catastrophic failure of the Enlightenment project.

Princhard

The attack on the Enlightenment is made explicit by Princhard (RI, 66–71).[36] Princhard's speech combines two of *Voyage*'s most important aspects, being both polemical *and* educational. Not for nothing is Princhard a history teacher (RI, 63). His role is not just to attack the Enlightenment, but to provide for future generations of French young, an explicit history lesson. 'Je suis payé pour la connaître' [I'm paid to know what I'm talking about], as he himself says (RI, 67). The use of their own language, the language of the street, coarse, energetic and full of slang is perhaps his and Céline's greatest educational tool.

The symbolic *mise en scène* of Princhard's speech is openly anti-Enlightenment.[37] Bardamu finds Princhard 'essayant des lunettes contre la lumière [...] au milieu d'un cercle de soldats' [trying on some sunglasses [...] in the middle of a circle of soldiers], before they repair together to the hospital terrace where 'l'après-midi rutilait splendide sur Princhard, défendu par ses verres opaques' [the afternoon rippled splendidly over Princhard, protected by his opaque glasses] (RI, 66). Princhard's speech begins with a denunciation of

Voyage's obvious targets, 'la Patrie' [the Fatherland], 'la folie des massacres' [the craze for massacres], the sacrificial cult of the hero — 'on va faire [...] un héros avec moi !' [they are going to make a hero of me!] (RI, 67) — 'la République' [the Republic] (RI, 68), whose leaders Princhard describes as 'nos tyrans d'aujourd'hui' [our current tyrants] (RI, 69). Princhard gives his 'pupil' a history lesson which begins with 'le roi soleil' [the Sun King], Louis XIV, and Louis XV, before projecting itself towards the Revolution and rooting itself in a denunciation of the Enlightenment. In true didactic style, Princhard declares:

> Les philosophes, ce sont eux, notez-le [...] qui ont commencé par raconter des histoires au bon peuple [...]. Ils se sont mis [...] à l'éduquer... Ah ! ils en avaient des vérités à lui révéler ! et des belles ! [...] Qui brillaient ! Qu'on en restait tout ébloui ! (RI, 69)

> [It was the philosophers, note it well [...] who began by spinning tales for the people [...]. They began [...] to educate the people... Ah, yes! They had truths to reveal! And fine ones! [...] Truths that shone so brightly! They dazzled everyone!]

The anti-Enlightenment symbolism does not need to be underlined, but in any case Princhard launches an accusation which summons the greatest names in the Enlightenment firmament, Voltaire, Diderot, Goethe.

Princhard's lesson is circular. It begins and ends with an evocation of the war. Its climax suggests the fate that awaits 'les Pacifiques puants, qu'on s'en empare et qu'on les écartèle !' [the stinking Pacifists, let them be taken hold of and ripped asunder!] (RI, 70). He leaves his 'pupil' with a final observation. Commemoration, overseen by '[le] Ministre' [the Minister] and 'le Préfet' [the Prefect], is based on exclusion from memory, where 'des lâches sans idéal' [the cowards without ideals] are separated from 'les morts convenables' [the decent dead]. History, he suggests, has come to this, institutionalised forgetting and official discourse which does nothing more than 'frémir de la gueule' [shout its mouth off] (RI, 70). The fate of the history teacher repeats the evidence of his discourse. He disappears in darkness to become one of the 'disparus' [disappeared]. The irony of this word, used to describe casualties of war whose bodies or identities have not been recovered — there were over 100,000 disappeared at Verdun, where the Douaumont Ossuary is their enduring monument — contradicts society's claim to remember and is as eloquent a statement as could be wished for of the finality of the 'brilliance' of Princhard's Enlightenment.

Les maîtres

Writing from Africa in 1916, Céline quotes, in what is an apparent movement of incipient anti-Semitism, Urbain Gohier's view that French literature of the future will be 'plus juive que jamais' [more Jewish than ever].[38] Ten years later, *L'Église*'s Act Three portrait of a globe manipulated by Jews provides real evidence of anti-Semitism. Yet, *Voyage* itself seems characterised by an absence of any direct anti-Semitic content. Philippe Alméras, however, has made much of 'trois petits mots' [three little words] in *Voyage*.[39] The words 'négro-judéo-saxonne' [negroid-Judaic-saxon] (RI, 72) Alméras argues, are clear evidence of the anti-Semitic content of *Voyage* and provide the missing link between *L'Église* and the pamphlets. The removal of the term 'civilisation judéo-militaire' [a Judaic-military civilisation] contained in the *Voyage* manuscript,[40] but not in the published *Voyage*, where it is replaced by the term 'commercialo-militaire' [commercial-military] (RI, 156), confirms Alméras and shows that there is, indeed, a calculated process of suppression or repression taking place, by which overt anti-Semitism is being occluded.

However, *Voyage* has, hidden in its patterns, a much more direct and obvious target. What emerges most forcefully from *Voyage*'s language and imagery is a clear accusation launched towards one of the principal architects of the Enlightenment and Republican France: the Freemasons.[41]

The Freemasons originated in the mid-seventeenth century in societies formed by architects and builders. An international, philosophical society, in the Platonic tradition — 'the true mason [is] a philosophe', it was said[42] — they grew in importance and counted members from the most powerful strata of society. They became a pre-eminent force in French political, commercial, artistic and army life. Organised into countrywide 'loges' [lodges], overseen by 'La Grande Loge de l'Orient' [the Great Lodge of the Orient] in Paris, the Freemasons are considered to have been inseparable from the French intelligentsia from the time of Louis XV to the establishment of the Empire.[43] The French Revolution was perhaps their finest moment.[44] They played 'incontestablement un rôle éducatif pour la génération politique de 1789 [...]. Pendant près d'un siècle, il avait enseigné "l'art de rendre les hommes égaux"' [without question an educational role for the political generation of 1789 [...]. For almost a century, they taught 'the art of making men equal'].[45] The revolutionary motto, *Liberté, Égalité, Fraternité* [*Liberty, Equality, Fraternity*], was identified with masonry and acclaimed during their rituals; the revolutionary anthem, *La Marseillaise*, was sung before the singing of masonic songs.[46] Freemasons referred to their fellows as 'frère' [brother]. They espoused and promoted Enlightenment values, referring to themselves as 'children of the light'.[47] Voltaire, Diderot and Condorcet, central figures of the Enlightenment, were Freemasons or espoused Freemason thinking. The Freemasons emerged from a tradition of alchemy and their inherited spiritual and material goal was the perfect state: 'l'*Or*' [Gold].[48]

After the Revolution, the Freemasons continued to exert their influence. By the time of the Third Republic, the Freemasons constituted 'une véritable classe dirigeante' [a veritable ruling class] in France.[49] The founder of the Third Republic, Léon Gambetta, was a Freemason.[50] In the years preceding the Great War, numbers of Freemasons doubled.[51] Nine members of the first French *Union Sacrée* [Sacred Union] war cabinet were masons.[52] The Great War was led by Freemasons. Marshal Foch, the French army commander during the Great War, was one, as were Lord Kitchener in Britain and General Pershing in the US. After the war, masonic membership continued to grow, reaching its highest ever level in 1930 as Céline was writing *Voyage*.

Masonic art had its own character. Masons, of course, were prominent in architecture and the society itself was imagined as a 'building'. The favoured literary style was the 'discours des orateurs' [orators' discourse]. The 'livre d'initiation' [the novel of initiation] was standard, as were theatre, poetry and song, all used to spread masonic ideas. Masonic writings had two dimensions: initiation and ideology.[53] The masons favoured geometry, astronomy, music and arithmetic, dialectic, rhetoric and grammar. The Freemason rhetorician was expected to possess 'la science des *rythmes* et des *sons*' [the science of *rhythms* and *sounds*], while his grammar, 'art d'écrire et de parler correctement, repose sur quatre principes [...] : la raison, l'ancienneté, l'autorité, l'usage' [the art of writing and speaking properly rested on four principles [...]: reason, tradition, authority, and usage].[54]

What was perhaps most notable about the Freemasons is that they were a secret society, whose members were sworn to inviolable silence.[55] Members were initiated in a series of highly ritualised ceremonies, which often took place in an underground cavern, lit by lamps and candles.[56] The candidate, the 'profane', wore a blindfold during the ceremony. The purpose of initiation was to '*apprendre à mourir*' [to learn to die].[57] In a ritual of death and resurrection, the former personality of the 'profane' 'dies' and is replaced by a new one.

In the course of the initiation the 'profane' undertakes a number of 'voyages'. On his voyage, he is guided in a circular journey to the south and east, returning by the north to his original position. The attendant Freemasons, kitted out with ceremonial sword, make a noise of rolling thunder with their feet.[58] The candidate must spend some time in the 'Cabinet de Réflexion' [Room of Reflection], representing Hades, 'le royaume des morts' [the Kingdom of the Dead]. The walls of the 'Cabinet de Réflexion' were painted black and inscribed with the letters V.I.T.R.I.O.L.U.M signifying: *Visita Interiora Terrae Rectificando Invenies Occultum Lapidem Veram Medicinam* or 'Visit the Interior of the Earth and in Rectifying you will find the Hidden Stone, which is True Medicine.'[59] This was the philosopher's stone which turned base metal into gold and which guaranteed immortality. Leaving the 'Cabinet', the candidate undergoes trials by water, air and fire, rituals of purification and empowerment over these elements. To lose his 'personality' he drinks 'l'eau d'oubli' [the water of forgetting][60] and later is given another drink, 'l'eau de mémoire' [the water of memory], which remakes him as 'un Maçon militant' [a militant Mason], a representative of the collective. At the end of the ritual, he is placed 'debout, face à l'Orient' [standing, facing the East],[61] and receives 'la Lumière' [the Light]. Masonic ritual is punctuated with long silences.

Freemason ritual was highly symbolic. Central symbols were the sun, the triangle,[62] an empty circle representing the sun, the eye, also representing the sun, and the egg, symbol of the cosmic egg of Orphic myth, whose shell was the night.[63] The letter G was central. It stood for 'Gnose' [Gnosis] or knowledge, and represented 'le Grand Architecte' [the Great Architect], the creator of the Universe.

Voyage's anti-masonic character is clear from its very first pages and is ever-present in the novel's anti-Enlightenment imagery. To begin with the novel itself is a 'livre d'initiation' [novel of initiation], which goes 'de la vie à la mort' [from life to death] (RI, epigraph) and ends with Bardamu facing the dawn. Bardamu himself will tell us that he has been initiated into death. 'Moi, je savais bien comment on meurt. J'ai appris' [Me, I knew well how to die, I had learned it] (RI, 388). Writing *Voyage* involves Céline in a symbolic dissolution or death of his own personality, to be reconstituted as a collective personality (see 6.1 *The Mask*). Bardamu's journey takes him to the south, Africa, to the east, America, and he returns via the north, 'l'Autre Monde' [the Other World] (RI, 237), symbolically the place of death, where the sun never appears.[64] His journey is a quest for gold which takes him into successive undergrounds while incessantly he pronounces his own death. All of this is evidence that the world of *Voyage* is a masonic world, shaped by masonic values and rituals.

Céline's vision of 'personal evil' in *Voyage* is thus 'les maîtres' [the masters]. The title of a full Freemason was 'maître' [master] and by calling those who direct the war 'les maîtres' (RI, 9), Céline points the finger directly at the Republic's 'classe dirigeante' [ruling class]: the Freemasons. This is hardly surprising given their guiding role in French society at the time of the war and in the decades leading towards new catastrophe. The anti-Republican dynamic of *Voyage* must perforce be directed against the values, ideals and practices of the group which constituted the essence of that Republic. The world of *Voyage* becomes an immense parody of Freemasonry, its ritual, its literature and its architecture. The large buildings that recur throughout *Voyage* evoke masonic architecture. For example, Bardamu's New York hotel, 'tombe gigantesque […].

Une torture architecturale gigantesque' [a gigantic tomb [...]. A gigantic, architectural torture] (RI, 205–206) or the Mairie [Town Hall] situated, 'dans un étang de lumière [...] cette clairière' [in a pool of light [...] a clearing] and surrounded by, 'des monstres et des monstres de maisons' [monsters and monsters of houses] (RI, 193). It is not for nothing that so many of Bardamu's journeys lead him towards large and threatening buildings.

The theme of the 'monster' and the 'monstrous', so central to *Voyage*, and evoked particularly through the use of the word 'grand' [big/great], indirectly suggests the 'Grande Guerre' [Great War]. The use of the word 'grande', in phrases like 'Grande déroute' [great rout] (RI, 239 and 279), in a world where *les grands* [the big] oppress *les petits* [the small], operates within this logic, where the capitalisation of the letter G is significant and refers the reader back again to 'la Grande Guerre' [the Great War], never mentioned directly by Céline, as well as evoking the masonic G. *Voyage*'s 'gigantism', which can be seen as an aspect of its totalising logic, is equally an indirect reflection of the masonic G, implicit in the evocation of the monstrous, and explicit in the use of the word 'géant' [giant] in expressions like 'la misère est géante' [poverty is gigantic] (RI, 217). The Ford factory at Detroit becomes 'cette géante multiforme' [that multiform giant] (RI, 231) while later Bardamu's Paris hotel is, significantly, 'un monstre à loger' [a monstrous lodging house] (RI, 358). Through *Voyage*'s gigantism the Freemasons are shadowed forth as a race of giants devouring both the earth and mankind.

The characters who populate *Voyage* are also representative of a masonic world. Bestombes and Baryton are characterised as 'masonic' by their oratorical style. Bestombes's 'yeux [...] surnaturels' [supernatural eyes] signal his appurtenance (RI, 86). Bardamu's military superior, Pinçon, does not like food but must eat 'ses œufs à la coque' [boiled eggs] at the General's table and is mockingly described as 'jaune' [yellow] (RI, 22). General des Entrayes, for his part, is associated with lamplight, 'sa table était mise, la lampe à sa place' [his table was set, the lamp in its place] (RI, 25). The arteries in his temples are clearly visible 'à la lampe' [in the lamplight] (RI, 26). Sainte-Engence's 'sabre' [sword] is equally, ceremonially, masonic (RI, 31). Robinson, blindfold, is not just the image of a soldier awaiting execution, or with wounded eyes, he is also the caricature of a 'profane', blindfold in a cavern lit only by a candle (RI, 325). Candles and lamps are ubiquitous in *Voyage*, of course, as is the cavern.

The description of France as a vast theatre, directly points to masonic influence on the totality of French life. The sustained theatrical metaphor of *Voyage* is inspired by the word 'loge' [lodge], while Bardamu in one scene appears himself in a 'loge' (RI, 100).[65] The theatrical evocation of Napoleon, for example, derives its sustenance from the Freemasons' adulation of the Emperor.[66] The 'belle subventionnée' [lovely actress] from the *Comédie Française* is Céline's joking recognition that its actresses provided the first female Freemasons.[67] Céline too is trenchantly anti-masonic in his oral style which subverts the masonic ideal of perfect grammar and the authority of the written word. Here Céline is employing the same strategy as with his challenge to Plato and the Enlightenment: reversal, distortion, and imitation or caricature.

Voyage is simply packed with references to Freemasons and Freemasonry. Littré, of *Voyage*'s epigraph, was a Freemason. Voltaire and Carnot, mentioned in Princhard's speech, were Freemasons. Goethe was one, or at least an honorary one, as was Napoleon, who was adored by the Freemasons. Painters evoked or mentioned in *Voyage* such as Fragonard (RI, 54) and Watteau (RI, 74) were notable Freemasons. It is likely that the initials of Arthur Ganate (RI, 7) conceal a reference to Arthur Groussier the most prominent Freemason and Labour Minister in inter-war France. The first pamphlet against Freemasonry, *Masonry Dissected*, was penned by Samuel Prichard in London in 1730. *Voyage*'s very own pamphlet writer, the history teacher, Princhard — the distortion of the name is quite in keeping with Céline's style[68] — is, indeed, one of the clearest indications given by Céline that he is attacking the Freemasons.

Return to 4 mai

Voyage, however, is at its most anti-masonic in its aura of darkness and secrecy, its use of silence and ritual. It can, indeed, be said that *Voyage* behaves like a secret organisation. Or, as a parody of one. *Voyage*'s evocation of the memory of Verdun is relevant here. Lord Northcliffe's March 1916 report on his visit to

Verdun, described it as so cut off from the world and so difficult of access that it was 'as secret as a Freemason lodge'.[69] Whether or not Céline knew of Northcliffe's description of Verdun — the likelihood is that he did[70] — there is every possibility that *Voyage* is shut up 'like a lodge' to purposefully mimic this reality of Verdun, where the French Army was being slaughtered in an atmosphere of secrecy and darkness in a France controlled by Freemasonry. That is, Céline suggests, that secret, ritualistic Verdun, and the slaughter of '4 mai', is the direct outcome and expression of a France shaped by Enlightenment and Revolution and whose principal architects were the Freemasons. In *Voyage*, Verdun and *Mort-Homme* become the symbol and meaning of a France controlled by Freemasonry [see 1.3 *Verdun*].

The link between Freemasonry and Verdun is a terrible one and yet it makes perfect sense when one bears in mind the explicit condemnation of Freemasonry in Céline's pre-Second World War pamphlets. The scale of the denunciation, however, when one finally grasps it, is nonetheless overwhelming.

'C'est le compte entre moi et "Eux"! au tout profond...' [It's the dispute between me and 'Them'! to the deepest level...] Céline wrote in his 1949 preface to *Voyage* (RI, 1114), thereby acknowledging *Voyage*'s adversarial character. It is now clear that *Voyage* is directed not just at the French Republic or the Enlightenment, but at the figures who, operating in silence and shadows, helped to engender both: the Freemasons. For all that those 'trois petits mots' [three little words] of Alméras signify, 'la race sémite n'existe pas, c'est une invention de franc-maçon' [the race of Jews does not exist, it's a Freemason invention] Céline will proclaim in *Bagatelles* (BM, 191) and it is, indeed, the Freemasons who are the most obvious and direct enemy of Céline's anti-Republic.[71]

9.3 BEYOND VOYAGE

This last section traces Céline's memory of the Great War after *Voyage*. It seeks to answer the question: what happens to Céline's memory of the Great War after *Voyage*? And what happens to his efforts to achieve death mastery? It is a vast enterprise and this section can offer only a brief sketch, in epilogue form, of some of the more salient points in Céline's journey to the end of memory.

Mort à crédit

Mort à crédit (1936) is a prequel to *Voyage*. It recounts Céline's early experience of death, the death of his grandmother, death of his class, death of his world, lost forever in the Great War. Beneath its black layers of comedy and obscenity it offers a sustained lament for a world that is gone, what Nicholas Hewitt calls Céline's 'golden age'.[72] The death of Céline's father in 1932 undoubtedly informs much of the grief that is at the heart of his second novel and undoubtedly accentuates Céline's need of and efforts at death mastery while he writes his second novel.[73]

Before embarking on his childhood tale, the narrator, Ferdinand, reminds the reader of his veteran status and the world of mental instability it has plunged him into, 'depuis la Guerre ça m'a sonné. Elle a couru derrière moi, la folie...' [since the War it's been ringing in my ears. It's been chasing after me, madness...] (RI, 536). He evokes his prestige as author of *Voyage*, a gesture which represents a clear consolidation of self as well as announcing an ongoing pattern of re-enactment. Evoking 'le Bébert du Val-de-Grâce', he comments, 'il lisait le *Voyage* celui-là' [the Bébert from the Val-de-Grâce read *Voyage*] (RI, 532). From this point on the memory of *Voyage* is subsumed into Céline's project.[74] One of Céline's first acts then, as author of *Mort à crédit*, is to establish a clear linear connection to *Voyage* and in doing so ensure its memory.[75] The linearity this creates points in two directions, backwards towards *Voyage*, the Great War and Verdun, and forwards towards death, the *north* which provides the direction of Céline's life and work and which is made explicit in the last trilogy.

Returning to his childhood,[76] Céline has little to say about the war. This is how he wants it. The setting of the pre-war world guarantees his commitment to moral silence (see 5.2 *The Temptation of Silence*). Yet, the Great War inevitably shadows all of *Mort à crédit*. Céline's return to the pre-war world enables him to depict it in its true colours, as a world destined for disaster.

In *Mort à crédit*, there is a significant recall of Céline's father's desire to make him join the army, 'ce qu'il aurait voulu [...] c'est que je parte au régiment' [what he wanted [...] was for me to join the regiment] (RI, 829), 'qu'il voulait plus me recauser [...] avant que je parte au régiment' [he didn't want to talk to me anymore [...] until I left to join the regiment] (RI, 856).

Re-entering the world of his childhood, Céline brings his father out of his silence, only to symbolically kill him. In doing so, Céline once again draws on myth to negotiate his present. This time it is the myth of Oedipus which allows Céline to enact a past drama of betrayal, of the younger generation by the older who urged it to war, and to settle scores with his father. Ferdinand's savage typewriter-assisted attack on his father becomes a staging of Céline's own attack on the power and authority of the French Republic (RI, 822). Where *Voyage* formulated an accusation, *Mort à crédit* enacts the 'capsizing of the ship of state' in mythical and metaphorical terms.

We have seen that one of Céline's aims in *Voyage* is to denounce the Freemasons. The world he condemns in *Mort à crédit* remains a masonic world revealed through Céline's use of language and symbol. In a rather disingenuous way, Céline brings his preoccupation with the Freemasons out into the open, when describing his father's rages:

> Il se voyait persécuté par un carnaval de monstres... Il déconnait à pleine bourre... Il en avait pour tous les goûts... Des juifs... des intrigants... les Arrivistes... Et puis surtout des Francs-Maçons... (RI, 651).
>
> [He imagined himself persecuted by a carnival of monsters... He spouted endless drivel... He had something for everyone's taste... The Jews... the intriguers... the Arrivistes... But especially the Freemasons...]

As Céline restates his father's griefs he exposes his own, bringing to the surface of the novel what simmers beneath it.

A striking stylistic innovation in Céline's second novel is his rampant use of suspension points. Even prior to publication he was criticised for using them.[77] There is much to be said about Céline's 'trois points' [three dots]. They are immediately distinctive and confer a visual uniqueness on Céline's text. They thus symbolise the originality of his work and his enterprise.

Céline's 'trois points' offer him a route to direct emotion.[78] His 'trois points' enable him to heighten the emotional intensity of his writing, to maintain an unflagging, breathless sense of urgency, to enliven his text and make himself feel more alive. The 'trois points' are his lifeline of emotion made visible, part of his effort to throw off his 'death imprint'. In addition, the 'trois points' open his text to silence. Abrupt movements of silence now interrupt almost every sentence. Within these silences, and more visibly than ever before, lies all of the finality of Céline's witness. The 'trois points' signal a world in constant disintegration, where the breach with the past is being constantly re-enacted and the failure of memory surges constantly to the surface. The 'trois points' are Céline's evocation of the failure of language, of memory, of the impossibility of communication, of understanding. They are a sign of the presence of the incomprehensible and unspeakable. They contain all of Céline's vast 'non-dit' [what is unsaid], all that he cannot say or is unwilling to say, all that has not been said or cannot be said. Ultimately they are, like all of Céline's silence, the visible sign of his 'death imprint', an enlarged presence for death in his text, transformed into a life-affirming likeness of lace, 'un beau suaire brodé d'histoires' [a beautiful shroud embroidered with stories] (RI, 537).

Mort à crédit is, if anything, more determinedly obscene and scatological than *Voyage*. However, while clinging to an orality which remains the guarantor of Céline's witness and truth, it enacts a number of significant stylistic advances. Céline's wholesale embrace of the octosyllable introduces a recurrent and incessant rhythm while ultimately claiming linear descent from a core French tradition.[79] Echoing writers as diverse as Villon, La Fontaine and Théophile Gautier, the octosyllable is the supreme emblem of Céline's connection to his literary past. As such, it has profound death-mastering connotations while providing at the same time an affirmation of Céline's 'idée française' [French idea] (see 4.1 *Africa*) and of his own Frenchness. It imposes order and rhythm on Céline's prose and is not without echoes of children reciting poetry in classrooms. It perhaps recalls memories of Céline's own classroom days, but in any case, the octosyllable can be readily attached to Céline's didactic purpose as well as representing a return to and evocation of a sense of 'right order'. The octosyllable is meant to reverberate in the mind as it is read and to induce a mental rhythm rich with a cargo of Céline's truths of tradition, nationality, race and literature. It is intended to return the French mind and language to its roots in poetry and is part of Céline's efforts to 'heal' language and in doing so heal self and heal France.

Moving Céline's prose towards poetry, the octosyllable marks a further shift towards a new means of truth-telling, a reverse echo of the thirteenth-century movement from poetry to prose, while in addition creating a mnemonic effect to complement the use of pleonastic 'rappel'. The octosyllable as a vector for memory underlines the role Céline is carving out for himself, in his art, as a guardian of memory. The affirmation of race implicit in the choice of the octosyllable underlines the heroic character of Céline's literary effort which seeks through regeneration to confer symbolic immortality on himself, his world, his people and his race (see 1.1 *The Hero*).

Céline's quest for the buried treasure of his own immortality continues in *Mort à crédit*.[80] The word *or* [gold] is visibly concealed in words such as 'G*or*loge' (a marvellous composite) and 'M*or*t' itself, and sometimes emerges to play a central musical role in Céline's text.[81] Deep within, however, the novel is marked by Céline's characteristic pessimism and futility. This must inevitably be the case when writing of a past world he knows predestined to horror, from the heart of a present en route to even greater carnage. When he finishes *Mort à crédit*, Céline is four years closer to the coming cataclysm of the Second World War. His death-mastering enterprise is more endangered than ever and demands of him even greater, and more protean, efforts.

Casse-pipe

There is no sense of nostalgia for war in Céline but there is very much so for the barracks. His unfinished third novel *Casse-pipe* represents a return to the world of *Maréchal des logis* Destouches with its rich, robust and often excremental vocabulary and imagery.[82] Like *Mort à crédit* it is a lament for a world destined to disappear in the Great War.

For Nicholas Hewitt, *Casse-pipe* provides an ironic and anguished counterpoint to Psichari's *L'Appel des armes* (see 1.1 *Ernest Psichari* and 7.6 *The Anti-Psichari*).[83] At the same time, Hewitt notes a progression towards a positive view of self and army and describes Ferdinand as eventually looking back with 'unalloyed nostalgia' at his 'unit'.[84] It is, indeed, in *Casse-pipe* that Céline articulates a first clear sense of reconciliation with his own soldier past. This acceptance will see the affirmation of his veteran self in the pamphlets where it will be reinforced by fervent anti-Semitism.[85]

As far as we know, Céline's lament for the cavalry remained unfinished. It is likely that, exhausted in the wake of *Mort à crédit*, he had not the heart for the immense effort demanded of him to tell this new story of disaster and the Great War death of the cavalry lost what would surely have been an enduring literary memorial.[86] It is also likely that with the Second World War increasingly imminent Céline needed to find a new death-mastering formulation which would take him beyond the claims of memory. The 1936 embrace of the pamphlet represents, for Céline, a first real breach with the memory of the First World War and a determined facing towards the Second.

Mea culpa

Mea culpa is a key turning-point for Céline, reminiscent of *L'Église* in the mid-twenties (see 4.1 *La Société des Nations*).[87] While *L'Église* recorded the failure of the League of Nations and world hopes for peace, *Mea culpa*, written in the wake of Céline's visit to Russia in 1936, records the failure of the Russian Revolution and the new society that has emerged from it, 'c'est encore l'injustice rambinée sous un nouveau blasé' [once again it's injustice kitted out with a new emblem].[88]

The manner in which *Mea culpa* interrupts the writing of *Casse-pipe* shows the inadequacy of the novel form to deal with the increasing tensions of Céline's pre-Second World War world. If the pamphlet was not his vocation, it became so. *Mea culpa* shows Céline the death-mastering possibilities of the pamphlet. Most of all, it enables him to grasp more firmly than ever Robert Jay Lifton's lifeline of rage and so pushes his work towards that extreme of emotion where it becomes pure invective.[89] As war approaches and death exerts more and more pressure on him, Céline is pushed altogether into the role of pamphleteer:

> C'est peut-être ça l'Espérance ? Et l'avenir esthétique aussi ! Des guerres qu'on saura plus pourquoi !... De plus en plus formidables ! [...] Que tout le monde en crèvera...[90]

[Maybe that's what Hope is? And the shape of the future too! Wars until no one has a clue what for!... More and more formidable! [...] Enough to do the entire world in...]

Inevitably, *Mea culpa* becomes the model for what is to follow: *Bagatelles pour un massacre* [*Bagatelles for a massacre*].

Bagatelles pour un massacre

Bagatelles pour un massacre (1938) confirms Céline's protean shift from novelist to pamphleteer. It marks a further movement on his part out of the silence of 'non-dit', from ironic satire to pure invective, and towards that extreme of tragic-irony in which his vision of 'personal evil' is fully articulated. In *Bagatelles*, Céline attacks Russia, communism, the Freemasons, Léon Blum's Popular Front party, the French middle-classes, and the evils of cinema, translation and alcohol. Most of all he attacks the Jew.[91] '*Man's deepest inner conflicts — those related to primal emotions about annihilating and being annihilated — become readily attached to the issue of race,*' writes Robert Jay Lifton.[92] This insight places Céline and *Bagatelles* once again at the heart of a struggle — no matter how corrupt or corrupting — for the immortality of nation and race, whose essential structure belongs to the heroic mode crushed in the Great War (see 1.1 *The Hero*). Race is, indeed, the organising principle of *Bagatelles* as Céline gives way to his most violent delirium. 'La fièvre me vint' [fever took hold of me], he writes (BM, 16). 'Tu vas voir l'antisemitisme !' [I'll show you anti-Semitism!] (BM, 41). Open, virulent anti-Semitism now occupies the centre of his vision of a world dominated by war and death. It provides a unifying principle by which death can be apprehended and by which the world can be saved. Céline offers this unifying principle to the French people as an assurance against death,[93] writing 's'il faut des veaux dans l'Aventure, qu'on saigne les Juifs ! c'est mon avis !' [if calves are needed for the Adventure, bleed the Jews! That's my view!] (BM, 319).[94] My death, our death, must be transformed into theirs, Céline is saying. In *Bagatelles*, the Jew becomes Céline's scapegoat.[95]

Céline's vision of the war to come is haunted by the last one. Behind his rage hovers the spectre of Verdun.[96] 'Fallait pas partir à la guerre, on s'est suicidé... Pour chaque Français tué à Verdun il est arrivé vingt youtres' [We shouldn't have gone to war, it was suicide... For every French soldier killed at Verdun, twenty Jews arrived among us] (BM, 309). Death favours the Jew, he insinuates, who triumphs in turn over the death of France. 'Ils deviennent également français !' he writes, adding, 'tu parles ! pas à Verdun !' [They are becoming equally French! Give me a break! They weren't equal at Verdun!] (BM, 71). The meaning of Céline's anti-Semitism is provided over and over by his memory of the Great War.

More than any other work of Céline's *Bagatelles* is threatened by, 'la prochaine guerre' [the next war] (BM, 88), 'la guerre prochaine' [the war to come] (BM, 94), 'l'immense tuerie prochaine' [the coming immense slaughter] (BM, 133). The memory of the Great War, however, remains its unrelenting backdrop and defines the war to come, a war of 'tranchées' [trenches][97] and 'barbelés' [barbed wire] (BM, 138), a war of futile heroism — 'le culte des héros c'est le culte de la veine' [the cult of the hero is the cult of the lucky] (BM, 138) — a war in which the French race is destined to be destroyed and forgotten. Céline has projected his memory of the Great War into his future. It now stands behind and before him, encircling him.

Céline's ultimate defence against this vision is vilification. His vilification of the Jew is unrelenting, page after page regurgitates the same horror, until he comes to resemble one of Robert Lifton's Nazi doctors, a 'half-educated', 'half-intellectual' wallowing in death-infatuated impotence.[98] The tragedy of Céline is that the author who, in *Voyage*, had enacted his ritual memory of ritual sacrifice and given it enduring literary form for the entire world should in *Bagatelles* be at the forefront of a new frenzy for sacrifice in calling the wrath of the entire world down upon one part of it. *Bagatelles* reveals a Céline whose mind is organised around and for war; who, indeed, is at war, fighting with all his genius for invective against his enemies, against death in the forms in which it appears to him, ex-soldier and veteran of the Great War.

At the centre of Céline's obsession there is, as ever, gold, the treasure he sought in *Voyage*, the stuff of his own immortality, the gold which was extracted from the 'men of gold', the soldiers sacrificed in the Great War. It is, of course, the Jews who have taken possession of this gold. The Jews are, 'avec de l'or [...] les maîtres absolus du monde' [with their gold [...] absolute masters of the world] (BM, 62). 'Ils ont tout l'or' [they have all the gold] (BM, 66). To dispossess the Jew of his gold is to rob him of his power over life and death. 'Sans or pas de guerre' [no war without gold], Céline writes (BM, 133). Gold which, as in *Voyage*, Céline converts into excrement, 'la merde juive [...] l'exquis caca juif génial ! [...] la divine fiente' [the Jewish shit [...] the exquisite, ingenious Jewish caca! [...] the divine droppings] (BM, 71). Gold, excrement and Jew are all subsumed in the same substance: death. In a corruption of one of *Voyage*'s key phrases, he writes, 'la vérité : le Juif' [the truth: the Jew] (BM, 49). The echo of 'la vérité [...] la mort' [the truth [...] death] is clearly heard, the equivalence unmistakeable.

The vitalising power of anti-Semitism can be seen in its effect on Céline's art. Here is soldier speech at its most exalted (see 8.2 *Soldier Speech*).[99] Nowhere is the transposition of emotion into language more successful as Céline forces self and language into an annihilating paroxysm of rage.[100] The sort of annihilating rage we have already seen in our portrait of the traumatised soldier (see 5.2 *Silence and Self*):

> J'ai la dent !... Une dent énorme !... Une vraie dent totalitaire !... Une dent mondiale !... Une dent de Révolution !... Une dent de conflagration planétaire !... De mobilisation de tous les charniers de l'Univers ! Un appétit sûrement divin ! Biblique !... (BM, 289).

> [I have a hunger!... An enormous hunger!... A truly totalitarian hunger!... A world hunger!... A hunger for Revolution!... A hunger for planetary conflagration!... For mobilisation of all the mass graves in the Universe!... A surely divine appetite! Biblical!...]

The howling wound of Céline's memory exists within the ever-tightening circle of war and death and nowhere in Céline's writing is the destructive, adversarial, indeed, fabulously homicidal, rage of the traumatised soldier more openly expressed.[101]

L'École des cadavres

In *L'École des cadavres* [*School for Corpses*][102] Céline returns with the same urgency to the themes established in *Bagatelles*. These themes are enunciated within the same pressing and now familiar dynamic of past war-future war, 'nous sommes pour ainsi dire en guerre...' proclaims Céline, 'on y est dans la "reder des ders"' [we are, so to speak, at war... we are in the latest 'war to end wars'] (EC, 20). His is a vision rooted in his earliest memory of horror, of 'tous nos cadavres épars sur les champs de la Meuse' [all our corpses strewn on the battlefields of the Meuse] (EC, 46, see also 3.3 *The Battle of the Marne*). Céline's educational purpose is explicit in the title. His 'école des cadavres' is one in which the Great War dead are the only teachers. 'Vive le Racisme ! On a compris à force des cadavres' [Long live Racism! We've learned thanks to our cadavers], Céline rails, juxtaposing his survivor's preoccupation with race and the death immersion of the Great War (EC, 223).

Céline's memory remains one of haunting repetition, '93, 70, 14, l'Espagne' [Spain], and premonition, 'la Grande Prochaine' [The Great Next One] (EC, 98). Céline foresees 'des prochaines hécatombes' [coming massacres] (EC, 35), 'de nouveaux Verduns !' [new Verduns] (EC, 51), 'Cinquante millions de cadavres aryens en perspective...' [fifty million aryan corpses in prospect] (EC, 28). 'Elle va durer combien d'années la prochaine "dernière" ?' [how long will the next 'last' one last?], he asks, predicting 'la prochaine nous coûtera au moins dans les vingt-cinq millions de morts' [the next war will cost us at least twenty-five million dead] (EC, 78). His is a memory haunted by the death of France itself, of a 'France anéantie par disparition des Français !' [France annihilated by the disappearance of the French] (EC, 79). 'Ça sera le suicide de la Nation !' [It will be the Nation's suicide!], he sings provocatively (EC, 91). 'Une autre victoire comme 18 et c'est la fin' [Another victory like '18 and we're done for] (EC, 94).

Céline continues to rail against 'la République maçonnique' [the masonic Republic] (EC, 30) and 'le Grand Pouvoir juif' [the Great Jewish Power] (EC, 27). 'Les Démocraties veulent la guerre' [Democracies want the war], he pronounces (EC, 25). And, 'en politique démocratique c'est l'or qui commande. Et l'or c'est le juif' [in democratic politics it's gold which gives the orders. And gold means the Jew] (EC, 180). More anti-Semite than ever, more virulent than ever, Céline demands, 'l'expulsion de tous les juifs' [the expulsion of all the

Jews] (EC, 98). 'Le juif doit disparaître' [the Jew must disappear], he writes (EC, 109). 'Désinfection ! Nettoyage ! Une seule race en France : l'Aryenne !...' [Disinfection! Cleansing! One race alone in Europe: the Aryan!...] (EC, 215). He voices his admiration for Hitler. Against the coming slaughter, 'une alliance avec l'Allemagne [...] c'est la seule solution' [an alliance with Germany [...] is the only solution] (EC, 283).

No work of Céline's is so marked by futility. It ends with one last jeremiad directed against the French themselves, against humanity in general, and against an entire world in which the re-enactment of war is the only certainty:

> La Roue tourne. Elle en écrasera, sûr, encore, des hommes et des hommes. Des millions et puis des millions. Ceux-ci, ceux-là et puis bien d'autres, ça n'en finira jamais.
> Ils fonceront toujours aux tueries, par torrents de viandes somnambules, aux charniers, de plus en plus colossaux, plantureux.
> Y a pas de raison que ça se termine. C'est leur nature. (EC, 295)

> [The Wheel turns. It will crush, certainly, again, humans upon humans. Millions of them and more millions. Those here, those over there and plenty of others, it will never end.
> They will always rush to slaughters, in torrents of somnambulant flesh, to ever more colossal, and lavish, mass graves.
> Why should it ever end. It's in their nature.]

The evidence of *Voyage* has not changed. Within one year of the publication of *L'École* in November 1938 the world will once again be at war.

Les Beaux Draps

Les Beaux Draps [*A Fine Mess*] is Céline's last pamphlet and as such marks a transition back to what is his ideal, immortalising form, the novel.[103] The brevity of *Les Beaux Draps* is evidence that Céline believes he has exhausted the potential of the pamphlet. It also indicates that there is less pressure on him to produce the immense works of denunciation that were *Bagatelles pour un massacre* and *L'École des cadavres*. Indeed, the worst has arrived and it has not been as bad as foreseen. The French army has been ignominiously defeated and the Third Republic has collapsed. The sought after alliance between France and Germany is now in place, under the command of the hero of Verdun, Philippe Pétain. The Great War has not repeated itself; there have been no trenches, no barbed wire, no massacre of France. While the Great War is not forgotten in *Les*

Beaux Draps the tension inherent in the past war-future war dynamic within Céline's memory has been dissolved. As such, *Les Beaux Draps* releases Céline from the imprisoning circle of his memory of the Great War.

Ever since *Voyage*, Céline has had an obsession with the suffering of children. *Voyage* itself is a world which, while it seeks birth, is without birth, a world in which the abortion and miscarriage reign. The death of Bébert characterises *Voyage*'s pessimism. *Mort à crédit*, which follows, is a lament for the world of Céline's childhood, but also a lament for childhood itself. *Mort à crédit* reveals childhood as one of Céline's major themes. Until *Les Beaux Draps*, however, the failure and death of childhood in Céline's work is one more element in his lacking death mastery. With *Les Beaux Draps* childhood suddenly regains its death-mastering potential.

Childhood is a major concern of *Les Beaux Draps*. 'La France [...] elle va crever [...] qu'elle produit plus assez d'enfants' [France [...] will die [...] because it no longer produces enough children], wails Céline (BD, 49), later proclaiming, 'l'enfance notre seule salut' [childhood is our only salvation] (BD, 57). Only the child can redeem the past. 'Plus d'enfants, plus de France,' Céline writes. 'France éternelle aura vécu [...] Verduns pour rien...' [No more children, no more France. Eternal France will be done for [...] Verduns for nothing...] (BD, 50). The child becomes the basis for a remodelling of man in which 'le petit rigodon du rêve... la musique timide du bonheur, notre menu refrain d'enfance' [the little rigadoon of dream... the timid music of happiness, our slender refrain of childhood] is primordial (BD, 55). Céline's affirmation of childhood is the springboard for the pamphlet's final pages where he once again reaffirms his status as healing doctor of his race. He summons, on the heels of *Voyage*'s 'la mère Henrouille' and *Mort à crédit*'s Caroline, one more vision of an old woman braver than death, who follows her own 'petite musique' [little music] into the winter night, 'les personnes de cet âge !... elles sont un peu comme les enfants' [persons of that age!... they are a little like children] (BD, 75). Céline himself falls under the charm of 'l'appel des Cygnes [...] qui bouleverse le cœur !' [the call of the Swans [...] which overturns your heart] (BD, 75). For the first time he leaves his readers with an exultant vision of hope in the future, a death-mastering vision as his text dissolves in luminous *féerie*:

> C'est fait ! la chose est faite ! la vie partie !...
> Diaphanes émules portons ailleurs nos entrechats !... en séjours d'aériennes grâces où s'achèvent nos mélodies... aux fontaines du grand mirage !... Ah ! Sans être ! Diaphanes de danse ! Désincarnés rigododants ! tout allégresse ! heureux de mort ! (BD, 77)

> [That's it! the thing is done! life has gone!...
> Diaphanous emulators let our entrechats carry us elsewhere!... in sojourns of aerial graces where our melodies fade... to fountains of the great mirage!... Ah! Without substance! Diaphanous dances! Disembodied rigadooning! all joyous! happy death!]

With this newfound death mastery Céline renounces the pamphlet and returns to the novel.[104] His next work will prove his great novel of death mastery: *Guignol's band*.

Guignol's band

Guignol's band (1944) is Céline's novel of death mastery.[105] This novel returns Céline to World War One London, to an overwhelming sense of having escaped the war and of still being alive, 'je trouvais la condition magique après ce que j'avais connu !...' [I found it all magic after what I'd been through] (RIII, 137, see also 4.1 *London*). Nowhere is the memory of the Great War more present in Céline's work as page after page evokes the wartime atmosphere of the English capital amid a raft of hallucinatory episodes, the product of Ferdinand's war-traumatised mind, 'troubles de mémoire [...] séquelles de choc et trauma' [troubles with memory [...] consequence of shock and trauma] (RIII, 626).[106]

Ironically, Céline's most haunted work is his most celebratory. Its lasting impression is of an exalted desire for life itself as it describes Ferdinand's infatuation with the English girl, Virginie. Its emblem is the songbird, a bright, singing symbol of transcendence.[107] Laurens Van Der Post's description of birdsong, one of his 'bird memories', might very well describe *Guignol's band* as an expression of:

> ultimate harmony and beauty, asserting itself in its most vulnerable and defenceless form, relying for its own authority and impact solely on the beauty and its necessities of order and measure and the lucidity of its voice. [...] It was free of all physical and material barriers and

impediments of personal pain and injury, as if it were fulfilling directly the measure of the will of creation invested in that little body of a small bird, un-wounding itself there and regaining its full sense of being, with its heart in its throat.[108]

Anyone who has read *Guignol's band* will know how appropriate this description is and that it truly is the novel of Céline's 'un-wounding', which sings 'with its heart in its throat'.

It is hardly surprising that in a novel so replete with images of transcendence and death mastery that gold, normally hidden in the world of Céline's imagination, is visibly and tangibly present. One violent and hallucinatory scene shows the merchant, Van Claben, being stuffed with gold before being murdered by Ferdinand and the anarchist Boro as they attempt to make him regurgitate it (RIII, 220–224). This gold flies and dances in the air like a bird:

> Jamais j'ai tant vu de pognon !... Si ça clignote dans l'atmosphère ! tout pimpant ! frétillant ! volage !... ça illumine toute la boutique !... d'or et de reflets... ça tintille !... (RIII, 218–219)

> [Never had I seen so much dough!... It flickers in the air! all flash! quivering! flighty!... It lights up the whole shop!... with gold and reflections... it clintillates!...]

Ferdinand later washes his hands in this gold, 'c'est le moment de se laver les poignes !... On plonge tous les trois dans le magot, Boro, moi, Delphine...' [it's time to wash our hands ! We plunge all three of us into the loot, Boro, me, Delphine...] (RIII, 219).

In another scene, the corpse, Mille-Pattes, pulls gold out of his innards while entertaining Ferdinand and Virginie in a restaurant, 'des poignées d'or qu'il s'extirpe [...] ça fait des petits amonts de louis d'or' [fistfuls of gold he pulls out of himself [...] making small piles of gold coins] (RIII, 485). These scenes are richly symbolic of a Céline who has regained his 'treasure', who has achieved death mastery, who has come back to life and reconnected with his own immortality.

What can explain, in the midst of a world at war, this joyous outpouring of creativity on Céline's part? What are the elements that make up his death mastery? They appear myriad. Is age, for example, a factor? Has Céline become reconciled to his war past and found inner acceptance of his own heroism? Have the pamphlets freed him of his domination by death? Have their limitless invective brought him finally to a full sense of being alive? Have they allowed him to successfully shift his 'death imprint' on to the shoulders of the Jews? All of these and, of course, the fall of the Third Republic, are major factors in Céline's death mastery.

A major thrust of Céline's writing since *Voyage* has been to avoid a second slaughter through 'capsizing the ship of state'. The threatened slaughter has been avoided. It has petered out in a 'phoney war', followed by the collapse of the French Republic and the institution of the Franco-German alliance Céline has so desired. On 13 August 1940, the French Government passed legislation outlawing secret organisations, legislation directed chiefly against the Freemasons. Already on 7 August, Arthur Groussier, now the leading French Freemason, had informed Philippe Pétain, leader of the new government, that the lodges were dissolving of their own accord and would cease all activity. Action against the Jews was soon to follow. The effect of all this is, for once, to truly release Céline from the cycle of re-enactment of his own traumatic experience. *Guignol's band* offers real evidence of healing.

There are also profound personal enhancements of Céline's death mastery at this time. Has, for example, his new relationship with Lucette Almansor released him?[109] It is certainly a factor. Victor Frankl tells us that one of the ways meaning is found is through 'encountering someone'.[110] 'Je t'ai choisie pour recueillir mon âme après ma mort' [I chose you to gather my soul after my death], Céline told Lucette,[111] and the evidence of *Guignol's band*'s portrait of Virginie, also points us in that direction. However, Frankl tells us that the creation of a work also confers meaning, and the evidence of the exultant final pages of *Les Beaux Draps* is that Céline believes he has successfully created a meaningful and enduring art form, leading to a sense of his own immortality and a renewed form of heroic transcendence.

Féerie pour une autre fois

Between *Guignol's band* and *Féerie pour une autre fois* [*Féerie for another time*] there is a dark shadow of interruption representing one of the most significant turning points in Céline's literary career. In *Féerie*, Céline's memory of the Great War is overtaken by events at the end of the Second World War, by his flight from France on the heels of the Vichy government, his journey north to Denmark and his imprisonment in Copenhagen. Returned to France from exile, Céline's narration is delivered from the depths of his Vestre Fængsel prison cell.[112] No longer is he solely the veteran clinging to his memory of an earlier war. He is Céline, exiled and imprisoned, traduced and condemned. His anti-Semitic past is occluded. His memory of the Great War recedes under new onslaughts. As such, Céline's memory of the Great War reflects the experience of collective memory, also interrupted by the Second World War.

For Henri Godard, *Féerie* and *Voyage* 'ont bien les mêmes points de depart : guerre pour guerre, et la même volonté de rupture avec le discours auquel les lecteurs sont habitués' [share the same points of departure: war for war, and the same determination to break with the discourse which his readers have gotten used to].[113] That there is a parallel is clear, 'la guerre 14 toujours dans l'oreille — Poëlcapelle la cellule' [the 1914 war still ringing in my ear — Poelkapelle the cell], wrote Céline in an early draft of *Féerie* (RIV, 582), assimilating his experience of imprisonment to his experience of war.[114] In the finished version of *Féerie*, Céline makes the parallel strikingly clear at the very outset as his epigraph echoes *Voyage*:

> L'horreur des réalités !
> Tous les lieux, noms, personnages, situations, présentés dans ce roman, sont imaginaires ! Absolument imaginaires ! Aucun rapport avec aucune réalité !
>
> [The horror of realities!
> All the places, names, persons, situations, presented in this novel are imaginary! Absolutely imaginary! No relation with any reality!]

The epigraph fulfils two important functions. Firstly, reminiscent of the epigraph to *Voyage* it recalls *Voyage* itself as a reference point in memory,[115] which will continue to be an important dimension in Céline's later work. Secondly, it places

Féerie in the same context as *Voyage*, as an effort to transcend through writing, 'l'horreur des réalités' [the horror of realities], the horror of memory. However, the task of memory in *Féerie* is, if anything, even more arduous than in *Voyage*. *Féerie* is a reflection of a world shaken by two disasters, where one menaces the other with oblivion. Céline's moral commitment to remember the Great War, in and beyond *Voyage*, is compromised by the pressure of more recent memory. The stylistic shift in *Féerie* is one which embraces this new reality of memory, subject to even greater disintegration than before, and results in a frantic art form which is the embodiment of disruption of place and time, 'confusion des lieux, des temps ! Merde ! C'est la féerie vous comprenez... Féerie c'est ça... l'avenir ! Passé ! Faux ! Vrai ! Fatigue !' [confusion of places, of times! Shit! It's féerie you understand... That's what it is, féerie... the future! Past! False! True! Fatigue!] (RIV, 15). *Féerie*, Pascal Ifri writes, is a text, 'à l'origine duquel se trouvent des impressions physiques qui déclenchent chez le narrateur un flux de souvenirs, lesquels constituent le récit en question' [rooted in physical sensations which unleash a flood of memories which form the narrator's narrative].[116] Ian Noble calls it a work of 'minimal narrative coherence'.[117]

There is a point in writing *Féerie* where the breach with Céline's memory of the Great War becomes visible. It occurs early on in the movement from draft manuscript to final version, as memory itself is reworked. In the published *Féerie*, receiving a visit from Clemence Arlon (modelled on the wife of Albert Milon, Branledore in *Voyage*, Marcel in *Féerie*), Céline recalls their first meeting in Val-de-Grâce hospital during the war:

> C'est loin le premier jour qu'on s'est vus... J'ai de la mémoire, je grave les choses, je peux rien oublier... C'est pas une preuve d'intelligence... C'est pas à se vanter la mémoire... enfin c'est ainsi... Je dis donc la date, le mois, mai 15, au Val... l'hôpital, le Val-de-Grâce... C'est loin le Val !... Je veux pas vous perdre dans mes souvenirs. (RIV, 8)

> [The day we met is long gone... I have a good memory, I engrave things in it, I can't forget anything... It's not a proof of intelligence... It's not something to boast about, memory... that's the way it is, that's all... And so I can give the date, the month, May 15, at the Val... the hospital, the Val-de-Grâce... It's distant, the Val!... I don't want to lose you in my memories.]

The claim to memory ends here in an abrupt turning away from memory. However, the draft version of *Féerie* developed this memory of Val-de-Grâce over more than forty pages (RIV, 888–931).[118]

In the finished text, the struggle with memory continues, 'plus de "guerre de 14 !" en parlez plus !' [no more '1914 war'! talk no more about it], Céline writes as he embarks on a fantastic detour to 1944 Montmartre dominated by his portrait of the painter, Jules (RIV, 168). *Féerie I* then ends with the aerial bombardment which will occupy all of *Féerie II*. It is tempting to see the entirety of *Féerie II* as a transcription of Céline's days under bombardment at Poelkapelle and of the 'music' of Hazebrouck, 'le canon tonne encore [...] mais c'est une musique à laquelle il est familiarisé' [the cannon thunders still [...] but it's a music he has become used to], his father wrote when visiting him in hospital,[119] a music in *Féerie* breaking through his silences and the layers of more recent memory which dominate his consciousness.

D'un château l'autre

Céline's final trilogy recalls his flight from France in the wake of the collapse of Vichy. This journey from castle to castle, from town to town, from train to train, across a landscape of ruin and devastation, is Céline's ultimate journey in his quest for gold. His goal is both literal, a reserve of gold deposited in a Danish bank before the war, and figurative, his own literary immortality. The quest, the journey north, is paramount and provides a clear linearity despite the confusion of landscape and memory.

In the trilogy, Céline continues the process of creating a specific landscape of memory. In a world in which memory itself is in disintegration, he points towards the work of memory as his real subject. 'Je veux remémorer !... [...] voilà ! tous les souvenirs !...' [I want to recollect!... [...] that's it! all the memories!...] (RII, 92). Gripped by fever, he forgets his present to remember the past, 'je rassemble mes souvenirs historiques...' [I'm gathering together my historical memories] (RII, 117). He establishes an historical context in which his own present is to be read. The trilogy marks his reinvention as 'chronicler' of a world in ruins, the last of his protean self-transformations. He announces his own role, 'on est mémorialiste ou pas !...' [you're either a memorialist or not] (RII, 92), and the power of his memory, 'ma mémoire est pas modérée, elle ! vache !... elle agite... s'agite !...' [my memory is not moderate! It's nasty!... it unsettles... it unsettles itself!...] (RII, 100). The will not to forget, the refusal to forget, remains as much a part of the trilogy as it is of *Voyage*.

As the trilogy carries him northwards, Céline directs his readers towards a forgotten past, in which the Great War and Verdun hold a privileged position. 'On a bien oublié Verdun [...] Ypres veut plus rien dire...' [Verdun has been forgotten [...] Ypres no longer means anything], he writes (RII, 38). Verdun remains the focal point of memory. 'Sérieux est mort, Verdun l'a tué ! Amen !...' [Serious is dead, Verdun killed it! Amen!], Céline proclaims (RII, 43). Each evocation of Verdun reminds the reader of a lost heroic identity, of a France that died in the Great War, and of Céline himself as the guardian of memory.

In the trilogy, and in *Château* in particular, the memory of the Great War and Verdun becomes one with the story of the death of Vichy. As such, part of the purpose of the trilogy is to assure the memory of Céline's 'founding myth' in *Voyage*.[120] By virtue of this link to his own literary memory, together with a chain of references recalling *Guignol's band*, *Mort à crédit* and others, all of Céline's *œuvre* is subsumed in the trilogy into a linearity oriented towards the north and the accomplishment of Céline's lifework. On the other hand, as the narrative carries the reader northward, he is constantly referred back, as in a *jeu de miroirs*, not just to past historical events, but to Céline's own story of those events, and particularly to *Voyage*:

> C'est le *Voyage* qui m'a fait tout le tort... mes pires haineux acharnés sont venus du *Voyage*... Personne m'a pardonné le *Voyage*... depuis le *Voyage* mon compte est bon !... (RII, 51)

> [*Voyage* is to blame for all my troubles... my most determined hateful pursuers come from *Voyage*... Nobody has forgiven me *Voyage*... Since *Voyage* I've been a marked man!...]

By referring text and reader back to *Voyage* in this way, and signalling that it is his *key* text, Céline suggests that *it* is the key to understanding the trilogy. *Voyage* is thus the subterranean memory of the trilogy, just as '4 mai' and Verdun were the subterranean memory of *Voyage* itself. Text, narrator and reader of the trilogy remain, as ever, within a logic of 'rappel'.

Nord

The evocation of *Voyage* continues in *Nord*. Robinson himself is summoned from the shadows (RII, 440). Elsewhere, Céline uses *Voyage* to satirise his critics, 'depuis le "Voyage" il est illisible !... le "Voyage" et encore !' [since *Voyage* he is unreadable!... the *Voyage* and then!] (RII, 563). In doing so, Céline indirectly provides *Voyage* with their imprimatur. His own war experience continues to constitute his own imprimatur, 'depuis septembre 14, je suis renseigné ! pas dans les livres, par l'expérience...' [since September '14, I've learned! but not from books, from experience...] (RII, 406).

Céline's remembering is, as ever, confused and tactical. All of his landscapes and cityscapes are designed to cover his tracks, and to represent a world of memory in which only he who truly remembers can find his way. As always, he is at pains to make a labyrinth of memory, in the image of post-war, twentieth-century memory, but he also painstakingly leaves clues for the reader to make his way back to *Voyage*, to the Great War, to '4 mai', to Verdun, to the memory of monstrous sacrifice, to the truth. Céline's memory is labyrinthine. The reader, like Céline, must use a mental compass to direct himself. Drawing the reader ever deeper into a world and past in disintegration, Céline reveals his strategy but accompanies it with the command to the reader to remember, to make sense out of the world he has inherited:

> Maintenant voyez où nous en sommes [...] entrés dans le désordre pour toujours !... donc trouvez assez naturel que je vous raconte l'hôtel Brenner, Baden-Baden, après le *"Löwen"*, Sigmaringen... où nous ne fûmes pourtant que bien après !... faites votre possible pour vous retrouver !... le temps ! l'espace ! Chronique comme je peux ! [...] moi là, historique, il me serait dénié de coudre tout de traviole ? [...] retrouvez-vous !... (RII, 318–319)

> [Now look where we are [...] entered into disorder forever!... well then you should find it natural that I tell you about the Brenner, Baden-Baden, after the '*Löwen*', Sigmaringen... where we were much later! do what you can to place yourself! time! space! I'm chronicling it as best I can! [...] me, here, historical, am I not allowed to tell it every which way? [...] Find yourself!...]

Determined to give a faithful impression of 'cette titubation dans les heures, les personnes, les années...' [that stumbling of hours, people, years...] (RII, 330), Céline creates a mélange of time, events and memories. His is a world which has 'perdu le nord' [lost the north]. His quest is to find it, to impose order on disorder, disorder which begins in 1914, 'la raison est morte en 14, novembre 14... après c'est fini, tout déconne...' [reason died in '14, November 1914... after that, it's finished, everything gets crazy...] (RII, 457).

There comes a point, however, where there is a need to surrender memory. The journey north demands it. In what is a valedictory to his memory of the Great War, Céline announces 'assez !... assez !... je vous parlerai pas de la guerre 14 !' [enough!... enough!... I will speak to you no longer of the 1914 war!] (RII, 604). This is his last overt reminder of his origins and the origins of all, his last 'rappel'. The abandonment of speech announces the death of oral memory. Céline ceases to speak; his literary witness is all that is left. When next his memory of the Great War is heard, with the publication of *Rigodon* [*Rigadoon*] in 1969, he himself will have become part of memory.

Rigodon

Since *Voyage* two themes have co-existed side by side in Céline's work, the rescue of memory from oblivion and the search for gold and immortality. Both themes reach their culmination in *Rigodon*. *Rigodon* is Céline's last landscape of memory. It is a landscape which, like nearly all Céline's landscapes, and like memory itself, is in constant danger of frittering away to nothing. As Céline journeys north, guided by his compass, he surveys a world in ruins. Painstakingly he tries to reconstitute a past which escapes him, 'souvenirs qu'il me faut... et je peux pas me souvenir de tout... choses et personnes... je m'y retrouve plus' [I need memories... and I can't remember everything... objects and people... I can no longer place myself] (RII, 855). The landscape of memory itself is being rewritten, 'villes et villages ont changé de noms' [towns and villages have changed names] (RII, 757). The journey through memory is a journey through 'ces pays disparus' [countries which have disappeared] (RII, 767).

As Céline's work has developed it has become more and more like memory itself. The frailty and uncertainty, the hesitations and detours of *Rigodon* are a far cry from the organised 'rappel' of *Voyage*. In *Rigodon*, memories spill together in an eclectic mix. Memories of Céline's childhood and his mother (RII, 847), 'ces enchantements d'autres temps' [those enchantments from a time past] (RII, 857), weave together with those of the Cameroon (RII, 825), and Verdun (RII, 863). The memory of the Great War appears to have no special place here. Verdun stands beside Stalingrad in a line from Azincourt to Algeria, way-stations of history, the history of the white race, 'le blanc [...] créé pour disparaître' [created to disappear] (RII, 729).

Verdun, however, retains its emblematic, central place in Céline's memory. In a movement aided by 'l'odeur de brûlé' [the smell of burning], Céline's first and last novels weave together, *Rigodon* becomes one with *Voyage* (see RI, 34) and 'le ravitaillement [...] dans la Woevre' [the re-provisioning [...] in the Woevre] in 1914 surges from the past:

> Je vois encore ce pont-levis de Verdun... debout sur les étriers j'envoyai le mot de passe... le pont-levis grinçait, s'abaissait [...] Nous entrions donc dans Verdun [...] on ne savait pas encore le reste, tout le reste !... si on savait ce qui vous attend, on bougerait plus, on demanderait ni pont-levis, ni porte... pas savoir est la force de l'homme et des animaux... (RII, 863)

> [I see again the Verdun drawbridge... standing in my stirrups I gave the password... the drawbridge creaked, lowered itself [...] We entered Verdun [...] we knew nothing of what was to come, all that was to come!... if you only knew what was ahead of you, you wouldn't budge anymore, you'd look for neither drawbridge nor gate... not knowing is the strength of humans and animals...]

Remembering, Céline stands once again at a point in time where all was about to change utterly, and stands once again face to face with the irrevocable and the irreversible. The only way to efface the past, 'pas regardable ce qui a existé !...' [not fit to be looked at, what's existed!] (RII, 827), would be never to have existed. 'Toujours bien eu le sentiment que j'aurais jamais dû exister...' [Always felt I should never have existed], Céline writes (RII, 763), echoing *Mort à crédit*'s, 'c'est naître qu'il aurait pas fallu' [being born was the mistake] (RI, 552). Writing becomes a substitute, a form of not existing, which at the same time offers immortalising possibilities, just as it has been from *Voyage*, where the struggle towards death and towards life, towards silence and towards speech were equal. The goal of writing remains, for Céline, death and the transcendence of death, the dual nature of the heroic 'man of gold'. Writing has become a metaphorical sacrifice enabling Céline to claim symbolic immortality. Céline's writing is directed like a compass towards that goal, 'toujours ma boussole, je l'ai autour du cou' [my compass, I always have it around my neck], 'on est lancés, on s'arrêtera pas ! Nord !... Nord !... aucune raison qu'on s'arrête' [we're on our way, we're not stopping! North!... North!... no reason to stop now] (RII, 886).

Writing at the end of his life in 1961, Céline marks the culmination of his life's work by remembering in *Rigodon* his arrival in Copenhagen in 1945. Here is the culmination of his quest for gold:

> Tous les droits de mes belles œuvres, à peu près six millions de francs, étaient là-haut... pas au petit bonheur : en coffre et en banque... je peux le dire à présent *Landsman Bank... Peter Bang Weg...*(RII, 886)
>
> [All the royalties from my fine works, almost six million francs, were there... not left to hazard, in safe and bank... I can tell you now it was *Landsman Bank... Peter Bang Weg...*]

At the end of the journey, Céline recovers his memory, 'je retrouve la mémoire !' [my memory comes back!] (RII, 920). In a deserted Copenhagen park, 'absolument personne autour' [absolutely no one around] (RII, 922), Céline and Lili confirm their secret, echoing *Voyage* once more, 'nous n'avons parlé de rien, jamais...' [we had spoken about nothing, never] (RII, 920), in the false bottom of Bébert's basket, 'notre trésor dans le double fond' [our treasure in the false bottom] (RII, 922). The long movement through a landscape of ruin and devastation gives way to an efflorescence of apocalyptic harmony. The park is suddenly filled with exotic birds, supreme emblems of transformation:

> Un ibis [...] et une 'aigrette' !... [...] un paon maintenant... ils viennent exprès !... et un 'oiseau-lyre' [...] encore un autre !... cette fois un toucan... [...] comme ça entourés d'oiseaux si il venait quelqu'un il se demanderait ce qu'on leur fait, si des fois nous ne sommes pas charmeurs... charmeurs d'oiseaux... (RII, 923)
>
> [An ibis [...] and an 'egret'!... [...] then a peacock... they're coming on purpose!... and a 'lyrebird' [...] and another one!... this time it's a

toucan... [...] surrounded by birds like that if anyone comes he'll wonder what we're doing to them, if perhaps we're charmers... bird charmers...]

Céline has recovered his 'trésor' [treasure] and his transformation into 'man of gold' is complete.[121] He can now face his own death with equanimity, 'et au tramway !... je vous ai dit, au "terminus", d'où nous sommes venus... on va se retrouver...' [to the tramway!... I told you, to the 'terminus' we came from... we're going to find ourselves...] (RII, 923). Memory has completed its work and the quest is over. A day after putting the finishing touches to *Rigodon*, Céline entered into possession of his immortality.

Conclusion

Céline's embodiment as modern Er signals both *Voyage*'s role as memory and Céline's redemptive role as witness to the death of heroism. His engagement with Plato's *The Republic* signals not just his purpose in deflecting the soldiers of the French Republic from new massacres but also represents a sustained adversarial targeting of the French Republic's philosophical and political basis. *Voyage* constitutes a systematic attack on the values which underpinned the Republic and which lay at the heart of the Enlightenment project, attack which culminates in an unparalleled literary act of accusation and denunciation. As *Voyage* tilts towards polemic, its imagery, symbolism and ritualistic content direct the reader inescapably towards the leadership of the French Republic and Céline's vision of 'personal evil': the Freemasons. A novel written under the sign of Verdun and '4 mai' climaxes with a vivid denunciation of the group Céline considers most responsible for the death of heroic France and for the disasters befallen his world. In this sense, *Voyage* is both novel and pamphlet. And it is here, in its aspect of political revolt, that the lifeline of rage grasped by the traumatised soldier Céline culminates in savage and enduring accusation.

Beyond *Voyage* and until *Les Beaux Draps* all of Céline's work inhabits a no-man's-land between war past and war future. The release from memory which follows on the collapse of the Third Republic is soon countered by new realities. After the magical *Guignol's band*, Céline's Great War memory is eclipsed by events at the end of the Second World War. The struggle with memory goes on, however, while the death-mastering effort of his work remains intact. Each novel becomes a further step on the ladder leading to immortality, Céline's *scala philosophorum* to the long sought after, ideal state of gold. *Rigodon* marks Céline's final triumph over death, which is nothing less than the triumph of his art over the silence of memory.

---

[1] Céline cited in Bellosta, p.17. See the first chapter of Bellosta, where she makes the case for *Voyage* as 'roman philosophique' [a philosophical novel], the basis for her thesis that *Voyage* is in fact a rewriting of French literature's archetypal 'roman philosophique': Voltaire's *Candide*.

[2] See *Le voyage au cinéma*, p.53.

[3] There is simply not space here to dwell on the many parallels between Plato and Céline, between *The Republic* and *Voyage*. In summary, however, it can be said that Céline may have identified with Plato, who was obsessed with the condemnation to death of Socrates and who made it central to his condemnation of the Athenian state, just as Céline makes the murder of French soldiers by their own army central to his attack of the French Republic. Beyond the direct interaction of these two books there is a broader interaction with Plato. For example, Céline's choice of an oral register recognises Socrates' preference for the spoken word expressed in the *Phaedrus*, calling to mind his assertion that the written word cannot act as memory, but only as a reminder of what has been (275a): Céline's 'rappel' (see 4.3 *The Function of Rappel*). Furthermore, Bardamu's alienation in a world of separation from an heroic ideal he cannot remember forcefully recalls Plato's theory of Recollection, also expressed in the *Phaedrus* (250a). The link between Céline and Plato is reinforced if one remembers that Céline's *Progrès* bore the original title *Périclès*. Périclès, to whom Plato was directly related, was the architect of Athenian democracy. Despite Céline's own express contempt for philosophy and the philosopher, the philosophical dimension of *Voyage* is clear and there is a case for examining Céline and *Voyage* in a broad philosophical context which would embrace his interaction with other philosophers. Nietzsche would undoubtedly occupy a prominent place among them. Indeed, through his incarnation as an anti-Plato, Céline embodies, in *Voyage*, Nietzsche's call for *'new philosophers'*. That Nietzsche's call is made in the context of an open denunciation of democracy is of striking relevance where Céline is concerned. See Nietzsche, *The Complete Works of Friedrich Nietzsche*, ed. by Dr. Oscar Levy, 12 vols (Edinburgh: Foulis, 1909), V: *Beyond Good and Evil: Prelude to a Philosophy of the Future*, trans. by Helen Zimmern, p.129.

[4] See Daryl H. Rice, *A Guide to Plato's Republic* (Oxford: Oxford University Press, 1998). Says Rice, 'it is not unusual for philosophers to give a forecast of what they are going to do, do it and then remind us of what they have done.' See Rice, p.116.

[5] Rice describes this type of conversational overture as 'showing that philosophical questions emerge in the course of ordinary life' and 'among people very much engaged with ordinary life'. See Rice, pp.2–3.

[6] See Plato, *The Republic*, ed. by Desmond Lee, 2nd edn, rev. (London: Penguin, 1987), note 2, p.364. This notion of art representing the 'ghosts' of true reality is a further clarification of Nicholas Hewitt's thesis that *Voyage* is a song sung by ghosts (see 6.1 *Donning the Mask*).

[7] Plato, p.67.

[8] Plato, p.194.

[9] Plato, pp.196–197.

[10] Plato, p.78.

[11] See particularly Plato, pp.81–88. Plato excises passages such as 'and expose to mortal and immortal eyes the hateful chambers of decay that fill the gods themselves with horror' or 'his disembodied soul took wing for the House of Hades, bewailing its lot and the youth and manhood that it left'. Passages, among others, which resonate powerfully with *Voyage*.

[12] Plato, pp.81–82.

[13] Plato, pp.83–84.

[14] Plato, p.84.

[15] Plato, p.85.

[16] Plato, p.85.

[17] Plato, p.113, also describes what makes a 'good' doctor, saying: 'the best way for a doctor to acquire skill is to have, in addition to his knowledge of medical science, as wide and as early an acquaintance as possible with serious illness; in addition he should have experienced all kinds of disease in his own person and not be of altogether healthy constitution. For doctors don't use their bodies to cure other people's bodies [...] they use their minds; and if their mental powers are or become bad their treatment can't be good.' It would, indeed, be interesting to know how a traumatised Doctor Destouches reflected on this passage in Plato.

[18] Plato, p.86.

[19] Plato, p.132.

[20] Plato, p.365.

[21] Plato, p.98.

[22] Plato, p.369.

[23] Plato, pp.370–371.

[24] Plato, p.373.

[25] Plato, p.132.

[26] Crocq, p.360.

[27] See Plato, *The Republic*, Appendix II, p.400.

[28] See Plato, Appendix II, p.404.

[29] See Plato, Appendix II, pp.400–401.

[30] Plato, *The Republic*, p.246.

[31] See Plato, Appendix II, p.401. There is also a view that the Er myth provides an account of a Near Death Experience (NDE), characterised by a vision of white light when close to death.

[32] Fussell, *The Great War and Modern Memory*, p.131.

[33] See Canetti, p.403.

[34] Pierre Verdaguer, *L'Univers de la cruauté: Une lecture de Céline* (Geneva: Droz, 1988), p.74.

[35] Verdaguer, p.76.

[36] The original *Voyage* manuscript describes Princhard's discourse as a 'pamphlet' and reveals that the war passage in Céline's first chapter (RI, 9) was taken directly from it. By moving it forward in this way Céline makes it an element in the musical overture of *Voyage*, and thus highlighting it underlines its importance. See Henri Godard, 'Une nouvelle lumière sur le *Voyage au bout de la nuit*.'

[37] Rosemarie Scullion places Princhard's speech in this anti-Enlightenment context and makes it an example of incipient fascist discourse in *Voyage*. See Scullion, 'Madness and Fascist Discourse in Céline's *Voyage au bout de la nuit*', *French Review*, 61, 5 (April 1988), 715–723.

[38] See letter to Simone Saintu on 25 October 1916, *Cahiers Céline*, 4, 134–139 (p.134).

[39] See Philippe Alméras, *Je suis le bouc: Céline et l'antisémitisme* (Paris: Denoël, 2000), pp.101–102.

[40] *Voyage* manuscript, fol. 256.

[41] As with our discussion of Plato, we can offer here only a brief sketch of *Voyage*'s anti-masonic character.

[42] This remark might well be kept in mind when considering Princhard's accusation directed against '*les philosophes*' (RI, 69). See Margaret C. Jacob, *Living the Enlightenment: Freemasonry and Politics in Eighteenth-Century Europe* (Oxford: Oxford University Press, 1991), p.146.

[43] Jacques Brengues, Monique Mosser, Daniel Roche, 'Le monde maçonnique des Lumières', in *Histoire des Francs-maçons en France*, ed. by Daniel Ligou (Toulouse: Privat, 1981), pp.97–158 (p.117).

[44] In 1925, the academic and Freemason, Gaston Martin, declared that the French Revolution had been the 'grande œuvre maçonnique' [the great Masonic work]. Cited in *Histoire des Francs-maçons*, p.172.

[45] Jacques Brengues and others, p.116.

[46] See Margaret C. Jacob, p.175.

[47] See Margaret C. Jacob, p.145.

[48] See Robert Ambelain, *Scala Philosophorum ou la symbolique des outils dans l'art royal* (Paris: Prisme, 1975), p.48.

---

[49] Daniel Ligou, 'Le Grand Orient de France (1771–1789)', in *Histoire des Francs-maçons en France*, pp.69–95 (p.95).

[50] See André Combes, 'L'École de la République (1861–1939)', in *Histoire des Francs-maçons en France*, pp.241–296 (p.251).

[51] Membership of the Grand Orient increased from 17,000 in 1882 to almost 31,000 in 1910. Membership of the Grande Loge increased from 4,000 in 1903 to 8,000 in 1912. These figures are taken from André Combes, p.273.

[52] See André Combes, p.285.

[53] See Jacques Brengues and others, pp.120–121. The most famous example of Freemason art is Mozart's *The Magic Flute* (1791). A letter Mozart wrote to his father in which he proclaims 'death is the ultimate purpose of life' is often cited as proof of his embrace of Freemason theories and philosophies of death. See Paul Nettl, *Mozart and Masonry* (New York: Capo, 1970), p.23. The resonance with Céline needs no emphasis. In this context, Céline's own reference to himself as the maker and player of a flute is of especial interest. See Ostrovsky, *Céline and his Vision*, p.201.

[54] See Robert Ambelain, *Scala Philosophorum*, pp.62–65.

[55] Of course, the Freemasons continue to exist. Our discussion of them, however, refers to their organisation in the past tense as a means of orienting their relevance to Céline's *Voyage* towards its proper historical context.

[56] Information on masonic ritual here is from a variety of sources, most notably two works by Robert Ambelain, *Scala Philosophorum* and *Cérémonies et rituels de la maçonnerie symbolique* (Paris: Laffont, 1978).

[57] See Ambelain, *Cérémonies et rituels*, p.89.

[58] Ambelain, *Cérémonies et rituels*, p.93.

[59] Ambelain, *Scala Philosophorum*, pp.25–26.

[60] See Ambelain, *Cérémonies et rituels*, pp.91–92. 'Vous deviendrez un autre être' [you will become another being], the candidate is told.

[61] Ambelain, *Cérémonies et rituels*, p.101.

[62] It is worth noting here that the boat structure of *Voyage* identified by the Damours (p.15) matches the symbolic triangular or pyramidal structure of the masonic '*Grande-Œuvre*' or of the purification 'des neuf *Sens*' [nine *Senses*] as reproduced in Ambelain's *Scala Philosophorum*, p.47 and p.70. In *L'École des cadavres* Céline scathingly refers to the cycle of wars which have devastated Europe since the French Revolution as 'grands abattoirs' [great slaughterhouses], 'Œuvres du Triangle' [Works of the Triangle] (EC, 98).

[63] In Orphic myth, Chronos or Time produces Chaos, or the infinite, and Ether, the finite. Their union creates the cosmic egg whose shell is the night, the same egg no doubt that sits in the sun-baked café terrace on the very first page of *Voyage* (RI, 7), and which recurs throughout Céline.

[64] See Robert Graves, *The White Goddess* (London: Faber and Faber, 1961), p.98.

[65] In French, the word *loge* [lodge] is also used in the expression 'loge de cochon' [pigsty] where it coincides with *Voyage*'s 'cochon' [pig] imagery.

[66] See Pierre Chevallier, *Histoire de la Franc-maçonnerie en France*, 3 vols (Paris: Fayard, 1974), I: *La Maçonnerie, école de l'égalité* (1725–1799), 18–19.

[67] See Margaret C. Jacob, p.127.

[68] See the distortion of names in Godard, *Poétique de Céline*, pp.302–303.

[69] Lord Northcliffe's commentary on Verdun published on-line at the following Internet address, http://www.lib.byu.edu/~rdh/wwi/1916/verdun.html, retrieved on 10 March 2002. This text was originally published in Northcliffe's *At the War* (London: Hodder & Stoughton, 1916).

[70] At the time, Northcliffe's report was widely translated and reproduced in over 3,000 newspapers. See *At the War*, p.161.

[71] Louis-Ferdinand Céline, *Bagatelles pour un massacre* (Paris: Denoël, 1938).

[72] See Nicholas Hewitt, *The Golden Age of Louis-Ferdinand Céline*, p.2. Of course, we have already related this 'golden age' to the soldier's experience of trauma. Robert Lifton describes the holocaust survivor's psychological idealisation of a golden age of childhood as representing: 'an effort to reactivate within himself old and profound feelings of love, nurturance and humanity, in order to be able to apply these feelings to his new formulation of life beyond the death immersion. Inevitably these relate to early childhood, a universal "golden age".' See Lifton, *Death in Life*,

pp.565–566. That Ferdinand's childhood in *Mort* appears more an 'excremental age' is a product of Céline's awareness of the destiny of his 'golden age' as well as an expression of his conflict with a debased present.

[73] Céline's father died on 14 March 1932. See Gibault, I, 302.

[74] Henri Godard provides a full itinerary of the recall of *Voyage* in Céline's later works. See *Romans*, I, 1286–1288.

[75] See also Hewitt, *The Golden Age of Louis-Ferdinand Céline*, p.120. Writes Hewitt, 'he is careful to establish himself at the beginning of the novel as a writer, not merely of legends, but also of *Voyage au bout de la nuit*.'

[76] Céline's controversially squalid depiction of his childhood can also be attributed, in part, to his engagement with Plato, who describes 'representative art' as 'an inferior child born of inferior parents'. This makes the family portrait in *Mort à crédit* a metaphor for, or symbol of, Céline's artistic project. See Plato, p.371.

[77] Céline's publisher Denoël tried vehemently to dissuade him from using his characteristic suspension points. See Poulet, p.94. The initial reaction to *Mort à crédit* was to be one of deep hostility. 'Une très grande majorité des comptes rendus est défavorable ou hostile' [a very large majority of the reviews were unfavourable or hostile], says Henri Godard, see 'Notice', in *Romans*, I, 1309–1416 (p.1401). In 1999 a specially convened Goncourt jury chose *Mort à crédit* as one of the twelve indispensable works of French literature. *Voyage* was not included.

[78] See Céline's own assessment of the contribution of his 'trois points' to his 'style émotif' in *Entretiens avec le professeur Y* (RIV, 541–545). See also Poulet, pp.93–94.

[79] Paul Nizan sees Céline's obsession with the octosyllable as leading to the failure of his style. Noting that the oral displays a tendency to verse, Nizan describes Céline's use of the octosyllable as imposing 'un rythme mécanique' [a mechanical rhythm] on *Mort à crédit*. 'Cette soumission à une machine du langage est très exactement le contraire d'un style' [this submission to a language machine is exactly the opposite of a style], writes Nizan. See Paul Nizan, 'Au royaume des artifices symboliques', p.58.

[80] One of hapless inventor and balloonist, Courtial des Pereires's outrageous money-making schemes is a competition to recover treasure from the bottom of the oceans (see RI, 943).

[81] See Hewitt, *The Golden Age*, p.109.

[82] 'La prédominance de "merde" dans *Casse-pipe* est significative' [the predominance of 'shit' in *Casse-pipe* is significant], Catherine Rouayrenc tells us. See Rouayrenc, 'Céline entre juron et injure', *Classicisme de Céline: Actes du XIIe Colloque international Louis-Ferdinand Céline 3–5 juillet 1998* (Paris: Société d'études céliniennes, 1999), 265–288 (p.287).

[83] See Hewitt, *The Golden Age*, p.128.

[84] Hewitt, *The Golden Age*, p.134.

[85] An American veteran of the Vietnam War, Séan Doherty, in conversation with myself, has remarked that in his experience it can take twenty years for the ex-soldier to come to terms with the experience of war.

[86] For an account of the unfinished status of *Casse-pipe*, see Henri Godard's 'Notice', in *Romans*, III, 878–880. Godard evokes the possibility of a lost version of *Casse-pipe* as long as *Mort*. The most recent news from Céline studies circles is that a full-length manuscript version of *Casse-pipe* does indeed exist.

[87] Céline, 'Mea culpa', *Cahiers Céline, 7: Céline et l'actualité 1933–1961*, ed. by Jean-Pierre Dauphin and Pascal Fouché (Paris: Gallimard, 1986), 30–45.

[88] 'Mea culpa', p.43. For a fuller treatment of Céline's Russian sojourn and his representation of Russia and communism in the pamphlets, see Tom Quinn, 'Postcards from Russia: the vision of Russia in Louis-Ferdinand Céline's early pamphlets', in Jane Conroy, ed., *Cross-Cultural Travel: Papers from the Royal Irish Academy Symposium on Literature and Travel*, National University of Ireland, Galway, November 2002 (Peter Lang: New York, 2003), pp.377–387.

[89] Merlin Thomas's observation of an intensification of Céline's use of the 'three points' as he writes the pamphlets is evidence of their increased emotional intensity. See Thomas, p.122. Alice Y. Kaplan notes that Céline even modifies borrowed texts by replacing semi-colons and full-stops with his 'trois points'. See Alice Y. Kaplan, 'Sources and Quotations in Céline's *Bagatelles pour un massacre*', trans. by Rosemarie Scullion, in Rosemarie Scullion and others, eds., *Céline and the*

Politics of Difference (Hanover: University of New England, 1995), pp.29–46 (p.46). This explanation of a shift in Céline's writing towards an extreme of invective in order to more firmly grasp Lifton's 'lifeline of rage' may go someway towards responding to Malraux's call for an examinination of how 'Céline est passé d'une expérience véritable à une expérience de l'invective' [Céline went from a real experience to an experience of invective]. In Grover, p.87.

[90] 'Mea culpa', p.45.

[91] A cursory examination of *Bagatelles* cannot do justice to its complexity. *Bagatelles* is shaped by its historical context. It is triggered in particular by the election in 1936 of the Popular Front, a left-wing political coalition, hostile to Germany, led by the French Jew, Léon Blum. For Céline, at this juncture, France was a country colonised by the Jews as Ireland was colonised by the British (BM, 311). The concerns of *Bagatelles* are many and its form multifarious. It is perhaps Céline's most protean work.

[92] Lifton, *Death in Life*, p.451.

[93] 'Victimising others can [...] be understood as an aberrant form of immortalisation,' writes Robert Jay Lifton. See Lifton, *Home from the War*, p.199.

[94] This quote alone contradicts Nicholas Hewitt's assertion re *Bagatelles* that, 'Céline is not [...] inciting the French to murder the Jews [...]. None of the thrust of the work goes in the direction of even envisaging physical retaliation.' See Nicholas Hewitt, *The Golden Age*, p.157.

[95] Writes Robert Jay Lifton: 'Scapegoating formulations [...] emerge from struggles between inner and external blaming, and create for the survivor an opportunity to cease being a victim and to make one of another. [...] These formulations [...] are difficult to sustain as coherent entities, and readily disintegrate into amorphous bitterness. [...] Yet a process at least bordering on scapegoating seems necessary to the formulation of any death immersion.' See Lifton, *Death in Life*, p.562. The tendency of the scapegoating formulation to become amorphous can be readily seen in the range of Céline's accusation in the pamphlets.

[96] The 1937 Exposition was inaugurated by the president of the French Republic on 4 May. The date, with its reminder of Verdun and *Voyage*, would have had a powerful resonance for Céline. See Vitoux, *La Vie de Céline*, p.306.

[97] *Bagatelles* was sold with a wrapper reading 'pour bien rire dans les tranchées' [to have a good laugh in the trenches]. See Philippe Alméras, *Céline: entre haines et passion*, p.184.

[98] Writes Lifton: 'Professionals who kill and professional killers in many ways merge. One link is the 'half-educated man' or 'half-intellectual' common among the Nazis. He can assume prominence in genocide by bringing to the project certain necessary elements: the smattering of knowledge that can enable one to ideologise radically the professional sphere and to embrace wholeheartedly false theories.' See Lifton, *The Nazi Doctors: Medical Killing and the Psychology of Genocide* (London: Macmillan, 1986), p.492.

[99] Publicity for *Bagatelles* issued by the *Centre de Documentation et de Propagande* described the pamphlet as a 'réquisitoire puissant contre les juifs écrit dans le style cru des tranchées' [a powerful indictment of the Jews written in the crude style of the trenches]. Document consulted at the *Institut mémoires de l'édition contemporaine* (IMEC), Paris.

[100] The neologism is the most striking evidence of Céline's increasing linguistic vitality. Merlin Thomas notes eight neologisms in the first half-page alone of *Bagatelles*. See Thomas, p.98. According to Eric Seebold, 'le néologisme est le trait marquant des pamphlets où il pullule littéralement' [the neologism is the main characteristic of the pamphlets which literally teem with them]. See Seebold, *Essai de situation des pamphlets de Louis-Ferdinand Céline* (Tusson: Du Lérot, 1985), p.97.

[101] Passages such as this one perfectly illustrate underground themes of 'cosmic violence' and 'cosmic retaliation' described by Robert Jay Lifton in his work with Vietnam veterans. See Lifton, *Home from the War*, pp.152–153.

[102] Louis-Ferdinand Céline, *L'École des cadavres* (Paris: Denoël, 1938).

[103] Céline, *Les Beaux Draps* ([n.p.]: [no pub], 1975, originally published in 1941).

[104] It is worth mentioning here Michel Déon's description of *Les Beaux Draps* as 'le plus émouvant cri de douleur de Céline' [Céline's most moving cry of pain]. See Déon, 'Les Beaux Draps', *L'Herne*, 325–326 (p.326).

[105] The second volume of *Guignol's band* was finished during Céline's post-Second World War Denmark exile and published posthumously in 1964. See Henri Godard's notes to *Romans*, III.

[106] Henri Godard writes that 'la Première Guerre mondiale [...] est comme le cœur invisible' [the First World War [...] is like the invisible heart] of both *Casse-pipe* and *Guignol's band*. He adds, 'cette guerre [...] n'est nulle part dans l'œuvre aussi concrètement présente que dans *Guignol's band*, à travers les souvenirs de corps déchiquetés qui hantent Ferdinand' [that war [...] is nowhere in Céline's work so concretely present as in *Guignol's Band* in the memories of sundered bodies that haunt Ferdinand] (RIII, pp.xviii–xix).

[107] See Joseph L.Henderson, 'Ancient myths and modern man', in *Man and his Symbols*, pp.104–157 (p.151).

[108] Van Der Post, p.83. Interestingly, Van Der Post believes the bird sings so beautifully because it is caged and recalls Lear's remark to Cordelia that they will sing in prison like birds in a cage. He is then told that the bird has also been blinded and so the beauty of its song is the result of a 'double separation' (p.84). We recall here that Céline's initiation into death has been symbolised in the epigraph to *Voyage* as a form of blindness, 'il suffit de fermer les yeux' [it's enough to close your eyes], a second separation added to the initial one resulting from his death encounter. Elsewhere, and not without relevance to Céline, Van Der Post reminds us that Plato thought of the mind as a cage of birds. He would not have marvelled, writes Van Der Post, that for the Bushman, 'the bird is never far from the storyteller's imagination [and] represented inspiration, the thoughts that come into the mind of man, winging of their own accord out of the blue of the imagination and demanding to be acknowledged and followed' (p.221).

[109] Céline met Lucette Almansor in 1934 and they married in 1943. Writes François Gibault, 'Céline connut, avec Lucette Almansor et jusqu'à la fin de sa vie, une aventure qui lui apporta les seuls moments heureux d'une existence qui allait être de plus en plus tumultueuse, puis de plus en plus solitaire' [Until the end of his life, Céline lived with Lucette Almansor an adventure which brought him the only happy moments of an existence destined to be ever more tumultuous, ever more solitary]. See Gibault, II, 192. For an account of their wedding see pp.330–332.

[110] Victor Frankl, *Man's Search for Meaning*, trans. by Ilse Lasch, preface by Gordon W.Allport (Boston: Beacon Press, 1959), p.115.

[111] Véronique Robert and Lucette Destouches, p.50.

[112] For an account of this period in Céline's life, see Gibault, III, 103–128.

[113] See Henri Godard's preface, in *Romans*, IV, p.x.

[114] Writes Henri Godard, 'rien ne pourrait dire mieux que ce rapprochement "Poëlcappelle la cellule" le parallélisme des deux expériences de la guerre et de la détention pour Céline' [nothing speaks more eloquently than this linking of 'Poelkapelle the cell' of the parallel nature of the two experiences of war and detention for Céline]. Godard, *Féerie pour une autre fois*, Appendice I: Notes et variantes', in *Romans*, IV, 1387–1412 (p.1405, note 3 to RIV, 582).

[115] Writes Nicholas Hewitt, '*Féerie* is fully conscious of its position as a descendant of *Voyage*.' See Hewitt, *The Life of Céline*, p.263.

[116] Ifri, p.207.

[117] Noble, p.55.

[118] Henri Godard offers this long passage in *Version C* of *Féerie* as a revisiting and expansion of the Val-de-Grâce episode in *Voyage* (RI, 85–86).

[119] Letter of Céline's father on 5 November 1914 cited in François Gibault, *Céline*, I, 148.

[120] Writes Henri Godard, 'rien ne montre mieux la puissance de l'imagination qui gouverne l'œuvre romanesque de Céline que la continuité dont témoignent ces derniers romans par rapport à celui dans lequel elle avait pour la première fois trouvé à s'exprimer' [nothing shows more the power of the imagination which governs Céline's novelistic creation than the continuity of the later novels in relation to the first one in which that imagination had expressed itself]. See Godard, in *Romans*, II: *D'un château l'autre, Nord, Rigodon* (1974), p.xvii.

[121] The search for gold was destined in reality to remain a Célinian metaphor. Henri Godard notes: 'Ces droits, convertis en or et contenus dans une boîte à biscuits, avaient bien d'abord été déposés, dans un coffre de banque à Copenhague, mais, au cours de la guerre, la menace d'une saisie des coffres par les Allemands avait amené Céline à charger une amie danoise de retirer la boîte et de la dissimuler. Cette amie n'étant pas à Copenhague lorsque Céline et Lili y arrivèrent, ils ne purent

rentrer en possession de l'or.' [These royalties, converted into gold and kept in a biscuit box, had indeed been deposited first of all in a Copenhagen bank safe, but, during the war, the danger that they would be seized by the Germans led Céline to ask a female Danish friend to recover the box and hide it. That friend being absent from Copenhagen when Céline and Lili arrived there, they could not gain possession of the gold]. It eventually transpired, after some confusion, that much of the gold had been spent. The rest was eventually placed in the keeping of Céline's lawyer in Denmark. 'Quant à l'or, que l'avocat ne pouvait mettre en circulation au Danemark, il l'emportait, dissimulé dans les roues de sa voiture, et l'utilisait lors de ses séjours à l'étranger. Si bien que Céline et Lili ne virent jamais cet or' [As for the gold, which the lawyer could not put into circulation in Denmark, he took it away, hidden in the wheels of his car, and used it during his stays abroad. So that Céline and Lili never did see the gold]. See Godard, 'Notice', *Romans*, II, 1191.

CONCLUSION

Céline was the only modern novelist who recognised that the first World War not only destroyed an epoch but would destroy the capacity of a civilisation to remember what war did to our entire century, the century of war.

Jerry Zaslove[1]

Le cauchemar historique que nous vivons tous a trouvé en lui son seul chroniqueur exact. [...] Céline n'a pas cessé de crier une vérité dont nous mourrons tous.

[The historical nightmare we are all living found in him its only true chronicler. [...] Céline never ceased to cry out a truth from which we are all dying.]

Philippe Sollers[2]

Céline, vous n'avez pas vaincu la mort qui nous tourmente [...]. Mais vous avez fait reculer un peu la mort, et c'est quelque chose.

[Céline, you have not beaten death which torments us [...]. But you have pushed death back a little, and that's something.]

Elie Faure[3]

Trauma

Louis-Ferdinand Céline was traumatised by his experience of war in 1914. Even before he was wounded at Poelkapelle, body, mind and imagination had been shaken by the revelation of the Great War's unprecedented horror. His witness at the Battle of the Marne is fully informed by his awareness of a world in free-fall into death and destruction. At Spincourt wood, death played hide and seek with him, and opened the lid on his fear of being killed. At Poelkapelle, his terrifying death encounter swept him into a maelstrom of breakdown and fever. At Hazebrouck, he endured days of delirium and terror, lacerating headaches and humiliating physical breakdown, hours of dark forgetfulness in which his heroic self dissolved and vanished. He felt guilt over survival, over abandonment of his comrades, and intense doubts and anxieties over his perceived failure of manliness. He felt he had become a coward. He had discovered that he was afraid to die. He was no longer who or what he had been before. He had ceased to be a hero.

As time went by the guilt, the fear, the horror, the trauma deepened. The war continued seemingly interminably and, at a remove from it, he was painfully aware of its absurdity, its hypocrisies and its degradations. In the wake of war the exalted, rarefied memory of these things sustained the official memory of the war, intolerably for him, who carried a sense of his own death and of the death of his country inscribed in the deepest depths of his troubled mind and soul, his 'death imprint'. He could never forget, never accept, never forgive the cruelty of the war's sacrifice, the folly of its blood-letting, the staggering, belling brashness of its lies, the pantomime of its pretences, the awfulness of the truths it revealed about humanity. And in that uniquely darkened place between two wars he was cursed with an awareness that the seeds of renewed conflict and untrammelled mass murder were sprouting from the political machinations of the present, from a rotten peace bedded in the soil of commemoration and the traditional narratives of warrior glory. His memory of war, so long a prisoner to silence, could not be held at bay. *Voyage* surged from beneath Céline's own traumatic memory of death, replete with its cargo of fear and nightmare, static, circular, horrendously unrelenting and unforgiving, informed by the unique genius of his own despairing art.

All of his trauma is there, in *Voyage*, all of his trauma, and all of his desire. For *Voyage* is a novel full of desire, desire for healing, for release, for regeneration, for transcendence, for memory, for immortality. Its depthless despair is matched only by its limitless hunger for a release from death and the menace of death. If, in the world between wars, with ten million corpses behind and sixty million to come, 'la vérité de ce monde c'est la mort' [the truth of this world is death] (RI, 200), 'je ne veux plus mourir' [I do not want to die anymore] (RI, 65) is the answering, appealing cry of Céline and *Voyage* against 'la sentence des hommes et des choses' [the sentence of men and things] (RI, 13). Born from the violent point of rupture with self and past, from an explosion at the very core of being, full of the pain of separation from an ideal death-mastering self, *Voyage* aches for understanding and meaning, while it struggles against the twin dark stars of 'disparu' [disappeared] and 'inconnu' [unknown], words which dominated the discourse of its time, and which signalled death, secrecy, mystery and forgetting.

Memory and Forgetting

Suicide might well have tempted Céline,[4] the temptation to meld his sense of inner deadness, his sense of hovering between life and death, his sense of being a ghost, with the dead whose voice resounded in him. Like Hamlet, however, he answered the deepest human question, the question of existence, with a spirit of rejection and revolt. He chose to live and to fight against forgetting. He chose to remember. In *Voyage*, profound act of memory, Céline remembers. He remembers the loss of his own heroic condition, remembers the sacrifice and suicide of his country, remembers the debacle of heroism and the imposed cowardice of technological warfare, remembers the flight of the soldier into the ground, the monstrosity of death unbound and rampant upon the earth, remembers the incompetence, indifference and sheer malignant stubbornness of the war's architects and leaders in the face of limitless human waste and suffering, remembers the uncounted treasure of life lost and the hidden treasure churned from the bowels of destruction, remembers the awful madness of war, its grotesque absurdity, remembers Poelkapelle, remembers Verdun, remembers '4 mai', remembers *Mort-Homme*, remembers the Great War.

Céline remembers and he speaks, speaks out of failed silence, speaks heroically to deny death its triumph. He speaks to tell his story of forgetting, of lost memory and lost identity, of lost heroism and lost death mastery. He speaks — calls out rather — to recall from the darkness of forgetting the memory of the past and to remind his listeners of the disasters that have befallen them. He speaks to summon from the shadows, the veteran, the forgotten, the marginalised, the wounded and the dead, speaks to summon them to his remembrance, his 'call to order', his mobilisation. He speaks to commit to memory, to fix in time his story of the past, for it is a story, made of his own loss of memory, of his own loss of heroic identity, and of the lost treasure of his own life. He speaks to enact a ritual of memory, speaks to provide a ritual incantation of protection against death and the architects of death. He speaks to voice his rage, to cry out his desire for vengeance, to roar his rejection at the rulers of the world of death, to bellow his dissent at the lie of commemoration, to inform, to warn, to educate his listeners, the poor, the young, the powerless, of the dangers that surround them. He speaks to point back towards the war that has decimated his race and half the world, speaks to point forward to the war that will crush what remains. He speaks to ask for a new way of living and being, where death will not be King. He speaks to summon the living and the dead to rise up against the tyranny of death. He speaks to heal, to mend language and in so doing to mend the mind and heart of the world. He speaks finally to forget, to step outside of his own death and that of his world, speaks so as to be able not to speak, to recover his silence, filling the world of *Voyage* with a sea of it, so that it overspills the edges of his fiction to drown the world.

And while he remembers, he forgets, forgets himself, so that he can say all this and do all this and arrive at the end of it all, and be silent. That silence which is so much a part of Céline's remembering and his forgetting.

Truth

What truth then is there in *Voyage*? Other than the truth of memory manipulated to ward off death and 'capsize the ship of state'? What does Céline remember? He remembers the debasement visited on self and world by the Great War. He remembers death stealing darkly over the earth to possess it. How does he remember? He remembers by creating a story, a dark-bright fiction hung upon the world and his time. Why does he remember the way that he does? Out of desire for healing and transcendence, out of a passionate determination to lend form and substance to the inchoate nature of traumatic experience, out of an insatiable hunger to render the 'unsayable' tangible and real, out of an urgent need to record what was, to bear witness, out of a great didactic intent to use bewitching fictions to enthral the world and make it listen and understand, out of desperate rage to refute and denounce, out of an unquenchable thirst for meaning and for truth, out of a restless dream of immortality forged in 'the smithy of [the] soul'.[5]

Bardamu is not Céline, but the symbol of Céline. *Voyage* is not his life, but the symbol of his life, the autobiography of his sensibility, his temperament, the map of his time and place in the world. *Voyage* is not the real memory of lived events, it is a symbol of memory, what Leslie Davis calls, 'Céline's Great War metaphor'.[6] Céline has filled these symbols and this metaphor with his witness, his truths, and the rest is silence.

What are Céline's truths? They are a soldier's truths. Robert Lifton, writing of the truths of Vietnam veterans, whose kinship with the soldiers of the Great War he acknowledges, describes their truth. This truth is also Céline's. It is a truth made of the 'hidden secrets of the places in which they have trespassed [...] the truth they have touched at its source'.[7] It is a truth which is partly 'the simple, unflinching rendition of grotesque, empty suffering', partly admiration for the enemy — in Céline's case, the Germans — partly 'the most terrible realisation of all', that it just wasn't worth it. Lifton writes:

> The ultimate truth at the source has to do with the ease with which a man [...] can become both victim and executioner; with the malignancy of the romantic and ideological deceptions about the war; and with the further source of these deceptions and victimizations in the deep recesses—

of 'America and Americans', writes Lifton of his Vietnam veterans, of France and the French, or indeed, of humans and humanity, we might say in the case of Céline.

Lifton recognises the ambivalence of the soldier, confronting 'starkly' his own destructiveness. 'That truth,' he says, 'can be frightening, even blinding.' Also part of the truth is the realisation that in society at large 'nobody wanted to hear the truth at source', and the inevitable doubt the veteran feels as to 'whether truth at the source is possible — for others, for himself, or as an entity at all'. We have seen all of this in *Voyage* and in Céline, the fear, the blindness, 'il suffit de fermer les yeux' [it is enough to close your eyes] (RI, epigraph), the helplessness. We have seen too the urgency, described by Lifton, of the 'truth-telling' mission of the soldier who having seen war feels he is in possession of a certain truth, an urgency which 'can lead to an intolerant righteousness', the 'sanctimoniousness [...] of men who, [have] crossed over to the other side and returned'. These men, Lifton says, 'understand that one never quite gets to "the truth" and that the struggle to approximate it is unending'. There is a struggle to master this truth, to make the telling of it authentic and a source of renewal. This too is one of the springs of Céline's renewal of language, not just death mastery, but truth mastery.

Witness

Céline's witness is protean and manifold. Through the creation of a universal fiction, firmly set in its intertextual matrix, Céline succeeds in representing, that is, in giving vibrant witness to, the complex reality of his time, culture, society and world. Through the cycle of re-enactment he represents the static and nightmarish entrapment of his own trauma, of the Great War and of the world between wars, haunted by death, caught up in a compulsion to repeat its disasters, saturated through and through with ritual. Through irony, humour and obscenity, and much, much more, he is witness to the emergence of 'modern memory' and gives it its most complete artistic expression. Through his art, through innovation and deliberate duality, he bears witness to the breach in time and consciousness, memory and identity, which is the Great War, falling like a shadow over the world of the human.

Céline's language is perhaps his greatest witness. Through the creation of a new language he succeeds in creating an unprecedented art form with which to represent an unprecedented event. He succeeds in drawing his readers into his witness. He succeeds in creating a new language of 'truth-telling', oral and democratic, through which to voice his memory of war past, his denunciation of the present, his horror at the future. This new language marks his distance from the world which has given birth to and sustained the Great War. It marks his moral commitment to enact change and to break out of the destructive cycles of violence that have swamped his world. It marks his engagement with his own cultural traditions, and with the shibboleths of the Enlightenment and the entire Platonic tradition. 'Il est celui qui tire un trait là-dessus' [it is he who draws a line under it], says Henri Godard of Céline's refusal of his inheritance of effete, positivist philosophies, 'et qui bracque le projecteur sur ce qu'il y a de contraire en l'homme [...] des principes de violence et d'irrationnel en nous' [and who fixes the projector on its opposite in humanity [...] those principles of violence and irrationality which inhabit us].[8]

Céline offers a supreme witness to human violence. Céline and *Voyage* both have their origins in the days of violent bombardment that heralded his death encounter at Poelkapelle. It is this violence which as Henri Godard puts it 'enclenche une explosion nouvelle par laquelle il pouvait franchir les limites d'une langue' [unleashes a new explosion enabling him to go beyond the limits of a language]. Céline's writing bears direct witness to the effect of violence on the human mind and on language and on imagination. Céline's witness to violence is multiple. As Henri Godard perceptively observes:

> Il examine toutes les formes de violence que nous pouvons subir [...] toutes les violences sociales, toutes les violences du monde, la violence radicale, celle qui tient à la mort, la violence que nous exerçons [...]. Il sent [...] que dans la violence que nous subissons [...] il y a une espèce de consentement à la mort.

> [He examines all the forms of violence we are subject to [...] all the forms of social violence, all the forms of world violence, radical violence, the violence of death, the violence we exert [...]. He senses [...] that in the violence to which we are subject [...] there is a form of consent to death.]

The world between the wars was a world given over to violence and to death. 'How many had seen, really seen?' ask historians Stéphane Audoin-Rouzeau and Annette Becker. How many had really understood the meaning and the import of this violence and where it would lead?

> De 1919 aux années trente, bien des choses furent montrées et dites sur la guerre et sur l'après-guerre. Mais les contemporains ont-ils 'vu' les conséquences profondes du conflit dont ils avaient été parties prenantes ? [...] Les générations de l'entre-deux-guerres n'ont pas perçu l'irradiation du monde par la culture de violence issue de la Grande Guerre. Il n'ont pu voir à quel point sa brutalisation les avaient rejoints irrémédiablement, à quel point elle s'était désormais inscrite au cœur des sociétés occidentales.[9]

> [From 1919 to the 1930s, a lot was shown and said about the war and the post-war. But, at the time, did people 'see' the profound consequences of a conflict in which they had participated? [...] The inter-war generations did not perceive the irradiation of the world by a culture of violence issued from the Great War. They were unable to see the extent to which its

brutalisation had become irremediably part of them, the extent to which it was from then on written into the heart of western societies.]

Céline did see. And who but a soldier, who had been to the violent heart of darkness of war and back, could have done so? In a world where commemoration had become a form of blindness and forgetting, Céline's witness shadowed forth the meaning of the past, not just for the past, not just for the present he inhabited or the future he feared, but for the entire concept of human civilisation.

The Memory of Louis-Ferdinand Céline

When all is said and done, *Voyage* utters the most intense cry of pain and protest at separation from a sense of ideal, death-mastering self. It is an intensely personal record. Its pain is so private that the real memory of Louis-Ferdinand Céline is veiled in secrecy, in forgetting. It is only through his genius that he manages to speak, for self and for world, while clinging to an intensely moral silence. *Voyage* is testament to the wound in the fabric of Céline's own being, but as if that were not enough, it is testament too, to a world gored with its own dark wound and dying in slow agony, a world standing in the midst of death and destruction, a world between wars. Which is to say that Céline has assumed the memory of his world and made it his own. He carries it like a cloak wrapped about him. His own memory walks within, reached by insight, intuition and strange leaps of the imagination. The cloak which guarantees invisibility is *Voyage*.

In the final pages of his *Sites of Memory, Sites of Mourning*, Jay Winter evokes Paul Klee's *Angelus Novus*, an angel flying into the air, his gaze staring back at a world of piled destruction behind him, as he is flung backwards into the future. This 'backward gaze', says Winter, is emblematic of the aftermath of the Great War and the 'universality of grief and mourning in Europe from 1914'.[10] Céline too was a prisoner to this 'backward gaze', but perhaps what most distinguishes his memory of disaster, is his escape and flight from the arms of the angel:

> Je refuse la guerre et tout ce qu'il y a dedans... Je ne la déplore pas moi...
> Je ne me résigne pas moi... Je ne pleurniche pas dessus moi... Je la refuse
> tout net, avec tous les hommes qu'elle contient, je ne veux rien avoir à
> faire avec eux, avec elle. (RI, 65)

[I reject the war and everything in it... I don't deplore it... I don't resign myself to it... I don't snivel over it... I reject it outright, with all of the men it contains, I want nothing to do with them, or with it.]

Out of all this pain, and in the face of overwhelming cataclysm, before and behind him, Céline created a myth of self, his own memory of who he was, of what he had done and what had been done to him, and of what his hopes and dreams were, when the nightmare loosed its grip. Deep down he desired transformation and redemption for himself and the world. Deep down he wanted a world of justice, integrity, beauty, compassion, love, peace. His desire could be as passionate and destructive as his lifeline of rage but it was nonetheless real and as pure as it could be in a mad and murderous world which was not a world of his invention or his choosing. His sin perhaps was his deadly pride fired by the 'sanctimoniousness' of the soldier in possession of the truth he burned to communicate. This pride prepared a terrible fall. He was aware of its dangers from early on. 'En un mot je suis orgueilleux est-ce un défaut je ne le crois et il me créera des déboires ou peut-être *la Réussite*' [In a word I am proud is it a fault I don't believe so and it will create problems for me or perhaps bring *Success*], he wrote, young cavalryman, at Rambouillet before the war (see 3.2 *La Réussite*). This pride ruled him and all but destroyed him. And still somehow, by the power and magic of his art, he survived.

Every survival is something of a miracle. Céline's art is in its own way miraculous. It tells the story of the strangest of miracles. The story of a soldier home from war, who has encountered death, and whose life has fallen back into his hands almost by accident. The story of a man who having escaped from a hell which still claims him, seeks to acquit himself of his debt to the living and the dead, and who is Er, Eros, Sisyphus, Proteus, Orpheus, Oedipus and Perseus all in one. The story of a soldier who, having lived war, has given up war and abandoned his physical weapons forever. The story of a soldier, whose only weapon, when all is said and done, is the liberating and transforming power of his art.[11] The story of a soldier whose art bears the enduring stamp of a survivor of the Great War and the immortal stamp of a man of gold.

[1] Jerry Zaslove, 'The Death of Memory: The Memory of Death, Céline's Mourning for the Masses...', in *Understanding Céline*, ed. by James Flynn and Wayne Burns (Seattle: Genitron Press, 1984), pp.187–241 (p.188).

[2] Philippe Sollers, *L'Herne*, p.429.

[3] Elie Faure, 'D'un Voyage au bout de la nuit', *L'Herne*, 438–442 (p.442).

[4] 'Why not commit suicide?' was the question Victor Frankl asked of his fellow prisoners on the edge of despair in Buchenwald. 'Je n'ai jamais pu me tuer moi' [I was never able to kill myself], Bardamu answers (RI, 200). But Frankl found one of the answers was to keep alive 'lingering memories worth preserving'. The Er myth, retold in *Voyage*, shows that Céline indeed found sustenance in the work of memory itself. This memory work is inextricably part of the meaning of *Voyage*. The search for meaning, Frankl says, is the prime motivator in human life (see 4.2 *The Search for Meaning*). And meaning, he says, is discovered in three ways, one of which is by, 'creating a work'. *Voyage*, in this sense, is both Céline's quest for meaning and the expression of that meaning. Meaning is also discovered, says Frankl, in the 'attitude taken to unavoidable suffering'. By transmuting his broken and debased symbol system into an art form, which is resolutely polemical, educational and innovatory, Céline manages to strike an attitude to suffering which is vitalising, both in its exploitation of emotion and rage, and in its creation of meaning. Frankl's third source of meaning, as we have seen, is in meeting someone who confers life with meaning (see 9.3 *Guignol's band*). See Frankl, p.115.

[5] James Joyce, *Portrait of the Artist as a Young Man* (London: Everyman, 1991), p.257.

[6] Leslie Davis, 'Re-writing the Rules: L.-F. Céline's Great War Metaphor', *Journal of the Institute of Romance Studies*, 6 (1998), 305–315.

[7] Robert Jay Lifton, *Home from the War*, pp.309–310 and following pages.

[8] This and following quotes are from Henri Godard's intervention at the conference on Céline organised by and held in the Bibliothèque nationale de France (Tolbiac site) on 19 September 2001.

[9] Audoin-Rouzeau and Becker, *14–18 retrouver la Guerre*, p.259.

[10] Jay Winter, *Sites of Memory*, p.223.

[11] There is a striking and fascinating interpretation of Céline's metaphor of the stick to represent his art (see 9.1 *The Anti-Plato*). Robert Jay Lifton recalls a scene from Alfred de Vigny where a soldier who has killed a child by accident in war now carries a stick which he has vowed will be his only weapon. It is more than likely that having read Vigny, Céline, ex-soldier, saw the stick of his art in this sense. See Lifton, *Home from the War*, p.122.

BIBLIOGRAPHY

Only texts referred to in this work are noted in the bibliography.

PRIMARY DOCUMENTS
Manuscripts
Journal des marches et opérations du 12ᵉ Cuirassiers, Le Service historique de l'armée de terre, Bibliothèque archives militaires, Château de Vincennes, Paris.

Voyage au bout de la nuit, Service des manuscrits, Bibliothèque nationale de France, rue Richelieu, Paris.
Printed
Historique du 12ᵉ Cuirassiers: au danger mon plaisir ([n.p]: [n.pub], [n.d]. – circa 1920–1925).

WORKS BY CÉLINE
Romans, I: *Voyage au bout de la nuit, Mort à crédit*, ed. and annot. by Henri Godard (Paris: Gallimard, 1981).

Romans, II: *D'un château l'autre, Nord, Rigodon*, ed. and annot. by Henri Godard (Paris: Gallimard, 1974).

Romans, III: *Casse-pipe, Guignol's band I, Guignol's band II*, ed. and annot. by Henri Godard (Paris: Gallimard, 1988).

Romans, IV: *Féerie pour une autre fois I, Féerie pour une autre fois II, Entretiens avec le professeur Y*, ed. and annot. by Henri Godard (Paris: Gallimard, 1993).

Bagatelles pour un massacre (Paris: Denoël, 1938).

L'École des cadavres (Paris: Denoël, 1938).

L'Église (Paris: Gallimard, 1952).

Les Beaux Draps, originally published 1941 (n. p.: n.pub., 1975).

SHORT TEXTS BY CÉLINE
'Hommage à Zola', *L'Herne: L.F. Céline*, ed. by Dominique de Roux, Michel Beaujour, Michel Thélia (Paris: Cahiers de l'Herne, 1972), 22–24. This volume is a reissue of numbers 3 (1963) and 5 (1965) of the Cahiers de l'Herne devoted to Céline.

'L'argot est né de la haine', *L'Herne*, p.39.

'Le baptême du feu de 1914 raconté par Céline en 1939', recorded in writing by P. Ordioni, in *Romans*, III, 77–79.

'Les Carnets du cuirassé Destouches', *L'Herne*, 10–12.

'Mea culpa', *Cahiers Céline*, 7: *Céline et l'actualité 1933–1961*, ed. by Jean-Pierre Dauphin and Pascal Fouché (Paris: Gallimard, 1986), 30–45.

'Rabelais, il a raté son coup', *L'Herne*, 44–45.

LETTERS

Lainé, Pierre, ed., *Lettres à Joseph Garcin: 1929–1938* (Paris: Monnier, 1987).

COLLECTIONS DEVOTED TO CÉLINE

L'Herne: L.F. Céline (see above for publication record).

Cahiers Céline, 1: *Céline et l'actualité littéraire 1932–1957*, ed. by Jean-Pierre Dauphin and Henri Godard (Paris: Gallimard, 1976).

Cahiers Céline, 2: *Céline et l'actualité littéraire 1957–1961*, ed. by Jean-Pierre Dauphin and Henri Godard (Paris: Gallimard, 1976).

Cahiers Céline, 3: *Semmelweiss et autres écrits médicaux*, ed. by Jean-Pierre Dauphin and Henri Godard (Paris: Gallimard, 1977).

Cahiers Céline, 4: *Lettres et premiers écrits d'Afrique 1916–1917*, ed. by Jean-Pierre Dauphin (Paris: Gallimard, 1978).

Cahiers Céline, 7: *Céline et l'actualité 1933–1961* (see short texts by Céline section above for publication record).

CONFERENCE PROCEEDINGS

Actes du Colloque international L.-F. Céline de Paris 1976 (Paris: Société d'études céliniennes, 1978).

Actes du Colloque international L.-F. Céline de Paris 1979 (Paris: Société d'études céliniennes, 1980).

Actes du Colloque international L.-F. Céline de Paris 1992 (Tusson, Charente: Du Lérot and Société d'études céliniennes, 1993).

Classicisme de Céline: Actes du XIIe Colloque international L.-F. Céline 1998 (Paris: Société d'études céliniennes, 1999).

La Démesure: Actes du XIVe Colloque international L.-F. Céline de Paris 2002 (Paris: Société d'études céliniennes, 2003).

THESES ON CÉLINE

Dauphin, Jean-Pierre, '*Voyage au bout de la nuit*: étude d'une illusion romanesque' (unpublished doctoral thesis, Paris IV, 1976).

Day, Philip Stephen, 'Le Héros picaresque dans *Voyage au bout de la nuit*' (unpublished M.A. in French Language and Literature Dissertation, University of Toronto, 1963).

Lainé, Pierre, 'De la débâcle à l'insurrection contre le monde moderne: l'itinéraire de Louis-Ferdinand Céline' (unpublished doctoral thesis, Paris IV, 1984).

Loselle, Andrea, 'Traveling in the Work of Louis-Ferdinand Céline' (unpublished doctoral thesis, Columbia University, 1990).

BOOKS ON CÉLINE

Aebersold, Denise, *Céline: un démystificateur mythomane* (Paris: Lettres Modernes, 1979).

Alméras, Philippe, *Céline: entre haines et passions* (Paris: Robert Laffont, 1994).

—, *Je suis le bouc: Céline et l'antisémitisme* (Paris: Denoël, 2000).

—, *Dictionnaire Céline: Une œuvre, une vie* (Paris: Plon, 2004).

Bastier, Jean, *Le Cuirassier blessé: Céline 1914–1916* (Tusson, Charente: du Lérot, 1999).

Bellosta, Marie-Christine, *Céline ou l'art de la contradiction: lecture de Voyage au bout de la nuit* (Paris: Presses Universitaires de France, 1990).

Blondiaux, Isabelle, *Une écriture psychotique: Louis-Ferdinand Céline* (Paris: A.G.Nizet, 1985).

Carile, Paolo, *Louis-Ferdinand Céline: Un allucinato di genio* (Bologna: Pàtron, 1969).

Carson, Jane, *Céline's Imaginative Space* (New York: Peter Lang, 1987).

Chesneau, Albert, *Essai de psychocritique de Louis-Ferdinand Céline* (Paris: Lettres Modernes, 1971).

Combessie-Savy, Christine, *Voyage au bout de la nuit de Céline* (Paris: Nathan, 1993).

Damour, A.-C. and J.-P., *L.-F. Céline: Voyage au bout de la nuit*, Études littéraires (Paris: Presses Universitaires de France, 1994).

Dauphin, Jean-Pierre, ed., *Les critiques de notre temps et Céline* (Paris: Garnier, 1976).

Day, Philip Stephen, *Le Miroir allégorique de Louis-Ferdinand Céline* (Paris: Klincksieck, 1974).

Derval, André, ed., *70 critiques de Voyage au bout de la nuit 1932–1935* (Paris: IMEC, 1993).

Gibault, François, *Céline*, 3 vols (Paris: Mercure de France, 1985–1986).

—, I: *1894–1932 Le Temps des espérances*.

—, II: *1932–1944 Délires et persécutions*.

—, III: *1944–1961 Cavalier de l'Apocalypse*.

Godard, Henri, *Poétique de Céline* (Paris: Gallimard, 1985).

Hewitt, Nicholas, *The Golden Age of Louis-Ferdinand Céline* (Lemington Spa: Berg, 1987).

—, *Les Maladies du siècle: the image of malaise in French fiction and thought in the inter-war years* (Hull: University of Hull, 1988).

—, *The Life of Céline* (London: Blackwell, 1999).

Hindus, Milton, *The Crippled Giant* (Hanover, NH: University of New England Press, 1986).

Ifri, Pascal A., *Céline et Proust: Correspondances proustiennes dans l'œuvre de L.-F. Céline* (Birmingham, Alabama: Summa Publications, 1996).

Juilland, Alphonse, *Elizabeth and Louis: Elizabeth Craig talks about Louis-Ferdinand Céline* (Stanford: Montparnasse Publications, 1991).

Kaminski, H.-E., *Céline en chemise brune* (Paris: Plasma, 1977).

Knapp, Bettina, *Céline: Man of Hate* (Alabama: University of Alabama Press, 1974).

Kristeva, Julia, *Pouvoirs de l'horreur: essai sur l'abjection* (Paris: Seuil, 1980).

McCarthy, Patrick, *Céline: A Critical Biography* (London: Allen Lane, 1975).

Monnier, Jean, *Elizabeth Craig raconte Céline: entretien avec la dédicataire de Voyage au bout de la nuit* (Paris: Bibliothèque de Littérature française contemporaine, 1988).

Mugnier, Jean-Paul, *L'Enfance meurtrie de Louis-Ferdinand Céline* (Paris: L'Harmattan, 2000).

Muray, Philippe, *Céline* (Paris: Denoël, 1984).

Murray, Jack, *The Landscapes of Alienation: Ideological Subversion in Kafka, Céline, and Onetti* (California: Stanford University Press, 1991).

Noble, Ian, *Language and Narration in Céline's writings: The Challenge of Disorder* (London: Macmillan, 1987).

Ostrovsky, Erika, *Céline and his Vision* (London: University of London Press,

1967).

Poulet, Robert, *Mon ami Bardamu: entretiens familiers avec L.-F. Céline* (Paris: Plon, 1971).

Richard, Jean-Pierre, *Nausée de Céline* ([Montpellier]: Fata Morgana, 1973).

Robert, Véronique with Lucette Destouches, *Céline secret* (Paris: Bernard‡ Grasset, 2001).

Scullion, Rosemarie and others, eds., *Céline and The Politics of Difference* (Hanover, NH: University Press of New England, 1995).

Seebold, Eric, *Essai de situation des pamphlets de Louis-Ferdinand Céline* (Tusson: Du Lérot, 1985).

Smith, André, *La Nuit de Louis-Ferdinand Céline* (Paris: Grasset, 1973).

Szafran, Willy, *Louis-Ferdinand Céline: essai psychanalytique* (Brussels: Éditions de L'Université de Bruxelles, 1976).

Thiher, Allen, *Céline: The Novel as Delirium* (New Brunswick, New Jersey: Rutgers University Press, 1972).

Thomas, Merlin, *Céline* (London: Faber and Faber, 1979).

Vandromme, Pol, *Louis-Ferdinand Céline* (Paris: Editions Universitaires, 1963).

Verdaguer, Pierre, *L'Univers de la cruauté: une lecture de Céline* (Geneva: Droz, 1988).

Vitoux, Frédéric, *Misère et parole* (Paris: Gallimard, 1973).

—, *La Vie de Céline* (Paris: Bernard Grasset, 1988).

ARTICLES ON CÉLINE

Bastier, Jean, 'L.-F. Céline en 1914, d'après les archives de l'armée', *Actes du Colloque international de Paris 1992*, 35–50.

Bataille, Georges, 'Une signification humaine', in Jean-Pierre Dauphin, ed., *Les critiques de notre temps et Céline*, pp.29–30.

Blondiaux, Isabelle, 'Louis-Ferdinand Céline et le diagnostic de paranoïa', *Actes du Colloque international Louis-Ferdinand Céline de Paris 1992*, 79–90.

—, 'La représentation de la pathologie psychique de guerre dans *Voyage au bout de la nuit*', in *Roman 20-50: Revue d'étude du roman du xxe siècle*, dossier critique : *Voyage au bout de la nuit* de Louis-Ferdinand Céline, études réunies par Yves Baudelle, 17 (June 1994) pp.105–115.

Brochard, Marcel, 'Céline à Rennes', *L'Herne*, 203–206.

Daudet, Léon, 'Voici un livre étonnant', in *Les critiques de notre temps et Céline*, pp.21–26.

Davis, Leslie, 'L'Anti-monde de L.-F.Céline', *Actes du Colloque international de Paris 1976*, 59–74.

—, 'Re-writing the rules: L.-F. Céline's Great War Metaphor', *Journal of the Institute of Romance Studies*, 6 (1998), 305–315.

De Boisdeffre, Pierre, 'Sur la postérité de Céline', *L'Herne*, 303–309.

Déon, Michel, 'Les Beaux Draps', *L'Herne*, 325–326.

Donley, Michael, 'L'identification cosmique', *L'Herne*, 327–334.

Faure, Elie, 'D'un Voyage au bout de la nuit', *L'Herne*, 438–442.

Geoffroy, Georges, 'Céline en Angleterre', *L'Herne*, 201–202.

Godard, Henri, 'Une nouvelle lumière sur le "Voyage au bout de la nuit"', *Le Monde*, 11 May 2001, p.14.

Kaplan, Alice Y., 'Sources and Quotations in Céline's *Bagatelles pour un massacre*', trans. by Rosemarie Scullion, in Rosemarie Scullion and others, eds., *Céline and the Politics of Difference*, pp.29–46.

Kerouac, Jack, untitled text, *L'Herne*, p.423.

Lévi-Strauss, Claude, Review of *Voyage*, from *L'Étudiant socialiste*, January 1933, in André Derval, ed., *70 critiques de Voyage au bout de la nuit 1932–1935*, pp.119–121.

Llambias, Robert, 'Guerre, histoire et langage dans le récit célinien', *Revue des Sciences Humaines*, 204 (October–December 1986), 89–105.

Luce, Stanford, 'Increment and Excrement: Céline and the Language of Hate', *Maledicta*, I (1977), 43–48.

Nizan, Paul, 'Au royaume des artifices symboliques', in *Les critiques de notre temps et Céline*, pp.55–60.

Ostrovsky, Erika, 'Mythe et subversion de mythe chez L.-F. Céline', *Actes du Colloque international de Paris 1979*, 83–91.

Pike, D.L., 'Céline and Dante: From Golden Bough to Charon's Oar', *Lectura Dante: A Forum for Dante Research*, 12 (1993), 65–74.

Quinn, Tom, 'The Death of Compassion in Louis-Ferdinand Céline's *Voyage au bout de la nuit*', *The Irish Journal of French Studies*, 1 (2001), 67–74.

—, '"Une immense, universelle moquerie" : mémoire démesurée de guerre démesurée — Céline, *Voyage au bout de la nuit* et la Grande Guerre', in *La Démesure: Actes du XIVe Colloque international L.-F.Céline de Paris 2002*, 217–231.

—, 'Postcards from Russia: the vision of Russia in Louis-Ferdinand Céline's early pamphlets', in Jane Conroy, ed., *Cross-Cultural Travel: Papers from the Royal Irish Academy Symposium on Literature and Travel*, National University of Ireland, Galway, November 2002 (New York: Peter Lang, 2003), pp.377–387.

Racelle-Latin, Danièle, '*Voyage au bout de la nuit* ou l'inauguration d'une poétique "argotique"', *Revue des Lettres Modernes*, 4 (1976), 53–78.

Rérolle, Raphaëlle, 'Le Manuscrit du "Voyage au bout de la nuit" vendu pour 11 millions de francs', *Le Monde*, 17 May 2001, p.32.

Rouayrenc, Catherine, 'Céline entre juron et injure', *Classicisme de Céline: Actes du XIIe Colloque international L.-F. Céline 1998*, 265–288.

Schilling, Gilbert, 'Les "descentes" de Bardamu', *Actes du Colloque international de Paris 1976*, 41–58.

Scullion, Rosemarie, 'Madness and Fascist Discourse in Céline's *Voyage au bout de la nuit*', *French Review*, 61, 5 (April 1988), 715–723.

Sollers, Philippe, untitled text, *L'Herne*, p.429.

Spitzer, Léo, 'Une habitude de style, le rappel chez Céline', *L'Herne*, 443–451.

Trotsky, Léon, 'Céline et Poincaré', *L'Herne*, 434–435.

Winter, Jay, 'Céline and the Cultivation of Hatred', in *Enlightenment, Passion, Modernity: Historical Essays in European Thought and Culture*, intro. and ed. by Mark S. Micale and Robert L. Dietle (Stanford: Stanford University Press, 2000), pp.230–248.

Zaslove, Jerry, 'The Death of Memory: The Memory of Death, Céline's Mourning for the Masses...' in *Understanding Céline*, ed. by James Flynn and Wayne Burns (Seattle: Genitron Press, 1984), pp.187–241.

BOOKS ON GREAT WAR

Association des écrivains combattants, *Anthologie des écrivains morts à la guerre 1914–1918*, 5 vols (Amiens: Edgar Malfère, 1924–1926).

Audoin-Rouzeau, Stéphane, *à travers leurs journaux: 14–18 Les combattants des Tranchées* (Paris: Armand Colin, 1986).

—, and Annette Becker, eds., *La Grande Guerre 1914–1918* (Paris: Gallimard, 1998).

—, *14–18: retrouver la Guerre* (Paris: Gallimard, 2000).

Babington, Anthony, *Shell-Shock* (London: Leo Cooper, 1997).

Barbusse, Henri, *Le Feu* (Paris: Flammarion, 1916).

Becker, Annette, *La Guerre et la foi: de la mort à la mémoire 1914–1930* (Paris: Armand Colin, 1994).

Becker, Jean-Jacques, *1914: Comment les Français sont entrés dans la guerre* (Paris: Presses de la Fondation Nationale des Sciences Politiques, 1977).

—, with the collaboration of Annette Becker, *La France en guerre (1914–1918): la grande mutation* (Paris: Complexe, 1988).

Becker, Jean-Jacques and Serge Bernstein, *Victoire et frustrations 1914–1918* (Paris: Seuil, 1990).

Bergonzi, Bernard, *Heroes' Twilight: A Study of the Literature of the Great War* (London: Constable, 1965).

Bloch, Marc, *Souvenirs de guerre 1914–1915* (Paris: Armand Colin, 1969).

—, *Réflexions d'un historien sur les fausses nouvelles de la guerre* (Paris: Allia, 1999).

Blunden, Edmund, *Undertones of War* (London: Penguin, 1982).

Brittain, Vera, *Testament of Youth* (London: Virago Press, 1978).

Canini, Gérard, *Combattre à Verdun: vie et souffrance quotidienne du soldat 1916–1917* (Nancy: Presse Universitaire de Nancy, 1988).

Cecil, Hugh and Peter Liddell, eds., *Facing Armageddon* (London: Leo Cooper, 1996).

Cendrars, Blaise, *La main coupée* (Paris: Denoël, 1946).

Coker, Christopher, *War and the 20th Century* (London: Brassey, 1994).

Cooperman, Stanley, *World War I and the American Novel* (Baltimore: John Hopkins, 1967).

Cru, Jean Norton, *Témoins* (Nancy: Presses Universitaires de Nancy, 1993).

—, *Du témoignage* (Paris: Allia, 1997).

Cruickshank, John, *Variations on Catastrophe: some French responses to the Great War* (Oxford: Oxford University Press, 1982).

Dorgelès, Roland, *Les Croix de bois* (Paris: Albin Michel, 1919).

Ducasse, André, Jacques Meyer, Gabriel Perreux, eds., *Vie et mort des Français 1914–1918* (Paris: Hachette, 1962).

Eksteins, Modris, *Rites of Spring: The Great War and the Birth of the Modern Age* (London: Papermac, 2000).

Ferguson, Niall, *The Pity of War* (London: Penguin, 1998).

Ferro, Marc, *La Grande Guerre, 1914–1918* (Paris: Gallimard, 1969).

Fussell, Paul, *The Great War and Modern Memory* (Oxford: Oxford University Press, 1975).

—, *Abroad: British Literary Travelling between the Wars* (New York: Oxford

University Press, 1980).

—, ed., *The Bloody Game: An Anthology of Modern Warfare* (London: Scribners, 1991).

Gilbert, Martin, *The First World War* (London: Weidenfeld & Nicolson, 1994).

Graves, Robert, *Goodbye to All That* (Oxford: Berghahn, 1995).

Gregory, Adrian, *The Silence of Memory: Armistice Day 1919–1946* (Oxford: Berg, 1994).

Guéno, Jean-Pierre and Yvès Laplume, eds., *Paroles de Poilus: Lettres et carnets du front 1914–1918* (Paris: Librio, 1998).

Hemingway, Ernest, *A Farewell to Arms* (London: Arrow Books,1994).

Horne, John, ed., *State, society and mobilisation in Europe during the First World War* (Cambridge: Cambridge University Press, 1997).

Hüppauf, Bernd, ed., *Modernity and Violence* (Berlin: De Gruyter, 1997).

Hynes, Samuel, *The Soldier's Tale: Bearing Witness to Modern War* (London: Pimlico, 1998).

Jünger, Ernst, *The Storm of Steel*, trans. by Basil Creighton (New York: Howard Fertig, 1975).

Keegan, John, *Soldiers: A History of Men in Battle* (London: Hamish Hamilton, 1985).

—, *The First World War* (London: Hutchinson, 1998).

Leed, Eric J., *No Man's Land: Combat and Identity in World War One* (London: Cambridge University Press, 1979).

MacDonald, Lyn, *The Roses of No Man's Land* (London: Penguin, 1980).

—, *To the Last Man: Spring 1918* (London: Viking, 1998).

Meyer, Jacques, *La Biffe* (Paris: Albin Michel, 1928).

Miquel, Pierre, *La Grande Guerre* (Paris: Arthème Fayard, 1983).

—, *Les Poilus: La France sacrifiée* (Paris: Plon, 2000).

Montague, C.E., *Disenchantment* (London: MacGibbon & Kee, 1968).

Moran, Lord, *The Anatomy of Courage*, 2nd edn (New York: Avery, 1987).

Mosse, George, *Fallen Soldiers: Reshaping the Memory of the World Wars* (Oxford: Oxford University Press, 1990).

Offenstadt, Nicolas, *Les Fusillés de la Grande Guerre et la mémoire collective 1914–1999* (Paris: Odile Jacob, 1999).

O'Neill, Terry, ed., *Readings on All Quiet on the Western Front* (San Diego: Greenhaven Press, 1999).

Pedroncini, Guy, *Les Mutineries de 1917* (Paris: Presse Universitaires de Paris, 1983).

Prost, Antoine, *Les Anciens Combattants et la société française 1914–1939*, 3 vols (Paris: Presses de la Fondation Nationale des Sciences Politiques, 1977).

—, I: *Histoire.*

—, II: *Sociologie.*

—, III: *Mentalités et idéologies.*

Remarque, Erich Maria, *All Quiet on the Western Front*, trans. by Brian Murdoch (London: Vintage, 1996).

Riegel, Léon, *Guerre et Littérature* (Paris: Klincksieck, 1978).

Rieuneau, Maurice, *Guerre et révolution dans le roman français 1919–1939*

(Paris: Klincksieck, 1974).

Sassoon, Siegfried, *The Complete Memoirs of George Sherston* (London: Faber and Faber, 1972).

Service historique de l'armée de terre avec le concours du Service d'information et de relations publiques des armées, *1916: Année de Verdun* (Paris: Charles-Lavauzelle, 1986).

Strachan, Hew, *The First World War* (London: The Historical Association, 1993). This text is a short pamphlet not to be confused with the following large volume.

—, *The First World War* (Oxford: Oxford University Press, 2001).

Weldon, Robert Whalen, *Bitter Wounds: German Victims of the Great War 1914–1939* (London: Cornell University Press, 1984).

Winter, Jay, *Sites of Memory, Sites of Mourning* (Cambridge: Cambridge University Press, 1995).

ARTICLES ON GREAT WAR

Audoin-Rouzeau, Stéphane, 'Quand les enfants font la guerre', *L'Histoire*, 169 (September 1993), 6–12.

—, 'L'Épreuve du feu', *L'Histoire*, 225 (October 1998), 34–43.

Becker, Annette, 'Aux morts, la patrie reconnaissante', *L'Histoire*, 225, 50–53.

Becker, Jean-Jacques, 'Mourir à Verdun', *L'Histoire*, 76 (March 1985), 18–29.

—, 'Plus jamais ça !', *L'Histoire*, 225, 56–59.

Blin, Jean-Pierre, 'Le Christ au champ d'honneur', *L'Histoire*, 225, p.52.

Church, Richard, '*All Quiet* Perfectly Transmits the Experience of War', in Terry O'Neill, ed., *Readings on All Quiet on the Western Front*.

Crocq, Louis, 'Et puis, c'est vous qui montez à l'assaut…', interview recorded by Bruno Cabanes, *L'Histoire*, special issue, 'Les hommes et la guerre', 267 (July - August 2002), 68–69.

Delaporte, Sophie, '15,000 Gueules Cassées', *L'Histoire*, 225, p.40.

Faron, Olivier, 'Une catastrophe démographique', *L'Histoire*, 225, 46–48.

—, 'Les pupilles, enfants chéris de la nation', *L'Histoire*, 225, p.48.

Holmes, Richard, 'The Last Hurrah: Cavalry on the Western Front, August–September 1914', in Hugh Cecil and Peter Liddell, eds., *Facing Armageddon*, pp.278–294.

Horne, John, 'Introduction: mobilising for "total war", 1914–1918', in *State, society and mobilisation in Europe during the First World*, pp.1–17.

Hutton, Will, 'The Terrible Slaughter that Changed the World', *The Observer*, 8 November 1998, p.14.

Meyer, Jacques, 'Vie et mort du soldat de Verdun', *Verdun 1916: Actes du Colloque international sur la Bataille de Verdun 6–7–8 juin 1975* (Verdun: Association Nationale du Souvenir de la Bataille de Verdun, Université de Nancy, 1977),18–29.

Mosse, George, 'Two World Wars and the Myth of the War Experience', *Journal of Contemporary History*, 21 (1986), 491–513.

Quinn, Tom, 'La Gloire guerrière et les images d'Epinal', *The Irish Journal of French Studies*, 3 (2003), 79–93.

Read, Herbert, 'Why War Books are Popular', in *Readings on All Quiet on the Western Front*.

Shephard, Ben, 'Shell-shock on the Somme', *RUSI*, 141 (1996), 51–56.

Vincent, Gérard, 'Guerres dites, guerres tues et l'énigme identitaire', in Philippe Ariès and Georges Duby, *Histoire de la vie privée*, V: *De la Première Guerre mondiale à nos jours*, ed. by Antoine Prost and Gérard Vincent, pp.201–249.

Winter, Jay, 'The Great War and the Persistence of Tradition', in Bernd Hüppauf, ed., *Modernity and Violence*, pp.33–45.

BOOKS ON MEMORY, SURVIVAL, AND TRAUMA

American Psychiatric Association, *Diagnostic and Statistical Manual of Mental Disorders: Version III* (Washington: American Psychiatric Association, 1984).

—, *Diagnostic and Statistical Manual IV* (1994).

Antze, Paul and Michael Lambek, eds., *Tense Past: Cultural Essays in Trauma and Memory* (London: Routledge, 1996).

Caruth, Cathy, ed., *Trauma: Explorations in Memory* (Baltimore: John Hopkins, 1995).

—, *Experience: Trauma, Narrative, and History* (Baltimore: John Hopkins, 1996).

Chambers, Ross, *The Writing of Melancholy: Modes of Opposition in Early French Modernism*, trans. by Mary Seidman Trouille (Chicago: The University of Chicago Press, 1993).

Connerton, Paul, *How Societies Remember* (New York: Cambridge University Press, 1989).

Crocq, Louis, *Les traumatismes psychiques de guerre* (Paris: Odile Jacob, 1999).

Des Pres, Terrence, *The Survivor* (New York: Oxford University Press, 1976).

Erikson, Erik H., *Childhood and Society* (London: Vintage, 1995).

Ferenzi, S. and others, *Psycho-analysis and the War Neuroses*, intro. by Sigmund Freud (London: The International Psycho-analytical Press, 1921).

Frankl, Victor, *Man's Search for Meaning*, trans. by. Ilse Lasch, preface by Gordon W. Allport (Boston: Beacon Press, 1959).

Freud, Sigmund, *The Standard Edition of the Complete Psychological Works of Sigmund Freud*, trans. and ed. by James Strachey in collaboration with Anna Freud, 24 vols (London: The Hogarth Press and the Institute of Psycho-analysis, 1955, 1958, repr. 1964).

Hendin, Herbert and Ann Pollinger Haas, *Wounds of War: The Psychological Aftermath of Combat in Vietnam* (New York: Basic Books, 1984).

Jung, Carl, *Memories, Dreams, Reflections*, recorded and ed. by Aniela Jaffé, trans. by Richard and Clara Winston (London: Fontana Press, 1995).

Lang, Berel, ed., *Writing and the Holocaust* (New York: Holmes & Meier, 1988).

Langer, Laurence L., *Holocaust Testimonies: the ruins of memory* (New Haven: Yale University Press, 1991).

Lifton, Robert Jay, *Death in Life: The Survivors of Hiroshima* (London: Pelican, 1971).

—, *Home from the War: Vietnam Veterans, neither Victims nor Executioners* (London: Wildwood, 1974).

—, *The Nazi Doctors: Medical Killing and the Psychology of Genocide* (London: Macmillan, 1986).

—, *The Protean Self: Human Resilience in an Age of Fragmentation* (Chicago: The Chicago University Press, 1999).

Power, D. J., *Military Psychology including Terrorism* (Chichester: Barry Rose Law Publishers, 1991).

Rank, Otto, *The Double: A Psychoanalytic Study*, ed., trans., and intro. by Harry Tucker, Jr. (New York: New American Library, 1978).

Ricœur, Paul, *La Mémoire, l'Histoire, l'Oubli* (Paris: Seuil, 2000).

Semprun, Jorge, *L'écriture ou la vie* (Paris: Gallimard, 1994).

Solomon, Zahava, *Combat Stress Reaction: The Enduring Toll of War* (New York: Plenum Press, 1993).

Terdiman, Richard, *Present Past: Modernity and the Memory Crisis* (Ithaca: Cornell University Press, 1993).

Van Der Post, Laurens, *The Voice of the Thunder* (London: Penguin, 1994).

Wilson, John Preston, and others, eds., *Human Adaptation to Extreme Stress* (New York: Plenum Press, 1988).

ARTICLES ON SURVIVAL, TRAUMA AND MEMORY

Antze, Paul and Michael Lambek, 'Introduction: Forecasting Memory', in Antze and Lambek, eds., *Tense Past*, pp.xi–xxxvii.

Atkinson, Roland M. and others, 'Complicated Postcombat Disorders in Vietnam Veterans', in John Preston Wilson and others, eds., *Human Adaptation to Extreme Stress*, pp.357–375.

Caruth, Cathy, 'Interview with Robert Jay Lifton', in Cathy Caruth, ed., *Trauma: Explorations in Memory*, pp.128–147.

Des Pres, Terrence, 'Holocaust *Laughter*', in Berel Lang, ed., *Writing and the Holocaust*, pp.216–233.

Freud, Sigmund, 'Beyond the Pleasure Principle', in *The Standard Edition of the Complete Psychological Works of Sigmund Freud*, XVIII (1955, repr. 1964), 7–64.

—, 'Memory, Repetition and Working Through', in *The Standard Edition*, XII (1955, 1958, repr.1964), 145–156.

Kirmayer, Laurence J., 'Landscapes of Memory: Trauma, Narrative and Dissociation', in *Tense Past*, pp.173–196.

Lambek, Michael, 'The Past Imperfect: Remembering as Moral Practice', in *Tense Past*, pp.235–254.

Laub, Dori, 'Truth and Testimony: The Process and the Struggle', in *Trauma: Explorations in Memory*, pp.61–75.

Lifton, Robert J., 'Understanding the Traumatized Self', in *Human Adaptation to Extreme Stress*, pp.7–31.

Parson, Erwin Randolph, 'Post-Traumatic Self Disorders', in *Human Adaptation to Extreme Stress*, pp.244–283.

Ricœur, Paul, 'Memory and Forgetting', in Kearney and Dooley, eds., *Questioning ethics: debates in contemporary philosophy*, pp.5–11.

—, 'Imagination, Testimony and Trust', in *Questioning ethics*, pp.12–17.

Van Der Kolk, Bessel A. and Onno Van Der Hart, 'The Intrusive Past: The Flexibility of Memory and The Engraving of Trauma', in *Trauma: Explorations in Memory*, pp.158–182.

Zelizer, Barbie, 'Reading the Past Against the Grain: The Shape of Memory

Studies', *Critical Studies in Mass Communications*, 12 (1995), 214–239.

MISCELLANEOUS BOOKS

Ahmed, Rollo, *The Black Art*, intro. by Dennis Wheatley (London: Arrow Books, 1966).

Ambelain, Robert, *Scala Philosophorum ou la symbolique des outils dans l'art royal* (Paris: Prisme, 1975).

—, *Cérémonies et rituels de la maçonnerie symbolique* (Paris: Laffont, 1978).

Amis, Martin, *Time's Arrow* (London: Penguin, 1992).

Ariès, Philippe, *L'Homme devant la mort* (Paris: Seuil, 1977).

—, with Georges Duby, eds., *Histoire de la vie privée*, 5 vols (Paris: Seuil, 1987).

Campbell, Joseph, *The Hero with a Thousand Faces* (London: Abacus Books, 1975).

Camus, Albert, *La Peste* (Paris: Gallimard, 1947).

Canetti, Elias, *Crowds and Power*, trans. by Carol Stewart (London: Penguin, 1981).

Carson, R.A.G., *Coins: Ancient, Mediaeval and Modern* (London: Hutchinson, 1962).

Cellini, Benvenuto, *La Vita*, intro. by Guido Davico Bonino (Turin: Giulio Einaudi, 1973).

Chartier, Roger, *Les Origines culturelles de la révolution française* (Paris: Seuil, 1990).

Chateaubriand, *Mémoires d'outre-tombe*, preface by Julien Gracq, ed. by Maurice Levaillant, 4 vols (Paris: Flammarion, 1982).

Chevallier, Pierre, *Histoire de la Franc-maçonnerie en France*, 3 vols (Paris: Fayard, 1974).

—, I: *La Maçonnerie, école de l'égalité* (1725–1799).

Condorcet, Marquis de, *Esquisse d'un tableau historique des progrès de l'esprit humain* (Paris: Librairie Philosophique Vrin, 1970).

Dante, *The Divine Comedy*, 3 vols (London: Penguin Books, 1949).

De Rougemont, Denis, *L'Amour et l'Occident* (Paris: Plon, 1939).

Doyle, William, *The Oxford History of the French Revolution* (Oxford: Oxford University Press, 1989).

Frazer, J. G., *The Golden Bough: A Study in Magic and Religion* (London: The Macmillan Press, 1983).

Frye, Northrop, *The Secular Scripture: A Study of the Structure of Romance* (Cambridge: Harvard University Press, 1976).

—, *The Anatomy of Criticism* (London: Penguin, 1990).

Graves, Robert, *The White Goddess* (London: Faber and Faber, 1961).

Grover, Frédéric, *Six entretiens avec André Malraux sur des écrivains de son temps* (Paris: Gallimard, 1978).

Guerber, H.A., *The Myths of Greece and Rome* (Ware, Hertfordshire: Worthsworth Editions, 2000).

Hobsbawm, Eric, *The Age of Extremes: The Short Twentieth Century 1914–1991* (London: Michael Joseph, 1994).

Homer, *The Odyssey*, intro. by Peter V. Jones, trans. by E.V. Rieu (London: Penguin, 1991).

Howard, Michael, *The Invention of Peace* (London: Profile Books, 2000).

Im Hof, Ulrich, *The Enlightenment*, trans. by William E.Yuill (Oxford: Blackwell, 1994).

Jacob, Margaret C., *Living the Enlightenment: Freemasonry and Politics in Eighteenth-Century Europe* (Oxford: Oxford University Press, 1991).

Joyce, James, *Ulysses* (New York: Vintage Books, 1961).

—, *Portrait of the Artist as a Young Man* (London: Everyman, 1991).

Jung, Carl G., ed., *Man and his Symbols* (London: Aldus Books, 1964).

—, *Memories, Dreams, Reflections*, recorded and ed. by Aniela Jaffé, trans. by Richard and Clara Winston (London: Fontana Press, 1995).

Kearney, Richard and Mark Dooley, eds., *Questioning Ethics: Debates in Contemporary Philosophy* (London: Routledge, 1999).

Lejeune, Philippe, *L'Autobiographie en France* (Paris: Armand Colin, 1971).

—, *Je est un autre* (Paris: Seuil, 1980).

Ligou, Daniel, ed., *Histoire des Francs-maçons en France* (Toulouse: Privat, 1981).

Lukács, György, *The Theory of the Novel*, trans. by Anna Bostock (London: Merlin Press, 1971).

Nietzsche, *The Complete Works of Friedrich Nietzsche*, ed. by Dr. Oscar Levy, 12 vols (Edinburgh: Foulis, 1909).

—, V: *Beyond Good and Evil: Prelude to a Philosophy of the Future*, trans. by Helen Zimmern.

Nettl, Paul. *Mozart and Masonry* (New York: Capo Press, 1970).

Plato, *The Republic*, trans. and intro. by Desmond Lee, 2nd edn (London: Penguin Books, 1987).

Rice, Daryl H., *A Guide to Plato's Republic* (Oxford: Oxford University Press, 1998).

Sellier, Philippe, *Le Mythe du héros ou le désir d'être dieu* (Paris: Bordas, 1970).

Seymour Smith, Martin, *Robert Graves: His Life and Work* (London: Bloomsbury, 1995).

Sirinelli, Jean-François, ed., *La France de 1914 à nos jours* (Paris: PUF, 1993).

Sun Tzu, *The Art of War* (Hertfordshire: Wordsworth Classics, 1998).

Terrou, Fernand, Claude Berranger, Jacques Godechot, Pierre Guiral, eds., *Histoire générale de la presse française*, 5 vols (Paris: Presses Universitaires de France, 1969–1976).

—, III (1972): *De 1871 à 1940*.

Vilar, Pierre, *A History of Gold and Money 1450–1920*, trans. from the Spanish by Judith White (London: NLB, 1976).

MISCELLANEOUS ARTICLES

Brengues, Jacques, Monique Mossor and Daniel Roche, 'Le monde maçonnique des Lumières', in Daniel Ligou, ed., *Histoire des Francs-maçons en France*, pp.97–158.

Butler, Samuel, 'On Compassion', in *The Age of Enlightenment*, ed. by Simon Eliot and Beverley Stern, 2 vols (London: Ward Lock Educational, in association with The Open University Press, 1979), I, 37–43.

Combes, André, 'L'École de la République (1861–1939)', in *Histoire des Francs-maçons en France*, pp.241–296.

Denby, David, 'Civil War, Revolution and Justice in Victor Hugo's *Quatrevingt-*

treize', *Romance Studies: Images of War*, 30 (1997), 7–17.

Henderson, Joseph L., 'Ancient Myths and Modern Man', in Carl G. Jung, ed., *Man and his Symbols*, pp.104–158.

Jacobi, Jolande, 'Symbols in an Individual Analysis', in *Man and his Symbols*, pp.272–303.

Jung, Carl G., 'Approaching the Unconscious', in *Man and his Symbols*, pp.18–103.

Kant, Immanuel, 'Toward Perpetual Peace', in *Practical Philosophy*, trans. and ed. by Mary J. Gregor, The Cambridge Edition of the Works of Immanuel Kant (Cambridge, U.S.: Cambridge University Press, 1996), pp.311–351.

Ligou, Daniel, 'Le Grand Orient de France (1771–1789)', in *Histoire des Francs-maçons en France*, pp.69–95.

Steiner George, 'Silence and the Poet', in *Language and Silence: Essays 1958–1966* (London: Faber and Faber, 1985), pp.55–74.

Von Franz, M.L., 'The Process of Individuation', in *Man and his symbols*, pp.158–229.

POEMS

Gurney, Ivor, 'There are strange hells within the minds war made', in Paul Fussell, ed., *The Bloody Game*, p.195.

Thomas, Edward, 'This is No Case of Petty Right or Wrong', *Poets of the Great War*, read by Michael Maloney and others, Naxos CD, NA 210912, 1997.

DICTIONARIES

Le Petit Robert: Dictionnaire de la langue française (Paris: Le Robert, 1989).

FILM AND VIDEO

Carroll, Anne, dir. and prod., *The Mind at War: Post-traumatic stress disorder*, Services Sound and Vision Corporation Production, for the British Ministry of Defence, 1993.

Kubrick, Stanley, dir., *Full Metal Jacket*, Metrodome, 1987.

Poirier, Léon, dir., *Verdun*, Gaumont, 1927, 1928 and 1930.

Ricœur, Paul, writer and narr., *Mémoire, oubli, histoire*, dir. by Stéphane Ginet, Arts et Éducation, France, 1995.

TELEVISION

Harrington, Julia, series producer and dir., *Shell Shock*, Blakeway Productions, Channel 4, 1998.

Holmes, Richard, writer, presenter and narr., *Western Front*, dir. by Albert Herman, BBC Television, 1999.

Knapp, Hubert, dir., *Ils ont tenu 1914–1918*, TF1, 1978.

Pivot, Bernard, pres., *Bouillon de Culture*, Antenne 2, broadcast on TV5 on 11 November 2000.

Wright, Patrick, pres. and narr., *A Day to Remember*, dir. by Ian McMillan, Illuminations, Channel 4, 1999.

CDs

Berlioz, *Benvenuto Cellini*, BBC Symphony Orchestra, Chorus of the Royal Opera House, cond. by Sir Colin Davis, Philips CD, 416 955-2 PH3.

Owen, Wilfred, and others, *Poets of the Great War*, read by Michael Maloney and others, Naxos CD, NA 210912, 1997.

INTERNET

Cadé, Michel, 'La Grande Guerre dans le cinéma français : une mise à distance', retrieved at http://www.ags.fr/d3/actesducolloque/frame325139.html. Text originally published in *Traces de 14–18: Actes du Colloque international tenu à Carcassonne du 24 au 27 avril 1996*, ed. by Sylvie Caucanas and Rémy Cazals (Carcassonne: Les Audois, 1997).

Lord Northcliffe's 'Commentary on Verdun', retrieved at http://www.lib.byu.edu/~rdh/wwi/1916/verdun.html. Text first published in Lord Northcliffe, *At the War* (London: Hodder & Stoughton, 1916).

Sebald, William G., 'The Questionable Business of Writing', interview retrieved at http://www.amazon.co.uk/exec/obidos/tg/feature/-/21586/026-3158445-1515666.

South African War Virtual Library, at http://www.sawvl.com.html.

INTERVIEWS AND LECTURES

Bach,General André, interviewed in *Libération*, 11 November 2001, p.17.

Deane, Seamus, public lecture, Dublin City University, 18 February 2000.

Gibault, François interviewed in Paris on the 25 November 1999 by myself.

Goggin, Lieutenant Colonel Colman, interviewed on various occasions in summer 2000 by myself.

Horne, Professor John, in conversation with myself at Trinity College Dublin in 1999 and 2000.

Rouaud, Jean, public lecture, Trinity College Dublin, on 12 December 1998.

Vitoux, Frédéric, interviewed in Paris on the 23 November 1999 by myself.

NEWSPAPERS

France Soir, 11 November, 1999.

Le Figaro, 10 November 1928.

Le Figaro, 11 November 1928.

Le Figaro, 12 November 1928.

Le Monde, 11 May 2001.

Le Monde, 17 May 2001.

Libération, 11 November 1998.

The Observer, 8 November, 1998.

My acknowledgement and thanks to the estate of Louis-Ferdinand Céline for permission to cite extensively from Céline's pamphlets.

INDEX